EVENING WOLVES

A NOVEL BY
LUKE TAYLOR

The characters and events described in this book are a work of fiction and any similarity to real persons or events, living or dead, is unintentionally coincidental.

Evening Wolves Title and Text copyright © 2014 by Luke Taylor

Scripture quotations taken from the Amplified® Bible, Copyright©1954, 1958, 1962, 1964, 1965, 1987 by The Lockman Foundation
Used by permission (www.Lockman.org)

ISBN 978-0-692-25338-0

Cover design by Laura Gordon

"Their horses are swifter than leopards, and are fiercer than **evening wolves**: and their horsemen spread themselves *and* press on proudly; yes, their horsemen come from afar; they fly like an eagle that hastens to devour. They all come for violence: their faces turn eagerly forward, and they gather prisoners together like sand. They scoff at kings, and rulers are a derision to them; they ridicule every stronghold, for they heap up dust (for earth mounds) and take it. They sweep by like a wind and pass on, and they load themselves with guilt, (as do all men) whose own power is their god."

-Habakkuk 1:8-11 Amplified® Bible

This work is dedicated to my family with love and gratitude

EVENING WOLVES

ONE

The man in the brown dining chair awoke from the murky depths of unconsciousness to find himself bound and gagged. Blinking away the fog, painful shafts of light pierced his eyes. His skull echoed with the thick, dull pain of medical narcosis and felt like a blacksmith's anvil at day's end.

Where was he? What happened?

Why was there nothing to recall but only a few seconds of memory?

Fear was a quick companion to the dryness in his throat and the numbness of his hands.

He tried to move. He tried even harder to think. He had to move, instinct told him so. But his hands were behind his back and God knew how long in the rigid chair had sent his tendons and muscles into some kind of stress-induced lockdown.

A shudder ran through him.

The room was a neutral-colored rectangle with white crown molding and a door directly before him, half-open. A single table lamp cast shadows across the couch to his right and the mahogany bookcase opposing it. To his left, a small table of the same wood, and one stoically placed dining chair implying there should've been two. A room for sitting and waiting; for killing time.

The man gasped. A body lay dormant on its

side, facing him; forever gazing into a question with no answer.

Shock sent him backwards, unbalanced. His head spun, the room spun. The chair crashed to the ground ungracefully. Nauseating floods of pain rushed to the space between his eyes and gravity sent it ever so slowly to the back of his head. The tightness of his body prevented his head from touching the ground but he might as well have been hit with a baseball bat.

Now his stomach was sick. *Deep* inside.

Something was terribly wrong.

The man tipped the chair to the right and scraped his feet to rotate his viewpoint, wincing as he did so, stopping once the deceased was in view.

It was a woman; once beautiful, now forever cold and distant. She was Caucasian, with black hair and jewel blue eyes, in evening wear, and the red puncture in her neck was her permanent undoing. Her blood had spread across the carpet like a glass of cabernet sauvignon carelessly swiped from a dinner table.

The man stared hard at the woman for a few seconds, hoping she would blink or say something but down deep where he knew something was irrevocably wrong he made a decision with every fiber of his will, no matter what the hurt, confusion or fallout, he would make his way out of the mess alive and figure out what the hell had gone down in that twelve by eight room with tan walls and white trim.

The man rolled over onto his knees with a great series of grunts and groans and stood as tall as the situation would permit. The window that spread before him and had been to his back as he had come to consciousness was dark and revealed a lawn and a fence of trees in the distance as muddled and incoherent as his own memory and he shuffled away from the window as quickly as possible. His head was pounding but it was in rhythm now, in concert with his heart, sending scared red blood cells to every square inch of his body.

With much difficulty the man made it to the solid mahogany bookcase and began to smash the chair against the space between the bookcase and the wall. Each blind thrust aggravated his head with a renewed agony, jolting his back, shoulders and hands, and he took every shattered fragment of hurt and anger and threw the chair into the wall until the legs split off and the back separated from the seat.

His hands still bound, he let the back of the chair fall free and worked his hands under his legs, leaning against the wall for stability. Through near-sighted squints he could see the plastic mockery of a zip tie.

Someone had been thorough...they had gone through great lengths to make him a prisoner.

Who was it? Who would possibly want to do this to him?

And the woman! What about her?

But there was no time for that now. He freed himself from the gag. His mind wanted to run away but his chest heaved. There was nowhere to run. Every street corner was an unmarked path to a dead end.

Dead.

He quickly went back to the woman and crouched. As soon as he did, a sharp pain flared in his crotch. The man stood and with great difficulty worked his hands down his waistband.

Then his body went cold.

Hidden between his scrotum and penis was a key wrapped in a piece of paper.

The pain seemed to go away as numbness took its place-the dissonance of being lost and alone and afraid, not only for his breath and his heartbeat but his life, as it was a name, an identity, who he was...

The man looked to the woman as she lay lifeless and then to the key wrapped in paper. Just as he was about to examine the key he heard the whir and woop of police sirens.

"What have you done?" He said. To the woman. To himself.

Then he ran.

Officer Braden eased the squad car to a halt just before the main gate of the Mansion. Perhaps it was quite beautiful in the daytime but at half-past two in the morning in had an ominous, monolithic quality to it, like a giant factory with no one at work, no movement or noise. Maybe it was the weather rolling in, too, or the fact there was one lone light on in the whole place.

The other car carried two Officers and pulled in behind his. Their names were Sheridan and Thom. Sheridan was an ex-Marine and was going to be a traffic cop next year. He was built thick and always wore a tactical jump suit. Thom had a gruff appearance too, short flaxy hair and a simple face that bore signs of Rosacea, but she was a sweet lady and did a lot of volunteer work at the community center. She was also a fierce racquetball player and had claimed victory in several Inter-Departmental tournaments.

Thom spoke first when they were all out.

"Some place."

"Yeah." Braden took one look at the computer dominating the squad car console before shutting the door. "Suspicious activity."

"Should we get Peters? He's nearby."

"Naw..." Braden hitched up his utility belt. "There was a big party here earlier tonight and the place is supposed to be vacant. The event planner drove by an hour ago and called in 'cuz that one light was on."

"So somebody fell asleep." Thom mused. "Or maybe the party's still going if you know what I mean."

"If it's that easy then we can all go to lunch."

Sheridan hadn't said a word and moved toward the gate. It opened with ease.

"Shouldn't this be locked?" He asked.

"Don't know. Let's hope the front door isn't." Braden said as he led the way up the wide paved drive to the front door. It took several minutes to cover the distance at a comfortable pace. Before entering he looked back at the vast expanse of manicured grass and could barely see the gate and the trees that lined it. The red and blue lights from the squad cars gave an eerie luminescence to the fog that had begun to fall.

"Have you ever been inside Fircrest Mansion before?" Thom asked.

"No." Braden put his hand to the door. "Let's see what it's like."

The man clomped into the hallway with wild eyes. He couldn't explain it to the cops, he just couldn't-even though he was innocent...or was he? He couldn't remember. There was nothing *to* remember, nothing there at all, like the grounds of the Mansion- foggy, wet, and greenish-black like deep-sea algae.

The man paused. He could make it out the back and over the fence. The cops would search room by room, wouldn't they? Maybe not. Maybe one was patrolling the yard. How many were there? Three, four? Too many questions, no time!

The man continued down the hall to a circular staircase. His feet were quick at work and his bound hands balanced his uncalibrated weight on the rail.

He found himself in an atrium, and fought a memory that began to float to the surface. There was no time to remember. *No time!*

His feet took him through a narrow hallway where he slipped on a long rug. Flashes of pain rattled his head and he scrunched and displaced the expensive rug as his feet and bound hands scraped for leverage. A minute later he was in an open kitchen with a set of French doors standing between himself and freedom.

He tried the handle. It was locked.

A deep breath filled his chest and he threw his weight into the door.

The door rattled with a mocking noise and stayed shut. Pain gripped and squeezed his face.

Without thinking he rushed the door again and embraced the cold, rough concrete of the patio through an explosion of shattered glass.

Rolling on the wet grass he gained his balance and scampered across the sea of green toward the fence. Surely the cops would be on him, any second. They had to have heard.

His body sent adrenaline to every muscle and ligament, though the closer he became to the brick and wrought iron partition the further away it seemed, like some treadmill dream sequence.

He ran without looking back; awkwardly, unevenly, and when he hit the brick and iron fence his lungs caught up with him.

He cast a glance at the Mansion, the giant monstrosity of riches it was, and to each side of the structure in search of dark blue justice.

Nothing.

The man threw his hands up and grabbed at the iron lines and spires, his feet slippery on the brick. It was no small feat to get up and over. As soon as he was, the jingle of Government Issue equipment followed the bouncing beam of light that began to snake around the left side of the house.

The man shrunk within himself and dropped down from the fence, now in the cover of the trees.

It was a cop, tall and muscular, and he paused to peer across the great sea of foggy darkness before turning his attention to the back patio and broken door.

The beam of light darted from the corners of the door to the patio of broken glass.

The man in the trees caught his breath as he watched.

The cop was about to inspect the glass for something, perhaps blood, but his radio hissed and chattered and he skirted the glass and lumbered inside the house.

The man in the trees sighed and muttered curses under his breath as he ran through the evergreens to find a road.

Sheridan found Braden in the small room with the light on. A woman in eveningwear was dead on the ground.

"The ME's on his way."

"Somebody's out there." Sheridan puffed. "We need the chopper."

"Thom's on it."

"I'm going back out there."

"No." Braden raised his voice, albeit just for that one word. He seemed to hear himself too and in the presence of the deceased, lowered his voice. "This is too big. Thom's calling every available officer. Homicide too."

"What are we going to do then?"

Braden's face was taut as he stared at the body.

"We are going to leave everything how it is."

Sheridan let out a lungful of air.

"There's no way I can find whoever was just outside in this weather anyway, at this time of night.

This place is so huge. They could be anywhere."

"I know." Braden surveyed the broken chair and the gag. "But somebody was here. Definitely. We just missed 'em."

"So much for lunch." Sheridan joked, though there was no humor in it. No laughing. Whatever had transpired at the Mansion was far more than suspicious activity. It was murder, maybe more. It was a case that would take thousands of man-hours, millions in payroll, and who knew if the truth of it all would ever come out.

Braden put his hands on his hips.

"Erland will figure it out."

Sheridan nodded and walked down the hall to wait.

TWO

The trees emptied to bushes and more grass and finally the landscape crested and ended with a sprawling view of a highway made distant by the disembodying fog.

It was his only chance.

As he surveyed the evergreen surroundings and caught his breath he noticed his shoulder and the shard of glass that was imbedded into it. He pulled it out with tender difficulty and a sour face.

Then he had an idea.

He pushed the fatigue from his lungs and made his way down the long rolling hill into more trees, using the sharpness of the glass to cut the ties free. It took some doing, but the unforgiving white plastic bands fell into the darkness. He checked his shoulder and the bleeding was minimal. He let the glass go too. Again, adrenaline and the dull ache in his head were the forces propelling him on. Fear's terrible grip wasn't as muscular now that he was away from the Mansion, even though the soft amble of cars on wet pavement tried to bring it back. There was another dip in the earth before it vaulted up again to the retaining wall of the highway.

The man peeked his head over. Not many cars. Not many at all.

The wall was easy enough to manage and he

struck a weary yet confident stride forward, whatever
direction that was, toward whatever was at the end of
forward. It didn't matter. It was away from the
Mansion.

Time to think was all he had before him, time to
process and chew on the shadows inside, but with every
car that passed, so would slip away his trails of
memory, so tender and fleeting they were; into the fog,
into the night.

The only thing he could hold onto was the grand
atrium at the bottom of the staircase. It held more
familiarity than the rectangular room.

And the woman.

He sighed for her. As much as he wanted to help
her he had to help himself. He couldn't do a thing for
her now but walk away from it all and try to remember.

People. Lots of people. Talking, talking, talking;
different levels of volume.

A car brushed past and tore it all away. It was
just too hard, his heart still thumping like a kick drum.
He needed peace and quiet to stop and think, to sort it
all out. He wished he knew his name and where he
lived. It would all be so easy then, wouldn't it?

The man felt for his wallet. He had none. Keys,
none-save the one, buried where no one would ever
think to look.

Buried?

Hidden...

The man stopped and it came to him. He had
been lying on the couch, groggy and sleepy, from what
he didn't know, and the woman had bent over him and
hid the key, and in the blink of an eye she was gone.

It got his heart beating faster, to bring it back. A
soupy, cloudy memory but so definite and real. Then
what?

Talking...

He had rolled over on the couch and...talking, men's voices. Her voice.

A car drifted past him and he fought to keep the memory alive.

Her voice.

What did she say? What did she say to those men so...so that they killed her?

What did she say...

"Excuse me, Mister..." The man looked up. A woman in a suede jacket had pulled her car to the shoulder some feet ahead and was resting her arm on the roof. "Are you okay?"

The man blinked. He walked toward her, unaware he had been a statue on the side of the highway.

She was not afraid.

"Are you okay?" She repeated. "Do you need a ride somewhere?"

The man swallowed hard and fought a frown. *What kind of woman would...*

"Would you believe me if I told you I had amnesia?"

Her eyes narrowed. She didn't speak immediately.

"Yes I would."

"Why?" The man asked. "Why would you believe me?"

The woman smiled.

"Because it's a terrible pickup line."

The man smiled too, but stayed put.

"Would you like to go to the hospital?"

"No...no thank you."

"Do you know where you live?"

"No...I don't."

"Well, you can't just stay out here. You'll get sick. Then you'll be lost and cold and sick and not remember where you live."

The frustration of confusion and circumstance in the man's face dissipated when he saw the wry grin that covered hers.

"Get in."

The man heard the gargling of chopper blades in the distance and walked toward the car.

Erland was in the shower when the call came. His cross-trainers were still warm from the late night run when he stepped back into them. He grabbed his khakis, a long-sleeve polo, and a waterproof jacket. Then he freed his Glock 17 and badge from the safe and said goodbye to the two-bedroom apartment he called home. He never thought at forty-one he'd be all alone, but he also never thought at forty-one he'd be the best Homicide Detective in the state. It balanced out. Work was work. Everything outside of work was to make work easier. That's why he was nearly religious about running and eating healthy; about living spartan and cheap and leaving life's dainties to those who knew no better and would wait in line for them like fluffy sheep.

Work was life. Life was work.

Erland rolled his early millenium Toyota Camry to the Mansion in just over half an hour from receiving the call. Yellow tape barred the gate but it was the formality. From what he had been briefed the crime scene was well locked down and a manhunt was underway. Forensic specialists were in the process of scoping the entire Mansion for evidence; room by room, floorboard by floorboard. Every light in the place was on and with the fog it looked like some giant imagination.

Erland sighed. It was the mother of all homicides in its own right. The little boy that read mystery books on the way home from school was enticed and intrigued, and the young law student was zealous for justice. But the largest portion of him, the spartan realist, the tireless worker and consummate professional aged four years in what was left of his soul.

Officer Braden greeted him with a handshake.

"Mike."

"Bill."

Bill Braden's small smile was in the fact that Erland held a certain charisma one had to be born with and had an American face that reminded anybody and everybody of somebody they could never quite place. His blue eyes still sparkled after all these years of Detective work and contained an understanding and kindness that made him easy to talk to.

"Take me to the room, fill me in."

"The ME's in the room, forensics are taking pictures and samples. Nothing's been touched. They're also inspecting the glass in the kitchen door and the helicopter's on IR scanning the surrounding property."

"Who else is coming?"

"A second ME, four more forensic scientists and eight Patrolmen."

"Think that'll be enough?"

"I don't know." Braden shrugged as they reached the door. "You're in charge now."

"I could always use an extra hand." Erland smiled and followed Braden through the grandeur of the structure.

"Erland's here." Braden called out once at the door of the crime scene. Three men and a woman filed out and acknowledged the Detective's presence. They were Craig, Delaney, Paxton, and Hardy, respectively.

Erland took a deep breath and entered the room alone. The woman was on her left side. The puncture in her neck was on her right. There was a slight twist to the way she fell, but not enough for a wound that would've been inflicted in a fight and flight manner, with force and movement. Her body looked either gently laid or deliberately placed in the position she was in now. She must've been held. The ME would check for microbrusing. With the naked eye Erland saw none on her bare arms. There was also something to the fact that her eyes were open, blue eyes as cold and deep with beauty and danger as Lake Baykal. Either it related to an exchange of communication or a defiance of death. Perhaps both. There was no shock frozen on her face. It was as objective as a face could be, still worthy of a magazine cover even in its lifeless state.

"There was a party here earlier?"

"Yes." Braden looked in from the doorframe.

"What kind?"

"It was a black-tie reception for a Libertarian convention slash dinner."

Erland nodded.

"Guest list?"

"We're working on it."

"She's wearing Luciano Del Rey..." Erland noted, thinking aloud. "And no necklace..." With her straightened raven black hair and sultry appliqué of makeup she had a face Erland swore he'd never forget. But it was her eyes, especially, and what he imagined they'd be like if she was still alive.

"Pardon?" Braden was writing on a notepad.

"Just talking to myself, as usual."

"That's what happens when you live by yourself." Braden joked. He was flying solo, too. A divorcee, but still solo. He saw his daughter twice a month and she didn't mind that he paid mom the money the court said to. She was going through her *nobody gets me* phase and Braden was just hoping she'd take his advice on college.

"How long have I known you, Bill?"

Braden's bushy eyebrows came together. He had kind of a bulldog face, as it was.

"Ten, eleven years."

"Why don't we pull an odd couple?"

The Officer chuckled.

"Yeah, why don't we?"

Erland noticed the two-chair table only having one next to it and scanned the room.

"Interesting."

A gag rested among the fractioned pieces of the chair. Scuffmarks were on the wall.

"Have they swabbed the gag yet?"

"No."

Erland stepped into the hall.

"Whoever was in that chair was there when you arrived." He said, his voice low and contemplative. He motioned for Craig and Delaney to continue their forensic work.

"I would think so because of the kitchen door."

"But you didn't see anyone in the window?"

"Nope."

"You didn't hear the chair breaking?"

"Nope."

Erland mushed around his mouth.

"Okay, let's go to the kitchen."

Braden took the Detective down the surrealist painting-lined hall to a grand staircase. Erland eyed the crystal chandelier and Sheridan stood where Erland wouldnt've wanted to in an earthquake.

"You heard the glass and went around back?" He asked the muscular cop.

"That's right, Sir."

"Lead the way." Erland tipped his head.

As they walked, Braden paused at the hallway that stretched from the atrium to the kitchen.

"We noticed the rug was like this."

"Pictures."

"Yessir."

The kitchen was full of granite and the stainless steel appliances were restaurant grade. If any food had been prepared in the kitchen earlier in the evening, there was no sign of it.

Braden stepped aside.

The doors had flung wide open and the glass in them shattered. One of the doors was off its hinges on the ground, the other frozen in time.

Each door had a handle.

"Have you checked the handles for prints yet?"

"No."

Erland was extremely cautious where he stepped in regards to the glass and removed a pen light from his jacket to inspect the fallen door.

Along the top left corner, there was blood.

"This is second priority. When you're done with the room, have them come down here."

Erland turned to Sheridan.

"How long did it take you to get here from the time you heard the glass break?"

"Thirty-five, forty seconds."

Erland nodded.

"Whoever it was was in good shape. I probably wouldnt've gotten up."

The Officers chuckled. Erland had blonde hair gone grey hair and when he got leave he usually let the five o'clock shadow become a real beard which aged him a few more years but everyone on the force knew he was all gristle, a real boxer type. Maybe that's because he actually had been an amateur boxer in high school and college and had twenty-six bouts under his belt.

Erland was about to say something suppository

when Braden's radio chirped. All of them made their way back to the room.

Craig, a lanky forensic analyst with tortoise shell glasses met them at the door.

"The deceased has no fingerprints."

Erland swallowed and eyed the two Patrolmen. Braden's radio chirped and he excused himself by a few feet.

"When do you think she died?"

"Last three or four hours, I'd say." Craig said, checking his own watch as he did so.

"And the party was over..." Erland looked to the taller Sheridan.

"11:00, I believe."

Braden came in.

"Yes, 11:00."

"I see."

"Sparky's here." Braden added and walked down the hall.

"I'll be back in a minute." Erland smiled to Craig and the other forensic techs. "Or two."

The Detective and the two Patrolmen made their way down to the front door.

"Sheridan, you still with Thom?"

"Yessir."

"I thought you were being transferred?"

"Not effective until February, Sir."

"Ah...know what you're going to do with the boost in salary?"

Sheridan smirked.

"I've got my eye on a new truck."

"An admirable goal." Erland said warmly.

"I'd blow it on a vacation somewhere." Braden chimed in as they left the Mansion "Some once in a lifetime kind of thing."

"I've already seen the world." Sheridan nearly

mumbled. "It ain't that great."

"You were a Marine..." Braden interjected and Erland distanced himself as they began to discuss Sheridan's views of other cultures. The K9 Officer in charge of Sparky was named Veracruz.

"Hello." Erland smiled. "Hello Sparky."

"Detective." Veracruz nodded. She was older than she looked and was mostly Mexican amongst a few other things. Her eyes were like shiny green olives and her smile, when she let it out, was bright and contagious. Several months ago there had been a ships passing in the night experience between them that had ended in some kind of gridlock.

"You..." Erland said and the Officers flanked him. "Need to follow us."

The four of them worked around the side of the Mansion. The fog had settled in and the air was damp and chilly. Sparky's tag dingled and dangled and his droopy bloodhound features looked wise in the dimness.

The rolling cackle and buzz of the chopper could be heard overhead and pulled from one side of the property to the other.

"There's some broken glass where the blood is." Erland finally said as they approached the patio. "Be careful."

Veracruz nodded. Then, in a sweet, high-pitched voice, she asked Sparky if he was ready.

"Over there." Erland pointed and stopped walking. Braden provided light, as did Sheridan.

"Go Sparky." Veracruz urged and let out some leash.

The bloodhound bent his head and sniffed and sniffed and turned quickly.

"He's got something." Veracruz called out, now in a quick walk, behind the specialist.

"Come on." Erland motioned. Beams of light bounced across the grass as the Officers followed. Braden fell in behind with Erland and Sheridan in step with Veracruz.

"Not too close." She said. Erland avoided contemplating the statement on a deeper, more personal level and they reached the brick and wrought iron fence, seemingly straight, as it were, from some English castle. To get to the fence took exactly seventeen seconds of fast walking. Sparky had a wailing and at the same time breathless bark and let the Officers know that he wanted *through* the fence. There was blood on it, no denying the suspect was there.

"We'll go around." Veracruz said.

"No." Erland began to climb; a matter of two or three movements to be up and over. "We'll carry him. There's no time."

Sheridan was quick to climb the fence in an easy hopping manner but Veracruz and the Detective made an interesting team as they grunted and groaned the slobbering barking specialist over the fence.

Braden's radio chirped. He was not climbing the fence-maybe he would've tried a few years ago, but since the divorce his after shift ice-cream intake had nearly tripled.

"News crew is here."

"I'll talk to 'em." Erland said from behind the dog's head. "Just not now." Sparky went from Veracruz' arms to his. "Make sure they stay well beyond the perimeter."

"You got it."

Braden clomped off.

"Sparky's as heavy as you are." Veracruz said too quietly for Sheridan to hear. Erland couldn't catch her face in the light.

"Okay buddy, down you go."

Sparky barked twice before Veracruz made it over and took the leash from Erland. All three followed the dog with flashlights of various sizes and strengths. The terrain pulled through some random groupings of evergreens and stopped, almost abruptly, on the crown of a hill Veracruz had no time to survey because Sparky continued on with his nose buried in the turf.

Erland noticed the lights of the highway and clenched his teeth. He paused to think for a moment before following Veracruz into the green puzzle that sat between the crown of the hill and the highway. Hopefully there was a corner piece somewhere in between. His grandfather always told him to get the corner pieces first, then to fill out the border and work outside in. He was a small town Sheriff and had been Erland's first teacher, many years ago.

Sparky barked and Sheridan whistled. Erland rushed down the hill. Sheridan's light was bouncing hurriedly between two spots and Veracruz continued on toward the highway and disappeared amongst limbs and fog.

"What is it?"

"Bloody shard of glass and a zip tie, which looks to be cut by the glass."

"Good work. Call for the next available forensic technician." Erland tapped the cop on the shoulder and pushed through the foliage.

He found Veracruz calming Sparky by the vaulted earth of the highway's retaining wall.

"Up and over?" He called out.

"The suspect, yes. Sparky, no."

The dog barked.

Erland took two steps and gracefully crested the retainer wall, standing tall. Traffic was a slow formality entombed in the soft and stilling tunnel of weather.

"God knows where he went."

"Do you know it's a he?" Veracruz asked, giving Sparky a treat.

"No." Erland sighed. "Not yet."

"Can you..." Veracruz offered, then withdrew.

Erland hopped from the wall and ruffled the back of Sparky's head a few times before resting his hands on his hips. Yes, they had DNA. Yes, they'd find the suspect. But the race just went from a sprint to a marathon and the wear and tear of it all was shifting gears between them.

"Well," Erland sucked in a lungful of cool air. "Time to go talk to the camera."

Veracruz smiled something in the corner of her mouth and walked back towards the roots and limbs poking through the fog.

THREE

The BMW took a right and left the highway.

"Where are you going?" The man asked.

"Home." The driver said. The man shook his head.

"No, I couldn't burden you."

"I want to help." She said with subtle kindness. "I really do." Then she looked to the man, in his despondency, gazing out the window. "Don't you want me to?"

"No more than you want to."

It didn't mean much.

"My name is Tanya."

It was a good place to start, although, she didn't know his name and he didn't either.

She looked to him expectantly.

"I thought it might help you remember. You must've said your name a thousand times...or seen it written. Heard it."

"Yeah..." The man stared as the trees gave way to the artificial lights of buildings.

"Are you thirsty?" She asked, as if the thought just flew into her head. They came to a red light. She answered her own question by turning and reaching in the back seat. The scrunch and smootch of the leather seat made the man turn. He saw her shirt was low cut and with the odd glare of street lamps he saw a delicate and simple gold necklace dancing as she moved.

Immediately, he remembered the woman, draped over him, key in hand. He remembered her dress, her bust line, the curve of her neck, her faintest hint of a chin cleft and her beautiful face. And the necklace she wore. Brilliant gold, thin and simple...

"Here you go, drink up."

The man blinked it away and took the bottle. No, it wasn't the same necklace, but it was the same idea. But when he saw her dead on the floor, she wasn't wearing a necklace. It was so strange how the image of the woman finding the water triggered a memory so short but so bold and vivid, yet in a way it conflicted with his strongest memory of her...on the ground in her own blood, still and motionless.

It was as disturbing as it was comforting. At least he had locked onto something of the near past that moved, that had color and shape. But still, whoever killed her wanted that key, the key he now had; and for whatever reason, they must've taken her necklace.

The more time went on the more bits and pieces would fall into place. Bigger links and strands would connect themselves at the speed of light.

He twisted the top and took a sip.

"I remembered something."

The woman's hair flipped as her head turned.

"What?"

"Nothing, just a woman."

"Your wife? Girlfriend?"

"No."

"Someone you can talk to who would help you remember?"

The man took a swig.

"No."

"Where was she?"

"I know things will come back, bit by bit. It was

your necklace, actually. She had one similar. Small, gold."

Tanya tapped her chest.

"Oh."

The man pulled at the vanity mirror and studied himself. Brown hair, brown eyes, stubble, wide nostrils, and a generally well-proportioned face that looked as foreign to him as Chinese writing.

Writing? What about the key and the paper? Maybe there was writing on one of them. Or both.

The man's hand was quick in his pocket to check if it was still there.

Of course it was, where would it go?

The man flipped up the vanity mirror and finished the water.

"What do I look like?" He asked.

"Pardon?" The car turned left across an intersection.

"What do I look like? Like a job, or something..."

Tanya shrugged.

"You could be anything."

The man jerked his head back and slacked into his seat.

"Thanks."

Rows of fast food establishments and their well-lit signs glared against the passenger window.

"What about you?" He asked. "What do you do?"

"I'm a lobbyist." She said.

"Oh, what party?"

"Libertarian."

The man's head took a memory like a bullet. The Mansion was host to a reception for a Libertarian party convention followed by a dinner with keynote speakers, fifteen hundred dollars a plate, limited invitation to the reception at the Mansion following...

"Did you go to the party?"

"The party?"

"I mean..." The man rubbed his head. How it hurt. His mouth wanted to move and his mind wanted to go and get it all out before it was gone. "There was a convention today, right?"

"Yes." She said with some brightness. "Are you a member?"

"Just, just..." A hand went up. "There was a convention...downtown, at the Arena, then a dinner at the Metropolitan Grand, then a private reception at Fircrest Mansion."

Tanya nodded then it hit her as it had hit the man how much he had strung together, how much detail was there.

Tanya focused on the road.

"You...you were there?"

"Yeah...all three." The man stared out the window. "I'm a journalist." He flipped the mirror down and disgustedly flipped it up again just to see what a reporter looked like. "I'm a lousy journalist."

"Hey." Tanya smiled. "We make a good team."

The man chuckled.

"Yeah..."

"With the way things are going, you'll have your memory back in no time."

The woman dead in the room. The key in his pocket. Why wasn't that comforting?

"Yeah..."

The man turned to her. She was mid-thirties, mildly attractive, somewhat athletic looking but cute enough. She seemed to straddle the line between several types of women without belonging to any of their groups. He guessed her to be intelligent, but not in a self-centered way. Her most resounding sensibility was hope, oddly enough, and perhaps that was his twisted perception in the moment but she seemed to be full of a hope that made her dark eyes starry when she spoke. He could see her, in full perky, waving little American flags in the audience of a great speech, or afterward, handing out flyers with a smile. She was everywhere, everywhere he was. It was that time of year, and he had seen her a lot, reporting on the primaries as he was. She was a common sight, the shell of her-but *she* had stopped the car. Why? In all of her polish and overachieving salesmanship, all of her tireless volunteer work and justified do-good service, why would she stop? She was best at brushing people off and staying on the go; avoiding one on one eye contact and close proximity. She was consumed with crowds and rallies and the frenzy of human emotion and volume. Why did she choose the stillness of the night and the intimacy of the BMW when she could've zipped on by?

Fear tickled his heart with a switchblade's edge. Was she in on it, whatever grand conspiracy he was sinking to the murky bottoms of? Or was he just jumping to false ends on the roller coaster of assumption?

Maybe she wasn't like everyone else. Maybe she was just Tanya and Tanya just wanted to help.

Boy how his head hurt.

"Why are you doing this?" The man asked.

Tanya pulled the car to the shoulder.

Her eyes met his. They blinked at each other a few times and then she pointed behind him.

"There's a gas station and mini-mart back there, next to it's a laundry mat, a Teriyaki place and a nail salon. Across the street there's a local branch bank, a fabric store and an old record shop where you can still get 38's for some reason. Up this street a half a mile's my place. It's quiet and suburban. I'm not married, I don't have a boyfriend, and I don't have any weird ideas. If *you* have any weird ideas just know I do Kickboxing twice a week and I'll have no problem using you for a heavy bag. I like to think I'm a Good Samaritan and that's all there is to it. I think if you do good things to people, whether they're good *or* bad, it will come back to you. Who knows when, but they do. I could let you out here, or you could come to my place and rest for a little bit longer till more comes back to you."

There was eye contact and silence between them.

"Aren't you afraid?"

"No." She said with a firm softness. "No I'm not."

"You don't know who I am." The man looked at the sleepy businesses around him. "*I* don't know who I am."

"I'm not afraid."

The man sighed.

"You sure it won't be a burden?"

She shook her head.

The man settled back in the seat as the BMW motored toward the clutches of the quiet neighborhoods of Wayilow.

Hands cozy in his pockets, Erland marched along the outside of the fence to the general staging area. The private access road that curved in front of the property was chock full of department vehicles of all shapes and sizes and in the shadows of the mist it became a strange carnival of light and sound.

A red and blue news van was at the very end of the line and three people were leaning on the vehicle, a woman and two men. The woman was familiar, she was

Jessica Birchall, a local TV news reporter. She was
always a bit glamorous for Erland's taste but she wasn't
just another average face trying to look pretty. She had
been on the grind for three years and the facts were
always her goal. The facts and trying to look good. She
had more colored overcoats than an outlet mall and
usually wore a tremendous amount of makeup. Today's
was an appropriate ruby red. It was a fine contrast to
her exclusively brunette hair that smelled of vanilla.

  One of the cameramen gave her a heads up.

  "Detective Erland?"

  He nodded. They shook hands.

  "Didn't recognize me without my tailored suit?"

  "Very incognito." She smiled at his obvious
sarcasm and her notepad was out. "Would you like to
make a statement to the camera?"

  "Have you already shot?"

  "No."

  "I'll tell you what I can and then we'll do it on
camera if the situation permits."

  "See Todd." She called over her shoulder.
"Good things come to those who wait." And then to
Erland as her eyes grew bigger for a second. "It's
freezing out here."

  "A woman was found dead in the east wing of
Fircrest Mansion, we believe it to be murder. The cause
of death was a single stab wound to the neck and she
was dead sometime between eight or nine PM to twelve
AM, and discovered at two thirty-four. We also believe
her to have been in attendance to the party that was held
here earlier. We are searching for a possible witness
slash suspect at the moment but we cannot release a
description of the suspect slash witness or any
information about the deceased."

  Birchall scribbled and scribbled.

  "Can you give us any details about the search

for your suspect?"

The Detective rubbed his chin.

"It's difficult to say, given the weather and the time of night, but we have complete faith that we will find the witness slash suspect due to the fact that we believe he or she sustained an injury to the upper body during the course of his or her leaving the property."

Birchall nodded in big slow movements as she wrote and a few things clicked in her mind.

"So the body was discovered at two thirty-four?"

"Yes."

"When did police first arrive at the scene?"

"Two thirty-one."

"Did..." Birchall begun and then frowned. "So they saw someone but can't describe them?"

"One of the Officers heard the sound of broken glass in the back of the property and rushed to investigate but could not get eyes on the suspect due the circumstances, such as the size of the property and the time of night, etcetera, but there is *conclusive* evidence to place at least one person at the scene of the crime when the officers arrived.

"At least one? Does the evidence support *more* than one?" Birchall's eyebrows jumped and her hand moved faster.

"As you might imagine, there's far too much evidence to go through to give you a detailed picture. We'll have another report for you, hopefully before the eleven o'clock news."

"Eleven?" Birchall flipped a page. "Howabout five?"

"I can't rush science. Or helicopters."

She smiled.

Officer Thom clomped up to Erland.

"Detective."

"Thank you Ms. Birchall. I won't be able to go on camera now..."

"Thank you Detective..." The reporter finished writing and began making preparations with her crew as another news van pulled up and Erland disappeared from view.

"We found the murder weapon." Thom said as they passed through the gate.

"Where?"

"In a garbage can in the bathroom next to the sitting room where the woman was killed. First room on the left, facing the hallway."

Erland digested the information.

"What was it?"

"It was a spike about the size of a number two pencil. Paxton said it was made of carbon fiber."

Erland chewed on his lip. A woman with no fingerprints stabbed in the carotid artery with something untraceable in a metal detector, perfectly concealable in a black tie event and ideal for assassination.

What was going on?

"Prints?"

"No, they're suspecting the use of latex gloves, but they could be nitrile."

"Keep your eyes out..." Erland was about to say, then, "Nevermind. I'm sure we'll find them...in a potted plant or something."

"Pardon?"

"Nothing, just talking to myself about where the gloves were. I'm sure they have latent partials if not the whole thing. It takes a heck of a grip to stab someone..."

"Oh," Thom chuckled and showed small dimples as they reached the door. "I hear you do that a lot."

"Talk to myself? Stage Two Batcheloritus. Curable, but still chronic."

Braden came to the door.

"Oh there you are. The Captain wants you to know he's been in contact with Washington D.C."

A wormy feeling began to bore its way into Erland's stomach.

"And?"

"And some people will be here as soon as possible."

Erland and Thom both checked their watches. It was almost four. Thom's was a digital job and Erland's an old Seiko.

"They don't mess around, do they?" Erland's hands found his jacket pockets and he spun around slowly. "Alright, let the Patrolmen go except you three that got here first. Have the ME take the body to the morgue and call off the helicopter. Is the sketch done yet?"

"Almost. What about VC and Sparky?"

"They can stay. That should clean it up."

"Right." Braden said, and headed for the gate, talking into his radio.

"Keep it up." The Detective nodded to Thom and she went inside. "Washington D.C., huh?" Erland let his eyes roll around the misty scene. "I hope they like puzzles."

FOUR

Tanya's home was a small rambler from the eighties and reminded the man a lot of his own home, or rather, the kind of home he would have wanted if he could remember where it was. It *felt* like a home, like the one who owned it let everything outside of it go the moment she shut the door and kicked off her shoes. It was in this sense of privacy and security, this separation of home and work that the man received not only a sense of cool stillness but an alarmingly awkward gift of trust.

He wasn't a murderer, was he? No, of course not! But she didn't know, why would she even consider...jeopardizing such a rare and beautiful thing to the unknown?

"There's a bathroom down the hall..." She said, slipping off her purse on the dining room table and taking off her jacket too. She had a healthy figure and was just over five foot five.

The man stood blankly by the door. There was an open kitchen, a dining room table with four chairs and next to him a small sectional and a TV. The hallways pulling away from this living space to the left and right were in darkness and mystery.

He could steal her purse, he could steal her car. He could go through her cupboards and eat all of her cereal. He could do anything he wanted and the possibilities ran through his head like voices through an underground cable. So he stood in the entranceway, knowing that he would be unable to further the journey until he made a conscious step in the only direction that would lead him to salvation. He could ask her why, again, or he could just say thank you and sit down and cool off, and let all of those accusations and assumptions leave, and be, not what he wasn't or who he thought he had been, but who he wanted to be right now.

Right now.

"Thank you again." The man said, letting himself all but collapse in the dining room chair that took the head of the table.

"You're..." Tanya's smile faded as she saw his right shoulder. "Bleeding."

"Yeah..."

She got a rag from the kitchen and ran it under cold water.

The man in the chair winced as she dabbed the stickiness away from the wound.

"You must've been in a car accident or something." Tanya surmised as she went to the bathroom to get a gauze pad and some tape. The lights flashed on in the hall. The man could see the soft carpet and an end table with a vase of intentionally fresh flowers on it and a photo of her and a youthful man with graduation attire. The door to the bedroom was half open.

The lights went out again and she came forward, hands full.

"I'll get the news on, maybe they'll say what happened."

"No." The man waved his hands painfully. "It's better for me to think when it's quiet."

Tanya began working. The man was wearing a

black cotton jacket and she removed it. His shirt was of the white collared variety and formally acceptable but nothing fancy. She unbuttoned it enough to get access to his shoulder, about halfway.

"Besides," The man smirked distantly, his head pounding. "It gives me a good chance to talk to you about politics."

"Libertarianism isn't politics." Tanya applied a bit of pressure to make sure there was no more bleeding. "It's a way of life."

"Can it really work, I mean, for everybody?"

"Sure it can." She placed a cotton ball on top of a bottle of hydrogen peroxide and tipped it over, then dabbed the area gently.

"How does it work for you?"

She didn't say and he looked up at her. Her face held a wry satisfaction.

"Now." She said. "Now is what it's all about to me."

"How so?" The man watched her deftly work with the gauze, scissors, and medical tape.

"Say we're at a ball game. Nice day, thousands of people, and there's an earthquake. A big one, like in those disaster movies from the seventies. How many people's number one thought in that moment is to care for someone else?"

The man shrugged.

"Not many."

"Right. Because all of their life, they're living in pursuit of their own pleasure. Taking, seeking to take. So when adversity or even tragedy comes, they'll trample each other down to make it out alive. Well, think of economics like that." She rubbed the tape flat and smiled. "Everybody's ready to run over each other to get out of something bad. In my mind, their discontent in their freedom leads them to a possessive capitalistic and epicurean, nearly colonial lifestyle. If they were truly free, they wouldn't seek to take so desperately."

The man frowned not in disagreement but in contemplation.

"Go on."

"With complete freedom, complete...liberation, comes an irreplaceable satisfaction. This nation was founded on just that. The joy of liberation."

"It came through war, though."

"Yes, but it became the land of the free, and that wasn't good enough. It really bugs me that a child can grow up here with access to the best of everything and abuse it so easily...and complain and expect and demand so much when they were born with a right to choose to be anything they wanted and they chose to be ungrateful."

Tanya was right. But the man remembered a lot of bellyaching at the convention.

"But the party..."

"Yes, we do pick and choose what we like of Republicans and Democrats as a party and the whole convention talked about how this isn't the way we want it or we're not quite there yet in such and such agenda, but we're as close to the middle as I can think of. We represent the most liberty."

The man swallowed. Tanya sat down across from him.

"So now, libertarianism is about now, what does that mean?"

"It means because I'm so happy I'm free I can concern myself with the needs of others."

The man chuckled and shook his head.

"You're not a libertarian. You're a saint."

Then he looked to his shoulder. It was better than hospital work, these days, with the health care system in a greedy shambles.

"I used to be a nurse." She smiled warmly and took her tools back to the bathroom. The light came on for a brief second and he saw the picture again. She must've seen the picture dozens of times a day, he thought, and if she sat where he sat when she ate dinner then she could see it the whole time.

Tanya came back and stood close.

"It's going to be okay." She said with a confidence all her own. "Whatever happened, whatever you can't remember."

The man bunched his hands.

"What if it's not?" He looked up at her and her soul was in her dark eyes. "What if it's not okay and I did something awful?"

"Did you?"

"I don't know." The man crashed his head into his hands. "I just can't remember."

Tanya dropped to one knee and put her hand on the back of the chair.

"Don't you think you would know if you did? Wouldn't your conscience tell you?"

Another bullet of memory hit the man at full speed. Slowly he turned to her.

Conscience? No, Constance...a name. Constant? CONSTANT.

Her eyes jumped around his face.

"What did I say?"

"Conscience, but that wasn't it." Her eyes still drifted around his face, looking for answers. "Look, I can remember things but they're not helping."

"What would help?"

The man's face softened from the frustrations of amnesia.

"Sometimes I wonder if this is a dream."

"A bad dream?"

"No...you don't make it so bad." Tanya smiled. "If I could just remember my name and where I live, I could be out of your hair."

"You're not in my hair."

"But it must be three in the morning."

"It's half-past four, but who's counting?" Tanya corrected, moving to the kitchen and getting two glasses of water from the tap.

The man watched her painfully. He did not want to say what bubbled up inside of him but it was a logical explanation and he had to.

"Are you helping me because of him?"

Her head spun around.

"Who?"

"The picture at the end of the hall. The college kid."

Tanya's face lost some color and the glass of water she held overflowed and ran across her wrist. She said nothing and busied herself with pouring water out of the glass and drying both the outside of the glass and her shirtsleeve.

She served the waters and sat down and hugged herself.

"I'm sorry." The man offered, but it was little more than that. He truly wanted to know. He had as many questions about her as he did himself.

"No, I deserve it." She took some water. "He was my fiancée. It was nearly five years ago, now. I met him through the University's Youth Congress program. I had just finished pre-med and was seeking a position at Corazon but I was also feeling the call to politics...to changing the world. We hit it off right away. I was a few years older than him but that didn't matter, we were kindred spirits." Tanya paused and a thin smile curled the edges of her mouth but it faded as she continued. "To make a long story short he got into...addictions and I couldn't see the signs. I was blinding myself, afraid if I reached out to help him I would be the one getting hurt. He didn't make it. He took his own life in a backhanded way, driving drunk...he didn't have the hope that I had, he was too overwhelmed with life and debts and not strong enough to go through it on his own. Everyone at University had debts...I did too, but he didn't know how to handle it...I didn't give him enough of myself for him to know he wasn't alone. I blame myself for it. If I would've known what I know now he'd still be here. I keep his picture to remind me, to motivate me, I guess, so his life won't have been in vain."

The man pushed the knot in his throat down with some tap water. It had a bitter, metallic aftertaste to it.

The very action of tipping the glass back ignited some picture of last night. He looked at the glass, the beads of liquid.

Ice?

Vodka on ice.

His head hurt again. It was the reason for his passing out on the couch. The open bar. How many had he thrown back? Seven, eight? Probably skipping dinner after the long day to boot...

His stomach gurgled.

The man looked up and Tanya was staring at him through watery eyes.

"No you know. I don't see how it changes anything."

"It doesn't. You're still a diamond in a field of mud."

Tanya smirked.

"And what about you?"

"I don't know what I am."

"What do you want to be?"

"It's not that easy."

"Do you know how many people are aching for a fresh start? To forget everything that was and be something completely brand new and totally different from what they were?"

The man sighed. She was impossible to argue with. From the moment he saw her on the side of the road he couldn't say no. And in her home and in her presence he felt no judgment, no peril, no shame. What had been had been, she was right, but the key was in his pocket and the vow had been made in his heart. Now, the truth was survival, and survival was the truth.

The man stood with great heaviness and walked to her.

"I'm grateful for all you've done." Her eyes blinked and blinked as his frame blotted out the overhead light and shadowed her face. He placed his right hand on the top of her head. "I won't forget you."

The man took his jacket and headed for the door.

"Where are you going?" She called out in the stillness.

But her answer was the sound of the front door softly clicking shut.

Brock had his eyes on a few different sets of TV's in a small, dark room. A few computer screens, too. Information and images streaked and bleeped through his brain at lightning speed. His hands were quick on a keyboard and paused only to tip his baseball cap backwards a fraction of an inch.

"Courtland."

Heavy booted footsteps could be heard from another room. Courtland was a stocky, middle-aged man of no determined nationality, which made him distinctly American. Brock was American too. So was

Kirke and Pitts in the next room. Kirke was kind of tan and Pitts was black and they were as American and homogenous in the urban environment as gray buildings and pavement.

"They're going to run the story on the five AM news."

"Which channel?"

"Two."

"They the only one?"

"So far."

"Still local?"

"Still local."

"Good." Courtland hitched up his pants, something he did a lot, and with the kind of money he made he might've been able to get pants that fit.

"Notify Jupiter."

Brock nodded and reached for the headphone/microphone set that was lying dormant in his lap.

"Let's hope we did a good enough job..." Courtland mumbled as he rubbed his blunt nose with calloused fingertips. Brock made a gesture of agreement although he didn't understand Courtland's hint of doubt. Team Io hadn't made any mistakes as of yet. If they had, they'd all be dead.

FIVE

Delaney was just finishing up the sketches when Erland came in.

"Quickly as possible."

"Just done." The grey haired man affirmed to the grey blonde Detective.

"We need to get her to the morgue."

The ME was right behind Erland with his assistant. The gurney was a tight fit in the hall. Despite Fircrest being a palace certain halls were still narrow.

"There'll be some...Feds coming and they're going to be asking a lot of questions, just so you know." The analysts in the room made eye contact with Erland and nodded. They all remembered the Morrison case. "I'll be in the foyer awaiting their arrival."

Erland moseyed down to the dramatic entrance space of Fircrest Mansion, replete with lavish displays of wealth, including creamy white marble pillars which gave it a Greek overtone and the stunning artistry involved in the hand laid hardwood floor of ballroom quality, which created a design of Penrose Steps made only legible from the top of the staircase, due to the sweeping size of it. The corner of the foyer, also, was appropriately armed with a shiny black Steinway Grand Piano that cost more than Erland's car at current market value and could no doubt play itself.

He heard the padding of dog feet and the jingle

of a collar.

Veracruz smiled.

"Got something you should see."

He followed Veracruz and Sparky up the long and winding staircase. She was perhaps conscious of the fact that Erland was choosing to look at his own feet on the way up instead of what was apparently eye level. She walked slowly enough to send the message and Erland was far from stupid. Sparky tugged on his leash and gave a breathless choking, though pleasantly eager sound and his stubby feet took him up the heights.

The room was all the way on the left wing towards the rear of the Mansion. It was a small anteroom to a much larger billiard room and it had a door to the billiard room, the hall, and a rear property-facing deck, perfect for smoking or having a semi-private conversation while watching the occasional polo match, or whatever spectacle the grand flatness of the rear grounds had to offer.

"Sparky sniffed the deceased and came here like a rocket."

She reached into a pouch on her utility belt and pulled out a key ring in a plastic evidence bag.

Erland's eyes tightened for a split second.

"Did Craig look at this?"

"Yes, he bagged it."

"Why didn't he tell me?"

"I said I would take care of it."

"Sarina, you know how it works."

"It's in the log."

"Sarina..."

Her hand went to his arm.

"I wanted to talk to you, Mike."

"There's nothing to talk about..."

"That's not true."

"Sarina..." He looked her squarely in the eyes.

They were emotional, soulful eyes. "I called you after what happened and got the message you weren't interested."

Veracruz shrugged as if trying to remember who that person was.

"I wasn't ready."

Erland's eyebrows jumped.

"And you're ready now? Is *now* a good time?"

Sparky sat on the floor and let his eyes meander around the room.

"I want to see you again."

Erland's lips came together and he reached out and held her arms near the elbow.

"Sarina..." He spoke slowly. "We can't do this now. This is why I had such a hard time with what happened. I can't let it pull at me when I'm working. This job hard enough as it is."

Erland bent down and ran his knuckles across Sparky's head. The bloodhound seemed pleasantly indifferent.

"I know..."

"When's your next day off?"

"Sunday." She said with hope.

Erland rolled his eyes around the room and she smiled in the corner of her mouth, as she did.

"I'll let you know when I can talk." He looked up and continued rubbing Sparky's head. Then he stood. "Since that night I never knew how you felt. Now I know." He put his hands in his pockets. "I *do* want to get to know you, Sarina, but I think we started off the wrong way. I'm not twenty-one."

"No." She nodded and curled her hair behind her ear. "I understand."

"I'm too old for a one night stand."

Her green eyes were full of something that hovered between compassion and longing.

"I'm not twenty-one either."

Erland gazed wearily upon her face and it was a mirror of sorts. Sparky went to lie down and began sniffing.

"Back to the evidence."

"It's just a key ring." Veracruz said, blankly. "Generic looking."

"It had her scent on it, huh?" Erland studied it. He held it up to the light and saw something minute, but obvious.

"It's scratched up."

"Really?"

"Yes." Erland turned it in the light to examine the pattern of the mark. "Not from age, either. Like...maybe a key was removed in a hurry or..."

"Or what?"

Sparky barked and followed it with a long, low moan and looked around.

Erland's eyes danced around Veracruz' face as he thought.

"What's wrong, Mike?"

"I don't know, have him smell the body again."

"Where is it?"

Erland rushed out the door.

"Come on!"

They caught up with the gurney in the main foyer. It was a matter of minutes from entering the ME's vehicle.

"It wasn't easy getting her down that many stairs." The lanky Craig joked as Erland came rushing up.

"Hold on."

Veracruz brought Sparky to the gurney and gave him two commands. Sparky sniffed and sniffed and then pulled away and went back up the stairs.

"Okay, go, quick." Erland ordered and scuffed

up the steps. Veracruz was in a quick shuffle and disappeared the opposite way they had come.

"Hurry up!" Veracruz called as she followed the dog down the winding mazes of opulence.

"Must be hard on the little guy, all of the scents in here..." Erland mused as he attempted to catch up.

He found the dog some three minutes later clawing at a door that was shut.

"This is it." Veracruz said.

"Call Braden."

Veracruz did. Sparky wouldn't stop sticking his nose the crook of the door, as if smelling as intensely as he was would open it.

"What's behind door number two?" Veracruz joked and tried the knob. It was locked.

"Call any available forensic technician that isn't involved in the kitchen door and is still on site."

Veracruz pulled Sparky back and talked in her radio.

Erland gave the door a firm shoulder and it snapped open.

Erland squinted and slowly entered the mess of a bedroom. A four-poster bed was violated of its comforter and its sheets and mattresses were torn with slashes. A chest of drawers had been spilled sideways and a painting that had hung above it was impaled on an open drawer. Decorative pieces were splayed right and left and navigation of the mess looked near impossible without injury of some kind.

Sparky shot past and Veracruz too.

"Sparky..."

Erland caught her hand and let the leash free.

"Let him go."

The dog ambled through the wreckage and went under the bed. A few seconds later he barked and uttered his jowly noises.

Erland carefully tiptoed through the destruction to the edge of the bed and saw a cream leather clutch on the far side.

"He's a good trooper, that Sparky."

Veracruz got on all fours to make a swipe under the bed for the leash.

"Let's get forensics in here, quick."

"That won't be necessary." A thin male voice called out. Erland turned to see a slick haired man in a blue suit. His skin was unusually tan for early November.

"Who are you?"

"My name is Tallifer. I'm from Homeland Security." His hand made a deft movement for a badge that shined in the light as if he cleaned it every time he had a smoke break. "I'm here to lock down the crime scene."

"It's already locked down."

"No, you misunderstand me, Mr..."

"Michael Erland, Detective First Grade, Crescent Police Department."

The handshake between them was uneasy and tense.

"You've issued a statement to the local news, I gather?"

"Yes."

"Nothing, not one letter of further information on the events that occurred here are to be released without Homeland's authority."

Erland pushed his lips out thoughtfully and nodded.

"Anything else?"

"Homeland is taking control of this case."

Erland blinked a few times.

"Let's talk about this outside."

"Fair enough." Tallifer slinked through the door.

Veracruz went to follow and Erland caught her arm and whispered so close she could feel his breath.

"Get someone to go over this as quickly and quietly as possible."

Veracruz understood and Erland beat her out the door.

"You alone?" Erland asked Tallifer, blocking Veracruz' exit from the agent's vision.

"Nope. My partner is in the foyer, probably drooling over that piano. Is it evidence too?"

"Follow me," Erland said. "We'll talk down there."

Erland was going to be brusque but he saw right away it was heading nowhere. Tallifer was on his own time and playing on his own field. If Erland wanted to join up he'd have to get the list of rules first.

Once they were at the staircase to the foyer Tallifer made a motion for his partner to come up so Erland did not succeed in conducting the meeting away from the area of traffic.

"This is Ratner."

The man was thin and gray haired, balding but not quite there yet, and wore wire rimmed glasses that he might've thought made him look more intelligent when in actuality they added to a natural severity that didn't need amplified. He looked like a Ratner, whatever that meant.

"He's very detail oriented."

"Congratulations..." Erland's head gave a stiff jerk toward him and he focused on the small and very tanned agent. "The call was suspicious activity from..."

Tallifer held out a hand.

"We know everything you know, Detective. We actually know a whole lot more, that's why we're here. To make an assessment of just how much information has been realized and therefore, leaked."

"Leaked?" Erland couldn't stop from scrunching up his face.

"Don't play dumb, Detective. You knew we were on our way. You knew she had no fingerprints. This isn't your average jealous husband homicide, okay?"

Erland took in some oxygen to prevent himself from taking that last crack personally, trying to demean his everyday job to say how important this one was, to place him somewhere far below Tallifer and his crew on the food chain.

"I didn't *leak* anything."

"No, you have done everything according to your standard operating procedures, but like I said, not one speck or spot of further information is coming out of this thing."

Tallifer turned to go back to the wrecked bedroom.

"For how long?" Erland queried him in a hope to stop him.

"Forever." Tallifer said over his shoulder as he walked. Erland took a step forward to follow and Ratner blocked him.

"Where's the body?"

"At the morgue."

Ratner's yellowing teeth showed as he saved himself from cursing.

"Tallifer!" He shouted. The agent turned. "She's at the morgue."

Tallifer squinted and came back with a half-twisted and bent over gesture as if to say he wasn't hearing what he was hearing.

"When?"

"When did I send the body or when did the body arrive at the morgue?"

"When did you send the body?"

Erland didn't like Tallifer's tone but wasn't afraid of him. His bark or his bite.

"Before I knew you were coming here."

Was that true? Not entirely. The deceased was on her way to the morgue, the Agents must've just missed her in the confusion of the entrance and the Detective wanted to know what it was all about and would've had a shot if the news of their coming wasn't delayed.

Tallifer made himself a little taller, still not to Erland's nose, and Erland was a normal size of just topping six feet.

"You'd better be right about that."

Ratner held a hand between them to quell his partner's increasing frustration, the lid for which had never been on too tight to begin with.

"Have they begun the autopsy yet?" Ratner asked.

"No, not without me there."

Ratner gave the tensest smile Erland had seen in years.

Hardy came up the stairs. She was a mildly overweight forensic specialist and seemed to work more hours than anybody else on the force.

She excused herself through the tight Mexican standoff at the top of the stairs and proceeded toward the newest scene with a bag slung over her shoulder.

"After you." Erland offered.

"No, please." Ratner insisted so that Erland would be in a Homeland sandwich.

The walk to the room was both directionally confusing and verbally silent. Erland didn't know what to make of the two Agents save the fact they were serious to the point of being overwound. Obviously they were bad at hiding the gravity of the situation, the implications all of it could have and whatever niceties

Tallifer had decided to come with were already out the
window.

"It was a purse." Erland said at the door. "A
clutch."

Tallifer gave him a flat glare and procured a set
of plastic gloves from Hardy's open bag on the floor.
After she had taken a few pictures he took the purse.

Erland bit his lip as the agent flipped through it.

"Yup. It's hers."

He gave it back to Hardy who accepted it
gingerly.

"What do you make of those?" Erland leaned on
the wall.

"Hmm?" Tallifer removed the gloves. "Oh, the
bed? Knife marks. There was obviously a fight in here."

"Obviously." Erland echoed.

"A knife and no blood." Tallifer's head bobbed.
"She's good.

"Was." Ratner added, as if it was necessary.

There was no small silence and Braden popped
his head in.

"..."

Erland pushed himself from the wall.

"Gentlemen, if you want to continue our
conversation down in the foyer..."

The odd trio filed down the hall and Tallifer's
phone sent an obnoxious tone into the atmosphere.

"I'll catch up."

He took out his phone and faded into an open
room, one of many in the ridiculously oversized
structure.

Ratner spoke up as they came to the staircase.

"That's some piano."

"Yeah..." Was all Erland could manage. His
mind was on the one who called Tallifer. That and what
was in the purse, and the way the Agent rifled through

it. Perhaps there was something that should've been *in* the purse and wasn't, and the man wasn't a cop. The reasons and motivations behind his actions were...different.

"I used to be a music teacher."

"Oh?" Erland smirked. "What changed?"

"Better pay. Better use of my brain."

"I see..." Erland made a funny face privately.

"Besides, jazz at the high school level is butcher's work."

They had reached the front door when Tallifer came rushing down the stairs.

"Detective."

Erland turned with an appraising glance, as if he didn't want to look but was compelled to.

"Yes."

"By the order of Homeland Security and the State Department you are hereby relieved of your duties relating to this case, effective immediately."

Erland stared with a thick, dull gaze at the man he could more than likely send skidding and sliding across the floor with one well-placed punch.

"What?"

"You will be placed on paid administrative leave and asked to return home directly from the crime scene and do not under any circumstance speak to any one of the press or any other members of the police force about this case or anything involving Fircrest Mansion lest you incur criminal charges for which there is no defense."

The thick, blockheaded gaze drifted from Tallifer to Ratner and back. There was so much to say, spit and vinegar but he felt like falling sideways on his lumpy apartment couch in apathy. If there was any fight to fight, now was not the time.

Besides, his old boxing gloves were in a storage

unit.

His nose, however, wasn't. It was as good as Sparky's and it smelled the foul spices of conspiracy, cover up, and crucifixion.

The latter, hopefully, not being his.

Erland swallowed, blinked, and wordlessly opened the door. The fog was heavier than ever and his watch said he really should've hit the sack a long time ago but in his line of work, time was something that never stopped and waited for anybody to catch up.

Erland's feet were hollow and solemn on the long paved walkway to the gate and then to his car.

The Detective took one last look at the sprawling monstrosity of opulence that was Fircrest Mansion and knew it wouldn't be the last time he saw it face to face, eye to eye.

SIX

No certain emptiness found a home in Tanya's stomach. She sat on the sectional, with what...a hope the man would come back? No, with a hope that she had done the right thing, done something good. For years now she had been living in modesty, volunteering here and there, living on what was left of her grandparent's inheritance; sowing seeds she might not ever see the fruit of.

Tanya shrugged it off. At eight o'clock she'd be putting together campaign signs for the printer. If she had to, if things got to be too tight, she could always go back to nursing. There was never a shortage of work for a nurse. Never. And it definitely was a job that helped people. Was she escaping it for some reason, because it reminded her of Robbie?

She found the remote and would let the small moving pictures lull her to sleep. One of the local channels ran a show early in the morning with shots of nature, Bible verses and baroque music. Perfect.

The TV set powered on seeing as it was an older model and a picture came to color of Jessica Birchall on a hedge-lined street at the bottom of a swollen hill pocked with jagged evergreens, standing before the up-lighted carved stone sign that read *Fircrest Mansion*. Behind her in the eerie distance stood the great luminescent block of the twenty-five thousand square foot structure.

Fircrest, that's where the reception for the black-tie dinner was. Tanya rubbed her forehead. How she would've loved to have been there. So many movers and shakers, so many open sets of ears tired of hearing the same old tripe.

What was Birchall reporting so early about it for? And since when did she cover politics? That was Nathan Albertson's job.

Tanya hit the volume a few times.

"Again, earlier tonight there was a reception for the fifteen hundred dollar a plate dinner here at Fircrest and we believe the victim to have been a guest of that party."

Victim?

"We are doing our best to acquire the guest list of that party, we don't know much information about the woman except she was murdered with a single stab wound to the neck."

Murdered?

The emptiness in Tanya's stomach spread throughout her bones. She was avoiding the inevitable.

"Police are searching for a suspect, male, perhaps female, someone who has sustained an injury to some part of his or her body, most likely a cut or gash of some kind during the course of an escape from police. It could be to the upper body or to the legs, but again, some kind of cut or gash...uh, if you have seen a person fitting this description near the Fircrest area, please call 911 or there is also the designated police tip hotline..."

Birchall checked her notes.

Tanya was stick to her stomach. Not because she had seen and helped the suspect in question, brought the man into her home and spoke to him, but because she knew he didn't kill anybody.

She knew!

But he had amnesia, right? Said he had it...she'd been lied to before, who hadn't?

He wasn't a murderer, he couldn't have been. *Could he?*

He was the man, all right. Admittedly at the party, right time of night, picked up in close proximity to the Mansion, and injury to his shoulder...but why? Why wasn't he guilty? What had he done or said to make Tanya so sure?

Nothing. He had done nothing. Guilt would've done something, said some comment, made some defense in fear-but innocence, innocence needed no defense, no explanation.

It was true. A thin thread linking her mind to her heart, but it was true.

And time would tell.

Tanya grit her teeth and locked the door. She was an optimist, an altruist, a cursed hoper. But she wasn't stupid.

Tanya dialed 911 and when the dispatcher spoke she felt her mouth go dry.

The man kicked at stones as he walked alone through the wilted suburban neighborhood to the main road. A mutt began to bark in a nearby yard and the man's head snapped to the direction of the noise. The thick condensation hung in the air almost low enough to jump up and grab and clung to every shake rooftop and bare tree branch.

The air was wet in his nose. Rain would be along soon, unless it blew over or burned off. Whatever light came from randomly placed streetlamps caught the fall reds and yellows in the spindly young trees dotted in and around the green shapes of the lots.

The man reached the main road and it was

nearly void of cars. But soon, the work crowd would be up and at the daily grind. Maybe, he thought, just maybe the amnesia was the best thing that happened to him. Because now, he had nothing but the moment, and in the short time he was with Tanya he gathered that all life before that time had somehow now been segregated and boxed up and sent somewhere to archive. He never remembered anyone really caring about him, really looking into his eyes and being so present and clear in the moment.

A possible murderer...

The man picked up the pace. She would know soon. Everyone would know. His face would be plastered on TV screens and printed in newspapers, the irony of it all! But he couldn't let them find out before he did, or else it would all be lost, whatever that woman tried to pass to him, whoever killed her would get away with it because he would be the bad guy for long enough to write the cover up. No wonder he had been bound and gagged and not killed along with her. He was the grand diversion while they regrouped, whoever they were, one man or a whole nation, he had what they wanted, what they couldn't find.

The key.

And if all of the pressure was on him he'd give it up or lose it somehow and they'd swoop right in and return to the darkness from which they came with impunity.

He couldn't pursue it just yet. Time was running short, yes, but he couldn't pursue the key before he knew his own name.

He did have an idea.

The man made his way to the mini mart attached to the gas station. He knew it had cameras. That was okay.

The doorbell gave a ring ring and the

Vietnamese attendant gave a despondent pair of eyes his way before returning his attention to a guitar magazine.

The man quickly found the newspapers. They were stacked in cubbyholes, organized by publisher.

That's what he was after, the publisher. Who on earth did he work for? If he could get to the publisher he could get to his house, if he could get to his house he could go after the key...

But the time...and his skin burned with each paper he rifled through, knowing the electric eye was watching his every move, just like the song. Time was going to be a poor diet for the next however many hours. He didn't care. He was going to run until it all caught up with him, and even then, he would run until it tripped him and smothered him.

The cover picture plastered across one of the papers looked vaguely familiar and he pulled it out. It was the Community Times, a monthly endeavor full of special interest stories usually harping on more than one emotion at a time.

The man frowned. He *had* worked for Community Times when it began printing; what was that, fourteen years ago?

It was the paper under Community Times that held the answer.

The Crescent Modern Journal, the CMJ. A largely political publication. Weekly printing with a special statewide electoral annual that made NFL draft magazines look like child's play.

His name was in there, especially with the upcoming elections, he had been run ragged covering the different angles.

His head hurt again. The paper had paid for him to be at the convention, the dinner, and the reception, and paid quite a lot. He would be expected to deliver the lion's share of material on the libertarian party.

His head...

What had gone wrong at the party? It couldn't have been *just* the vodka...

The man flipped though the paper and found the address of the main offices. It looked incredibly familiar, like it was something he had to write down for people all the time.

He put the paper back.

"How far is Crescent from here?"

"Ten mile." The attendant said without looking up.

"South?"

"North. Follow interstate. You notice skyline."

The man left.

Crescent, ten miles north. So he must be in Wayilow. Tanya lived in Wayilow.

He began walking back towards the residential area but on the other side of the street. Wayliow was the lower class and Eavesdale was the middle class. Fircrest sat between them on its high horse and acted as a silent judge between them. Crescent was the big city where they all went to work and eat and play and shop.

Ten miles, too far to walk in the time frame. The man kept his eye out in the yellowy grass yards of the ramblers and the shanty carports as he walked.

He would need wheels.

The man passed old pre-fabs and split-levels and clomped down a small hill. The houses were dice rolls of color and condition, all of them being like vegetables in the supermarket someone usually moved to find something better. But they all represented families and lives and hopes and dreams and the suppressed relinquishment thereof.

He got his wish in a rambler where periwinkle paint was blistered and splitting and vehicles of all

levels of rust and *restoration* were stashed in the yard.
It wasn't his first choice, but it was his only choice.

The bicycle was a BMX model, black and red
with cute little flames, suited for an overgrown preteen
but it worked and was light and he gave the seat an
adjustment with a stiff punch of the heel of his hand
and began riding, trying to follow the confusing
neighborhood signs after he pushed the large toy up a
hill.

Making it back to the fast food alley of
Wayilow's one street of commerce, he pedaled north,
towards the sprawling Metropolis of Crescent.

The stocky man named Courtland came from
the bathroom of the small rambler drying his hands
with a light blue towel.

"How's the shoulder?"

"She dislocated it." Kirke shook his head. "It
doesn't feet great."

"It's back in?"

Kirke had a sinister looking face to begin with
and it was twisted and unhappy in the dimly lit living
room that held nothing more than an old couch and a
card table across the dark wood floor.

"Yeah it's back in."

"You wanna drop out?"

"No."

Courtland walked across the squeaky wood
floor to the room where Brock had all of the electronics
humming.

"Good, because when Jupiter calls we have to
be ready."

Kirke grimaced and gently rolled his shoulder
around as a pitcher would.

Pitts said nothing through all of it. His eyes
were closed in some kind of meditation. He had learned

it serving overseas for the Army sometime ago.

Brock turned as Courtland occupied the doorframe.

"Two is now exclusive with the report on Fircrest. Homeland is on the scene."

"Who?"

"Ratner and Tallifer."

"Really..." Courtland stared a hole in the floor, letting his mind hold a semi-intellectual conversation with itself. Several minutes later he asked, "Jupiter?"

"Nothing yet."

Courtland made his way to the card table to examine the items lying on it yet again. A man's leather wallet, thick with business cards, credit cards and the like, also the man's keys, all of which had been thoroughly examined and found to be innocuous. There were some other small effects of the man's, like a tin of mints and some cheap pens and an even cheaper watch, but strangely no cell phone. Finally, there was a delicate woman's necklace, which was the left half of a heart in twenty-four karat gold-it could've been an angel wing too, as interpretation went but looked more like a heart.

The two bedroom apartment was exactly the way he left it; cold, distant, and inhuman. Artless and spotless, a barren void of emotion.

Erland put his keys in the dish on the kitchenette countertop. Was he like that? A cold fish already filleted under the skin? If he was, what did it matter? Life was work, work was life.

But then there was Sarina. Someone who desired to be with him. Maybe it was just the case and the timing of it all. Erland had an incision somewhere inside of him and gravity was beginning to pull him apart and separate his guts from his heart. He'd been running on one for so long the other had grown hard to the touch.

He could give it all to the case or to Sarina. There was no way to balance it out.

And now, Homeland had ripped the surfboard from under his feet before he could hit the big wave and ride the pipeline to the shore.

Erland scratched his head and ran a hand over his balding spot in the back.

The sun would be up soon. He would need some sleep. He'd probably have to talk to the Captain or one of the Lieutenants about it and there would be a mile of paper work to back it all. Not that he was touchy, it wasn't his case, it wasn't his state, but it was his job, and it was weird that two suits from somewhere else had shut him down like a malpracticing doctor or a negligent restaurateur. He'd been at it a long time and never been booted out during the most important stages of such a wide-open investigation.

Erland shuffled to his bed and threw off his shoes and khakis with some disgust, then, neatly arranged them where they belonged as if another person had invaded his body for a moment.

He would keep his notes and observations sharp in his mind and play the game.

He certainly wasn't going to forget someone committed murder. It was his own sworn duty to bring the guilty to justice.

Erland drifted into his own fog and thought of Sarina. Where was she? Had she been placed on administrative leave too? Did he really want to share a bed with her, share a life with her? Or did he really like his own little snow globe where nothing got messed up no matter how quickly the earth tipped and turned because it was all frozen solid and glued shut.

He was a loner's loner, and everyone's pal at

arm's length. He was a good Detective and he never gave himself enough time to think if that alone made him happy or not.

The Detective tried to make himself comfortable on the stiff mattress. As of now, time was all he had.

SEVEN

It had been some time since the man had ridden a bicycle but there was a saying about that. He was reminded of a time in China covering a political summit but the scene that came to his brain was a blurry thing that smelled of gasoline. From his writer's perspective there had been as many bicycles in Beijing as blades of grass. The world was an amazing place; so diverse and beautiful, yet at times so hideously ugly. Maybe *that* had been his call to journalism; to explore and expose, both the good and the bad, to tell it like it was the best he could through the color of his own lens. It was all so distant now, but it was beginning to fall into place; who he was, why he was, and what he was going to do with the moment he held in his hands.

He was going to throw his cards to the wind. No time to cry, no time to think.

Crescent was a city split in two by a river, even though the river ran along side the city and there wasn't a bridge to be found in the city. The division was in the sea of people, and the shifting current of water that ran between them. The sides were North Crescent and South. South was mostly industrial and North had all of the niceties packed neatly inside of it. As the streets became strangely more and more familiar, the man realized his paper was located in South. If Crescent was a bust, the South was the shoulders and the North was

the head. The South had come first in the city's
evolutionary rise from muck and mud and given way to
the expansion of the North, but the South never had the
money put back into it. It was loaded with the revolving
doors of small business owners and their fight to
survive and its generally bland and stony grey shell was
organically dotted with the local color of such places as
the Benchmark Motel, Manga Teriyaki, and King's
Brewery, as well as The Riverfront School of Dramatic
Art for Youth. Not every light bulb was working nor
every window fully cleaned, but the heart was there and
it showed.

The North was a clinical display of architecture,
technology, and generationally invested revenue. Every
piece of greenery had been strategically placed in its
planter box and every statue and fountain had someone
else's name on it. There was an air of repressed
aggression and entitlement in each and every street
corner as if to say that the way it was just wasn't good
enough and a new tower of offices or residences needed
to be built higher and better than the last one.

The man stopped at a group of black men
playing dice in front of a small coil and spring factory.

"Excuse me, where is the Crescent Modern
Journal?"

Three were really into it, two were leaning on
the wall of the building, perhaps waiting for it to open.
One was smoking a Kool.

"In Crescent." The smoker said. All of them
laughed and one of the leaners jokingly pushed the
smoker a few times.

"This way?" The man pointed up the street.

"That way." The smoker pointed more to the
man's left. "Two blocks, can't miss it."

"Why's that?"

"'Cuz it's a dump."

The group cackled again.

The man sped off. Traffic was very light and the not yet risen sun was doing its best to burn off the fog but failing. The man was beginning to work up a light sweat when he saw the building. It was a three story block, perhaps a refurbished apartment unit or hotel from the thirties-a tawdry and dusty excuse for a business. Even calling itself the *Crescent Modern Journal*, the title of which was appropriately stenciled in a creamy white faded and cracking script clearly visible on what would be the top floor, the paper was trying to speak for *both* of Crescent's neighborhoods, only the North had forgotten to speak for *it*. Just looking at the giant brick oven he remembered how hot it could be in the summer.

The man ditched the bike and walked a block on foot. It would take him that long to figure out how to get in. As he walked, he eyed the structure in all of its magnificence, and proposed, due to its age, it would have to have a door or window somewhere that didn't quite close all the way. He didn't have his watch with him but knew his co-workers would be arriving soon. They were a very early crowd.

Was he ready for that? Could he bluff his way through one of those casual conversations of pleasantries without the co-worker knowing his brain was scrambled eggs? If it was his only way in, he'd have to chance it, whatever feelings of sickness came into his stomach and mushed around in his guts as if a baker had stolen them to make cinnamon rolls with.

A station wagon of the German variety rolled past him and parked in one of the twenty or so official spots alongside the building. After thirty seconds of walking he would make irrevocable contact. He wouldn't be alone.

The man squeezed his hands a few times and

took a deep breath.

How his head hurt.

The woman was coming from her car, putting her keys away. She was a short brunette with short hair and wore a modest pantsuit that, was, if anything, monochromatic. She had a pleasant but serious face and wore thick black vanity frames that some men found to be attractive.

She looked up and he made sure to smile.

"Oh, hey Darren."

Darren? What kind of name was that?

"Hello..." He reached for her name and didn't find it. She looked vaguely familiar, but everyone did, in a way. Especially the longer he looked blankly at their faces in search of clues about his own.

"You're here early." She said quickly, before he could trip over his own tongue.

"I forgot some things."

"Oh." She went for an electric key card from her purse. "Like this guy?"

"Yeah."

"It was your big day out." She smirked in a mildly flirtatious manner, perhaps because it was only the two of them and it was reasonably dark, which made it somehow understandable from her perspective. There was no danger of any of her co-workers seeing her act as such. Then, as he was waiting for her to swipe the key card she looked up at him again. "I wish I got to go." Her eyes swelled. "There was even a *murder*."

The man made a face of sure confusion as his co-worker entered the building. He watched her walk into the lobby, which was some strange hybrid of a public school and an old hotel without the funding of either. For a split second he didn't want to go in after her because it was going to be rough. The steps were going to get higher and higher until the oxygen ran out and the fall from it all would be a brutal, bone-crunching reality from which there was no waking up.

But he'd made a promise in that room; to himself, and in a way, to that woman. She had trusted in him. *He* had to trust in *himself*, and in the dice of life.

The man walked through the door just as the weight of it caused it to sweep and click shut behind him. He followed the sounds of her heels on the exposed concrete subfloor that had a strangely glossy sheen to it. Before them was a stretch of steel surplus desks ensconced in shelves and cabinets with an exposed staircase against the far back wall that lead to a bank of private offices. The space was large because the higher floors had been knocked out and brick pillars ran all the way up to the ceiling, but it was a narrow rectangle, due to the fact that a small but highly efficient printing press was located directly next to the writer's desks and partitioned with a soundproofed wall that looked somewhat like frosted glass.

So his name was Darren, and one of these rat holes belonged to him.

"What did you forget?" His co-worker asked.

"I forgot where my desk is." Darren rubbed his eyes with no need to act. "I had a lot of booze last night. I barely made it out of there."

The woman held a nervous smile and just when Darren was about to begin walking to make her think it was a joke she pointed. He finally sat down in a desk that looked to be the messiest of the bunch and felt the scrutiny of her nervous gaze.

"You had a lot of...booze, you said?"

"That's right."

She half-turned over the back of her chair.

"What about AA?"

Darren blinked through trying to remember and

nothing came.

"What about it?"

"You said you were going to quit."

"It's just a really stressful time." Darren shrugged, going with the vibe he was feeling inside, like an improv actor; but nothing about it felt, in any way, false.

"I know, that's why you don't want to have any dependency."

Dependency? *Alcohol* dependency? What was she going on about? And why didn't it...*feel* like play-acting?

"Your rough is due at five." She turned back to a hunched positioned at her desk.

"I know."

Darren began to dig around his desk, but it was so messy it was hard to focus. Not that he knew what to look for if he could, and he just pushed a few trinkets around and moved a stapler and a stack of papers.

Through this he could feel her investigative gaze and he looked up at her dumbly.

"What did you forget?"

"My keys."

The woman's eyes took on a pitiable appraisal of him. In a glance, he read her reasonably plain face and it felt sorry for him.

"Did you have them last night?"

He shook his head.

"It was such a long day, I mean, I could've dropped the somewhere at the convention...or...at Fircrest."

"Your house keys?"

"Yes, my everything keys. I was riding with...I was carpooling, so I didn't think about them."

"You didn't go home?"

"No, I was at a friend's before the convention."

A bit of a ripple went across her eyebrows, like she was offended or something.

The woman turned around and turned on her PC and the process sounded like a crop duster coughing to life for an early morning run.

Darren continued rattling doors and lifting papers. Then he got a knot in his throat when his own voice shot across the semi-silence of the room.

"Would you do me a favor?"

The woman turned. Her face was hard to read, and even more familiar than before.

"You know I would."

"Could you drive me home?"

She looked at him with stony eyes.

He didn't realize until after he had asked the question she might not've known where he lived. Then he would be exposed.

His skin burned under her eyes.

"Home?"

"I think it'd be better if I work on the rough from the comfort of my couch." He offered.

She continued to stare.

"On one condition. You go back to AA."

Darren smiled.

Ratner entered the converted tour bus Homeland called a Tactical Mobile Field Operations Vehicle. It was slightly larger than a tour bus and was irreplaceable in the capacity it served. The rig had its own satellite receiver dish, a secure mainframe computer system with several high definition screens, an armory of H&K's of all sizes, enough firepower to do some damage if need be, and a seating area for strategy and table work. Rollins, the computer technician, was at work piecing together the current state of evidence and entering various bits of known information into processing models and algorithms for the purposes of creating a clear idea of what happened, why it happened, how it happened, and most importantly how to proceed as the future unwound its deadly fuse.

Tallifer had removed his suit jacket, rolled up his sleeves, and was elbow deep in every available Police report as well as a few other things the Police had no idea of.

"A woman in Wayilow reports picking up a hitchhiker along the highway adjacent to Fircrest." Ratner sat down and the leatherette swivel chair squeaked. "He had an injury to his shoulder and also claims to have amnesia."

Tallifer's tanned face passed from pensive to rigid.

"When?"

"She picked him up some time before three, she guessed."

Tallifer shook his head like he just won the lottery but lost the ticket.

"That's him..." The Agent bit his finger then shook it at Ratner. "We have to let the locals get him. We have way too much to clean up. We have to work on Jupiter."

"You know it was Jupiter?"

"Confirmed? No, but that's why she was there. Something crazy happened...it was never supposed to go this way, you know?" Tallifer let his eyes drift to the window for a second or two, not enough to really see anything. "We have to know what went wrong."

"It happened." Ratner shrugged.

"I know, that's why I want to leave it and work on Jupiter. If he was there, we'll know it. We'll also know what she did with the key."

"Yeah..." Ratner bounced his smartphone in his hand. "It wasn't in her purse."

"It could still be in that house. There's no way any of Jupiter's group got it."

"Hmm..."

"You said he had amnesia?" Tallifer pushed the papers in front of him aside, as if they were a meal he was no longer interested in.

"Yes."

"And he was the one bound and gagged?"

"DNA will confirm that but it definitely points that way."

"He must've been in the room at the time of her murder."

"I thought as much."

"Do you think he saw her...die?"

"Knowing Jupiter, he wouldn't be alive if he did. That *is* if Jupiter or his group killed her. I know it's obvious but there's so much information here for us to assume incorrectly and to be wrong about such important details could prove to be fatal."

Ratner set the phone on the table and Tallifer turned his eyes again to the window.

"He must've been unconscious."

"It's probable. They would've checked."

"Why didn't they move him? If he was unconscious he wouldn'tve known. There was a bathroom nearby."

"Time. If Jupiter was there and his killers were, she would've known right away they were going to take the key and kill her...obviously, as stealthy as possible, but as forcefully as possible too. The time of death was between eight and twelve. The party ended at eleven. Their timing couldn't have been better. Either she hid the key and gave herself up, or she hid the key and failed in trying to escape. It happens."

Tallifer for once was bothered by his partner's lack of emotion, but that's what made them a good team. He had it. Ratner didn't.

"We would know for sure if they had the key. Hill's been on guard. You know him."

"Yeah..." Ratner fidgeted with the phone, the color and text of the computer screens nearby reflecting off of his small, round glasses. "It's hidden somewhere. It's going to be virtually impossible to find. I don't want to guess the odds on that one."

"But we know how she thinks, and how she was trained."

"Yes, to a point, especially with her, but we also have to see how the op was such a drastic failure."

Tallifer clenched his teeth.

"I know, you don't have to tell me."

Rollins, the tech, minimized a number of screens to make way for an uploading video link and removed his headset.

"Conference."

"Okay." Tallifer threw on his jacket and straightened his tie and made his way to Rollins' chair.

The image on the screen was of Don Bartleson, Tallifer's superior, a former US Army General and Iraq War veteran, coming in choppy and delayed real time from his Q clearance office in Washington D.C. His face held less emotion that Ratner's and bore a strange resemblance to Hiram Ulysses S. Grant.

"Before you give me a sitrep you need to know Marland is enroute and will be wheels down within the hour. Marland will now have complete authority. Reinforcements will be ready for deployment in Crescent soon after. Fircrest will be locked down and you will be able to coordinate with the locals as per her instructions."

Tallifer swallowed. Marland. He knew it was coming. So now he was being supplanted as he had done to the Homicide Detective.

"We are aware of the witness." Tallifer began. "The locals are working on it. We have not performed an autopsy yet but she is at the morgue."

"Good." The voice came before the image. "Wait for Marland."

"Right."

"Do you have the key?"

"No."

"How bad was the leak?"

"We can only begin to know if we interview each and every party guest to figure out who's who, which we will do once we get the guest list. The witness claims to have amnesia."

"Let's hope he does."

"It *is* my belief that he was not conscious at the time of her killing."

There was a pause and Bartleson's chin jutted forward.

"Go on."

"So we may have less to go on with this lead than hope would dictate."

"Considering the claim of amnesia is real?"

"Yes."

"Considering he's not one of them?"

"Yes."

Bartleson paused and the humming of the computers hard at work could be heard in the tense space of stale air.

"I suggest," Tallifer continued, "that we pursue the murderers with more vigilance. We have the murder weapon and if we get the guest list I know we can single out Jupiter's agents." Tallifer's face was hard and serious. "Sir, I believe if we can convict one of his agents of murder they will give up Jupiter on a plea bargain."

Bartleson nodded.

Tallifer smirked.

"It could be the best thing that happened to us."

"Dammit, Ryan!" Bartleson nearly spit through the screen. "We lost an *irreplaceable* Agent and are already suffering the consequences. Your job is to assess the damage-don't you dare go beyond it. Marland will be there before you can say transfer to Omaha and your team better be ready to give her all of the help she needs because this is so far from over we'll be lucky to clean up the fallout before Elections."

Tallifer nodded and the picture went black. Rollins, pinching the heavy nose that sat above a black goatee, hesitated for a moment because Tallifer was in his chair, sitting in contemplative silence. Then it occurred to Tallifer and he sulked to his original seat, allowing the tech to bring all of the programs and applications he had running back to life.

Tallifer eyed Ratner who had snagged his phone and begun to dial.

"Autopsy?"

"And Tanya Wilson."

Tallifer nodded heavily as his partner left the TMFOV. Typing and clicking was a fading sound in his ears as the wheels of his mind rolled round and round.

He wanted Jupiter so bad. Jupiter was an evil man, the scum of the earth. And like scum, he was everywhere. Invisible. A germ. But he had his weaknesses.

He had to. Or else there'd be no way to get him.

Marland would be taking over soon. He would do what he was told. But he and Marland never saw eye-to-eye or nose-to-nose. She was always a lone wolf...of sorts. But this game, this dance of good people and bad people; right people and wrong people, was more of a Rubik's cube than a chess match, and more of a game of cards than a title bout.

He took immense pressure for it all. He thought about it day and night, and maybe, just maybe, the opportunity to cut the head off of the dragon would present itself.

If it did, he would strike like lightning.

EIGHT

Tanya was staring at the ceiling trying to rest when the phone rang.

"Hello."

"Tanya Wilson?"

"Speaking."

"Hello Ms. Wilson, my name is Jared Ratner, I'm with the Department of Homeland Security."

Tanya's spine tingled and she sat up slowly.

"Yes?"

"I'd like to ask you some questions about the man you helped earlier."

"Yes..."

"Ma'am, are you aware that helping or aiding a terrorist in any way affiliates you with that terrorist and thus makes you eligible for the same punishment?"

"..."

"Ms. Wilson?"

"I'm...I'm not a terrorist."

Ratner's tone softened noticeably.

"I don't think you are, ma'am, but the man you helped earlier tonight might be a threat to national security and we have to find him as quickly as possible."

"Yes...but, I'm not a terrorist. I was just...I just picked up a hitchhiker, and I have nursing experience, so, I thought..."

"Yes, ma'am, I understand...I just need to know
if he told you anything."

Tanya frowned and shook her head.

"N...no, he had amnesia."

"Amnesia?"

"Yes."

"And you knew this how?"

"He told me...and I'm a nurse, I have experience
in..."

"Where did he go?"

Tanya nervously looked out the window as if
she heard something.

"I...listen, I told the police all of this already. I
told them everything I did, everything I know."

There was a pause on Ratner's end and a few
clicking noises.

"Ma'am, don't go anywhere. We'll have
someone over to you as soon as we can to ask you more
questions. Your cooperation is vital to national security
and if you could, try not to move anything in your
house because it might have DNA on it."

Tanya nodded slowly, letting the gravity of the
Agent's dry words fall on her.

"I understand."

"Thank you, Ms. Wilson."

The phone was heavy in her hand and her arm
sagged to the couch.

What had she done?

The one called Jupiter was sitting in the
stateroom of a one hundred and twenty foot yacht that
was meandering around a chain of islands nearly sixty
miles from the mouth of the Targus River. The room
was not wood paneled and nautical as was to be
expected. Everything in it was white; nothing in the
room was any color other than white. The rest of the

yacht was as nondescript as a boat of its size could be. The yacht's name was *Divide et Impera* and was an ancient language for a deadly maxim. Jupiter was an ancient name itself but the one that bore it took no credit for it.

Jupiter studied the screen of a small notebook computer and reached for a cellphone, one of four on the desk. Each cell phone was white, as was Jupiter's clothing, and one would have a hard time telling the phones apart.

Not Jupiter. His brain was a computer in and of itself, a two teraflop processor and a sixty-acre mainframe of information free from the risk of being hacked into.

"Ganymede." He spoke into the phone in a voice that could best be described as belonging to no English speaking country in and of itself but being a product of several of them in varying ratios.

"Yes."

"Move into position two and await further instructions."

"Yes."

Jupiter placed the cellphone precisely where it had been and went for another.

"Europa."

"Yes."

"There's a woman named Tanya Wilson, her address is being sent to you. Homeland wants to question her about the Fircrest suspect. See that you do it first."

"Yes."

Jupiter placed the phone where it had been and moved to a wet bar for bottled water from Himalayan springs and two different medications.

Who really knew how much damage had been done? Jupiter would soon find out, and then, assess if the time was right for more damage.

Whatever it took to get the key. It was only the beginning.

Jessica Birchall applied pressure to the spots next to the bridge of her nose. Her sinuses were killing her. The doctor had said the infection was immune deficiency related and came from stress and a poor diet but could be easily rectified if she took some time off and ate a home-cooked meal for a change. A nice long bath with a good cup of Rooibos tea was all she wanted but it was as far away and improbable as a week of vacation given the current situation. The long day had only just begun and she was willing to do what it took to see the story through. At the moment, she was taking a time out in the privacy of her Subaru in the parking lot of the Channel 2 News studio in North Crescent, waiting to go inside and speak with her producer about Fircrest.

It was some story, so many unknowns and to her knowledge, the other two local stations had been unable to pick up the story as of yet.

It was *going to be* some story...but it could wait for a few minutes. It wasn't even six yet.

There was a rap of knuckles on the passenger window.

Birchall peeled an eye open to see Francine, Director Hodge's secretary.

"What is it?" She asked, after leaning over the stick shift and opening the door.

"Hodge wants to see you now."

"Okay..." She yawned. "Tell him I'll be in in a minute."

For a second frustration flashed through Francine's face, but only for a moment, because Francine was one of the sweetest people in the world.

She was Vietnamese and always smiled from the depths of her small body.

"No. Right now. He sent me out here."

Birchall snagged her purse and left a half empty latte gone cold to guard her Subaru.

"What is it?"

"I don't know." Francine said as they walked. "But I heard something about Homeland Security."

"What?" Birchall squinted at the converted Hospital complete with helipad that was their news studio. It sat deep in the heart of urban Crescent but the size of the lot made it feel more like a rocket launch pad in the middle of nowhere.

"It was very urgent. It was about your report."

Birchall thought about it and stared at the concrete in front of her feet and the stubs of car bumpers and wheels as the sound of four heels hurriedly clacked across the lot to the door.

"Has anyone else picked it up yet?"

"No."

"Not national?"

"No."

What on earth would Homeland Security want with...

Fircrest, it had to be...something tied with the election, the murder was tied to the election. Well, if they thought they were going to kill her story, for whatever reason, they had another thing coming. It was *her* story and free speech was *her* career.

Hodge was a tough guy, he knew how to play hardball. And she wasn't exactly a lightweight when it came to dealing with *politics*.

Birchall opened the door for Francine.

The bath would have to wait.

The drive was incredibly quiet through the

awakenings of South Crescent. Once past the rail yard, the old homes and businesses of small immigrant communities began to blend into each other.

It was as if Darren's co-worker wanted him to say something. He could feel it. He was content to look out the window and search for familiarity. It came in a bagel shop here and a street sign there, but nothing that really mattered. Just junk, stuffed way back in his head, that amazingly weird and weirdly amazing thing the brain was. So full of nothing with a potential for everything all at once, keeping vital organs and senses running like a clock even when he didn't know his own name and yet keeping from him all of those details he considered so vital to remember.

It would come.

The traffic was ever so slightly increasing as the grainy, industrial bits and pieces of South gave way to the suburb of Mossyrock, one of the oldest parts of Crescent. Houses were hodge podge; some kept and some relatively abandoned looking-each one having a character of its own while maintaining a historical similitude with the neighborhood.

There was a small Jewish community in the nicest part of Mossyrock and Darren's face fell a bit as they drove past.

"Do you remember the last time I drove you home?"

"No."

She looked at him and made a disappointed face.

"It was when you bet your holiday bonus on a horse that broke its leg in the Breeder's Mile and had to be put down the following week." Darren smirked. "You were drowning your sorrows in the parking lot with some Peppermint Schnapps."

"I wasn't going to drive home, was I?"

"I wouldn't let you. You didn't have money for the bus, either. You spent it all in that office pool for the Breeder's Mile you and Trenton were so crazy about doing.

"Well..."

"And do you remember what I said when I dropped you off?"

Darren shook his head and it lolled over. She had both hands on the wheel, perfect and rigid.

"No."

"I said," She didn't take her eyes off the road. "Don't make me do this again."

"I owe you one..." Darren offered and it occurred to him with as much as he said it in his life the interstate Powerball lottery wouldn't cut his debts.

"Two, but I'm not counting."

"I fell off the wagon." Darren said, not knowing he had been on a wagon, not remembering trying to not drink, not that it was easy to remember anything...

"And when you fall, you fall hard."

Darren felt a self-righteous jab. But he bit his lip. After all she knew where he lived. It was the price of admission.

"Was it rum this time or are you back to vodka?"

"It was vodka..."

The woman made clicking noises and shook her head. She slowed and signaled and Darren hoped they were getting close.

"I guess it couldn't be helped. You were thrown into the buffet line after having starved yourself."

What could he say? *Drive faster, please.*

"If everyone jumped off a bridge, as the saying goes..."

His head really hurt and the key burned in his pocket. He couldn't deal with her little jabs, not now, he had to stay focused and work as quickly as possible.

"I won't tell Mackie, but if you write drunk, he'll know." Mackie was a co-editor of the CMJ, one of four. "He didn't go himself because you begged to go, you were practically on your knees."

"Okay..." He almost went to say her name but couldn't think of it. "I get it."

The car stopped. The woman curled her hair behind her ears and turned to him.

"AA Darren."

"I got it."

"So what do I do if we're here again?"

"That's your choice." He said as he opened the door. The street was narrow and packed with small houses and cars stuck on either side of the street would make through traffic very difficult. The house the woman parked directly in front of was a blocky two-story that had been thrown in the dryer and placed back on its foundation somewhat unevenly. It was an oatmeal color with white trim and windows and doors. The left side of the property was segregated by a brown privacy fence and pair of fir trees and the right side of the property spilled directly into the neighboring house with only the junk from Darren's empty carport to separate them. The grass in the front yard was lacking vibrancy and the bushes near the door were overgrown.

The mailbox read D. Reston

So it was his.

"Thank you very much." He said and actually meant it.

"Aren't you forgetting something?" She asked. He stood on the curb with a dumb and simple face. "How are you going to get in?"

"I have a key hidden somewhere."

"Do you need help?"

"Always." He smiled.

She followed him to the front door.

"Should I look under the mat?"

"Look wherever you think is appropriate." Darren smirked as he approached the carport. She thought he had a hangover. Amnesia was some kind of hangover, wasn't it? And to tell he had no keys when all he truly had was a key was a wrinkle of irony only a writer, if even a hack political reporter for a hack political paper could appreciate.

Darren eyed the bits and pieces of the carport. Lots of tools and a few tires, different cans of oil and a jack. Either he was a mechanic or he was a wannabe. So what did he drive?

Darren sighed and took it in. He was Darren Reston. This was his house. This was his carport. Those were his tools.

It clicked. He reached in one of the toolboxes and lifted the tray to find the spare key in a pile of greasy nuts, bolts, and washers.

He may have been a mess, but he understood his way of life, or at least it made sense when he tried not to think about it and just let it go.

Darren came back to the front door where his fellow journalist was digging through the bushes.

"I got it."

She looked up, her hair now out of place.

"I thought I was going to have to work a little harder."

Darren put the key in the door and opened it.

"Thank you again."

"You know Darren," her heels clicked on the concrete pathway as she walked to her car. "All some women want is a man who has a job and doesn't drink."

Darren blinked at her. The subtext was mighty thick. He really didn't know what to say.

So he didn't say anything.

She left with a silent wave and Darren sighed.
He walked through the open door and reached for the
key in his pocket. It was smaller than his house key as
he compared the two in each hand, respectively.
Perhaps it belonged to a safety deposit box or a very
small vehicle.

His house was a wreck. The door opened to a
linoleum-lined entrance that visually stretched into a
galley kitchen with a washer and dryer at the end. A
hall ran to his left and was covered in pickled oak
wallpaper and hid a staircase covered in blue carpet. He
shut the door behind and walked to the right. There he
saw a small living room dining room combination, also
the same knotty blue carpet. Nothing matched and there
was a dusty banana plant in a terra cotta pot stuffed
next to a floor to ceiling window. Every tabletop and
empty corner was occupied by some kind of paper or
box of papers or book or a stack thereof. There was no
space to rest the eye, but somehow, again, it made
sense.

Darren walked back to the hall. The carpeted
staircase looked creaky and a few framed pictures hung
alongside the steps, uneven against pickled oak
wallpaper. There was a bathroom and an office coming
from the hall. Darren let out a gutted sigh when he saw
the office. It looked as if it had been ransacked even
though he knew it had not and the walls were tomato
red.

After using the bathroom, Darren walked into
the kitchen and saw an empty bottle of rum on the
counter. His face showed certain sadness as he opened a
cupboard to find a bottle of vodka behind a collection
of spices and staples like flour and sugar.

So he really was an alcoholic. A drunk hack
writer. Darren Reston, single. Thirties. Total failure.

Darren went back to the bathroom and looked

himself in the eye.

Why didn't he know this Darren Reston? A better question would've been, why did he have to continue being this Darren Reston?

He took a shower and found some clothes. Tanya had done a nice job and the wound was healing so he had removed her bandage and slapped a simple Band-Aid on it. He found some bread that wasn't moldy and made toast and as he ate it, considered the key.

It sat on the countertop with the paper wrapped around it.

So this was it, the woman's dying gift, hidden where no one would find it. What brilliant desperation.

He removed the paper and read it.

Mutual Cherry 410.

Darren blinked and it occurred to him his mind was working best when he was trying his not to engage it. So he ate his toast and listened to the humming of the overhead fluorescent light.

Mutual was an upper-middle class branch bank in the western United States. That would fit with the guess of a safety deposit box.

Cherry...was that a name it was under? Box 410, on Cherry? Or the address was 410 Cherry.

Darren ate his toast.

410 Cherry Drive or 410 Cherry Way East would be an address, but the 410 came after the word, not before.

Leaving the toast for a moment, Darren found a phone book. There was a Mutual Bank in North Crescent on Cherry Street and the address was 2600.

410 had to be the box number.

But what name? Was Cherry the street name and the name the box was under?

Darren finished the toast.

The woman could've been named Cherry. She
passed the key to him because she was keeping
something hidden. He was therefore going to be an
impartial agent of whatever was in Mutual box 410 on
Cherry.

That was it, had to be.

What name...did it matter? No, the key
mattered. A scribble was all they needed. They were
hourly servants that didn't see past basic procedure.

Darren scuffed upstairs to his bedroom. He
would have to dress appropriately for the next phase of
the operation, it would probably be the longest. He
would go to Mutual and get whatever was in the box
and take it to the Police and answer all of their
questions.

Darren chose his most comfortable and familiar
clothes. Blue jeans, white tennis shoes, a collegiate
hooded sweatshirt and a hooded waterproof jacket.
Then he scrounged around and found several things of
importance, perhaps more so in the future as it was an
unknown and potentially dangerous environment. A
pen-sized Maglite, a Swiss Army knife, a plastic one-
time lighter, some pocket change and small bills. He
also found an expired driver's license in an old wallet
and put his house key in there too. Even though the
driver's license picture showed him with glasses it
would have to do.

Before leaving he wrote a note and hid it
somewhere he knew someone would find it if they
looked.

Then he grabbed a granola bar and bottled water
and began walking to the nearest bus stop.

A part of him wanted to go back into his cozy
rat nest and sleep it all away-he'd been sleeping and
drinking and stumbling through life for as long as he
could ascertain. Even though it was an echo compared

to how he felt inside now, it made sense, it was an easy way out.

But it was as if when he had woken up bound and gagged, he had woken up a new person only to find who he *was* not who he had *been*, and however he got to be that way he had no idea. He understood what he saw in the mess of his house but if he were to start over it wouldn't ever be the same.

He promised himself the truth, and in a way, the promise extended to the dead woman as well. She had given him some form of new life, and it was enough for him to reach out and grab it with both hands. She had passed the key on to him and he was now running with it.

The cobwebbed clutches of sleep broke with the sun and three sharp knocks on the door.

Tanya Wilson took a deep breath and blinked it away. She slept light anyway, and the blinds were twisted just enough to let the cold golden yellow of fall cut through the darkness of yesterday. The knock, impatient, sounded again. It was a man's hand; authoritative, but not impartial like a delivery driver that had other things to do. Perhaps it was the man from Homeland. How long had it been since he called? She would check on the phone, after she let the man in.

So Tanya pushed herself up and opened the door. By then it was too late to reason, to think, or to change what she had done.

The man at the door was *not* from Homeland Security, and his hand coming toward her face was the last thing she expected to see. The shock of it was so gripping she failed to react when the man was most vulnerable.

Tanya stumbled backwards and the man fell on top of her. He was a large, burly man and wore black

from head to toe. He had done nothing to hide his
hawk-like nose or small eyes but it was of little
importance to him as he struggled to flip Tanya over on
her stomach.

She squirmed and struggled but the man was too
strong. He had straddled her and was in the process of
pinning her shoulders when Tanya wriggled free from
his legs and smashed her foot in desperation where she
knew every man was painfully sensitive.

Air came out of him in a wheezing gush and as
he hunched on the floor to collect himself Tanya
scampered to her feet to get the phone, seeing the man
rise as she did. By the time she reached the phone on
the couch he had jumped over it, small eyes burning
with the repression of pain. Tanya rushed to the kitchen
with the man on her heels. She snagged a frying pan
from the counter and came to a defensive position in the
small space between the couch and the dining set. The
man slowed from his clomping movements to see his
quarry would not be an easy target. She held the phone
in one hand and the frying pan in another, and before
calculating which one was more dangerous he feinted a
lunge.

The frying pan flinched. He saw no fear in her
eyes. She couldn't dial with the pan in her hand, she
would try to knock him out and lock herself somewhere
to call the cops.

That couldn't happen. Absolutely not.

A smirk wrinkled the man's lips and he threw
himself back to the kitchen, just what Tanya didn't
expect. She looked to the left and to the right trying to
anticipate what side the man would launch himself
from, but then she heard the rattling of drawers and
understood. Boldly she advanced toward the dining
room entrance but it was too late. The man in black had
acquired a knife. It was a German made Santoku knife

and the high polish steel glinted in the light spilling from the blinds.

"What do you want?" Tanya's voice trembled.

"*You.*"

The man lunged and she swiped the frying pan in desperation feeling the reverberation of the hideous clanging noise the two weapons made. The man didn't care that he had lost the knife. He leapt at her and tackled her into the small coffee table. Tanya lost her air as she received the violent sandwich and the man rolled off into the television set by the force of momentum he had accumulated and the box fell from its stand and on the back of his neck. His legs, too, had struck some kind of lamp or decorative piece and the sound of destruction lasted nearly three seconds. The man with the hawk-like nose struggled to get free of the damage and when he stood upright he saw the woman on the table, chest heaving and searching for air.

Perfect.

The man rushed to shut the door and reached in his jacket for a small leather wallet. He approached Tanya without hurry and removed the syringe from the wallet. With all of her might and lack of oxygen Tanya stretched her left arm toward the phone on the ground. The smirk was back on the man's vicious face as he smashed the phone to bits with one firm stomp.

Tanya shook her head in pleading as the man grabbed her arm, rolled up her sleeve, and emptied the contents of the syringe into her bloodstream.

NINE

Francine picked up her stride to get the door of Hodge's office so that Birchall would not have to break hers. Francine saw it in her eye and so did everyone else in the station that had looked up to say *good morning* or *excuse me*; it was the eye of some kind of jungle cat. Birchall was known for it, though she herself knew nothing about it or its reputation. No one had the guts to approach her about it.

Denton Hodge heard Birchall's heels on the tile floor and removed his reading glasses. He was a slight man of undetermined age with the guess being seventy-one, and still looked spry albeit a bit stressed. He had but a combful of hairs left on his head and they were wispy and white and sometimes they were swept all the way to the left, other times, all the way to the right. The three most popular jokes made on the matter were that he either forgot which direction he combed it last when he woke up in the morning and after several minutes of staring at himself in the mirror, he finally *remembered*, or that it was a secret indicator which way the network was slanting politically at the moment, and finally, that his wife of forty-eight years was playing a mean trick on him and he didn't know.

"Yes?"

"Homeland wants to kill Fircrest?"

Hodge had a gleam in his eye because Jessica

always shot straight. Sometimes, too straight, and he believed, even though the world was supposed to be a judgment free and undiscriminating place, that her looks saved her-not that she was naturally pretty, but the package she had molded herself into preyed upon men's dreams as much as the words that came from their lips. No one would answer the questions of a woman that was not only pushy, but ugly, and because of her deliberately painted shell, her *pushiness* was seen as *desire, ambition, or hunger.*

"What did Francine tell you?" Hodge's voice held hints of the Deep South where gators swam freely in lakes and little boys swung freely from rope swings into those lakes without their mothers standing on the banks in fear.

"Nothing."

"Well then it's better that way." Hodge motioned for Jessica to take a seat, which she did so reluctantly and somewhat mechanically, because her focus was on her superior. His face, his voice, his words. "Because I don't know much myself."

"You don't know or you can't say?"

"Now Jessica, I'm not on trial here. The investigation is closed, the crime scene is closed, the whole enchilada is locked up and done with."

The jungle cat eyes narrowed.

"That's from the network or from the government?"

"From Homeland Security. We're not going to report anything about it at all-just as if it never happened."

Hodge bounced gently in his chair as Birchall chewed it all up in her mind, and he knew she was doing just that. He could almost feel it.

"Doesn't that make you..." She finally said. "Intrigued?"

"Jessie, by the time you get to be my age, you've learned that compromise is what makes the world spin in the direction it was spinning before you showed up and keep it spinning that direction long after you've been laid to rest. I know a woman died, but there's no reason why you should jeopardize your career over one woman's death."

Jessica's eyebrows came together and her spine shivered. There was a detached coldness, a precision laced in his choice of words. Inside she snapped to attention. Her article began *now*.

"Who said anything about losing my job?"

"I'm just saying you don't want to tango with the wrong partner."

"It's my job. Dancing with cops, lawyers, criminals *and*, occasionally stars."

Hodge sighed. Birchall was not often sarcastic and he was getting nowhere with his choice of colloquialisms.

"Jessie, don't do anything you'll regret. They told me not to pursue it. There are plenty of stories out there and there will be plenty of material to keep you busy. If you do anything, *anything* to pursue the Fircrest story, it won't be on my orders or company time and don't be surprised if you don't work here anymore after you do so because it was never my call in the first place..."

Jessica Birchall pinched her sinuses and nodded. The message from Denton Hodge was as clear as the shroud surrounding Fircrest Mansion was *un*clear.

The truth was the truth. There was *no* changing it. But both the truth and what ever happened up at that palace was being zipped up in a body bag.

Tallifer was smoking a Marlboro when the gargle of helicopter blades rattled through the green blanket of Fircrest. The fog had burned away. He took a generous sigh, letting the smoke go and ground the cigarette into the walkway and walked in the direction of the front gate. By the time he got there the jet black Bell 407 was twisting down toward the natural helipad the overly large circular driveway had created. On the green lawn against the newborn sunrise it was a striking image.

The person that emerged from the helicopter was an even more striking image.

She was as tall and athletic as she was as graceful and elegant and the pinstripe black pantsuit framed her form with a professional distinction. But it was her face and her jewel blue eyes especially that resonated with an exotic and rare yet completely wholesome and natural beauty.

She was truly one of a kind.

Tallifer squinted against the new light to see her.

Actually, two of a kind.

Her name was Sierra Marland. Her sister, her twin, her identical counterpart and closest confidant in the whole wide world, Magnolia, was the woman who had been slain at Fircrest.

"Sierra." Tallifer nodded.

"Ryan." They did not shake hands, and an observer would note there was no affection between them. Tallifer looked up to her even though she couldnt've been over five foot nine.

"Where's Maggie?"

"She's at the morgue. They have not performed the autopsy yet."

"Are all of her effects there too?"

"Yes."

Sierra took in the vastness of the estate for a moment and then turned back to wave off the chopper.

"Lead the way."

Tallifer got doors for her and did all of the gentlemanly things but it was forced. A side of him wanted to tear into her about the foolishness of the operation but he knew what it was like to lose a sibling; his brother was killed in Mosul during a second tour. He knew her grief to a point but it did not negate the present, and the present was all their doing. Bartleson and the Marlands. It was all *their* fault.

Sierra ducked under the crime tape and studied the room. Tallifer wondered if she was going to cry or if she already had.

"Maggie was here?" She pointed.

"Yes."

Sierra stared at the blood on the carpet, so much her own blood, her own DNA, blood that could've been hers.

"I guess it was her turn..." She said, softly.

"Here are the pictures." Tallifer gave her the tablet he had been working on and she would be keeping it now that she was in charge. Every bit of information between the work the cops had done and what Homeland had accumulated and already knew was on it. He watched her face as she took it in, pictures of her embryonic double slain in cold blood.

"What else can you tell me about the scene?"

"We're working on piecing together a scenario of the potential possibilities surrounding her death. We can't be sure. We know it was a stab wound to the neck. It was obviously Jupiter's crew and there's the witness. That's all."

Marland walked over the blood to the window and stared through it at a few different angles and then saw the broken chair in the corner. Her eyes went from the table and chair to the corner and back.

"I can't wait to talk to him. He must have the

key."

"Pardon?"

"The key, Ryan. She gave it to him."

Tallifer's arms crossed.

"We can't be certain."

"*We* don't have to be. *I* am. *We* think the same way." Marland took a glance out the window to the main gate and back to the tanned agent. "And if *we* are going to get some resolution here you're going to have to let me assume a lot of unknowns. I'm not disregarding your MIT perspective or the work you've done so far but there's no one on planet earth that knows Maggie better than me. She did what I would do. That's why *we* are in SAB."

Tallifer nodded. There wasn't much he could say. Without raising her voice she established a great deal and if Tallifer questioned her again he knew she wouldn't hesitate to put him exactly where she wanted him. Still, he couldn't resist. The operation was a disaster from before the word go.

"Okay, I get it. But, I knew the moment you two and Bartleson cooked this thing up it was doomed."

"That's why you don't work in the Special Assignment Branch, you *think* too much. You'd be better off as an auditor."

Tallifer bit his lip as Marland brushed past and her perfume held an intoxicating suggestion that made him dislike her all the more. She and her sister had become these untouchables, these superstars and although for the obvious reasons, he was tired of looking from the outside in knowing he'd worked his way up from spit in the Department with his own two hands and Marland's success seemed to come from some kind of magic. When Tallifer reached the atrium he saw Marland conversing with Ratner, who had been placing a number of calls. Then she left out the front.

"We're going to the morgue." Ratner called up as he spotted Tallifer leaning on the bannister. "She wants you to wait here for the forensic team and to begin as soon as they arrive."

Tallifer nodded with pursed lips and distant eyes, like he was a part of a football team that was losing the game and still calling the same old plays.

Sierra Marland did things her way. Not his way. Maybe she wanted Jupiter as bad as he did, maybe for different reasons; but whatever happened, he wasn't going to let her ruin the operation any more than she already had. Jupiter was falling through the endless space of justice and all of its black holes and Ryan Tallifer was going to be the one to yank the chain around Jupiter's neck to break it once and for all.

The obnoxious bleating of the cordless phone pulled Erland out of some grey dream that he couldn't remember the half of but made so much sense just a minute ago. It occurred to him as the phone cast its alarming noises into the atmosphere that he had actually been sleeping, and that wasn't something he did a lot of. Resting was not sleeping, resting was like a car idling at a stoplight. Sleeping was actually turning the car off and taking the keys out and sometimes, forgetting where the keys were. He pushed his way up slowly and reached for the phone.

"Yeah..."

"Mike..." The voice on the other end was quiet and distant though it wished to be closer and still maintain its quietness.

It was Veracruz.

"Sarina..."

"Did I wake you?"

"Yeah..."

"I'm sorry."

"No, it's okay." Erland pushed up a little more and his head found the cold wall to lean on. "Have you been put on leave too?"

"..."

"...Did they tell you not to talk about it?"

"Yeah..."

"It's okay, Sarina, even if they were listening, I'm not afraid of them. I'm not afraid of losing my job. I'm not afraid of anything anymore."

Erland could hear water being turned on in the background, the squeaking of the faucet handles and splashing of liquid.

"I'm not either." She said, but who knew how much she meant it.

The Detective took a big wake up inhale.

"Are you hungry?"

"...Not really."

"Do you want to come over?"

"Yes."

Erland nodded to himself. She didn't want to talk. She wanted to talk.

"I'll be here."

A pause preceded another squeaking noise, but longer than the one before. Perhaps a shower curtain.

"Adios."

The phone beeped.

Erland sighed. It had been so long since he'd been the desire of a woman. That was the oddity of it. He'd never consciously been romantically wanted. In the fuller scope of homicide work as well, it was always the man that sought out the woman, and many times over the rejection of the one sought, from mother to wife; sister, daughter, girlfriend or co-worker, could lead to terrible ends. So what did Sarina seek? Shelter and security? Stability? Passion, pleasure? Did she seek to take or seek to give?

Or maybe just to abide together in silence so the sounds of loneliness wouldn't be so loud.

At any rate, it was too early in the morning to think. It was a new day, sort of, and work wasn't life. Work had been cut out of the day with a surgical precision and there was no routine to fall into-not that the job didn't have its variances, nuances, subtleties and extremes, but it was a way of life and today wasn't it.

He couldn't even remember his last *true* vacation, where he said forget it and dug his toes in the sand or got lost somewhere and didn't care about anything. Maybe because that *just* wasn't Detective First Grade Michael Erland. He had to care about *something*.

Someone.

He kicked his feet out of bed and rubbed his eyes.

Ready or not, that someone was Sarina Veracruz.

TEN

Ratner didn't even attempt small talk during the car ride after the obligatory apology for her loss and sentiment about the United States losing a great asset. It wasn't her loss, Sierra thought, as Crescent began to swell around them. It was Maggie's loss, and wherever she had gone she had lost whatever the rest of her life had in store. Maybe a family, kids, and a little coffee shop back in their hometown on the East Coast. Maybe unicorns were real too. After all, every minute of their lives was now something in memorandum with no present to laugh about it. The secrets they shared had passed from life to death, the camaraderie only *they* possessed was now severed and torn. And how many times had they told each other how they knew it could happen at any moment but never did they expect it would. Perhaps that was their pride and it had not broken their fall. Sierra's to despair, and Maggie's to death.

And now Sierra was going to the morgue to beg Maggie's corpse for an answer.

It was all so wrong.

Shouldn't they've gotten out of it all? Could they? As perfect a team as they were, an ideal fit for Special Assignment Branch with military service, criminal justice degrees, foreign language cognizance and amateur acting skills, shouldn't they've just turned the lights off and became someone else?

Sierra blinked rapidly as Ratner pulled the car up to the graying building on Dunham Street.

She would have to harden herself to make it out alive, harden herself even harder in places inside than she already was to see the course of justice through and break the tape.

Harden she would, but not just yet.

The walk to Maggie's body was somber. Sierra waited in the wings like a civilian as Ratner mumbled something to the coroner and filled out single sheet of paper with a carbon copy even though the coroner was well aware of Ratner's privileges. Part of Sierra wanted to get it over as quickly as possible, while the other, wiser part of her, Maggie's influence, no doubt, wanted to leave no stone unturned both in her heart and on the case, hoping never to return to this place of pain again.

"Would you like to be alone?" Ratner asked as the coroner moved through the small anteroom to the bank of steel doors.

"Yes."

The coroner opening the door reminded Sierra of going to the refrigerator late at night. He pulled out a thin slab covered in a white sheet. Sierra didn't smell the bleach or the antiseptic or see the blue lights glare off of the walls of white bathroom tile and stainless steel. She was new to it all, it was a virginal experience; like falling out of a plane or giving birth. She was giving herself to it, fully, opening up and letting it reach every crack and hole in her soul.

Sierra pulled the sheet back to see herself, pale and beautiful, void of color and full of peace. She tried to fight the urge to weep. She could not.

If it was thirty-seven seconds it was an eternity, and wherever Maggie was, it truly was an eternity, and Sierra wept from a very dark and burdened place in her guts.

When she rose from bended knees, perfect makeup stained and streaking, she still saw herself on a slab of steel. It was as if now, *she* had to be Magnolia. Part of Sierra had to stay on that slab. Only one of them could live on in the real world. Whether it was the Special Assignment Branch Homeland Security Agent or the woman who loved to cook and paint watercolors of gardens and beaches she could not decide.

She wanted Maggie to decide for her, to speak from beyond the grave some blessing or guidance, some veiled direction which way to go. The Department would understand if she quit. Completely, who would blame her? CONSTANT was nearly a pile of scraps as it was. She could lay Magnolia to rest back in Fulton Bay and live a life of peace in a house where the Atlantic was only a barefooted walk across the rolling dunes of lemony straw grass and ashen brown sand away. She could sleep every night in the arms of a simple man who loved her for who she was and forget what cruel and inhuman evils the world was full of.

But the fact that Magnolia was dead was the product of these evils and she had to stay the course, to see it through-to justify Magnolia's passing with the vindication of retribution, to wipe out once and for all the terrible menace they had toiled so many years to track.

The choice was hers and hers alone, but it had already been made for her.

Sierra bent gracefully at the waist and kissed her sister on the forehead.

"Goodbye, Maggie." Sierra wiped each eye with her left hand and smiled, patting Magnolia's hair. "I'll have the necklace now." She then added with a broken smile, savoring the gentle beauty of her twin's bare neck and shoulders, even considering the small red wound that signified her final moments.

Then she kissed her sister's forehead again and pulled the sheet over her head.

She took a minute at a mirror and returned to the anteroom where the men were talking around a desk that had a box on it.

"The coroner can begin the autopsy now." Her head nodded to the box on the table as her arms crossed. "Her effects?"

"Yes."

"Remember her clutch is being processed by forensics."

The coroner opened the box. It was empty.

Sierra's head twitched.

"Where...was the necklace in her purse?"

Ratner didn't say anything and shook his head painfully.

Sierra stood in the blue light, staring a hole in the box. Her jaw tightened and then her nostrils flared as she ground the guilty party into dust in her mind.

"Sierra..."

"It's okay. I'll get it back."

Mutual Partners Bank on Cherry was a daunting sight. It wasn't in the subtly aged brick facade or the two sets of revolving doors or in the fact that it took up four stories and just sat there in the middle of the block like a mausoleum; it was that Darren Reston had to go in as one thing and come out as another. There was an ancient reference there, Rubicon, it was, and as worthless as that was shards of minutiae like that were the only thing running through his head as the bus pulled away and the bodies of early morning environmentally conscious North Crescenters walked their environmentally conscious viewpoints and bodies to work.

The key was hotter in his pocket than it had ever been, a secret literally dying to come to life.

So Darren jaywalked through a space in the traffic. As he approached the revolving doors he wondered if he should've picked a more affluent appearance for this phase of the operation. The blue jeans and sweatshirt were not exactly common on Cherry, save the presence of construction workers retrofitting the Pinnacle Building. No matter, the key meant the box was his and if he looked like a royal prince or a cross dresser it wouldn't change the duty of the banker to give him the box. For what is was worth, every article of clothing on his body was perfectly clean.

Darren pushed his weight into the door and examined the broad space of the bank with his fractured writer's eye. Suits both masculine and feminine milled about but it wasn't as busy as he had hoped. It must've been after eight now.

He strode forward, knowing the cameras were on him, and human eyes, too, but all still objective and unknowing the heart underneath the thick cotton was beating madly in fear.

There were well-built wooden desks to the right with a smattering of personal investors preparing their strategies to siphon away two to three percent of net worth from their gullible middle class clients and a line of tellers behind a marble countertop replete with bulletproof glass. To the left there was a sitting room that visually blocked a hall of elevators and no doubt the athletic looking man reading the paper was a plainclothes security guard. Who read the paper anymore? Amnesia had taken away the number of subscribers to the Crescent Modern Journal from him at the moment, not that he knew that information to begin with.

Darren swallowed hard and chose the logically obvious teller. She was Indian and her name was Parmindy. She had very straight black hair and her choice of attire was an off white blouse of the British persuasion.

"Hello, what can I do for you today?" She asked with a smile that was as genuine as it was obligatory.

"I would like to get my safety deposit box." Darren said before correctly lining up the words in his mind.

"Alright, what name is it under?"

The writer froze for a second. Then it struck him an honest lie was the best choice and once the lies began to flow there was no turning back from there.

"It's not mine, it's not under my name I should say. It belonged to my second cousin who just passed. We weren't very close...but she willed me this safety deposit box." Parmindy's eyes were wide and unforgivingly hard to read. "I'm sure it's just a little memento or something, but I'd really like to put the whole thing to rest."

The teller gave a gesture of affirmation.

"I'll be right back."

The uneasiness in Darren's guts was working its way into full-blown panic sickness. How awful would it be to sink upon sight of the shore.

She returned expediently with a form.

"Alright, please fill out the highlighted areas." She said as the pen in her hand deftly circled several numbered lines and spaces, crossing out one box entirely.

As he began to examine the document, Darren realized just how much information he had to fill out about his second cousin, the owner of the box, the dead Ms. Fircrest. Slowly did the pen hover over the information about himself as well.

"It's box 410."

Parmindy affirmed and punched some things into her computer.

"Lacey James-Henderson."

"Yes, that's her." Darren smiled. "LJ, we always called her."

Then the teller frowned.

"She passed, you said?"

"That's right." Darren refused to look up and kept scribbling.

"When?"

"Two days ago."

"What of?"

"Suicide."

Parmindy's face fell.

"That's tragic. She was so beautiful."

Darren looked up.

"Did you set up the box for her? Maybe you could tell me what's inside and I wouldn't have to go through all this trouble."

"No, I'm just looking at her license picture here." Parmindy twisted the flat screen monitor and Darren saw an extremely photogenic picture of the woman he was now referring to in his mind as Ms. Fircrest, the late Ms. Fircrest. Her beauty was evident even through the thick glass. This was all because of her, God knew why.

"Yes, it's one of those things. She had everything going for her, you know..."

Darren passed the paper back under the slot in the glass.

"And your license, please."

It was an inevitable request and he reluctantly complied. Parmindy left wordlessly and Darren avoided looking around and appearing suspicious. The hardest of it was over.

Parmindy returned with a set of keys.

"Follow me, please."

He walked parallel to her until they reached a small gate at the end of the marble counter. She unlocked the gate with a plastic security pass and opened the gate for Darren, returning his license as she did so. He followed as Parmindy's heels made hollow clacks on the marble floor. The hallway was well lit and most inconspicuously filmed by a quartet of black bubbles hanging from the ceiling. Darren swallowed as they took a left turn into a room that was more of a post office looking set up than he expected.

"410 is over in the corner." She smiled. "I'll give you a minute."

"Thank you." Darren wasted no time and made his way to the corner with the key.

He shoved the key in the hole and twisted it with no small violence but hesitated a moment to open it. What was it, what was all of the secrecy for? What did this beautiful woman pass on to him and give her life for?

The answer was a memory card, for too small for a computer port, more than likely for a handheld device or some form of special platform he was unaware of, more than likely.

A little innocent piece of plastic-so easily corrupted or destroyed, lost or misplaced or forgotten about.

But not his one, it was like some coveted diamond or the famous jewel-encrusted raptor of the silver screen. It was death, and before he thought about it he reached down to tie his shoe and slipped it down the length of his left ankle, snug against the bone in a shroud of white cotton.

Information? Secrets? A map? A list of names or pictures? He was a writer after all, a political

reporter; maybe more of an opinion-spewer, or rather,
an *editorialist* but he could still put two and two
together and smell the smoke when there was a fire.
Fircrest, the convention, the murder. He didn't know
who the woman was but he did know the memory card
meant a great deal to her.

Darren closed the door to the box and walked,
hearing the quiet squeakings of his basketball shoes on
the slick floor. Parmindy gave him a smile to match the
first one and opened the gate for him. From there,
Darren walked every so slowly and normally to the
door and the street. And as he put his weight into the
revolving door, head full of ideas and what not, he did
not see the unusually athletic looking man reading the
paper on the cafe au lait colored leather couch had risen
to follow him.

The cellphone was out before Marland had left
the morgue. Tallifer was on the other end.

"I'm..." He was about to add to Ratner's
apologies.

"I've been going over the case on my tablet."
Marland said as they reached the car. "I want Detective
Erland to work with us."

Tallifer rolled his eyes on the other end.

"I'll have to talk to Bartleson."

"Ryan, you're forgetting you're second. I tell
you what to do and you do it. I talk to Bartleson."

Tallifer hung up before a curse came out.

Marland was pushing things around on her
tablet when Ratner fired the Department Issue Lumina
and spoke up.

"Do you think it's wise to open this up?"

"If I didn't I wouldn't." Marland squinted and
wondered if they resented women in authority or if they
just didn't like her.

"What we do and what a run of the mill Homicide Detective does..."

"Read his file if you think he's run of the mill. The records don't lie."

Ratner sighed as he merged into traffic.

"Bartleson *won't* declassify CONSTANT."

"Green lighting a local Detective to solve a murder won't ruin national security and it certainly won't hurt my process to have someone around who's not so stuck to Homeland protocols he can't get a cup of coffee without running a palm scan."

Ratner didn't say anything to that.

Sierra put the tablet to sleep and smoothed out her pants.

"I'm into statistics," Ratner began.

"If you're thinking," Sierra cut him off before anything long winded had a chance to inflate itself. "Think about the case. Lord knows Maggie deserves it."

Marland saw people of every race, color, and creed as the Lumina pulled through North Crescent in search of the looping highway return to Fircrest and added, "Everyone does."

Erland was laid out on the smoky blue couch that ate up most of the living room when the room echoed with three raps. He pushed himself up and opened the door. Veracruz had chosen the tightest civilian clothes she could find which were not only a distinct contrast from the tactical jumpsuit she usually wore but the loose sweat pants and t-shirt Erland had on. Sarina was ready to go to the club and Erland to the gym. Her hair was also damp and smelled of shampoo in a strong and appealing way, but forcefully so.

"Hey."

"Hi." She said, and he stood aside. She walked

in delicately with both hands holding the strap of her purse so it dangled in front of her as she walked.

"Would you like some coffee?" He asked. "I have one of those machines..."

"Sure." She said, but he knew that'd be the answer even if he had to ride a donkey down to Columbia to get the beans himself.

"Take a seat." He said, and began to busy himself with the process of the individual brewing machine, something cup it was called, a present from Bunko squad. Working the machine didn't take any degree of mental devotion, but he needed time to remember, to remember why.

There had been a long stretch of murders, particularly gruesome, and even though that was his career there were moments where he would pick up a stack of photos and still go a little green somewhere inside. Maybe it was a sign of age. He'd done his time, that was for sure, and no one expected him to go forever, but it just wasn't like it used to be, and it hadn't been for a good seven or eight months. What was once a sense of duty and justice had become a heavy weight.

So Sarina Veracruz had been...a pain reliever. Could he tell her that? One night after a couple of drinks and dances at the Nexus was no foundation for everlasting love. And love was something he truly had for his job. *Had.* It was becoming difficult to do, a labor like walking in knee-deep water on a sandbar in south Florida, unknowing to when the sandbar would end and the endless depth of sinking water would begin. He *wanted* to tell her he saw something in her eyes that triggered something he always wanted-a sense of kindness or whatever, but he couldn't lie. All he had seen at the Nexus was a curvy shape. And come to find out that the person it belonged to worked in the same building as he did and looked up to him as many did. It was some kind of lottery.

Erland brought Sarina her coffee.

"What kind is it?"

"Uh...something not too strong. I think. Cream or sugar?"

"Yes." She took it and set it on the side table next to the wall and the window where the blinds were still shut but since they never quite shut properly light was peeking through.

Erland went to the refrigerator. There was no more time to think.

He brought the cream and sugar and set it on the side table before coming around to the opposite end of the couch and taking a seat; not insecure, but most definitely unsure.

He had used her, like some kind of forbidden injection, and while he wasn't holding himself to some saintly standard it really bothered him. He had crossed a line inside of himself he didn't know was there.

"You're not having any?"

"If I start too early I don't stop."

Sarina administered the proper amounts of cream and sugar.

"So what are you going to do now that you're not working?"

"I haven't thought about it. I' d be drooling all over my pillow if you hadn't called."

She smiled but something clicked inside of her, behind her eyes, like it was time to move on. Perhaps it was the reference to sleep or the location of where sleeping was done.

"What can I say, Mike?"

"I don't know. Part of me knows that I reached out to someone in pain, and I can't avoid the core of it. Especially now that time is *all* I have."

Sarina's green olive eyes widened, saying *you*

have me too, if you want.

"I can't forget that night." She said. "Can you?"

Erland inhaled and shook his head.

"Sarina, all I do is forget. If I didn't, I'd be a basket case." Then his eyes went to a spot in the carpet no distinction from any other spot in the floor. "That said I can't. I remember it like it was yesterday."

"I'm sorry for not calling." She said. "I meant to, but I just didn't know what to say. I didn't know you were in pain about it..."

Erland smiled.

"If I didn't keep my cards *real* close they'd fall on the floor." Then he began to wring his hands. "...I, I've been having such a hard time with work, especially leading up to that night with the Granderson case and the two girls in Park Ridge, then Miller and Dobbs and that shooting at the school..."

Sarina nodded, her face screwed up.

"I can't imagine, Mike..."

"I have to look at pictures of blood and their dead bodies and the bloody murder weapons for hours, and dig into the personal lives of less than exemplary people with an unrelenting skepticism..." He looked up at her. "I'm cracking." He blinked and her face didn't change. It was still twisted, in empathy. "I'm shocked it's taken me this long. Maybe the timing of it was providence, whatever that means. I'd been slipping and no one saw."

"But you reached out to me."

"I reached out in the dark for something to make me feel better, to make all of the junk I carry around go away for a night, but it didn't." Erland stood and walked to the window. "Someone out there right now is getting murdered. Maybe not in this city, or this state, but somewhere, someone somebody loves is no longer on this planet."

Sarina stood and slipped her arms around him. On her toes she could place her chin on his shoulder.

"You just need a break."

"No, I need to stop." He stared in her olive green eyes. "While I'm still a human being."

A hand cupped his chin. Sarina's eyes were close to his.

"You are, I know you are. Don't give up on yourself. You're good at your job, and if you can't do it anymore, then that's because you've done your part and there's nothing more for you to do."

Finally someone understood his life had become some consuming study of death and the scars of morbid memories ran deep but not deep enough to cause permanent ruin. Even if his reaching out to her had not come from a place of purity, it had come from a place of humanity, and confirmed to him he was not past the gateway of becoming one of the morbid and emotionally destroyed criminals he was forced to live with inside.

The cordless cut through the apartment with an obnoxious tone.

Maybe she was going to kiss him. Maybe she wasn't. Erland left her arms and got the phone in the bedroom. He heard Sarina take a seat as he answered.

"Yeah?"

"Erland?"

"Who's this?

"Tallifer."

"What, d'you have bugs in my apartment?"

There was a space of time long enough for the Agent to roll his eyes.

"My superior, Marland, wants you to work with Homeland Security on the murder."

Erland chewed on his lip as he loafed back to the living room.

"You do? Why's that?"

"It's her call, not mine. I just do what she says. If you don't want to, you'll have to take it up with your Lieutenant, because he's fine with it. She was impressed with your record and we need all hands on deck."

Erland and Sarina exchanged glances.

"Where do I report?"

"Fircrest."

"Okay."

The call ended as abruptly as it started. Erland juggled the phone as he entertained a few thoughts, then tossed it on the couch, the thoughts along with it.

He was going to say something.

"I know." Sarina said, instead. She collected her purse and stood. "I think *you* should have that coffee."

"Lord knows how long the case will take."

"But at least you'll be able to walk away on your own terms. I saw the look in your eye at the gate. It was like you actually wanted to be there, marching through the forest at three in the morning." Sarina came closer. "Just remember what's waiting for you at the end of the road..."

Erland smiled to himself as she left. Then he went to find some more appropriate clothing, taking Sarina's coffee along with him.

ELEVEN

After requesting to take the day off, Jessica Birchall walked the parking lot with the silence of her thoughts. Was it, whatever *it* was, worth losing her career? She considered the question, and all of its temptation. Sure she had elbowed her way into a few stories and chased down those who originally wouldn't answer her questions, but all she did was report occurrences, events, and happenings. Car crashes, shootings, fires and occasionally those fuzzy-inside stories she wrote herself.

Never had she tangled with anything remotely career compromising, like labor unions, pharmaceutica, or the US Military. She was just a run of the mill pretty face on the tube that got to wear different colored overcoats and say all the right words for a few minutes per newscast.

Birchall reached her car and got a messenger bag from the trunk, one of two. So there was something Homeland Security didn't want the public to know at the Mansion. Yes, who the woman was and how she died, and especially *why*, but was it on the count of the upcoming elections? Or was it something bigger?

The reporter continued along the lot to where the lot ended in a line of stickly alder trees that had shed their leaves. When she saw no traffic she jaywalked across Woodward Avenue and walked to where it intersected with Pointer. There, a phone booth, a true scarcity these days, was stashed against a crusty looking smoke shop, also increasingly rare. It wasn't her ideal place to hangout, but she was going to be quick.

First, she called Precinct Three who was handling the case. She did not give her real name. She knew that was where Erland worked because she had covered the school shooting *and* the Granderson case before that. When she asked to speak with Erland the voice on the other end said he had taken the day off.

Birchall hung up after that and recorded it all on her notepad with her own unique shorthand that no one else could even begin to decipher. Why would Erland take the day off? He had worked almost fourteen hours days and God knew how much at home for twenty-six days to put Granderson behind bars. Erland *wouldn't* take the day off. He couldn't. He wasn't that kind of man.

It was strange but not conclusive.

Her next call was to the Libertarian Campaign office in Crescent. She called to inquire the name of the woman who was killed at the Mansion and the brush-off they dealt her was that the Police were handling it and all questions about it should be directed to them. The Party had no knowledge of the subject except for its occurrence and would be getting any information about it the same time the public did. And while it was true the Party had no special investigative powers that Jessica knew of, they knew quite well exactly *what* name on the guest list belonged to the deceased because everyone of the guests was some kind of heavy donor or staunch career member.

After hanging up, Birchall chewed on her lip and wrote. It was a very...*rehearsed* response and the Party member who answered the phone never bugged her about who *she* was, in other words, didn't care. The Party was in shutdown mode, and whatever reports may begin or had already begun to bubble around about the timing of the convention and the death would be answered with a shrug.

Was that their doing or had they been told? Instructed?

Ordered...

Birchall then called the consortium that owned Fircrest Mansion, Bellamy Family Financial, which amusingly worked out to become a very popular texting acronym and was three or four spots down on an Internet search if the acronym was typed in the engine.

Posing as a potential renter for a very expensive wedding, she learned from the extremely polite receptionist that Fircrest Mansion would be unavailable for a length of time unknown to them, due to the recent events. The receptionist further confided that the murder really hurt the Mansion's image, although she was surprised more hadn't been said about it in the news. Also, that despite Fircrest being one of their most prestigious northernmost properties, they also had a mansion, albeit half the size, on a lake near Mount Turbus.

For some reason that call got her to think more than the first two. Well, perhaps the first two got her to *assume* and the call to BFF got her to *think*.

Why hadn't this story erupted in the social eye? It was a politically related murder, wasn't it? If anybody heard convention and murder in the same sentence or saw it in a headline their imagination would run wild ever before the facts got out.

Well, she had been first to report it, and to her knowledge Thornton and Bravey from Four and Five respectively never talked to Erland, because he had gone back in the house. And, when she had shot her story, the small bit that it was, for the five AM slot, Thornton and Bravey were still waiting. She left shortly after that.

So Bellamy Family Financial was told something to the effect that Fircrest was locked down and no one could rent it out until it was officially deemed no longer a crime scene. Perhaps that was true but it seemed more intense than that, like an authoritative body had *taken over* the Mansion, and while the Police did close somewhere down for investigation there was usually more of an attempt at humanity to it.

The next call was to Thornton, just for the fact that she didn't like Bravey. He was nosy and rude. Not about facts like she was, but about personal information and stuff that didn't matter.

"Hello?"

"What's got three legs and no eyes?"

"Excuse me, who is speaking?"

Birchall laughed and the man on the other end no doubt shook his head. The answer was a bar stool, and it was a horribly clumsy attempt at a pickup line joke Thornton had witnessed a man lay on Birchall one night they had gone for drinks after reporting a recent warehouse fire.

"Jessica, what's with you? Call me on your cell, you know how I hate unknown numbers."

"Well I was out and about..."

"What's the deal?

"What?"

"With the story?"

Thornton cut to the chase. He was a former collegiate quarterback at a small school and was the kind of guy that had everything in life because he went and got it-but, the kind of life he went and grabbed was a fifty-seven thousand a year job with a stressful marriage. He was direct, whereas Bravey was accusatory, and Thornton was precise, where Bravey was statistical. Not to mention Thornton had a cheesy sense of humor and it made it easy to get him on a lighter side and keep him there.

"Fircrest?"

"Yeah, you were the only one who got to do it."

"Really? Wait, where are you right now?"

"I'm on my way to Wayliow, actually."

"Wayliow..."

"Yeah, there was a reports of a possible abduction."

"Oh, I thought you'd still be waiting for Erland to come out."

"No, he left. It was weird. These two suits came in, I don't know, about four, quarter past, and then all of the cops left. All of them. We had to leave too."

Jessica stared through the dirty and streaked glass for a moment and then began to scribble furiously, changing the phone from her left ear to her right, so she could pinch the phone between her shoulder and her ear as she wrote her illegible shorthand which was closer to cuneiform than English.

"Did they say why?"

"No. I think they were the FBI, maybe because it was the convention, you know. I'd be working on it but my editor told me just to take the next exclusive and wait on it."

"Did Bravey leave too?"

"Yeah, we both did. He said something about a lost hiker at the base of Mount Turbus."

Birchall flipped a page and stopped.

Wayliow was *really* close to Fircrest.

Abduction...

Was it the Fircrest suspect, the one with an injury...

"Hey listen Jessie, I gotta go."

"Hold on Danny, I'll be there in a little bit."

"It's my exclusive."

"I know, it's not about that. I'll tell you when I'm there..."

"Okay..."

Birchall hung up the phone and sighed. Whatever story was out there, it wasn't Fircrest. If Fircrest could end her career it could also make it. Those two suits weren't dusting for prints they were dusting Fircrest.

Birchall stuffed the notepad in the messenger bag and hugged herself as she walked back to her car. The angles were spreading themselves now, the cast of the crime was filling out. To catch a murderer was a story. To cover up a murder was a story. However it related to the convention was a story. Now the puzzle was little more than a game of sliding the pieces into place as they developed. That, and avoiding Hodge's warning as an extension of Homeland. They were the shutters, the lockers, the zippers. They were closing down everything and everyone related to the case, whatever the proximity.

It was only a matter of time before whatever they were rushing to keep the lid on was going to explode. It was the way of nature, and in an age where information was all but instantaneous, no government agency could hide the truth, no matter how hard they tried.

Jessica fired her Subaru and put it in gear on a path for Wayliow.

The Department Lumina pulled up just behind the TMFOV and Marland was met by Tabitha Grey, a young Agent they called T. She was the leader of Crescent's small division and had been enroute. She took off her sunglasses and shook Marland's hand. Marland knew from a short operation in Crescent years ago that T was a former Olympic gymnast though she never made it to the games and she had an All-American look and was a natural blonde. She wore brown slacks and a black leather jacket. Her hair was in a tight ponytail. It was because of Marland's recommendation that Tabitha was in the position she was.

"Hi Sierra, it's been awhile."

"Good movie." An Agent piped up in the background. There were three behind her, all men, lined up as if ready to be drafted.

"Hello Tabitha, how's your mother?"

The young Agent couldn't hide her surprise as she put her sunglasses back on. They were Serengeti.

"She's doing okay, thanks for asking. Thanks for remembering, I should say."

"Bring along some friends?"

"Yes," Tabitha turned and held out her hand, which she was unaware of how artistic the movement was, and all of her movements in general. "Let me introduce you."

"I'll be in bus." Ratner said, cellphone in hand. Marland nodded.

"From right to left; Luis Jimenez, Keith Quinlan, and Henry Morell."

Marland smiled and appraised them. Jimenez was a compact and healthy looking Hispanic of perhaps nearly forty, and her guess was he was either Cuban or Puerto Rican, and had a great deal of life experience that he drew on for his work in the agency. Quinlan was the tallest of them by nearly four inches and he carried a very intelligent undertone, from the perfect cropping of his auburn hair and the crispness of his suit and shininess of his shoes. Perhaps he was another MIT grad. Finally Morell, who was chewing gum and had yet to stop checking Marland out with his proud black eyes, was no question a smooth talker and an expert at extracting information from subjects that would be difficult for others. He knew what to say to who and when to say it and Marland looked forward to his attempts at her in the future, knowing they would be entertaining at best.

"Hello." Marland said genially and took in a breath of fresh air and turned to Tabitha. "Have they been briefed?"

"Not exactly."

"Okay, I'll make this part short so we can get to work. Don Bartleson in SAB is my boss. I answer directly to him. Homeland SAB Agent Magnolia Marland was killed during the course of an SAB operation here last night. Yes, she is my sister. Don't worry about it. Also, I know none of you are officially SAB cleared but what we have to do here won't jeopardize any sensitive material, and as long as you run everything you do by me and do exactly what I say, none of you will have any long IDD's after this is over, Lord knows how we hate those. Magnolia was attempting to make contact with a hacker we know only as Jupiter, who we believe was in attendance at the party here last night. Once we obtain the guest list, which should be any minute, we will have a very narrow field of players. It is imperative that you stay factual in your assessment of everything you do, remove all emotion from the picture. We are dealing with cold, ruthless people whose only incentive and reward for their work is money. *Always* keep that in mind. Also, we are searching for a suspect who was a witness to Magnolia's death. I will delegate these tasks between you, but both of these angles are of the utmost importance. Do your job like it's the *only* job. Okay?"

There were nods.

"Yes ma'am." Jimenez smiled.

"You'll get up to speed real fast once you're in the bus. One more thing, I don't have time to read your files so I'll just ask a few questions and lets go down the line. Okay?"

Nods again.

"I could send them to your tablet and you could read them later." Tabitha offered.

Marland shook her head.

"Okay, languages." Marland pointed her finger and went down the line.

"Spanish, English, a little French and Italian if I try very hard." Jimenez said.

"English, and a good deal of Latin." Quinlan smiled.

"Just American." Morell shrugged.

"Military?"

"No."

"No."

"US Army."

So Morell and Marland had something to talk about. Marland logged that bit of information.

"Specialty?"

"Latin American gangs and Immigration."

That was no surprise.

"Computer surveillance systems, mainly tracking, monitoring..."

"Interrogation...excuse me," Morell smirked, "Interviewing."

Marland sighed. Her guesses were pretty good, but that was the bulk of her career in a nutshell.

"Tabitha, where would they fit best?"

As she thought, Tallifer walking from the gate with his hands in his pockets.

"Jimenez on tracking the suspect for sure, and

then the rest of us on the guests."

"I agree completely. How many vehicles?"

"Two, but we can get more."

"I'll let you know if we need 'em. Okay T, take 'em in the bus, I'll be right there. Oh, one more thing..." The group paused and turned. "We will be giving provisional status to a local Homicide Detective who will be here shortly, so treat him like he's one of us for the time being. Okay? Thank you."

Tallifer scuffed up to Marland giving a dirty eye to the newcomers.

"T's in charge now?"

"Yes."

"What happened to MacEndell?"

"Uh...I think he...moved to Florida."

"Oh. Well, Rollins just got the guest list and we got something you should see in the house, so..."

"I'll come see what you have first."

"Okay."

"You want to tell me about it as we walk?"

"Sure." Tallifer reached in his jacket for his Marlboros to find he only had four left so he put them back. "We found a very small but sophisticated security camera near the bar."

"Really?"

"Yes. When I called Bellamy Financial about it, they said it was because they had a problem with caterers stealing alcohol. You know, it can garner thousands of dollars if done right, but, anyway, if it has anything we can use, it'll be a big score."

"Is it like a CCTV?"

"Not really, it just records to a memory card. I gather it's only used when the bar is used. We should be able to format a reader. If my research is correct the little guys film non-stop for a month, unless you set automatic shutoffs, then God knows how long it'll film for."

Tallifer got the front door for Marland.

"Are there any more cameras?"

"They wouldn't say."

"What do you mean?"

Tallifer stopped in the grand entrance and lowered his voice though it didn't matter because no one was listening.

"I have a theory that they don't want to tell us about the *other* cameras because then they'll have to let us see what was on them."

"You think there's damming evidence on BFF? Wouldn't they destroy it if there was?"

"No, not them, on someone else. I mean, who wouldn't take an illicit tumble in one of those bedrooms, or whatever the case was..." Tallifer lowered his voice even more, "At any rate, we know what to look for now, and we're in the process of ripping this place apart right after we dust if for prints, so we'll find the cameras...I just hope there was one in that room."

"How many do you have working now?"

"Four. Ten more are on route with the Mobile Crime Lab. We've done everything we can with the crime scenes until the MCL comes."

"Excellent. Don't bring the camera to the bus, yet. Wait till you have all of them and we'll log them separately all at once."

Tallifer nodded and Marland left. He stopped for a moment to think, eyes searching around the grandeur, wondering how many electric eyes were eyeing him back. It was strange, since he was a Homeland Security Agent and had worked in surveillance and with all of the gadgets they employed and knew good and well the power of observation available not only on the national level but in the private sector, that he had never really thought about who was watching him.

He turned to the open door frame to see the slowly shrinking shape of Sierra Marland on a line of gray in thick borders of green and her feminine grace had a way of making nearly everything around her feel like a living painting.

The eyes were watching him watch her. But who was watching them? And yes, all of it was recorded and stored, documented and detailed.

It was bigger than him. Bigger than he'd ever be, but at least he was on the right side of it. That's why he hated Jupiter so badly, because Jupiter was in the electric eye business and somehow always knew where the traps were and where the exits were. That's why he had slipped out of Fircrest. The eyes were on *his* side.

The Homeland Agent known as Hill followed the man who suspiciously entered Mutual Partners Bank through the mild pedestrian traffic of seven ten AM. He wasn't sure what set the man apart from others he'd seen, or if Hill was the only one being suspicious, but after three blocks of pursuit, Hill was convinced the man who had entered the bank had something to do with the box.

Hill advanced as quickly as he could without alerting the man. On the corner of Brooks and Fourteenth, Hill passed the man and shot four quick profile photos with his phone before the man nervously looked around to those who were awaiting the crosswalk with him.

Hill left the man and placed a call, walking back to the bank.

"Yes?"

"I'll send you some pictures. Tell me who this is."

The Agent sent the pictures.

"Got it. Call you back."

"Thanks."

Hill confidently strode through the bank lobby to Parmindy and flashed his badge.

"Ma'am, may I ask you what the man in the blue jacket wanted just now."

The woman was surprised at first and complied.

"Yes, he wanted a safety deposit box."

"410?"

"Yes."

Hill pushed off the counter and began to run, grabbing his cell phone and hitting a designated speed dial.

"This is Agent Luther Hill, Homeland Security, Go code 518, I am requesting Police pursuit on a possible murder suspect and confirmed threat to national security, suspect is advancing south southeast on Fourteenth, suspect is potentially armed and must be subdued non-violently with extreme prejudice. Suspect is white male, mid-thirties, wearing a blue raincoat and white athletic shoes."

Hill struck a fast jog, peeking left ever so often for a sight of the man. He was about three blocks away, in a rough L-shape, and though he didn't know where the man was going, or what his pattern was, he had an educated guess. Hill was drawing upon his time as a bail bondsman as well, where he hunted many a bond skipper through the urban jungle. There was a predication to it, a calculated assumption. A feeling, almost.

The Agent cut across Brooks and ran up Thirteenth, hoping to catch sight of him in the crosswalk. Even in the crisp and chilly early-November morning, Hill was beginning to perspire. He was in good shape and ran a couple of miles a week but the treadmill was not the hard, cold pavement, dodging lumps of clothing and waiting for traffic lights.

He caught sight of the blue jacket all the way over on fifteenth but still heading south southeast and after taking a second pause in his run, confirmed it was the target and sped off.

The cellphone rang in his hand.

"Go."

"His name's Darren Reston, he's a reporter for the Crescent Modern Journal."

A reporter? Holy...

"Tell Jupiter, quick, I'm going to get him before the cops do."

"The cops?"

"I had to...if we lose him we lose what was in that box." Hill waited for the light. "We can always take him once he's in custody."

"You...fine, just get him. Io out."

Hill settled back into his jog. He would be on Reston in a few minutes. Police sirens entered his ears from blocks away, it was impossible to tell from which direction. Hill cursed himself, his timing was off. Precinct Four was within spitting distance of the Pinnacle building. Was that where the man was headed, back to Cherry? No, he was going south.

Capital Station. The suspect could board a subway to a number to any number of locations or handoff whatever was in the box either on the train or even before. It would be an insurmountable loss if a third party reporter blew the whistle. Playing both sides as he was, Hill knew if the government got the man and whatever was in the box, they'd recess into a false sense of security and try to sort it all out in the organized chaos they called due process, and if he was patient, he'd be able to get whatever information Jupiter wanted so badly, and perhaps even more. If he got to the man before the government did, then, the contents of the box would be his and the man would be dead. It was the ideal situation. But if the reporter took dynamite to the whole thing, there'd be no end to the fallout of it.

Hill skipped across the dashed white lines and almost hit a bicyclist in a yellow rain suit, turning up Fifteenth. He held for a second and scanned for his target and spotted him near the entrance of Capitol Station. As Hill dropped into a dead sprint, the man paused at a newspaper stand. The sirens increased and Hill saw a squad car dangerously flying around the corner of Parkway just missing a passenger bus that had pulled to the side.

Running on to the street from the sidewalk Hill pulled out his badge and the car swerved to a stop, the door opening almost simultaneously. Traffic ahead and behind had either slowed or stopped altogether. Pedestrians too, were beginning to gum up the sidewalks.

Hill knew the entire thread of the plan either being a success or a failure was in the space of two or three heartbeats.

"Have the next car hold the entrance. If he runs, we will pursue; if he splits, I'll stay on him and you two cover the subway."

The two Officers rushed from the car, drawing their Glocks. Hill drew his Sig-Sauer and there were a few gasps. Strangely the man in the blue raincoat hadn't moved from the newspapers, his hand was touching one of the boxes, near the quarter slot. Was he trying to blend? Or was he hiding something?

Did he know he was being followed?

Before Hill could figure it out they were on him.

"Homeland Security, put your hands up!"

The man looked up and without hesitating ran into the station.

Hill leapt the curb and rushed in after him as
sirens from the second car preceded the squealing of
tires. One of the Officers stayed back to inform the
newcomers and Hill knew by the jingle jangle behind
him the other officer was close on him.

The steep stairs were hard to manage and Hill's
eyes darted between his feet and the dark blue jacket,
not even one hundred yards ahead. Once they entered
the small flat terminal, Hill took a chance.

"Stop or I'll shoot." He yelled as the man ran
for the turnstiles.

"Get down, get down!" The cop with him
shouted. Screams and compliance came from the scant
pedestrian traffic.

The man did not stop and Hill was not going to
shoot. An Officer Involved Shooting investigation was
the *last* thing he wanted. The man hopped the turnstile
with a vaulted-motion that slowed him down and
dodged to the left behind the sweep of a wall.

"Go, cut him off." Hill pointed and the Officer
ran left, and would potentially cut him off in a matter of
minutes if the reporter named Reston continued toward
the southerly subway platform. Hill had to get him
before then, so much depended on it.

Instead of vaulting the turnstile with his hand
assisting as Reston had, Hill leapt over it like a track
hurdle. He took the corner at a sharp angle and ran into
a pedestrian, sending her into the wall.

He had Reston in his sights, he wasn't going to
the south platform.

Perfect.

Hill holstered his gun and ran as fast as he could
down the causeway, closing in on Reston. His lungs
were burning with pain but the fire of his contract with
Jupiter burned in the steel of his mind and was stronger
than any pain he felt or could feel.

Reston took a right. He was trying to get back to street level.

Hill sped around the corner and as Reston reached the stairs, Hill leapt and snagged the reporter's foot. Hill's face ground against Reston's white shoes as they stood in place and Reston put out his hands to block his face from the pain of the concrete steps. Reston grunted and wriggled as Hill leapt on top of him in a standing straddle. Hill's Sig-Sauer made a clicking-sucking noise as he ripped it from its holster and stuck it in Reston's face.

"Where is it? Give it to me."

"Where is what?"

"Homeland Security, dammit, give me what was in box 410!"

The reporter's nose began to trickle blood, slowly.

"What?"

"Did you pass it off?" Hill wrenched a wad of jacket and shook violently. "Hmm? Where is it?"

The jingle jangle of Officers preceded their heavy footsteps at the top of the staircase.

Hill blinked as if it was a mirage and let his breath catch up to him, his body unwinding ever so slowly until he pushed himself up and held the gun limply in his right hand.

"I got him."

Hill wiped his nose and stared at Reston as Reston stared at him. Then the cops flipped Reston over and his hands went together.

"I want a lawyer." He said, face to a floor that smelled of urine.

"You have the right to remain silent..." One of the Officers spoke.

Hill placed his Sig back in the holster and went for his phone.

"It's contained. He's in police custody."

"..."

Hill distanced himself by a few feet as the cops put the cuffs on the writer.

"I don't know what it is yet, I don't know if he still has it, but it'll come out..." The double Agent's eyes darted around and he held his breath for a beat as the Officer who had followed him into the station at the pursuit's origin came rushing up to assist the arrest. "But it just got a whole lot harder."

Hill put the phone away and wearily followed the Officers to the morning daylight as they escorted Reston to the nearest squad car in the sight of the entire city block. As badly as Hill wanted to flash his badge again and take Reston to Homeland's office on Seventh he had no car, and once Tallifer knew he had the suspect from Fircrest he'd want him immediately-it was too risky, too much on the line to blow.

The Homeland Security Agent named Hill would wait, and be patient.

TWELVE

Sierra Marland opened the door to the TMFOV and the hectic sound of communication. Tabitha Grey turned as Marland took the three steep steps slowly. On one of the screens she could see the face of a somewhat nondescript and normal looking man. His name was Darren Reston and he lived at 134 Place just outside of Mossyrock. The photo was from his driver's license. Also on the screen were seven stills taken from Mutual Partners bank on Cherry.

"The box was opened." Tabitha said, seeing Marland was watching the screen and listening to the work her team was doing, hearing bits and pieces of the phone calls and conversations.

"Then she passed off the key."

Tabitha turned to the screen.

"He was at the party."

Sierra received a paper from Grey. It was the guest list, printed out, faxed directly from the local Libertarian Party office that had helped coordinate some of the logistics and grunt work of yesterday's long string of activities. Reston's name was circled. Her eyes couldn't help notice Lacey James-Henderson a few spots away. It was Magnolia's cover name, and since they were identical in nearly every way and switched in and out of operations many times for many reasons, it was also like seeing her own name.

"Who's got him?"

"Crescent PD."

"What Precinct?"

"Three." Marland squinted and thought as Tabitha asked, "Do you want him transferred to our building on Seventh?"

"No. The cops are keeping him for now...what did they charge him with?"

"Attempted murder."

Marland frowned and turned quickly like she had forgotten something and then looked back.

"Did they have a description from the investigation?"

"No, Hill called in a go code."

"He did?" Marland couldn't hide her surprise. *Hill?* He used to track people down for a living. There was no way the conversation was private and Jimenez' ear perked up and he half turned before going back to his work on a man with a Russian name.

"Well, keep 'em corralled and I'll take some help down there. What's Erland's ETA?"

"Five minutes, give or take."

"Re-route him to Precinct Three. I'm sure he knows where it is-he's got a desk there. Send his Provisionals over there."

Marland was about to leave when Tabitha stood from her seat and came closer.

"So..." Her voice was low and her Midwestern accent was somehow more noticeable, "Is it an *attachment* provisional or an *inclusion* provisional?"

"Attachment."

The former gymnast smiled broadly and her teeth couldn't have been more photogenic.

"Thank God."

That meant Erland would still be a Police Detective but be in the loop as little or as much as she saw fit. The other option would make him a Homeland Security Agent, with limited power and privilege but a whole lot more than a city police detective. While she would reserve the right to *deputize* Erland in a manner of speaking and make him a provisional Homeland Agent, she knew doing so straight away would ostracize him from the team. They were not the most humble collection of characters in the judicial branch to say the least and were very proud of having *earned* their power.

Marland left and saw Tallifer speaking to Ratner about something by their car. The conversation stopped when she arrived.

"I'm going to Wayilow to bring in the woman who spoke with the witness."

"His name's Darren Reston. He's a journalist." Both of the Agents knew what that meant. "He had the key. He got the box and Hill called in a go code to get him. He must've run. He's gotta be the guy alright, I'm sure he was in the room with Maggie. He's down at Precinct Three and I'm going to carve him up like a spiral cut ham if I have to."

Tallifer had some kind of glee on his face.
"Excellent."

"I'm going to take Morell with me and we're going to meet Erland there and give him his provisionals." Upon hearing this Tallifer's face fell to a faintly bitter grimace. There was no question *he* wanted to interrogate Reston, but *he* was the only one on site not only qualified enough but *capable* enough to administrate the investigation of the monstrously opulent crime puzzle that was Fircrest, leading the charge from the front. In a way, Marland had given him the most unglamorous and at the same time important job of the entire investigation.

Ratner reached for the keys of the Lumina and

dismissed himself.

"Morell." Tallifer shook his head.

"Interrogation is his specialty." Marland turned to stride back to the bus. "A workwoman knows her tools."

As she turned her back and entered the bus Tallifer bit his cheek and sulked back to the Mansion to continue searching room by room, inch by inch for black cameras no bigger than a mechanical pencil.

Once Marland entered she came to the mainframe bank and rested against it for a beat as she called for Morell.

His head snapped up and at the jerk of hers he was up from his place like the seat of his pants was on fire. He caught up to Marland just outside the door.

"Don't forget your sidearm." She said.

Morell cursed and ran back in the bus. Sierra continued walking and smiled to herself. So Tallifer thought she was preferring Morell for his skills. Little did either of them know the role Morell would be playing. It never ceased to amaze Sierra to what ends a person's mind would go so quickly over what, a comment? A gesture? An unspoken thought? In her time working with Tallifer, he seemed to always take things very hard, personal things, like another Agent being selected for a task over him. Perhaps he hadn't had that one good life lesson yet about being rejected. Or maybe he *had* gone through it and hadn't learned much.

Morell wouldn't hear one word of the interrogation. Not a single word. He wasn't briefed *or* cleared. Marland knew as she walked toward the team's vehicles that the deeper the investigation went, the more she'd have to shield and segregate and manage the differing levels of sensitive information between her team members. Tallifer had the hardest job and he knew of CONSTANT. He knew of the box and what was in the box. He didn't know what she or Bartleson knew *about* CONSTANT, but he knew Jupiter was the target. He knew Jupiter a little better than most of Homeland did, but he didn't know everything. Tabitha on the other hand knew box 410 was important but had no idea what was inside of it. She knew nothing of CONSTANT. None of them did, except Ratner, Tallifer, Marland and Bartleson, who she pulled out her phone to dial.

Morell came thumping up.

"Sorry 'bout that, Sierra."

The beautiful Agent stopped at a white Suburban and turned to him. He squinted at her as the sun shone over her right shoulder.

"If you ever forget your sidearm again you *will* be sorry, and although my name is Sierra, I never gave you permission to use it."

He smiled an easy breezy thing in a boyish way that matched his remotely boyish face.

"I'm..." He was about to apologize again and held up a thumb angled toward the bus. "It's just that Tabitha's real lax about that and I heard you with her, so..."

"I don't care if you guys practice yoga while you're doing IDFT's, we do it *my* way, understood?"

"Yes...Agent Marland."

Morell dug in his pocket for the keys to the Suburban. He held them out.

"You drive."

Morell's head lolled with cockiness all his own.

"Yes...Agent Marland."

Sierra made a quick call to her superior outside of the white Suburban as Morell fired the engine.

Hopefully her plan would work.

The frail and decrepit figure dressed in a soft green sweater and slacks made his way through the office from the elevator. The office was well lit and immaculately clean and held no more than twenty spacious cubicles, only a few of which were filled.

The secretary looked up from her day planner as the man approached.

"Ah, Mr. Bellamy, you're in early today."

The old man smiled and continued walking. He was Robert Bellamy the Third, President of Bellamy Family Financial. The secretary smoothly rose from her seat and opened the door for him. Her name was that of a flower, Bellamy didn't remember which. Iris? No, Lily...

"Thank you."

"Your son should be returning from his trip from Toronto today."

"Oh, is he?"

Bellamy continued the aged shuffle to a giant leather throne that seemed insignificant behind the table that stretched before it.

"And there's a...Mr. Polis to see you."

Bellamy perked up and sighed once he settled in the chair.

"I'll see him now."

The secretary adjusted her eyeglasses and nodded.

Bellamy sighed again and rubbed an arthritic hand over his heart. It had been a week since the specialist had diagnosed him with arrhythmia and while the medication had been helping, he feared it was getting worse.

Mr. Polis was a compact man with a strong chin and stiff, gelled hair that had been dyed a shade too dark for his skin. There was a hardness in his eyes and strength in his fists that Bellamy had not seen for some time. He was in top physical shape for being close to fifty years old and wore a leather blazer. A gold Rolex was visible on his wrist and held more sentimental than monetary value.

When the secretary had closed the door behind her, Polis spoke in a voice sounded as if it was laced with French, when in actuality he was of Flemish birth and there was a difference, subtle though it was.

"What is the job?"

"Fircrest Mansion."

Polis ambled closer, letting his fingers glide across the top of the smooth table.

"That won't be easy."

"It won't be the hardest thing you've ever done."

A smile bit into the side of Polis' face, more of a sneer.

"You're right." He crossed his arms. "Do you want me to plant something? Or to steal it?"

"There's a small surveillance camera in a bedroom on the east wing. I need you to get it before Homeland Security does."

Polis shook his head.

"I thought cops handled murders."

"I don't know what's going on, but they've taken over the Mansion and they *cannot* find that camera. You won't have much time. You'll have to do it tonight."

Polis shook his head again.

"Rush fee."

"I know! I don't care!" Bellamy raised his voice no more than a decibel and put his hand on his heart and blinked his eyes a few times. "If you don't get the camera I won't be able to pay you anything. Not now, not ever. My secretary will give you a blueprint. The room is designated F-Thirty Four."

Polis came around the table and put a calloused hand on old Bellamy's shoulder.

"Don't worry. I'll get it." The professional thief moved to the door and paused. His jacket made a scrunching sound. "Are you alright?"

"No." The financial genius shook his head. "Robert is coming in today. I'm going to tell him."

"You are going to retire?"

The old man chuckled and it was a wheezing, breathy laugh.

"You could say that."

Polis smirked and pointed his finger at the old man.

"Have I ever let you down? Same time, tomorrow."

Bellamy nodded, and if Polis didn't return with the camera, Bellamy didn't know if his heart would make it through the turmoil that would follow.

Courtland slammed the front door to the small rambler behind him.

"Ten minutes!" He called out and the team began to flawlessly snap into action. Even Kirke, face still warped in a snarl from his encounter with Magnolia Marland, rushed to help Brock disconnect and pack up the electronic equipment. A black Yukon and a small moving van of the same color were parked outside of the rambler and the team of four was quick and systematic as they made necessary preparations.

Courtland checked his watch as he sat in the passenger seat of the Yukon. Eight minutes ten seconds elapsed time.

Pitts took the driver seat and Courtland eyed the rear view mirror. Brock gave a thumbs up from the driver's seat of the moving van and Kirke put a stick of chewing gum in his mouth.

"Hit it." The stocky leader told the former soldier. "We're going to PierHouse."

Team Io was on the move. Team Callisto would be there too. Team Europa was running critical field operations and Ganymede was preparing the exchange site. Jupiter was coming to land and the "moons" would be surrounding him, spinning and orbiting, waiting for his command to take the program to the next level. If the timing was right, then Homeland Security's dangling carrot would be their own demise, and Jupiter would be able to use their own momentum against them, like judo, and turn their world upside down and take what they held most valuable in one smooth, seamless strike.

Kelly Barnett was at her desk when the phone rang.

"Is Darren in yet?"

The voice on the other end was the editor, Mackie. She wasn't aware Mackie had come in yet. Her desk faced the door and she'd been watching.

"He's working from home."

"Not today he's not. I'll call him. The deadline for the rough's been moved up. It's not my decision. I want him on the floor. Jorgensen will give him a hand."

Barnett looked around, and curled her hair behind her ears.

"He's...a little tired."

"Of course he is, that's why Jorgensen will help."

"Jorgensen wasn't even at the convention, let alone the dinner."

There was a pause from Mackie, then the sharp honking of a horn. He was in transit, perhaps stuck in the thick bottleneck of the Interstate. The commute alone was enough to cause ulcers at times and Mackie

was under a great deal of stress with private funding
meetings coming up in December.

"No, but he's a good support writer."

Barnett stood with the phone and squinted as the
door opened and a group of four came in. They were
the Democrat writers and had biked to work.

"Darren doesn't like Jorgensen."

"I don't care, Kelly...this city..." The honking
continued and the editor swore. "You call him, okay.
Get him in before eight and if you don't he'd better be
in before nine with something on paper."

The writer swallowed.

"Yes Mr. Mackie."

Kelly dialed Reston's home. She waited and
waited and got the answering machine. She hung up
and called again and chose not to leave a message. She
tried his cellphone and got the voicemail.

Kelly Barnett slammed the phone down and
grabbed her jacket, running to the door. If Darren was
negligent on this one he would *lose* his job. The CMJ
had given him a gift on a silver platter and he had
chosen vodka instead.

No matter, Kelly would save the day again. She
cared about Darren more than he knew. Maybe for once
he would see that.

Thoughts rushed through her head, things to say
if she saw him pathetically wrapped up in a blanket on
the couch or bent over on the kitchenette table. Was he
worth the space in her soul? Was he worth the effort?

Part of her was determined to find out. She
thought about him *way* more than he thought about her,
if he ever *did*. She had even cut her hair short because
he made a comment about wondering what it would
look like and she had taken to wear the vanity frames
because of overhearing a conversation Darren had with
a co-worker about how women that wore glasses looked

more intelligent.

She was tired of his inconsistency and his mediocrity. As a writer, he had the tools to be not only compelling, but effective. And as a man, well, not only did she find him attractive, but charming and thoughtful, and she wasn't looking for that former athlete who still tried to be the man in a co-ed league, or that failed intellectual who hosted dinner parties to satiate his own ramblings, but a man she could...*love*. They'd had dinner more than once and on two separate occasions he'd spilled some dreams of his. Perhaps it had been the Merlot talking. If he had won her over in a moment or it was the proximity of working together for three years, she couldn't tell-her emotions were tumbling around inside over it all.

If she kept breaking his fall and covering his back he'd never change. But she cared too much to watch him fall, to see him disgraced.

Kelly slipped into her station wagon and fired the engine. The radio sparked to life as well, a drowsy country number spilled from the speakers with a woman's drawl over steely slide guitar.

She shut it off. Silence would be her companion on the drive to Mossyrock.

THIRTEEN

The drive was quiet until Morell couldn't stand it any longer. Sierra Marland had been a stoic statuette, gazing thoughtfully out the window. She knew his disposition was in high gear on the count of her beauty and that it might not have registered to him that she had just lost her best friend in the entire universe. She had read his file-not the file that Tabitha put together, but the one on the SAB computer. It was as if he didn't have a choice. He was *driven* to women. And while it hadn't yet interfered with the job he had done thus far at Homeland, it sat like a cloud over his true potential and it was not only unnecessary for the job demanded of him at Marland's side but quite simply unacceptable.

"I see you don't carry a side arm." He began with a slick carelessness.

"So you were looking."

"No..." Marland could feel the temperature rise in the car as Morell's face flushed. "I didn't..."

"So you were looking?"

Morell pursed his lips and smirked. His eyebrows came together to say, *why not.*

"Yeah, I was."

Marland nodded and returned to examine the scenes that passed before the window, rich and poor intermingling on First, waiting for the twice a day ferry up the mouth of the Targus River to Christmas Island.

"You're not the first."

"Not the first what?" Morell was quick.

"Numbnuts who thinks there are those that are crazy about you and those that are about to be."

Morell's face twitched and he reloaded.

"Does that mean you're not into guys or something?"

"I'm not into numbnuts guys like you."

Morell's face was redder than ever and it wasn't because of the commuter traffic beginning to pour in through North Crescent from the Interstate.

"You know I could report you for harassment."

"Then you'd be proving my point about what you're lacking downstairs."

The haughty Agent turned to her.

"What's your trip anyway?"

Marland was as calm as could be.

"Because I'm not easy now you're going to get mad at me?"

Morell's mouth wiggled around a few times and he clenched his fist and stared out the window as the Suburban came to a halt.

There was silence until the light changed and the trickle of traffic began to unthaw.

Marland sighed. Enough of the game.

"I know more about you than you think I do, Henry." The Agent's ears perked up at the use of his first name. "I know about your...relationships, that's not to say that I'm a voyeur or an abuser of my office in anyway...I bring it up because I know how good you *can be* at your job, and how easily distracted you can get."

Marland turned from the window. Morell met her quietly intense gaze. His eyes then darted between hers and the road as he searched his vocabulary for an apology.

"I..."

"I need you to be focused, Henry, like never before. What you do off duty is up to you, but once you punch your timecard all of that has to go. There's more at stake here than you can imagine, and it's going to take a lot out of you-there's going to be times where your mind wants to slip and you have to be rigid with it, like nothing else in the world matters but what you're doing and what you're ordered to do." Marland sat back in the seat and took a deep sigh eyes to the soft tan of the roof. "Anything less than that and you could die, or worse, get someone *else* killed."

Morell didn't say anything for a few minutes. Then he nodded as a young man would having received instruction from an elder.

"Thank you, Agent Marland."

"Call me Sierra." She smiled. "And besides," She tapped him warmly on the shoulder. "I'm spoken for."

Morell chuckled at himself and turned into the parking garage of Precinct Three.

"What's his name, if I may ask?"

"I'll let you know when I meet him."

Precinct Three was one of the few buildings in the department that had benefitted from last years' cigarette and alcohol tax increase and had been not only fully retrofitted with new technologies and fixtures but radically redesigned while somehow maintaining a continuity to CPD's other stations and buildings.

Erland slowed and signaled and his Toyota turned and dipped down to the entrance of the parking garage, stopping at the gate.

"Hello." The Officer said from the booth. "May I see your ID?"

Erland gave him his badge.

"There's a spot reserved for you near the elevator, Sir." The Officer returned Erland's ID. "The desk sergeant will get you situated."

"Thanks."

Erland eased the Toyota forward. The top floor was the motor pool and Erland saw two SWAT vehicles being washed as the car dipped lower. On the third level he found the spot reserved for him and parked next to a white Suburban.

He looked to the console and the mug he brought from home and took the last swig of the coffee, even though it had gone cold. Remembering his moment with Sarina, he locked up the car and took the elevator.

Not knowing what was in store for him, he chose to wear a generic yet timeless blue suit and white shirt, no tie. He always had to fiddle with them to get them right and after thinking it actually was right he would work through the day and see himself in the mirror hours later and the tie would be askew once more. It wasn't a case of vanity, but rather, efficiency, and anything that required so much maintenance was not worth it, unless of course protocol required it. Then, the protocol itself was a case of vanity.

The lobby was a broad yet narrow space that was clean on the eyes and was the hub of many hallways.

Erland came to the desk and tapped it.

"Hello, Detective Erland..."

The desk sergeant acknowledged him and reached for a red folder next to the computer monitor.

"You have your badge and your sidearm?"

"Yes."

The desk sergeant opened the folder and handed the detective a glossy clip on ID and two papers.

"Fill these out and sign these please."

Erland did.

"I don't think I've been here since the remodel...my old desk is stashed somewhere in this place but I've been hopping around Precincts."

The desk sergeant smiled and obviously didn't recognize Erland though he got the feeling she took pride in remembering names and faces.

"I like it..." She said, eyes wandering around. It was new, and clean, and the plants weren't from the eighties, but there was little to really *like*.

Erland signed the papers with a series of scratchy pen marks.

"Is that it?"

"Yes." The desk sergeant collected the paper. "They're expecting you in the Observation Room, it's in B4, to your left about a hundred yards on the right."

"Thank you very much."

Erland walked and made sure to breath deep and think absolutely nothing. He debated making an attempt at a bury-the-hatchet-speech if he saw Tallifer in the observation room although they were both just tools of the process and it really was nothing personal. Perhaps Tallifer could've been less suspicious...and a lot more gracious.

Erland arrived in Hall B, and saw a man of boyish looks chewing gum as he paced in front of the door to B5. He was wearing a black suit. As Erland walked up the man stared at his chest.

"Detective Erland?"

"Yes."

"Henry Morell, Homeland Security."

They shook hands.

"Are you in charge?"

"No." The Agent smirked. "I'm security. The Agent in charge will be along soon, you can wait in the observation room."

Morell got the door and as Erland stepped in the room he felt an immediate temperature change. The small room was a cloudy color and at the moment, had absolutely nothing in it, except for the overhead light that cast no more light than was necessary to see through the two-way mirror into the Interrogation Room. If Erland had any time to question whether or not there should've been recording equipment it would've been wasted. He was working with a new animal now, and was a guest of a party of a different culture. Anything and everything in his mind was going to be carefully filtered before being processed.

The man in the arctic white Interrogation Room was a mid-thirties man who looked to be as Crescent as one possibly could, that was to say he was a white American and was simply a normal looking person who more than likely enjoyed a good microbrew or watching his favorite sport on TV. Maybe he had a motorcycle. Maybe he was divorced. Maybe he had a special talent but the odds said he didn't, and he was more than likely as simple and plain as low-fat yogurt. He was wearing a sweatshirt that Erland couldn't read the writing on and white tennis shoes that were a few smudges away from being brand new.

Erland put his hands in his pockets. He was in the dark. Was *this* the man who had escaped through the woods? Or was it someone else?

The doorknob rattled in Interrogation and a woman stepped in. Erland couldn't see her face but she was about five foot seven, slender, and had very healthy, dark hair that caught the overhead light as if it came from a TV commercial.

The man handcuffed at the table looked up.

His eyes flared, gripped with shock and fear.

"No, it can't be!"

The man pushed himself back from the table

and fell awkwardly on the floor.

"No, it's a ghost...God help me..."

Erland squinted and the woman walked around the table. He was still unable to see her face.

"I'm not a ghost, Mr. Reston."

"God help me..." The man was covering his eyes, and the random breaks in his voice denoted an immense burden of stress.

"Mr. Reston..."

"My mind is shot..." Reston pulled his sleeves away from his eyes and stared at the woman, blinking with, in his mind, no small amount of bravery at what the spiral of his life had become.

"God Almighty..." Reston covered his eyes. "I'm going insane!"

Reston pressed his wrists into his face and began to cry.

The woman crossed her arms and walked back around the table.

Erland chewed on his lip. What on...

The doorknob rattled and the woman walked in.

Erland's heart skipped a beat and his body flushed, sending goose bumps and heat in a nuclear flash across every square inch of his body.

The woman *was* the murdered woman of Fircrest. There was no difference between them, save that one was dead, and the other was very much alive and standing in front of him. Reston might've thought he was insane but Erland knew he wasn't.

They were the *same*.

She saw the shock on Erland's face and shut the door, wordlessly walking to stand next to him.

"I have a lot of explaining to do, I know." She turned to the two-way mirror. "It's not what you think it is."

"I don't know *what* to think." Erland said.

"Who..."

"My name is Sierra Marland." The beautiful woman offered her hand. "I believe you've already met my late sister, Magnolia."

Erland's head rolled back slowly and his faced relaxed as he shook her hand, which was a firm, confident one, but naturally so and not trying hard to be.

"Mike Erland...I'm very sorry."

"So am I Detective." She turned back to the glass. "That's why you're here. You see, Maggie was in the middle of a very dangerous operation and there's a lot at stake if we don't figure out who killed her."

"Is that why you brought me in?"

"It's more than that, Detective. More than that."

The woman left again and so did Erland's calm and composure. He was still a bit shaken inside to see so vivid and alive what had been etched in his investigative memory as so irrevocably dead. As he watched her enter Interrogation he kept shaking his head how perfectly precise of a copy she was. Flawless.

"Stop crying..." She said to Reston and picked him up by the shoulders and put him back in the chair. "Come on."

Reston grimaced at her with red eyes.

"What is this? What's the point of all this?"

"Listen to me, Mr. Reston. I *know* you're innocent." His head twitched and he blinked at her, face still twisted. Erland crossed his arms and squinted. Marland spoke slowly and clearly like she was speaking to a child. "The woman you saw in that room was my twin sister. I *know* you did not kill her. Clear?"

The reporter nodded in a disembodied way.

"She gave you the key to that box before she died. I need what was in that box. Do you have it?"

The reporter nodded again.

"It's in my left sock." He said, with a sticky, dehydrated mouth.

She moved around the table to get it. Erland determined they had only patted him down and stuck him in the room, handcuffed. A strip search would've compromised the security of what the Marland sisters were doing. In a strange way, their crazy mission that he wasn't even beginning to try to figure out had been a success, albeit, with a tremendous sacrifice.

Marland retrieved the memory card and stood behind Reston, hands on his shoulders.

"Thank you, Darren." She bent down and spoke in his ear. "She did right by you and you did right by her. I'll be right back."

She left and his head flopped forward, loose and relaxed and he let out a thick sigh.

Erland put his hands in his pockets as Sierra returned with the memory card.

"I need you to do a service for your country." She said, standing next to him and looking into the room. "Because it's about to be under attack like it never has before."

Erland's head bobbled with sincerity.

"I will. I'm yours now."

Sierra looked him in his eyes and then her eyes went to the ID on his chest and back. Her mouth gave a small twitch and she cast a glance back to the door before returning her confident gaze to the Detective.

"I'm in a branch of Homeland that handles special assignments. For over three years now, *our* information has been compromised at a low level. I'm not talking about teenage hackers making Pyrrhic assaults on the White House homepage, I'm talking about our own secure network data-that's all of our work at a lower level, being compromised by a hacker we know only as Jupiter." Marland turned back to the mirror. "Well, he's more than a hacker. He's an information broker. He steals our information and sells it to the highest bidder. For example, remember when we were tracking the man responsible for the Embassy bombing last year?"

"Yes. It was all over the news that he was killed by his own men."

"It was made to look that way. When we found out he was here in the United States, we moved as quickly as we could but since our network had been severely compromised, Jupiter sold the information to an unknown party that wanted to exact revenge on the bomber on behalf of one of the people he got in the blast. We felt it on all levels. Members of the media accused *us* of killing the bomber ourselves and eschewing due process, but we knew the worst of it was that our sovereign borders were the site of a multi-party execution brokered by a faceless hacker who used *our* information without us knowing about it. I'll never forget the look on my boss' face after he met with the President. We knew what the public knew. With all of our cameras and satellites, we were so far in the dark it was farcical."

"And your sister..."

"We decided to bring Jupiter into the open with a temptation that would be too great to refuse. The operation was called CONSTANT, which stood for Criminal Operations Network Satellite Tracking and Notation Test. That's all it was, a giant test. We know he has insiders in our Department and it was known we were using a massive four billion dollar grant to upgrade our system into one all seeing eye that sat above the United States like a space station. We went as far as to launch a rocket into space to convince Jupiter that we were progressing with the upgrade earlier than scheduled-even though what we did launch is still sitting there in orbit pumping out radiation like Fukoshima and there's no practical use for it but Jupiter's thinks otherwise, because the bait we used was real. Only four people knew the fullness of the operation-only four people in Homeland know how worthless that system upgrade grant would be if we didn't catch this guy-it would mean the most advanced surveillance project on earth would have a Titanic flaw in its construction and the very enemy it was designed to keep out would be dealt a winning hand at the house table every time."

Erland shook his head. Marland looked down to the ground.

"Maggie...volunteered to float the bait. The convention soiree at Fircrest Mansion was the arranged location. We made sure Jupiter knew she was trying to *sell* the information herself, counting on the fact that not only is he a true capitalist, he is extremely possessive about controlling the United States' compromised information flow, trying to corner the market so to speak. I'm not sure what happened since Maggie was supposed to assassinate him outright. Maybe he got spooked. Anyway, Maggie was able to hide the key to the safety deposit box where this was." Sierra held up the memory card. "This *is* CONSTANT. It's the hard memory of a secure computer terminal in Washington DC, completely free to view on a high powered mainframe-linked computer without fear of encryption, tracking, or Trojan horse virus spiking. You wouldn't believe what's on here. It's everything we have that wasn't compromised. The value of it is...priceless. It's the only thing that would've drawn him out..."

"And *he* had it?" Erland asked, his head jerking toward Reston in the other room.

"He had the key to the box that held it. Maggie

acted in desperation. She passed it to him. Jupiter's men must've browsed his pockets and what not. She hid it well." Sierra got a twinkle in her jewel eyes. "I think I know where. At any rate, it was a safer bet than swallowing it, or throwing it out the window. It brought a human unpredictability that Maggie figured I could catch up with and bring under control before the other side breached it."

Marland stood very close to Erland, nearly nose to chin and looked in his eyes, her voice was decibels above a whisper.

"I can't trust anybody in the Department. The whole thing is corrupted. My boss isn't even sure about the President himself. I need *you* to be the only one I can trust. Can you do that?"

Erland studied her flawless face. It was impossible to say no. But why did he want to dance with death and destruction when he was only a Homicide Detective? He put puzzles together after all of the evidence was collected and neatly sorted and organized, he didn't play secret agent and leap over tall buildings in a single bound.

"Why me?"

"Because you are who your file says you are. You're a good man."

"How do you know I can't be paid off?"

Marland squinted into his soul and smiled.

"If *you* can, then this country's screwed. You're the only hope this place has. You and people like you. People like me."

Marland took Erland's hand and placed CONSTANT into it and closed his hand around it.

"Thank you for your trust." Erland said, after staring at his knuckles and thinking about what power there was in that small memory card. "But what if I say no? Can I say no?"

"You can," Marland nodded. "But you won't. You don't want this place to become a third world country. You don't want the land of the free and the home of the brave to become weak and full of fear. You've given everything you had to put one killer at a time behind bars so little girls could ride their tricycles in their cul-de-sac like they did when you grew up, when people left their doors unlocked at night and kids could walk to school without the fear of something happening to them. You *can't* say no."

Erland swallowed and looked at the memory card.

"You've done your research."

Marland jerked her chin at the memory card.

"No one knows you have it. The case report will state that it was destroyed until we can secure our network and rebuild it. Until then the Department's information gathering will be in a sort of cold freeze. We'll hide it at a later time but we're playing a game of magic with our enemies, and you're gonna be the rabbit that I pull out of the hat."

Erland took in a breath.

"I'll do what you say...but I'm just a Homicide Detective. I don't know how much help I can be."

"You're all the help I need. Just stick to me like glue, and if you have to, be a bastard."

Marland's warm smile was comforting and spread heat inside of him like a warm soup on a cold day, but as she left, the dread and gravity of the situation was beginning to fall on him and as he stared at the crushed figure of Reston he understood the writer's breakdown. Life could be a tornado, or a volcano, but it was what you did moving forward that made you a victor...or a victim. So America's information was under attack, being stolen from the very ones who gathered it. From the lowliest housewife to the most prestigious athlete, everyone was at risk of being compromised-their phone calls and text messages, credit cards and Internet searches. All of it could be stolen and sold to someone who could use it to cause extreme destruction, not to mention the threat it posed to national security in the war against terror.

What a nightmare. Erland never thought when he parked his Toyota in the Mansion's circular drive that it would lead to this.

Sierra Marland entered the Interrogation room again and sat down opposite Reston.

"I've been informed you have amnesia, Darren. We'll get a Doctor in here soon to give you an examination and give you some medicine that will help relax you."

"I'll be okay." He croaked.

*Amnesia...bound and gagged, running for his life in confusion...*the more Erland tried to visualize what it must've been like for him the more he sympathized with the writer.

"I need you to tell me everything you remember, starting with seeing my sister and we'll back track, and if there's anything you don't remember just take a minute...try to answer my questions as best as possible."

"That's the first thing I remember...I was in a chair, with a gag in my mouth...my hands were tied. I saw her on the floor there and I broke free when I heard sirens."

"Why did you run?"

"I didn't know what to do. I had the key and the paper. I didn't know if I killed her or what..."

"She gave you the key, didn't she?"

"Yes. I was kind of...passed out on the couch. I remember her...leaning over me and putting the key in my pants. I can still see her necklace dangling and catching the light."

Marland sighed at that.

"Did you hear anything or were you too drowsy?"

"No, I heard men's voices, more than one, like a group of them in the room. One must've come and checked on me but I was...drunk..."

"Did you hear them say anything in particular, anything you remember?"

"Just a single word, constant."

Erland's eyes narrowed.

"Do you remember what they said about the word, or was it in a sentence?"

"I just remember that word. The rest is a jumbled mess. When I woke up my head hurt really bad. It still does, the pain comes in spurts."

"We'll get a Doctor to look at you soon, I just need you to answer a few more questions."

"How did you know where the box was?"

"It was written on the paper."

"What was written on the paper?"

"Cherry 410."

"And from that you ascertained that the key was for box 410 in Mutual Bank on Cherry?"

"Yes. I'm not that smart but it seemed obvious."

"How did you get it?"

"I made up a lie about ownership. I'm sorry but I had to get it."

"That leads me to why you did it."

The writer's eyes searched around the arctic white room and his hand tapped on the table.

"I thought it would prove I was innocent."

"Why did you run if you were innocent?"

"Because someone set me up...I wanted to go to the cops when it was all laid out."

"But the cops came to you."

"They didn't want to hear what I had to say, that was for sure...in fact, the guy who chased me down, a guy in a suit, big athletic guy, he asked me where it was."

"Where what was?"

"I...that chip thing."

"Did you tell him?"

"No. He backed off when the cops came. It was like he wanted it, then when the cops slapped the cuffs on me he backed off."

"Did you hear him make a phone call?"

"No, but he very well could've. I was listening to my Miranda rights and I still haven't had my lawyer."

"You don't need a lawyer, Darren, you need a Doctor. You were the victim of circumstance. You're not a criminal and anyone who thinks you are will have to answer to me."

The writer watched in some reserved awe as Marland left the room. A moment later she came to Erland's side.

"Something's wrong."

"What?"

"Hill operated outside of protocol twice. The cause of it is too suspicious to be coincidental."

"What did he do?"

"He was tasked with sitting at the bank. He would've known when the box was being accessed because he has a two-way transmitter ear insert that would've alerted him and synced him with the support group in Washington. There wouldn'tve been a chase if he had done so. So, he must not've used the device. Second, he asked Reston where it was. He didn't know *what* was in the box, it could've been nothing. That wasn't his place. Then he backed off when the cops came. And he called in a go code...an emergency protocol, reserved for only threats to national security."

"You're right, the chase sounds avoidable, like he could've stopped Reston in the bank."

"Unless he didn't want to be seen or cause a scene that witnesses could corroborate, which would explain a few things."

Erland cupped his hand on his mouth and lowered his voice.

"Wait, so you mean you believe this Hill is working for..."

"Jupiter. I can't be sure, but the rules of this game we're about to play are that all parties are guilty *until* proven innocent."

"What about Reston, then?"

"There's no way he has the *capacity* to kill Maggie. She's a level two Shotokan black belt. She could've killed those men in that room but it would've been a brutal fight. She died because she gave herself up in hopes that I would be able to snag the big fish. *His* actions were consistent with a hopeless attempt to rectify the confusion of the situation. He knew he was set up as a stall tactic and someone was trying to get away with something. He's a writer, a political writer at that. He's not stupid but he's not that smart. In retrospect though, I'm glad it worked out this way...I mean, considering what Maggie chose to do, I know we at least have a fighting chance to win."

The Detective took it in. It was gambling and magic, chess and capture the flag all rolled into one endless period of play from which there was no reprieve.

"So what now?"

"He's going to get an examination and you're going to stay with me. Remember, you don't owe anybody anything. Keep your thoughts to yourself, don't let anybody even *think* you know what's going on."

"Yes ma'am." He acknowledged.

"Please call me Sierra when we're together, but not in front of anybody else. It'll help keep you on a lower status in their mind, believe me, little things like that go a long way."

"Got it."

Sierra turned to the door, buttoning her pinstripe jacket.

"We're going to have a conversation with Agent Hill. You ready?"

Erland nodded, and in the pit of his stomach felt like he did when they had announced his name for the weigh-in at the Continental Plaza Hotel before the Hugo Marquez fight in the final round of the Golden Gloves tournament.

Hopefully, the outcome would be far different than it had been that night.

FOURTEEN

When Jessica Birchall eased the Subaru to a halt, it was a good hundred yards from a small suburban rambler that was flanked by Police cars, yellow tape, the Channel Four van and a few spectators.

Birchall slung the messenger bag over her shoulder and struck a straight course to Thornton who was filming an exclusive. She heard the details once within earshot.

"Witnesses describe a man dressed in black uh, all black, a white man, mid thirties or forties, strong build, dark hair, enter this house behind me and come out minutes later with a woman slung over his shoulder. The man placed the woman in a van which was a...white Chevy van, witnesses did not get the license plate. We believe this to be a kidnapping, and the woman, as you're seeing a picture on your screen, is twenty-eight year old Tanya Wilson, a libertarian party campaign assistant, according to neighbors had no known boyfriends or...neighbors, a close neighbor I should say, stated she was not in a relationship of any kind that she knew of and so this does not appear to be an issue of domestic, uh this is not a domestic issue...if you see the woman on your screen, please call the 911 or the designated tip hotline."

Birchall hugged herself and rubbed her arms. It was colder in Wayilow than it was in Crescent, perhaps that was the altitude. As she waited, Birchall threw a weary glance at the burdened and laboriously tired dwellings. One home in particular, a brown rambler of a little more than a thousand square feet sat behind a long driveway where the concrete was cracked and grass was growing through. On the edge of the property which was about three feet lower than the property next to it, sat a toilet amongst a group of sandbags. The front yard of the house was taken by two truck canopies as they slept in waiting and the back yard was dominated by a large maple that stretched over the roofline.

"Um...yes," Thornton continued after receiving a question from his earpiece. "It is believed by Police and eyewitness reports that Tanya Wilson was still alive at the time of her alleged abduction even though she was over the man's shoulder in a way that would suggest otherwise, it is our guess that she was incapacitated in a manner of speaking. Initial Police reports suggest there was a struggle in the house, but there is no indication of any serious injury, again, on those initial reports."

The reporter bided her time as Thornton nodded and stepped away from the camera and the boom microphone.

"Hi Jessie." He said after he gave the audio man his earpiece. "I just finished my segment."

"Do you think it's related to the Fircrest murder?"

Dan Thornton distanced himself from his crew and he walked toward Jessica's Subaru. She followed.

"The only thread I can see is the connection to the Libertarian Party. I don't think the woman was at Fircrest last night but I know she was at the convention."

"But there were seven thousand people there."

"I know."

"Why would someone want to have her kidnapped if it wasn't related to the murder? There's a conspiracy, here, can't you see it?"

"Jessica, I can't talk about it unless you give me a piece of the Fircrest murder."

Birchall's head snapped back.

"It's not about a story, Dan, don't you find it odd that someone gets killed and the best Homicide Detective in the state gets sent home?"

"Yes, but I can't let you in on this if you can't let me in on yours."

"There's nothing to let you in on, Dan!" Birchall raised her voice and then stepped closer and nearly whispered. "Denton Hodge told me if I don't drop Fircrest I'll lose my job."

Thornton wiped a broad hand across a nose that had been broken in college.

"...Well what do you want to do?"

"I want you to do *your* job and keep your eye out. There's something Homeland Security wants hidden in that place. If this is related, we'll know more about what they're hiding. I heard your report too...sounded fairly sinister."

"Yeah..." Thornton looked around and half turned to face the crime scene. "I don't like it..."

Birchall walked around him and put her hands on her hips.

"I think it's related to the elections, personally. I'm going to pursue that angle. If you find anything that links this with what happened at Fircrest, call me."

"On your cell phone?"

"No. I'll give you the number later."

Birchall walked to her car. As she was about to unlock the door, a silver Lumina streaked past and pulled onto the curb near one of the squad cars. The man that emerged out of the car looked familiar. It was his profile, and his coldly intelligent demeanor, the boniness of his face.

She remembered.

The reporter crossed the street again and caught up with Thornton as he was working something out with the cameraman about a shot angle for the next story.

"Do you see that man?"

She all but pointed as the man in the black suit dug into his jacket for a badge and engaged in dialogue with an Officer.

"Yeah?"

"He was at Fircrest, wasn't he?"

"Maybe...I thought you'd left by that time."

"No, I hadn't."

"So...he's not FBI?"

"No, Homeland Security. They're the ones who shut me down. Make sure you speak with him. If you get a runaround, you'll know what I'm talking about."

"I'll ask him if the two are related."

"Go for it." Birchall turned to cross the street. "I don't think he'll like it."

Not more than three hundred feet away, the Homeland Security Agent named Ratner confirmed with the cops something he had feared once he knew of the woman's involvement with the Fircrest suspect. Ratner reached for his cell phone as he stepped inside the humble home and saw the signs of battle.

"Tallifer. I've got some bad news."

The tanned Agent listened. Collateral damage had already begun. Jupiter had abducted Tanya to hold leverage.

What a piece of filth.

Tallifer cursed and speed dialed Marland. If Jupiter wanted to use innocents as pawns he was bringing a far different curse upon himself.

Reston's home looked no different than it did earlier, not that it should've. Kelly Barnett left her car near the curb and marched to the door with no reservations. She knocked and the door creaked open.

"Darren!" She shouted as she clomped through the home. There was no answer.

She took the steps to the second story quickly. Darren Reston was *not* in the house. He was *supposed* to be, but he wasn't.

It was a mile to the nearest coffee shop. And where was his GTO? He babied that thing like a little girl did her favorite stuffed animal.

Kelly let out a sound of frustration. It was his fault. All *his* fault. Mackie would be tearing the pages out of phonebooks with his teeth to learn of Reston's negligence seeing as the paper had paid nearly five thousand dollars at the end of the day for Darren's big night out.

Kelly stormed from the home and slammed the door. As she was cutting across the lawn she saw something out of the corner of her eye. It was a bottle, near Darren's toolboxes in the carport. Barnett was so mad she wanted to break it over his head and since he wasn't there she at least wanted to kick it so she could hear the sound of it smashing back against some dark corner, like the one Darren had crawled to. When she came within striking distance she found the bottle was empty and it had a piece of paper rolled up inside of it. Before the hit song could come to her she grabbed the bottle and wiggled her fingers inside to get the paper. It took some doing, but she managed to remove the paper. She read it aloud.

"I have amnesia, I've been set up for murder. I don't know what happened at Fircrest but I didn't do it and I'm going to prove it."

Darren's co-worker frowned at his signature on the bottom. She looked to the area where she found it to see there were *no* bottles in the carport anywhere, and the bottle was coincidentally close to where he had procured the spare house key.

The more Kelly thought about it, the more it confused her. Was he talking about the murder? If it was true, then he *hadn't* been drinking and he was only making her think so. But why didn't he tell her? None of it made any sense.

Kelly took the steps to her station wagon slowly and carefully. Covering for him as he slept off a binge was one thing, throwing her hat in with such an insane claim was another. If Darren was in trouble, she wanted to help, but again, her feelings towards him were not reciprocated. He *could've* asked for help and he didn't.

So what could she do? If he was gone, he was gone; and where he had gone he had not wanted her to follow.

Erland was on Sierra like glue as they cut through the hallways to the cafeteria. It was a pleasant thing with tall windows that bore resemblance to the University's.

"Grab something if you want it, this'll be a social call-if he wants it to be."

From there they split and Erland reached for a plate and waited in a line of three. The Officer in front of him looked at his badge and up at him and turned around. She recognized him but didn't want to talk. He didn't remember seeing her before but it went like that. Not everyone was chummy. Even people Erland had worked with for going on five years, sometimes they did little more than grunt obligatory greetings. Erland watched Marland go to the hot bar and fidget with a cup while staring across the seats to an athletic looking man in a black suit with dark hair. The Detective took a pair of buckwheat pancakes and didn't mind that they weren't organic. He tried his best when he could but there were times where it was unavoidable. Eating healthy was one of the reasons why he could work so hard and not keel over.

As he left the line Marland caught stride with him.

"That's Hill." She said in a voice only he could hear in the room of nearly thirty on duty Law Enforcement Officers and Officials.

"I know."

"How do you know?"

"I saw you stare him down."

"You were watching me watch him?"

Erland shrugged.

"When you put it that way."

She smiled and they reached the table where Hill was seated. He had a paper and a cup of coffee. A bowl of what was either oatmeal or cereal was empty next to him, wiped clean.

"Hey Luther."

The Agent looked up.

"Marland?" He was genuinely surprised to see her. He stood up and shook her hand. "What are you doing here?"

"I could say the same thing!"

Erland noticed the immediate change in her tone and mannerisms. She had applied a veneer of social levity that she had not had in their conversations in the Observation Room or even in the slightly flirtatious joke she had made only seconds ago. Erland could tell she was playing a game now. It was obvious to him, hopefully it wasn't to Hill. That let Erland know that he was dealing with the *real* Sierra and whatever she was giving him was authentic.

"I'm here on Detective Erland's behalf."

Hill looked to Erland and offered his hand.

"Detective."

"Pleasure." Erland complied.

"You didn't come for the food, that's for sure."
Hill sat down again. "My apologies, Detective."

"It's alright." Erland took a seat with his
pancakes. "It's to be expected."

Marland held a smile at her partner he didn't see
as he began the daunting task of eating the thick, gluten
gut bombs without butter or syrup, to make them, if
only, a bit healthier.

"So, Luther, I'm here on business."

"Yeah. I was just about to leave."

"What's the rush? Have another cup of coffee."

"I'll get it for you..." Erland offered, half
standing up and Marland grabbed his arm with a
surprisingly firm grip, eyes locked on Hill. Erland sat
down.

"It seems we have some things to talk about."

"I don't think I follow."

"Darren Reston."

Erland took a bite and watched Hill's face. Hill
was searching for a flight path for his line of defense.

"The guy in Interrogation? What about him?"

"Why'd you call in a go code?"

"Because I knew how important he was."

"Really? Who told you?"

"It was the box, Marland, he got the box."

"But you found that out *after* you left the bank
to tail him."

Hill frowned.

"Wait, why are you being so accusatory? I was
acting on DC's order."

"The same people who gave you the two way?"

Hill's eyes bounced from Marland to Erland,

who sat chewing on the pancakes like some kind of pasture cow.

"You're not in charge of this, Marland, talk to Tallifer if you have a problem with the way I did my job. I'll write a report for you."

"Wrong. I *am* in charge. Tallifer answers to *me*. *You* answer to *me*."

"He never said..."

"Why didn't you use the two way to confirm? You could've taken him in the bank..." Marland leaned in. "Why did you call in the go code and make up a line about attempted murder?" She snarled.

There was no viable lie for him to spew. The two way was working perfectly, and Marland had not chosen to corner him with the testimony of a possible amnesiac but with the procedure the Department had agreed on. If they had to they'd check his phone and he wouldn't have any time to clear it. He hadn't used the two way because he had made calls on his phone he didn't want DC to hear, and more than likely, he was using a phone they had nothing to do with.

He was gutted, cleaned and cooked on the spot-barbecued by Sierra's blue eyes.

Marland was still leaning in and continued to whisper, bearing teeth in disgust of what was before her.

"I know you're working for Jupiter and if you're not man enough to face life in prison with a possible death sentence for treason you'd better pull your sidearm now and take a shot at me in front of all these people because it's the best chance you're ever gonna get."

Hill's face was flushed red and Marland pushed herself back. Erland swallowed with difficulty.

"I wouldn't do it." He added.

"Now I'm going to go tell Lieutenant Ross who

he's got in his cafeteria and we're going to make sure you're locked so far in deep freeze you won't see the sun till the day you die."

The beautiful Agent left everything but a pool of blood behind as she departed. Hill watched her jog from the cafeteria.

"So what's your angle?" Hill probed.

"What do you mean?"

"You can make half a million g's if you let me walk out."

"You're a fool." Erland cut a wedge and then stared at the man. "Your only way out is a plea bargain, give her Jupiter's location, his contacts, everything you know."

Hill chuckled.

"I fear him more than her."

"Do you fear the lethal injection?"

Hill shrugged.

"When you're in this life you know it's coming sometime so you live it on the edge. When you get what's coming to you, it's not as much of a surprise as it is a disappointment."

Hill stood up and buttoned his jacket.

Then he bolted.

Erland pushed off the table and stumbled after the speedy Hill. As the double Agent reached the mouth of entrance Erland snagged a mug from the hot bar and threw it at him, which made a thick ringing sound as it struck him in the back of his large head and made a hollow clanging noise on the tile floor. There was a murmur amongst the onlookers and voices began to put words to thoughts as they watched, unsure of what to do.

Erland fell on Hill as Hill flipped over and went for his gun. Erland smashed his fist across Hill's face and swiped the gun away. The double Agent's face wrinkled in pain and blood began to drip from the corner of his eye.

At the violence, several officers surrounded the men and Erland stayed poised to strike for the space of a few heartbeats.

When he relaxed, convinced Hill was subdued, the Agent threw his fist toward the Detective who dodged and smacked him on the other side of his face.

Again, Erland poised to strike and saw in the back of Hill's eyes he had given up, and was almost compelled, despite his damning position, to give an escape a shot.

"Make a hole, make a hole." It was Lieutenant Ross with Marland. Erland looked up to see Ross reaching down to personally detain the traitor. Marland had her arms crossed and her face was cheeky with satisfaction.

"Nice work, Detective." Ross said, and called for two more Officers to help him. The rest of the uniforms dissipated from the scene, returning to what they had been doing or moving to do something else, asking those with them what had happened.

"Yeah, nice work Detective."

Erland pinched and pulled at his shirt a few times to give himself some ventilation.

"Did you know he was going to run?"

Marland shrugged.

"I don't really *know* much of anything, I guess a lot and I'm right more than I am wrong."

"Did you hope he would run?"

"I hoped those pancakes wouldn't slow you down if he did." Her laugh was a small and joyful gesture that bunched her shoulders and tipped her head back. Her eyes saw the mug on the floor. "I see you improvised."

"Well he got the drop on me, and he was a little

younger...and in a little better shape."

Marland reached low for the mug and placed it back on the hot bar, placing a graceful hand on her blouse as she did so to keep the blouse from revealing anything.

"We have to wait for the Doctor to finish with Reston."

"What about Hill?"

"He won't break."

They began to walk from the cafeteria.

"Could you confuse him?"

"No."

"Use him as bait to lure Jupiter out?"

"No."

"So you'll just leave him?"

"For now. He doesn't know as much as you're hoping he does. Jupiter uses secure groups, teams or even individuals. All of them are routed through his computer system and have no contact with each other, that we know of." Marland stopped by a door that looked no different than the ones next to it. Her voice lowered. "We've been through this before. We caught one of his doubles and did all but pull his fingernails out to find out most of what we know now. If Hill's going to talk, it's because he wants to, and what he has to say will be worthless since Jupiter changes everything so drastically from...we can only guess week to week. But it could be daily."

Erland shook his head. It was a far different process than finding a murderer, but he had to approach it the same way, the way his grandfather had taught him. Get the corners, and fill out the border and the inside of the puzzle would take care of itself.

"You said he has teams or groups." Erland put his hands in his pockets as Marland opened the door.

"Yeah, we call 'em *moons*. Cute, huh?"

The room was dark and Marland stepped into the void, Erland could hear her footsteps. He followed her and shut the door.

The metallic sound of a naked bulb with a pull chain was unmistakable. It reminded Erland of the basement in the home he grew up in outside of Garden Grove.

The room was a small janitor's space and had a rack of shelves that held cardboard boxes of cleaners, sponges, rags and the like. There were also mops and buckets in the corner. Marland's target was the janitor's locker.

"What's in here?" He asked.

"This is where we're going to hide it."

"Why here?"

"Because we could come back ten years later and find it here. Janitors are creatures of habit and this building just got an update, so it won't be moving anytime soon. It beats the heck out of a private third party like a bank where you need names and papers and all that, and there's no way I'd bury it in the woods."

"What about Homeland back in D.C.?"

"It's be safer in a museum on display."

Erland gave her the memory card and stared at her silky black hair and the artistry of her figure as she bent down and slipped it in the behind the angled metal construction of the industrial locker wall. No one would know it was there unless their names were Sierra or Mike. She pulled a card from her pocket that looked to be as identical to CONSTANT as she was to her own sister and gave it to Erland.

"Is this a phony?"

"Yup."

"Why?"

"Because if for some reason you are singled out as the one I trust, then it'll give me enough time to get to you before they pull *your* fingernails out."

Erland had been examining the card and his eyes darted up to hers at that statement. She was as serious as she was slender. The pause in her gaze spoke to Erland that it wasn't too late to bail out.

"I see." His eyes went back to the card.

"If we play it right it won't come to that, I just want you to be prepared. It seems Jupiter has raised the stakes and now has a hostage, the woman that picked up Reston on the highway. I'm convinced he'll do anything and it won't be long till he knows about you."

Marland tapped him on the shoulder and walked around him. Erland studied the room briefly. Sierra had left the locker exactly the way it had been when they came in, door slightly ajar.

Erland followed the Homeland Agent as she walked back to the Observation Room. Thank God he was on *her* side.

FIFTEEN

The mechanical hum of a generator or something like it bore through Tanya Wilson's ears. Her eyes were open and saw nothing but darkness. The room or enclosure she was in was as humid as it was dusty. Her head reeled with the gripping force of whatever the man had injected into her arm. It clung to her skin in a thin and eerie way and made her shiver inside, disconnected from the past and future in the mystery of the present.

Her mouth was dry and the sound of the humming was growing stronger, either that or her ears were warming to the fact that her brain was now engaged and trying to run for its life.

Though the darkness was as black as deep space she could feel her hands. They were tied, above her head, to something that felt like a steel pipe.

The more she thought, the more it hurt, in a slow and dull, irrefutable way. For whatever reason, she was a captive.

Tanya sat in silence for what could've been ten minutes as easily as it could've been an hour, listening to the humming and whirring.

Then a shaft of orange light cut through the darkness to her right, in the top corner of her vision. The size of it told her it was a fair distance away. She tried to focus her eyes but they didn't want to work very well.

As the light dissipated she could hear heavy steps on what sounded like a steel catwalk. From her guess it was a small army.

Even though her mouth was free she couldn't scream. Her throat was far too dry, a feeling that snaked all the way down to her kidneys, and who would hear her in the darkness over the mechanical humming?

Minutes later the footsteps came near her and a flashlight beam hit the ground. Before she could follow the light up to get a view of the body that held it, the light was in her eyes. It was a piercing and painful weapon in her vulnerable position.

"Don't say anything, Ms. Wilson, just listen. I'm not a bad man. I don't want to hurt you and I won't unless you make me." Tanya pinched her eyes closed as she listened. The voice had a northeastern accent and was intentionally calm. "If all goes according to plan you'll be able to be back home shortly. Whatever you do, do not try to escape. I will not hesitate to shoot you. If you understand, nod your head. If not, I will repeat myself. Do you understand?"

Tanya nodded slowly.

The beam clicked off and the steps marched along the metal back to the place where they had come from, though Tanya couldn't see the orange light as she had originally because of the blinking spots burned in her eyes.

At least he didn't want to hurt her, to do things to her that would scar her for life. Or so he said. But there had been more than one? Could she trust her ears? There was definitely more than one. And why would the man shoot her if she tried to escape? She was a prisoner.

No, a *hostage*.

Tanya tried to collect herself and rested her head

against the cold steel pipe.

There was no way out.

Tabitha Grey stepped from the TMFOV bus and scanned the scene for Tallifer. When she didn't see him she walked toward the Mansion. As a child it had been a dream of hers to have a giant house and be the royal princess of it all but the older she grew that dream had slowly faded and Tabitha realized she didn't have to be the person she was *told* to be and the princess wish was something thrust upon her, almost as culture. As the youngest of seven she had very little space to call her own and through the proximity of team gymnastics and the logistics of college, she had learned to operate with little or no space at all and even now rented a very small loft apartment in Crescent with an incredible view of the Targus River emptying into the Bay. She had really fallen into Homeland Security by accident. It began as a unique intern program at the University, only four on the entire campus had been selected from a screening of two hundred, and interest alone had spurned her to sign up. The more she observed the various positions and spent time with the Agents, she began to convince herself it was the only job she would be happy in. That was going on three years ago, and even though she was in leadership only because MacEndell had recently retired and she would be replaced by a senior Agent in a matter of weeks, T was very pleased with the way things were going to the chagrin of her parents, who insisted that she be a Doctor, a Lawyer, or worse, a Dentist, like the path of her incredibly competitive and overachieving elders. However, unlike her elders, she had no debt and lived a simple life that didn't involve two dogs, three cats and arguments about who set the keys where. Even as her mother was slowly succumbing to Hodgkin's

Lymphoma, she still didn't see the wisdom and
fortitude of Tabitha's solitary path. Her mother's only
concern was grandchildren, as if it were a number that
should equal her age. T had no children and no prospect
of them. Many of the men she encountered in the job
were either afraid of her petit cheerleaderesque
appearance, or assumed she was something she wasn't.
True, the evidence stated she was an All-American do-
gooder ideal for the cover of a cereal box as much as a
moisturizer commercial, but the woman that lived
inside of that bright and bubbly shell was a much
different animal. She had been spending a great deal of
time at the range lately, and she knew if she ever had to
pull her sidearm and drop someone, the grit would be
there. So she wasn't looking for a man at the moment
with how much the job sat in her life, but if she were
he'd have to be a *real* tough guy, because that's who
she was. No one knew how painful Olympic level
gymnastics was except those who stayed the course,
and again, no one knew the tireless and lonely
dedication it took, save those that woke up, chalked up,
and hit it for the hours that it took to be *perfect*.
Retrospectively, it was a shame that with all the blood
and sweat she had poured into it, Tabitha's end was as
an alternate's alternate and she never got to travel to the
games, even despite her Romanian-style balance beam
routine.

      Tabitha found Ryan Tallifer in the kitchen,
knees on a countertop, head in a cabinet. One of
Homeland's forensic technicians was working on the
door.

      "MCL here yet?" Tallifer asked, peeking his
head from the cabinet enclosure only for a glance.
There must've been an entire oak tree's worth, stained a
rich reddish brown. With all of the veiny grey granite
and stainless steel it was just another wealthy *looking*

space, and to Tabitha's oddly sparse disposition it was nearly sickeningly so, like having butter on a rib eye steak.

"Not until around nine, I'd say."

Tallifer swore and snapped his hand back. The tip of his finger was bleeding. He put it in his mouth.

"What are you doing here?" He asked, after he pulled it out for an examination.

"I just wanted to tell you Marland and the Detective will be back within the hour."

"Erland."

"Pardon?"

"His name's *Erland*." Tallifer opened another cabinet. "And he's one of the best."

"I read the file." Tabitha shrugged and looked around. Her voice was a quick rapid fire of words. "It's still not right, I mean, this is what we do, this is our job. We can solve it without him, we needn't jeopardize the mission-I mean, the way we work, just because he's more practiced at it than we are..."

"Think of him like a specialist imported from D.C. You know how they do that. There's always some specialist flown in for some extremely small and detailed part."

"I know..." Tabitha moseyed over to the broken door and the geometric glass puzzle of evidence it had become. "It's just that...he's not one of *us*, you know."

Tallifer made a noise of not caring and sighed, shimmying from the painful position on the granite.

Tallifer swore again. Tabitha turned around and eyed him as he was rubbing his kneecaps.

"You gonna make it or should I perform a field medical exam on you?"

The tanned Agent threw her a sarcastic face. An FME was a *very* hands on procedure.

"You're not my type."

It was true, they were probably the last two people on earth who would be in a relationship, perhaps because they were inwardly so different. Though Tallifer would never admit to it in a group setting, he wrote memoirs and studied philosophy in his spare time. However, he never let that influence or interfere with his job or even slip out on a personal level. To him, it was his religion, and he kept his dedication to it very private. His outward appearance would lump him in the same category as Henry Morell, and Tallifer did have the *look* of a man that chased just about anyone who had a heartbeat and wasn't the same gender, but it was far from the truth. In fact, any woman that tried to play the game with Tallifer received a frosty reception.

"That doesn't matter." Tabitha leaned on a countertop as Tallifer moved to the drawers.

"How so?"

"How many people do it because it's convenient?"

Tabitha was slightly amused by the Agent's interest. His brain was half or less than halfway connected to the conversation. She liked to toy and play with men she respected, just like one of her gymnastics teammates. They only problem was, they were men, not women, and the men she respected didn't go in for that sort of thing, and the men that *did* go in for that she didn't respect.

"Do what?"

"Get in a relationship."

"Sure...uh, a lot, I guess."

"So what about it, why aren't we the two point four dream? You're tan, I'm blonde, together we'd make the next President of the United States."

Tallifer didn't laugh.

"Don't you have something else to do?"

Tabitha shrugged and removed her hands from

the counter, saving a joke about carpooling. Her body
was such a dream of perfectly perky Middle America,
and in so many ways, the gestures she had absorbed in
gymnastics by repetition drove the point home. But the
soul that was Tabitha Grey hated pink and kittens and
craft projects that involved raffia or felt; she didn't
needlepoint or bake pies or play the piano. She lived on
smoothies and shakes and worked out for an hour and a
half every day and turned off the lights in her loft
apartment to practice putting her sidearm together from
a pile of pieces as the world around her fell asleep to
the TV.

"Just think how lucky you'd be if I was Tabitha
Tallifer. My middle name is *Isabella*, by the way."

The Agent shook his head as the woman left.
Women required a space of time he didn't have to offer,
and in the gears of his mind, it was better for both to
remain at a distance. Intelligently, he understood the
humor in what she had said but all of it was a big shrug
to him.

When Tallifer had finished with the drawers he
swept the rest of the kitchen and found no camera.
Bothered that there was none, he climbed the
countertop and looked above a built in buffet. Aside
from being extremely dusty, which he didn't expect,
Tallifer found nothing. Still atop the counter he looked
back and forth letting his eyes dart around to the
different angles in the room.

Then it hit him.

On the opposite side of the room under a small
table ideal for a vase of flowers angled perfectly so that
it could capture everything that went on in the space
was a shaft of electronic surveillance no bigger than a
mechanical pencil. Not only was it inches from ground
level, it was colored in a way that camouflaged it
perfectly.

It was only the fifth camera he'd found in what
felt like as many hours, but it was a start. If the five
were any indication the Mansion held somewhere in the
hundreds and they were about as easy and logical to
find as a squirrel nuts.

The figure in white known as Jupiter walked the
steep ramp that not only removed him from the safety
of *Divide et Impera*, but placed him back on the soil
where he was most vulnerable. It was imperative-there
was no avoiding it. Jupiter's operation was on the
strictest of timelines and the setback at Fircrest
Mansion had all but knocked it sideways. Knowing he
was being set *up* to buy the single most valuable cache
of information the world had ever seen come to market,
he had placed in motion a once in a lifetime deal in
hopes that Fircrest would've ended differently. Despite
the target he now had on his back for having exposed
himself to his enemies without them actually knowing
what he looked like, the prospect of the potential capital
gained from the deal had become a salacious desire in
his mind. What hope he held onto for the information to
still become his came from the dangerous obsession
that put him into business to begin with.
The love of money.
The middle-aged Jupiter, surrounded in some
kind of oblong honeycomb shape by beefy guards of
the paramilitary variety, nondescript in varying shades
of urban garb, entered the modern construction that was
PierHouse. Most of it was glass; heavy soaring sheets
of it, some frosted, some clear, and what wasn't was a
golden or pale maple, and the designer's goal had been
to fuse the liquid energy flow of the Targus River with
the gravitational power of the distant but ever looming
Mount Turbus. Jupiter didn't care all too much about
that, nor that the building was little more than an

oversized art gallery, he only needed a place to strategize with his *moons* before proceeding with the next phase of the operation. He had planned to have the information already and the second and third parties involved would be expecting the same thing.

Callisto was with him at all times. They were Dannigan, Sung, Brown, Halstan, and a man they called Kix who could see better out of one eye than most people could out of two.

Io was waiting, seated in a room that was supposedly shaped like a blue whale and was again, nothing but wood and glass, a juxtaposition of straight lines and waves, filled with texture and void of anything else but just enough seating to hold a meeting.

Courtland stood and hitched up his pants.

"Sit down." Jupiter said. "Hill isn't with us anymore."

There was a small ripple of reaction in Team Io. They all knew if they blew their job in any way, Jupiter would cut ties with them. It was the price they paid to be in his face to face employ, as one of his moons, getting paid nearly two million a year for a job that on any other crook, thief, or criminal's payroll would add up to maybe a quarter of it after special bonuses.

"What's the plan?" Courtland asked. Jupiter's plans were very extreme things, detailed to the last point leaving nothing to chance.

"I will proceed with the arranged meeting with our broker. I want *him* to proceed as if we *have* the information ahead of tomorrow's sale. Ganymede will continue preparing the site and even though Hill is no longer with Europa I will trust them to retrieve the information from the side of Homeland Security while your team, Courtland, pursues the information from the *other* side."

The stocky man hitched up his pants even

though he was seated.

"What do you mean?"

Jupiter reached in his specially made jacket and removed one of four phones and told Courtland and the rest of Io team exactly what he meant.

"We have to time it delicately, but we're about to turn the heat up on our enemies. If it's done right, they'll be begging *us* for mercy."

A smile pulled across the thinness of Courtland's lips as for the next half hour or so, Jupiter set the foundation for what would transpire from the moment the conversation ended to the time of the planned information auction.

Sierra Marland had a graceful walk that Erland determined one had to be somewhat born with. He, as a young boxer, had been informed by his trainer, that he had what the trainer described as *heart* and the trainer then spent the next twenty minutes about how he couldn't explain what heart was but Erland had it. Michael *The Machine Gun Man* Erland. It was a good name. The trainer gave it to him because of his hand speed. Hand speed and eye coordination he'd been born with too, just like the elegant smoothness that Sierra Marland moved around Precinct Three with.

Agent Morell turned as she approached the doors of Observation and Interrogation.

"The Doc should be finished in a minute."

"Good. I'll talk to him." Marland turned to see if Erland was next to her, which he was. "Also, there'll be an Agent Hill in with Lieutenant Ross right now, they're speaking with Bartleson in D.C. I want you to...*interview* him after the Doctor is done with Reston and we begin to process him."

A smirk slowly spread across Morell's face. He took a toothpick from his pocket and put it between his teeth the same place a cigarette would go.

"No kidding?"

"*No* kidding, Morell. So you'll stay here. I'll take Detective Erland back to Fircrest with me and the MCL should be there so I'll get him to work on the evidence."

"I'll let you know if I get anything."

The Police Doctor exited Interrogation.

"I'll be waiting." Marland passed Morell and Erland followed. "What's the diagnosis?" Marland asked the Doctor, who was a kind looking black woman with a soft and almost sleepy voice.

"Well, there is no question the patient had amnesia, but it's a strange combination of retrograde and post-traumatic amnesia. I'm still awaiting the results of a blood test, but I do believe, since he suffered no physical trauma that would merit it, the condition was pushed over that boundary by chronic alcoholism. There was a...very small area of irritation on his neck behind the right ear, and I could examine that area further but I'd need to move him to Regional Hospital to do that."

"How big of an area?"

"An eighth of an inch, maybe."

Erland eyed Marland and her face was grave.

"Could it have been from a violently administered injection?"

"That is definitely possible. I couldn't see a needle mark but if it was done some time ago that would explain it."

"Do you think it was STRIC-R?"

The Doctor swept through the file cabinet inside.

"That would explain the symptoms, migraine, dry mouth, and the fact that he was admittedly a heavy user of alcohol might have interacted with the drug to create the perfect environment for amnesia...seeing as memory loss is the most prominent debilitating side-effect...but the blood test will either confirm or deny the presence of STRIC-R, and the human brain is never predictable when it comes to how amnesia was first triggered and later developed. I do think he threw up not too long ago as well, there was a great deal of acid in his mouth."

"Alright..." Marland scratched her eyebrow with her pinky. "How much longer till the blood test will be done?"

"Forty minutes to an hour."

"Call me at this number." Marland showed the Doctor the number from her phone and the Doctor wrote it down. Erland turned to look behind him while they did this and did not see the Agent named Morell anywhere.

"I'll do that, hopefully it will be sooner."

"It's okay if it isn't." Marland shook the Doctor's hand and tapped Erland on the shoulder.

"Yes?"

"You looking for celebrities?" She was already at the door to Interrogation. "I'm going to have a word with Reston. He'll stay here and Morell will talk to him later. Wait for me in the car."

She tossed Erland the keys and he fumbled the catch and dropped them. When he reached down for them and stood up again he spotted the faintest glimpse in her exotic eyes, a pleasant gleam, but it was only a flash as it was swallowed in hair with the turning of her head and the presence of the door frame.

Sierra Marland took the seat opposite Reston and spoke to him as she had before, in the calm and patient voice an elementary school teacher would use to explain to a child something that was beyond their comprehension.

"You doing okay, Darren?"

"Yeah..."

"What happened to you is hard to describe so I'll say it this way, your brain shut down part of itself to save itself from getting damaged. When it went to start that part up again, it forgot where it put the keys."

"That sounds right. Physically I feel great, except the headache." Darren pointed a finger to the IV on wheels that was next to him and stuck in his left arm. "I'm not as thirsty now."

"That's good, I'm glad...it seems someone poisoned you."

"Really?" The writer's eyebrows jumped. "Is that what knocked me out?"

"We believe your alcohol dependency and the poison caused your memory to shut down. The poison does just that, targets the brain."

"God, that's horrible." Darren's shoulders rolled and he wiped his forehead. Sierra hoped he wasn't going to cry again. "I don't know what happened."

Marland leaned forward and a serious undertone slipped into her voice.

"I know Darren, and you're not under any suspicion anymore but you *have to remember*."

"I..."

"Do you remember the open bar?"

"Yes, of course." Reston smiled, glad it was an easy question.

"Did you have any drinks?"

"Yes, quite a few."

"Do you remember having quite a few or do you assume that you did since you passed out on the couch?"

Reston's mouth flew open to answer and sealed shut again.

"Now that you say it, I clearly remember

ordering the vodka on ice, it was Polish, actually, I can tell the taste difference between it and Russian, and that French stuff of course, and then turning around because someone brushed past me."

Marland hid the excitement on her face as she attempted to keep Reston's mind on the path.

"Okay, do you remember who was next to you at the bar?"

"Like their names?"

"No, gender, colors they were wearing, any distinguishing features, size, whatever you can."

"Well, it was a man that brushed past me, dark suit...pretty much everyone was in a black suit, lot of tuxes...but I remember coming to the bar to talk it up with this one lady...it was her dress, I think. It really stood out."

Sierra nearly bit her tongue to remain calm.

"What color was it?"

"Her dress?"

"Yes, you said it stood out, what color was it?"

Reston shook his head and scratched his arm where the IV had been inserted.

"Gosh...blue green, green blue. Turquoise, teal, I don't know, it had almost a flip flop, uh, chameleon effect like hot rod cars, you know."

Marland stood up, the subtlest smile on her lips.

"Thank you Darren. An Agent Morell will be in with you shortly to continue talking to you about what you remember and he will record your statement. After the Doctor clears you to leave you will be processed out and free to return home."

The writer seemed to nearly wilt at the prospect of being removed from the present and being thrown to the wolves of his past routines.

"Yeah, I've just been sitting here, running over everything in my mind and little by little the movie keeps getting longer..."

"What's wrong?"

"It's just that...I don't know where my car is, I don't even know *what* my car is...and the CMJ paid almost five grand to get me to hob nob with all of these movers and shakers and I can't remember any of it. I have an article to write and I can't write spit...this is the biggest time of year for us and this is one of the most important things that's happened to me that I can ever remember and I can't really do anything about it..."

"Is there anyone that can help you, any friends or co-workers?"

Darren rubbed his head.

"Yeah, there is one that I know of. She'll never believe me, though..."

"Really?" Marland smirked and went for her phone. "What's her number?"

Reston twitched nervously.

"You're going to...call her?"

"Yeah, why not?"

"...Could I do it?"

"If you want to..." Marland put her phone away. "How about this, you can call her after you're done with Agent Morell, to give you some time to think about what you want to say..." Marland went for the door. "Give you some time to get hydrated."

Sierra walked through the busy mill of the Precinct and debated tossing her new partner around in her thoughts. No file could say it all. There was definitely something about him paper and ink could not capture. Before she could begin to consider who and what he was the elevator to the garage was opening before her and her feet were taking her to the white Suburban. The Detective was leaning on a Camry next to the Suburban. It was an unfortunate champagne green color.

"I didn't know if you want me to ride with you or follow behind, even though you gave me the keys..." She came up to him and threw a glance in his car. It was nearly mint, almost brand new for being nearly ten years old.

"You can leave your car here but now that you mention it I should drive."

Erland held out the keys and did not throw them to her like she had to him. When she held out her hand Erland took that hand in his free hand and squinted.

"Just like your sister..." He said and stared at her.

He released the keys and she pulled her hand back, not knowing what he meant by that. She understood once he'd walked around the back of the Suburban to enter the passenger seat.

"You mean my lack of fingerprints?"

"Yes." He looked straight ahead.

Sierra's face became serious for a moment.

"We shared many things, Detective. And we had a lot in common...that doesn't mean we were *exactly* the same."

Marland fired the SUV and let the cold bright sun take the somber feelings away as she began to drive the simple but congested route back to Fircrest Mansion.

"What do you mean by that?" Erland said at the second lengthy red light.

"She was a level two Shotokan black belt and I won't tell you what color I was...we were both in the Army but had different jobs."

"You were in the Army?" Erland was shocked. A woman of her femininity didn't seem to carry the hardness of military training.

"We were Officers. We worked in the Pentagon."

"Well, there's the Army, then there's...the Army. I guess I thought for a minute of you in the jungle."

"I did Basic. I got mud on my face. I cried and puked and all that. Maggie didn't. She was older. Tougher. Smarter. I was always the more sensitive, artistic one, better at dancing and acting in high school you know how it goes with siblings."

"Yes and no." Erland was leaning on the window armrest, hand mindlessly rubbing his chin as if he had a beard. He had no siblings but had studied them to no end and knew that they could be closer than married couples and on the other side of the coin be bitter, mortal enemies.

"We shared the same things only in different ratios. She liked to paint but I was just way better at it. I really enjoyed lacrosse but she was a natural. One of the best in the school district."

Sierra was skirting around that which was sensitive to describe, how they were identical on the outside but their hearts beat so differently. Sierra had followed Magnolia but never measured up to her, and all that Sierra naturally leaned toward had little or no place in the business. If there were lovers, and fighters; then they had found their living examples in Magnolia and Sierra Marland, and while it was obvious Maggie was a fighter, Sierra's very substance and deepest core had been locked away and only kept alive *by* her relationship with her twin sister.

"Lacrosse?"

"Yeah. We're from the Northeast, it's just something we do there."

"I was always a baseball guy..." Erland smiled.

"I believe Agent Hill is aware of that but that's not what your file said."

"I'm sure mine says as much about me as yours

would about you."

"Yes and no." Marland echoed with a smile, meaning Erland had obviously never read Marland's file but knew that there was far more to her than it would've said if he had.

"If you're referring to my illustriously brief boxing career then, yes, I did it, but I hate to be one of those old guys that brags about what he did when he was younger."

"You're not old." Marland signaled to get out of the city.

"I know, but, what's the average age of your Agents?" As Marland thought the Detective continued. "And all of the cops nowadays, it's not like when I first started in Mountain County, the sheriff was sixty-five and the deputy was fifty-eight!"

"Is that where you grew up?"

"Don't you know?"

"I got enough from your file to know you were the only man for the job." The statement was not entirely true. Marland just didn't want to talk about her and Maggie anymore, afraid of going soft where she was trying to become hard, especially considering how easy Erland was to talk to.

"No, I grew up in Garden Grove. It's in the next state over, right on the border...it's basin farming, from the Turbus Mountain plain...loads of hops and apples, even blackberries and asparagus. They had a great joint there too, the Red Clover Diner. Breakfast all day, Saturday night special was always all you could eat London Broil and garlic green beans for four ninety-nine. Don't know if it's still that much. Haven't been to Garden Grove since I took this job."

Sierra spotted the twinkle in his already charismatic blue eyes. Seeing a printed name or word in a file could never have the color or depth of the human experience. So even though Marland technically *knew* what Erland either said or was about to say, she was also, in a way, hearing it for the first time.

"So you must like fall, then?"

"Yeah. We used to have a harvest festival in the town square, not anything special, but, all the caramel apples you could possibly imagine and live music-country and blues stuff, square dancing, just kind of like it used to be when our parents generation grew up."

"I only hear the stories, though. Sounds like you got quite a slice of it."

"Yeah." Erland shifted positions in his seat.

"Do you miss it?"

"No, I'm not sentimental. It was a different time, I know that. Just like boxing. That was one period of my life, and when I left Garden Grove for college and ended up coming back to be a small town county Detective was another. I've been in this...season I guess is the best way to say it for years now, and..."

"What?" Marland said, accelerating to freeway speed, having broken through the clutches of the streets.

"And after this case I'm going to retire..."

"Really?"

"Yeah...I talked it over with my...girlfriend earlier."

Marland noticed the lack of confidence in that last statement compared to what he had been saying earlier. It was as if he had to convince himself that was the appropriate label for the woman he had made the decision with. Whether she was a woman he had email contact with or slept next to, the file had not said anything about it and Sierra therefore, couldn't know just yet. It surprised her in a way because of its inconsistency with her study of him and she would let the matter steep in her mind.

"Well, now's not the time to press you...but I

know we can use good leadership in Homeland moving
forward. I don't know how long it'll take to clean out
the wolves' den that it's become but I guarantee you I
would regret not making you an offer. There'll be some
empty seats in Washington D.C. and if you asked me
real nice I'm sure I could reserve you an office that
looks onto the Potomac."

     Erland didn't say anything. Now he didn't want
to talk about a sensitive subject any further, lest his
focus be removed from the task at hand. Sierra was just
so pleasant and intelligent and personable, and it didn't
hurt how she was one of the most beautiful people he'd
ever seen. It was as if he'd known her for a long time,
like they'd been friends in a past life, and he didn't
want to let that sidetrack him from a job he'd already
made up in his mind would be far from easy.

     "We'll cross that bridge when we get there,
Sierra."

     Yes, they would.

SIXTEEN

In a clean commercial rental space on Schwartz and Eleventh, Jessica Birchall located the local branch of the Libertarian Campaign Office. It was little more than a heavily populated floor covered in boxes, tables, and many more boxes. The reporter gathered it was an extremely important day for flyers, pamphlets, posters and signs because the populace's vote was most vulnerable the week after the convention and this year's volunteers were consumed to do better than last year's. While wading through the miasma of rubber bands, paper clips, and positive energy, she caught the attention of an unusually tall woman and after some trouble Jessica remembered she used to be a professional basketball player. She was searching for the name, trying to get a picture of the back of the jersey...it was framed in a sports bar on First.

"Hello, can I help you?"

"Yes, my name is Jessica Birchall, I'm from..."

"Oh, yes, I knew I recognized you."

She was *very* tall and had hands that completely engulfed Birchall's, delicate as Birchall's were. Her milky coffee colored skin was obviously of a mixed race and she complimented it well with a radiant blouse that was the color of raw salmon.

"Are you doing a feature on potential Congressman Felix? We believe he has all tools to serve District Seven with distinction."

"No, well, not yet anyway." Birchall waved a hand. "I'll bring it up to my producer. No, I was wondering if I could profile exactly what's going on right now."

Jessica broke eye contact as she said so and let her sight wander around the veritable beehive of activity.

"Yes, it is something isn't it? Single moms, *working* moms, college kids, we even have a former ER nurse...although I don't see her at the moment." A woman brushed past with a stack of what looked to be painter's stir sticks. Perhaps they would double for signposts. The former power forward stopped the woman by draping a hand on her shoulder. "Linda, have you seen Tanya?"

"No, she hasn't come in yet."

Though Jessica was thinking about her angle of attack to get her hands on the guest list a knife of chance pierced her memory and the nasally words of Danny Thornton rattled through her ears like wind shaking a rickety screen door. *We believe this to be a to be a kidnapping, and the woman, as you're seeing a picture on your screen, is twenty-eight year old Tanya Wilson, a libertarian party campaign assistant...*

It *had* to be the same woman.

"Tanya?"

"Yes." The volunteer promotional materials manager turned as the woman with the box marched off. "Do you know her?"

"Tanya *Wilson*?"

"Yes." Then the woman's face changed as she gazed down into Birchall's. "Why, what's wrong?"

"Tanya Wilson was just kidnapped in Wayilow."

"Oh my God, when?"

"This morning."

The tall woman was visibly distraught as a tremor pulled at the outside of her mouth so much so that even the size of her hand could not hide it.

"Excuse me." The woman turned and walked toward a closed door some thirty feet away. Birchall took in a brave lung of air and followed. When the manager opened the door and went to shut it she felt the resistance of Birchall's thin shoulders and bones and turned around startled.

"Oh..." Tears burned her eyes. "I'm so sorry, please Ms. Birchall I can't talk right now, please excuse me."

Birchall tactfully shut the door and spoke calmly.

"Ms...Sheyrie..."

"It's Anderson now," The tall woman reached for a tissue on the desk that occupied the corner of the small room by a window that surveyed the floor space and took in some of the natural light from the floor to ceiling windows that ran along Schwartz Avenue. The woman blew her nose and sat on the end of the desk.

"Mrs. Anderson, the kidnapping of Tanya Wilson is *directly* related to the murder that I reported earlier at Fircrest Mansion."

Directly? Jessica had no evidence to support that but how could it not have been?

"Ms. Birchall, I don't want to talk about it...Tanya of all people..." Anderson's brown eyes welled with tears and she reached for another tissue.

"You don't have to *talk* about it, you just have to help me out."

"How, I don't know anything? And I certainly won't go on camera."

"You don't have to."

Anderson let her head hang back and blinked at

the acoustic tiles of the ceiling.

"Why does this have to happen now, why? We can't take the hit!"

She was obviously referring to the party, and how, even if there were a randomness or a happenstance to it all, the public would dumbly lump the two together. First they would see a murder, and then a kidnapping, and soon, whenever anything Libertarian was referenced, their minds would go straight to those issues and the clouds they cast. And who knew if there would be more?

"If you help me, you can help the Party. I don't want the public to misinterpret the information they're getting."

The look that fell upon Birchall from the woman's face was a combination of shock and disappointment.

"You *are* the information they're getting. Your channel's one of the worst about cutting us out of the argument. It's either red or blue for you, we don't even get a chance."

"That's far from my responsibility to begin with, I just report car crashes and fires..."

"So why are you here?" Anderson crossed her arms as those tears she hadn't dabbed already were drying on her cheekbones. "You didn't come to tell me about Tanya. I'm sure I would've found that out pretty soon. What do you want?"

"I want the guest list to the party at Fircrest Mansion."

"Why?"

"I'll tell you why..." Birchall crossed her arms as well and toed an imaginary line that stood between her and Anderson. "Because the honorable and venerable Department of Homeland Security shut down my reporting the murder at Fircrest Mansion and if I do anything further to investigate it I will lose my job."

Anderson squinted and slowly released her arms until they supported her leaning position on the table.

"Come again?"

"I want to know what happened."

"Why?"

"The Party is owed an answer. The *people* are owed an answer."

Anderson ran fingernails back through her hairline several times and Birchall could hear the scraping sound that it made.

"If...Homeland Security shut it down they had a good reason. I don't want to be involved."

"You don't have to. If you showed me where the guest list was, then I could copy it." Birchall moved to the window and took in the frenetic pace of the workers, all fourteen or so of them. "Or, in this chaotic environment you could've...*lost* the guest list."

Anderson's arms crossed again.

"What makes you so sure I have one, and what are you going to do once you have it?"

"Do you *want* to know?" Birchall said with a calculated coldness and looked over her shoulder.

"Are you really going to do it for the Party?" Anderson asked as she wiped her nose.

Birchall sighed and shook her head as she walked to stand close to the desk.

"Look...I've already decided I wanted to find out what happened, I'm fine with the consequences...so, if I *am* going to lose my job, I at least want to know the truth before I do."

Their eyes met and from her defeated posture on the edge of the table, Anderson still cast a shadow on Birchall's face.

"Fair enough." She said, and reached out to remove a stack of sample flyers, the various trial and error formats that had come back from the printer only to be rejected, thus creating the last minute frenzy.

As Anderson's large feet made hollow clops across the floor on her way to the door, Birchall saw that *under* those scraps of paper destined for the recycle bin was a list of names printed on white paper in black ink, size ten font.

When Tabitha Grey opened the door to the TMFOV and stepped back in to the darkened walls that were lit only by the computer monitors, smart phones and tablet screens, Jimenez was quick to approach her.

"We've narrowed down the guest list to thirteen names."

The Agent ran through the names and as he did so his stilted East Los Angeles English was only subtly apparent. He had worked for many years on improving it.

"What's the possibility of Jupiter and his men coming in as staff?"

"The more names we cross off the list, the more likely it becomes."

T put her hands on hips that were cocked to one side. One leg was rigid, straight out and the other was a right angle to it.

"Do we know who did the catering, linens, music, any of it?"

"Quinlan is having trouble with that. The guest list came from the Libertarian office and that's all the involvement they had."

"That's strange."

"Yes...it seems the party was essentially paid for by George Benton Silverstein, and since he's half of Silverstein and Murphy International Law Firm we know he has plenty of money and plenty of receipts. This was a big tax write off for him. He's been a Party

Member for several years and I doubt he had any knowledge of the staffing."

"So Quinlan's trying to contact his offices?"

"Yeah. That'll be a big mother to tackle. So far they've been unavailable."

"Jupiter and crew didn't just roll in."

"Just about. You know how easy it is. Security is a joke."

"Was there any security?"

Jimenez nodded his head repeatedly as if once wasn't enough.

"There was but really no more than a concert. It was a private event. That's probably why it was chosen."

"Yeah..." Tabitha made goldfish lips as she thought. "Good thing we have the cameras."

"Cameras?" Quinlan piped up. He was hunched over a tablet that he had convinced the tech Rollins to synch with the TMFOV's computer.

"Yeah. Bellamy Family Financial had caught people stealing alcohol and went crazy. Tallifer's getting beat up just looking for them all."

"How's the forensic team?" Quinlan took a moment to rub his eyes, having not seen the light of day since stepping into the bus.

"They're at a stand still to *process* evidence until the MCL comes, but there's still years worth to gather." Tabitha's hips cocked to the other side as she placed her hands on them again. "Give me the first three names."

"Natalie Pierce."

"What about her stood out in particular?"

"A couple of DUI's, that's all. Wait staff, arrived at four o'clock, stayed till eleven-clean up really started at ten."

"Kyle Rayal...Rayali? How do you say that?"

"Ra'alai." Tabitha corrected as she saw the sheet. "It's Samoan. Let me guess, misdemeanor drug possession-he parked cars."

"Yeah, right on. Another one is Tim Wolcek. Guest, not staff-no criminal record."

Tabitha frowned. Not on the count of the name, but on a thread entering her mind.

"Are we operating under the assumption Jupiter and all of his team were men? Let's say they were, what about insiders, spotters, pass offs, ancillaries...like how'd they get that carbon fiber spike? Did they come in with it? We have to assume everyone in the whole place was bad until we can prove they weren't." She ran a finger down the tip of her nose a few times in a movement that mirrored the speed in which she talked. "How did you narrow it down to these thirteen?"

"We were trying to do just that, seeing who may've had either criminal records, or may have been *ab*normal in any way, such as Wolcek *was* the only disabled guest at the party...and I think their security so to speak *was* the guest list, the prestige of it. But that said, there was a discreet metal detector at the main door and *responsible observation* was provided for by Bellamy Family's own Insurance Agents. It's a fancy name for a couple of lurches that mill around and speak into their wrists and give the guests the illusion that they're being protected. If anything like, say, a hostage crisis were to happen, they'd be as effective at stopping crime as a plate of fish tacos. They don't even carry guns."

Tabitha's stomach gurgled at the thought of a fresh fish taco with crispy cabbage and some tangy mango salsa with red onions and cilantro. Her diet didn't permit such lusty delights and it hadn't since the days of Olympic gymnastics-still, as it were, food was a growing passion of hers and whenever vacation came her way she made sure to indulge in the making of and eating those dishes she had been *saving up* in her mind.

"Well then we have to pull the scope *way* back, we need to get into bank accounts and phone records and make sure all of the good people really are good people, and that means more than just what's on the guest list. I'm sure this hacker has connections like we wouldn't believe."

Quinlan coughed twice and did not cover his mouth. Tabitha looked past Jimenez to see Quinlan adjust his position as he was bunched up and folded into the most uncomfortable seat in corner, which, for a man of his stature must've been difficult.

"What are you doing back there, playing Tetris?"

"It's not Wolcek. He's in a wheelchair."

"Isn't that why you singled his name out?"

"I just don't think he could've killed a Homeland Security Agent since he's been semi-paralyzed for ten years now."

"That makes him *more* suspicious in a way-just think about it. The carbon fiber spike could've been *in* his wheel chair. He could've been their spotter."

Jimenez moved a foot or two to stand over Rollins and could see the tattoo that ran up his back through the open collar of his green shirt.

"Can you open a new tab and work on Wolcek for a minute?"

"Sure."

There was the swiping and smashing of keys.

"Where does he work?"

There was more typing.

"Sugar Hill Elementary. He's the Principal. First disabled Principal in State history."

"No kidding? My niece goes there...my brother's kid..."

Tabitha turned sideways to slide past Jimenez and became a statue in front of Quinlan. He was painfully scanning through police documents on the DUI of Natalie Pierce.

"You know, even if they won't let you smoke anymore, the Government still demands that you take a break."

Quinlan smirked and kept reading.

"Then why don't you?"

Their time in the TMFOV was far from the beginning of their day. They'd been on alert ever since Magnolia Marland entered Crescent and while they hadn't known Magnolia personally or been cognizant of the depths of the operation, they were beginning to feel the weariness seventy-hour standby had caused. It meant they got to be home and for all intents and purposes be very normal people but with the call to action always pulling at the back of their minds it never let them fully enjoy a hot meal or a deep sleep. Since eight o'clock last night they had been on Status One, which meant any second they had to be ready to hop into the fighter jet, hit the throttle and take off.

The process had been easier for T than it had been for the others-her life of somewhat solitary athletics culminating in a series of extremely scrutinized command performances trained her for the job in some ways *better* than the military. Even former Sergeant Morell, in all of his applied smoothness and suaveness wouldn't have the *energy* to charm someone, even if they were as rare of a vision as Sierra Marland, because his mental capacity for battle readiness was limited to *physical* performance, whereas all of T's energy fit into the perfection of the *routine*, a symbiotic partnership of muscular strength and the control of mental accuracy. Tabitha, though a bit hungry, was actually very well rested. She had learned to take power naps in the back of uncomfortable buses and the tight corners of sweaty gymnasiums and was riding the wave of one such nap. For some reason the protein shake was burning off quicker than usual.

"I'm fine Keith, but you look like death in a steamer tray."

Quinlan stood and stretched.

"You may be in charge..." Quinlan yawned. "But you can't order me around. So don't try to stop me as I take a walk around this fine establishment and get some cold air between my ears."

Tabitha smiled and reached on her tiptoes to tap his shoulder.

"Attaway."

Quinlan buttoned his suit jacket and brushed himself free of the semi-imaginary dust and debris that might've accumulated on his fine Italian suit. As he left the TMFOV, his last image was of the three Agents pooled around the bank of computer screens in deep study of the one named Tim Wolcek.

Once free of the bus, Quinlan walked hurriedly along the circular drive until it ended near the palisade of trees and the actual brick and wrought iron fence that began to frame Fircrest's extensive lot.

If they were onto Wolcek, it was only a matter of time.

Once Quinlan had marched all the way along the line of the fence and found the corner, he went for his cell phone and made a speed dialed call.

"Wolcek." Was all he said.

"Right..." The voice on the other end responded. Quinlan could hear the clap of hard soled shoes on flooring. "Are you ready?"

"No. I'm not." Quinlan began to walk along the fence line. "And what are we going to do about Marland?"

220 Luke Taylor

"Don't worry about Marland, she'll be last."

Quinlan spoke quietly even though there was no need. He was surrounded by trees and the forensic busybodies were quarantined to the monstrous building.

"You're endangering the whole operation if you mess with her. We need to take her out before she gets to you."

"If it's too hot for you, you can always leave." The voice on the other end was calm and became even calmer. "Otherwise don't ever question my decisions again."

Quinlan swore and let his eyes beadily snap between the treetops.

"It's just that she's too smart."

"She's my only *real* enemy, she always has been. When I finally realized that she was behind the operation it was a blessing as much as it was a curse. I know how hard she plays. I knew her bait would be real. She was as tempting of a target as CONSTANT itself."

"Her and her sister."

"And it worked out, didn't it? One down, one to go."

Quinlan sighed.

"Yes."

"Only, I would say, I had hoped it had been Sierra at that party. She's more dangerous than Magnolia ever thought of being...so don't worry. Just do your part and Sierra will join her sister and take the blame for all of it."

Quinlan swore again.

"I hope you're right."

"I am."

"One more thing, Fircrest has cameras."

There was an unnatural silence. Jupiter's mind was *extremely* sharp and a pause with him was never more than three seconds. As the pause was approaching ten seconds and just when Quinlan was debating asking if he was still there he heard the voice calmer than it had ever been.

"You know what you have to do then."

"Should I wait till they get all of them?"

"Do what you think is best, what you know won't be traced back to you. Just don't wait too long."

The phone went back into his suit jacket. He breathed deep and rubbed his hands together and continued walking. Sierra Marland *was* their only enemy. By any means necessary they had systematically *removed* their enemies at every level until only the finest of them remained. They had known about the Marlands, but from their perspective, they were more legend than fact. From their days in the Pentagon as young intelligence analysts to their classified operations with the State Department. That was until the Marlands targeted *them* as the planet's ultimate enemy, Jupiter and his shadowy moons, the pinnacle of terrorism, having ascertained that so many of America's problems stemmed from leaked and compromised intelligence sold to the highest bidders. And against Quinlan's best wishes and hopes, Jupiter had wanted to dance with the beautiful sisters, and made had it far worse on himself and all those in his employ by killing only *one* of them.

Mike and Sierra pulled up behind the Department Lumina that belonged to Tabitha and once free from the Suburban's seat belts, advanced up the circular drive.

"Tallifer's looking for ribbon cameras, you could help him out before the Crime Lab shows up, then you can do your magic."

Erland smirked and scratched his head back

where the balding spot was.

"Tallifer was...discourteous our first meeting...I don't think he's changed any."

Marland hugged herself, trying to hide an observation that was colder than she remembered.

"Tallifer can only do the job one way. He knows how important you are, and as long as neither he nor anyone else see you as I see you, everything will be fine."

Sierra watched the Detective's face after she said that.

"Do you think...there are more like Agent Hill?" He asked.

"I have my doubts about everyone, Mike. I always have. That's why I'm not dead yet. I've been in this strange business for long enough to know that everyone has a price."

"What about you?"

Marland smiled and turned her head back toward the vista and the tops of the trees as they cascaded down the slope of the hill. Below the cold clear blue sky and the pale sun ran the snaking line of the highway and beyond that the poky black bits of North Crescent's towering wealth and the gray and brown spillover of South's industrial parks and commercial properties.

"What I want, money can't buy." Her exotic eyes became even more distant, like she was looking past the skyline, beyond the river to whatever desire dreamers saw in the curve of the horizon. "If I could have it, I'd be gone."

"So is anyone here...playing for the other team?" Erland changed the subject quickly, making note of what Sierra had said, and with what grave honesty she had said it. She quickly threw him a glance and returned her attention again to the vista.

"I don't want you to know what I know. I don't want you to think the way I think. I want you to be as impartial as you possibly can." She spun on her heel slowly and came to stand close to him, as she had in the Observation Room. "I brought you here for Maggie's sake, to solve a murder. Now I'm beginning to realize how much more you have to offer...and...I don't want you to get caught up in it." She sighed and stared down at the buttons of his suit. "I want to keep you out of harm's way. You haven't sworn the oath that I have and I don't want you to suffer the same consequences."

"Sierra." Erland said with a smile. They made eye contact and she saw the twinkle was still there. "Tell me what to do and I'll do it...but promise me that you'll never put *my* personal safety above *your* mission."

Sierra's jewel blue eyes were solemn.

"I promise."

"Okay then." Erland put his hands in his pockets and winked. "Catch you later."

Marland watched him until he was lost behind the giant gate.

Erland made up the distance between the gate and the door in solitude. It had been hours and he was back as if nothing had happened. But so much had happened, and the timing of it was all at once; a landslide pulling down old growth trees in his soul. His thoughts drifted toward young Veracruz, not even thirty; how she pulled at him...she was like an anchor, a big heavy anchor, and to think of her brought him way down to the murky bottom of a memory where it was just her and him, alone, sunken to the sediment of the ocean floor where there was no light and the current was too strong to fight.

Then he thought of Marland just now, on the edge of the hill, how the newborn sun flamed over her shoulder, having burned through the fog of the night; how the tops of the trees were beneath her feet and the city of Crescent was small enough to fit in the palm of her hand. Her face could change like the sky itself and like the sky never lost its radiance and beauty. Sierra Marland was a facade with no end and yet she had been as genuine and true to him as the heavens were blue.

Or so he believed, and would believe it to his grave, because he had been in Law Enforcement long enough to see all there was to see, climbing into the maze of lies that sat in pools behind people's eyes. In hers he saw a shield of fists in a veil, and what that defense protected was something *beyond* value, and still miraculously tender and untouched after years of service in secret.

Erland entered the Mansion slowly and walked to the piano. He found a great heaviness sitting upon his chest, heavy as the glossy black piano itself. He stared at the contrasting color of the keys and couldn't refuse their comparisons to the two women.

Why now of all times...

He didn't fight it. A lucid moment took him as he stood, and he wrote a poem in his head for a woman who had stirred in him something as new as it was lost and forgotten.

"Detective?" Erland cast his eyes to the balcony. The tanned Ryan Tallifer was holding a small cardboard box in one arm. "Come on up."

Erland wasted no time and left his thoughts at the piano. Marland needed every tool in his arsenal as a Detective, and certainly he would have to draw on the experience of all of the cases he had tried so hard to forget.

The box switched from Tallifer's right to his left as Erland skipped up the stairs.

"Detective. Glad you're aboard."

Erland shook Tallifer's hand and while it wasn't as tense and rigid as their first meeting it was in no way as honest as Sierra's.

"Are those the cameras?" Erland referenced the box and the dark pencil-like objects in it. There were about thirty or so.

"Marland briefed you?"

"All she said was I could help you look for them until the MCL arrived, then I would be handling the murder investigation with forensics."

"Is that all she talked about?"

Erland remembered their conversation in the Observation Room. It was his first opportunity to play the role she had asked him to, that of Switzerland, with a hidden allegiance to her alone. He had no problem lying to Tallifer and he had been in positions previously where he had to speak a truthful lie and had not forgotten how to do it.

"She asked me where I grew up, asked me about my days as a boxer."

"You were a boxer?" Tallifer's lips pursed and he turned. The jerk of his head ordered Erland to follow. "What weight class?"

"Middleweight."

"Professional?"

"No, Amateur. Second place regional Golden Gloves tournament. I fought in Municipal Arena."

"Really?" Tallifer laid the box to rest outside a door that looked no different than any other. "You get a medal for that?"

"I did. It's in a shoebox in my closet."

"Who got first?" Tallifer opened the door to an empty room. "Did he go pro?"

"Hugo Marquez."

"Hugo The Hellhound Marquez?"

Erland smirked, standing at the door, as Tallifer

did all but sniff the room like Sparky. There was absolutely nothing in it, but he was going to make triple sure.

"One and the same. You a boxing fan?"

"I wouldn't call myself a fan but I definitely try to follow sports..." Tallifer came back to the door. "Other guys would think I was a dick if I didn't talk sports, and you never know what sport a guy's into, so I try to keep up on all of 'em. Even sports that aren't sports."

Erland chuckled.

"I get ya."

Tallifer snagged the box with his foot, sliding it across the hall and trying the door opposite. It, too, was empty.

"He was a southpaw, right?" Tallifer inspected the room anyway.

"Yes."

"I did see the title fight he had against..."

"Jones?"

"No..." Tallifer picked up the box and walked down the hall. Erland followed. "Max something."

"Maxie Kramer?"

"Yeah," Tallifer passed two doors and set the box down. "Mad Maxie Kramer. Boy did Maxie get beat up...did you get beat up as bad as he did?"

The chuckled returned. Tallifer tried the door and it was locked.

"Worse."

"You're modest for an old dog. Most guys your age have inflated their younger days so many times they've forgotten what actually happened." Tallifer reached for the lock pick kit that was sitting in the box. He squinted at the Detective. "You're pretty for a boxer too. You're not pulling my leg are you?"

The Detective moved closer to watch the Agent

pick the lock. He had a two handed method and changed picks a few times.

"Not at all. I bet it's on the Internet now, one of those video sites. I'd be the skinny white guy in the white trunks-by the end of the fight, they were white and red. If you're calling me pretty referring to my nose and my ears or scar tissue and all that, for one, I was *extremely* defensive. I wasn't a slugger. I would dodge and move and throw flurries-just enough to win rounds. My style was very technical...my trainer was Irish. And...I guess I was young and healed quickly."

Tallifer changed picks again. Then the door opened. Again, the room was empty.

"Before you ask, Detective, I'm checking all of the empty rooms to see if they really are. After we learned that the owners of this place had cameras here, and they wouldn't tell us where, we got a copy of their...statusing of the rooms for lack of a better word, so right now I'm going through all of the ones marked empty."

"So what about those two we passed?"

"They're both supposed to be half baths. There's three in this area that are guest rooms, three empty, two half baths, and one master room they had designated by the word media."

"So the cameras, what about the murder room?"

"First place I looked in once we learned of the camera's presence, and I don't know how many people have been in there, looking for evidence and such. I gave up hope for it, but if you want to look, go ahead. Otherwise, follow me. Next stop is the media room."

"Lead on, MacTallifer."

The Agent grabbed the box with both arms and marched toward the end of the hall. Erland could almost feel him thinking.

"Was that a...rip off Shakespeare? MacBeth?

Lead on MacDuff?"

Erland nodded.

"Yes, I believe it was."

Tallifer set the box down in the corner, near an end table that was made of what looked to be soapstone.

"Do you read Shakespeare?"

"I only know enough so that I'm not a dick to guys who like Shakespeare."

The tanned Agent smiled broadly. He even laughed.

SEVENTEEN

Messenger bag over her shoulder, Jessica Birchall walked down Schwartz till she reached the intersection of Tenth. On the corner was an Internet Cafe, stuffed underneath a larger gastro pub. The restaurant was named Millard's and was up a flight of stairs that ran behind little more than a library-style row of segregated cubes of chairs and slow and old looking desktop computers. The only users at the moment were a pair of foreign students with tanned skin and black hair that spoke to each other in a language Birchall wasn't familiar with as they pointed to various images of a distinguished looking figure of American History Birchall knew was responsible for writing the Constitution but couldn't place which one. The cafe was little more than a long strip of space and had four two-person tables in the back near a door. Only one was occupied at the moment, filled by an overweight homeless looking man who ate a sandwich that smelled of canned tuna and guarded a cache of paper plates and Styrofoam cups. A small woman with red hair was behind a counter that held only enough room for two industrial coffee pots and all of the necessary accouterments.

"How much to use a computer?"

"It's free if you buy an eight ounce coffee."

Since it wasn't worth a sigh, Jessica reached in

her messenger bag and gave the small woman a dollar more than the coffee was worth and chose the one that said French Roast. Upon tasting it, it was not French Roast, and if it was, then it had been brewed incorrectly.

Setting the coffee beside her, and conscious of the foot traffic up and down the stairs from the gastro pub, since not only the bubbles and spikes of breakfast conversation spilled down the steps but also the clangs and crashes of dishes, Jessica found a search engine and went to work on the guest list. Some of the more prestigious attendees she knew by name, some needed confirming, and others made sense once she searched them. No more than twenty minutes into it she hit a block.

The name Lacey James-Henderson did not merit any direct search hits, and what came close Birchall would have to try to bend to see if the highlighted people would have anything to do with any of the other guests.

In Birchall's mind, Lacey James-Henderson could only have been one of two people. The victim or the suspect.

The reporter moved to the state's official site and searched public records directly for Lacey James-Henderson and attempted to find anything to go on.

Her reward was in a notice of address change. Both addresses were in Crescent and by her knowledge of the city one was near the river and the other was close to a block of hourly rate hotels and motels. Birchall searched them and found their dichotomy could not be any more obvious. The first address *was* an apartment in the Regency Tower, one of the tallest residential towers in Crescent and the rent couldnt've been cheap. It had views of the Targus as it poured into the bay on one side and a sweeping perspective of the rest of Crescent and the rolling evergreen foothills on the other. The second was dead in the heart of Crescent's own little daytime Las Vegas. Though she wasn't looking forward to it, she would have to check that one first.

Rollins was following Jimenez' train of thought in their research of Tim Wolcek when Bartleson's D.C. support center beeped an alert.

"Go." He said.

"We located a computer in Crescent searching for Lacey-James Henderson, and as we isolated it and scanned its history we found it's been searching the guest list too."

Rollins half turned in his seat, pulling on his black goatee.

"Jimenez get..." He shouted and saw Marland standing next to him. "Oh, I didn't know you were back."

"I just stepped in, what's wrong?"

"Someone in town is searching for Lacey James-Henderson *and* the guest list."

Marland frowned. Her eyes drifted around and said much to someone who knew the rules of the game and knew that the searching of the names and especially that one was *not* something Jupiter would do, even as a distraction.

This was the result of an outside pair of hands, a very nosy pair of hands.

"They won't find anything." Marland blew it off, turning back to the door. "Is Ratner still out?"

"Yes."

"Has he had any leads on the kidnapping?"

"No."

"Get the location of the computer and reroute him."

Ratner was only a few blocks from the location and parked the Lumina thirty feet from Millard's and the Internet Cafe that was stuffed beneath it.

He was on the phone as he shut the car door.

"How many are online?"

"Three."

"Okay." Ratner paused before the entrance and affixed his Bluetooth in case of a chase and actually looked like a character from the famous space movies of the eighties. "Ready."

The severe looking Agent entered the space with a strong push of the door and to his immediate right, two Bengali teenagers were studying James Madison. A few computers down a woman in her late twenties sat with a messenger bag. She had dark brown hair and was engrossed in the screen.

"Could I have a coffee, ma'am?" Ratner said to the small red haired woman behind the counter that was almost the same size. He let his eyes drift to the handwritten chalk menu of specialty coffee offerings to be natural and inconspicuous and turned once he heard the pounding of footsteps.

"She's running!" Ratner shouted and began pursuit.

"Do you need Police assistance?" Rollins offered, back in the TMFOV.

"No!"

Ratner sped after the target in a lurching movement. She was no more than seven feet away when an overweight man that had been sitting near the wall stood up and collided with Ratner. The result was an explosion of paper plates, napkins and Styrofoam cups. The Agent flipped over the man as he had slid from his seat in a still semi-seated position and the world was a dark rumble of shapes and colors as Ratner slid and crashed to a halt. He gained composure as quickly as possible considering his glasses were gone and so was his Bluetooth. As he pushed to his knees he saw the back door swing closed and he helplessly fumbled for his glasses.

"Aww, man I'm sorry..." The man who had caused the damaged waddled slowly toward him and smelled of urine.

"I'm fine!" Ratner shouted and scraped and clawed toward the door. His knee was in searing pain and didn't want to cooperate. He limped out the back and was mocked by the emptiness of the alley, and considering it was a corner lot, the woman had four different ways to go and he couldn't see her anywhere and it would've been a slow and painful hobble to the intersection.

Ratner grabbed his phone.

"She got away."

"She? Can I have a description?"

Ratner sighed and limped back inside to look for his glasses and Bluetooth and try to get a description from the Internet Cafe barista.

Jessica Birchall was running for her life. She finally slowed when she reached her car, and as she fumbled with the keys she told herself that she was doing the right thing. But as she threw herself in the car and fired the Subaru, she wasn't so sure. The balding man with the glasses had forced her to run. She had seen him shut down the investigation at the Mansion and then he had been at the scene of Tanya Wilson's house. He was everywhere, everywhere she was and fear had been a snapping reaction to seeing him only a breath away in the Internet Cafe.

The reporter breathed nice and slow, her hands losing their excited trembling. She had broken a sweat and dabbed her forehead with a fast food napkin from the glove box.

The Subaru entered traffic and Birchall convinced herself the truth was worth the peril. One had died and another had been kidnapped, all because they knew something the government was hiding. Who was next? Congressional Candidate Felix? Another congressional candidate? Who was big enough that they had Homeland Security on their side? Was someone in the government planning to alter the elections...or was one of the candidates going to blow the whistle on the government and Homeland was the strong arm snuffing every candle related to the truth?

If they caught her, they'd throw her in jail and she'd lose her job but she knew that wouldn't be the end if she had evidence.

And as she directed the car toward South Crescent and the address in the seediest neighborhood of the city, Birchall hoped to find just that, if not, to find Lacey James-Henderson herself.

The door opened to a slate gray room that was little more than a small movie theater.

"Wow..." Tallifer took it in as his feet made no sound on the carpet. The center of the room was occupied by four rows of seats, twenty-four in all and against the near wall stood what would've been an entertainment center in a normal home, necessary to house the projector, sound system, and all of the power and adapter cords that it took. Directly across from that and on the wall facing the seats was a pull down projection screen that Erland would've felt lost in had it been a sleeping blanket.

"What does one do with this?"

"Whatever one wants." Tallifer shrugged. "Are you an electronics guy?"

"No."

"Good, so then I won't have to act like I know the specs on any of this stuff." Tallifer began with the projector screen wall. "The cameras look like mechanical pencils, check the box if you need to."

Erland took the opposite wall and began to rummage around the projector system in the entertainment center.

"If there's one in here, it's probably angled in a way to get most of the room."

"I used to think that until I found them in some pretty strange places." Tallifer pulled down on the screen and it slid up and then he ran his fingers along the back behind it, where it was mounted to the wall.

Erland continued to dig around the unit as Tallifer conducted his investigation. It was perhaps three minutes later when Tallifer stepped into the frame of the door and went cold.

"Hey, do you have the box?"

"No." Erland called from a half-seated crouching position, running his hands along the back panel of the unit.

"I set it right here." Tallifer motioned to the soap stone end table. Then he cursed and walked off.

Erland paid no thought to it since they had been talking and he might not've set it where he thought.

Tallifer walked down the hall and came to the balcony that overlooked the entrance floor. There he saw one of the Crescent Homeland Agents with the box.

"Hey!" He called out. "Where are you going with that?"

The Agent turned.

"Into the bus."

"Why, I'm not done yet?"

"We're going to store them there."

"Like hell..." Tallifer skipped down the stairs nearly sideways and clip clapped across the floor. "I'm in charge of that."

He put his hand on the box.

"Take it easy, Tallifer."

"And what's your name again?" The tanned Agent asked the man who was *much* taller than him.

"Quinlan."

"I'll bring the cameras to the bus once I've got all of them. I've got a system going and you're messing it up." Tallifer took the box back and stuffed in under his arm like a pro football.

Quinlan watched hopelessly as Tallifer skipped back up the stairs.

It wouldn't be as easy as he hoped.

When Tallifer returned with the box, Erland heard him mutter a litany of curses amongst the word *flunky*.

"What happened?" The Detective asked.

"Procedure. Tabitha must've told him I needed help." Erland presented a clock to the Agent. "What's this?"

"There's a camera inside of it. I don't think it's like the ones you've got there, but it has a camera in it for sure-there's a kind of fisheye lens reflection above the number twelve."

Tallifer set the box down between his legs where he stood and pried the back off of the clock. He followed the wires and pulled the camera out of the clock.

"Nope. It's the same...only smaller." He let it dangle and set it into the box. "Where'd you find it?"

"On the top of the entertainment unit."

"...Obviously..." Tallifer mumbled and brushed past the Detective for another room. They were doubling back and had passed the pair of half-baths when Tallifer's phone buzzed in his breast pocket. He set the box down, again, between his legs where he stood.

"Yeah?"

"Mobile Crime Lab has arrived." Tabitha said on the other end and hung up.

"Detective." Tallifer smiled. "You're on."

Courtland led Team Io down to the garage of PierHouse, which was a veritable stockyard of vehicles. Each one of them was in uniform of the national private security firm known as RepMax and was walking toward a pair of RepMax wrapped black Mercedes vans that had been carefully outfitted for the Team's needs, which consisted of tactical assault gear down to the last thread of ripstop and enough Semtex to blow one of Crescent's most famous buildings to the ground. Each and every one of these items was packed and stowed away in black duffel bags that also had the RepMax markings and from the untrained eye, held no suspicion in themselves. Brock gave Courtland, Kirke and Pitts their wireless communication units and checked the levels.

"Green, go."

"Red, go."

"Blue, go."

"Black, go."

"Jupiter, Io is a go."

The man in white sitting in a very small alcove in PierHouse only inches away from an emergency exit door answered via the microphone on his small and thin laptop computer.

"I'll be watching." Was all he said, and leaned back in the rolling office chair and powered on a wall mounted flat screen television for the local news.

The Homeland Agent named Hill scratched his bullet-shaped head as he waited in the stuffy room reserved for suspected criminals in Crescent PD's newly renovated Precinct Three. He had examined every square inch of cheap pine molding and the rip in the carpet near the door a hundred times if he'd done it once. Apparently they had overlooked the holding room, or had run out of money. The walls, too, were far from a perfect white.

Waiting was a horrible thing, knowing that his game was all but over and in the same token not knowing what he was waiting *for*. The fact that Jupiter had cut ties with him was inevitable, but he couldn't avoid the thought of skydiving into the black hole of justice without a parachute. The sight of Sierra Marland was not only a surprise but painful reminder that Jupiter's group, even being a group of shadows and ghosts, was in an uphill battle against the totalitarian regime the United States Government had become. The only way to defeat their iron grip of information hoarding was to steal it from them and hold *them* at ransom. In that manner, Jupiter was a Robin Hood figure to many around the world, those who could pay, those who the Government had forced into debt or hiding, or those who had been held at ransom themselves by the eyes in the sky. If the populace only knew what the satellites their tax dollars paid for could actually do they would hesitate even going to the mailbox, let alone posting their entire lives on the internet and throwing away to the cloud their most intimate privacies and personal details.

With Jupiter, all of the information was in good hands. He was a middleman and a broker, a holding company determined to let that information go like a laser-guided bomb strike to where it would do the most damage to those who *did* the most damage. Even though Jupiter's moral compass was solely calibrated by money and wealth, his own twisted sense of vindication hid behind his information sales, as if to say, only the corrupt will be exposed, in the process, thus corrupting more than anyone had before him. Jupiter would hold ransom auctions in private to see who would bid more for damming and exploitative evidence, the blackmailer, or the victim, and more often than naught it was the victim who would take a bank loan out on their soul to keep the evidence locked away forever. Still, the news was fraught with such things, things that caused popular figures to fall from grace and public consensus on key issues to be poisoned, and it was in this fickle and contorted limelight that Jupiter saw the power of nations.

All he had to do was to control the court of public opinion and he held the world in his hand. Hill knew the ascent of his business was for just that, to be the most powerful man in the world. Not the richest, but the most powerful. That being what it was, his love of money was only a means to an end.

The Agent named Hill saw his meaninglessness in the sight of that, knowing full well Jupiter would rise as a god of war in the information age and there was now nothing he could do for it or against it. He was merely another warrior waiting in the holding pattern for his eternal fate to be decided.

The door opened and a man in a dark suit like his own sat down opposite him, toothpick in his mouth. The Agent had a smart phone in his hand and was staring at it, opening some application.

"Can I talk to Marland?" Hill asked.

"No." The man said. "I'm the only chance you've got." As the man said it, it was as if he didn't care either way, still looking at the phone.

"Chance at what?" Hill snarled. "I'm dead and

you know it."

"You can tell me where Jupiter is..."

"And how do I know that?"

"How did you contact him?"

"By carrier pigeon."

The Agent looked him in the eye and smiled.

"Why do you want to talk to her?"

"She would understand. You're just a little fish."

"We're all little fish Hill, that's why we're here."

"Marland's not. She's the one you have to watch out for."

"Why's that?" Morell leaned back in the chair. With the way Hill was cuffed hand and foot and bolted to the floor Morell could've taken a nap and been in perfect security.

"Because she's got everyone at SAB wrapped around her little finger, she can do whatever she wants and get away with it."

"She's SAB, Hill, that's like saying the President said to do it himself. We all know the autonomy of SAB, and the authority, and how damn hard it is to get in and how damn good you have to be to stay in."

"Yeah," Hill leaned forward, "so I was working with Jupiter, but what about you? She says *boo* and everyone pees their pants. She so much as *implies* someone is dirty they'll lock them up and throw away the key."

"Are you trying to threaten me?"

"I'm trying to *warn* you. There's a difference."

"Warn me of what?" Morell removed the toothpick from his mouth and pointed at Hill. "That I'm going to be sitting there?"

"Marland won't tell anybody what her plans are,

will she?"

"She's not supposed to."

"Bartleson doesn't even know what she's got up the sleeves of that pinstripe pantsuit."

"And how do you know that? Did Bartleson talk to you about it? He's buried so deep in D.C.'s top clearances you wouldn't even be able to *stand* next to him without getting a pat down and a debrief and you want me to believe that you know what Marland's supposedly planning and her boss *doesn't?*"

"That's what you think." Hill leaned back and crossed his arms with somewhat of a defiant face.

"Fine, you pitched and I'll catch."

"I want a plane to South America before I tell you anything else."

Morell laughed and his boyish dimples were apparent. He laughed again.

"Is that what you wanted to tell Marland? I'm going to make you think I've got some dirty dirt so get me the next plane to Acapulco?"

"Acapulco's in Mexico, you idiot."

"Whatever." Morell stood up and buttoned his suit, leaving his phone. "When I come back I'm going to bring a Doctor with me and we're going to determine just how much pain you can handle." Morell leaned in very close. "And I'm *not* bluffing."

The Agent left and the worms of doubt started chewing on Hill's stomach. He had to figure out if Morell was bluffing before Morell figured out if he *was*.

Only one of them actually was.

EIGHTEEN

       Morell spent nearly an hour with Darren Reston and not only concluded that he was the victim of a terrible coincidence but was a hopelessly boring person. Not that everyone had to lead the life of excitement that Henry Morell did, work hard and play harder, but he would think that Reston would be more...something. Ambitious, maybe? Opportunistic? Considering his steamed white potato life, Morell found it quite amazing that the journalist actually *had* mustered the moxie to do the things he had, and both of them attributed it to the amnesia.

       "I think we're all finished then." Morell put the small voice recorder in his pants pocket.

       "The longer I sit here the more I remember."

       "Well, you can't stay but you don't have to leave."

       "What does that mean?" Reston scratched around the area where the IV was still regulating his bodily fluid.

       "It means I'm sure they'll let you get something in the cafeteria if you want but you're going to have to get some help to start your life back up again."

       "Yeah..." Reston's eyes drifted around the room. "Do you have a phone by any chance?"

       "Not with me right now, do you need to make a call?"

"Yeah...I tried to earlier and it just didn't work out, but I think I'm ready now. I'm ready to go back to life...you know, start over."

"Well," Morell stood up and checked the IV drip by giving it a couple of gentle flicks. "No one can ever *really* start over. There's always something that catches up to you. You have to look it in the eyes and tell it to go away before you can, as you say, start over. Running away from it will never make it change."

"Hmm." Was all Reston said and looked and the veins in his hands.

"If that's not clear enough I'm talking about alcohol. When I was a teenager my older brother got hooked on it-said it made him deal with stress. He's not alive anymore. I've been to a hundred clubs and bars if I've been to one but I won't touch the stuff. Not since that night he did what he did. Just think if you hadn'tve had that drink at the party you wouldn't be here now."

"I know..." Darren nodded. Then again, "I know."

"I'll get you that phone." Morell shut the door, and as he did, his face changed, because he was going back to talk to Hill.

When he opened the door he found the Doctor on the floor and his phone missing from the table.

Morell cursed and crouched, reaching for the Doctor.

"Are you okay?"

She was alive and it seemed like Hill had given her one good punch when she hadn't expected it.

Morell, without alarm, stood quietly and slowly and closed the door behind him, scanning the hallway that ran ahead of him and curved slightly to the left.

Then he pulled the cell phone from his pocket that had *not* been fitted with a Hyperactive Geosynchronous Transponder and speed dialed Sierra

Marland.

Luther Hill made a quick path to the restroom he had spotted on his way to the holding room. His pulse was racing, being completely trapped in a den of blue wolves.

Once in the men's restroom, he locked himself in a stall and removed his jacket, and rolled up his sleeves. His jacket went behind the toilet. Once at the sink he splashed water on his hair and radically changed its shape and profile so he would look far less like the man that had been arrested in the cafeteria. Still, so many Police Officers and department officials milling around, one was bound to spot him. He needed a disguise.

Hill left the restroom, conscious of the cut that Detective had caused by punching him and felt it with the trembling tips of his fingers. As he walked he expected any second to be found out.

Cautiously, the double Agent maneuvered around the back end of the Precinct, conscious to avoid the densely populated areas near the front entrance and the north side of the building. He was inwardly grateful that the holding room he'd been stashed in was located in the deadest part of the structure. He passed several innocuous rooms in which records were stored and as much as he hoped for the armaments room to attempt a hostile escape, he found something much better, the janitor's closet.

Without hesitation Hill entered the room and was hit with the choking assault of chemicals and industrial cleaners. He quickly located the light. Scanning the room he found a locker and advanced toward it. The door was opened, but barely so, and he wrenched at it and was met with a metallic screeching and clanging. His eyes hurriedly darted around inside and located a spare set of brown pants and jacket. Even if they didn't fit they were his only chance. As he was changing and throwing his eyes to the door in fear, he spotted something shiny catching the light from the single overhead bulb.

He reached for it and found it to be a small memory card.

For a moment, the haphazard sense of panic left him and he considered the card very carefully.

Was it? No, it couldn'tve been. Sure it was the size and shape of what Jupiter was supposed to have purchased from the seller at Fircrest that turned out to be Magnolia Marland, but what were the chances of it being in the janitor's locker in Precinct Three?

Hill swallowed hard and nearly gagged as the chemicals began to get to him. He was over thinking it. It was probably a memory card the janitor had stuffed in his pocket to take to work to print family photos and things, there was no way Sierra Marland would've done stashed the card there, assuming she *had* the information, and it wasn't locked in some nuclear bomb proof vault in a national park in Utah.

Chuckling to himself, Hill took the memory card anyway, but left the phone. Marland knew he was going to escape, and had nearly tempted him to do so more than likely prompting the Agent to *forget* his phone. Getting out of the building wouldn't be easy, but Hill knew, if Marland had cooked up some crazy plan like she was legendary for, by leaving the phone he'd let her know he was playing the game but not by her guidelines. There was a way to take a carrot from a trap without dangling from the noose for doing it.

Morell was in no hurry walking around Precinct following the signal from a distance. When it had stopped for more than three minutes, he decided to get a closer look. As he approached the janitor's closet, it made sense.

The Agent entered the room with his hand on his pistol and found the small space to be vacant. He saw the change of clothes was gone from the room and the phone was sitting in the locker. Upon closer inspection the memory card was gone.

It was *exactly* how Marland had told him he would find it, and though he had no idea what was going on, he was confident in her abilities and plans, no matter what that desperate traitor had to say.

"He's got the clothes and the card and left the phone." He told the SAB Agent as he moved to the doorway.

"Good." She said, all the way over in Fircrest, thinking as she did. "Inform the Lieutenant and he should be seen exiting on one of the cameras, then we'll start tracking him and he'll lead us to Jupiter. There's already a plainclothes Officer at each exit. The SWAT team is on standby."

"And if he doesn't?" Morell asked, already in a jog to contact Lieutenant Ross.

"He will."

"Alright...I'll keep you posted." Morell stuffed the phone in his pocket and on his way passed by the Doctor who looked to be as healthy as could be, despite taking a punch. There had been some play-acting on her behalf.

"He used the metal clip from my ID to break out." She said.

"Follow me." Morell said as he jogged. As soon as he reached the Lieutenant's office, the Agent felt a knot forming in his stomach. He knew they were closer than they had ever been to capturing Jupiter even though he had no idea of how many times they'd tried or how close they'd ever been. It was just that gut

feeling that something irrevocably serious was going to
happen and strangely enough the only time that knot
ever came up was when he knew a girl was going to
dump him. Thus far, it had never *ever* been wrong.

"Lieutenant Ross?"

The man behind the desk was a thick black man
formerly from Miami-Dade County Police.

Henry Morell gave him the details.

"Right. I'll take it from here. Marland said
you're staying put so I'm putting you in observation
with the SWAT team so she can coordinate. She said
you were Army?"

"Third Stryker Brigade, Second Infantry
Division, Bravo Company." Morell said as he came to
attention.

"Good, then you won't mind getting suited up
for combat, will you?"

The knot in his guts aside, he most certainly
would not. Lieutenant Ross went for his desk phone and
began to issue orders.

The Doctor was there at Morell's side and
seeing her reminded him.

"Did you get the results of the blood test?"

"Yes."

"Was it what Marland suspected?"

"STRIC-R? Yes it was."

Morell didn't know what STRIC-R was but he
knew Marland did and once again she was right. On the
last two instances alone she had falsified Hill's claims
that she was doing her own thing or about to and
somewhere inside Morell changed gears so that he
would be able to suit up with the SWAT team and if
need be, do his part to take Jupiter down once and for
all.

The Mobile Crime Lab was a sixty-foot trailer pulled by a bright red Mack truck. The squeal of the air brakes and the grumble of the diesel engine were unmistakable. Erland waltzed from the Mansion and stopped at the gate, as Tabitha Grey stood overseeing the deployment of the trailer. Since it was so large and the TMFOV bus took up the room that it did, the trailer was placed on the grass parallel to the drive as it ran up the sweeping hill, providing easy access to whatever vehicles would come and go. Having done that, the driver aided the forensic scientists that emerged from the MCL in securing the trailer with blocks and wheel locks due to the steep angle of the hill, and because of the sheer size of the circular drive it was a good two-hundred feet away from the main gate.

Erland walked and passed Tabitha.

"You guys like your toys big."

"It's far from a toy, Detective." Tabitha fell in pace with him. "It has everything a private crime lab would have...except a restroom."

The Detective observed how many people were milling about the trailer.

"More guests to the party."

"Now we have fourteen total forensic analysts, technicians, scientists, artists, whatever they want to call themselves, we have them, so not one scrap of evidence should go unnoticed or unprocessed and you can nail the bastard that killed Agent Marland."

There was an edge in Tabitha's voice; a biting frost, like the breeze that swirled around Fircrest ever so often to remind everyone outside that it was that time of year.

"Can you give me a tour?" Erland offered as friendly as possible.

"No. Roshie will do that."

Tabitha left and took the cold air with her.

Erland held back as the Mack laboriously pulled away from the trailer and after crushing a fair amount of neatly manicured grass, found the long strip of pavement that lead down the hill like a ski jump launch ramp. Erland watched the truck and surveyed the geography. The hill emptied into a very small shelf of land that dropped straight off into the slant of the highway, which, as it curved around the looming hill, gained some height. The altitude difference between the area where Reston had entered the highway and the small line of the highway below the hill had to be a hundred feet. It was strange, but that was the nature of the area, lumps of green cut by rivers with splats of residential areas carelessly thrown in between. Some day, hopefully not tomorrow, the metropolitan area of Crescent would struggle from the weight of growth and be unable to support the high volume of citizens on its curvy roads and highways. Crescent rush hour was already a national travesty. He knew it living just outside the big city to the north in a district known as to the locals as Pill Valley, due to its overwhelming concentration of clinics, dentists, drug stores, and apartment complexes, not to mention Corazon Hospital. Its formal name was simply, Valley.

Erland spotted a foreign looking woman who couldn't have been over five feet tall giving orders to some of the others. None of them were in lab coats as he would've expected, and on a whole, they actually had the appearance of a mountain climbing expedition. As he thought about it, they had approached from the south, perhaps from another state where it was warmer.

"Excuse me." Erland stopped. The woman turned.

"Yes, can I help you?" Her voice was high pitched and carried a British accent. Face to face he determined she was definitely Pakistani, at least he assumed so because he had Pakistani neighbors and she could've been one of their near relatives. There was a small community of them in the Griffin Park area of greater Crescent, and he had spent a great deal of time there with the Granderson case. She was a friendly little figure in a puffy North Face jacket and a knit beanie but more than likely a fierce tyrant as a leader when it came to the toil of evidence processing management.

"Detective First Grade Michael Erland, CPD," He offered his hand. "I'm on special...authorization from Homeland Security to assist you."

"Oh." The woman smiled and shook his hand as one hand held her knit beanie hat on. "I've been reading about you on the trip up. Glad to be working with you, Sir."

"You would be Roshie?"

"Yes, yes." Her face lit up. "When can we begin?"

"Oh," Erland shrugged. "I'm not in charge of that, I'm really only here as an outsider. You would want to speak to an Agent Marland about that, she's the brunette, not the blonde." Erland pointed with his thumb. "I was heading up the Police investigation here earlier so I know the scene pretty well, and quite a few of the questions I had at the time have been answered but the case is by no means close to a solid lead."

Roshie took off her hat and had very short, almost buzzed black hair and small black opal stud earrings not only on her lobes but also on her cartilage. She peeked around Erland and her mouth fell open.

"That's the biggest building I've ever seen..."

"I know." Erland said. "We'll take it one room at a time."

He was just about to turn when he heard a familiar and welcome voice.

"You must be Roshie..." Sierra Marland shook

the small woman's hand.

"Yes, yes."

"Welcome. You and all of your companions are going to make a big difference."

"Well, we've covered all of the bases. We're prepared to process any type of evidence you may have."

"Excuse me, Roshie." Marland smiled and then to Erland. "Detective?"

They took a few feet and Roshie marched back to the trailer.

"Yeah?"

"We're in the middle of a fox hunt right now, I just wanted to tell you about it because I don't want you to be out of the loop but if anybody asks or says anything you have to act surprised."

"Got it."

"We let Hill escape and we're hoping he's going to lead us to Jupiter's location. Morell will ride with the SWAT team. I'll be running the operation from the bus when the time comes and if you want to see it you'll be notified, otherwise, I'll let you do what I know you do better than anyone else."

Sierra didn't smile like usual but she did transmit a tremendous amount of confidence through her eyes.

"I won't let you down." Erland nodded.

Sierra's eyes said he couldn't, but by the way she walked with her head down back to the bus he knew the weight of the world was on her shoulders.

Unsure was the only word that could accurately describe the look on Kelly Barnett's face as she was admitted past the desk sergeant and escorted by a Doctor Patrice to the room where Darren was located.

"Mr. Reston suffered a hybridized form of

amnesia due to several different factors, one of which being chronic alcoholism." The Doctor informed her as they walked.

Kelly pushed her glasses up on her nose.

"That figures."

"But the result of what happened was the cause of a potent drug called STRIC-R. I don't have time to explain it to you, but STRIC-R is the equivalent of a temporary mental straightjacket. He's been through a lot and is handling it very well." They reached the door. "I don't know exactly what he told you but he will need help moving forward. He's in no condition to work and depending on the amount of STRIC-R is residually in his system, he could have lapses."

The CMJ journalist pushed her lip out.

"Is there anything you can give him to help?"

The Doctor shook her head and her voice was a softening brush on Kelly's rough nerves.

"I've done what I can. I'm in contact with a specialist about further treatment but it might take some time. Don't worry. All he needs is a good friend. Just don't let him drive home."

Kelly smiled and it faded as she opened the door. She hid a small gasp to see the IV in Darren's arm.

"Hi." She said quietly and sat down to face him. He looked tired and used up, but still the same Darren she wished to know better. It was his reaching out to her that had made up her mind that he felt the same way, seeing as he could've called one of his fantasy football drinking buddies and didn't.

"Kelly..."

"You remember?"

"Yeah..." Darren smiled and scratched his ear. "How could I forget?"

Kelly returned his smile and a warmth grew

inside.

"If you need *any* help at all Darren, I'm here."

At first, it was a timid gesture, but Kelly placed one of the hands that held each other in her lap on the table and it found its way to rest on top of Darren's. Her other hand curled the hair behind her ears.

"Thank you, Kelly. I mean it..." Darren nearly teared up which was something Kelly didn't know he was capable of amidst his wily sarcastic fits and humorous insights. "There was a woman in Wayilow that helped me...maybe it's because of what happened but I never really felt like anyone cared about me until she did what she did..." Kelly blinked as she listened. "But the longer I sat here the more I thought about you and all of the times you helped me and I took it for granted or I just didn't see it...all of the times I was too deep into the bottle to know the difference."

Kelly mashed her lips together and nodded. Her fellow journalist looked her in the eye and a single tear rolled down the side of his cheek. His brown eyes said he was tired of being lazy and pathetic and wanted to be serious. About work. About life. Maybe those times they had gone out to dinner he had only been half present, not caring too much about her because he thought she didn't care about him.

She squeezed his hand. Now those passing comments she had planted made sense to his foggy memory, those times at work when he caught her looking at him and she had looked away.

"I can take you home." She said.

Reston nodded. It was the only place *to* go.

The Subaru came to a halt across the street from a washed out apartment block that had *Palisades* written in light blue script across the face of the building and perhaps would've satisfied a beach bound bohemian in a sunny state but slapped up against the gray pavement of used car lots, small casinos, and hourly motels that quantified the area of South Crescent known as Quintero, it looked positively out of place. What should've been a row of palms flanking the underwhelming entrance was a row of poplars and there was a trio of neon colored balloons tied to a sign that advertised the monthly price, which was still quite high, considering. For a second, Jessica Birchall contemplated leaving her ruby red overcoat in the car but it was still too cold for that and since there wasn't much to her she needed the jacket, despite the attention that its vivid color drew to her.

The episode in the Internet cafe had startled her and brought her to a very suspicious place. A heavy frown had taken up residence on her face and with the messenger bag at her side she looked as hard and as formidable as one of her delicacy possibly could. Her eyes were quick to dart back and forth in wary glances for anything that would provoke a hasty retreat to the car.

The entrance was little more than a pair of glass doors that jingled like the portal to a second hand shop and an unattended administration area that Birchall bypassed for a long hall that lead to a bunched up zigzag staircase. The steps were a very coarse brand of carpet that had been cleaned one too many times and had streaks and spaces of color deficiency and once on the second floor Jessica walked until she reached forty-seven A.

Forty-Seven A, as it turned out, was unlocked, and to her shock, completely empty.

Jessica carefully walked around the nearly seven hundred square foot dwelling and the silence of it was disturbing. She expected to find a dead body in the shower or for someone to leap out of the closet and couldn't even find a fingerprint in the dust of the windowsill.

It was a resoundingly heavy strikeout.

That was until she spoke with the apartment manager, a half-bent over man with a matted whitish beard whose shirt said his name but the sewn-on tag was too curled to read. The man smelled of unhealthy sweat and lacquer thinner. He was in the middle of maintenance and was wrangling a wheeled bucket and mop through the front door and all the jingling and grunting that followed when Birchall accosted him.

"Is Lacey in?" She asked.

"Who?"

"Lacey James-Henderson, Forty-Seven A."

"Oh...Lacey? No, the man said his name was Quin...Quinlan."

"No, that apartment belongs to my friend Lacey," Birchall made an show of reaching in her bag, looking for something that would drive her acting job home, some slip of paper or something tangible. "She gave me the address...we were going to have lunch with some friends and pull some slots at the All-Star..."

"Nope, nope, forty-seven A, that apartment belongs to Mr. Quinlan and I'll show you if you don't believe me, young lady."

The man waddled to his desk and began to hunt and peck on a computer several years older than the ones in the Internet Cafe. He squinted painfully as he operated the machine and finally struck a proud look.

Jessica leaned over the counter and saw the apartment had been paid for a month by the name Quinlan, Keith, not James-Henderson, Lacey.

Not knowing exactly what that meant, Birchall quickly left *Palisades*, crossed the street and fired up the Subaru for the Regency Tower address in North Crescent.

NINETEEN

Cutting through what law enforcement officials he did encounter with a strident pace and his head toward the ground, Luther Hill made his way to the stairs for the parking garage. From the heaviness of his brow he could see cameras in nearly every corner of the building the closer he became to freedom and did his best to avoid them. Once he was out of the building he would adopt a final change of clothes. He took the stairs to the ground level of the parking garage as quickly as he could without being in a suspicious hurry and wondered when the alarm would be raised that he had escaped, if ever. Just as he was approaching the parking gate, he heard the alarm.

The desire to fall into a dead sprint and hop the flimsy looking metal swing arm and the retractable steel spikes below was suppressed immediately and Hill kept his confident pace. The clamor had all of the makings of a fire alarm but held a different cadence. It filled the hollowness of the garage with a piercing and jarring racket.

"Excuse me, Sir, there's been a lockdown, you're not allowed to leave yet." The Officer at the gate said as Hill was a few feet away. The Officer was on the phone and turned away from Hill for a split second. It was enough time for Hill to silently skip up the concrete curb and force his way into the small booth.

Before the Officer could react, Hill was on him and had
knocked him out by smashing the Officer's head
against the counter several times. In a crouched
position, alarm still banging and ringing wildly, Hill
looked over the waist high counter through the
Plexiglas windows of the enclosure to see if anyone
was on to him. When he saw nothing he took all of
three minutes to change into the Officer's apparel, and
though the Officer had a gun, he also had a radio, and in
many ways that was going to be more of an important
tool as the escape progressed. Throughout the process
Hill had thrown glances back into the orangey darkness
of the garage and to the different fixed angle cameras
that would foil his disguise.

      Hill left the small parking enclosure for the
street and once out of view of the cameras, fell into a
flat sprint for the nearest alley. There, he ditched the
Officer's jacket as he had stuffed it over the brown one.
The web belt went in the garbage and he kept the gun,
the radio, and the badge, and stuffed them all in the
brown janitor's jacket.

      He knew he had been caught on camera and
now they were looking for him, but he had the
advantage. They were looking for an Officer, not a man
in black pants and a brown jacket, and it would take
them too long to figure it out because he doubled back
the other direction, striking a course for PierHouse. To
add to it all he found a green baseball cap in the
dumpster where he stuffed the jacket and though it
smelled like drunken urine he pulled it down tight on
his head, keeping the volume on the Police radio he had
stuffed in the breast pocket of the jacket high enough to
hear as he walked through the morning foot traffic of
North Crescent.

Kincaid, a plainclothes Narcotics Detective with an overbite and a beer belly, spoke into his cell phone from the cab of a white Ford Ranger.

"I've got him. Brown jacket, green hat, black pants, heading east on...Foster. Pursuit?"

"Not yet, keep an eye on him." Lieutenant Ross said from the integrated intercom system in the Command Room of the Precinct, a small room that spilled over from the dispatch room. Ross was standing watch over the computer that had every operative positioned and identified on a grid-like map. The goal was to both scare Hill with the Patrolmen and lead him into a false sense of security at the same time, letting him hear the radio chatter and in his mind and *assume* that he was evading them, while letting the plainclothes Officers hang back and report on his location.

"Fiedler, move up to Wallinder...if he doesn't take it, go to Fourth."

"Copy..."

Henry Morell walked in, suited up in SWAT black, with level II body armor and knee and elbow pads, bulletproof helmet in hand. A camera was mounted to the helmet and had a small transmission antenna.

"SWAT's ready, Lieutenant."

"Good." Ross answered without looking. "You got your camera?"

"Yes."

"Okay. Is Homeland ready?"

"Yes." Morell nodded and told the woman at the computer a few technical things about the link so that they would see the same feed and listen in on the details of the SWAT assault.

"So once we pinpoint the location, we'll begin to set a perimeter." Ross stood tall and stretched. "Marland's in charge of the assault."

The way he said it was a backhanded manner to
remove all of the responsibility from his end in case
anything went wrong. Deep down inside, he wished he
was the one coordinating the assault, but he was more
than happy to defer to a higher power and was
confident in the Homeland Agent's ability considering
the kind of operation she was running. If there was
anything Ross hated it was a traitor and would do
anything to see one brought to justice. To let the bird
fly the coup to find the nest was more than a perfect
trade off for a few bumps and bruises, seeing as both
the Doctor and the gate Officer had not sustained any
serious injuries, although the traitor had been more
violent with the gate Officer and he had a mild
concussion, it was all gravy in the face of capturing, as
Marland had put it, the most dangerous man in
America.

"Both SWAT teams will be on the road in five."
Morell said as he left the room.

"Kincaid, begin pursuit."

"Roger."

Lieutenant Ross studied the map and any points
of importance within walking distance.

"Begin triangulation as well."

"Roger."

Ross spread his legs and braced his hands on his
kneecaps like a college football coach in crunch time.
He listened as the Patrolmen began to rattle off the
street names of their routes, knowing that Hill was
hearing exactly the same thing.

Morell didn't have enough time to perform his
superstitious pre-combat ritual and in the back of his
mind convinced himself this was different than
Baghdad and therefore he didn't have to do it. Even so,
seeing the hardened steel in the eyes of the two SWAT

teams of eight split into squads of four, he couldn't help but feel like he was about to be in the belly of the beast again, the diesel motors churning and throwing dust and feigning death, cutting through the narrow streets of the ancient city, looking for adventure as the song said.

He strapped his helmet on tight and checked his weapons. He had an M4 carbine and his service pistol, two flash bang grenades and one smoke. The man next to him was the breach man and was loading his automatic shotgun with shells.

"This your first time out?" Morell asked as he adjusted his chinstrap.

"No. Second...I was support team at the Bowers High School shooting."

Morell nodded and assisted the man by reversing the direction of one of the smoke grenades in his web belt.

"This'll turn out differently." Morell smiled but how could he possibly know? Combat, SWAT or street sweeping in Baghdad, day or night, it was all riding the lightning, becoming one with the split second instinct and the radical force of adrenaline that a soldier counted on like a spouse, to be there always at all times, never to leave.

Morell was the last to get in the armored SWAT car after the order was given to leave the Precinct. The adrenaline had chewed him up and spit him out and left him for someone else, someone younger and better suited to handle the volatile relationship. It was more than likely the reason why he couldn't actually commit to one of the many women he'd been with, he was afraid they'd be taken from him too, like his life in the Army had, and because of that very lack of commitment, they always did leave.

The Agent let his reservations fall on the cold concrete of the parking garage and armed the M4 as he leapt in the back of the armored car.

Hill was in a group of pedestrians waiting for a crosswalk to turn favorable when he heard the chatter of the Patrolmen on the radio. The main cluster of them was searching in a three-block radius around the Precinct. So far there had been no coded comments about the dumpster.

Content that he was in the clear, the Agent ceased his zigzagging and headed for the Targus. It took all of ten minutes before he could smell it.

The Targus River was a thick blue-green vein of industry and always had been. Three blocks from the Waterfront, Hill could see the line of logging barges in their weekly trudge to the Mill in Ram's Head, up the river coast to the north. He spotted the orange cranes of the warehouse district and knew PierHouse was close.

A block away from the artistic structure Hill stopped stone cold in a corner-viewing alley and listened to the radio, his eyes hawk-like in scanning the streets for anything that remotely resembled a plainclothes or undercover Officer. Once satisfied, Hill removed the radio and badge from the jacket and threw it in the alley, boldly jaywalking the street when traffic permitted. PierHouse was the product of a wealthy company's investment in the Waterfront and was strangely close to the greasy angles and washed out colors of the shipping container yards and warehouses. It had the magnificence of the Sydney Opera House as a movie model ship did to film of a real ship. The result was nevertheless an effective boost in the Waterfront's much needed prestige and even with the expensive restaurants that followed several hundred feet away there was no denying the Targus, as beautiful as water could be, was still just a logging pipeline with a bi-weekly visit from shallow draft cargo vessels and the ferries to the northern islands.

Luther Hill came to the daunting entrance of sharp angles and didn't even bother with the stout pair of wooden doors. A pair of XY axis cameras, one mounted above each corner of the door, studied him thoroughly for all of a minute and a half before one of the doors pulled open.

Hill entered PierHouse and the door shut behind him.

Parked in front of Riviera's on the opposite side of the street, Kincaid reported the act to Lieutenant Ross.

"Suspect entered alone. No visual on who let him in."

"PierHouse it is." Ross crossed his arms, knowing what a SWAT siege of such a beloved structure would do to the city. He scratched his cheek as the feed from Morell's helmet camera was up and running on the computer screen in concert with the map and the SWAT's tactical bandwidth was humming through the speakers instead of the Patrolmen's bogus triangulation. Ross studied the ticks and blips as the perimeter fell around PierHouse like a net and the armored SWAT car punched straight through the middle of the net.

Dannigan had the Skorpion submachine gun fixed to a swivel-holster and concealed in his jacket. They all did. Hill didn't know it as his feet made thick clomps on the wood floors.

The dark haired former contract killer named Dannigan and the bald man named Halstan escorted Hill to the whale room where he waited. Dannigan and Halstan stood at his right and left shoulder, respectively, and said nothing as the man in white entered the room nearly two minutes later with the one-eyed Kix. It was then they stepped back a few feet and took on a rigid and defensive posture with their legs spread and their arms crossed.

"Why'd you come here?" Jupiter asked. He was not a small man but he was by no means a large one, and even though his face and the size of his body was quite forgettable his physical presence had nothing to do with the deadly aura of intimidation that was his alone. The power was in his eyes, little black eyes that sat under the faintest lines of eyebrows, black eyes that saw everything.

"I have it." Hill lied.

"Have what?"

"What Reston took from the box. The memory card."

"How'd you get it?"

Hill swallowed and made a move to take off his hat. Immediately the Skorpions were exposed from behind the fabric of the bodyguard's suits, and each killing machine was trained on the thickness of the front his body.

"Woah...Jupiter, what are you doing?"

"You blew it, you know what happens. The fact that you're here puts me in jeopardy. I should have them shoot you right now."

"But I've got it! I got what you wanted to get at Fircrest!"

"You were compromised. How do I know you weren't followed? How do I know they didn't turn you? Or they didn't put a tracker in that memory card?"

"You've got to be kidding man," Hill's face stretched, hiding worry. "I've worked with you for three years. I helped you put away Congressmen Davies and the CEO from the Rodell Corporation, and I embedded myself in Homeland without their knowledge!"

Jupiter wasn't having it, true as it was, Hill was a valuable asset but his judgment had been poor in the relative autonomy of performing the job that he had been assigned.

"How'd you get it?"

"I took it from him when he was in holding." Hill lied, hoping Jupiter would buy it, at least giving him enough time to figure out something else to get back in the crew. If the card were as he thought and just the janitor's family photos or emails then he would be able to make up a story about Marland switching it.

"And when did Marland find you out?"

"I broke protocol."

Jupiter's teeth ground together and sent little pulses through the flesh of his cheeks.

"Why?"

"It's hard playing both sides, I got rattled..." Hill took the smelly green hat off and threw it on the floor. "You know how it is...and have these guys put the guns away. It won't happen again."

Jupiter's chin jerked toward Hill.

"Let me see it."

Hill smiled.

Before Jupiter could see the memory card, his phone buzzed in his back pocked. He reached for it and his blood fell to subzero temperatures when he saw the camera feed from the security system.

Erland was wondering what the inside of the TMFOV bus actually looked like and opened the door. What greeted him was a gallery of intense glares as a handful of people were fanned out before an appropriately large flat screen monitor, arms crossed or bracing and leaning on whatever objects were behind them. The air in the bus was thick and claustrophobic.

Before anyone could say anything voices of the

SWAT team came in warbled tone from the speakers.

"Falcon One in position."

Erland took a spot next to Sierra Marland, who stood directly behind Rollins as he sat in operation of the computer system.

"We believe Jupiter is in PierHouse. Morell has the camera. We can't afford to confirm, we have to move now."

The screen was a shaky and grainy view of four men in black body armor approaching the front entrance of the structure, two thick wooden doors flanked by closed circuit security cameras.

"Falcon Two in position."

There was the space of a heartbeat.

"Go." Marland said.

"Go, go." Rollins, the computer technician repeated.

The man in the front of the line of SWAT soldiers raised the barrel of his shotgun and with two booming blasts, blew the hinges from the door. He stepped aside as the next man in line rammed his foot against the door. It fell like a domino. The man behind him threw a flash bang grenade in the sliver of a hallway visible from Morell's helmet viewpoint and there were shouts after the snapping concussion of the grenade rocked the hall.

"Go! Go! Go!" The squad leader named Rodriguez shouted. He was the man before Morell.

A fair distance away there was the sound of another flash bang and it was followed directly by the cackle and pop of small arms fire.

"Falcon One, taking fire...engaging hostiles...rear atrium."

Erland and Marland watched the motion sick video as the SWAT team with the designation Falcon Two shuffled down the long hall of maple flooring and wavy frosted glass in silence, as the noises of battle raged some unknown distance away.

"Clear!" The point man shouted.

But it wasn't. There was the sound of a gun cocking, the unmistakable metallic choking and arming of an automatic, followed by the high-pitched whine of a small and remotely operated motor.

It wasn't until the wall of frosted glass exploded in deadly shards Falcon Two knew where the sound had come from. Not thirty feet away, in a different room, a six-barreled gas operated belt-fed Minigun with a laser sight and extremely prejudicial targeting system had fired to life, sending 7.62mm rounds into the hallway at the rate of three-thousand a second.

Erland covered his mouth as Morell ducked and the bodies in front of him thudded with bullet after bullet and the wall behind them splintered with sawdust and the spray of blood.

The killing took maybe seven seconds.

Morell swore and pushed himself backwards.

"Murphy! Murphy!" He shouted.

Marland pressed her lips together. The responsibility was on her shoulders. But it wasn't supposed to be a capturing. It was supposed to be a killing.

It was war.

Pain welled within Marland's heart as Morell's helmet camera showed the lifeless bodies of beloved family members-husbands, fathers, sons, brothers. Their sacrifice would not be in vain.

"Falcon One!" Morell called out. "Falcon Two is down!"

"Roger, Falcon Two, threats neutralized, heading to your position."

"Negative, negative! Falcon Two was taken down by a remote Minigun, laser sight, heat-signature...east hallway main door. Continue pursuit of target and be advised."

"Roger."

"You getting this?" Morell called out. The laser sight pulled back and forth across the wall and held in the middle, as if waiting for a new target.

Marland nodded. She let go of a heavy sigh and the air ran right back in her lungs with a sharp breath.

At the end of the long hall, a man in white stood in the doorframe for a split second before rushing to his left.

"That's him!" Marland shouted, not knowing for sure because she had never seen him but the punch in her gut to the image on the screen was the only confirmation she needed.

Morell swore and pushed himself up behind the safety of the wooden wall.

"Falcon Two pursuing target, east hallway."

Morell held for a beat and then took a running leap at the hallway. The minigun responded by whining and tracking to follow the heat signature before the bullets began to fly. Chunks and splinters of wood became sawdust as the thuds and snaps of bullets bit into the wall. Morell broad jumped over the bloody mess of bodies and landed on his belly with a grunt, skidding across the floor and sliding to a stop against the doorframe where he saw the man in white. Out of the corner of his eye with the helmet cocked as it was, Morell saw half of a white pant leg and shoe passing through a doorframe at the end of another hall just as the door closed.

The sense of desire was tangible in the TMFOV. Erland could feel the intensity bubbling inside of Tabitha and Jimenez. The tall Quinlan held a cold and tactical face and Sierra Marland's beauty was being overshadowed by the gravity of the situation. Her eyebrows were twisted in disbelief and the line of her mouth was drawn downward, pulled by two jutting tendons in her neck.

Morell scrambled for momentum and took off after Jupiter. He was to the door in three seconds.

The group in the TMFOV watched wordlessly as the door opened to a darkened staircase that was tight and sharp and just large enough for Morell to stand in.

There was a plastic click clacking and the zipping sound of fabric as Morell swung the M4 around to his back and reached for his service pistol and a flashlight.

"Falcon Two in silent pursuit." He radioed. There was no confirmation from Falcon One.

"Where does this lead?" Marland asked Rollins who had the blueprint schematic loaded on a smaller screen.

"It doesn't exist." The computer technician said behind a frown.

"Where's it close to?" Marland reiterated.

"There's a causeway that leads to the dock...it runs under the structure...that could be it."

"What about the garage?"

"It's possible..."

Their eyes darted between screens. Morell was still descending, and doing so cautiously considering the fate of Falcon Two.

"Talk to me Henry."

"I'm blind down here." He whispered.

Then the steepness of kneecap tearing stairs ended and two halls of darkness ran as a right angle to each other, one straight ahead of Morell, the other to his immediate left. There was no indication of Jupiter's presence and no way to see more than seven to ten feet ahead due to the weakness of the flashlight beam.

"Two halls, true north and north northeast."

Marland studied the schematic for a brief second.

"True north." She took a chance. "It should lead to the dock."

"Roger."

"Have Police advance the perimeter with extreme caution. No one gets in *or* out, I don't care *who* they are."

"Yes." Rollins began to type, wiping his nose quickly before resuming the pounding and tapping of keys.

Morell shuffled until he came to a heavy steel door.

"It's locked..."

He tried his shoulder.

"There must be something blocking it on the other side." Marland offered, wiping her forehead with the back of her hand.

"Roger."

Morell reached in the pocket of his left leg for a small lock detonator.

Jupiter ran along the maintenance ramp that snaked its way under the creosote slathered wooden posts that were the sole foundation of the Waterfront dock system. There had to be thousands of them, thick brown tree trunk-like support beams reinforced by steel bolts and cross braced steel rods. The man in white crouched once he was secure behind a wall of half-empty barrels that designated a small maintenance deposit of various bits of greasy tools and items.

His small black eyes were trained on the green steel door no more than three hundred feet away and the knob and lock of the door blew off with a small explosion and a puff of smoke. The cinder block in front of the door didn't move and inch and after several thrusts and bashes the door bent from its hinges and flipped over the top of the cinder block and became a ramp from the darkness of the emergency passage of PierHouse. The man that emerged from the darkness, clambering over the obstacle as he swung the M4 from his back into a tactical position, was a figure in SWAT gear, the very same that had survived the failsafe in the entrance hall.

Jupiter tucked and bunched himself up even more to see the man advance and scan the scene. It quickly struck the man as Jupiter had hoped, and once the man leapt into the water to chase *Divide et Impera* as it began to gain separation from the dock and fire the propellers that would push it toward the middle of the Targus in direct path of the shipping lane, the man in white named Jupiter moved off along the maintenance ramp to the space where it came to the surface near the Waterfront's busiest area, Sailor's Quarter. There he would get lost amongst the Police evacuation of the arcade, the carousel, the ticky tack shops, and all of the restaurants as his enemies in Homeland chased the ghost ship that once was his beloved home.

The camera shorted out the moment Morell leapt into the water. Marland rubbed her eyes.

"Do we have audio?"

"Nope."

"Hold the perimeter tight. If Jupiter's not on that yacht we can't let him go."

Rollins typed and typed. Marland could hear Tabitha grinding her teeth together. She looked over at Erland and his eyes were on his shoes in contemplation.

Exactly seven Policemen advanced through the blockade of cars, cones, and Police tape heading due east along the Targus and the businesses that sat on the

Pier system built into its rocky banks. The situation was far from contained due to the noises of violence that had rattled and echoed through PierHouse for all of six and a half minutes. Bystanders were already flocking to the secure side of the street and the Officers from West Quadrant were going to have the behemoth task of sorting through the wealth of locals and tourists pressed into Sailor's Quarter.

As they approached the first restaurant, a steak and seafood place named Horatio's, there was a deafening concussion from the east and the ball of fire and smoke that followed it killed their chances of controlling what would become a miasma of hysterical and chaotic humanity.

Morell squeezed his eyes shut and threw his hands in front of his face as the giant white yacht with the Latin name erupted in a deadly blaze. Razor sharp shards and spikes of glass zipped in every direction and everything from bits of white plastic to chunks of deck wood caught the air fluttered to the uneven surface of the water with a random similitude.

His face and hands bleeding, Morell gasped for air in the frigid water. The weight of the heavy SWAT gear was pulling him under. He kicked and thrashed in a misguided backward paddle, scraping at the straps of his body armor as he did. He was nearly eighty feet from the hundred and twenty-foot yacht when the second explosion buckled the boat and cracked it in half like a snack pretzel.

The force of it snapped the Agent's head back and pressed it under surface of the Targus. The explosion was the last thing he saw.

The seven Officers spread out as they hit the sidewalk, rushing for the entrance of each structure to establish control. They were too late. The panic and pandemonium of the yacht explosion on top of the flash bangs and the gunfire sent customer and staff member alike dashing for safety and the flood of bodies proved to be too much for the Officers to handle and as they shouted for back up in the face of the overwhelming mob, they failed to identify the middle aged man in white that was swept past the yellow tape and cones by the sea of faces.

TWENTY

The ride through Mossyrock was not unlike the first trip of the day, with Reston staring out the window and observing the smallest slices of life as they were unfolding around him.

"Would you like some music?" Kelly offered.

"No thanks." Then he shook his head. "What am I going to do about the article?"

"Mackie will understand."

"No he won't...I'm as good as dead."

"Don't say that, Darren." Kelly frowned and her eyebrows were lost in the frames of the glasses. "You're lucky to be alive."

"It's a figure of speech..."

"I know, but...we're writers, we can do better."

The use of the unified pronoun *we* in place of the accusatory singular *I* or *you* made Darren grin.

"I'm sorry. Old habit."

"Well old habits are out the window." Then a look of pleasure spread across Kelly's face. "Maybe that means you'll let me drive your GTO."

"My what?"

"You haven't forgotten *it* of all things, have you?"

Darren's eyebrows pulled together and he plucked at his lip.

"You mean my car? I have no idea where it is."

"Oh my..." Kelly signaled and turned onto Darren's street. "This is serious. I swore the day you stopped babying that car was the day aliens had replaced you with a lookalike."

"Aliens?"

"It's a figure of speech." Kelly winked.

"Oh..."

Darren opened the door as the car came to a stop and surveyed his house again. It was technically the same way he left it but there was something about it that now comforted him. Perhaps it was Kelly's presence, and the house was just that, a house. It was the familiarity, the end of it all, whatever weird dream it was, and now the lights of normalcy were switching back on again.

"You got your key or do I have to stick my head in the bushes again?"

"No, I got it." Darren said as he moseyed to the door. "So I drive a GTO?"

"A Nineteen and Seventy Pontiac GTO, Verdoro Green with a six point six liter four-hundred cubic inch v-eight."

Key in hand, Darren turned with a bewildered face.

"What?"

"You've only told me about it so many times. I don't know how many times I've been in it and seen the glee on your face as you fired it up. You took me to the Pinnacle Grille before they began the remodel, and remember how small the spaces were in the parking garage on Eleventh? You were convinced that some smart car that parked next to us had nicked it and you bought that infomercial scratch remover and took the weekend off."

Darren shrugged and laughed.

"No I don't remember."

"That's okay...that's why I'm here."

Darren stared at her as she walked closer.

"No, Kelly, that's *not* why you're here. You're here because you love me."

The journalist stopped. She blinked and removed her glasses.

"I'm your friend, Darren."

He closed the distance and wrapped his arms around her and she reciprocated with a soft sigh, squeezing him back, letting the vanity frames fall to the ground.

"Thank you." Darren said, in her ear, and held her in silence for several seconds. "Why don't you come inside?" He asked, after the hug had ended and they stood at arms' length.

"Are you sure?"

"I need some serious help, Kelly, and you're the only one who I want to help me." He slipped his arm around her and they began to walk to the door. "The rough draft is due at five, I haven't had a real meal since God knows when yesterday, my baby is missing and the house is a mess."

"I'll do anything you want, Darren."

"*Anything?*" He held a wry smile.

"Anything."

"What about Mackie?"

Kelly smirked.

"Mackie will understand."

Sierra Marland left the TMFOV bus with a pale and ashen complexion. She struck a course for somewhere that was anywhere away from the cramped darkness of the bus, a place where the wind could run through her ears and the coldness could surround around her soul and remind her how human she was and how fragile the threads of life could be.

She hugged herself and walked and reached the corner of the brick and wrought iron fence. It was time for lunch. It was time to reset and reboot. Bartleson had been informed and the Waterfront was a zoo with bits of a multi-million dollar yacht bobbing in the Targus, a veritable mess; the intelligence community's version of an oil spill. PierHouse had been handled poorly, but with a target as dangerous and elusive as Jupiter there was no *good* way to do something, there was only the way of the dice.

"Are you okay?"

The voice startled her. It was Erland. For some reason she hadn't heard him approaching.

"Yes." She said, turning back to gaze into the trees.

"When's the last time you slept?" He asked, not moving.

"I...don't remember."

"Tabitha's ready to take over the world and I've got enough evidence to process till she actually goes through with it. Why don't you take a breather?"

"It's not that easy." She called over her shoulder. "The moment we went through with it we knew there was no turning back."

"Yeah..." Erland came to stand next to her. "But you're no good to anyone if you're running on empty."

"PierHouse was not a case of me being tired."

"I'm not talking about PierHouse, Sierra, you're a *human being.*"

Sierra shook her head and buried her face in her hands.

"You're right."

"I mean, your twin sister just died, the least you could do take a few hours away from it all."

"You're right." Sierra said again, not removing her face from her hands.

"How long have you been going like this?"

"This is hour fifty-two...I couldn't sleep on the flight from D.C."

"Is there anywhere you can go you can get a shower and a hot meal?"

"Yeah...I've got a place across the hall from Tabitha." Then her eyes became distant again. "Magnolia used it to get ready for the party."

Erland looked to the same distant spot out in the river where she was gazing. The smoke from the explosion was rising behind the Crescent skyline.

"That teal dress she was wearing was Luciano Del Rey, wasn't it?" He said, changing the subject as only he could.

"Yes it was." Sierra turned to him. "How'd you know that?"

"A lot of little things get stuck in the gears, it's just how my brain works."

It was an answer that meant nothing, as true as it was.

"She wanted to wear red..." Sierra remembered, her exotic eyes weary and downcast above perfect cheekbones. "I told her it was bad luck. So we settled for that dress. It was supposedly the same one that one actress wore when she won the Oscar last year...same style, I mean."

"She was one of the most beautiful women I've ever seen." Erland said, with his hands in his pockets, and didn't walk away until Sierra Marland knew exactly what he meant.

It was three o'clock when a knock on the door grabbed Sierra's attention from the depths of sleep. She had showered, eaten, and fallen in near narcolepsy on the twin bed in the comfortably furnished apartment atop the Regency Tower. The knock reverberated through the small apartment once more and Sierra pushed herself from the bed. Perhaps it was Erland.

As hopeful as she was the peephole said otherwise.

Sierra opened the door and it locked at a scant distance as the chain prevented it from swinging any further.

"Hello, my name is Jessica Birchall." The woman in a ruby red overcoat said as she stood in the hall.

"Can I help you?"

"Is your name Lacey James-Henderson?"

So it made sense. This was the one searching the guest list, the third party that had nothing to do with Jupiter...or did she? Was she a diversion, a distraction? Marland would play along.

"Yes."

"Oh good." Birchall sighed. "I only want to ask you a few questions."

"Just a minute."

Sierra shut the door and the chain made a tell tale sliding and clinking and the door opened wide.

Jessica moved forward into the small living space, which was centered around a large window that faced the spread of Crescent and captured the rolling evergreen hills behind it. As she moved to the window she didn't see the woman studying her messenger bag, and even her walk and her stance.

Jessica turned around. The woman was wearing only a man's white collared shirt and panties of the same color and she sat on the edge of the couch that faced the window, her legs closed together. The size of the shirt preserved her modesty considering her startling femininity made her appear like some kind of exotic model-not only meriting the lack of clothing, but making it obviously mundane. Jessica determined the woman did not rent the apartment alone by her wearing of the man's shirt and decided to be brief.

"Were you at the party at Fircrest Mansion last night?"

Perhaps that was the cause of the man's shirt. It was white and would've been perfectly acceptable at the party. The reason for her still being in it at three o'clock was left to the imagination.

"Who wants to know?"

"I told you, my name is Jessica Birchall."

"But *you* want to know or someone *else* wants you to know?"

"I work for Channel Two news if that's what you're asking but I'm not under any contractual inquiries."

"Off the record." Sierra yawned intentionally and covered half of it.

"Yes."

"How'd you find me?"

"Your name was on the guest list."

Sierra's eyes wanted to squint. It was a reaction like flinching. Whenever she was playing a mind game squinting was a tell of hers that she had received a piece of information that she never had before. Maggie told her so when they were playing chess once. Sierra rubbed her hand across her eyes to hide it and yawned again.

"But *how* did you find me?"

"The Internet."

Sierra shrugged. Tabitha had handled the booking of the two apartments under the false name, the Regency and the one in Quintero, perhaps she had delegated the task and it had been done incorrectly.

"So...the party?"

"Yes."

"Lacey James-Henderson was there." Sierra

nodded.

"Do you know anything about the woman that was killed, do you know who she was?"

Sierra tilted her head and continued the act of drowsiness, although it wasn't the hardest act she'd ever had to play, she felt as if she could've gone another couple of hours comfortably before the stress of it all would begin well up in her brain.

"Want some coffee?" She asked.

"No thanks."

"Well, it's a brand new day for me." Sierra slinked away from the couch and Birchall followed her. The kitchen was the largest space in the apartment because of the adjoining dining room.

"Please, Miss Henderson, I don't want to take up very much of your time."

"Oh, it's okay." Sierra slurred and poured water from a pitcher in the coffee pot and once satisfied with the level, poured the pot into the top of the coffee maker. "I don't mind. And you're not in a rush, are you?"

"No, but I don't have much time."

"Don't worry." Sierra smiled a dreamy thing. "Take a seat."

Birchall walked past and removed her messenger bag, sitting in the seat that faced the kitchen, one of four.

"So do you know about the woman that was murdered or not?"

"What if I do? What's it to you?"

"I'll relay your story to the Police."

"What if I don't want the story relayed to the Police."

Birchall thought and lines wormed their way across her forehead and her delicate hands held one another in her lap.

"If you know something you *have* to come forward."

Sierra plugged the machine and pushed a button. Coffee and filters were already next to the pot.

"Says who?"

"Because there's a conspiracy that may damage the whole election," Birchall nearly pleaded. "Someone died in that Mansion and the Department of Homeland Security doesn't want anyone to know, now if you don't come forward with what you know about it someone else's life could be at risk. First a woman is murdered, then another one is abducted, you could be next!"

Sierra Marland smiled as the coffee muttered and spit its dark liquid of life into the pot.

"Is that what you think?"

Jessica Birchall studied the face before her for a moment and was unsettled.

"What do you mean?"

"You've got it all figured out and that's what you think?"

"Why..."

Marland held up a hand and came to take the seat opposite the reporter.

"How much do you want to know?"

"I want to know all of it," Birchall said and reached in the messenger bag for a notepad and pen. "Start at the beginning."

"I am the Homeland Security Agent in charge of the investigation."

Birchall's delicate face was pale.

"Really?"

"There's a thousand ways I can prove that if I needed to but I'll just say that the balding man with the glasses that chased you in the Internet cafe was none too happy about losing you and his right knee really hurts."

If it was possible, Birchall's face lost even more color. Perhaps it was her dark hair against red overcoat.

"Well..."

"Just listen." Marland said as the coffee maker began its process. "It's not what you think, not at all, and though I commend your efforts thus far, I believe you were ordered not to stick your nose in it, am I right?"

"Yes, you're right."

"Your superior's name is...Denton Hodge, isn't it?"

"Yes."

"Who do you think *gave* him that order?" Marland said as she went for a mug in the cupboard.

Birchall let out a heavy sigh and buried her head into her hands.

"I...I only wanted the truth."

"And you think it had something to do with the elections? In the Libertarian Party?" Marland scoffed. "That's reaching. You know this area's as democratic as they come. Half of the people at the convention came from out of state."

"It's my fault..."

Birchall rested her head on her hand on the table as Sierra left the room. Birchall was tired, it had been a long day, and now to find out she had been chasing the wrong trail with all the fervor she had was disheartening to say the least. She thought about what she had told Danny Thornton, and what all of it was really about but the legality of her actions had her wrapped and bundled up in confusion. If she could've left well enough alone she would've been able to cover the Waterfront Incident as it was now being dubbed by the media she was potentially no longer a part of. Jessica ran the events over in her mind beginning with

the late night run to Fircrest and the meeting with
Detective Erland in the cold...how could twelve hours
feel like such a long time?

"You did no harm." Sierra said as she reentered
the room a few minutes later, only now fully clothed in
soft and supple mid-calf reaching brown calf-skin
boots, stylish dark blue jeans made of Japanese
selvedge denim, a pink knit sweater and an olive green
cotton jacket with a furry hood. Though Marland didn't
need the help the clothes fit her perfectly and she
looked as if she would be at home on the streets of
Crescent as an upper middle-class self-made
professional.

"I'm very sorry...I'm not going to lose my job,
am I?" Birchall asked, genuinely worried.

Sierra sat down with a cup of the freshly brewed
coffee.

"Not if you do what I say. You can keep your
job if you earn it."

"What do you mean?" Birchall tilted her head.
"Please explain, I...I don't want to go to jail."

"I want you to investigate something with the
same tenacity you pursued what you thought was this
deep conspiracy about the convention. You won't do it
alone, though. You'll have some help. That is if he's up
for it."

Birchall nodded before she knew what Marland
was getting her into.

"Go on."

"I'm in the middle of one hell of an operation
right now and I was debating about going guerilla and
you've convinced me. You and Reston."

"Reston?"

"He was the suspect at Fircrest, the man with
the injury."

"Really?" Birchall's face showed the revelation

honestly.

"Yes. He's a journalist for the CMJ. He was there to cover the party for his paper, unknowing that's where the operation I'm involved in began. He was a victim of circumstance, kind of like you are. He stumbled right into it. The woman who was kidnapped in Wayilow was kidnapped because she helped him. My partner had passed on a bit of information to him without his knowledge of it and the people I'm trying to take out were trying to get him and anyone close to him. What happened earlier today at the Pier was a result of...poor leadership in pursuing the bad guys but nevertheless, we were inches away from getting one of the most dangerous terrorists in America."

"My goodness..." Birchall nodded. So they were all connected.

"And if you want to keep your job, and no doubt if Reston wants to keep his, you'll do exactly what I say and we'll use the media to throw our target in the corner."

"Would that work?" Birchall rubbed her forehead, "I mean, haven't you tried that before?"

"No...all of what we've done has been in secret, that's the nature of intelligence work, CIA, FBI, the like. You see the results of it in the news or hear about what happened years later but I'm going to turn the tables on our target and *you're* going to be the ones to do it. We're going to use the news and social media and everyone that he's put in jeopardy to hunt him down. I don't know why I've never thought about it before but I've never been this desperate either. If we do it right he'll fold up like a two dollar watch."

Birchall tapped her fingers on the table and thought.

"Will we be in danger?"

"No. You'll be able to work from here and I'll

have an Agent assigned to cover you at all times, whether in this apartment or the one next door."

"Okay..." Birchall kept tapping her fingers.

Marland came over to her and put a hand on her shoulder.

"Relax..."

"I'm trying to." The reporter nodded, and her hands moved from tapping the table to wringing each other. "It's just...this is the biggest story of my life and I don't want to mess it up, even though the fact that I'm here is a mess up. I mean, I ran from a Federal Agent, I could go to prison."

"You're not going to prison," Marland put her arm on the back of the chair. "Calm down already, all you have to do is be an investigative reporter, okay? You'll have help, and you'll be protected."

Birchall ceased any and all nervous gestures.

"Okay."

"Good." Marland left for the bedroom and came back with a purse that was kind of a pale cream in color, also leather. "I'm going to give you my number and I'm going to leave the door unlocked so that if you want to, you can go get some things and come back, or you can stay here and rest. If Reston agrees to work with you, he'll come here and once you're together I'll brief you and you can begin working."

Jessica Birchall nodded solemnly as she watched the woman who she had assumed was Lacey James-Henderson stick her ID and badge in the breast pocket of her jacket and conceal her service weapon in a back holster.

"I have everything I need in my bag."

"Take a nap then." Marland smiled, then, she strode the distance to the table and offered her hand. "My name's Marland by the way."

The reporter shook her hand, still somewhat

rattled down inside and watched as the graceful woman snagged the cup of black coffee and headed out the door.

The man in white was no longer. He had been able to not only steal a new pair of clothes from a poorly monitored and too good for themselves boutique garments store along the opposite side of the Waterfront but also a car from one of the lots where travelers overpaid to park their vehicle for three hours. The ride was an old Lincoln Mark IV colored a brownish red and he had unlocked the door using the wire hangar from the garments store. Once inside the safety of the car, he was able to hot-wire the ignition. The car had about a half tank of gas.

It was imperative that he keep his meeting with the broker, not only to preserve the appearance of having the information to sell, but put it out there how dangerous it had become to be the man known as Jupiter and since there had been nothing but death and destruction since the information had come to market it was well worth the price of admission. Jupiter knew once he had sold the information, he would be able to move out of the business for good, and move up the ladder, to a more comfortable and more powerful position where he could apply all of the knowledge he'd learned over the years, all that was necessary for manipulation. But Team Callisto was no longer. Their blood had been spilled in defense of PierHouse.

Before he pressed the car into the ease of the afternoon traffic, he made a call. He still had all four phones.

Courtland answered promptly.

"Have you heard?"

"Yes."

"Proceed with the plan. You're on your own."

"I understand."

The call ended. Courtland was a fierce man. He would die for the plan. It was his twisted sense of patriotism and Jupiter didn't care. He made another call.

"Yes?"

"Destroy the cameras at any cost, we're moving ahead with Sugar Hill."

"What about the fallout?"

"It's a necessary evil."

"Okay..."

That call ended. Jupiter wasn't concerned with Quinlan's reservations about Sugar Hill Elementary School. The slow burning would catch fire. He didn't know what Marland was cooking up because she was keeping it all to herself but he was certain it wasn't as painfully catastrophic as what he had set in motion. If she wanted to play his game she was going to have to bleed and if she were the last to bleed then she would have to deal with the pain of watching everyone around her do so till there was no one left.

TWENTY-ONE

Darren Reston was on the couch in and out of snoring when the throaty low-pitched grumble idling in the driveway pulled him from dreams. He took a breath and let it out in peace as the car door shut and the clip clopping of Kelly Barnett's heels came to the front step. The door swung open with a characteristic squeak and once he heard it knew he'd never forget it as she came to sit on the edge of the couch.

"It was down at the Arena. You had a spare key in the trunk, under the carpet liner."

"It took you all that time to get it?"

Barnett playfully hit Reston in the foot.

"I had to talk them out of towing it."

"But you got to drive it." There was a light in Darren's eye. "How'd you like it?"

"Well you know me, I have an Audi that's never gone over forty-five."

"You didn't romp on it?"

Kelly shrugged and curled the hair behind her ears.

"Maybe I did." She laughed and Darren laughed because she did. He liked her face when she laughed and the way she laughed was open and free. Her vanity frames were gone and she said she had lost them and couldn't find them because she wasn't wearing her glasses. He didn't remember her being so bubbly and funny but he didn't remember anything, and the newness of life was something he was finding out couldn't be any better.

"Maybe I can take you out to dinner tonight." The light had not left.

"What about your rough draft?"

"Nah...we can cook something up before the issue prints. We have two days, right? Two days and an editor that barely sees an inch beyond his own nose...I guess it's that time of the month for Mackie, he's just being a..."

"Remember we're writers, Darren, we have to do better."

"Oh yeah...well anyway..." His eyes pleasantly studied her face. "Dinner..."

"We can't go to Crescent, it's a mess with that yacht blowing up and the shooting at the Pier. Good thing the Arena isn't that far from here."

"I wasn't thinking about Crescent."

Kelly's left eyebrow jumped up and froze.

"Oh?"

The phone rang and Darren frowned. For some reason he had expected a different ring, something perhaps more...modern.

He flipped his legs off the couch and pushed a pile of papers out of the way to find the source of the noise. Kelly rolled her eyes and Darren finally found the phone in an old box of newspaper clippings next to a two empty fifty-milliliter bottles of amaretto.

"Hello."

"Darren?"

"Yes?"

"It's Sierra Marland, Homeland Security. Are you doing well?"

"Yes, I am, thank you very much." Reston looked to Kelly as he said so and her face held no expression either way.

"Listen Darren, if you're up for it, I need you to help me do something."

"Really..." Reston sat on the edge of the couch. "I mean, what could I possibly do to help you?"

"You're a journalist, aren't you Darren?"

"Yes."

"Well I have a story for you that will make your editor forget all about what you can't remember at Fircrest."

"What do you mean?" Darren's face became pensive.

"I can explain it in more detail once you come."

"Woah, woah, wait. I just got settled down, I mean, my brain is like a bag of hamburger and I don't want to rock the boat." Again he looked to Kelly and this time her eyes said *we're writers, Darren, we can do better.*

"You don't have to do it, Darren, but you would be completely safe and you'd be not only doing your country a great service but you'd be getting back at the people that set you up...and...killed my sister."

Darren's face changed. He moved his jaw left and right a few times.

"Why didn't you say so. I'll be glad to do what I can."

"Thank you Darren, I knew you would."

Marland gave him the address.

"I'll be there before five o'clock if the traffic permits."

"Did you...make that phone call okay?"

"Yes." Darren smiled. "Yes I did, thank you for remembering."

"See you soon." Marland hung up.

"Who was that?" Kelly asked.

"Homeland Security. She wants me to help her

but she didn't say exactly what she wanted me to do."

"Well don't do it, then."

"No, Kelly, I have to. I mean, she said I'd be helping get the people who did all of this; poisoned me and set me up like I killed that woman." Kelly saw in Darren's face there was no turning back. "That woman was her sister you know."

"The woman on the phone?"

"Yeah. It was her twin sister. Scared the daylights out of me when I saw her, I thought I had gone bonkers."

Kelly shook her head and looked at the floor, the mess of it, and her eyes drifted around finding no clean space to rest upon.

"Well, you can't drive. You don't have a license. I guess that means I have to drive."

Darren chuckled at her as he stood up and walked toward her.

"Now Mackie's really going to be steamed."

"Why's that?"

"Because I've kidnapped his best writer on some secret government mission."

"I'm just going to *drive*."

"No you're not." Darren pulled her close again. "I'm not doing it if you're not doing it with me. That's the deal. I'm not doing anything without you now and if you get sick of me, well then, that's that but I've got a new shot at it and I'm doing it right."

"Darren," Her voice was soft. "I could never get sick of you."

She rested her head against his as they embraced and Kelly smiled from ear to ear as she saw the afternoon sun shining on the waxy hood Verdoro Green Pontiac GTO.

The light shining through the third story window caught the various shades of the white of the hospital room. The privacy curtain had been pulled back to reveal the light and only one bed was taken. The television was off and a nurse was nearby preparing one of the other beds for a coming patient.

Henry Morell woke to the beeping of the EKG and began to cough and sputter, heaving and nearly choking from the half-upright position he was in. The nurse, a Japanese woman named Kawada, assisted the Agent by raising angle of the bed and calming him from the shock of life.

The nurse left as his airway was clear and his eyes drifted to the acoustic tiles of the ceiling. It wasn't Valhalla. He hadn't died a soldier's glorious death.

Footsteps caused his eyes to shift. He wasn't going to move anymore than he had to.

"Hey Sergeant." It was Marland. She looked different than the last time he saw her. She wasn't wearing professional government clothes and if it was possible she was prettier than ever but there was something to be said about the state of people in hospitals.

"Hey." A choking reflex wanted to bubble up and he was able to stop it by relaxing. His eyes drifted up and down her body helplessly.

"You don't have to say anything. I just wanted to check in on you on my way back to Fircrest."

"That's sweet." He said. "Did we get...him?"

"No. But we're closer than ever. You were pronounced dead at the scene."

A smile drifted across Morell's face.

"Can't get rid of me...huh?"

"Nor do I want to." Sierra was warm and put a hand on his head. His face was a brutal zigzag of cut and scrapes as were his hands and fingers. He had been dead for nearly ninety seconds on the dock and God knew how long he had bobbed in the water before Gilman of Falcon One had pulled him out and began CPR. The Doctor said his concussion had saved him from taking on more water and though she didn't quite understand it, she believed it. Henry Morell was alive, and though loss of life happened in her line of work, she always hated to be around it, to be a part of it.

Or to be the *cause* of it.

"You're officially out of the loop now," Sierra said, nearly apologetically. "But if you want to know what happens, just turn on that little box up there."

She winked at him and left.

Morell sighed and felt a bubbling in his throat. The nurse returned with a new pair of sheets for the bed. He felt like he could sleep for a year and still be far from comfortably rested, so he closed his eyes and when the time was right, he would ask the nurse for the remote.

Roshie and her team were professional to the point of comedy. Their quickly syncopated form of communication peppered with jokes that only a lifetime forensic scientist would find amusing was not only astoundingly harmonious to Erland's outside perspective, but incredibly entertaining. He could tell they did what they loved and loved what they did, and it reminded him of how he used to be, how he used to work with if he could dare say it, *joy.*

"This is a bloody mess." Roshie said, reverting to her adoptive English vocabulary. She was studying a series of latent partial fingerprints processed using ninhydrin in a comparison microscope because the computer they usually used to do that had grown confused.

"How so?" Erland asked as he stood next to her,

making an appendix of evidence by listing what belonged to who and where they were and so on. As each article was processed he placed it in a time log to see if it added up. At the moment he was juggling four different yellow pads because of the amount of bodies that had been in the Mansion, and even though they were only interested in a few key people, the volume of evidence was staggering to say the least.

"Take a look." She said. It was a genial professional consideration but if the expert said it was a mess then Erland would think it would be less coherent than that.

What he saw in the microscope was three separate fragments of purple lines. The ninhydrin did that, making the ridge of the fingerprint purple, and was used for lifting latent prints from porous surfaces. They were working on the fabric of the couch Reston had been laying on.

"We've matched the angle of arches...the one on the left looks more like a tent arch..."

Erland pulled away from the microscope and rubbed his eyes and went back in.

"Yet another puzzle..." He said, pulling back again. "How were they gathered?"

"They were spaced out, like they were all from the same hand, but...they're too symmetrical, perhaps because they're just partials. Fragments."

"Can you tell when this is from?"

"It's tough to say, I would say it's from the day of the party."

"And they're not Reston's?"

"Not at all."

"Do they match with anyone we've processed so far, anyone at the party from the kitchen staff to the Governor himself?"

"The computer had a tantrum when I tried them

so I'll have to do it all the old fashioned way. I'll take a picture of them and compare it with what we have processed through IAFIS."

"And these were the only prints in the room that we haven't identified?"

"Yes."

"What is your professional opinion they belong to a guilty party?"

"High. Considering the placement of the body, the one these belonged to was standing close to the couch and during the course of some conversation might have leaned or braced themself on the couch for a small length of time. We're running a few other tests right now...I guess there's only so much we can do with the space we've got."

Erland chuckled.

"You kidding? This little trailer is amazing. I'm used to waiting weeks or even *months* to get something from a crime scene processed and analyzed."

It was. Not only did it have ABIS but also a small variant of the SIMBAS blood analysis process, which used a microchip to separate blood cells. It helped that Roshie was on the team of SIMBAS inventors.

"How have you done on searching for the gloves?"

"Not too well. I'll keep trying, though."

They had detected the presence of latex on the murder weapon, the carbon fiber spike, and considering the ability of technology to remove fingerprints from latex, they were Erland's best hope to get a conviction for the murder of Magnolia Marland, which was the job Sierra had given him clearance to do.

Erland left the papers in the small corner he had been given to work on them, since he was all but exiled from the TMFOV bus by Tabitha and Tallifer didn't need any help with the cameras, he exited the trailer, blowing into his hands.

Four o'clock was approaching and the darkness of night wasn't far off. It reminded Erland of his younger days when he first came to Crescent and as a fresh new Detective would sign up for night ride-alongs with the Patrolmen to learn the neighborhoods and see the streets for what they were, even after his two years as a Patrolman on the night watch. In over twelve years of being a Homicide Detective in the Crescent Police Department he had never been to Fircrest Mansion, and wondered why, standing far above the city that he knew so well, anyone would want to live in such a congested anthill of humanity. The comfort of the trees and the freedom of the cold winds gave him thoughts of the long jogs around the hops fields at dusk and the way life used to be in Garden Grove. Quieter...still and soft. There was room to breath, room to move, and room to let the size of nature make him feel small and cozy as he walked to school or rode his bike three miles to the library for a book on the collected cases of Interpol or that one he read over and over about the Nuremberg Trials.

Erland passed through the gate and his concern grew for Sierra Marland. All of this time processing fingerprints and bits of hair and microfibers of clothing, running back and forth to the Mansion to visualize the picture of what had happened as he waited for Tallifer to collect and begin to process all of the film from the cameras, Sierra had been in the back of his mind. Something about the Waterfront assault had struck her deeply and he hadn't seen her since she left and wouldn't dare ask Tabitha if she had any guess on when Sierra would return because Tabitha saw Erland as an unnecessary accessory; dead weight. However, without Sierra, Erland felt less secure and safe, and though he

was on the more fearless end of the spectrum when it
came to personal security, Erland knew he'd never
fought in this weight class before, and Sierra was the
only person *he* trusted, given their conversations on the
subject. Upon first meeting her he saw some kind of
invincibility in her, perhaps the power of her
confidence, but the Waterfront assault convinced him
that her weakness was her own judgment, and though
she was playing some kind of game with Jupiter, she
couldn't throw away lives like he could and took loss of
life *so* hard. If she second-guessed and doubted herself,
she would hesitate or flinch when the next moment
came. It was just like boxing. Erland was one of the
best his trainer had seen at dodging punches at the *end*
of his career. Not the beginning. At the beginning he
had heart and had won fights on that alone. It took him
getting punched in the nose to learn that he wanted to
practice for hours in the gym so that he didn't have to
anymore. Sierra was a vastly experienced soul, he knew
that, but the death of her twin must've cracked the core
of her tactical psychology and emotional stability
concerning death. The paleness on her face was as if to
say she had killed those SWAT soldiers and ruined the
logging routes of the harbor for months. She had taken
on hell of a punch on the nose in Magnolia's murder
but it was like she was forgetting to duck and dodge
and move her feet, forgetting that *her* punches were
stronger and her corner was behind her.

      The next time Erland saw Sierra again he would
tell her his thoughts. It was a good analogy. Boxing
wasn't for everybody but it was the only sport that
related to life in every way, and there was only one
winner, only one champion, which was certainly true in
the fight against terror.

      Erland stepped into the Mansion and expected
to see Tallifer half-buried in the piano searching for a

camera but could only guess where he had gone. As the Detective scuffed up the staircase and walked the familiar route to the room where Magnolia was murdered, he tried to add up how many times his apartment would fit into the Mansion. Before he could finish the calculation, he was at the open door of the room.

He stood in the open door and squinted. He had seen the pictures and been in the evidence, but now he had to guess. He had to be a theorist and an artist, a director of moving pictures that were only as real as he could make them.

The couch was four and a half to five feet away from the beginning of the bloodstain, which was where Magnolia had been stabbed. The carpet was too hard and flat to find footprints, even trace ones. He searched again anyway.

Making a noise of frustration, Erland moved to the narrow hallway. To the left was a bathroom. He opened the door gently, using a pair of the medical gloves provided him by one of the forensic scientists back in the MCL trailer.

The bathroom was little more than a toilet and a sink and Erland examined the space as thoroughly as he could.

Then he saw it.

A smudge on the paint, a scuff, hidden from the dim overhead light by the edge of the door. Changing angles he almost couldn't see it. He dropped into a squat and gauged the height to be three and a half feet high. Running his finger gently over it he guessed it to be a rubber marking.

What was rubber and three and half feet high? Erland studied the doorframe again. He moved forward in the squat and slid his finger up and down each side of the wooden doorframe and found the smallest of

indents on each side of the wood. They were visible
from only about an inch away. They weren't scratches
but they were definitely made by applied pressure, and
again, they were perfectly even, about fourteen to
fifteen inches in height above the floor.

Erland smirked.

He walked back into the room of the murder and
pulled the chair that had been vacant at the table to the
couch, noting the area where the partials were taken. He
sat down in the chair and placed his hand on the area
where the prints had been lifted, looking over to where
the blood was. Then he stood up slowly, acting as if he
was rising from a wheelchair. The space was there. All
he would have to do is take a step and commit the act,
considering Magnolia had been held.

So that was his theory, the latent partial was
from the same latex glove used on the murder weapon,
and the prints were latent partials made confusing to the
computer because they had gone *through* the gloves due
to the pressure of bracing needed to rise from the chair.
Latex gloves were not flawless, powdered or otherwise.
Prints could be nearly embossed into the gloves if
enough time was given to wear them or could be
transferred considering the oils in the hand and the
pressure of what act had been committed in them.

Erland walked to the bathroom, eyes on the
floor for symmetrical lines. He moved down the hall
and finally at the crown of the staircase where the
carpet ended and the glossy hardwood began he saw a
smudge in the poly coating, perhaps from the twisting
of the wheel chair.

Back at the bathroom, Erland studied the area.
There was hardly any space for maneuvering the chair,
which was the reason for the scuff of one of the rubber
push handles against the wall. It took him a moment to
visualize the wheelchair in the small bathroom where

he stood.

Erland removed the lid to the water tank on the toilet and expected to see the gloves sitting in the water. The murder weapon had been found in the garbage next to the toilet, hadn't it? So wherever the gloves had been discarded it had been done in a hurry.

The hallway held no answer. He looked behind paintings and found himself back at the floor that lead to the crown of the staircase.

It had to be easier than that. It was all done in a flash.

Just as Erland debated giving up to go down and process more evidence he started over in a half crouch as if he *was* in the wheel chair. Upon reaching the door to the murder room he stopped and considered how difficult it was to *enter* the bathroom and did so. Why wouldn't the wheelchair ride on through to the murder room?

Erland stood up and stared blankly at the toilet. Then he reached out and flushed it. The result was a bubbling gurgle and the water level began to rise. The Detective stepped back as the toilet bowl overflowed and splashed water on the floor till the tank had emptied.

So that was it. The gloves were in the plumbing.

A smile spread across his face but it wouldn't be easy. The gloves held the incriminating evidence. If they could match the prints on the couch to the glove and the glove to the murder weapon they would have something solid. But the killer had in a way disposed of the gloves by soaking them in the water of the toilet.

Roshie would be able to get something, he was sure of it. And once Tallifer was done with the cameras they'd be able to see exactly who the wheelchair suspect was.

Erland stuck his hands in his pockets and

listened to the toilet go through its cycle of filling back up.

Then he heard the echo of a single gunshot.

The Detective sprinted to the window of the murder room and saw the lone available Department Lumina peel out on the circular drive.

Erland sprinted down the hall and took the stairs dangerously fast, hitting the door and reaching full speed on the concrete walkway that lead to the gate. The wind whistled in his ears and his breath came in controlled rushes. As he came to the gate, the image of the sixty foot Mobile Crime Lab unit lurching and rolling along the hill like a runaway train froze him cold where he stood. The Detective's mouth opened in silent horror as the trailer picked up speed down the hundred foot elevation drop of the hill and launched itself off the small ramp of earth into the air where it suspended for three eternal seconds until it came crashing down with a cataclysmic crunch of sparks and twisted metal, biting through the concrete highway divider and piling into cars in the southbound lane. The pre-rush hour traffic at highway speed could not stop fast enough and the shriek of rubber and the split second of silence before the jarring explosion of glass and plastic filled the highway, cars launching off the backs of those before them as they piled up in a mess of steam and smoke.

His breath came back to him and his eyes shot to the TMFOV bus. Through one of the bulletproof windows he could see Tabitha Grey banging the butt of her gun on the corner of the glass to no effect. Jimenez was behind her on his phone. He ran to the door. A crowbar had been shoved in the rectangular latch of the handle and Erland wrenched on it until it flew off with a metallic ping and sent him falling to the ground. He was back up as quickly as he could, seeing Tallifer on the ground near a pair of rubber skid marks, face up, a pool of blood running from the back of his head.

Tabitha was out at his side in a matter of seconds.

"Oh my God." She said to see Ryan Tallifer dead and then the constant hold of the horn directed her eyes to the highway. "Oh my God..."

Jimenez was calling Marland. He cursed and mashed the screen of his smart phone.

"She's not answering."

"Who was it?" Erland shouted. "Who did this?"

"I don't know," Tabitha's eyebrows quivered as she ran a hand through her hair. "I just looked up once I heard the gunshot and then MCL was rolling down the hill and we couldn't get out."

Erland reached down to Tallifer's jacket pocket and took his phone.

"Have Marland call me if you get through to her."

"Where are you going?" Tabitha asked.

"I'm going to get the bastard. Lock up the bus and secure the Mansion!"

Tabitha nodded and seemed to pull it together, securing her service weapon.

"Detective..." She called out after Erland as he began to jog down the circular drive. He turned, still jogging. "Be careful."

Erland gave a quick salute and ran down the hundred foot decline of the hill that stretched three quarters of a mile till the private drive met a public road that he could follow until a car suitable for confiscating and providing pursuit presented itself.

TWENTY-TWO

The name of the street was Thirty-First and it was void of traffic. Erland paused to look both ways as he came to the dotted yellow line and inwardly cursed the professional dress code he'd never been ordered to follow. Running a couple of miles in a pair of Mizuno's and a pair of Florsheim's were worlds apart and at his age, his feet knew the difference *real* quick.

Thirty-First was a wavy line that ran around nearly fifty percent of the hill and joined with several smaller roads as they led off to Wayilow and Eavesdale and even the highway. It was shrouded and buried in thick trees and was poorly lit at night because Fircrest came under County funding. Even though night hadn't fallen yet, he couldn't see much through the curving line of the road.

Erland snapped his head both ways several times. He had to choose. The solitude and silence of the empty road was sickening, considering the overwhelming rush of confusion and anger spilling into the knotted mess of his guts.

The Detective strained for noise and could only hear the distant bleat of the car horns and wouldn't let himself dwell on the highway's carnage. He chose to go down the hill, closer to the highway and the road to Crescent and began what he told his mind would be a marathon. Anything less and his body would start to shut down. His mind had to be strong and mechanical, like a piston. He couldn't think of Tallifer's blood spreading across the ground and Tabitha's horrified face, or the Olympic ski jump of the sixty-foot trailer to the highway. But as he ran, he couldn't remove the pictures from his eyes. The images were soundless stabs of shock and color and they wouldn't stop. Whatever had failed had failed and he couldn't fix it. The whole operation from start to finish was some horrible game of chess and the masters had left the pieces to fight it out themselves. Only there was no black or white, just the living and the dead, and the ominous fence of the forest trees to keep all of the game pieces locked in the board till there was no one left standing.

There was no victory in death, just death. To *live* through the chaos would be victory and it would come at an extremely high cost.

Erland let the images fuel him like the stinging punch on the nose that it was and he flew down the road in great clip clopping strides, his blue suit jacket flapping behind him and he ran for nearly two minutes before the symmetrically spaced glare of headlights bent around the street.

Instinct pulled his badge and waved his arms. The vehicle was a midnight blue minivan and came to a halt, the engine still running as the driver lowered the window. He was a bearded man in a sports uniform and his face was bent in concern. There was a passenger with him who looked like him and was perhaps a brother, also wearing a sports uniform but in a different color and number.

"What happened?" He asked.

"Get out of the car." Erland said with as much authority as his lungs would permit and noted the number of the front license plate.

"What? No...no...I'm on my way..."

"By the order of Homeland Security I'm commandeering this vehicle for pursuit, now get out." Erland said, putting his badge back in his pocket. The laminated Homeland Security card had stayed secure clipped to the outer breast jacket pocket of his suit. The man squinted at the print and the picture.

"Can I see your badge again?"

Erland pulled his service weapon and pointed it at the man.

"Get out of the van, now!"

"Dude!" The passenger cursed. "Let him have it!"

"Okay! Okay!" The bearded man pushed the door open timidly, his arms raised.

Erland pushed him out of the way and threw himself in the driver's seat. He ripped the shifter down to reverse and mashed the gas, and once a few hundred feet away from the bewildered sports fans, clicked the shifter up to drive and pulled a squealing U-turn.

Once the minivan was speeding to the intersection of Thirty-First and Rodgers Ave, Erland dialed 911 on Tallifer's cell.

"911..." The dispatcher said after a quick dial tone. Erland thought for a moment as the van came to a rolling stop before turning.

"Mary, is that you?"

There was a half-second of alarm from the dispatcher.

"Who is this?"

"It's Detective Erland..." And before Mary could respond he spoke rapidly as the minivan accelerated toward the buildings and shapes of Crescent. "I'm in pursuit of a stolen white Chevy Lumina in a dark blue Dodge Caravan, license plate on the Caravan is Lima Charlie Lima Six Two Zero, plates on the Lumina are government, suspect driving the Lumina is wanted for homicide, please get anyone available to assist pursuit, area of Fircrest."

There was a quick typing of fingers and keyboard discernible over the minivan engine.

"Okay, what direction?"

"I'm heading...east on Rodgers Ave. I don't know where the suspect is or what direction he went...his only options were north or south on Thirty-First."

"Okay..."

Erland kept his eyes open as he drove. As Rodgers Ave pulled away from the thick and green hill of Fircrest it ran parallel with the highway and made for a scenic approach to Crescent.

The dispatcher was about to speak when the phone beeped. Erland looked and before cursing about it being the battery he saw it was an incoming call from S. Marland.

"Sierra, Tallifer's dead and the MCL is in the eastbound lane of Two-Eleven."

There was no answer.

"Tabitha and Jimenez are securing Fircrest, I'm in pursuit."

When there was no answer again Erland twitched his head and blinked. Nothing but the sound of ringing in his ears.

"Who was it?" She finally said, in a voice that was hurt and controlled at the same time.

"I don't know."

"Did you see Quinlan?"

"No."

"Did you see Ratner?"

"No, no, I didn't see anybody! I was inside trying to figure out who killed your sister and I hear a gunshot and run outside to see the MCL rolling down the hill!"

Erland could almost feel Sierra drop her head into her hands on the other end.

"Then I see Tabitha and Jimenez are locked up in the bus and Tallifer's bleeding out from the back of his head."

Sierra was slow to respond.

"Was it Tabitha's car?"

"Yes, yes, I...called dispatch they're getting everyone on it."

Erland listened as Sierra processed. Then his eyes drifted toward the highway and saw the white Lumina driving westbound away from Crescent, slow and steady, hidden in the mass of boxed up traffic.

Erland cursed.

"I see him."

Him he didn't know who but snapped into action.

"Hold on..."

Erland tossed the phone on the dash and glanced at the road before looking back to the Lumina and then at the road he was on once more. The highway entrance was half a mile ahead.

The Detective increased his speed as he approached the small intersection. Over the course of the drive running parallel to the highway the trees had given way to the gray of the pavement and the stragglers of businesses and buildings found on the side of highway Two-Eleven.

The light was red for the three cars in front of him and he swerved around them and onto the curb of the sidewalk outside of a donut shop and caused the violent halt of an oncoming car as he pulled the minivan through the intersection in a looping screech, heading toward the on-ramp after rumbling through the tight underpass. Avoiding two more vehicles, the

Detective hit the on-ramp hard and worked the engine and the wheel to dodge and weave in and amongst the glue-like trickle of traffic.

When Erland guessed he was two or two and a half miles behind the Lumina and couldn't get past the gridlock, he changed vehicles. Not thirty feet ahead and two lanes to the left, next to the thin inside shoulder and concrete lane divider was a man in a padded leather suit on a lime green Kawasaki Ninja.

Erland snagged the phone and left the van. The smoking steaming crash site was two and a half miles away and an exit was maybe a quarter of a mile beyond that. Many were taking the exit even though traffic lightened and began to move further past the crash heading westbound. Eastbound traffic wasn't moving an inch and all of the westbound traffic had been reduced to rolling stop and go.

"I've got him Sierra, I'm switching to a motorcycle."

"Understood, Mike." She said, and he heard the sounds of an engine revving on her end as she did. "I'll handle the Mansion, just take him down if you have to."

Erland dropped the phone in his jacket pocket, sprinting to the bike before traffic advanced any further. He reached the Ninja and pulled his gun remembering the time wasted with the van.

"Get off the bike!"

Though he couldn't see his face through the dark shield of the visor, Erland was grateful the man gave a startled reaction and complied quickly. The gun back in its holster, Erland jumped on the Kawasaki and the engine began to ping ping as he took a wide curling route up the thin left shoulder of the highway, half standing to get a view of the Lumina.

The Detective spotted the Lumina in the far right lane, preparing to exit, inching ever closer to freedom. As badly as Erland wanted to coordinate with the police he couldn't possibly use the phone and drive the bike at the same time. The Yamaha One-Fifty he'd zipped around the hops fields of Garden Grove in had gathered dust a long time ago and if he jeopardized his *own* safety in anyway he would spill the bike and lose the Lumina for good, and being as generic as it was, the cops could've already pulled several over by now to find out they'd made a mistake.

He was cut off from Sierra, cut off from dispatch.

He *was* the pursuit.

Dipping his head back for a second he heard sirens but they were far enough out from the chaos due to the mess of the Waterfront for him to locate.

Erland cut across three lanes of traffic and ducked down into an aerodynamic position and snapped his wrist a few times, feeling the wind sting his eyes as the Six-Fifty began to whine and moan and the bike flew along the large shoulder off the far right lane.

A third of a mile away the Lumina responded, free of the clutches of the highway, and roared down the off-ramp, swerving to use the shoulder as well.

The chase narrowed to a matter of feet as the off ramp rolled and lowered toward a string of neighborhoods and twisting roads that ran along the river and split in a T-shape, left and right, with the Lumina swinging wide to the right before nearly fishtailing as the driver put all of his weight in the wheel to throw the car to the left. The car slipped from the road and spit chewed up clods of grass and mud in the air as it lurched back on to the gray strip of pavement that was as long as it was narrow, each branch and fork running from it to some congested cul-de-sac or dead end.

Erland shifted and leaned into the turn before

cranking his wrist. Two seconds removed from the turn
the driver threw a box from the window. The brown
cardboard arced hopelessly in midair before rolling
across the ground, spilling what Erland saw in the
passing blink of an eye were black rods no bigger than
mechanical pencils.

The cameras, Tallifer's box of cameras.

Erland smashed his teeth together and pushed
the Six Fifty harder, catching his quarry within a matter
of seconds and coming within what felt to be inches of
the bumper of the Lumina.

The Detective winced as the cold wind cut his
eyes and cheeks and his jacket flapped in the rush of air
like a flag. He strained to see the outline of the driver
through the slice of glass and the rattling of the Ninja
and only saw a shadowed male figure hunched at the
wheel. The shape of the driver moved twice, looking to
the rear view mirror and back to the road.

The boxing reflexes saved Erland's life as he
whipped the bike to the right only heartbeats before the
driver of the Lumina mashed on the brakes and came to
a furious and complete stop.

Erland zipped by and then slowed and came to a
spinning halt, letting the bike fall to the ground as he
stepped from it. The engine began to die with a wearily
unraveling whine and the back wheel continued to spin.

The Detective drew his Glock 17. The car held
its place for a moment of defiance as the whir of sirens
came swirling from the direction of the highway.

The driver's body was thrown backward as the
car laid rubber on the road.

Erland swallowed and began to fire.

The first three bullets bit into the plastic of the
bumper with hollow plunks and plinks and the fourth
shattered the windshield. Erland held for a breath as the
car charged his undefended position in the middle of

the road and reset his aim.

The Detective fired three more bullets and not forty feet away the right front tire popped in a shredded mess and a scatter of sparks from the shrieking grind of the axle and wheel scraping the pavement. The driver wrenched the steering wheel the other way but it was as if the car was on ice and inertia and momentum twisted its path off the road.

Erland leapt from the pavement toward the sidewalk and hit the cold bar of safety in a grunting roll as the back end of the Lumina smashed into the Kawasaki Ninja. The car skipped over the bike and gained air as it rotated once again and piled engine first into the strong steel of a streetlamp. The pained scream of the horn rattled his ears as his heart thumped in his chest.

The Detective pushed himself from the ground after what was ten or twenty seconds of gathering himself from adrenaline's nausea and trained his gun on the car. As he advanced the growl of an approaching squad car flared to the right but all of his focus was on the dead husk of the white Lumina.

His body was tense as he skirted around the vehicle to the driver's side. The hood was folded like a sheet of paper and the engine spewed gray and white fumes and smelled of sour fluids and rubber.

The sirens slowed and ceased and two doors whumphed shut.

Erland came to a sightline of the driver and held his ground, gun ready to unload whatever ammunition remained.

"Detective, stand down!" A blurb of blue-black called out as footsteps clumped toward him.

Another Officer passed before him, gun drawn, and saw the figure slumped in eternal rest on the wheel of the Lumina.

"Stand down, Detective." The Officer said. Nearer, calmer.

The Glock fell to his side and he watched as the Officers checked the driver's vital signs. He saw a shaking of the head pass between them.

Erland pushed the weariness out of his lungs and stared back down the road to see the chewed up chunks and bent front wheel of the lime green Ninja and further back the scatter of pencil cameras in the pale orange of the street lamps and the premature sunset.

Shutting the door to room One-Eleven, the thick man in the janitor's clothing pushed his cart of cleaners and rags down the hall.

"Red. Set." He said to the wireless communication unit, which was little more than a copper penny in his ear and caught his voice as well as transmitted the other voices of Team Io.

At nearly the same exact moment there was a crackling of words in the thick man's ear.

"Blue. Set."

It was as planned to the second, and the small straggling of teachers and staff that remained at Sugar Hill Elementary were all in the auditorium, preparing for the evening's winter concert.

Courtland continued to wheel the cart around the hall and left the cart outside of a bathroom.

He then made his way toward the auditorium, which was a quick walk underneath an eaves covered walkway lined with hand painted rocks and took the broom that had been left leaning next to the door and began to sweep.

Three minutes later Pitts approached him from the area of the playground. Pitts was wearing the black RepMax uniform. He was going to say something and the door to the auditorium opened.

"Oh, there you are Tom."

Courtland looked up from sweeping.

"Hmm?"

The speaker frowned, an overweight teacher with bleached hair, cut short and curled poorly.

"You're not Tom."

"No, ma'am, he had to go home sick. I'm just replacing him for tonight, because of the concert."

"Yes, yes." The woman flapped her hand for Courtland to follow. "The stage could use a buffing and the risers haven't been taken out of storage yet and we can't find the key."

"Alright ma'am, I'll be along in a minute." The teacher smiled and then turned to Pitts, who, for a black man, would've been put in her box as a clean cut athlete-type. "Who are you?"

"Thad Miller. RepMax." Pitts offered his hand. "Crescent PD has asked us to get a few men over here considering the recent events, they can't spare anyone and they want to make sure everyone's safe tonight."

"Oh!" The teacher's eyes were wide. "Yeah, that's horrible isn't it? I hope it won't hurt the turnout for the concert."

The teacher turned and left with a hurried walk.

"I think we should move the vans before the cars show up." Pitts said once the teacher was out of earshot. "And remove the RepMax wrap."

Courtland checked his watch. The concert was at seven-thirty.

"Okay, get it done quick."

Pitts nodded and jogged off with a clinking of keys. They would need every second of time to wire the auditorium.

The Gulfstream V was not two hours from landing when the man in the thick leather chair was brought to cognizance by the stewardess.

"Mr. Brown, your tea."

"Ah, thank you Olivia." The man named Mr. Brown nodded and closed his eyes. When they were open they were alert, pale green eyes and their intelligence was hidden behind thick glasses and puffy bags. No one would call Mr. Brown a good looking man but he did have a sort of earnest, trustworthy face that reminded one of a distant relative they forgot they liked to spend time with at a family reunion. Even though he wasn't much older than fifty he could've easily passed for sixty due to the stress diet and emergency scheduling, and Crescent would in no way work to reverse that. Crescent had been a disaster from the word *go* and Mr. Brown was not only surprised that it took the President as long as it had to begin to scrap it but a bit perturbed. He was a lawyer, a highly specialized one-the Cabinet's version of an insurance investigator, and could all but swing the gavel himself after his investigations were over. His job from the lips of the President was to find fault, straighten it out, and move on, and he was going to do just that, whatever way he saw fit.

The alert pale green eyes flickered open and Mr. Brown took a sip of tea. It was nettle leaf and wasn't everyone's...favorite, but he was used to being odd and outcast and being the enemy, and had cracked tougher nuts than Sierra Marland.

Though he was truly sorry for the loss of her sister and a great Agent in Magnolia Marland, the autonomy and sovereignty Dan Bartleson had bestowed upon her had been both presumptuous and dangerous, and the result was the lack of Bartleson's name on the door of the office he had been in for six years.

Mr. Brown didn't care *who* Sierra Marland was, but only what she did, and her track record aside, there was too much of a question mark in his academic point of view. The more Sierra pushed, the greater the catastrophe and the United States Government, let alone the city of Crescent, could take no more. To add a nuclear hazard to a fire that needed no fuel, Mr. Brown had learned only hours before takeoff of Marland's possession of the CONSTANT program's verified data. Dan Bartleson had in no small way misled the President to believe that the data being used as bait was not only outdated but also embedded with a virus. Upon learning the nature of the entire CONSTANT program once the President ordered Mr. Brown to probe its origins and its progress in the wake of the collateral damage, it became apparent the Marland's had taken to playing with a brand of fire no one had authorized and their actions were not only criminal, they were treasonous. They had, in a way, stolen the information to sell to a man that stole information only to trap him at his own game, and so far, it had backfired in the worst way. Yet, considering the Marland's SAB performance year to date and their track record in the business, they merited a hesitation. Whatever extreme outside shot Sierra had at pulling it all off was miraculous to say the least, but Mr. Brown had been ordered to stop her and do so in a way that drew no attention to himself so that whatever strides had been made in capturing Jupiter and stopping his fearsome grip of information terror could be expedited by the FBI.

Brown took another sip of tea. Jurisdiction would be what it was. *He* had the power and he was going to use it to its fullest extent.

When Courtland arrived in the auditorium with the buffer, he made eye contact with Kirke, who was also in RepMax gear, holding the ladder that Brock stood on as he changed one of the colored bulbs for the stage lighting. Knowing Pitts should be finished moving the vans and continuing to look obvious as he lurched around the campus with his radio in hand, Courtland schlepped the buffer toward the stage.

"Do you have your keys?" A thin woman with bright red lips and frizzy bleached hair asked.

"For the storage unit? Hold on..."

The woman bounced on her toes, looking around nervously. The auditorium was steeply angled and held maybe five hundred seats. The stage was a good ninety feet across and another thirty deep, and was stacked with moveable backgrounds, the most notable of which was a castle and spooky trees.

Courtland gave the woman the key, pulling it from the ring.

"Thank you." She said, all but running up the steps and clomping across the stage.

"If it's not that one I have another one." He called, pulling the buffer laboriously up the steps. "After all, I don't work here." He added, to himself.

As he muscled the buffer to the stage he noticed Pitts enter the auditorium and begin a stone-faced dialogue with Kirke.

Courtland checked his watch and powered up the machine. The noise of it caused Brock to turn and he promptly came down from the ladder, grabbing a black duffel bag that had been under one of the seats. Brock left the auditorium and exactly two minutes later, so did Kirke and Pitts.

TWENTY-THREE

The drive to the Regency Tower was solemn. The fact that he was back in his Camry held no comfort, a car was just a tool, but at least it was familiar. He had stayed at the crash as the Police began to close down the street and enter the procedures he was so accustomed to, but this time, he was on the *other* side of it. Lieutenant Ross had come to the scene personally and informed him of the OIS case that would be forthcoming and how the shooting at Fircrest had given the Police no choice but to close off the entire area with a barricade and armed guard. For the time being, Erland was on paid administrative leave and so it was the near history repeating itself only in much different circumstances. Sierra's Homeland operation had been brutally ripped apart and what was left were shells and husks of death and destruction. It was as if not only had their work been in vain but had made a royal disaster of what was before so effortlessly untroubled.

Erland paused to wait for a space in traffic to turn left. His part in it all was unavoidable. Playing the scenes over in his mind, he couldn't see an alternative. They'd been ambushed and blindsided, taken advantage of and left to deal with not only what to do moving forward, but the responsibility of what *had been* done. Eastbound traffic on the Two-Eleven wasn't going to move for days and the closure of Fircrest Hill also

Luke Taylor

created more problems on top of the ones already presented by the cleanup at the Waterfront. Erland had learned that only two forensic scientists survived the crash, Roshie and a man named Mendholssen, and they were both in critical condition.

He could feel it as he left the street and entered the Regency Tower parking garage. Crescent was a nervous wreck with all that had transpired, and it could only get worse. The news was constantly fraught with incidents across the country, shootings and crashes here and there, and only something like a natural disaster could pummel a city for days on end, but what if Jupiter's bloody power struggle didn't stop? What if the murders and explosions were only the beginning of something far worse? Crescent would become the most cursed city in the country if it wasn't already. What more could possibly go wrong?

The Detective couldn't think about it. Sierra had been painfully morose on the phone as she told him where to go. He had explained the episode with the chase. Quinlan had been working for Jupiter and shot Tallifer and stolen the cameras. Now the Police had the cameras and it was as if Sierra couldn't do anything about it. Ever since the Waterfront, she had been different.

The apartment was one floor away from the top and Erland held his fist at the door for a heartbeat before knocking.

The door opened on his second knock. The face that greeted him was the blonde American symmetry of Tabitha Grey. Her eyebrows were slightly twisted together, and she was wearing a black tank top and jeans. Her hair was free from the ponytail and fell past her shoulders.

She said nothing and nudged her head to her left, leaving the door open.

The loft apartment was a tasteful monochromatic design and lacked the coldness of modern architecture but in the same token was void of the homey touches of life, save a jacket tossed over the back of a chair near the door and a travel magazine half thumbed through on the circular dining table at it sat dormant between two mugs.

Tabitha moved across the open floor to where a triangle of yellow shot up to the ceiling and sat in the chair next to the lamp in a youthful slouch of depression. Not three feet away from her was an L shaped kitchen and the small round table and across a comfortable bit of floor space was a sectional couch and a large bookshelf. The couch faced what was a gigantic window.

Erland turned his eyes to the window and the figure that stood before it with arms crossed, staring into the anamorphic slurry of colors caught together in the burying of the sun as night fell like a jar of blue-black paint.

"I'm sorry." The words came from Erland's mouth, croaking and hoarse. Tabitha eyed him with a mixture of sadness and respect.

Sierra turned and her eyes lingered on the River and the boats and barges that had flooded the passageway to clean up the mess.

"It's not your fault." She said. "It's mine. I'm the one who's sorry."

Erland shut the door behind him and walked over to the window to stand next to her.

"I've been placed on leave because of a pending OIS investigation."

"I might as well be."

"What do you mean?" Erland let his gaze stay on her face before he turned his attention to Tabitha, who curled her hair as she sat bunched up in the chair.

"Bartleson, my boss in the Special Assignment Branch, has been deactivated. There's a man on his way from D.C. named Mr. Brown, and he's known in our business as *the Electrician* because after he's done with you you've been unplugged and you have no power." Sierra took a deep breath. "So we're next."

"But...there has to be something you can do," Erland's face twisted. "If you can't then Jupiter will get away."

There was a small silence and Sierra's jewel blue eyes locked on to the Detective's face for a moment before the faintest of grins pulled at the corners of her full lips.

"There is something we can do, but it's going to get hairy."

"What do you mean?"

"Bartleson told me before this operation started that we'd get to this point and I didn't want to believe him, but he's seen it all. He was counting on Maggie being here as I was, and though she's not, the tactics are still the same. Bartleson told me, Sierra, whatever happens, legal or otherwise, Jupiter *must* die, and if you do it with a badge or without one, I'll stand by you, and if I'm not standing anymore, than you'll have to take your chances, but we're all this country has left, and I'll be damned if I let it go because I'm afraid of breaking the rules."

The Detective let his thoughts be known.

"So you're going to...do what exactly?"

"We're going to finish the job ourselves."

Erland frowned.

"Just you and Tabitha?"

"And you."

The blonde gymnast stood and walked across the floor to sit on the edge of the sectional so that Erland was surrounded.

"But...I can't. I'm not a Homeland Agent, I don't have the leeway that you do, and not only that, I'm just a Homicide Detective, I don't have the qualifications."

"Tell that to Quinlan." Tabitha said. "If you hadn'tve reacted the way you did he'd be gone and we wouldn't have the cameras."

"But we don't have the cameras, the police do."

"It's the same thing." Tabitha shrugged. "Rollins will get them."

"No it's not the same. I'm bound by procedures and paperwork that stacks as high as this building. If you're talking about going some form of rogue on me they won't mind too much but if I do it I'll be all over the local news and be incarcerated faster than you can say grand jury."

The more Erland argued his point the denser their faces seemed to be. They were like mountains, cold, distant, hard and magnificent.

"You don't have to do it." Marland added.

"Do what?"

"What I want you to do."

"Which is what?" Erland said with some frustration, as if to say that what he had done already had proven what he felt about Marland's mission and he was in for good and the fact that she was still offering a way out was wrong.

"Follow me." She said and motioned toward the darkness that sat beyond the kitchen. Erland followed her and Marland quickly made her way over to Tabitha and whispered something in her ear to which Tabitha's face made no change and grabbed her jacket and left the loft.

The Detective followed Marland to the screen divided portion of Tabitha's apartment that was her bedroom, which was a queen-sized platform flanked by two built in units filled with clothes. Next to the bed was a pair of sliding doors that lead to a deck and in the corner of the bedroom space was a chair. Marland sat on the edge of the bed and he pulled the chair a foot from the wall.

"There's something you should know." She began. Erland didn't say anything. His arms were crossed and his head tilted to the right. "Jupiter wants the information to sell it."

"I already know that."

"So if we...let him have it, we'll be able to get everything."

"Everything? What do you mean *everything?*"

"I mean him, the seller, the buyer or buyers, all of his network...that was the whole idea, to lure him out with live bait so we could slay the dragon."

"But don't you get it Sierra," Erland leaned forward. "It'll never stop, first it's a Hill, then it's a Quinlan, then it's the Secretary of State or the President himself! What makes you so sure that you'll as you say *slay the dragon* with whatever you've got planned, how do you know it won't get worse?"

"I don't." The woman shook her head and pursed her lips. "Its' a gamble."

"And how can you gamble so freely when so many lives are at stake? The city's a torn up mess and you're gonna make it worse."

"Do you think I *want* to do this?" Her eyebrows twisted as she stood. "Do you think I *like* this? Do you think this is *easy* or this is how I *wanted* it to be?"

Sierra opened her mouth to continue and no words came out, like she had been attacked by a choking poison. She flared her nostrils and blinked her eyes to keep from crying. Then she fell to the bed, slowly, in a deflated hunch and fought the storm inside with a quivering and weak heartbeat.

"Do you think I *wanted* Maggie to die? Do you think I have a *choice*?"

Erland sighed as she sat before him and held herself together. They were both right. He could afford a modicum of self-righteousness because his side of the law was always after the fact. He figured out what happened and who was responsible. But Sierra's place was preventative. She was always far ahead of the game, desperately in a race to stop the unstoppable, and hindsight ate at her soul like an army of maggots.

Erland stood up.

"Forgive me, Sierra."

She stood as well and wiped her nose with the back of her hand, still blinking and keeping the horrid pain inside.

Erland wrapped his arms around her and closed his eyes, feeling her warmth and shape as she buried her head against his chest and began to cry. He could only imagine her burden as he felt the sobs being pulled from the marrow of her bones. Her best friend and twin sister had given her life to the gamble, and died in faith that Sierra could see the gamble through. Now Bartleson was gone, D.C. was against her with the best career killer they had to offer, and all that she had done was come within a leaping grasp of the elusive Jupiter only to fall flat on her face. As he held her the words in the Observation Room carried more weight. He was the hope that *she* had, that there still was someone in the world who wasn't either too scared, corrupt, or comfortable to do the right thing, risking all that was so glossy and smooth. Well, as Erland's record was a sterling example of perfection, the river raft was coming to a fall of no certain height. If America couldn't break Jupiter's iron grip of digital terrorism, then it was hopeless. Not only would the moms and pops of the here there and everywhere be vulnerable to assault, but the banks and the financial giants, healthcare and manufacturing. Sierra's fight was at a low enough level to handle, even considering Jupiter's massive stranglehold, and if Sierra fell it would only get larger and the cancer would spread until it infected every living cell of American life.

His eyes opened and journeyed around the space and landed on Tabitha's bed. How it looked so comfortable and plush with the fleece blanket on it. How long had it been since Mike had seen his own bed, and how simple and peaceful it would be to lay down next to Sierra in all of her radiant beauty and watch her sleep, knowing she was safe and free from harm.

But would that moment ever come? If it did it would be far removed from the bitter struggle of the present, in a world where Jupiter and his oppressive evil did not exist. That very peace and safety and freedom of life was what he had fought for as a member of Law Enforcement, and what he had forgotten about through the mess of blood, bones, bullet fragments and lies, because he had never had it at home to call his own. He knew it was real and it was out there, somewhere, like a dream or an idea, but he had never held it in his grasp and felt its rushing current of heat, energy, and life.

Until now.

Sierra squeezed the man in her arms and held him and pulled her tearstained face back to look at him.

"It pains me to ask you...you should've known the moment you saw me that your career was over."

The Detective smiled.

"I was going to retire anyway, remember?"

The smile mirrored on her face but so faintly so.

"I...don't know what it is about you." She said. "I can't keep it back. I just feel close to you and..."

"And what?"

The last bits of light in the sky caught the rich

blueness of her eyes.

"It's like you're an old friend or something...like I knew you in another life."

The Detective's hand found its way from her shoulder to her hair and he let a half curled hand brush it back from her forehead.

"If I'd ever seen a woman as remarkable as you I would've remembered."

The curling of her lips was genuine.

"Tabitha won't be back for awhile."

Their eyes said many things in silence before Erland spoke.

"It won't make you forget the pain, Sierra."

"Just when I think I never will, I think of you." She let her head fall against his chest. "In some ways you remind me of Maggie, so tough and responsible..." Her head pulled back. "Like a rock. She warned me about you, you know,"

"Hmm?"

"When we were planning this operation we knew we had to select an outside man, someone we could trust, someone we had hidden from the game board, someone the other side never suspected was in step with us the whole way. I must've looked through thousands until I found you."

"What made you choose me?"

The hint of a shrug bunched Sierra's left shoulder.

"It was a gamble. I guess I just knew."

"What did Magnolia warn you about?"

"That I'd built you up in my mind to be something you weren't, and if you were all that I thought you'd be, then I'd get too close, that I'd let what feelings I'd been building up for months cloud my judgment."

Erland cupped her face in his right hand.

"Impossible."

A flood of thankful pleasure broke from the borders of pain in Sierra's jewel blue eyes. It was as if she was letting him know he was the answer to the mystic statement she had made on the hill of Fircrest about having a price no one could match and if she had what she wanted she would be gone.

"Will you?" Was all she said.

"I won't Sierra, not like this."

"It's just us, Mike. All of it can go away for a little while."

"But it'll still be there."

She nodded and took him in with unsatisfied eyes. If she ever wondered what love was she certainly knew that if it didn't come by blood it began with respect; honor, even, and the way she felt about Detective First Grade Michael Erland had only been amplified by his maturity and integrity.

She closed her eyes and kissed him on the lips, only once, softly and gently.

Then a flash of fire came into her eyes.

"Just don't die, okay?"

"I promise." The Detective smiled. "I promise."

Jessica Birchall was resting on the couch when there was a knock on the door. She kicked her feet from comfort and took in a sharp breath of air. She wondered how long she had been out, seeing how night had fallen.

She looked through the peephole and saw three people, a man and two women.

Birchall opened the door wide.

"Hello." She said genially, her systems still wanting rest though she was well practiced in the ability to be friendly when she didn't want to.

Tabitha jerked her thumb toward the door and her eyes went to the hall. The man and woman entered

the apartment as Birchall stepped wide and Tabitha
entered last and bolted the door, reaching for her phone
as she did.

The three journalists naturally migrated to the
sitting area before the dark window and Tabitha held a
hushed dialogue in the small walkway that lead to one
of the bedrooms. Unlike her own apartment, the door of
which was not ten feet away, this apartment was a more
traditional design with smaller, more segregated rooms
and the main living area was only a seating area that
faced the window and the kitchen and dining room was
directly behind it, separated by a wall. The bedrooms
were off where Tabitha was conversing.

"My name's Jessica." Birchall offered her hand
to the woman first, only because she was closest. "I
believe we'll be working together."

"Kelly Barnett." The short woman with short
brown hair smiled and Birchall would've described her
in a blurb as bookish and intelligent, and Birchall
may've guessed she was Canadian.

"Darren Reston." The man shook her hand and
frowned. "Don't I know you?"

"Not that I'm aware of." Birchall crossed her
arms.

"She's on TV." Kelly said.

"Oh..." Darren chuckled. "My brain's still
coming up to speed."

Birchall held her professional veneer but
wondered how that would affect what the Homeland
Agent wanted them to do, which she still had not made
known. And to that, Birchall was grateful, because she
needed the rest, mentally and physically.

"Marland will be here in a few minutes."
Tabitha called out as she came from the hallway and
leaned against a small space of blank wall near the door
with her arms crossed and one leg planted firmly on the

floor and the other braced against the wall at an angle.

Kelly removed her jacket and took a seat and Reston followed her lead.

"You know, I could get used to this." She told the man.

"Pardon?" Birchall asked, standing near the window, examining a decorative shelf near the glass that held nothing of practical value.

"Working for the government, secret stuff. Beats the tar out of covering candidates as exciting as tapioca pudding."

"So you both write for the Crescent Modern Journal?" She asked. "Marland, the uh...Homeland Agent only said something about Reston."

"Darren's in no state to work without help." Kelly looked to him and placed her hand on his shoulder. "She knows what he's been through. If she has any objections about me then Darren can't work."

Birchall mashed her lips together and kept from saying something foolish. Marland had given her some kind of ultimatum to do what she said or lose her job and the partner she was going to be given was in a condition that needed a tagalong Marland had said nothing about. Wasn't that some kind of security risk?

"Well I'm not exactly sure what we'll be doing but I'm ready for it."

Reston said nothing to Birchall's comment. His eyes were on the window.

"I never thought going down to the convention yesterday I'd be here, today."

"Life's funny that way." Kelly said and Birchall noticed her demeanor towards him was like that of a girlfriend.

"I never thought when I was reporting on the murder that I'd be here talking to the suspect." Birchall said as she took a seat next to Kelly. No sooner did she sit down than there was a knock on the door. Tabitha checked the peephole with her hand ready to snag the gun at her back and began to work the noisy bolt.

Sierra Marland walked through the door with Detective Erland behind her.

"Detective?" Birchall's eyebrows came together.

The journalists rose and there was the huddle of an odd dinner party arrangement for a few seconds. Marland studied Kelly Barnett without her knowledge and decided she was okay. There was no evidence to support Jupiter had planted an agent close to Reston, he was only involved as a victim of circumstance. Still, Marland would watch her closely, despite her initial positive gut judgment that this woman represented the sincere phone call he'd had a hard time making.

"Hello Ms. Birchall." Erland nodded, and looked to Reston. "I know you but you don't know me. You had me on quite a chase at Fircrest. My name's Erland."

Reston shrugged as he shook the Detective's hand.

"So you know I'm innocent."

"Absolutely. You've been removed as a suspect from the murder of M..." Erland caught himself. "Lacey James-Henderson."

"It's okay, Mike, we're going to be sharing a lot of information with them to bring them up to speed but will in no way compromise the operation." Erland nodded and Birchall's twisted face merited an explanation. "Lacey was just a cover name." Sierra continued. "He means Magnolia Marland, she was my twin sister."

"I'm so sorry." Birchall offered.

"Should we?" Tabitha proposed with a nudge of her head her right.

"Absolutely...if all of you migrate to the dining room we'll have something to eat and discuss the plan. If you have any question, I'll answer them if I can."

The notion was not only logical but well received. The bodies left in a small ruckus of rubbing cloth and clacking shoes. Tabitha and Sierra stood alone.

"Where's Jimenez?" Sierra asked.

"I don't know. When you gave me the code Zeta I came back to my apartment, then you arrived right before Erland."

"He hasn't called you?"

"No."

"Rollins?"

"He's at Precinct Three, working on the cameras. At least he said he was going to back at Fircrest."

"What about Ratner?"

"Last I heard from him was in the bus when he was trying to get Birchall."

"It's not good." Sierra plucked at her bottom lip. Tabitha read her face.

"You don't think they're Jupiter's too, do you? Jimenez and Ratner?"

"I can't know until they turn. I just can't. I thought Quinlan was one of us. You've worked with him for two years. His profile is bleach clean...I mean, how can a guy that's done that much overseas charity work just turn on a dime?"

"What about Rollins?"

"Rollins had been with us since it started. He's the only computer geek we've had. Nobody knows the project like him-it's his baby just as much as mine. He designed the special memory card. It's good he's in the safety of the Precinct."

Since Marland had issued a code Zeta, which

was a procedure for pulling back from the theater of operation and disabling all connectivity with the network, Tabitha was the only Homeland Agent Marland had spoken to, other than Bartleson's final goodbye over the phone.

"You can never know what someone's really thinking..." Tabitha stared at Marland's boots. "You can only guess...and hope."

Sierra placed a graceful hand on the Agent's shoulder. They were once acquaintances and teammates, now they were friends.

"Don't take it so hard. That's *my* job. You had nothing to do with it."

"But Mr. Brown'll come down on me. It's my team, Sierra. I've been in charge of Homeland in Crescent since MacEndell left and I'm responsible for Quinlan, Jimenez, *and* Morell. I'm glad *he's* okay."

"If we work this right, by the time the bell tolls for us we'll show up with a wagon full of bad guys."

Tabitha nodded. Sierra was right. To take too much responsibility was to rob herself of her razor-edge focus. It was to shift her viewpoint from the operation and place the spotlight on herself, like she was back at the Olympic Trials.

"I hope D.C. sees it the same way. I kind of feel like...now that Bartleson's gone and you're on your own, like I did the first time I had a meet overseas. My parents couldn't afford to come. I was a wreck. I fell off the beam and messed up my bars...and I *never* fell off the beam in a meet, that was my best discipline."

"What happened?" Marland asked.

A warrior's face of victory hid behind her youthful features.

"I pulled the best damn vault routine they'd ever seen."

Marland chuckled.

"Of course you did."

Tabitha swore and shook her head.

"Thank God for Erland." The comment surprised Marland. Tabitha had made negative remarks about having the Detective on board and her desire to give him the lowest team clearance possible had been poorly covered. "He reacted when I just stood there, staring at Tallifer's bloody head. He ran down the hill and ended up putting Quinlan in a tree...I don't know if I could've done that. I certainly didn't expect it from him."

Marland crossed her arms as the blonde's face became contemplative.

"Well, T, we really need him. Jupiter doesn't know about him and until Quinlan flipped you didn't either, but I knew I had to have an ace up my sleeve."

"That's why you're in charge, and I'm not." The young Agent smirked. "And I'll follow you to the grave to take this bastard down."

Tabitha held out her fist. Marland looked her in the eye and hit the top of it with her fist, and then Tabitha hit the top of Marland's fist with her own.

"Let's do it."

Tabitha busied herself with preparing the meal as Sierra and Mike answered questions.

"So you want us to take this story you've outlined to the local news and on to the world news as well as social media?" Jessica Birchall inquired with professional candor.

"Yes. Jupiter doesn't *control* the news so much as he writes it by controlling acts of terror, and doesn't *own* the Internet so much as he takes full advantage of its powerful flaws." Sierra said, her eyes on five sequential pay as you go flip phones, and she was entering the corresponding numbers into each phone.

"He can try to manipulate our information once we dump it but it'll catch fire and he'll feel the heat instantaneously. We'll back him into a corner and force his hand. If there's anything he wants more than money it's his own privacy and by attacking that we're making it as personal as possible. Try as he might to run damage control the snowball will be too big before he could even begin."

"And how are you going to play both sides?" Reston asked the Detective.

"Until the OIS Investigation I'm a normal citizen, just as Sierra is until Mr. Brown comes to shut her down, that's why we have to put the pressure on him now because we don't know how much longer we'll have this kind of freedom. And unless we break the law, we won't be doing anything they can beat us over the head with."

"But you can't use the resources you were using to track him and get as close as you did at PierHouse."

"Right." Marland slid a phone to each person at the table save Reston. "But we'll get him. I'm sure of it."

"How?" Birchall asked.

"That's not your concern. You'll have plenty on your plate as it is."

"Yeah." Reston added. "Between texting, tweeting, posting and cut pasting, we'll be up all night."

Kelly laughed.

"You haven't *worked* all night since the last Republican Administration."

Erland chuckled and the fact he did made Sierra smile to herself. Hopefully it would be over soon, and he could keep his promises. Sierra's smile was stillborn as she remembered the promise he had forced her to make. *Never put my personal safety above your operation.* The two were potentially mutually exclusive.

She hid her face as it fell by busying herself with the tablet that was in her purse.

"All of the information you will need is on here."

When she looked up she saw Erland was eyeing her and the smile slid across his face as a plate of pasta and tomato sauce was set before her.

"The garlic bread will be here in a minute." Tabitha said, with four more plates in her strong arms.

"Very impressive." Kelly said as Tabitha walked around the table.

"I used to wait tables in college to help pay tuition. When my parents found out I wasn't going be what they wanted they bailed."

"You paid your way through school?" Birchall asked.

"Two years of it." Tabitha said as she reached in the oven for the garlic bread. "It wasn't that bad. The worst part of it was trying to find my way after gymnastics wasn't going to be an option."

"You were a gymnast?" Birchall's interest continued.

"Yes I was. A very successful failure." Tabitha sat down with the bread, content that everyone was settled, and before Birchall kept the line of questions going she said, "How about you? You weren't born a TV reporter."

"No, I kind of wanted to be a novelist, you know, trade paperbacks in the supermarket...but maybe later in life. I just followed the path and it took me here."

"I think you could be one now." Kelly laughed.

"And I have plenty of material for true crime if you're into that." Erland added with surprising levity.

Sierra nodded to herself as she began to eat. The pasta was a bit past al dente and she could feel the vibrant freshness of the tomatoes and garlic of the warm sauce striking its comforting chord within.

Erland was the first to finish after no more than ten minutes, and even then, he didn't clean the plate and stayed away from the garlic bread, as delicious as it smelled.

"Excuse me," he said, rubbing the back of his neck. "I'm not feeling well." Tabitha was concerned. "It's not the food, Tabitha, I think it's just the long day catching up to me. I haven't slept for a while. Do you mind?"

Tabitha stood.

"Oh no, not at all."

Since they would be working and planning their assault on Jupiter's public image or complete and utter lack thereof, it would be too noisy for him to rest in the dummy apartment and would have to do so in silence and seclusion of Tabitha's loft.

The young Agent led him to the door and opened it. Erland moved to the couch and took off his jacket.

As he turned, Tabitha gave him a fleece blanket. She must've had a stash of them.

"For the record, I owe you an apology." She said.

"No..." Erland shook his head. "Not in the least."

"Yes. I was wrong about you. I didn't want you here." Erland shrugged. Tabitha held her hand out. The Detective looked her in the eye and shook her hand.

"I appreciate it, Tabitha."

"If Sierra trusts you, *I* trust you, and it was good of her not to tell me about you until I actually did."

Erland nodded.

"Thank you."

She left and shut the door behind her as the

Detective removed his shoes and curled up on the sectional, and didn't fight the drowsiness that had come to cover the canyon the adrenaline had bored through his body.

The door opened again and he sat up to see Sierra Marland slide through with a paper shopping bag.

"I have some...operational considerations for you."

"Really?" Erland sat up and swung his feet around as she came to sit by him.

"You can't look like a cop."

"Oh I've got clothes at home."

Marland's face was quizzical.

"Humor me." She said. "Before you count sheep. And one more thing, I think I should have the fake memory card back to distance you from me during your OIS and whatever Mr. Brown might throw your way."

"Good idea."

He gave her the card from his pocket and watched her until she reached the door when she turned and added. "I hope they fit."

Erland checked the bag. She really had thought of everything.

TWENTY-FOUR

Tanya's head rose from its STRIC-R induced blackout. The mechanical noise was no more but nothing had changed save the darkness. Somehow, it had become darker. The smell was an industrial one of musty dirt, grease and grime but no definite shapes could confirm. Her hands had fallen asleep long ago, above her head, no matter how many times she had squeezed and flexed them, and the STRIC-R blackout brought her to some panicked state of life, as if she had been swirling under seawater and just broke the surface to gasp for air. If only it was just that. She tried to move her feet and they didn't work too well, either, curled up behind her. Sweat clung to her skin in a clammy film.

The metallic catwalk banged and clanged and rang louder in the space because of the lack of the mechanical sound, whatever it was. Tanya turned to see the bounces of the flashlights approaching and heard the semi-repetitive pattern of a scraping noise that ceased for a split second every two or three seconds.

As the group of bodies came to her, she saw the reason for the noise.

A balding gray-haired man in a black suit had been drug before her. She caught his face in the jumping shafts of light and it was cut and bruised from beating.

There was a rustle and shuffle of bodies and

clothes and boots that finally ended with the static
image of the man, spent on the ground, all lights on
him.

"Tanya, are you listening?"

She nodded slowly. In the light they could see
her but from her low angle she couldn't quite see them.
She didn't dare try to speak, her throat wouldn't have it
and she was conscious of choking.

"Good, I'm going to ask you some questions,
and every time I don't like the answer, I'll take it out on
this man. Do you understand?"

Tanya winced and went to cry but there were no
tears. She was a nurse and a volunteer lobbyist, all she
wanted to do was help people, but she didn't know their
answers, she didn't know anything.

"If this all works out, he lives, you live, and you
can both go home and forget this ever happened."

How could she forget? It had been hours if it
had been days, she needed water and food and the
restroom, how could she forget the agony and the
paralyzing sensations and random blackouts of the drug
the man had flooded her system with so long ago.

"Okay Tanya, first question. Where is
CONSTANT?"

Tanya shook her head with as much strength as
she had.

The speaker kicked the man in the left kidney.
He recoiled in pain and one of the other men steadied
him with his foot, face up, so that his next dose of pain
would be as squarely dealt as the last was.

"It's just a small little memory card, Tanya,
Reston must've showed it to you."

Tanya's face screwed up. Reston? Who were
they talking about? *What* were they talking about? They
must have had the wrong person.

"I'll ask you again, where is CONSTANT?"

The space of silence was only two seconds. The man kicked again.

Ratner recoiled and coughed.

"She doesn't know anything, dammit!" His voice was still strong and shrill, even after the kidnapping and the beating. "She doesn't even know his name. He got the memory card four hours after going to her house."

The man who had done the speaking and the kicking crouched low and Tanya got a glimpse of his face only for a brief moment before one of the flashlights moved. He was a swarthy-skinned man and had a pockmarked neck. His northeastern accent was more apparent the slower he spoke and he spoke *very* slowly to the man on the ground.

"I knew that...but I got you to talk. And if you stop talking, one of you's is dead and it's my choice which."

Ratner rolled and tried to sit up, which they let him as he struggled.

"My information dies with me."

Tanya squinted to see the balding man's defiance as some of the flashlights had fallen to the sides of them that carried them.

The sickening sound of a steel blade being unleashed from the sheath seemed to echo through the industrial space.

"You wanna see about that?"

Tanya heard no response for a second or two. Then the flashlights clicked off and Ratner's excruciating screams shook every beam and joist in the building.

Considering the recent events, certain parts of Crescent were *easier* to navigate due to the lack of people present. Also, the fear of what might happen

next had forced the casual metropolitans back in their
dens and hovels and only the people that were out were
those who had no choice and were either driving or
walking to whatever safe destination they called home.
On the edge of Quintero there was a gated building
secluded in red oak trees that, observing what was
around it, might've been out of place, as the Quintero
district ran between North and South with neither one
taking ownership for it, but the seamless fusing of the
structure with a small nearby park made sense to
anyone that looked at it even though most never did.

Jupiter parked the Lincoln Mark IV across the
street and quickly made his way though the front gate
and to the door. The building was confusing in that it
could've been a church but wasn't. It had the bones of
one, and perhaps the correct architecture of a late
nineteenth century mission of two stories and a bell
tower drove the assumption home but it was far from it.

The front door was unlocked and Jupiter entered
the claustrophobic staircase that was to his immediate
left near a coat closet. The staircase emptied after
twenty seconds or so to a balcony that overlooked the
large floor of the barn-like building. The pews had been
removed years ago. The walls were white plaster and
the floors a very dark brown. There wasn't much more
to see. It was usually rented for weddings but that was
about it.

Jupiter checked one of his cell phones for the
time and after no longer than three minutes wait he
heard steps.

A pale man with black hair slicked back and
bunched to curly bits near the upturned collar of his
woolen overcoat scuffed up the stairs followed by a
bulky man with a beard that barely managed to squeeze
himself through.

"Alone tonight?" The pale man joked and his

jokes were always bad, but what did Jupiter care. He cared for nothing but money, and the man named Killinger represented *just* that.

"Nevermind." Jupiter said. "Are they ready?"

"Do you have it?" The man walked to the edge of the balcony.

"Are they ready?" Jupiter reiterated.

"Do you have it?" The man turned, his black arched eyebrows nearly vampiric against his pale skin and the heavy collar of the overcoat.

"I don't." Jupiter's honesty was forced. Lying would've gained him nothing though he had no qualms with lying.

"Will you?"

"I will. I guarantee it."

"How can you be so sure?" Killinger continued his meandering around the balcony and it squeaked as he did so. Jupiter's gaze passed from Killinger to his bulky bodyguard who was blocking the only exit unless Jupiter was to leap off the balcony to the floor two stories below.

"My men are working on it. We believe we know where it is...getting it will be a problem."

"How big of a problem?" Killinger's eyebrows arched again.

"Big enough to merit thirty-percent from you, if you're patient and will fulfill your end."

Killinger didn't say anything until he stood very close.

"I *always* fulfill my end." He whispered. Then he continued his random pacing. "And what makes you so sure that I won't have thirty just because I want it?"

"That's not how it works." Jupiter crossed his arms.

"Times change, business changes. Even ours is a cyclical industry. One month it's Somali Pirates, then

it's Al Qaeda, then a fugitive bomber or a young
hacker. The business is unpredictable, and if you want
to stay...*alive*, then you have to change with it."

"What are you saying?"

Killinger stood at the balcony facing the large
floor below.

"I'm saying the amount of bidders has
increased, so my fee has too. The auction's bigger than
I imagined. You wouldn't believe how many more
companies want to protect themselves from this new
world war. Everyone's scared of losing money on the
public's emotional *reaction* to the news concerning
terrorism, not to mention losing money to terrorism
itself." He turned and came to stand next to Jupiter as
he continued. "Your recent activities in Crescent alone
have killed nearly ten percent of *all* the capital gained
last year of the five major companies headquartered in
this city. That's only one day of terroristic activities.
One day. Hundreds of millions of dollars. It's easier
than ever to manipulate the public with fear but that
also makes it that much harder on us to *control* it."

"What happened today would've been avoided
if certain things had been handled differently." Jupiter
said with certain coldness. "It wasn't my plan but my
business runs by any means necessary."

"A great road to failure." Killinger nodded and
crossed his arms. "I'll say this, Lawrence. The time has
come for us to part ways. I know the gravity of what
you're selling and that's why I'm a part of it. More for
you means more for me, but this is the last time we'll
ever meet like this. If you don't have plans to change
your business model after this sale, then you'll never
make another sale. You know I'm the only one that can
float your merchandise. Especially what you're selling.
We're not talking about a hit on some run of the mill
activist or exposing a dirty cop. This is what it's all

about, this is *why* we do business."

Lawrence, the man also known as Jupiter, attempted to swallow what dryness was in his throat.

"If it that's the way it is, I can't fight it."

"You know how big the beast is," Killinger added. "We're just merchants. Corporations are now far more powerful than countries and all we do is sell them information to protect their investments. So once it gets to a point where we can't do that anymore, we serve no purpose."

"It's not that bad."

"Yes it is. It's so unpredictable. The domestic terrorism we've manipulated is now only twenty-eight percent. It used to be seventy. It's grown. So much of it, we're not a part of anymore. And what are we going to do when the companies and corporations come to us for answers when we have none?"

"I don't know..."

"Terrorism is so bad now that we can't incite it ourselves so we in turn have to predict the next great calamity like nine-eleven, and if we can't *predict* the calamities, we can't sell them the information to protect them *from* the calamities. So it's up to them to fight over the scraps of whatever markets are left like evening wolves for a deer carcass."

Jupiter nodded. It was the end of an era. There were no more superpowers represented by flags and national anthems, but by dotcom names and brand logos. The true power of the world was in the trend, the opinion, and the hand of the consumer. Their currency was fear and faith, hype and hope. Manufacturing exclusivity had replaced landmass for a show of power and followers and friends had taken over for political party lines. Product launches of the newest technology wrapped in colored plastic merited life-halting waiting lines only for that same bit of plastic to be outdated in a

matter of months. What possessed insanity caused such
chaos when other parts of the world lived day to day
just to eat? And how many couldn't even eat? It was the
near omnipotence of the great system of the world and
it was a runaway freight train that neither man could
afford to ride to the crash.

"I'll have it. Don't worry."

"I'm not worried." Killinger smirked and moved
to the stand before his bodyguard with his head twisted
to squint Jupiter's direction. Only half of his face was
visible behind the woolen collar. "I'll keep in touch. If
you don't have it by an hour before the meet, then it's
off, and you're on your own."

Jupiter shook his head in compliance.

"One more thing. I'm not taking thirty percent,
I'm taking fifty."

There was nothing Jupiter could say. It would
take all he had to get CONSTANT and there was no
other way he could sell it than through Killinger.
Killinger had him by his testicles.

Jupiter nodded painfully and Killinger left in
silence. Jupiter reached for his phone.

The Porsche Carrera was charcoal frost metallic
in color and purred with German perfection as it pulled
close to the police barricade and the stretch of cones
blocking Thirty-First from any through traffic. The
professional thief named Polis gauged the entrance to
the Mansion being roughly a mile or two away and the
same held true for the other end of Thirty-First as it
drug around nearly half of the mountainous hill. A
military-looking Officer came from his car clutching a
flashlight capable of knocking a man out if swung
correctly.

The window of the Porsche lowered.

"I'm sorry Sir, you can't go through."

"But I have an important meeting," Polis thickened up his French accent. His dress, too, in a brown V-neck shirt and white dinner jacket was all he needed to elicit another apology from the Officer.

"I'm very sorry Sir, you might want to try Davis and Fortieth and cut through the Meadow Greens neighborhood."

Polis cursed in French *and* English in the same sentence and slammed his fist on the wheel. The window slid up and the Porsche grumbled away from the barricade, its glossy wax job catching the orangey orbs of the randomly staggered street lamps until it disappeared from the eyes of the guard. Polis noted the reserved frustrations of the Officer. The city was under some kind of siege and he was stuck in the dry cold night telling people to turn around. It wasn't in Polis' job description to read subtext but he was certain Bellamy's urgent request for the camera in room F-Thirty Four was directly related to the day's occurrences. There had been a murder at Fircrest, perhaps that was the cause of the desperate mission, and though Polis *was* not a man of a golden moral compass, he didn't want to think of himself as an extended accessory to murder. The Judicial system was prejudice against thieves, even though the US Government was fond of using men like Polis to do jobs they couldn't publicize, and Polis was a thief, and he was a good one, and fell under harsh penalties justified if caught. But never had he taken a life and wanted to continue in a fashion that ensured he never would. He had made a decent living by stealing mostly industrial secrets back in the day and the age of information had reduced his business to a form of cat burglary and he couldn't complain. Diamonds were a thief's best friend.

The Porsche came to a halt on the shoulder of Thirty-First across the street from an espresso stand that

held a space of gravel in between two lazy streets that
forked away from Thirty-First. It had closed for the
night. The Porsche was in a blind spot of overhead
lighting and the silvery gray color would blend in with
the fog if it came back. There, Polis removed his jacket
and stuffed himself in a skin tight black turtleneck and a
black vest. His tools were in a black neoprene bag and
his gloves were black neoprene as well.

     Polis exited the Porsche and locked it, sticking
the magnetic key ring underneath the driver's side
wheel. Then he began to take the steep and grassy
ascent of the green hill, adjusting the black balaclava
mask till it felt just right.

     Since Team Ganymede had finished preparing a
potential hostage exchange site for the woman named
Tanya Wilson, they turned their attention to Fircrest
Mansion.

     The plain white Ford van had pulled to the
shoulder of the highway whereupon its emergency
blinkers began to click and flash. Four men piled onto
the slice of road, one with a spare tire. The driver blew
on his hands as he walked to the side of the van and the
men appropriated duffel bags from the back. A few
words were said between them and the driver began the
process of removing the tire, and taking his time to do
so as he checked his microphone.

     "Ready?"

     The same word he had posed in a question was
returned as an answer in four different voices. There
was a pause, and then a fifth voice echoed the reply
with confidence. The fifth voice belonged to the driver
of the exit vehicle, parked on Dawson Place within
spitting distance of a westbound highway entrance.

     The four men dressed in tight-fitting black from
head to toe hopped over the retainer wall of the

highway and skidded down the vault of earth as it began to lead to the forest hill of Fircrest. No one had seen them do this-the seven o'clock traffic had miraculously dwindled due to citizen fear, and since no one bothered going eastbound because of the crash as it was still being cleaned and sorted out, the westbound lane was virtually empty.

"Ritter." The team leader whispered hoarsely. The man named Ritter looked up from his half crouch and nodded. He gave the other three men a quartet of liquid packets from a duffel bag that he then left in the small ditch that was made at the lowest point of the geography, which was still far higher than any point of access from Thirty-First. It was the same point in which Reston had escaped Fircrest Mansion, although none of Team Ganymede knew this.

"Kalil." The team leader whispered again. The man named Kalil issued items from his duffel bag as well, only they were incendiary canister grenades, four a piece, white phosphorus, and their military nickname was *Willie Pete*. The grenades could cause third degree burns in the blink of an eye and smoke inhalation from their fiery explosion was nearly just as dangerous.

"Greene." The team leader stood up and removed items from his bag as Greene did the same. When the equipping had finished each man was in night vision goggles and carried a silence Heckler and Koch Forty-Five.

The team leader, named Charlie, then gave two silent hand signals, and Team Ganymede launched their assault on Fircrest Mansion.

His dream was of a time when he used to hunt deer with his father near the timberline of Mount Turbus. He was seventeen and to have his own rifle was a feeling he'd never had before. The snow was packed

and hard and dusted with early morning powder. There
was no sound. They wore woodland camouflage and
looked for signs of deer removing their velvet on the
tree trunks. The marching was tiresome and after a
while the gun sagged in his arms. Then the stagger of
brown trunks and the sour smell of pine sap left as did
the clutching maze of the timber line and a white tail
silently walking across a snowy meadow clearing, head
down in search for bits of clover filled his eyes. His
father raised his rifle and Michael felt something on his
lower body, some clutching or grasping. He turned and
the bright white of the mountain dream faded for the
darkness of Tabitha's apartment.

Erland woke and it felt as if his veins were full
of cold syrup. For the briefest of moments he had
forgotten who and where he was. But his eyes had
opened to the feminine warmth of Sierra Marland's
enchanting face and the light from the lamp across the
room behind the couch was enough to highlight and
shadow her artistic features in a way that made him
think he'd woken from one dream into another.

"Time to go." She said, her hand on his hip as
he was curled on Tabitha's couch.

Marland stood up and Erland attempted to but
only accomplished a leaning-sitting maneuver, the
feeling of the deepest sleep shocking his mind but his
body, being too strung out from the moment of waking
did not care. Maybe it was a sign of forty-one.

"What time is it?" He said, blinking and rubbing
his eyes.

"About seven-twenty."

Erland looked down at himself as he removed
the plush fleece blanket. He had nearly forgotten the
clothes Sierra had provided for him. He had changed
into them before sleeping.

There was a smirk of pleasure in the side of her

lips as he folded the blanket and turned his attention to her.

"So I don't look like a cop now?"

Sierra squinted and took his head by the chin, gently turning it back and forth to see the five o'clock shadow. Then she ran a hand through his short haircut a few times and shook her head with pursed lips.

"Not at all."

Erland chuckled. The snug fit of the denim was comfortable but foreign. The long sleeve cotton t-shirt was also the same. Erland sat down again to step into and lace up the sneakers and they reminded him of running shoes but had an urban flair and were miles from gym wear. The jacket was on the back of the couch and was one like hers. As Erland threw himself into the jacket he began to understand Sierra's logic and her comments about looking like a cop.

"We're quite the couple." He said. "Where are we going?"

"I want to talk to Tim Wolcek." Sierra crossed her arms. "When you called me back there at Quinlan's crash you said you think the one who killed Maggie was in a wheelchair, and he's the only one on the guest list who was. I was thinking that if we can elicit a confession from him we could trade punishment for Jupiter's location. It's a long shot, but we don't have much else."

Erland nodded as he adjusted various aspects of the new wardrobe.

"You said that wouldn't work with Hill."

"Hill was just a foot solider. He was stupid enough to lead us to Jupiter. If Wolcek *did* kill Maggie then he's at a higher trust level-a deeper cover so to speak, even if by coercion of some kind, and he would know, if not exactly where Jupiter is or what he's doing, a whole lot more than Hill. Hill was just muscle."

"So Jupiter has muscle *and* brains." Erland walked to the circular dining table where he had placed his personal effects and items of necessity. "What makes you sure he'll fall for it? If he's brains, he'll know how to wiggle out of it."

"We'll have to play him in a way where he thinks his only option is to rat."

Erland looked at what had been in his pockets as Marland came over. He had his personal smart phone as well as Tallifer's. Then there was the simple phone Sierra had given him and the odd bits of things like breath mints and notes scribbled on scraps of paper, cash and coins and of course his wallet and keys. The badge and the holster for his Glock 17 were on the table too. The gun had been confiscated by CPD for the pending Officer Involved Shooting investigation.

Sierra singled out an item of interest and picked it up.

"What is this?"

It was a pocketknife that was brown but not wood. It was plaited with silver zigzags on one side and not the other. There was no symmetry to the brown body of the knife. One side was lumpy and the other smooth. The blade was only three inches.

"It was a gift from my dad. It's made from the antlers of the first deer we killed together by an old Blackfoot that had a corner shop in Garden Grove, his name was Sam Littlebear." Erland took it from her warm hand and studied it. "I don't remember the last time I used it. I'm always taking it out for the metal detector and every time I tell myself I'll leave it at home but I never do."

Sierra stuck out her bottom lip as she knew the reason why.

"When did he die?"

"About two years ago now. Lung cancer."
Erland said, putting the knife in his pocket. "I knew it
was coming. The Erland men don't have a high life
expectancy. They're working class, you know..."

Sierra gave Erland a firm embrace.

"You're different." She nearly whispered. It was
true. He had risen above the demons of his small town
blood and literally fought his way out of a certain
destiny as a chain smoking hops farmer to follow the
steps of his maternal grandfather and take up the mantle
of law enforcement. Boxing had given him a tiny but
reasonable scholarship and somehow he had ridden the
bare-knuckle rails to the Mountain County Sheriff's
Department to learn the ropes from the sixty-five year
old protégé of his since passed maternal grandfather
and had accumulated much in the way of wisdom and
patience. He was different. The Erland men had lived in
Garden Grove for five generations and here he was so
many years later in the big city as one of the state's
most prolific Homicide Detectives. And now he was
working hand in hand with a woman he felt he'd waited
for and knew was out there, a woman who in the same
strange way had held out hope for a man like him. Life
was odd that way, and a man couldn't question it, he
could only say yes or no when it presented its critical
questions.

Sierra released him and moved to the door.

"I'll be in the hall. You know where Sugar Hill
Elementary is?"

"Of course."

"Okay."

Sierra walked a matter of feet and knocked on
the door to the other apartment. Tabitha answered and
though she looked tired, the natural structure of her face
always carried a freshness to it and when she smiled,
rare as it was, one couldn't help but think of summer.

"We're going to leave now. I suggest that since you had Quinlan book the apartment you move them once they've begun to transmit. We can't know for sure if Quinlan told anyone about them. I don't think he would break cover like that."

"Where should I take them?"

"Do you have any Homeland buildings, safe houses? I didn't look that far in the brief because I counted on this one."

"Yeah, we have a few, but won't Mr. Brown have access to all that?"

"I'm not worried about him. Once they've flooded the news, their part is done and if they're picked up by Mr. Brown for questioning they'll be safer than if they're just hanging out there in the breeze while we go after Jupiter."

"I agree."

"Okay." Sierra nodded. "If I call you, it'll be an emergency."

Just as the door shut Erland came from Tabitha's apartment. As he approached a smile bloomed across Sierra's face because it stemmed from the trueness of her heart and she turned her head as it fell again because of what would happen to him if her gambling guess was accurate.

TWENTY-FIVE

The house in Mossyrock was a boxy unit from the seventies and needed a good renovation to reach full market value but the neighborhood alone sealed the home's value as a quiet retreat in the clutches of a span of old growth oaks that had changed from green to orange and red.

Jimenez had just about had it with his phone. It was as if the signal was being jammed or something. He tossed the phone on the low leather couch that squished every time he sat in it and marched across the croaky hardwood floor for the landline.

Not a light was on in the house.

The Homeland Agent threw a glance to the front window and the street. It was empty, save the homeowners cars that always congested the strip of concrete the city was passing as a street.

Since Tabitha had passed him the order from Marland for the Code Zeta he had left the Mansion. He assumed Tabitha and Rollins had commandeered cars as he had but hadn't seen either of them since that moment as he was the last to leave. He was breaking procedure by trying to contact them. But no matter what he tried his calls wouldn't connect.

Jimenez dialed a familiar number on the landline and scratched the back of his head. His house hadn't been the same since the divorce and his rebound

relationship had ended poorly, even then, he was sure
he could get Sarina Veracruz to come over and help
him since she was in Law Enforcement.

"Sarina?"

There was a pause.

"Luis?" Then Sarina's voice changed. "Luis
why are you calling me? You know it's over."

"Sarina, listen. It's not about that but I need you
to come over."

"What? There's no way."

Jimenez stared at the popcorn ceiling.

"It's about Fircrest, okay, I gotta talk to you."

There was another pause, this one longer than
the first.

"But...you're Homeland."

"I know, and it's complicated, so could you just
forget what happened between us for a moment and
help me out here."

"...I'm just a K-9 cop, Lui."

"It doesn't matter, you're the only one I can talk
to. I'll explain when you get here."

There was the sound of rustling on the other end
and a quick cough, like that of a smoker.

"Okay. I'll be there in five minutes."

But Luis Jimenez didn't respond. He saw a flash
of black at the back window from the faint castoff of
the streetlight in the front. He let the wall mounted
phone drop and dangle as he reached for his gun and
moved to the window. Someone was out there. Since
his thoughts had been consumed with the Code Zeta
and Quinlan's disastrous acts of murder, theft and
treason, he hadn't noticed the lack of Balboa's barking
in the back yard. The Beagle always barked once or
twice when he came home and he used to bark
incessantly to the complaint of neighbors. It was
Veracruz' off duty training of the dog that had led to

their relationship in the first place, a meeting of logical chance if there ever was one.

The Agent squinted and fell to a squat at the edge of the window. The silence pierced his mind and he expected the worst.

Polis sighed as he saw the back of Fircrest Mansion and its fullness through the spaces in the wrought iron fence. Every light in the building was on and the same was true for the small foot level garden lamps spaced around the property's edge and near the cropped foliage of the lowest floor. The back of it was a sprawling green field of turf and nothing else. No cover, no shadow.

He waited for ten minutes in the cold and checked the gold Rolex. A single Policeman completed a circuit of the Mansion in seven minutes and eighteen seconds. While waiting for the Policeman to walk the circuit, he had kept his eyes on the brightly lit windows of the Mansion and saw the dark blue of only one guard on the second floor but assumed one would be on the ground floor as well. No matter. Polis knew where he wanted to go.

The thief waited till the Policeman was past the halfway point of the building and hopped the fence. Once over he fell into a dead sprint in a flat angle for the fence near the corner of the property. He did this because at the far end of the structure, the Policeman took a second to specifically survey the furthest edge of the property before moving around the side yard and to the front to complete another lap of guard duty. Polis had to take this angle because the viewpoint of the second floor guard coincided with the outdoor Patrolman in a way that created a blind spot along the fence for ten seconds. Once at the fence, Polis ran along it until he reached the corner of the structure, whereupon he broke from his line and came to rest.

Polis pulled back the glove to see the Rolex again. It wouldn't be enough time.

The thief rushed to remove four separate objects, two of them cylindrical and metallic, one of them a spring and the other a tight coil of very thin polypropylene rope. When he had attached the rope to the two cylinders, he removed a launcher pistol no bigger than a smart phone from a small pouch on his belt and inserted the spring. It took strength to cock the pistol and he fired the first cylinder with a click and a muffled puffing noise to a strip of wood above the stony wall of the structure, just below the arching roofline. The cylinder bit into the wood and he shot the second cylinder in the same area only several inches away. The result was a v shape of rope. Polis took a breath and pushed it out as he leapt to grab the rope and began climbing up the side of the building. The chiseled shape of his upper body bulged and flexed in the skintight black turtleneck with the tremendous exertion. His lower body was squeezed in a ball below him as he shimmied up the rope with the strength of his arms, shoulder and back alone. The sheer size of the Mansion and the extremity of the roofline made him unable to brace his legs against the stone as a traditional climber would and as Polis reached the roof and flipped his legs around, laying flat against it with enough time to pull the rope to him before the Officer wound his way to the side yard.

Polis shook his head at himself. Another year older and he could still get it done. Now that he was in no man's land he took his time replacing the cylinders and rope in the pockets of the vest. He advanced in a low crouch up the angle of the roof to survey the front space of the property. In the clarity of the weather and the excellence of his surgically perfected eyesight, he

could see the cleanup effort on the Two-Eleven and
spotted only one cop car in the circular drive next to
what looked to be a tour bus.

The thief frowned at the tour bus and had no
time to figure it out. He ran like a monkey, hands and
feet guiding him along the bent spine of the angled roof
until he reached a desired point that looked no different
from any other spot on the roof. There, Polis removed
his vest, and spread it on the roof so it wouldn't slip off,
and pressed himself down on his chest with his feet
pointing toward the ground. He bent his legs up and
tucked them back, pushing with his arms. He slid down
the slick line of the roof with ease and as the space of
the roof ended some four seconds later he flipped his
legs down, spreading his arms to stop his momentum
and he dropped gently in the space of a small balcony
protected from two-story drop by a wrought iron
balustrade.

Once on the balcony, Polis nearly leapt to the
safety of the thin wall that sat between the glass door
and the edge of the balustrade.

The door was unlocked and once Polis was in
what looked to be some kind of small conference room,
he ran on angled tiptoes to the cover of the closed door.
There he caught his breath and checked his watch.

The target room was off a secluded hallway that
came from the grand staircase of the atrium. There was
little or no cover between his current location and the
target room and while he had been keeping the upstairs
guard's timing in mind he hadn't observed him long
enough to merit any concrete definition of his routine.
There was a certain calculated risk involved in any job,
but dealing with CPD or any Police Department for that
matter was far different from some stooge in a dark
jacket with a walkie talkie who made eleven bucks an
hour staring at nothing-not to mention the state of alert

CPD had been placed in under the day's hex of destruction.

Polis centered himself to chance a look into the exposure but the surprise of darkness nearly startled him. It was as if the power had been cut.

The thief ran to the window and checked. Every light in the house was off, and for that matter, even the service lights on the Thirty-First.

The driver of the van had not only replaced the wheel but had moved the vehicle in reverse along the shoulder and exited the highway, swinging the van around and crossing lanes. He had then maneuvered the van through a stranglehold of suburban streets to a gated transformer station at which he lobbed a pair of the white phosphorus grenades without even stopping.

Officer Sheridan blew warm air into his calloused hands. He had just come on shift from the Homeland initiated layoff at five AM and with all of the activities in Crescent he was frustrated he had drawn roadblock duty, considering his background as a Marine. Officer Thom, who was in the car doing paperwork, had joked about it being an early taste of traffic work, and strangely, Sheridan hadn't thought about how much standing in the cold he'd actually be doing.

As Sheridan paced back and forth the dispelled crack of a distant explosion echoed through the trees from the east. The Officer looked up to the direction of the noise and the street lamps went dark. He snapped his head to the right and left and spun on his heel. Thom noticed the lack of light.

"Transformer?" She said as Sheridan opened the door to get at the computer.

"Must be. We can't leave so I'll call it in."

Polis took advantage of the fallen darkness though he didn't want to admit what he believed the cause of it to be. His feet were quick and light as he all but danced through the open space of the top floor near the staircase and to the secluded hallway that was lined with impressionist paintings. Polis heard the clomping of footsteps up the stairs and made himself flat on the ground, as if he was riding a luge.

The Officer that had lurched up the stairs stopped at the end of the hallway, his flashlight beam shining into the floor. He was a tall man with a hard stomach that came from a poor diet and the Officer that came to stand before him was a short and compact man who appeared to be no older than twenty and spent what time he had left from covering extra shifts at the gym.

"All the lights out up here?" The tall one asked, the beam of his flashlight bopped around the broadness of the open portion of the second floor.

"Yeah."

"I'll call Sheridan, see if they have power on the street. Go get Markel and tell him to get his butt in here."

"Right."

The short youngster ran down the stairs as if his life depended on it. The tall Officer walked down the stairs after him on his radio.

Polis pushed himself up and advanced past the bathroom and turned his attention to the room, the door of which was open. He pulled an LED light from his pants pocket and flashed it only three times in the room. His eyes took pictures of what they saw and he walked straight toward the window in the darkness. He knew exactly where the hidden security camera was and took it.

The grainy green of the goggles colored the Mansion in a way that made it little more than a darkish blob of lines and angles. Charlie was up and over the fence quickly and having run to and alongside the breadth of the Mansion, spotted a tangle of Police Officers near the obvious entrance of the front. His head whipped around and gave the silent signal for Greene and Kalil to take them out.

Charlie moved the opposite way to the back entrance and Ritter was inches behind. The two men cautiously covered every angle as they approached the back.

"...Targets neutralized..." Kalil said over the comm.

"Proceed." Charlie came to the broken glass door of the kitchen and jerked his head. Ritter moved in.

From there, the team scattered into four quadrants of the house.

Charlie, still on the ground floor and in the right wing of the Mansion, was in a grand wood paneled room, which, in another era, would've been full of mounted taxidermy trophies. Now it was little more than a small ballroom for proms and whatnot. He removed one of the pouches of liquid from his pocket and emptied it in the room. The liquid was an even blend of high octane AV gas and nitro methane. The very fumes of it were highly combustible and it was a worthy propellant to the white phosphorus grenades. Charlie started in the room, sprinkling the contents of the pouch on the ground and walls till he was back in the kitchen. The pouch was two liters. He emptied the other three pouches in subsequent rooms and hallways.

"We have company..." Ritter muttered.

"Take him out!" Charlie snapped, raising his

silenced pistol and shuffling backwards out the door.

Charlie checked his watch. The police would be growing suspicious by the lack of radio contact. They could handle twenty more seconds of time at the most. Then they had to be over the fence and down the hill to Jens and the getaway van.

"Blow it and go!" Charlie ordered. "He won't survive."

Charlie didn't know if it was a he or she and he didn't care. The giant place would burn like hell.

Charlie held rear cover as Kalil ran through the kitchen past him.

"There's someone in there." He said.

"I don't give a damn, light it and go!"

Kalil ran back inside and toward the front.

Ten seconds had gone by. There was no more time.

"Fire one!" The team leader shouted as he took one of the Willie Pete's and ran to the window of the wood paneled room. It crashed and clattered to pieces with two shots and he ripped the pin from the grenade and threw it inside. He turned his back and ran to the broken door of the kitchen as the incendiary device splattered white hot phosphorus across the wood of the room in a fizzling flash of sparks and smoke. The ignition caught the gas and fuel with a whumpf and the resulting flames began to lick and twist through the Mansion.

A total of eight grenades were released in the Mansion in sequential order.

Team Ganymede met up in the side yard in somewhat of a dead sprint. By the time they were over the fence the searing and scorching heat of the flames had engulfed the entire Mansion, spurned toward the ultimate destruction by lacquered floors of inlaid wood, acres of expensive fabric, abundance of oil paintings, a heavily stocked bar of alcohol and the grandeur of oxygen rich open space.

Polis struggled with the closed window. The harsh smoke was creeping through the walls and burning his lungs. He held his breath the best he could and finally he broke the window with his elbow. The result was a jagged and bloody tear in his sleeve and the cold rush of fresh night air and freedom. But it was only a breath and he needed more, he needed a whole open skyline of it to escape the horrid fingers of the poisonous gas. His mind was racing with possibilities as to who would do such a thing and why and his body took all it had to keep his mind sharp as it was working harder than ever before fighting the astringent chemicals of the smoke.

The window had no balcony and he didn't care. What was a broken leg on the scales of life and death? Polis threw the shutters wide and judged the distance for a second before squeezing himself into a bunch and launching his muscular frame through the broken window.

The ground was an unforgiving reality and he sprained one ankle if not two as he landed ungracefully. The roar of the raging storm of flames and deadly fumes was a deafening catastrophe and he pawed and scraped at the ground to break free.

His back felt the heat as the living tongues of color and sound tore through the structure. Glass shattered in compressed explosions. Polis yearned for air, crawling toward the darkness of the cold night, unable to escape the clutches of the inferno.

The fight was left to his upper body now, his legs had given out on him. The tendons in his ankles must've snapped or torn and his upper body was already fatigued from the climb.

Polis dug his fingernails into the damp green sod and felt concrete. Then the backlight from the fire faded to an endless sea of black.

Sarina Veracruz parked the Chevy Silverado she was borrowing from her brother in Jimenez' driveway, surprised that his Lexus wasn't there. On the drive over she had been juggling Erland and Jimenez in her mind and it was exceedingly strange that he had called her today, of all days, in the very vacancy of a lonely evening she had been planning to spend with the Detective given their deactivation from the Fircrest investigation. Erland's choice to return at Homeland's request had created the void and the frozen pizza and cable television did nothing to fill it. Erland and Jimenez were both the same age, both in law enforcement, both dependable and reliable, but wasn't she just too young for an old man? Erland had already gone gray from the stress of the job and the fact that Jimenez was a Mexican from East Los Angeles made him virtually immune to gray hair but soon he would get pudgy drinking beer and watch baseball every night while that old leather couch of his was covered in Beagle fur.

She slid from the seat and shut the door. It was all a jumble inside. They each had their unique qualities and in retrospect she had made the breakup worse by that night in the Nexus club. In many ways she had lied to Jimenez and ultimately to herself by saying how she had met another man, even though, that's about all she had done, met and spent the night with the Detective. So for months she had been putting off a man she had been steady two years with for someone she was actually avoiding as they passed each other in the Precinct. And part of her heart still felt for Jimenez, if it was pity or otherwise, because he had lost nearly everything but his house and the shell of it in a bitter divorce and really only wanted someone to take care of him when he came home from work.

It had to stop, the confusion of it. Erland had given her his commitment, hadn't he? And so she was going to dive in to him with both feet. Or was she? Something about returning to that little brown house in Mossyrock brought back as many good memories as it did bad ones-still, so many *good* memories...

Her hand gave three thick raps on the door. She waited in the cold for what felt like two minutes and was closer to forty seconds and knocked again. When there was no answer she skipped down the steps and walked to the side yard. The brown and angular seventies-built dwelling was nearly adjacent to the house next to it on the right side and on the left it had a broad side yard that was gated to keep Balboa from terrorizing the neighborhood cats although the height of the matching brown privacy fence enabled them to thoroughly mess with him.

Sarina found the gate open and gasped.

Balboa was on his side on the grass, his little feet sticking out in a limp and lifeless manner.

Sarina's face was twisted in pain as she rushed to kneel on the grass. She loved dogs more than anything else in life, especially those she had trained. Ever since she was a young girl she had wanted to be a veterinarian and to see the precious Beagle void of life was a blow that forced all the air from her stomach. Her eyes welled with tears and her mind jumped to Luis, if he was in danger too. He had called her for help, hadn't he?

Veracruz stood and ran to the back door. It was open.

"Luis! Luis!"

She rushed through the sunroom in the back,

past images of last summer and to the blank space of the living room and the squeaky leather couch as it faced the fireplace.

Where was his TV? Where was he?

Sarina passed in front of the couch, heading for the short hall that led to the kitchen as it set directly opposing the neighboring house. Why weren't any of the lights on? *Was Jimenez even home?*

Her questions were answered in the blink of an eye. Jimenez was face down on the hardwood behind the couch and she nearly leapt backwards, startled. A hand wrapped around her mouth while a swift foot swept her balance from her. She fell to the ground, crushed by the weight of the figure on top of her.

There was no fight in her as much as she squirmed from the terrible grip of the poison flooding her veins. There was only darkness.

TWENTY-SIX

The man removed the inch long needle from the small space behind the woman's ear. Then he worked quickly in dragging her toward the body of Jimenez, laying her next to him. He removed a silenced pistol from his shoulder holster and leaned the Homeland Agent upright against the couch. He wrenched a strong hand on the back of Sarina's jacket and when she slumped down again grabbed at her shirt as well and pulled her up high enough to stick the gun in her hand and wrap her fingers around the handle.

The barrel of the silencer was not two inches away from the Agent's neck when he pulled the trigger. A clicking sound made way for a metallic slicing and squishing of blood and flesh. Jimenez' body fell at a sideways angle and hunched over the squeaky couch only to fall headlong and twist off the slippery leather to land with his back to the floor. Blood covered the couch and floor in a smeared mess of red slime.

The man let Sarina drop like a sack of potatoes. Her head smashed against the floor. The man took the gun and placed it back in Sarina's hands and left the home in the woman's Chevy having lifted the keys from her purse and taking the man's phone from the couch. He parked the Silverado a block away and walked a block more to his own car after making a quick call.

Sheridan was in a dead sprint to the patrol car as the cracking concussions rocked Fircrest Hill. Their sonic signature landed somewhere between construction explosives and fireworks and the suddenness of them spread through the frigid air as it hung, wet and heavy over the hill and startled him for the faintest of moments before the memories of combat kicked in. By the time he got to the car and threw himself in the driver's seat, Thom had frantically moved the cones and barriers enough to allow the car and subsequent emergency vehicles that would follow to pass through.

"Call Bridges!" Sheridan said at nearly the same time as Thom bunched herself in the seat next to him, both of them feeling the lurch of speed as Sheridan punched the accelerator. She ripped the walkie from her belt and called for the senior Officer of the Fircrest guard detail.

There was no response.

"Try Markel!" Sheridan squinted through the trees at the bright color burning through the density of the foliage. There was no way to see in any detail as the car wound up the side of the hill to the front of the private drive that ran straight up the peak.

"He's not answering either."

Both Officers saw exactly why as the car came to face the Mansion head on.

Thom didn't hesitate calling the fire department and any available back up as if there *was* any considering the events of the day.

The car roared around the drive and squealed as it stopped near the gate. Thom was out before Sheridan and the incredible heat pushed her back behind the door.

The Mansion cracked and groaned as wood split

and glass exploded. A thunderous roar consumed the structure and blackened the once gray-brown stone with an endless heat.

"Pull the car back!" Thom shouted and Sheridan couldn't hear. His eyes were on the body inside the gate.

He saw her lips move in a twist of his head as he pressed toward the inferno. The smoke and gas seared his eyes and they teared and begged for closure. It took every ounce of Jarhead training to reach the body and by the time he did he felt like passing out. The fumes of the fire were horribly toxic and a distinctive odor sat behind the blue-orange death that he had no time to try and place but they had crossed paths before. His hands grabbed at whatever blackness they could and pulled. The body was heavy and Thom helped him once he reached the gate.

The pulling ceased when they had reached the trunk of the car.

"Is he alive?" Thom yelled at the top of her lungs.

Sheridan checked. He was.

The former Marine wiped his forehead and strained against the cacophony to hear the frantic whir of the ladder truck.

Sugar Hill Elementary was one of North Crescent's crowning achievements as it was deemed a *bully free zone* and had the highest college enrollment rate of any elementary school in the state. Students were encouraged not only to participate in *random acts of kindness*, or what the school call the RAK-Attack, but were also quick to publicize the good deeds of others with commendations known as *Eye-See-You's*. The school itself sat somewhere between the Targus River and the green slope that spilled from Fircrest Hill

near the highway as the last bits of North Crescent were
squeezed and smushed into the residential
neighborhoods of Goldendale, Griffin Park, and Valley
and edged with three and four story dwelling blocks.
The buildings and units were all from a large budget
reform in the eighties and at the time had been state of
the art. Now, somehow, the school had the merits of a
private business park and a prison in equal doses. The
campus was gated not only by chain link but a generous
stand of alders and oaks, with a few silver birches
inside the grounds kids were told *not* to climb. Most of
the buildings were either white or brown and white and
the auditorium was a healthy domed structure that sat
behind a digital reader board and one of the busiest
parking lots in North Crescent.

Mike Erland pulled the champagne green Camry
to the curbside across the street.

"What's going on here?" Sierra asked.

"Probably a winter concert. What time is it?"

"Seven-thirty one."

"Yeah." Erland pulled at the knees of his jeans
and saw how many late arrivals were still trouping in
their fancied up children. "We should talk to Wolcek
before he gets involved with the festivities."

"Hold on." Sierra stopped the Detective and
handed him a new pistol she had stashed in her purse. It
was an H&K Forty USP. "I know it's not your Glock,"
She said, "but it still works the same way."

Erland's face said he'd rather not considering he
was in an OIS but was wise enough to know better. He
took the pistol and it was a perfect fit in his back
holster. The H&K carried a forty-caliber bullet and was
not only larger but gave more recoil than the Glock 17
nine millimeter. But, both of them held their hopes that
he wouldn't have to use it.

The man and woman exited the car and Erland

felt the cold from the water and stuffed his hands in the
pockets of the jacket. As he walked Sierra caught stride
with him and slipped her arm through the angle of his.

"I could get used to this." She said. He turned to
catch a sparkle in the blue of her eyes from the street
lamps. A swirling puff of night wind tousled the subtle
waves of her black hair.

They hit the sidewalk and she released his arm.
Erland got the door for her and once inside Sierra shook
her head. The place was a zoo. Parents and children,
children and parents, extended family and even a
service dog.

"Maybe they came for the snacks." Erland
nudged his head toward a table that sat amongst a few
others in the individual scholastic achievement lined
hall that lead to the auditorium. Sierra saw what was a
foldable table covered in pale tan sugar cookies in the
shapes of pumpkins and turkeys, as well as footballs
and stars, each one covered in a thick slathering of
either unnaturally colored frosting or bitty crystals of
similarly dyed sugar. Next to it was a table of hot cider,
and the sight of free food caused quite a backup on the
way to the Lester R. MacMurry Auditorium for
Performing Arts.

"Do you want to split up to find Wolcek?"
Erland offered.

"Never." Marland shook her head and they
politely cut through the gawking block of confusion.
"We're partners now." She added, once they were
actually inside the auditorium. "We don't split up."

The angled floor rose maybe twenty feet in
elevation at the very back and the curtains were drawn
on the stage. The ambient volume of the room was
spiked with false laughter and muttered mumbles and
the motif of the decoration was purple and gold, no
doubt the colors of the mascot, which was a forgettable

and somewhat imaginary bird.

"Do you see anyone in a wheelchair?" Erland nearly shouted even though Sierra was close enough whisper to.

She shook her head and caught the attention of a woman she had spied almost instantly. The elderly woman was a thin and wiry soul in a holiday sweater and the smell of her perfume nearly gave Erland a headache, even though he was very good about keeping his cool when it came to offensive odors having worked Homicide for so long.

"Excuse me, ma'am, where is Principal Wolcek?"

"Pardon?" The woman stopped and her penciled-in eyebrows arched inquisitively. She wore a sticky nametag that read *Doris*.

"Where is the Principal? I must speak to him."

"Oh, his office is on the other side of the school in the Admin building, near sixth grade, you can't miss it. Tell him we're running a bit late if you don't mind, I sent a page and I don't know what's happened to him."

"Cookies." Erland said to the not yet but about to be frazzled woman as they left.

Once out in the cool night air for the short walk around the front of the auditorium and by the playground Erland laughed.

"What?" Sierra said and said it again as Erland wouldn't stop.

"Nothing, I just thought of retirement." His face was as quizzical as hers had been when she was overseeing his judgment of the new clothes.

"What about it?"

"I just...couldn't see myself in the rat race, you know. I just don't get the point of it all."

Marland hugged herself.

"Go on..."

"I mean, what's better than a nice, quiet life?"

"Have you talked it over with...your girlfriend?"

The Detective stopped.

"Whoa, wait." He loosely held Sierra at arm's length. "What did you say?"

"You spoke of retirement in the car from the Precinct to Fircrest. You said you talked it over with your...girlfriend."

A flash of what could've been misconstrued as anger wrinkled through Erland's face before he released it to the brushing night wind and poor light of the campus.

"Sierra...that woman was little more than an acquaintance, I haven't even seen her for three months; it was just a one time thing. I didn't know what else to call her at the time." Erland sighed. It had been heavy on his soul but he was so skilled at compartmentalizing what he felt when he didn't think about it. However when he *did*, it had a way of bundling itself all together. "It's just that, we were working Fircrest together, she's in K-9, and after Tallifer gave us all the boot, she came to my apartment and wanted to know if I was serious or not."

Sierra didn't move.

"Sierra, please, you have to believe me when I say you're the only thing that's right about this whole mess. If I had known who you were years ago we wouldn't even be *having* this conversation."

Erland drew her to him and embraced her in the cold.

"I didn't want that moment at Tabitha's to end." He said quietly in her ear. "But I'm not free to love you till this is all over. I can't do it."

He held her unreasonably beautiful face in both of his hands.

"Understand?"

She nodded. Then she wrapped her arms around him.

"I'm so sorry Mike. I just thought...because you didn't want to...that you were just being nice to me...I was having a breakdown."

"No, Sierra, no..."

"I thought that the way I felt...feel about you was...is..."

Erland dropped to a knee from the embrace and held her hands in his.

"Sierra, I've never known another woman like you. Listen to me when I say that I want nothing more than to be with you. I'm tired of the lies and the pain and the suffering of this life and I know you are too. We give everything we've got to the job and come home to an empty house with little more than a pat on the back. It's only because I...respect so much what you've become to me that I wouldn't dare use it in such a causal...and careless way." The Detective smiled. "We *owe* each other peace. We *owe* each other the freedom of a quiet life where it's just you and me and a sandy beach. It means too damn much to me. I just want this all to go away and to spend the rest of my life with you, but I know that can't happen yet, and it sure as hell is worth waiting for."

The Detective rose and kissed her languidly on the lips and then looked her in the eyes.

"It's the *only* thing worth waiting for."

He pulled her along the walkway that ran from the open playground and on to the administration building as tears welled in her eyes.

"Now let's go find Wolcek, okay?"

Sierra nodded and wiped her eyes, feeling the strength from the grip of his hand on her shoulder and the heat from his body, the stability and power he had emanated from him and was as infectious as it was contagious. He was what she had always wanted and always dreamed about and knew was out there, just as she was to him and it made her skin crawl within her to forsake the true purity of her heart's desire with such a vulgar and devious betrayal. The real thing was before them both on a silver platter and the deceitful gambler was risking it all for the mission. She *had* to hear the pledge of allegiance from his own mouth especially because he had not chosen to sleep with her as would practically *any* other man in his position, she *had* to know his trust in her was complete. She had been watering the seeds of attraction since the moment they had laid eyes on each other and *had* to know that he was madly in love with her and thus, *blinded* by it.

For though she wanted nothing more than to magically fly away from what madness it was and spend the rest of her days in his arms, she knew the next phase of the gamble could ruin that forever but was the *only* way she could possibly imagine trapping Jupiter once and for all.

The struggle within her ripped a hole in her stomach. He had *made* her promise, hadn't he? And all he was saying was backing up the fact that Jupiter was to be destroyed by *any* means necessary.

Magnolia was right, damn her. It was too hard. She had become inexplicably tainted and intertwined with the operation as she had prophesied.

As they walked to the administration building Sierra sucked up the fear of losing what she had hoped to find her whole life and finally had in her arms. She had already lost Maggie. She couldn't lose Mike. It was all up to the dice, to the gamble, and though it severed her in half to risk so much it was all she had left on the table to gamble with.

The writer's convention of Jessica Birchall, Darren Reston, and Kelly Barnett was not without controversy as they continued to flood the news and social media with the story Marland had given them; though she had only been the architect, they were the artisans and builders.

"Say that again?" Birchall's face communicated her technical misunderstanding.

"Who, how, why, what, when, and where."

"That's absurd."

"No, no. That's how Mrs. Bleecher taught it to us."

Jessica was dialing a number on her personal smart phone in order to place the fourth call of about six or seven as she was arguing. Kelly was in a machine-like mode with the tablet Marland had provided and could not afford to so much as look up and break her concentration. Darren was writing a piece that would be able to be published in print.

"It's who, what, when, where, how, and why."

"Nope. Who, how..."

"Who *how?* Who did *what* how? Who did what when? Where and how did they do it and why?"

Before Darren could offer a rebuttal one of Kelly's furious hands slapped Darren on the arm. His mouth stayed shut. They were still at the table and coffee cups were half or nearly empty before them.

"Mrs. Bleecher could've been wrong." He said, rubbing his arm. "She was kind of old..."

"Hello?" Jessica stood up and began to walk to the bedroom. "Yes, my name's Jessica Birchall..." Her voice faded.

"Why'd you hit me?" Darren asked in a loud whisper.

"Because you were wrong."

"You could've just said something..."

Kelly gave him a sour look.

"Write, Socrates, write."

Darren looked down to the notes he had and to the nearly finished article. It would be passed to every major paper publisher, and its verification was that it came last in the slaughter of Jupiter's privacy. The print media would be *behind* the story and running to their board of directors in confusion, unknown to them that the true source would remain anonymous and the forest fire of publicity on social networking, data sharing, and media outletting had all been accomplished by one CMJ employee with a tablet. To bolster that, Birchall was going on the air for the eleven o'clock news with the story and was also baiting the producers with her attempts to set up an anonymous film interview with her clandestine source, Sierra Marland. Even if that *didn't* happen, Birchall was still going on the air and all of Crescent's questions would be answered, the dots connected. By now, the destruction in Crescent was national news and there was no real *reason* for it. Marland had provided the wrecking crew of reporters with a tangible prime steak profile of that very reason with the shot of Jupiter from Morell's helmet camera, as well as the images and rap sheets of the men that had been killed in defense of PierHouse; also the deceased Luther Hill and how he was a traitorous Homeland Agent and had escaped police custody. Not to be left out, Keith Quinlan, another corrupt Agent, destroying the Crime Lab and the evidence as well as killing fifteen people and attempting to escape. For good measure, there was the abduction of Tanya Wilson and the fracas caused by Hill as the police chased down and arrested an innocent man. Finally, the inciting event of the murder of a woman whose identity remained a guarded secret at Fircrest Mansion. All of it fell on Jupiter.

All of it.

The timing was right, the material was tight, the connections were seamless and without refusal. Marland had provided enough authenticated Homeland data of the classified variety to end her career several times over but by doing so exposed the amoral turncoats and set up a perimeter around the fugitive Jupiter so tight he'd have to start breathing through an aqualung. His face, pixilated but still legible, was now not only going to be on the moving pictures of the televised news but plastered all over the permanency of the internet, the very arena where he marauded and terrorized the American public in silence and secrecy with an iron fist. The ripple effect of the information release would spread like nuclear radiation and the fallout alone would poison Jupiter's operation with some permanency, but more than that, it would make him more desperate than he'd ever been before. He had backed Marland into a corner, and she had lashed out at him with a counterpunch to the body only moments after one of his own haymakers had missed her head. And the criminal hacker Jupiter, cut off from his network and on the run, would have no way to remove or alter the information flow in anyway, due to the sheer volume and timeliness of it.

"That does it." Birchall said as she came back to the table and set her smart phone near her coffee cup. "Denton Hodge says regional will want to fly me to New York next week for more on this story, since I was the only one in the *world* who covered the murder..."

"Isn't that the guy that told you you'd lose your job if you kept nosing around?" Reston asked, and in doing so, was in a way apologizing for his defense of Mrs. Bleecher's inaccurate teaching.

"Yeah..." Jessica finished the coffee and noted how much better it was than the car drippings from the

Internet Cafe. "I think Marland said something to him after she left...she's always making a call to someone..."

Tabitha Grey came running in the dining room. "All of you, come quick!"

The journalists saw the horror stretched across her face and nearly launched themselves from their chairs to follow her to the large window in the living space where the clomping ended in fearful awe.

There, speechlessness arrested them with an image worth at least a thousand words if it was once worth one hundred and seventy-three million dollars.

Fircrest Mansion, in all of its magnificent opulence and lofty seclusion was burning like a dark and endless fire of hell.

Checking his watch, Timothy S. Wolcek swore at his punctuality, or lack thereof. He was the leader of Sugar Hill, the Principal, the man in charge and was held to the highest standard not only by himself, but by the rigidity of the program and the children it produced. They were among the brightest and finest young minds in the country and never a cross word passed between them. Classrooms were places of encouragement and teamwork and scholastic unity was reflected in personal similarity. There was no comparison where there was acceptance and no acceptance to bullying or any other forms of psychological superiority. At Sugar Hill, there was only *equality*, and the vocabulary was as replete with uni-gender terminology as their education was with integrated smart technology.

Wolcek took his cellphone from the desk and stuffed it in his winter coat pocket, even though Mrs. Grensley had the heat turned too high in the administration building the run to the concert venue was chilly enough to merit the thick outerwear. He took his speech from the table as well, just a little something he had penned to praise the children before the concert.

The administration building was empty. His head was down as he rolled the wheelchair through the widened door of his office and down the oatmeal and butter colored hallway, lined, as it was, with thumbtack and paper ridden bulletin boards.

Wolcek looked up from the paper to turn right and head for the exit when a man and a woman stepped through the door bringing with them a frosty breath of night air. He'd never seen the man before but the woman made the blood leave his face as it flushed like a toilet. Wolcek spun the chair around with his head down and began to wheel the chair toward another exit.

"Excuse me, Mr. Wolcek." The man said.

The Principal stopped. Dread filled his lungs and stomach. How could he get out of it? Was there any other disabled school Principal by that name?

Wolcek slowly turned the wheelchair to face the approaching figures. There was no doubt in his mind, he was staring at the very woman he had killed only hours before.

"Yes?" He did his best to smile politely and felt the burning discomfort of guilt flare across every inch of his skin. His right hand nonchalantly slipped in the pocket of his jacket.

"Do you mind if I ask you a few questions?" The man began. He was a good-looking gray haired man in his early forties.

"Actually I can't right now, I have opening remarks to make at the Fall Concert tonight, and it runs on a *very* tight schedule."

"Well, they're running late due to the traffic issues caused by today's...events, so, I'm sure you can spare a few minutes." The man had a twinkle in his blue eyes and Wolcek could not so much as peek at the woman who stood confidently next to the man with her hands resting in the back pocket of her jeans.

"What is it?" Wolcek was unintentionally terse. Inside the jacket pocket he was texting his only option to escape.

"Were you at Fircrest Mansion last night?"

"Who wants to know?" The Principal's round face was shiny under the long bands of fluorescent lights. Shadows were cast around his deep-set eyes making them hard to read.

The man pulled a badge from his jacket.

"CPD."

Wolcek sighed.

"Yes. I was. What about it?"

"Did you kill my sister?" The woman said with all the subtlety of a dead blow hammer, yet with a detached and unemotional tone of voice.

The blast of revelation that the woman before him who was in no way different than the one he had stabbed in the neck was a sister rippled through the guilty man's face with a gesture as revealing as the squiggly lines of a court-ordered polygraph.

Mike and Sierra exchanged grim looks and their eyes became hard as they stood between Wolcek and the door.

"Wh...what did you say?"

"We have a partial print on a latex glove," Erland put his hands on his hips even though he didn't have the latex glove and all of the evidence from the case was in a steaming heap in the westbound lane of the Two-Eleven and they really only had the cameras at Precinct Three. "And I'm sure that we'll match the latex to a box in your office or some school supply room, not to mention we have a parallel indentation in the doorway of the bathroom adjacent the room of the murder and a rubber scuff on the wall consistent with the left handle of your wheelchair."

"But..."

"And finally, if I look *real* hard," Erland leaned on his knees to meet Wolcek in the eyes. "I'll find a hollow space for that carbon fiber spike on that lazy boy of yours."

The man in the wheelchair took in a deep swirl of oxygen and stared at Sierra, though the thickness of his brow prevented her from reading him. Regardless she reached in the breast pocket of her jacket and speed dialed Tabitha on speaker without removing her phone.

"Jupiter forced me to, for what it's worth." The man said with as much color as the very walls that were shrinking around him. "He somehow found out I've been falsifying test scores and fudging the budget for years...he said he'd forget it if I did him a favor at the Fircrest party-he was even going to pay me..."

Sierra's jaw was clenched tight and her blue eyes were barely visible as she listened.

"Go on."

The Principal wiped his forehead with the puffy sleeve of his free hand.

"Jupiter said no one would suspect a cripple...and they made it easy. They held her. I didn't think about it. There was no fight. She looked like she was already dead."

"STRIC-R..." Erland mouthed as Sierra passed him a glare.

"He knew I'd do anything...I've nearly broken my back to make this school what it is, from nothing, and with all of the ESL kids and foreigners pouring in our district I couldn't let them ruin our reputation."

Sierra pulled the H&K from her back holster and startled Wolcek by aiming at the lump of his body. Both of his hands shot up at right angles.

"No, no please, I'm sorry. Please don't kill me."

Sierra's face was frigid and glassed over.

"You can't shoot him, Sierra." Erland said.

"Tell me where Jupiter is and I won't."

"I haven't seen him!" The Principal's voice fluctuated and quavered. "You have to believe me."

"He was at the party, right?"

"Yes, yes he was, but I haven't seen him since then."

"Where's the exchange site?"

"*Exchange?* I don't know what you're talking about!"

Sierra thrust the gun forward as her arm became rigid and taught.

"The sale, Wolcek, *where is the sale?*"

The Principal's mouth stuttered open and closed and no words were audible.

Sierra cocked the gun and Wolcek jumped in his seat as if a bomb had exploded. One of his arms limply bent over his head in a feeble attempt to make it all go away.

Sierra's nostrils were flared and her lips bent low at the corners of her mouth as if she was preparing herself to euthanize a sick and pathetic animal.

She didn't have the chance.

Two armed men flashed behind Wolcek at nearly the same time as the exit not twelve feet behind Marland crashed open, two more men with pistols completing the hammer and anvil scheme with catastrophic perfection. Marland twitched her head to see Erland facing the opposite direction with his H&K drawn. It was four to two. Five if the simpering murderer counted. The hardness had not left Sierra's face. Magnolia's voice was finally crying out to her for vengeance but she had put all of her chips on the table and the gamble was playing out exactly as she had anticipated. The thought of what was next slid a shiver down her spine.

TWENTY-SEVEN

Tabitha Grey was trying with everything in her to shake the shock of Fircrest becoming a funeral pyre and Sierra's call did nothing to help. She was in the elevator with Barnett, Birchall and Reston on the long ride to the parking garage. She had heard the confession, and now she was hearing the standoff. Marland and Erland were in trouble and she now she was responsible to jump in support with no order from Sierra whatsoever. All of her life she had trusted her determination to the hands of a coach or a leader, knowing that whatever they said to do, she would do with all of her might. But she was the leader, and the more she looked for answers the fewer she found.

"Agent Grey, is that Agent Marland?" Reston asked from behind.

Tabitha sliced a negating hand through the air as she listened. Her eyes danced around the steel door and up to the highlighted number series and back down to the door.

Courtland was the first to speak. His silenced marksman's pistol would make no sound in killing anyone that stood in the hallway.

"Put it down, Marland."

The H&K sagged in her hand as surrender ran through her body. Erland caught her out of the corner of his eye and did the same, reluctantly. His posture was ready to fight, she could nearly feel the energy flying off of him, and the desire to protect her had somehow empowered him.

"You're not worth the air you breathe." Sierra nearly growled and stared a hole in Wolcek's face. He looked frail and weak even for a year away from fifty, as if one strong puff of mountain wind would knock him from the mobile chair.

"I know..." Wolcek's head fell.

"Drop the guns, both of you, on the floor." Courtland ordered.

Mike and Sierra complied. Kirke and Pitts, both in RepMax uniforms, moved closer, slowly, and took Erland's gun.

"Get it, Wolcek." Courtland was taking no chances, keeping his distance from Sierra with the human shield. The computer man Brock was next to him.

The Principal wheeled the chair forward, deflated. He stopped close enough to grab it and reached down.

Sierra flicked her fist down in a slash of lightning, striking with a twist of her legs and hips. Wolcek's head received the force of the blow like an old pillow and his body bent unnaturally as he collided with the wall with a muffled grunt.

"Get up!" Sierra shouted. There was no interference from Courtland or anyone else on Team Io. They understood.

Wolcek's head spun and he whimpered as his legs were tangled together underneath him. His hand stretched out for the H&K Forty and Sierra mashed her boot on his hand and ground it as he screamed in pain.

Then Erland's hand was on Sierra's shoulder and he said her name, softly and quietly. Just her name.

No more.

Sierra stopped and kicked the gun toward Courtland, who was a thick figure in the janitor's suit. His face was a broad and ugly thing, unhealthy too.

Brock reached down for the gun. He took it and stuffed it in the front of his pants after removing the chambered round and flicking the safety on. The spare bullet that popped from the gun made a pinging noise in the silence and he reached for it.

Erland moved forward to pick Wolcek up and propped the broken man in the wheelchair.

"You listen to me," He said with intense blue eyes. "As long as I'm alive you'll get thirty to life. And even if I'm not, justice *will* have its course."

Erland stood tall next to Sierra and directed the intensity of his eyes to Courtland.

Tabitha nearly sprinted from the elevator as the doors pinged and peeled open, the three journalists right behind.

"They're in trouble." She said as she reached the white Suburban that was only feet from the elevator door. The Nineteen and Seventy Pontiac GTO was parked two cars away from it. "I've gotta go."

The writers stood empathetically behind her as she removed a submachine gun and a bulletproof vest from the back of the Suburban. They knew this fight was far beyond their contribution.

"Where are they?" Reston asked.

"Sugar Hill Elementary."

Reston shook his head as Tabitha shut the bi-fold back doors. He stopped her with the keys to the GTO.

"You'll never get there in time." Was all he said.

Tabitha received them in silence and nodded.

She threw the Suburban keys to Kelly Barnett.

"One of us we'll call you. Don't worry..."

The journalists stood as helpless statues, their eyes offering what hope they had.

The blonde pushed herself into the green car and the goat fired with a maddened grumble. The squeal of tires twisted through the parking garage and the eight-cylinder symphony became quieter and quieter and quieter until the reporters stood in silence.

Barnett stared at the keys in her hand.

The thick one named Courtland pulled Wolcek out of the way. The box Team Io had Marland and the Detective in was no bigger than six feet by six.

"This is how it's going to be, Marland." Courtland began. "You're going to tell us where CONSTANT is or we're going to take this guy here and feed him his own fingers."

"My name's Michael Erland and I'm a Detective with CPD, Mr. If you screw with me you're gonna have every cop in the city looking to take you down."

Sierra said nothing. Courtland threw a nod to Pitts. The former soldier stepped forward and kicked Erland square in the nuts from behind.

The Agent hid the pain on her face as she watched Erland roll and squirm on the hard school floor in a scrunched up ball.

"That's only the beginning." Courtland smirked. "He'll have nothing left down there when we're all through."

"I won't tell you." Sierra said. "Our lives are nothing compared to the security of four-hundred million people. Do you know *how much* information is on that card? It's way above *your* pay grade."

"No, I don't, but Jupiter does, and he would kill

his own mother for it. And, if you don't care what we do to this guy, maybe you'll care about all those families in the auditorium, all those little children."

A plague of doubt washed through her body. "What?"

"That auditorium is wired with remotely triggered Semtex. The place'll fall straight down like a house of cards. That is, unless you want to hand over CONSTANT. Then, I'll just shoot you but the kids will be okay. He'll live too. He won't look pretty, but he'll live."

"I don't have it." Sierra's voice was flat. That much was true. But the gamble was nearly as much about bluffing as it was about predicting and assuming. It was a brutal, nasty game but if she played it right it would all be worth it. It was tearing her soul into little bitty pieces but it was worth it.

"You did what?" Wolcek whined from a foot away from Courtland.

"Shut up." Courtland didn't even look at him.

"You never said anything about...a bomb, you said you were here to protect me and would take me somewhere safe after the concert where Jupiter would pay me!"

Courtland turned and pistol-whipped the Principal and he fell from the chair unconscious.

"So," Courtland said, "We're going to split you two up, seeing as you've done a lot of damage today and you couldn't have done it alone. We're going to take *him* and see how far his spine bends until *he* tells us where CONSTANT is, and we're going to keep *you* here and wait till the cops come with the bomb threat they're about to get. You'll be convicted for the logical manslaughter of your sister's murderer and Mr. Brown'll have no trouble at all in stashing you away in the darkest corner the US Government can find. If you tell me where CONSTANT is before that, then, like I said earlier, you die quickly and everybody else gets to go home."

Sierra's eyes narrowed as she listened. Erland didn't know what to do as he stood and looked to her for a lead and saw the mask of the gambler.

"I won't kill Wolcek." She said.

Courtland half turned and pointed the silenced pistol at the Principal as he lay face down on the floor. The gun clicked and puffed once and the body jerked as it received the bullet to the back. Erland's teeth ground together as blood began to seep into the floor.

"You just did." Courtland turned the gun back to her. "So what's it going to be? Truth or consequence?"

Marland chose not to say anything to Courtland. Her blue eyes were full of a pain Erland had never seen in them before as she turned to him.

"Forgive me." She said.

Erland stared into the eyes without blinking as the two men pulled him away from her, away and through the doors into the cold black night. He wanted to say something but he couldn't. It was as if he understood in that space of seconds that she had knowingly predicted the moment and done nothing to stop it.

"Bring her here." Courtland said to Brock as he busied himself with removing the silencer from his weapon. Brock pointed his gun at her head and advanced toward her. Marland held her arms out.

She took a breath to center herself and closed her eyes, remembering all of those times on the mat where she had sparred with Maggie.

They would not be in vain.

Sierra opened her eyes as Brock was within inches of her right arm as he began to circle around her.

She slid directly toward him and grabbed his wrist with her left hand and flicked her right in a flat knife, connecting with his throat. She forced the gun hand straight up and Brock's reaction to the attack squeezed a round into the fluorescent light above. The pop of the gun caused Courtland to look up. Sierra grabbed Brock by the collar and swung him from the wall, driving him laterally across the hall as three twenty-two caliber bullets struck his body, arching him backwards. Sierra snagged the gun from his hand as he fell and lurched away from him in the swirl of momentum, sending four shots at the blur of brown Brock's fading shape had revealed.

Pressing herself from the dirty and now bloodstained floor, Sierra launched herself toward the wall as Courtland struggled for balance on his back. A bullet was in his right shoulder and another in his left leg.

Marland came to him and kicked the previously silenced twenty-two out of his hand before he could let it flop her direction and lazily spread rounds into the wall. It clattered and skidded to Wolcek's body.

Her knee pressing down on his painfully overworked lungs and the barrel of the pistol grinding into his forehead, Sierra asked one question through clenched teeth.

"Where are they taking him?"

Courtland gasped for breath and coughed up blood. Neither of them knew the bullet to the shoulder had ricocheted off of his scapula and passed through his aorta where it was lodged for good.

He didn't get the chance to answer, even if he wanted to. His eyes shut without warning and wouldn't open again.

Marland pushed herself from him, the adrenaline rising like the power band of a racecar before a shift to the next gear. The gun in her hand flashed to Brock and back to Courtland.

Dead.

Marland slipped the gun in her jacket pocket. It was a SIG-Sauer and had plenty of damage left. She rifled through Courtland's pockets for answers and got his phone, a wallet that belonged to Darren Reston and a set of keys on a leather keychain bearing the embossed letters *GTO*, two of them were most definitely old looking keys, as well as Courtland's wallet of phony ID's and his own keys, money, and the like. Nothing handwritten or singular but she had the phone. She was positive the Semtex could be triggered from it and one of the numbers in it belonged to Jupiter.

Then Marland pulled at the collar of the janitor's uniform and saw a thin gold necklace. She frowned as she worked the pendant to her hand and then her breath left her for a moment. It was *their* necklace, the twenty-four karat half of a heart that they used to trade like a race baton. Whoever was in the operation wore the necklace and its absence was devastating. Its meaning far outweighed its monetary value. Sierra took the necklace from the ugly man and solemnly placed it on her own neck. Then she ran the same procedure with Brock, retrieving her H&K from his pants and removing all of his pertinent items so that each body was bereft of identification or evidence of any kind. Finished, she ran the opposite direction of the exit they had taken Erland through knowing any minute the suspicion of the gunshots would be answered by the shock and screaming horror of the dead bodies and the blood seeping from them.

The blonde Homeland Agent had learned to drive a stick senior year in high school but the GTO was *not* her uncles' Volkswagen Golf. She had never felt not only the power of the V-Eight engine guzzling gas as she crushed the pedal but the addictive rush of driving dangerously fast.

Pushing the green muscle car east at nearly eight o'clock, the streets were all but vacant and would only become increasingly so as the bitter blackness of night blended into the void of early morning. Red lights, where she encountered them, were mere afterthoughts and not a block from Sugar Hill Elementary her cell phone buzzed her heart. The GTO had cut travel time in half, at least.

"Sierra?" Tabitha pinched the phone in her left shoulder and ear as she slowed for a right corner and downshifted.

"Tabitha, Jupiter's men have got Erland." Tabitha didn't say anything and slowed even more as Broad Street approached, the school visible. "I got two of them and have their phones. I got the leader, too."

The GTO stopped at the intersection on the southwest corner of the Sugar Hill campus.

"Where are they taking him?"

"I don't know yet. I'm on the north side of the school, administration building. Where are you?"

"Southwest, the intersection of Broad Street and..."

"Do you see them?"

Tabitha squinted.

"No, they're on you're side. They must be."

"Hang tight." Marland ended the call and left Tabitha to the grumbling GTO and the pounding of her heart.

Sierra Marland took cover behind the blue and orange plastic support beams of the jungle gym and the smell of bark was fresh against the twisting fingers of cold night air. She was free from the danger of the lights that ran around the property and hugged the essential buildings but the harder she looked for them the more frustrated she became. Perhaps the soundproofing of the auditorium prevented the innocents from hearing any of the gunshots, and being indoors the shots would've been distilled somewhat by the density of the concrete, but she was still surprised at the silence of the campus. It was as if nothing had happened.

But so much *had* happened, so much zipped through the neural pathways in her brain, making calculations and assumptions about the new information she had received and she wanted to leave it all on the jungle gym lest it spark the emotional turmoil mulching her soul and catch fire, burning her up to a place where she was no good; not for Erland, not for Maggie, not for the millions of Americans that depended on her even if they didn't know it.

Seeing nothing in the yard Sierra heard sirens and flit across the beauty bark and along a line of hawthorns to the wall of the administration building. The sirens were a ways off but in the stillness of the night the sound carried and it bounced along the cold angles of the atmosphere from some distance. As she strained her ears to listen there was a cracking noise nearby.

Instantaneously her entire body tingled with heightened awareness and she pressed herself against the frigid solidity of the building as if to make herself blend into it and its darkness.

Outside the property gate and cut by the geometry of the chain link fence, scruffy bushes and the sickly shapes of late fall trees were the bodies of three men walking across the street, having come from a dry leaf covered sidewalk.

Marland sighed something of relief and braced

herself for the next phase of the gamble. Momentum was rolling like a roulette wheel and she had placed her chips on the only number she could afford to.

"Tabitha." Marland whispered.

"Yeah?"

"They're getting into a black van. I think it's a Mercedes. I can't see the license plate. Northeast side."

The GTO roared to life for a few seconds over the phone and bubbled back down to an idle.

"Got 'em. Two vans...There's a driver in each. I can't follow both of them."

Anxiety welled within Sierra. The leader of the team had never planned on leaving. Jupiter had something else in mind with the Semtex-wired auditorium. At least she had the detonator, being the cell phone, or so she logically assumed.

"Hold on..." Sierra said, and reached for both of the phones. She checked the phonebook of each and made an educated guess on what number to call based on the ID they were logged under.

The smart phone in her hand rang as she held the burn phone with Tabitha on the other end in the opposite hand.

"Yeah?" It was a male voice, but which van?

"Erland..." Sierra attempted a male voice and even though she'd been taking acting lessons for years it never sounded good enough to her.

"Yeah, we're pulling out now. Meet you at Keller's."

The call ended and Sierra hid her shock as both vans fired to life and began to move in unison.

"Sierra, which one?"

"Keller's?" She said, exasperated. "Where's Keller's?"

"Is that a person's house?" Tabitha smooched the vinyl seat as she adjusted her position, ready like a racehorse to run.

"I don't know dammit, is it a business? Think!"

"Keller's..." Then Tabitha swore and the GTO powered up. "Keller's Ironworks, it's in South Crescent. The building was condemned last year."

"Which way are they headed?" Sierra began to run to the parking lot and the gate that lead to the freedom of the street and across from it, her only chance at pursuit.

"Still west." Tabitha shifted. "I bet they'll split at the intersection."

"You take the one that's going south to Keller's."

"What about you?"

"I'll follow the other one. I'll come once they take Erland in there."

"Talk to me, Sierra..." Tabitha urged as she came to a corner. "What's going on?"

"...Jupiter will be there." Sierra reached Erland's Toyota and broke the window with the butt of her pistol.

"How do you know?"

"Because I couldn't hide my secret player for ever, T. Jupiter will know I've confided in him and he's desperate. He'll hurt him to get to me."

"But does he know where it is?" Tabitha shifted as Marland attempted to hot-wire the Toyota. "I mean, you're the only one who does."

"Not exactly. I made him think I hid it at the Precinct."

"Did you?"

"No."

"So where is it?"

Erland's Toyota fired with a congested clicking and revved slowly in the cold.

"Call me when the van gets to Keller's

Ironworks and hang back, okay."

Tabitha nodded and threw the phone on the passenger seat, her face set against the challenge of holding back without letting go. The lack of automotive traffic would make it a dangerous duel of timing and assumption. And even if she could miraculously tail the black van in the only cherry Verdoro Green Nineteen and Seventy Pontiac GTO in all of Crescent without the black van's knowledge, she would then have to visually confirm Erland's physical presence in a part of town that was a confusing maze of industrial buildings and small business shanties, teeming with looters, loiters, losers and a complete absence of sufficient lighting. She hoped Marland had it easier and more than that, hoped Marland knew what the hell she was doing, because the whole thing was about two inches from falling apart and burning up like the giant matchbox of Fircrest Mansion.

The Gulfstream V touched down at Bay County Airport after maddening delays from the tower. Even though Mr. Brown had top clearance and was on a laser guided mission from the President of the United States, Bay County had been so affected by the disaster of Crescent as it was no more than twenty miles away from the last clutches of South's property line, the two runways were like anthills.

Mr. Brown was greeted on the tarmac by a cadre of cars, Agents and Operatives, and it was a veritable who's who of the local and regional powers. There was no initial handshaking. Mr. Brown pressed his hands together in a steeple.

"Mr. Brown," A pair of black men in their forties nodded. They both wore black suits and Mr. Brown was astute enough to notice the differences between them but there weren't many. Their names were Siller and Harrington. Theirs was a black Lincoln and they were FBI. To their left was a blonde-haired blue-eyed man who stood out from the rest in a tan suit and a blue shirt, no tie. He leaned on a white Mercury and smoked a nasty smelling Camel non-filter with black gloves. His name was Loomis and he said nothing. Didn't need to. He was CIA. The State Department had sent two women named Justine and Potter who were in competing-colored pantsuits and one had her hair in a bun and the other's fell to her shoulders. They made a point of shaking hands with Mr. Brown because they were low on the totem pole. Last was the Chief of Police and he had three Officers with him and they were all burly and thick in the tactical jumpsuits.

Mr. Brown stood before them with his assistant, a short man with a tablet whose name was Paul Chang as the Gulfstream V began to taxi. Mr. Brown made a quick speech about what needed to be done and how the President had given him the full power of the Executive Branch concerning the operation and as a lawyer he was well aware of the legal boundaries.

The target was Sierra Marland and all of her known aliases. She was in possession of extremely sensitive classified information and was no longer able, considering the circumstances, to perform the duties demanded of her and was to be apprehended by any means necessary *with* the modified memory card known as CONSTANT.

Mr. Brown said a few more things concerning the urgency of the operation and then took a step aside as Paul Chang gave the technical merits of Homeland's position to which Chief of Police Nolan was thoroughly knowledgeable and was able to then further inform the coalition team on the Crescent situation.

The blonde Loomis approached Mr. Brown with

a strut that he'd seen before and knew where it came from. The fact that the CIA had sent Loomis was evidence enough of their stance on the giant crater the operation to catch Jupiter had become.

"You're wrong." The man said in a west Texas drawl, taking a long drag on the cigarette. After so many years of sitting in rooms thick with its stale fumes Mr. Brown detested the smell. Thank God it was illegal to smoke in public buildings.

"Is that the Director's opinion, or yours?" The alert green eyes behind the glasses studied the devil-may-care attitude of the man before him. Even though Mr. Brown was on a mission from the President to prevent any more damage in Crescent, the forefront of which was to subdue Sierra Marland, the obvious pecking order in the different agencies was beginning to manifest. Loomis, as it was, was not *in* the struggle, but rather, *outside* of it. He wasn't present on account of *having* to be but *wanting* to be. The FBI, however, was in a saber-rattling duel with Homeland Security to see who did a better job protecting the country so that when budget time came, Homeland wasn't stealing anymore of what use to be all theirs. The State Department was in appearance more for legal support and because the Marland's used to be up in the rafters of the business there.

"I'm not going to answer that unless you tell me why you've rustled up a posse to go after the Cowgirl and not the Indian?"

"Jupiter is not the priority here."

"Why the hell not?" Loomis' accent was nearly sweet in all that it said and could in no way appear insubordinate.

"Because Jupiter doesn't have CONSTANT."

Loomis nodded and tipped his head up to release the smoke. He stood closer to Mr. Brown.

"You know, those two FBI clones are lickin' to make a good impression by cleaning up the mess Homeland's in...zeal and wisdom aren't too common together. I wouldn't trust them to handle with care..."

"So what's your angle?"

Loomis waved a hand and a squiggly trail of smoke followed like a magic wand. Loomis had a captivating subtlety and charm and was capable of more tricks than a sage in Pharaoh's court.

"Ah ah, I ain't finished yet. Both them two power tigers from State over there got passed for transfer and promotion by the Marland sisters for one of them coveted SAB positions, and you, my friend," The hand pointed two strong fingers. "Have been an enemy of the Special Assignment Branch of Homeland since the President created it for his top secret domestic dirty work."

Mr. Brown stepped aside and Loomis with him.

"All of that may be true, but it doesn't change who's died and who's about to. If we don't stop Marland from whatever she's got planned the damage will get worse and worse and worse and we can't afford that. So while you *may* and are *entitled* to think we've all got an axe to grind, we're just doing our job as Marland thought she was doing hers."

"I'm not questioning your orders, I'm questioning *the* orders."

Mr. Brown squinted as if he was a seven year old hearing his first curse word.

"You can't."

"I don't blame the President for getting queasy when one of the biggest cities in the country starts gettin' all chewed up because of public enemy numero uno but if she's that damn close I'd be throwing everything I had out there to help her get the guy. For cryin' out loud Brown, that Boston Marathon bomber shut the whole city down and it took every cop they had beatin' the pavement to wrastle a kid and we ain't dealin' with no kid. If you wanna get real, it was a flaw to *expect* the impossible from them by making the operation so damn small."

"But our network is *severely* compromised." Mr. Brown leaned in despite the cigarette smoke and spoke in a strained whisper. "We have no idea who is in Jupiter's pocket. The President is sitting in the Oval Office right now scared to even speak of the operation to his Cabinet because he doesn't know who Jupiter has a hold on."

"All the more reason you should let it play out. If she got that close she'll do it again. I know them Marlands, they'd take on a Diamondback with a pair of children's scissors if they had to. While this destruction of Crescent is painful, the black hats've been exposing themselves left and right, and the more time goes by, the more weasels will make a run for it."

"I can't give her any more time. Besides, she called a Zeta."

"Is that something like an op kill order? Walk away till Daddy comes to take you home?"

"Yes..." Mr. Brown agreed hesitantly. The Zeta code was far more technical than that. "Whatever she's doing now she's doing as a civilian. Bartleson gave her a heads up and she's gone night wolf on us, that's why we've got the Police involved."

"Does she have any help?"

"You know an Agent named Tabitha Grey?"

"No." Loomis dropped the cigarette and ground it with the heel of his python skin boots. "Should I?"

"We are operating under the assumption she is working with Marland despite the Zeta code. She had also enlisted the help of a CPD Homicide Detective to figure out exactly who killed Magnolia and pursue

Jupiter from that angle, a man named Michael Erland."

"Him I know. In name anyway. The Granderson Trial was national news. He was the guy that finally figured it out and put that whack job behind bars, right?"

"Yes. He's under an OIS investigation now and more than likely has nothing to do with Marland. Without his pursuit of one of our...traitors, we wouldn't have Fircrest's security cameras. One of our men is working on them as we speak."

"Good timing." Loomis chuckled and began to play with his brushed nickel zippo in an unconscious way as one gloved hand hung on his belt, the other was at his side. "The place'll never be the same."

That was putting it mildly. The eerie glow of the flames could be seen from miles away although Crescent's tall buildings prevented many on the street from seeing it, the knowledge of the fire was spreading as most of Crescent's population was indoors, glued to the news and a previously frozen meal.

"I have my orders, Loomis." Mr. Brown said as if to bow out of the conversation.

"Hold up." The Texan held out one of his large, mesmerizing hands. "I'd just like you to know that I won't be interfering with what you have to do in any way. The CIA is officially out of this one."

Mr. Brown nodded and his hands steepled. The Texan patted him on the back with a smooth and slick gesture.

Loomis watched him walk back to the group of hunters with a silent snigger, removing the glove as the distance between them grew. Loomis pulled out his cell phone and made a call, confirming the initiation of the CIA operation named *MERCHANT*.

TWENTY-EIGHT

The white Suburban pulled parallel to Jessica Birchall's Subaru. She stood at the driver door. The window of the Suburban was down and Kelly Barnett gave her a wave.

"Good luck, okay?" She said without clarity, considering Tabitha's speedy departure with assault gear.

"Good luck to you guys." Birchall waved and bent down to enter the car. She left for the Channel Two building and Kelly drove slowly toward the Crescent Modern Journal.

"What are you thinking?" She asked Reston as his eyes were on the road and the city as it fell to an eerie darkness.

"About all of it...the fire, how I was just there..."

"What about...what might happen to us?"

Darren's head lolled over. It would take him days, maybe even weeks considering the condition of his body to come to full recovery.

"What do you mean?"

"This guy, Jupiter, whatever his real name is, he's done all of this, hasn't he? And now *we're* targeting *him*. Marland said to attack his privacy was as personal as we could get. She also said we'd be protected...and the Agent that was doing that took your car because Marland's in trouble. So who's protecting *us* if they can't protect *themselves?*"

"Spit it out." Darren said, sitting up in the seat.

"I'm scared, Darren, I don't want to die. I want to help you and do what's right but...I'm just scared, you know?"

Darren put his hand on her shoulder and shook his head.

"I understand completely...but the guy that's afraid of death and dying and his own shadow got burned up in the Mansion. I feel like I *owe* it to her."

"But how? You don't owe her anything!" Kelly's eyebrows were twisted.

"She *exonerated* me."

"So she could *use* you *and* me."

"No Kelly."

"And that poor Detective, did you see the way he looked at her? He would follow her into a live volcano if she said so."

Darren closed his mouth and turned his head back to the window. The division and resistance he felt was tangible, like a wall of glass had risen up through the center console, in between the cup holders. Though Kelly's voice of reason and argument had a point it just wasn't what Darren felt inside, and since waking up bound and gagged that's all he had to go by, and it had not only proved to have saved his life but in some strange way prevented an intelligence community disaster, the bonus of which being new life to a relationship he had been unaware had grown stagnant.

"I don't trust her." Kelly said, flatly, her face a mirror of her voice.

"I do."

"I wanna go to the police, Darren. Agent Grey was supposed to be protecting us and she took your car."

"I gave it to her."

"And we're driving a Homeland Security vehicle...I mean, I just want to make it stop."

"Kelly," Darren leaned over the console and that imaginary wall of glass. "We can't do that. *You* flooded social media with the truth about who was behind the attacks, *you* posted the picture of Jupiter. Birchall's going on the air, *showing her face on TV*, I've written an article that will be printed in God knows how many newspapers; we've *all* done it *together*. If you were worried you should've said something."

"But Agent Grey was supposed be guarding us until it was over."

"It won't *be* over, Kelly, it's a war that'll take years and years. Didn't you listen to what they said? This Jupiter guy's got people everywhere."

"Aren't you afraid one of them will take us out?" Kelly nearly shouted, stopping the car in the middle of the empty street. Darren blinked at her face, stretched and strained, the ringer of following his spiral taking its toll. Perhaps the specter of danger, backed by every criminal act from kidnapping to murder to arson had thrown her over the edge. The woman Darren beheld before him was *not* the one he had embraced in the driveway of his home. She was a cracked shell of that confident strength, all that he had needed to face life in the wake of circumstance.

He wanted to reach out to her and catch her, support her in her struggle as she had for him but the fundamental disagreement sat between them like a border crossing. How could he say it was going to be okay if he didn't know it wasn't? Had he selfishly jeopardized her safety by his own newfound fearlessness?

"Say something!" Kelly was exasperated, the snowball of fear rolling unhinged inside of her.

Reston did not.

Kelly turned to the road and blinked but couldn't stop the tears of terrorism. She scratched at her eyes with her sleeve and began to drive.

"I'm going to the Police."

Darren bit his lip. The damage had been done from Kelly's part. She had already put it out there, the kindling and the accelerant to the fire in advance from Birchall's thick and slow burning televised news story and his print story which was more wood in reserve to sustain the fire as it grew and demanded more. He wanted to support Kelly and stand by her but he simply couldn't agree, at least not until the fullness of Marland's plan had been executed. It was actually *more* dangerous to back out at this point.

The struggle ate at the edge of Darren's mind as Kelly turned the car around. He couldn't. He just couldn't. Whatever warmth and happiness he had felt in Kelly's arms that afternoon paled in comparison with the thought of being a part of eliminating the most treacherous terrorist in the United States. The more Marland explained the more it made sense. His head was always in the news and news media, he was well aware of the scandal and destruction caused by the great unknown that now had a face.

But was Marland just spinning it her way? Was she as Kelly said, just using them all for her own gain? After all, the higher ups were coming to shut her down, weren't they? What had *she* done?

Reston could sit in the passenger seat and reason back and forth till Election Day, weighing each side in his damaged mind, being pulled ever closer to someone else's conclusion in the drunken stupor of rationale and explanation.

Or he could act, throwing off the gag and the zip tie and run for his life.

"Stop the car."

"What?" Kelly said, the exasperation still tainting her features.

"Stop the car, Kelly, let me out."

"What, why?"

"I'm not going to the cops. I'm going to CMJ."

"Darren..."

"Kelly," He looked her in the eyes. "I have to do this."

The car stopped.

"But Darren, I need you."

Reston held his ground with great difficulty. Was he saying he didn't need her by his disagreement? Was he abandoning her by taking the opposite path?

"And I need to do my part."

Kelly's lip trembled underneath reddened eyes. "No Darren..."

The journalist released his seatbelt and pressed his body into the door. A rush of cold air crept through the Suburban and bit Kelly's ears and nose.

Reston shut the door and turned his back on the white vehicle in a lonely march for the CMJ. When the rev of the motor powered through the emptiness of the street several seconds later it was not in an effort to follow him.

Darren threw a glance over his shoulder and blew in his hands before stuffing them in his pants pocket. If Kelly didn't understand then they had no business being together. For some reason, Darren's fractured mind drifted to Tanya, and the quiet moment they had together brought him some comfort as seemingly all of Crescent was his. Birchall had related the details of the abduction to him and Marland confirmed. Tanya Wilson was in the hands of Jupiter. While it angered him that some brute had ripped her from her home in broad daylight he wasn't surprised and was sure that those on the case were doing their very best to find her and maybe Marland would be able to find her before then. He wondered about Tanya and knew the only way to help was to do *his* part, even if it was a sure road to jeopardy and danger, what was there to lose? What else was there?

     Sierra Marland sat for a moment at an intersection as the van pulled away a block ahead of her and turned right. She had followed the van through the scraggly traffic of North and the business district and the randomness of small buildings and businesses of South were beginning to replace the swell of the skyscrapers.

     The slain leader's cellphone buzzed on the seat next to her and she took a breath to try and smooth out the stiffness that was attacking her throat before applying the male voice once again.

     "Yes?"

     "I'm going to Keller's. Blow the charges the moment the cops show up."

     Sierra juggled it in her mind before she realized who was speaking. It was Jupiter. It had to be. The voice had called the leader's phone, hadn't he? And the calmness and stillness of the diction could only belong to a man who had everything planned out to the detail only to have it ruined and was fighting with all he had to keep control. And the accent of the voice was...nonexistent, which made it unreasonably unique, as if every letter was carefully thought out to produce perfect English pronunciation.

     "Yes."

     "Has Marland cracked yet?"

     "...No."

     "Call me when she does."

     "Yes."

     Then the call ended as abruptly as it had begun.

Sierra's pulse was elevated and her body flushed with heat at what could've been.

The phone fell as her arm went limp on the seat and she sat at the intersection with one hand on the wheel, deep in thought. So Erland was going to Keller's. Jupiter was going to Keller's. She was tailing a van with no reason why. But the van had to hold some sinister purpose behind the glossy black exterior. Why else was it on the road? Certainly not for a diversion, because nothing in Jupiter's voice gave away the notion of being tailed, infiltrated, or potentially destroyed. For all intents and purposes his operation was still running smoothly. In his mind he had her at the hands of one of his brutes and a bomb at Sugar Hill and he was going to interrogate Erland himself or at least be present when he was while she was undergoing a frame up for killing Wolcek. So why the second van?

Sierra wasn't going to take any chances. Whatever Jupiter had in store with the second van, she couldn't risk ruining all she had gambled for.

The Toyota pulled a hard left from the intersection.

South Crescent's warehouse district was something to forget. Shells of old businesses that had run their course were always being jumpstarted again by a new endeavor that didn't even get the time to change the old name before falling out of function themselves. Keller's Ironworks was one of those buildings and it was four thousand square feet if it was six and the rusted and patina-toned exterior of the building hearkened back to a time when rails ruled the country and real men wore grease stained overalls and rolled their own cigarettes. Tabitha Grey slowed the GTO to a halt as the black Mercedes van stopped not two inches from one of the many entrance doors and

Pitts was as quick as he was cautious, opening the back to wrangle the floppy and STRIC-R loaded Detective from the van.

"Sierra." Tabitha whispered, though she was safely in the dark across the street near the high fences of a small junkyard stacked with totaled taxicabs. "They're taking Erland inside Keller's Ironworks."

"Okay..." Sierra responded with her attention elsewhere not five miles away. "Wait for Jupiter."

"You think he's going to show?"

"I know it...just hold on. I'll be there soon."

Pitts had no trouble carrying the hundred and sixty pound man up the stairs and to the catwalk that skirted around the edge of the building and overlooked what would have been the production area through the door dividing the production area from the smelter and the blast furnace.

His steps made hollow clangs and it didn't matter. No one was in the building that shouldn't have been. Pitts walked confidently toward the downward-pointing flashlight beam of the man from Team Europa guarding the stairs that descended to the guts of the blast furnace.

Once free from the stairs, Pitts dropped the Detective on the floor and Tanya Wilson's head lolled over to see the newest victim.

The man had been laid next to Ratner's bloody corpse and she studied the men as five more flashlights came on and hushed voices began to work with a small pouch and a syringe.

One of the men searched the good-looking gray haired man loosely and removed all of his things and put them on an overturned fifty-five gallon drum. A comment was made about a pocketknife. There was the clicking of a flip phone and the clinking of a heavy chain. Tanya absorbed the images and sounds as fast as possible, as fast as they came in slices and streaks, and after two minutes the man was hung up like Jesus Christ, arms out, feet three inches off the ground.

There was silence and one of the thugs injected the man in the neck and he awoke some four seconds later with a numb and expressionless noise, as if he was having his head compressed by some kind of merciless mechanical device.

"You'll get over it in a few minutes." A calm male voice said through the darkness. Tanya watched the man's face as five flashlights were on him. He blinked and twisted his head side to side to escape the piercing LED beams but could not. They burned his eyes like mirrors of the sun. The injection must've been some kind of intravenous reversal agent. As a nurse, Tanya had prepared her share of them for opioid overdose.

"How much?" The calm voice asked someone near him.

"One hundred cc's."

"Good, good..."

There was a rustle of cloth and the voice was handed a flashlight. The beam studied every square inch of the Detective.

"He didn't have it." A man from behind said.

"Strip him." The calm voice ordered and stepped back.

Tanya watched as the droopy frame was lowered from the chains and removed every article of clothing on his body.

The Toyota pulled directly behind the GTO and Sierra left the Camry and slid in the passenger seat of the Pontiac. Tabitha had already applied the body armor and was sitting with the H&K MP5 vertically between

her legs. She had the Forty-caliber pistol in her back
holster as well.

"See that maroon Lincoln by the van?" She
pointed. Sierra did. It was an eighties or nineties model,
no doubt stolen from somewhere near the Waterfront in
one of those pay for a day lots.

"Is that Jupiter?"

"Yes. He went in about five or six minutes ago.
He wasn't wearing white, but, he was a match from this
far away."

Sierra took a deep sigh and Tabitha studied her
face, then put a hand on her shoulder.

"It's okay. It won't be like PierHouse."

"To think this was all my doing..." She said in
the darkness.

"You only did what you had to."

"I risked an innocent life to play the game, T. If
this doesn't work out I'll never forgive myself."

Tabitha's American symmetry carried a faint
smile.

"I can see you care about him, Sierra. But if *you*
don't have faith *we'll* all die."

Sierra nodded and shook Tabitha's hand. There
was a great deal of firepower between them. But more
than that, they held the shock of the unexpected in their
grasp-even though they were parachuting into an unlit
warehouse of the unknown. PierHouse had been a
disaster for that very reason, and Jupiter hadn't been
expecting an attack then. But he also hadn't been
hounded and chased into a corner and forced to
improvise and conduct the savage business that
propelled him in secret. It was a dangerous place for an
enemy but a place, nonetheless, that left blind spots,
small though they were.

"The leader of the team knew about Mr.
Brown..." Marland said.

"Because he's dirty or because they've hacked the White House?"

"I can't say. I just know that our window shrinks every time we look out of it." Sierra flicked the safety from both guns, the H&K and the stolen SIG, and eyed her partner with due vigilance. "Alright then, T. See you on the other side."

All of his clothes removed, Erland shivered on the cold slab of a floor, being pulled from the deep recesses of STRIC-R unconsciousness to a horribly dark and painful reality. He tried to distinguish what voice belonged to what blur but the haze and the lack of light, save the laser-like stabs of LED flashlights that skipped across his face ever so often made it impossible.

"Loosen him up." The calm voice rang in his ears.

Two shapes approached Erland and rammed their feet against his ribs. The Detective curled in a ball to protect himself but the two men didn't care. Their heavily booted feet kicked and hacked at whatever was flesh, and in the syrupy clouds of the STRIC-R narcotic, he couldn't feel the pain as much as he would've without it, but his poisoned mind was running in exaggerations of a fear he didn't want to accept. Each blow was amplified by the thought of what was next and the inability to stop it was colliding with the anxiety of what had gone wrong.

Sierra had abandoned him. The specter of it was the cause for the chemical reaction in his soul. It was as if she had baited him and repeatedly tested him, all for this.

What had she done?

"Hold him down." A rough New England voice growled.

Two hands took his wrists and his feet and though he twisted and curled to fight it they stretched him out on the cold floor.

The feet went to work again, pummeling his belly, his kidneys, and his liver.

"When we're done," The New England voice sniggered through the blows. "You'll forget how bad you felt after the Hugo Marquez fight."

The beating was two and a half minutes if it was an hour. Even after their assault had finished, Erland still wriggled and reeled as if he was being attacked.

"String him up." The calm voice called out. Tanya Wilson watched in horror as the naked man slid across the floor to the chains, where it didn't take much to hoist him up to the crucified position once more.

"It's not here." A voice said from the same area as the calm one.

"Check his shoes." The equable tone answered back. "Take them apart if you have to. If he has a watch, rip that apart. Check the phone."

Then one of the flashlights stayed trained on Erland's face as the New England voice came within striking distance. There was a nod, Tanya saw it from the figure that stood next to the two men taking apart the shoes, the phone and the old Seiko.

"Where is it?" New England said. He grabbed Erland's face by the chin and shook it. "Where is CONSTANT?"

The man's lack of patience was apparent. He smacked the Detective before he could even respond from the mental delay of the narcotic.

Erland's face nearly spun off of its neck and the hand grabbed his chin and lined him up for three more punches before his head hung feebly and his chest heaved from the exertion of staying alive. The drug was compressing everything and slowing it down, making it hard to think and even harder to move, and even though it was suppressing the pain Erland had never felt so awful in his life. His guts were jello in some suspension between liquid and solid and his head was like a juicy piece of fruit being pressed between someone's hands and the fear of when it was going to explode was climbing up his spine vertebrae by vertebrae.

There was no hope. Sierra was *not* coming. Despite all he had in his heart toward her, this was the end of the game. His life had served its purpose on the squares of black and white and a more powerful piece was coming to knock him off his place to roll helplessly to the side with all the other victims.

Blood trickled from the cut above his right eye and fell down his chin to the floor in steady drips and drops.

"Didn't take you long to bleed, did it?" New England goaded, pacing like a caged tiger before him, waiting for his next assault to be Okayed. Tanya's eyes drifted in between the thick man who had hit the man in chains and the man near the overturned barrel. In the stabs and flashes of light she thought she could see him playing with a small pocketknife in contemplation.

The man glanced up from the knife and nodded again. Tanya only caught half of a face and an eye as black as the void that filled the dead warehouse.

Erland grunted and let out a low moan as the heavy fist connected with the cut over his eye. The swelling was unstoppable and the punishment would only increase the size of the cut with each bludgeoning strike.

"Where is CONSTANT?" The man shouted not an inch from his ear.

"I don't have it!" Erland nearly cried from the bottom of his naked toes as the man responded by mashing his fist against the cut. Blood flicked across

the ground and the man pulled the chin back to center
the Detective's head for another belt.

"Hold up."

Tanya turned and squinted as two of the
flashlights gave perfect illumination to the object in
question but a pair of bodies blocked her view of what
it was.

"Is that it?"

"It must be."

"We'll have to check. How can we check? The
yacht's gone."

"The helicopter will be here any minute."

"What about the school?"

"I don't know...Marland won't break." Then the
calm voice chuckled. "She must've thought that she
was hiding it from me..."

"More?" New England asked.

"No." Jupiter shook his head. "He didn't know.
She hid it...she used him."

The man that owned the voice of control
approached the battered Detective.

"Do you know what CONSTANT is?"

The man in chains mumbled something
incoherent as his head rolled from side to side. Even
Tanya strained against her fetters to hear.

"Do you know what CONSTANT is?" Jupiter
repeated as he stepped closer.

Erland raised his head and squinted through the
one, good eye.

"Do I know...what...what...is..."

"CONSTANT. It's an acronym. It's Homeland,
did they tell you what it was when they asked for your
help?"

Erland sighed in an effort to catch his breath.
The man before him was the same man as was in the
pixilated frame from Morell's helmet camera. He had

been studying pixilated faces for years and knew what to look for. Even with one eye swollen and the other cutting in and out of narcotic blurring, the light was good enough to see the face of the one who called himself Jupiter.

Why did he want to know? To spare the Detective? To find out how much CPD knew? What way did he gamble? And where was Marland for advice on speculative gambling, seeing as she knew how to wrap people's lives in those slender and womanly hands of hers and shake them all up and send them bouncing along the green felt war zone.

If he said yes, he could stretch it out and spook Jupiter about the merchandise, how hot it was, how it was diseased with some super worm and there was tracking material in it and legions of SWAT troopers were on their way to get him right now but then his reward would be a bullet in the head. So he said no.

"No...no..."

Erland gave himself to the lie, as if he was just giving up on the fight, and on life. His body had been gambled with and the numbers on the dice just weren't correct and he'd lost.

"Give me a gun." Jupiter said, flatly, as if asking for a straw at a drive-thru.

There was compliance and Erland could hear the cocking of it.

"I...don't..."

Jupiter moved to Tanya Wilson. All of a sudden lights came to Erland and Wilson, both of them squinting away the horrible blindness while attempting to look their fate in the eye.

The New England voice grabbed Erland by the chin and twisted his head to see Tanya Wilson, hooked up to a poorly painted metal pole, arms pulled above her head and locked with handcuffs. Her legs were

stuffed underneath her and her face was glazed with
turmoil and sweat.

"Do you know what CONSTANT is?" Jupiter
asked.

Erland shook his head and the barrel of the gun
sunk till it met the skin of Tanya's forehead.

"If you lie to me one more time her blood is on
your hands."

Erland's heart began to beat faster and his chest
hurt with a different pain than any of the other stings
and aches in his body. It was a bluff, wasn't it? How
could Jupiter know, how could he know one way or the
other? What was truth or the lie in the face of such
coercion and brutality?

Jupiter fired a shot and Erland flinched. The
sound of screaming pierced the dead blackness. The
shell pinged and rattled on the cold, hard floor.

"Just a few inches," Jupiter said. "Her blood is
on your hands."

He strained to see the woman's face as her chest
heaved from the scare.

A shot punched through the void of the building
and it wasn't from Jupiter's gun. The man with the
rough New England voice grunted as a bullet sliced into
his stomach. He fell against Erland and clutched at him,
sliding away to the space of darkness as the chaos and
cacophony of the blind shoot out captured Keller's
Ironworks with a startling fury.

Erland fell to the hard slab floor, the arms
holding the chains no longer able as they went for their
guns and all of the LED flashlights took off, bouncing
every which direction as the holders of them ran for
cover. A submachine gun spit nine-millimeter bullets to
the left in controlled bursts. Erland scraped for distance
and pulled himself across the smooth floor in a feeble
slide for Tanya. One of the flashlights had been

dropped and rolled to rest at her feet. Not a foot away, sparks flying from crates and pipes taking fire and return fire, the bloody hand of the New England voice latched on to Erland's ankle.

The Detective turned and the edge of the powerful beam caught the man's face. With the leverage he had gained from Erland's ankle, the man reached for more, for Erland's arm or his face, for the flashlight.

The Detective pulled his foot back and let it loose. It connected with the man's face but didn't slow him down. Erland kicked again and hit the man's neck. Erland kicked and kicked and slid forward until the hand and the face that it belonged to had fallen back to the recesses of black.

Erland made it to the woman in bondage and could do nothing about it. His heart was beating out of his chest and his lungs were burning with a fire he'd never felt before. Whatever they'd done to him, it held a dreaded permanency to it and the Detective reached for the woman and his head fell to the cold floor in silence as the zips and bings of ricochets bounced overhead.

Careful not to hit anyone else, Sierra and Tabitha ran in a half crouch back to the safety of the door as it was guarded by a large hopper of steel pipes. Bullets cracked and bit into the walls until someone yelled for a cease-fire and the sound of metal stairs banging and clanging with heavy steps filled the dormant forge. Tabitha checked around the backside of the hopper.

"Do you see anything?" Sierra nearly whispered.

"There's a catwalk." Tabitha spotted a train of lights. "They're leaving."

"I saw Erland. I have to get him. Go to the car."

Tabitha's head whipped around to plead with Sierra but she was gone. They had to work together. They were worthless alone.

Tabitha swore and ran to the door, hitting it hard and sweeping the gun around her sightline as the frigid night air greeted her with silence and emptiness. The nearest operating businesses were miles away but the sirens would be coming soon, no doubt about it. Tabitha pressed to the edge of the warehouse and she stood, eyes scanning, in the generous space of pavement that ran a long lane along Keller's and separated it from the neighboring building. Something caught her eye in the peering and she kneeled at the corner of the warehouse for protection.

There was a covered sky bridge that stretched from Keller's to a lower, flat-topped building some eight hundred yards away.

Tabitha swore again and launched herself into a flat out sprint, throwing the MP5 at her back and tightening the tactical sling to keep the gun from bouncing as the cold air stung her eyes.

TWENTY-NINE

Pressing along the lumps and blocks of darkness, Sierra reached the place she had taken the first shot from. Her heart fell in her chest as she spotted Detective First Grade Michael Erland face down on the cold floor in the static wash of the dropped flashlight. Next to him and helplessly cuffed to a metal pole was the abducted Tanya Wilson. She was alive. But what of Erland?

Sierra planted her hand and vaulted over the wall of crates she had used for cover and pressed through the darkness toward the light.

Her foot caught on something and she fell, spilling into the darkness and losing the SIG. It clattered along the floor and slid to the emptiness of nowhere and she pressed herself up and pulled the H&K from her back and rushed to the metal pole.

Training the gun at four different angles she saw nothing. Heard nothing. *Felt* nothing. Sierra pushed the frantic air out of her lungs and shot a single round into the cuffs, beginning the freedom of Tanya Wilson.

She fell sideways, away from Erland in a whimper and Sierra reached for the flashlight, directing it back to where she had came and what had tripped her up.

The light danced and caught the body of a muscular man next to a thick cord of heavy lifting chains. He was dead. Sierra had shot him in the stomach. His face, too, showed signs of beating. The light danced again and caught the body of Jared Ratner, face up, his white shirt slashed up with knife wounds and Sierra's stomach nearly turned inside of her to see the pale and bloodied corpse, mutilated.

Finally she turned to Erland and squatted, holstering the H&K, flipping over his naked body and pressing her hand to his neck. His pulse was strong, but his eyes were closed.

A dam of segregated emotion ached to explode within her soul to see the man she loved so beaten and bruised, his right eye swollen and his face reddened and streaked with blood. She reached to him and wrapped her body around his, kneeling and pulling and squeezing him into the heat of her heart with a face of anguish, lifting him from the cruel ground to the place where he belonged.

She rubbed his back and a wheeze was pressed from his lungs. He mumbled something and she didn't stop. She counted the seconds, burning like a fuse and didn't want to let go. It had been hard enough, but he was alive dammit, he was alive.

She removed her coat and laid him on it and turned her attention toward Tanya Wilson. She had drug herself in an arm over arm belly crawl to an overturned fifty-five gallon drum and Sierra understood why. On it were all of Erland's personal effects and his clothes were carelessly cast aside. The flashlight addressed each item and found the torn up sneakers, the bottoms of them sliced clean off and pried apart.

So they had it. Jupiter had found CONSTANT. The real thing; the cache of secure and un-hacked information of these sovereign United States. Names, dates, places, pictures, passwords, codes, and numbers; enough data to last a lifetime.

Jupiter had it.

"Dress him." Sierra ordered as Tanya struggled for balance. Sierra grabbed her shoulders firmly and pulled her vertical. Sierra stuck the flashlight in the cavity of the nearby stair railing that lead to the catwalk as the former nurse limped and hobbled to follow the command.

Marland removed her phone to dial Tabitha and got nothing. She grit her teeth as she grabbed her jacket and pulled her gun from the holster.

Her footsteps were soft and light as she hit the corner of Keller's to see the covered walkway in full view. Tabitha hadn't felt the phone buzz in her jacket pocket through the body armor as she ran it wouldn't have mattered if she did. The five or so men that darted through the sky bridge were in her sights.

Tabitha pushed all of the air from the sprint away from her in a visible puff of white and debated letting the MP5 shatter every inch of glass in that sky bridge but the glass was inside of what looked to be a steel cage of fine mesh and was outlined by thick rebar-like supports. Her only chance was the flat-topped building of three stories. The sky bridge led to the second story of the building and that would give her enough time.

Marland returned to Erland and Tanya by the time Erland was dressed in all but his shoes. He moaned and his head lolled as the former nurse had him propped up against the steel pole as she had been.

"Let's get him outside," Marland ordered, pointing. "Straight that way. There's a green Toyota Camry behind a green Pontiac about four hundred yards from the door to your left, on the corner."

Tanya was weak and unsure and gave it

everything she had, with Erland slumped against her, his bare feet all but dragging on the floor. They followed Marland as she pressed the phone to her ear, begging Tabitha to answer.

Then she heard it, through the amplification of the abandoned structure. The gurgle and grind of helicopter blades cutting the cold night air.

Marland cursed and ran to the stairs and the catwalk. Tabitha had to let them go! Marland called again and there was no answer.

That was the gamble! It was paying off even in all of its losses and imperfections but it would be for naught if Tabitha gunned them down, she had to let them go! If she wasn't at the car as ordered the whole operation from the moment Magnolia was murdered and Sierra re-calculated and rethought the strategy would be as dust. The gamble banked on the fact that Sierra would be able to give CONSTANT to Jupiter in a way that made him feel he had earned it through great duress which would in turn would force him to sell it as quickly as possible-then she would get the whole rotten damn round table of them, whoever they were, get them all and lock them up where the sun couldn't shine. She had sacrificed her relationship with Erland to do it, and less importantly her entire career, and Jupiter held CONSTANT in his sick and demented hands on the way to the quickly approaching helicopter.

Sierra's feet pounded the metal stairs to reach the catwalk. This very moment was the break in the wave she had dreaded; in it there was no bluffing, no cheating, no hoping. Only the dice.

Just before hitting the ground floor wall of the flat-topped building, Tabitha Grey caught the slick blue-black reflections and the on off on blink of the marker lights not two hundred feet in the air. The sound of the chopper cutting the cold air was nearly deafening. There was no time for a sweep through the building, and Tabitha ran another twenty feet to the fire escape. It took a leap to reach the bottom rung, and once latched on, Tabitha was quick up the ladder to the steep steps. Three feet from the top, she slowed and dropped to a crouch, sliding the MP5 to assault position. Her eyes cast a quick glance back to the warehouse, and from her position, she could faintly see the car, or at least, where it was supposed to be. No bodies, no people. Not Erland or Sierra Marland. Tabitha wondered where the Agent was and couldn't spend any time on it. Jupiter was going to get away and she could feel the pull of Tallifer's blank eyes staring into the sky, not to mention the forensic scientists dead on the highway and the thousands upon thousands rich and poor whose lives had been altered by Jupiter and his oppressive siege of the American highway of information that was little more than ones and zeroes.

It stopped here, with her, in a position no one on her side had ever been before, and if she was to die doing it, then that was her legacy. Marland had made her choice in the action and she was nowhere in sight. It was Tabitha's turn to write history.

The helicopter was a Sikorsky S-76 with a capacity of fourteen and landed at the furthest end of the building. Four armed men stepped from it in half squats considering the near-takeoff speed of the blades. Tabitha squinted as a pack of men rushed from the sky bridge, having taken cover in anticipation of the landing. Jupiter was screened by two men as their guns were out, stabbing at different angles in the dark for potential threats. At the very twitch of her head, lowering into the corner of the fire escape, she thought she had been made, but the group continued on. Tabitha held her position till they were equidistant from the sky bridge and the chopper and raised the MP5, charging into the flat span of the building and squeezing the trigger in tight bursts.

Erland took the steps mechanically in his bare feet, dragging the left one more than the right. He must've been wrong but in the swirl of STRIC-R he thought he had seen Sierra, heard her and smelled her; touched her as she touched him. Was that what a near death experience did? Had the deepest desires of his human fabric made an angel of a woman who was as cunning as she was exquisite? Was the poison warping every painful thing he had gone through in the day and made her the antidote for it? Or was he just hallucinating, stuck in a web of the drug's tangled fingers as they dug into his brain. The woman next to him with his arm wrapped around her shoulder was not Sierra and he needed to stop and sort it all out as the Detective that he was but the tide had left the beach and the tsunami had taken its place. All he wanted was to fall down and come back to consciousness in his apartment with the smell of bacon frying and Sierra in her pajamas working the cast iron skillet but he knew that if he did fall down, he would never wake up. And Sierra, had he not pledged his feelings to her in the swirling cold of Sugar Hill Elementary? Maybe that's all they were, feelings; clouds without water and trees without roots-just a great big set up and he was the fool of the ages for falling for it. She was the last thing in his mind through the beating and the pain but now that he was free and had caught the faintest whisper of her presence she was all he could think about. The stairs hurt his knees and his feet felt the pricks of the cold metal slats and his mind told him she was at the end of the stairs, and every step was one step closer, and whatever she had planned had worked out, despite his ignorance of it when in fact, his ignorance had been part of the plan after all. If he could only see her, talk to her, ask her why and look into those jewel blue eyes himself and see the truth, then he would know.

The woman jumped at the staccato report of gunfire, and in the soupy buzz it had the short, repetitive bursts of a distant techno beat, low and jumbled together, and brighter, higher pitched pops flew over the top of it with some random repetition. The gunfire chewed at Erland's ears with a disembodied ache and stopped nearly as soon as it had begun.

It clicked in his mind the woman was Tanya Wilson and as each stair passed underfoot the sensory straightjacket of STRIC-R began to leave slowly, like a clogged sink. Something was chasing it away from his body and though he didn't understand it he was walking from a dream into a reality.

He would know once the path ended if Sierra Marland was a part of the dream or the reality and if he had been dreaming his way through reality all along.

The Agent threw herself onto the flat roof of the adjacent building from the sky bridge, her gun darting left and right and back to the blue black Sikorsky as it pressed itself into the air and slung shards of cold and whining air on to the roof until the darkened sea of the sky received its slick shape. The helicopter left silence and death in its wake, and Marland saw nothing moving as she scanned the flat surface and the horde of bodies left there.

Her stomach felt hollow and barren as the gun sight stopped to her far right, near the fire escape. Face down on the ground was Tabitha Grey.

Marland sprinted to her and holstered her H&K. The MP5 was in her right hand and Sierra rolled

Tabitha on her back. Her eyes flickered to life and rolled over to greet her friend and partner till the end.

"I...g-got 'em...all..." She struggled with a gurgle in her throat. Two slugs stuck out of the bulletproof vest and a third had a ripped horrible palm of torn tissue and blood in her neck near the shoulder. A forty-five caliber hollow point had carved its deadly path through her skin, flattening on impact, and Tabitha's healthy body was pumping type B positive all over the ground as her heart raced to live.

"Don't talk." Sierra's eyebrows and lips were bunched together in an effort not to soak the roof with her tears. She couldn't handle the death, the blood, the violence and the damage it did to her soul to see a friend die. The distant light in Tabitha's eyes bore a tunnel through Sierra's spine and her hands and feet felt weak and unstable. Sierra kneeled and wanted to clamp her hand on Tabitha's neck to stop the bleeding but the size of the wound was too great. Even if they called an ambulance her chances of making it were virtually nonexistent. She had only seconds to live.

Police sirens whooped and wired blocks away and Sierra snapped from the horrible numbness Tabitha's ebbing spirit had forced upon her and stood to face the cold. She threw her head to the sky bridge and saw Erland stumble bare footed through it with Tanya Wilson and both of them stopped and stared, stricken to silence at the destruction and death.

Sierra didn't see Tanya's details as the former nurse slipped to her knees and covered her mouth; the woman somehow fell from focus and disappeared. Erland's sore and rejected face filled her vision, glazed with sweat and shame, right eye swollen and blood streaked.

The pain was too much. There was no answer for it or time to explain it. Not here. Damn what she had told Tanya to do, damn what she *couldn't* tell Tabitha to do. The Police cars were after her just as much as they were after the gunfire.

So she ran.

Erland watched as the shape of his dream disappeared down the fire escape. He ran to chase it and fell to a rough and stinging reality, and pushed himself to his feet only to come to Tabitha Grey's dormant body.

Her voice gargled in her throat as if it was a wind-up toy running out of energy. Her body was static and her heart was still working as hard as possible and her eyes were on the Detective. He stumbled to his knees and the tips of her fingers trembled.

Erland took her left hand and held it in both of his.

"T...take...care..." The Agent's mouth struggled to say as her body was becoming stiff and inoperable. "Ta...ke care of her...Mike."

Tabitha's last wheeze of life was in some kind of smile and Erland swallowed hard as he watched her spirit leave into the dry cold of the night and brushed his hand over her eyes to close them. Then he came to his full height with great heaviness and a skewed sense of balance and peered into the straightness of the distance where a lone figure stood beside a pair of headlights. Erland grit his teeth with a savage fury as the figure bunched into the car and drove off.

THIRTY

    Christian Lowery emerged from the Camaro all of six foot three and buttoned his blue sport coat, appraising the forgettable brown house in the middle of East Hawks Lane. If it wasn't for the gorgeous seclusion of the Mossyrock neighborhood and all of its old growth oaks, the house would've been a hard sell. The *for sale by owner* sign spread a bitter taste in Lowery's mouth considering the homicide.

    "You ready?" The redhead looked to Officer Braden who was in the middle of yawning as the question had been asked, leaning on the trunk of his squad car. "When do you get off anyway?"

    "Next Tuesday." The pudgy Officer joked and then held up his index finger.

    "An hour? Okay, let's make it quick."

    "A homicide's never quick. I know your IQ's like..." Braden rolled his eyes around. "Like as high as the top speed on that car of yours but remember what Erland told you about initial reactions at a crime scene. The quicker your mind goes the more conclusions you can jump to."

    Lowery shook his head with a former jock's carefree smirk. It was sweet the older guys were looking out for him but since this was his first murder in Crescent as the lead investigator, even though it was on the count of serious staffing reasons, he was not

going to let anybody down, least of all the man he
looked up to the most, Detective First Grade Michael
Erland. Maybe he was the new guy and low man on the
totem pole but everybody liked him and was cheering
for him to do well in life in their own strange way, even
if it meant dumping the brunt of their fictional water-
cooler horror stories, practical jokes, and sage advice on
him.

"Seriously Bill, you should go home."

"I know...I will soon. I'll just make sure you get
all of the facts here and then I'll shove off. Nguyen and
Kerns are already inside."

"How is the old man?" The Detective fresh from
the Maricopa County Sheriff's Department with a four-
year degree in criminal justice from ASU put his hands
in his pockets as he followed Braden across the street.
The lights in the house were on and the glow from the
street was poor. Lowery was also lucky to find an inch
of room for the Camaro in the congestion of the
driveway deprived avenue but the street had been
sealed off. "I heard he's in an OIS?"

"Saving the world." Braden joked as they
crossed the crime tape and approached the gate where
the dog was still laid out and had not been touched. "I
heard about the OIS but I don't know much else."

"That guy hasn't fired a gun in years." Lowery's
natural smirk increased and received a dirty look from
Bill Braden.

"That's what you think, kid. Don't let his
natural charm and lack of the usual B.S. deceive you.
Erland used to hunt White Tail deer in the Turbus
Mountain Forest. He still might but he doesn't talk
about it anymore if he does."

The young Second Grade Detective stood at the
nearly frozen beagle, waiting for some kind of point or
punch line.

"Yeah?"

"You're not from around here, are you kid?"

"I'm from Phoenix."

Braden chuckled as he eyed the dog.

"Mount Turbus is host to the largest grey wolf population in the world." The Officer hit Lowery in the chest with the back of his hand and pointed a finger an inch away from his nose. "Have him tell you the one about Christmas break when the sun went down." Braden reached into a pocket in his pants and gave the Detective a pair of plastic gloves and unleashed the brightness of his flashlight on the dog while the Detective put them on. "He doesn't exaggerate."

Lowery had a scoffing laugh and it somehow fit the permanent smirk and his big athletic frame.

"Every story is exaggerated. That's what makes it a story."

"Not this one, kid. If you don't believe it, you can check it out on the internet...the paper's called...the Evans Pass Observer or something like that...anyway, Evans Pass is a city over that way, 'bout four thousand feet up and they've only got one paper. I won't ruin the story for you so check it out before you forget. Okay?"

"Okay." The Detective nodded, seeing the Officer's growing excitement. "But first thing's first."

Lowery squatted to view the dog. There was no blood or any sign of blunt force trauma.

"Doesn't look that old to me." Braden said through another yawn.

"He's not. I'd say he couldn't be over five...I don't see any bruising."

"We can come back to him."

"Yeah..."

The pair walked around the back yard to the door, open as it was. The front door was locked and nothing had been touched since the yellow crime tape had been set.

Nguyen was on the radio and told Lowery and Braden the Medical Examiner was on her way.

"A neighbor saw the dog and came around back?" Lowery confirmed inquisitively.

"That's right."

Lowery checked his watch. That was nearly twenty minutes ago. Great response time, considering.

"Nosy neighbor..." The redhead chuckled and made his way into the house and through the sunroom, coming to a halt in the nearly vacant living room of dark hardwood floors and yellow-white walls.

"Holy cow..." Was all he said.

Braden glanced at Nguyen who had a serious face to begin with. The Detective slowly circled around the focal point of the murder investigation, the low couch, and the mess of it.

"So Veracruz was here?" He asked.

"Yes, right where you are standing."

"What kind of condition is she in?" The concern was obvious on all of their faces, most of all Lowery's. He had experienced an interdepartmental murder back in Arizona and every time the Police Department took a hit in the media it made the job that much harder and a murder was far and above the worst thing that could happen.

"She has signs of some kind of overdose of something and isn't sharp enough to get anything from yet. Kerns is with her in the bedroom and the ambulance is enroute. She's got a broken nose and the gun was in her hand. She was face down."

Braden nodded as Nguyen spoke rapidly. Only Braden knew Veracruz personally but she was one of them. She had more time in grade at CPD than Lowery did.

"I beat the ambulance?" Lowery smirked.

"A day like this shows you how understaffed a city can be." Braden was as blunt as he was cryptic. The siege of Crescent had fallen on CPD and all of its branch services like a Viking war axe. There was an unsaid feeling that the Waterfront would never be the same. The economic repercussions of blocking the Targus' shipping lanes and destruction of buildings like PierHouse and Fircrest Mansion would ripple well into the next decade if not longer. Fear had a way of killing business and the media had a way of rehashing it so it never left the public's subconscious. Future votes on taxpayer dollars would be reshuffled and distributed due to the clean up and restoration and the stigma of it all would haunt the city forever.

"Well," Lowery crossed his arms and came to stand before the two Officers. "Either she killed him or she didn't."

"Would you like to talk to her?"

"After the ambulance comes." Lowery walked back to the body.

"Who is he?"

"We don't know, he had no identification."

"Great..." The young Detective looked to the fireplace and the space of the wall next to it. "There's the slug. The shell casing must be under the couch..."

Braden and Nguyen checked and then affirmed and watched as Lowery juggled the angles and stood behind the couch where Veracruz had during the shooting.

"It's there." Braden said, stopping the Detective where they had found their fellow Officer.

"How did she get to be face down if she shot him?" The Detective proposed as he studied the angle of Jimenez' body. Braden shrugged and Nguyen squinted as Lowery continued. "He was obviously standing right next to the couch and the shot spilled him over and he slid but why did she break her nose?"

"Before she shot him?" Braden offered.

"But there's no sign of a struggle anywhere, is there?" Lowery corrected, some kind of intelligent glow lighting his face. "You found her face down with the gun in her...left hand, right?"

"Yes."

"Is she left handed, do you know?"

Braden shrugged again.

"We could ask her."

"Not yet...not yet..." Lowery's eyes danced around the room and stayed on the wall phone in the corner of the room that was hanging limply, unhooked from its base. It was as if he had been avoiding it.

"Have you checked the last number he called?"

"No."

"I bet you a half-dozen cronuts its hers."

Nguyen smiled and left out the back as the ambulance approached and began to weave its way through the congested street.

"It's too late for a cronut." Braden scratched his chin, which was a few years away from becoming a jowl.

"It's *never* too late for a cronut." Lowery's smirk was back, though it never really left, it was broad and pleasant as he hit the phone's redial.

A jumpy Latin hip-hop ringtone danced through the silence of the bedroom.

"I'll see you tomorrow, Bill." Lowery winked as he walked to the bedroom.

Sarina Veracruz was on the edge of a queen-sized bed that looked too well made to have ever been slept in. The bedroom itself was free of everything that wasn't absolutely essential and Christian wanted to relay that message to his wife but thought it might go over like a lead balloon. Especially since they had both decided to leave Arizona for good she was having some kind of decoration anxiety if that was even the condition for it and had spent nearly five thousand dollars in making sure their house in Ambler's Way three miles west of the Airport looked and felt like a home, even though a house in Ambler's Way didn't cost much more than a hundred and fifty g's.

"Sarina, you okay?" Lowery asked with his hands in his pockets and knocked his head toward the door so Officer Kerns left. Lowery squatted to see her face as it was buried in her hands and a bloody towel. He noticed a rip in her blouse by the collar as her body was bent and defeated and her olive green eyes were beady as they rolled over to meet his.

"Who are you?" She asked.

"Chris Lowery, Homicide."

"CPD?"

He nodded slowly.

"Thank God they didn't send Mike..."

"You wanna tell me who the man in the living room is?"

Her eyes faded shut and her lungs let out a burdened sigh. Two EMT's came into the bedroom with their essential tools and began to work as silently as possible.

"Luis...Jimenez."

Lowery nodded again, keeping his tone of voice reasonable and soft. He could tell she was rummy but connected to the moment and trying hard to keep herself that way. Nguyen had been too forceful or he would've known the information already.

"What does he do?"

Sarina sighed again.

"Department of Homeland...Security."

The young Detective stood and felt the ash come into his face. Sarina traded the bloody kitchen towel for the hands of an EMT named Rossington. Her twitching eyes sat balefully on his face and said how she knew she was hopelessly damned but didn't feel guilty about it. He wondered if that was because of the coldness of her heart or if she was so far deep into a set up that she had nothing to say but the straight truth even though she was speaking it through the mouth of an overdose of who knew what.

Christian Lowery returned to the living room and leaned on the wall near the fireplace, looking at the slug and the body of Luis Jimenez and then the Medical Examiner as she entered the house to make the bloody mess official.

Erland had asked him once why he wanted Homicide when he could work Vice or Fraud, and standing in the drafty seventies-built home with a four-thousand piece puzzle in his lap at eight o'clock when Kimmie was at home pouting because her new recipe for Panang curry was going into Glad containers for the evening, he actually understood the gray-haired Detective's brilliant words.

The fifth grade teacher whose name was Doris Polzine braved the cold darkness to locate Mr. Wolcek. She had held off as long as possible and attendance had been surprisingly high considering the day's events, and hopefully the songs of happiness and good times would warm the hearts of everyone in the auditorium. The children had been working on the concert since early September and took great pride in the musical program. Ms. Hu had really gone above and beyond this year and included choreography with the colored light display. The concert began late but the tone of the children's voices was as strong as it was beautiful and the walk to the Administration Building wasn't so bad.

Doris opened the door, her head still down and

was as unprepared to see the slaughter and death as one of her young students. Mr. Wolcek, the janitor-even one of the security men, where were the others? Sickness immediately welled up within her and she lost the two pumpkin cookies she had eaten minutes ago as she ran for the door. Fear was a terrible grip, clamping her every joint and ligament and she became stiff and afraid to move but still managed to run to the auditorium with a lurching limp to get the telephone because she could not bear to see the bloody floor and the spiritless bodies that covered it.

His breath came in dissipating white puffs as he pushed through the cutting cold. It wasn't the first time he'd walked alone and his march to the CMJ building was stirring more than uneasy feelings inside. For the first time since he had launched himself from the bondages of his old life that moment at Fircrest, Darren Reston felt horribly confused, and not on the count which direction he was going or what his name was. One word above all was nagging at the back of his mind and nothing could tear it out.

Loyalty.

He had seen Kelly's face when she sat opposite him in the Precinct with the IV in his arm. It was the face of one who'd been there before, who'd seen him low in the downswing of the bottle and to watch her drive off was almost harder than getting out of the car. It was as if her relationship with him only stretched so far, her *belief* only carried so much credit.

A blue car zipped by and Darren crossed Parkshead Avenue. Two blocks later he saw a street musician, a guitar player with a beard, sheltered from the wind in an alcove of the Targus County public library building. Something about the music made him stop. He could tell the man wasn't homeless or broke or

strung out on drugs, but then again, he didn't look like
he was anybody famous. The guitar case was open to
imply he was a street performer but there was no money
in it.

"Sounds good." Darren said and wasn't lying.
Perhaps it was in the...accuracy of it. The music
resonating from the sunburst acoustic personified the
feeling of a lonely city and empty streets yet carried a
hopeful undertone and a swing of freedom that only
someone living in the moment could feel.

The man nodded. His eyes were reddened, not
from drugs but tears.

"You okay, man?"

He nodded. He wasn't any older than thirty.

"Tough day, huh?"

The musician nodded again and Darren pressed
off. He could tell the man was sensitive and was
playing a painful lullaby to the city that he loved,
perhaps more as a way to communicate what was
welling inside than anything else.

In some strange way it was like divine
confirmation to Reston that to let it out and to make it
known was the only way to go, and if he was alone,
then, like the musician, he was alone, but he was being
honest to the tune inside. It was sad to see the streets so
empty and vacant and the closer Darren was to the
washed out brick of the CMJ building, the more he
believed that by publishing the story and doing *his* part
to make the truth known, he would be freeing each and
every square light of a skyscraper that was shut up in
fear and wonder.

At least on the street, in the cold, Darren could
see with his own two eyes that it was lonely, it was
empty, but it was certainly nothing to be afraid of.

The Channel Two building was unchanged through all of the day's events, and perhaps, the fact that it used to be a hospital had something to do with it. Nearly the same amount of cars stacked the broad lot and the sickly black trees that framed it hadn't even lost any more of their scraggly leaves.

Jessica Birchall parked the Subaru in a distant spot because she needed the walk. Denton Hodge knew she was coming and had already set aside the top media editor to help her with the presentation of the story, and it was slated for eleven, giving them a good hour and a half at least. Regardless of that, an uneasiness nibbled at her confidence. While Darren and Kelly were submitting almost numerical, factual data, she was going to be the face of this story; for Crescent, for the state, and for the whole world, until it ballooned as Marland promised it would. If this Jupiter wanted a target to take out, it would be her. Birchall hadn't felt the pressure in her sinuses since dinner and was grateful for whatever reason, but seeing the lot again and the looming hospital building of Channel Two News, the pressure came back. Perhaps it was just being outside and being cold despite the protection of the ruby red overcoat. The threat of death by this madman's hand was a very real possibility yet she just didn't think of it that way. What thoughts of fear and worry had every right to be clouding her mind had since blown past. In fact she was more worried her sinus problem would affect her speaking voice, seeing as she'd taken voice lessons for almost two years now to project her naturally feeble and soft tone and this would be her introduction to America.

Francine met her in the lobby and her sweet Vietnamese face carried a nervous excitement about it.

"Your career's never going to be the same." Francine rubbed Jessica's back quickly and warmly as women do.

"Thanks but I haven't even gone on air yet."

"I know but who do you think's been putting all of this together?" They began to walk to the elevator after Birchall signed in with the security guard at the desk and showed her credentials, even though their security wasn't much different than a local gym. "I knew that when I saw your tiger eyes you were going to get your big break."

Birchall frowned and smiled at the same time, as it was possible.

"Wait, what?"

"When you stormed in Hodgie's office." Francine beamed as the elevator door pinged open and they began the procedure.

"I still don't know what you're talking about, tigers?"

Francine's face lost its happiness, like she had ruined a joke for someone and just realized it.

"They've never told you?"

"No, they've never told me." Birchall crossed her arms as the elevator doors slid shut.

Kirke, having taken two painkillers for his shoulder in the solitude of the van, finished the longwinded route to Cherry Street and parked the black Mercedes van across from the Pinnacle Building. He leaned over in his seat to take in its impressive height and pulled up the collar of his jacket and ran two fingers over a freckled nose. The driving was more for timing that anything and he waited until in was nearly nine o'clock to see Team Ganymede's plain white van pull up to the curb thirty feet from the Pinnacle Building's darkened entrance and flash their headlights off and on and finally off as the vehicle came to rest.

The last surviving member of Team Io twisted

his head to see the payload of Semtex in the back of the van and waited for the black clad RepMax impostors of Ganymede to come over. Four crossed the street, one stayed in the van to keep watch.

The one named Charlie rested an arm on the driver window once Kirke had powered it down.

"We haven't heard about the school yet."

"Courtland has the trigger, Jupiter calls him. I'm out of it."

Charlie was a tough looking man and had a scarred up chin and a forehead that could crack stacks of pine planks but he was also handsome.

"Where's Pitts?"

"We had to split. We had a run in at the school but Courtland got it. We're still on schedule, aren't we?"

"Yeah..." Charlie cast a look along the street to make sure no one was witnessing the Semtex go in the duffel bags.

"Do you wanna call Jupiter?"

"I don't call Jupiter." Charlie's voice was as terse as his face. He was right. Ganymede was just a hammer and they did what they were told. There was no thinking involved, they were all former soldiers at the highest levels.

"Courtland hasn't called me so it's all good."

"Well..." Charlie tapped on the door. "Tell Pitts I said hey."

"Will do."

He knew they had served together but wasn't sure which branch of service, they didn't really talk about it. Kirke wasn't a former soldier like they were, he was just a pure criminal from way back.

Kirke bent his head low to watch the four RepMax impostors confidently stride to entrance of the Pinnacle building, covered and enshrouded as it was in the darkened recesses and supports of tarps and scaffolding behind a chopped up strip of concrete. Once they had disappeared, Kirke took a swig of water and checked his watch.

Kelly was a nervous wreck held together by cotton and foundation when she stopped the white suburban at the CPD building on Hartley. She didn't remember if it was Precinct Five or Thirteen, however that worked and it was a derelict building that hadn't felt the effects of the tax increases yet.

She left the Suburban dormant at the sidewalk directly before the door and entered timidly.

The desk sergeant was a fifty something year old man with a droopy face below a tuft of gray hair and his nametag read Macon.

"Excuse me." Kelly started and curled her hair behind her ears.

"Yes, ma'am." Macon set aside a crossword puzzle. The Precinct was nearly vacant because of the day's events. Officers were flung far and wide to not only clean up the desolation but prevent panic.

"This is very hard to explain, but...I would like to...turn in a Homeland Security vehicle."

The confusion had already begun to taint the Officer's face.

"Turn in?"

"Yes, I was...in an operation with a Homeland Security operative named Sierra Marland...and..."

Macon held out his hand and went to the phone.

"Hold on, let me make a call. You can wait over there."

Kelly noticed the area where he was directing her toward and her mind went to the airport and how one always had to wait. She crossed the dusty floor and sat in a long sectioned leatherette bench next to a

vertical magazine rack and waxy green plant that
needed water. The journalist felt cold and stared at her
size seven and a half shoes.

"Your name please?" Macon called out.

"Barnett, Kelly Barnett."

He nodded in thanks and his voice fell again to a
volume not meant for her ears.

Kelly's eyes worked around the whitishness of
the Precinct and the long runner of fluorescent lighting
that stretched down the hall to her right. Just as she was
about to search the magazines for something to take her
mind of the difficulty of what she had chosen to do, an
Officer and an EMT rattled a gurney around the corner
of the lengthy hall and came to her, stopping at the
Macon's desk.

"Is that Homeland Agent here yet?"

Macon shook his head and the EMT pushed the
stretcher to a small alcove near the door, away from
Kelly. Her eyes were wide. The man on the stretcher
was middle aged and dressed in black from head to toe.
He didn't look American and had his eyes closed,
receiving a steady flow of enriched air from an oxygen
mask. Kelly looked for burn marks because the man
brought with him a sour, bitter old smell of smoke and
death. The burning image of Fircrest lit up her
imagination.

"Did you hear about the shooting at Keller's?"
Macon asked as he was on hold.

"Yeah. Sounded like a warzone." The Officer
took a paper from the desk and got a pen from his
pocket.

"It's insane." Macon's face held a burned-out
disbelief and finally he hung up the phone and stood.

"Ms. Barnett?"

"Yes?" Kelly stood.

"There's going to be a Homeland Security

Agent arriving here shortly to receive something and he'll be transporting this man to Precinct Three," Macon was helpful yet the confusion was still in his face and Kelly couldn't help but feel as she was being passed off and she hadn't expected it.

"Will he take the car?"

"Yes..." Macon said with hesitation and left, tramping down the hall the gurney had come from. The Officer who had accompanied the gurney with the EMT occupied the chair to replace the Desk Sergeant. He was a Sergeant too. Kelly didn't see his name because the door opened and a goateed man of average height entered the Precinct. His eyes quickly assessed each person in the small entrance space before a formal word could be said. Kelly could tell he was intelligent, despite his casual wintry appearance.

The new Desk Sergeant looked up.

"Rollins." Was all the man said, not moving.

"Right." The Sergeant reached under the desk and produced a plastic bag with something that looked like a mechanical pencil inside. The man with the goatee took it greedily.

"And there's a white Suburban out there..." He threw a thumb.

"Yes," Kelly was bold before the Desk Sergeant could say a word. "It belongs to a Homeland Agent named Sierra Marland."

The dark eyes above the goatee stated that he knew as much but had plunged into some radical uncertainty.

"And you are?"

"Kelly Barnett, I was working with her...she..."

"Hold on." The man who she assumed was named Rollins took a step to speak with the Desk Sergeant. The EMT had stayed silent through all of it. Kelly blinked and resisted the anxious gnaw that was eating through her toes.

She saw the Desk Sergeant nod with surety and the man spoke to the EMT who wheeled the gurney outside to the cold.

"Come with me." He said.

Kelly followed and her eyes took a few seconds to readjust to the darkness.

"My name's Rollins," He offered his hand and she shook it tentatively as they walked to the white Suburban. "Do you have the keys?"

"Yes."

She gave them to him.

"Get in and tell me all about it." He moved around the hood and stopped as he saw her face and her reticence.

He chuckled to himself and reached inside the puffy winter jacket and showed her his identification.

"I know I'm not your typical Agent, Miss, but Sierra has trusted me with her life before and if you were driving her car and working with her then you can trust me the same way." Kelly stayed put as the man finished. "I don't know what happened because we've been out of contact but I've been working my ass off and Sierra knows the score. So if something happened to her, you have to tell me about it, for her sake, and for the sake of the operation, okay?"

Even though Rollins was someone she would want to avoid in everyday life, seeing as he had that grungy air of tattoos and punk rock she could see his dark eyes were far more intelligent than she initially assumed and his voice was as heartfelt as a voice could be.

Kelly nodded and got in the passenger seat and told him everything she could and Rollins filled in a few blanks in the timeline.

"So Tabitha went to Keller's Ironworks."

Rollins surmised as he pushed the car toward Precinct Three with the Ambulance carrying Polis behind him. "She must've. That was the cause for the shooting. I don't know all of it but I know there was a helicopter involved and seven are dead."

"What about Agent Marland and Detective Erland?"

"Possibly, but I don't know...she's been in and around all of the damage today. I can't bring her up because of Mr. Brown. He's supposed to be making Precinct Three his op center and if I keep my distance from her she'll get it all worked out."

Kelly nodded and saw Rollins roll his weary neck. She remembered the looming threat of Mr. Brown and how Marland wasn't sure if he was part of Jupiter's plan or not.

"But you've been working on the footage from Fircrest, right?" Kelly curled her hair behind her ears. "She needs to see it."

"I know but I can't communicate with her. She issued a Code Zeta...like an abort sequence..."

Kelly nearly jumped in her seat and took the burn phone from her purse. It just occurred to her and she could've kicked herself.

"This, you can call her on this. I don't know why I didn't mention it. You can call Agent Grey, too. And Erland. All the numbers are in there."

Rollins took the phone and nodded a long and decisive movement once he judged the device.

"That's like her...I'll do it, but not yet. Whatever happened at Keller's needs to cool off. If she's one of the victims we've got no chance in hell anyway."

Kelly sighed and felt lighter.

"You'll know when you call her, I guess."

"Yes, and it'd be best for you to get outta here."

Kelly's mind immediately went to Darren

Reston and how he was elsewhere, walking in the cold.

"But what about the others?"

"You did your job, they can do theirs. That's all Sierra wanted. The further you distance yourself from Crescent the better, considering once Mr. Brown gets a hold of you you'll have no life until you're fully debriefed and fully cleared to re-enter the world of the living."

Kelly thought for a moment of why she came to that apartment. Darren Reston. She was helping *him*. Agent Marland hadn't batted an eye at her, and why was that? Because her loyalty to Darren must've been lighting her up like a Christmas tree. She couldn't leave. He was the whole reason she was in the operation and to think of the time it would've taken them without her. She was a part of it alright, a big part...

"I can't leave. Darren's still here."

"Do you have a car?" Rollins asked.

"At Darren's house, Agent Grey has his car."

"Where do you live?"

"On Thirty-Fourth...but..."

"But what? I'll have an Officer take you there once we're at the Precinct. Or to Darren's."

"No...I'll wait...I have to talk to Erland."

Rollins paused at a red light and waited for thru traffic.

"You can't. You've done your job and have to distance yourself from it, okay? There's no option *not* to." The Suburban pushed on. "I'm sure Tabitha was going to take you guys somewhere but it got out of hand as it always does...just, just let me handle it with Sierra, okay? It's gonna work out."

Kelly sighed and watched the silent city brush past. Her mind went to Darren and Rollins' words echoed over the still images of his face.

Charlie was in the lead with the duffel of
Semtex over his shoulder and the intentional lack of
light in the lobby of the Pinnacle building coupled with
the stillborn progress of gutting and retrofitting looked
like something out of a horror movie.

Two rent-a-cop guards of no particular affiliate
were at a brand new enclave of serpentine marble that
was in the process of being chiseled to read *Pacific
Holdings Pinnacle Tower*, or so Charlie assumed,
seeing as it was casually covered with a drop cloth and
not yet finished. Charlie was a blonde man, not very
tall, with a good looking face that was, if anything,
made more so by the scaring on his chin and in the
tight-fitting RepMax black and black gloves he was
ready for business.

"You in charge here?" He asserted himself and
set the duffel down between his feet.

Neither security guard wanted to say yes and his
hard eyes juggled between them as he removed the
glove on his right hand.

"Yes." The one on the left finally said and he
couldnt've been any older than twenty-four but he was
muscled enough to get the job.

Charlie gave him a business card. It had a fake
name but was an official RepMax forgery, not that the
hourly worker would've known the difference.

"We're here to update the cameras."

"I wasn't told." The hulk shrugged.

"That's okay. I'm on time like I'm supposed to
be-whether you were told or not." Charlie checked his
watch and threw a look to Kalil who began to move
with his duffel to the small pool area where a new water
feature was being built tile by tile.

"Hold on, I'm going to have to call my boss."

Charlie left the bag and walked around the

serpentine enclave.

"Are the cameras in yet?"

"No, but..."

Charlie's left hand flicked like a knife to the bulky boy's neck and he clutched his throat, choking and gasping. By the time the second security guard had figured out what was going down Charlie's gloved left hand was on the back of his head and slammed the guard's face to the perfectly hard serpentine marble slab. He fell to the ground next to his friend and they both stopped breathing at nearly the same time. Charlie put his glove back on and nodded to Greene and Ritter as they were going to take the foundation with the heavy bags. Once the drop cloth from the marble had covered the two guards Charlie joined Kalil for the stairwell. Each one of them had donned a black baseball cap and even if there were any cameras and the security guard didn't know what he was talking about, they would never get the faces of the bombers. The mission was clear and concise, and if Crescent thought for one minute they had seen destruction they would find out when the light of day returned they were sorely mistaken.

Jupiter would hold their most expensive building at ransom until his sale was completed and whether the ransom was paid or not, the Pinnacle Building and all Pacific Holdings had sunk into it would be forever shattered and fall to a pile of dust.

THIRTY-ONE

     The Sikorsky S-76 was a blue-black specter in the night and rose to ten thousand feet before moving south over the rolling mound of Fircrest.

     "What about Dexter?" The pilot asked. Jupiter had a headset as it was impossible to hear without one.

     "What?" He asked, still grabbing his ankle as he had taken a grazing ricochet from the crazed blonde with the MP5. His mind was processing what had happened and while he knew Sierra Marland was behind it he never saw her and it worried him. He thought about calling Courtland again but reasoned that she had made her way out of it and wondered if *she* had set *him* up, using that Detective as bait. She *had* used the Detective, hadn't she? Perhaps she had hoped that he would be distracted by the memory card, if it was CONSTANT or not and she could kill him as he sat there twiddling his thumbs. It nearly worked. But he had escaped yet again and was not feeling so good for the next time. No matter what he threw at her she seemed to wriggle out of it and he was running out of moves. But if he really had CONSTANT he was waiting for the news of a lifetime, to hear the memory card was legitimate and Jenkins to his left was about to speak the verdict. Jenkins was all of twenty-two and had been unscathed in the assault as had Yarrow and Phillips. Other than that, the casualty rate had been high. Jupiter had thrown himself in the chopper before seeing if the blonde had died or not and as far as he knew the firefight could've still been going. He didn't care. He was gone.

Jenkins had hooked the card up to an adaptable reader via USB to his laptop.

"There's some kind of encryption just to access it," He offered with a quavering voice that was laced with Brooklyn. "It's definitely a Homeland algorithm, I can tell."

"Hold on," Jupiter held out the hand that wasn't around his ankle and looked to the pilot in the cockpit. "How far away is Dexter?"

"Two miles."

"No, further."

They had been scanning high schools to find a field to land the chopper. Jupiter knew the air was only so safe before voices on the radio would get wise to the fact that the chopper's presence was congruent with the warehouse district shootout. He wasn't biting his nails for Ganymede to finish with the Pinnacle Building but he was running out of Teams to take him to safety once on the ground. Yarrow and Phillips stayed in the helicopter at all times, so really, his only protection was Jenkins and he was a tech guy, not a stone cold killer like Charlie or even Courtland. Jupiter held off on calling Charlie and turned his attention to Jenkins.

"Do we have to hack it just to see if it's real?"

"I wouldn't know how. I've never encountered this kind of card before...its like it's been specially made, it probably holds as much data as a mainframe. The code's all weird too, like some old-school thing only way perverted."

So far so good. That's exactly what CONSTANT was billed to be.

"Let me see."

Jupiter took the computer from the young Jenkins who pulled the hair out of his eyes and watched the master hacker work.

Jupiter's fingers moved as fast as his mind in perfect synchronization as if there was no buffer between them. Jenkins saw four new windows open up as Jupiter grit his teeth with the searing pain in his ankle.

"I'm going to copy the start up file and change the access parameter...and make myself admin." Jupiter noted for Jenkins benefit. "And re-task the program to think it's the default...so when I infect the original with a virus, I'll have the other one to open the file bank."

Jenkins twitched and scratched his chest to hide the nervous burn in his lungs.

"But...won't you risk damaging all the data with a virus?"

"If there's already one on here what do I have to lose?" The hacker typed. "Besides, there's no connectivity in Homeland algorithms, they're like square blocks. If one goes, it's the only one, the rest'll be safe. If I can't get in with the default start up then it'll just take more time to find the back door."

"Can we get the encryption key?"

"I don't think there is one..." Jupiter studied the number sequences as he analyzed what would be the road map of the memory card's partitioning structure. He saw it was grouped into one-gigabyte chunks, stranded together by exactly four hundred and thirteen kilobyte chains that alternated pattern like a checkerboard.

"Chief Katonah?" The pilot asked.

"Yes." Jupiter said, not to the pilot but to the computer. He had discerned the weak spot in the algorithm and copied it to the corrupted startup file. The helicopter swayed and banked to move east for Chief

Katonah High in Landsbrook.

Jenkins watched the screen with wide eyes as Jupiter hit two keys, one of them being return. The algorithm that linked the separated one-gigabyte chunks vanished as the laptops processor clicked and chewed and the virus Jupiter had attached to the start up file did its work.

"Eh voila." Jupiter's smile hid in a wince of pain. He now had direct access to the information by killing the security chain.

"What did you do?"

"There was no key." Jupiter chuckled. "Instead they had these four-hundred and thirty kilobyte moats interlocked with dummy trails around the one gig partitions. It's just like disarming a bomb-you have to pick the right wire. It's ready for decryption."

Jenkins took the laptop back with a smile. In a strange way, he was like a son to Jupiter, in the manner that the hacker mentored him and the sense of awe Jenkins held for the man.

"I've never seen that before."

"I have..." Jupiter looked out the window to the sea of black and the smallest blips of yellowed light.

The hacker sighed at the pain as his body began the work of sending its natural opiates to his ankle. He called Killinger.

"Yes?" The answer was quick.

"I have it." Jupiter said as his eyes read one of the files Jenkins opened to see. It was a complete surveillance report of a foreign dignitary's visit to Washington D.C. The information was as legitimate as the helicopter they were flying in. CONSTANT was no lie and there was no virus embedded in it. Jenkins had already checked for surreptitious tracking and found none.

"Where do you want to meet?"

"Chief Katonah High School."

There was a brief second for a facial gesture Jupiter could only guess at.

"I'll be there in thirty minutes."

Jupiter pulled the phone back to check the time. Charlie and Ganymede would be done by then. He would stay off the phone to Courtland and Io in case Marland was trying to track him through signal. A track would only be possible if he placed a call. And even though he didn't want to give Marland another shot at retribution, he was positive it wasn't the last time their paths would cross.

Homicide's space in Precinct Three was no more than three sets of narrow office rooms separated by walls and doors and a conference area across the hall that spanned the length of all three but couldn't handle more than twelve comfortably. Lowery was heavy as he sat down at his desk cluster in the left corner of room Three-Eighty-One and spun idly in the wheeled office chair as he thought. His eyes drifted over to Erland's desk and built-in unit. Each room had four, one to a corner. His eyes sat also on Schultze and Romero's desks but they weren't the Machine Gun Man. If he had a penny for every time the veteran Detective did something on a case that he later wrote down in his notebook for study he'd be able to by a new notebook. Lowery looked down at the perfect cleanliness of his jam-packed desk and over to Erland's sparse workspace again, nearly expecting him to be there, hunched over, writing out questions with a number two pencil.

Officer Towns knocked on the door with a quick rap rap and poked her head in.

"Chris?"

"Yeah." Lowery spun in the chair.

"Mike was at Keller's Ironworks and he's in

rough shape."

"What?" The constant smirk twisted the Detective's face in an incredulous way.

"There was a shootout there, God knows what happened." Towns shook her head and wiped her small, slightly upturned nose a few times. "They'll be sticking him in HomCon until someone from Homeland Security gets here, just wanted to let you know."

Lowery acknowledged wordlessly and began another series of slow spins still processing the news. HomCon was short for the Homicide Conference Room across the hall. Lowery knew Erland had been brought on by Homeland to solve the murder at Fircrest but hadn't heard anything about it and was wondering what the man had gotten into considering the OIS. There was nothing good ahead of a Detective in an open OIS finding himself in a shootout. Nothing at all.

Just when Lowery was wondering if he had elevated the man above reproach he pushed himself from the spinning chair and headed for the cafeteria.

There he found a tightly wrapped sandwich of turkey and iceberg lettuce on white and took a pair of shelf-stable mayos and a bottled water. Edgar Bailer from Missing Persons was eating the same sandwich in the corner and Lowery gave him a nod. Bailer didn't really like Lowery because he was from Wisconsin and carried a grudge from some college football bowl game Lowery never saw, and college was almost five years ago for the both of them.

"You should've taken the ham." Bailer pushed the sandwich away from him, seeing as it was just the crusts and Bailer didn't like crusts anymore than he liked Lowery.

"Why? Turkey's dry?"

"No dryer than grandma's...can't wait to go back to Racine next week." The Detective held a sarcastic face, as if to say he was loathing the idea, when everyone in the Precinct really knew how he felt about his roots. He was a tall man with thin and bony features and enough freckles for eight faces but just a hair shorter than Lowery, so much so that he had to look up to him when they stood eye to eye.

"We don't do ham, Kimmie doesn't like it."

"Really?" Bailer asked as he stood. He was single and perhaps was always going to be that way, not because he was a tough outsider like Erland, but because he struggled to be honest with women and was constantly trying to impress; didn't matter if it was the ugliest duckling in the pond or a woman who swept him off his feet, he was going to ruin it with a bad joke or too heavy of a hand somewhere.

"Just because she says jump you say how high?"

Lowery said nothing and busied himself with the unceremonious unwrapping of the smushed sandwich as Bailer stood next to him with a hand in his pocket and the other mindlessly wadding up the garbage and making a squishing sound.

"Ham's not good for you."

"So it's not Kimmie, it's Erland. He's gonna have this whole place crapping green before he retires." The Midwestern voice resided in the freckle-covered nose. To him a real man wanted nothing more than a piece of dead meat.

"I didn't say I'm going to live on raw veggies and Wild Salmon," Lowery pushed the shelf-stable mayo around the dry white bread like a tube of toothpaste, evening it out with his pinky finger. "It's just that a pig lives in the mud and eats whatever it wants to."

"I'll have you know pigs are more intelligent than dogs...some of them."

Lowery looked down again to the sandwich

because he thought of the dead Beagle in the side yard of the brown house on East Hawks Lane. Then he thought of Veracruz and how nearly every word out of her mouth was about a dog or something related to them. They weren't a profession, they were a passion, and to know she wouldn't be with them for Lord knew how many years if convicted of the murder of Luis Jimenez, a six year veteran of Homeland Security, was a sad thought indeed.

The Missing Persons Detective wrinkled the plastic wrap in a tight ball and moved for the garbage near the exit.

Christian Lowery twisted in his seat.

"What'd you say about Erland's retirement?"

"What?" Bailer turned and nodded as the plastic fell to the bottom of the receptacle. "I just figured that a guy, no matter his skill...or popularity...wouldn't have much of a choice considering."

"What'd you mean exactly?"

"You didn't hear?"

Lowery shook his head and it wasn't a lie, because he had only been given the roughest of sketches, and in his line, that wasn't even enough paper to blow his nose on.

"There's seven dead up on the roof top of the building adjacent the old Keller's Ironworks, one of them had an MP5 and no one had an ID, except Erland, and apparently he looked like he'd gone ten rounds with a sledge hammer-barefoot and bleeding, whole nine yards, and guess who's hanging on him?"

"Who?" Lowery angled his body tighter to give Bailer his full attention.

"Tanya Wilson."

"Really?" Lowery's smirk was again incredulous. It was a tremendous set of circumstances that any investigator would have a thick time piecing together even with witness cooperation.

"Yeah, that's how I know. I've been working with Jerry and Welleby to find her and boom, there she is on the roof of an old slaughterhouse."

"Are they bringing her into HomCon too?"

"No. She's got a Patrolmen on each elbow and she's going to the hospital." Bailer came back to the table and Lowery sat normally again because it was beginning to hurt his back and he thought of giving in to Kimmie's demands that he do Pilates with her.

"What about Mike?"

"Nobody at the Precinct can even look at him until a Mr...Brown I think it is...yeah, until Brown shows up. He's a Homeland guy, I assume Homeland's the reason for the OIS and now this? But...your guess is as good as mine. I'm just happy Wilson can sleep safe tonight, you know? That's what I'm in it for..."

And Bailer left with Lowery debating whether she could. She had been in captivity for what, twelve or fourteen hours? Surely she would faint from exhaustion when the adrenaline ran out but horrors of captivity of any kind soon left no one, not even the bravest of souls.

Lowery took half of the sandwich and consumed a third of it in one bite, reaching for his phone. The first speed dial option was obvious. Kimmie made him wait till the third ring.

"Hello?"

"Hey baby, I'mna be late."

There was a sigh.

"Why?"

"Have you been watching the news?" Chris said without checking his tone and realized it was probably her way of worrying.

"Of course, I mean, I just wanna know you're going to be okay. It's been a long day, you know? I just wanna see you."

Lowery cursed himself. It had been a long day and their second anniversary was only a month and a half away and he was still feeling out the ropes of not only married life but how it intersected with work. Sure he should've gone home, Tyler could've taken the Veracruz/Jimenez case-but something inside of him, some kind of instinct knew there was a lot more bubbling than just that...or a murder at Fircrest and the subsequent fire. It had to be linked somehow, the spread of it was too close to be random. Crescent saw thousands of crimes a day from the petty to the extreme, but never such a devastating arc of crescendoing catastrophes like this, and he was determined with all of his youthful zeal to submit whatever piece of the puzzle his homicide was to the grand darkness of the greater mystery.

"I know baby but I'm on a Homicide now and it's real bad...I can't talk about it but someone here at the Precinct was involved."

"...Honey that's horrible." Kimmie empathized. "It's not Mike, is it?"

"No, no..." Lowery nearly laughed. She had been quite smitten with the forty-one year old Detective's reserved charm the couple times he'd been over for dinner and the one time just for beer and the Superbowl. "It's a K-9 officer, but I can't talk about it."

"...Well...when do you think you'll be home?" There was most certainly want in her voice.

"I don't know...Eleven, twelve?"

"...Okay..."

Lowery bit his lip. She had been home all day, home scared and he was young enough to let the Department work him to the bone, even though they were stretched thin and a lot of people from dispatchers to Patrolmen to EMT's, firemen and even clean up crews were all working longer shifts Chris had been practically eating and sleeping at his desk since transferring from Maricopa County in an effort to climb the ladder.

"No later than twelve, honey. I promise."

"...Okay..." He knew she was leaning on her left leg playing with the top button of her blouse as she did. "It's been awhile..."

"I know..."

"...I love you."

"I love you too baby."

Lowery let the phone drop in the breast pocket of his blue sport coat and contemplated the sandwich. It wasn't worth the time. Everything he wanted and needed was waiting at home and he had enough time before his promissory deadline to investigate the matter a little deeper.

After consulting his notes and what information he had gleaned and scrounged in casual conversation from Lieutenant Ross, two dispatchers and a handful of Officers, Lowery made a call to Brandino in Arson as he was lead in the monumental task of deciphering what happened at Fircrest.

"Chris...Lowe, was it?"

"Lowery, Sir."

Brandino used to be in the Chicago Fire Department. He was the kind of guy that made a great speech about needing everybody but was a real boy's clubber and looked down on those that weren't in the fold. At first glance he was gruff but when that blew over he turned long-winded and couldn't ever find the appropriate places to stop himself.

"Why do you wanna know the cause of the fire? I mean, the whole place's a big lump of charcoal now, it's gone."

"I'm investigating the murder of a Homeland

Agent who worked there earlier in the day and I understand he worked in some kind of RV or something? I just want to know if it's still in tact."

"Oh yeah, it's alright. I'm looking at it now. Not a scratch on it. Plenty of evidence inside, I'm sure. The fire never touched it."

"Good, good." Lowery nodded as he was leaning on the wall next to the door of HomCon and heard swearing and coughing. "Are you okay?"

"No, it's that damn peroxide gas."

"The what?"

"Phosphorus Peroxide gas is a side effect of the grenades. There's no doubt they were used here but they doused the place some kind of wicked accelerant- just a few grenades wouldn't do it. I'm smelling gasoline, kind of, but simple gas wouldn't do it. This place went up, real hot, *real* fast. They knew what they were doing."

"They?"

"Yeah, there had to be a group. No witnesses of course, 'cept their scorched compadre they left for dead. I'm gonna have a word with him when I'm done here. He's gonna have a rough night."

"Are they brining him here?"

"He should already be there. Go check and see that he is, alright? I'll be in maybe 'round eleven, twelve."

"Yessir."

"Alright, good man."

Lowery held the phone tight as he walked. The two sections of holding cells or holding areas were seemingly miles apart. The standard jail was not forty feet from the entrance but a number of small rooms, some of them for interrogation complete with two way mirrors and cameras and others just rooms to make somebody sweat in were stashed in the back corners of the Precinct where the remodeling budget had failed to reach. Lowery spotted Doctor Patrice walking down the hall toward him.

"You still here?" He asked in passing and stopped.

"Yeah. I'm treating the Fircrest survivor for third degree burns. They're absolutely horrible."

"Third degree?" Lowery plucked at his lip with his red eyebrows arched. "White phosphorus burns?"

"Exactly, how'd you know?" Doctor Patrice's smooth and calm voice repeated in her big brown eyes even though she was surprised.

"What else burns that hot? Can I see him? I have to ask him about an RV that's there-a Homeland vehicle-I'm investigating the murder of one of the men that worked there earlier and I need to know if he broke into the RV or not."

"Um..." Patrice shrugged. "He's lucid but still in a great deal of pain...you might want to try the Homeland Agent that brought him in though." The Doctor was quick in diagnosing Lowery's face. "You haven't spoken with him yet?"

"No. This case is still pretty fresh and with all that's happened today it hasn't been a very...traditional investigation."

The Detective crossed his arms. It had been pulling teeth piecing together that Jimenez was Crescent stationed and had been a part of whatever investigation Erland had and they worked in an RV on the Fircrest lot and he wondered quickly in front of the penetrating eyes of the Doc why the giant trailer had hit the highway like a failed ski jumper and the mansion turned to ashes and the RV hadn't a scratch on it. Still, with all the information he had, no one had told him or bothered to contact him as lead investigator to let him know a Homeland Agent was in fact, in the building.

Protocol? Lack of respect? The stress of circumstance?
    Conspiracy?
    No option was out and Lowery checked his
watch to make sure he wasn't going to let Kimmie
down. She had eaten dinner by herself too many times
this fall, she deserved better. And even for being
newlyweds of a sort, he hadn't seen too much of her
and they couldn't have that first child he knew she
wanted so desperately if he was always so damn busy.
    "Do you know where he is?"
    "His name's Milton Rollins, he should be...I
don't know, try Dispatch."
    Her smile was a welcome sight but it was
Kimmie's bottle blonde hair that smelled of peaches
that filled his mind and put a kick in his step. He felt his
heart moving faster than usual and cast off what Erland
was always telling him about being relaxed while
working. It was as if he was trying to unravel the whole
day's colossus of crime in a matter of hours and some
how the zeal that twisted his mind to work seemingly
endless shifts was actually convinced of the possibility.
    He had broken a light sweat after being rejected
by Dispatch who had never heard of a Rollins or a
Milton Rollins of the Department of Homeland
Security.
    He was working his way back, defeatedly, to
find the burn victim of the Fircrest arson when he ran
into Lieutenant Ross in civilian clothes.
    "Hey, slow down kid."
    Lowery stopped in some kind of stun for a
second, realizing he was running around like a headless
farm animal and wasn't helping the redheads in the joke
department.
    "Do you know where I can find Rollins?
Homeland Agent Rollins?"
    "Yeah, he should be in Four-Eighty, just him

and a couple laptops and a soda."

"Thanks." Lowery turned and a wise hand grabbed his arm.

"He has a standing order not to be disturbed."

"It's about the Homicide."

"Whatever it is, it can wait."

"But we can't just let Veracruz sit in a cell until we get around to talking to a guy that's in the building."

Lieutenant Ross' wise face changed and he crossed his arms. The entire Police Department was under an extreme amount of stress and the second guessing and finger pointing would continue until long after all the messes had been cleaned up. Mayor Geffington had already made a speech calling for patience and diligence and several other words that didn't mean a dime's worth of difference to a pack of scared animals huddled together in front of their TV sets waiting for the moving pictures to show them the next tragedy. The stress of the entire city showed in Ross' dark eyes, especially in the puffiness underneath them and he ran a hand over the short nubbins of his fading hair to calm himself.

"First of all," Ross' voice stayed firm and was laced with a razor sharp intensity. "Veracruz hasn't been charged yet despite the damning situation she was found in. Secondly, she's not in a cell, she's on a couch with a bottled water in Five-Zero-Eight with a Psychiatrist. And finally," The Lieutenant's voice jumped in volume, unable to hold back, "None of this would've happened without Homeland to begin with, so if you have something to say to the guy, go do it, but don't be surprised what comes your way, because they don't live in the same world we do, they live outside of it and don't know that *we* have to deal with and clean up the consequences of *their* actions, we have to live with the people once they're gone and while they're here they can just tell us what to do but when they leave they make us look like the ones responsible."

Lowery bit his lip and put his hands behind his back. Ross was releasing a truckload of pressure. The wise, coach-like superior sighed and glanced around at the thinned presence in the causeway they stood in and put a hand on shoulder of the taller man.

"Listen bud, I'm sorry but I missed my daughter's eleventh birthday today and my wife's been calling me nonstop about what's been going on because the kids are scared to death and think that Daddy's not going to come home. We just got word of a shooting at Sugar Hill Elementary...they found a bomb there too..."

Ross swore to himself with his hands on his hips and his weary eyes bore a hole in the ground.

"Anyway," He came back from contemplation. "I have to wait till a Homeland high-up named Brown gets here, then I can go home." One of the hands came back to Lowery's shoulder. "Just keep it cool and don't rock the boat, okay? Sarina's innocent until proven guilty and that's a big enough job for any Homicide Detective."

"Even Erland." Lowery affirmed as he stared at the same point in the linoleum that the Lieutenant had.

"Brown won't let me talk to him. I know he had nothing to do with the shooting but I can't figure out why he was there...I told him to go home. You'd think with the OIS he wouldn't even go to the corner mart till it was over."

"If Brown told you not to talk to him then he still must've been working with Homeland." Lowery crossed his arms and something clicked on Ross' face but he kept it to himself.

"I'll be in HomCon. Erland should be here soon. I'll get in a few words before Brown shows."

Lowery nodded a quick thing with just his chin

and made his way toward Five-Zero-Eight, a small room with a couch used for waiting family members and relatives and plenty of tears had been shed in the tight space.

The Detective knocked before entering and saw Doctor Patrice with Veracruz, who was wearing a thin white t-shirt that was a size too small and black jeans. The Doctor was examining the K9 Officer's scalp and hairline, as well as her ears.

Lowery watched in silence, something he had learned from Erland, not to speak right away and to let the scene develop before taking an angle.

Sarina's olive green eyes hadn't lost their woe and her right arm was hooked to an IV. Lowery squinted to see the back of her shirt was torn near the collar.

Doctor Patrice spotted the Detective out of the corner of her eye and came to the door, motioning for their conversation to be held outside of Veracruz' earshot.

"She has a needle mark on her neck behind her right ear near the lobe." The Doctor said in a hushed tone as the door was still open.

"Needle mark?"

"Yes, same exact place as Darren Reston, the suspect of the Fircrest manhunt. Although I'm sure his injection was so long ago an irritation developed around the area and hid the insertion point."

Lowery was silent and plucked at his lip.

"Will you be able to check Mike when he comes in?"

"Yes."

"Do you know what it is? The injection?"

Doctor Patrice moved a few steps from the door and began to whisper. Lowery had to bend down to hear her.

"It's called stenitolribouzinecephimate type regular. STRIC-R. It's like an intensified benzodiazepine, with all the refinement of what parts of the brain it targets but the side effects are more like a barbiturate. It's illegal and hits quicker than a flash flood in the desert."

Lowery completely understood the desert reference.

"She doesn't seem too bad though..."

"It matters on the dosage. Reston was a chronic alcoholic and the dosage lead to a form of amnesia but her reaction would lead me to believe she's dabbled in recreational drugs before...even if it was a very low dosage she should be incoherent without some form of reversal agent."

Lowery frowned.

"You mean she has a resistance?"

"Yes, probably from an analgesic like codeine...but that would take testing. It would also mean she lied to a certain extent in the interview process."

"So you know it's...STRIC-R without a blood test?"

"I'm positive, especially if Mike and Ms. Wilson have similar marks and side effects."

So, if Erland and Wilson had STRIC-R in their systems it would link all of their crimes together to whoever had the drug.

"Where do you get this STRIC-R?"

"You don't get it, you make it."

"Make it? Like meth?"

Doctor Patrice mashed her lips together.

"No, you'd have to have a very advanced scientific laboratory to fabricate such a delicate chain fusion. It's very volatile and susceptible to corruption until it's set in the stabilizer matrix which is usually dimethyl sulfoxide and propylene glycol."

Lowery made a face at the nastiness. Drugs and all of that medical stuff gave him the woozies, and that wasn't anything like blood or guts, that he could handle. But to think of a pile of man-made chemicals running through your veins and targeting specific areas of your brain to shut them down or warp their function really weirded him out.

"Have you seen the autopsy report of the woman that was murdered at Fircrest?"

"No." Doctor Patrice shook her head.

"How much do you wanna bet both the woman and Luis Jimenez have STRIC-R in their systems too?"

"Nothing would surprise me at this point. My boyfriend's been texting me all day with what's happened. He's in Houston right now and wants to hop on a redeye and I told him there's no good in that, the Airport's backed up, stay where you are, I'll be fine."

She was so helpful and stable. Lowery wanted to hug her and just smiled.

"I'll get back to you on that...can I have a minute with Officer Veracruz?"

The Doctor nodded and left, her chocolate skin catching the runners of fluorescent lights.

Lowery stood in the doorframe for a second. Veracruz was dabbing her nose which had stopped bleeding. Her green eyes lazily drifted from the drip of the IV to his tall frame as he came to stand next to the arm of the couch.

"How did your shirt get ripped?" He asked. He had to know if she had struggled with Jimenez.

"I don't know." She said. "I must've been out."

"And he was on the floor when you came in?"

"Yeah, we already went over this, I was out in seconds."

"Listen, Sarina, there's an illegal drug in your

system and it's strong enough to take out a bull elephant. The fact that you're not a bowl of jello right now lets me know you have a history of using painkillers and you wouldn'tve gotten this job if you told the truth about it. If I find no other evidence to support the fact that you were set up or framed in any way, I'll be forced to put in a recommendation for involuntary manslaughter at the very least. If there is so much as a *hint* of anything stronger I don't know *what* court in America would overlook murder one."

Sarina's eyes welled.

"I didn't do it."

"That won't fly. I have to know, why did he call you over?"

"I already told you..." Veracruz' voice broke, the stress on her face causing her lip to tremble. "He said he needed to talk to me about Fircrest."

"But what about it?"

"He didn't say! I just went over there, I didn't know he was dead-I would've called the cops but I didn't know..."

"But what could've happened at Fircrest that made him go back to his house and believe the only person he could talk to about it was you?" Lowery squatted down as the K9 Officer cried silently. "You have to understand how suspicious it all looks. And I have to dig into your personal life to determine the state of your relationship at the time, where you were at. It's going to be rough but you have to be completely honest with me."

Lowery put his hand on her back and she nearly peeked at him from the shield of her hands.

"I didn't do it..."

"Then it will be obvious." Lowery offered sincerely. "The evidence doesn't lie."

The Detective stood by the door for nearly thirty

seconds until Doctor Patrice rounded the corner with the Psychiatrist, a small and plump woman nearing sixty with very dark hair and heavy silver earrings. Her name was Chirzen and Lowery wasn't sure what nationality she was but she did have an accent.

"No question's off the table." Lowery said to Chirzen after making eye contact. "I wanna know everything."

The Psychiatrist nodded and Lowery took to the hall to locate the burn victim from the Fircrest inferno.

THIRTY-TWO

Feeling like a newly convalescent patient from some dramatic major surgery, Detective First Grade Michael Erland entered Precinct Three with slow steps and a suppressed anger at who had turned his world upside down.

Sierra Marland.

The drowning sirens had swallowed his body and the red and blue lights had pierced his eyes-hands had grabbed him and moved him to the back of an ambulance for treatment only to leave him surrounded by a wall of dark blue with a thousand questions.

And here he was, in the very building he first came to after being transferred from Mountain County Sheriff's Department, and like the building he had changed a great deal.

Every eye was upon his battered face and bare feet as he was escorted through the halls, all in judgment of some sort, some form of bias whether for or against, others averted their glares and made a point of looking away. What was it, twelve years? Twelve years of his life, changed in one day.

A woman caught his eye and she rushed to him only to be halted by the two Officers that were accompanying the Detective to HomCon.

"Detective Erland...wh..."

"Ma'am please!" The one to his right pushed

Kelly Barnett away with a strong hand.

"Don't say anything, Mike." The one on his left added.

The Detective shook his head in frustration. Another bystander caught in the wash of Sierra's sinking ship, chopped up in the propeller blades and sucked into the spreading wake. Her magnetic pull was like some kind of supernova in outer space, a brilliant bloom of otherworldly beauty forever linked with catastrophe.

Erland looked forward, at the ground, dejected and guilty until the floor ran out and gave way to the hard tan carpet of HomCon.

The two Officers were surprised to see Lieutenant Ross in civilian clothes and with nothing more than a nudge of his head the door was shut and silence rang in Erland's ear.

The Detective took the nearest seat and said nothing, zoned in thought.

"What happened Mike?" Ross came from the podium where presentations were made and spun one of the folding chairs to sit opposite him, and the fatherly Lieutenant did so with his legs spread, resting crossed arms on the back of the chair. "What the hell happened?"

"I didn't go home-I went to Tabitha's...one of the Homeland Agents. I was working with Homeland still...it was all so harmless one minute and then it snapped..."

"What happened?" Ross' tone was understanding as Erland stared a hole in the wall with a zombie's gaze.

"Sugar Hill Elementary...I knew from six points of evidence that Tim Wolcek killed Agent Magnolia Marland...we just went to talk to him..."

Ross' face took the information with a swirled

reaction of compassion and regret.

"Wolcek was killed earlier tonight. Shot."

"I know. I was there. I watched it happen..."

The Lieutenant's head slumped as if it had lost all ability to hold itself upright. He swore to himself and one of the arms that was crossed over the other drifted to the nubbins on his head which he rubbed a few times before speaking.

"Listen Mike, I know you better than anybody here...I know you were deputized by Homeland and you were doing the right thing in your mind and I stand behind you...I'm sure given a few days of debriefing I'd be able to hear the whole story and prove myself right but I'm not in charge."

Erland's head twisted slowly and he eyed the Lieutenant with his good eye, the other one was completely sealed and puffy.

"Then who the hell is?" He said without color of any kind.

"A man named Brown from Washington D.C. He should be here pretty soon and let me tell you, he's got the full power of the Executive Branch behind him. I don't know what kind of operation you got into but you have no idea what kind of hornet's nest you stirred up."

Erland's mind could've taken it a thousand ways but he was prepared. Brown. Mr. Brown, as the leader of the team at Sugar Hill had called him. And Jupiter, did he know Mr. Brown? Did he *send* Mr. Brown?

As much as he didn't want to admit it, Sierra was out there, alone, in the cold, against a raging pack of wolves, surrounding her on every side just like that one ill-fated hunting trip to the Turbus Mountain Forest, and she had predicted the moves correctly and escaped only to leave behind a hurricane.

But Jupiter had the memory card, didn't he? No, the real memory card was stashed at the Precinct, he had watched her do it, CONSTANT was in the janitor's locker. So what did Jupiter have? And what was Sierra's play? To convince Jupiter he had CONSTANT by hiding it on the Detective and letting him get tortured while the hacker's men found it?

If it was the case then why didn't she say so, damn it, why didn't she trust him like she kept saying she did, what was all that in the apartment and at the school-was it all an act? How could he take her word again if he had the chance to ask?

Then Erland remembered their flawed promises.

Don't put my personal safety above your mission...I promise...

Don't die...I promise...

Erland humorlessly saw the fruit of their fracture and hated himself for being so selfish and narrow-minded. Sierra must've pulled her hair out in an effort to convince herself her plan would work and the only way it would've was if he didn't know. He had seen her heaviness after the PierHouse shoot out, bearing the burden meant for her sister on top of the *loss* of her sister, what was a little beating in the face of saving the United States from Jupiter's grip? He was the only one *she* trusted and she had sacrificed that for the mission only to be vindicated by her gamble.

Then why did Erland feel so guilty? And Sierra, in whatever dark and lonely place she was, running for her life, she *must've* felt guilty.

What about Tabitha? In some strange way she had died without bitterness, died with understanding as only a submitted servant could.

And he had made a promise to her, hadn't he? At least he would've until the cord of life unraveled before her eyes.

Take care of her, Mike...

Erland shook his head and let it hang on his tight shoulders. He didn't understand it. God it was such a mess.

The door flew open with a smacking sound and man of sixty-something with glasses and a sharply dressed Chinese-American assistant surveyed the scene before speaking.

"Which one of you is Michael Erland?"

The Detective turned his head and said nothing. The shut right eye was enough to answer the question.

"Who are you?" The man who must've been Mr. Brown asked Lieutenant Ross.

"Marvin Ross, I'm his superior."

"Leave."

"Anything you say to him you can say to me."

Mr. Brown stood with loose fists but fists nonetheless. Erland saw this and his good eye darted between the face of him and the Lieutenant.

"This is *way* above your pay grade Lieutenant." Before Ross could figure out how Mr. Brown knew he was a Lieutenant as he was in civilian clothes the man continued. "Erland was statused as a provisional Homeland Agent and falls under our jurisdiction and authority and ours alone from the *moment* he signed that waiver, every single twitch of his thumb is Homeland and you have nothing to do with it."

Ross stood.

"What about the OIS? Where were you when my man had to commandeer a POV and risk his life to chase down one of your rogue Agents and save whatever screwed up operation you were in the process of losing?"

"That falls under Cat Six Article Twenty-Seven A of the Provisional Deputization of LLEO's..." Brown turned his eyes to Paul Chang for a brief enough gesture to merit the assistant's furious use of the tablet he held.

"So you mean there is no OIS?" Ross was as intense as he was succinct. "He just shot up a Homeland car resulting in the death of the Homeland Agent inside the car and poof, Article such and such erases all of that?"

"Mr. Ross."

"It's *Lieutenant* Ross damn it, and I've earned every damn ounce of it doing my job keeping this city safe and all of a sudden your Agents come in for some secret operation and throw around the words national security a few times and half of the city's either blown up or on fire!"

Ross stood with wide eyes, his lungs recoiling from the exertion of shouting.

Mr. Brown waited for an uneasy set of beats and Erland's good eye danced between their faces to gauge them.

"Lieutenant Ross, if you don't change your tone *and* your attitude, you won't *be* a Lieutenant any more."

"Is that a threat?" Ross crossed his arms. Erland wanted him to stop, righteous though he was, there was no reason for it. Ross was just going to get himself in trouble, especially if this Brown was affiliated with Jupiter in any way.

"I don't make threats. I don't need to."

Mr. Brown was as sanguine as an albino snake and Ross took a deep sigh before tapping Erland on the shoulder and leaving the room.

Kelly Barnett nearly sprinted from her seat near the door as she caught a flash of Rollins. He was on the move and was taken aback when he saw her face.

"What's wrong?" He asked as they walked to room Four-Eighty.

"They brought Detective Erland in like he's a criminal."

"What?" Rollins frowned and then pulled Kelly aside as they reached the privacy of an empty hall. "Did you see Brown?"

"I don't know, what does he look like?"

"I mean," Rollins corrected and spoke slowly. "Was Erland with uniformed Officers or someone that resembled a Homeland Agent?"

"He was with Officers." Barnett nodded and tried to calm herself. "I knew this would happen. If they got him then Darren and Jessica are next."

Rollins checked his watch. It was a little after ten.

"If Brown's here then I'm about to be deactivated." The tech swore and ran a pensive hand across his goatee before making a hasty decision. "There's something that you have to do for all of us, for the mission, for everything. If my guess is right it'll be the battle that wins the war."

If any nervous energy had since departed it rushed back into her face in splotches of red.

"Anything."

Rollins held his tongue for a moment to determine if she was capable and convinced himself Sierra was a good judge of character-Kelly had made it this far and had reached the point where she was the only option.

"Follow me."

Polis opened his eyes from the long, deep wince of agony to see the frame of a tall redheaded man in a blue sport coat with tan pants and a white shirt. The master thief blinked to life and his chiseled face still held the grimace of pain as he stretched out, immobile on the cot, shirtless and hooked up to an oxygen mask and an IV drip. A portable EKG was blipping peacefully beside him as well.

"Could you bring me a cup of coffee?" The red-haired man said to a much shorter Officer, a stout man who had been assigned to guard, as he had heard through their mouths, the Fircrest Arsonist. He could see it in the news, he would forever live in infamy for a crime he didn't commit.

The cop left and the redhead took a seat next to Polis.

"My name's Chris Lowery, I'm a Detective." Though he didn't specify what avenue it was obvious to Polis he was in Arson. "I need to ask you a few things and then you can get back to rest."

Polis knew he had to tell the truth at some point, whether it was going to be believed or not, and to see the lack of hardness in the man's face was reassuring.

Polis looked down at his oxygen mask several times. His hands were at his sides in restraints to the edge of the gurney and on his stomach with the gaping hole in his back it was a position even the best magician couldnt've escaped from.

Lowery removed the oxygen mask and studied the phosphorus burn. It was as if a splat of lava had clung to his back like glue and the deep laceration that was a result was red and tender and the skin around it yellowed and nearly diseased looking. Lowery wondered why the area was not bandaged and saw how it glistened with some kind of chemical.

"I didn't set the place on fire." Lowery heard the man say with a strong accent, perhaps French. The Detective chewed on his lip as he listened and was reminded of Veracruz. Innocence needed no defense but in the miasma of due process it had its moments of being the worst defense.

"Let me start with your name and what you do."

"My name is...Jean-George Polis...I am a thief."

Lowery had taken a pad from his sport coat and paused in writing.

"Excuse me?"

"I am a thief...I was hired by Robert Bellamy the Third to retrieve a camera in one of the rooms...I just happened to be there when the arsonists were..."

Lowery blinked rapidly and sat back in his seat. Just like Veracruz, how was he supposed to prove that?

"And where is this camera?"

"The Homeland Agent with the goatee has it."

Lowery didn't know if that was Rollins but assumed it was.

"And what's on this camera that made it so important for Bellamy to hire a thief so that Homeland Security wouldn't find it?"

"How do I know?" Polis' sangfroid was as obvious as it was second nature. "I did my job. I don't know who the hell those guys were but there can't be anything left of that place now."

"There's not." Lowery confirmed as he wrote. "Can you describe these guys?"

"More than one, no more than six. They wore black and had...NVG's...Willie Pete's and wireless comms..."

"Sounds like an action movie..." Lowery watched the sedated face as it ran through the images stuffed inside.

"They were para-military...they spoke English, sounded American. Other than that I can't tell you anything..."

"No names?"

"No."

"What time was this?"

"Ach, merde-je ne souvenir pas..."

"Excuse me?"

"Look at me, Detective, I can barely breathe from the inhalation of the gas and my back feels like there's no skin on it. I can't give you any more than that and if you talk to Bellamy he'll deny every word but I have no reason to lie...those men shot at me and I escaped with my life. I'm not one of them."

Lowery pursed his lips and affixed the oxygen mask back on Jean-George Polis' face. The Detective figured him to be about fifty-two and eyed his well-muscled condition. His words were certainly possible but still needed a great deal of corroboration. And who would want to burn Fircrest Mansion to the ground? Would Bellamy want to destroy his own property after having stolen the camera to make it look like someone else was responsible? What was on this camera that was so damning and why didn't the prior Homeland search locate the camera?

Too many unknowns, but less than Veracruz. It wasn't his case anyway but he kept the details back in the studious recesses of his mind, utterly convinced the conspiracy lurking in the shadows was some kind of painfully large fire-spitting dungeon dweller and was way out of his league.

Lowery stood.

"The evidence doesn't lie." He said objectively, a statement neither for nor against the self-admitted thief.

"One more thing," Polis added through the mask and Lowery pulled it out just enough to hear the request. "I have a gold Rolex...very special to me."

"It's in evidence."

"See that it stays there, s'il vous plait."

Lowery checked the time and broke into a light jog once free from the room.

Mr. Brown leaned against the wall with his arms crossed. The door was shut and Paul Chang stood, guarding it in some strange way in all of his slightness.

"Now then, Erland, where's Marland?"

"I don't know." It was not a lie but he knew his answer would be pressed regardless.

"I could've bet the farm you'd say that, so I'll ask it again and you'll have to do better."

"I saw her go but I don't know where she went."

"What was she driving then?"

"A green car." Erland said quickly.

"Green? There must be thousands of those on the road, howbout a make and model?"

"I couldn't see damn it, I was shot up with STRIC-R and beaten within an inch of my life and it was like eight-hundred yards away."

Brown pushed from the wall and his eyes jumped to Chang.

"How do you know it was STRIC-R?"

"Magnolia had it. Reston had it. I had it. In the neck right behind the ear."

"I asked you how you knew."

"Isn't it obvious?"

"Did Sierra talk about it?"

"She knew Reston had it. It's an MO for crying out loud, d'you think I'm stupid?"

"No, Mr. Erland, on the contrary." Brown drifted around the conference room with his eyes on the floor. "I know you're a reasonably...intelligent man with a sterling record and I'd hate to see it blemished right at the end."

"What d'you mean?" Erland looked up at the man through his good eye.

"You're *never* going back to Detective work *ever* again. You will be permanently deactivated from *any* work involving the United States Government of *any* kind whether it be State Representative or a Cooks Assistant in a high school cafeteria." Brown sat next to Erland whose vision rested on the chair in front of him where Ross had been and spoke with vitriol so concise it seemed pre-planned. "And I'm going to rip apart *every single* aspect of your life from the day you were born up until now and have you debriefed by *every single* acronym I can think of until I damn well satisfied that you've told the truth and were acting as an honorable public servant under the authority of a dishonorable *untrustworthy* psychotic *witch*."

It took all of the control Erland had learned as a boxer not to flatten the man in the emotion of the moment and all the more wisdom he had gained as a Detective to not let that struggle show on his face, but from the slanderous words and accusations, Erland knew he still loved Sierra. Despite her nearly magical abilities to control and manipulate she was the furthest thing opposite of a witch he could think of and he couldn't defend her as much as it burned within him to do so, he had to stand-alone. Whatever she had done, he understood it now. The enemies were circling, no matter their motives or end roads, their enemies had pushed them back together.

"Why do you want her so bad?" Erland asked.

"She has CONSTANT. Do you even *know* what that is?"

Erland paused, cursing himself for diverting the conversation to something far more damning than his relationship with Sierra.

What the hell...

"Criminal Operations Network Satellite Tracking and Notations Test."

Mr. Brown let a wash of what Erland would describe as sinister pleasure drain from his face before speaking.

"Does she have it?"

"No."

"Who has it?"

"The real one or the fake?"

"How do you know there's a fake?"

Erland let his lungs calm because they had crept up on him. His heart pounded in his chest from holding back the desire to break Brown's nose and yet he felt as if he was being lead like a dog into the kennel of Brown's choosing and not only couldn't stop it, but couldn't fight it.

"Sierra gave one to me but she took it back. She hid one somewhere. There could be a hundred of them for all I know. She probably has the real one in the cup of her bra."

"Reston had the real one from the Mutual Bank on Cherry, box 410. Where'd it go? There's no record of it in evidence from Reston's processing. Surely you witnessed her Q and A session with him, you must know a *lot* more than you're telling me."

Erland's face felt as hard as slab granite.

"I don't know but the one Jupiter has is a fake."

Brown stood quickly and walked behind Erland to speak with Chang. Erland couldn't see Brown's face and didn't know if he was with Jupiter or not. It was impossible to read into the maneuver-whether he was sending his minion off to contact Jupiter or some other type of psychological diversion was in the works and Erland sat in the pool of his own thoughts for nearly five minutes or at least until a heavy drum of knuckles filled the room.

Chang answered the door. Erland turned to see Rollins.

"Are you Brown?" Rollins asked Chang.

"I'm Brown, who are you?"

"Milton Rollins, Homeland Security SAB."

Mr. Brown's spine straightened and Rollins had a burning look buried in his dark eyes.

"Interesting."

"I'm the..."

"I know who you are."

"Then you'll want to see the footage."

"Yes."

Mr. Brown turned to Erland.

"I'm not going anywhere." The Detective shrugged. Mr. Brown told Chang to watch him as if he was going to make a run for it and the Detective dumbly gazed at the dapper Chang and made him so nervous he moved to the podium and busied himself with his tablet.

The door was open a crack and Erland didn't see Lowery sneak in.

"Hey I brought you some coffee."

Erland turned to see his protégé.

"Thanks man."

"You can't be in here." Chang told Lowery who was taller by nearly a foot and a half. The assistant rushed from his place with a defiant face.

"I'm just bringing my friend a cup of coffee- that's common courtesy around here."

"Okay, then leave the coffee and don't say anything." Chang slashed his hand as a woman came through the half open door. Erland spotted her movement before it was too late but with the after effects of STRIC-R and the beating, even with the reversal agent, his mouth wasn't yet as connected to his brain as he would've liked.

Kelly Barnett collided with Lowery and the full eight ounces of hot coffee received the shock with a gulping delay and sloshed from the cup as Lowery tried to correct it, making whatever remained in the paper cup splash over his sleeve. That which didn't drench

Chang's handheld tablet fell to the tan carpet and splattered pants and shoes. Erland pulled his feet back as a sip or two landed on his bare skin.

Chang swore and Lowery was speechless.

"Oh my gosh I'm so sorry I didn't see you!" Kelly reached into her purse for a napkin and went to her hands and knees on the carpet.

"Who the hell are you?" Lowery puffed, pants looking like he'd lost control of his bladder and the one sleeve not helping the cause. Chang left in a hurry throwing liquid off the tablet screen with flicks of his hand and cursing that the web pages were changing as he did so.

"Barnett, I work with Rollins..." Kelly said quickly and Erland squinted as she worked her way over. "I'm *really* sorry..."

"Son of a..." Lowery shook his head. "Kimmie's going to kill me. I just got this back from the dry cleaners...she says she won't let me have a real suit till I come home without a spill somewhere..." The redhead set the cup down on the floor and let his easy smirk go. "I know she's only kidding but this won't help."

Kelly had inched closer on her hands and knees and was a hair away from Erland's foot.

"Tell her you can't get a promotion unless you have matching pants and jacket set that's either blue or blue. Preferably...blue."

Lowery nodded and chuckled and didn't see Kelly's closed hand push a thirty-two gigabyte flash drive under Erland's foot. The look in her eye was all the Detective needed. A sparkly blue eye winked at her and Kelly Barnett left as quickly as she came to the tune of Lowery shaking his head. He watched her leave and then shut the door.

"What the hell happened Mike? You look horrible."

"I can't talk about it."

"Can you talk to me about Luis Jimenez?"

Erland didn't expect to hear that from Lowery and his face showed it.

"Why, what about him?"

"Did you know he was murdered at around eight thirty?"

"What?" Erland was caught in the trap of his own thoughts and the disorientation of it spread across his body with looseness in the uncomfortable seat. Jupiter was everywhere, his fingers were in everything, and the fact that Kelly Barnett and Milton Rollins had teamed up gave him a world of confidence in Sierra's choice to sell him out and make Jupiter think the lone Detective had been a foolish pawn in the grand scheme. He had an assumption about the thumb drive under his foot, and it burned inside of him to see if he was right but he would have to be patient.

"Yeah, he was shot in the neck."

"Who shot him?"

"Sarina Veracruz."

The words gutted Erland's stomach with a clean cut and he was left to watch it all spill out. Furious questions rammed his mind with why's and how's and he held back being sick.

What on *earth* had gone wrong? The Detective stared at the floor, the zombie eyes returning.

"Dear God..."

"You worked with Jimenez at Fircrest, didn't you?" Lowery's head sunk in his shoulders as if someone was listening, his speech quick and tight.

"Yes, but..."

"He called her over to his house to talk about something that went wrong at Fircrest and when she showed up the dog was dead and he was dead and that's the last thing that she remembered."

Erland's eyes darted between Lowery's interlocked hands and his face and back.

"Was she doped?"

"STRIC-R? Yeah, how'd you know-you got it too?"

"Yeah."

"Then she didn't do it. I bet Jimenez was loaded with it too. And I asked the Doc about it and it can only be made in a special lab."

"Of course not but that's not enough."

"It has to be, especially if we get the autopsy report of that the murder victim from Fircrest."

"Magnolia Marland? Brown would never let that go. She was an SAB Homeland Agent, and the mission she died on is what started this whole mess."

"No kidding..." Lowery pulled back and stared at the ceiling in a gesture of frustration. "I...I gotta get Cruzie out man...the gun has her prints on it and she was in position to pull the trigger."

Erland looked to the door and hesitated as if it was going to fly open.

"But there has to be something else...if she had STRIC-R in her system she wouldnt've been able to move."

"She said she blacked out but she seemed okay at the scene."

"That's not good-the stuff's way to strong..."

"Patrice said she had some kind of resistance. God knows how cognizant she was at the time of the shooting."

"Genetic?"

"No, like a prior history with drugs, specifically painkillers." Erland swore to himself upon hearing the answer and looked away and Lowery leaned in.

"There's gotta be *something* man, you worked with both of them that day-you gotta have *some* perspective that I don't."

Erland held his mouth closed and the thumb drive felt as if it was made of molten lead under Lowery's proximity. Mr. Brown said he would rip into Erland's life and if so, he certainly would know they had slept together albeit just that once several months ago and it would be enough to taint a case that needed no more confusion. It would be all but a dead lock if Sarina had any kind of personal relationship in the same way with Jimenez...and Erland didn't want to admit the logic behind why Jimenez called her of all people.

"Just dig deeper..." Erland said, not completely focused and then came back. "And consider the angles..."

"Her nose is broken but I don't know if it's from falling or from an altercation with Jimenez. It's too hard to tell. Her t-shirt was torn by the collar, same dilemma."

Lowery stood as Paul Chang returned.

"The Doctor is on her way to give you a quick examination before Mr. Brown returns." Chang stated, as official as was humanly possible and glared at the tall red head.

Erland nodded and Lowery left with the cup and an air of hopeful regret because it was time for him to go home.

Rollins hunched at the small table in room Four-Eighty to tap a few keys on the laptop before spinning the computer to favor Mr. Brown's viewpoint. The Homeland Deactivator shut the door and watched the spliced tape with attentive pale green eyes. With the assistance of a searching matrix and hybrid facial recognition software, Rollins had taken the hard-copied footage from every camera Fircrest had to offer and made a short movie surrounding Magnolia Marland.

The final camera, retrieved from the smoldering body of the professional thief by Officer Sheridan, was all the evidence needed to confirm an eternal conviction of the guilty and vindicate the innocent, because it had been hidden in the very room the murder had been committed in. Rollins never knew why Tallifer couldn't find it but that was beside the point, and his dark, deep-set eyes juggled between the screen and the face of the man who studied the screen in veiled perplexity.

The video was less than ten minutes and Mr. Brown was silent for another minute and a half after its final frame.

Then he put his hands in the pockets of his wooly gray suit jacket like chicken wings.

"Destroy it." He said.

"Pardon?"

"You heard me. Destroy the video and all of the cameras. Everything. In fact, Mr. Chang will accompany you to the incinerator here in the Precinct. I want you to even destroy the computer you did the work on."

Rollins nodded somewhat effusively.

"Yes Sir."

Mr. Brown grabbed the doorknob and turned slowly.

"Did Marland try to contact you after the Code Zeta?"

"Not at all. I've been here with the cameras since, the desk sergeant will verify...I left to get Polis and the camera in his possession and came right back."

"I know...considering your position in this failure...you were just a pawn and were operating under immense circumstances regarding not only Bartleson's negligence but the Marland's as well. I will, of course...overlook your designing of the CONSTANT memory card and compliance in the operation as a senior SAB Computer Systems Analyst in exchange for your testimony against them when the time comes."

Rollins held a stony face and judged the man in his mind. One Marland was dead, the other nearly several times over and now a fugitive to those who employed her, and the old man in charge of it all was on his way to a job counting paperclips in Alaska or a grand jury, whichever fit Mr. Brown's fancy.

"And the Detective, for that matter."

"...I will..." Rollins nodded with all the conviction he had to offer and sighed something deep and heavy after Mr. Brown left Four-Eighty for HomCon.

Doctor Patrice entered the conference room with a small bag and went right for the spaces behind Erland's ear just behind the lobe to find the needle mark in his neck.

"I knew it." She said. Erland's eyes were solemn and he knew it too.

"They gave me something to wake me up."

"Yes..." Patrice gently checked the Detective's eyes with a penlight. "Probably a triple concentration of Xenolaine...I don't have any with me but I know they do at Corazon. It should keep you going for a bit. I'll go call the hospital and tell them to send some over."

"No," Erland twitched his head to negate the offer. "I don't want any more needles in me...please."

"Detective." Patrice was firm. "Short term memory loss *will* hit within twenty-four to forty-eight hours if you're not properly stabilized. If I was in charge I'd send you to Corazon and put you on..."

Mr. Brown entered the room again and Patrice took some form of defensive posture with her hands on her hips.

"Can you tell me why I can't move Mr. Polis or

Detective Erland to the hospital but Tanya Wilson is already there? *Before* I got to examine her?"

"That's my call, Doctor. How is he?"

"I won't know exactly until I get him to a hospital." Patrice was increasingly succinct as her frustration with the bureaucracy increased by the second.

"Was he given STRIC-R?"

"Yes."

"Is he okay now?"

The Doctor nodded her head slowly as if she was reasoning with a five year old.

"Yes, but he won't be *unless* he can get the proper treatment."

"What kind of window do you project?"

"It depends on the body...a perfectly healthy male of his age, maybe a day or two? But that's not..."

Mr. Brown held up a hand.

"Detective Erland will be sent home and kept under guard where he will be retrieved for later debriefing. If he is cooperative, he will get the treatment."

"You can't do that!" Patrice held out her hands. "This is the United States. He has a right to treatment."

"And he gave *up* that right when he aided a fugitive in stealing classified proprietary technology and endangering the *entire* Departmental database!" Mr. Brown nearly shouted his glasses off.

Doctor Patrice was not only disarmed but dismayed. Her eyes fell to the Detective in disbelief.

"Don't worry." Erland gave her half of a smile. "I'll be fine."

"What about Polis? He could have long term organ damage from phosphorus poisoning."

"Can you treat him here?"

"I'd need some things..."

"And you'll have them."

The Doctor sighed and looked to Erland with a defeated apology.

"Is there *anything* I can do?" She asked.

Some hope filled the Detective's face.

"Could you spare a pair of socks?"

The Doctor nearly sprinted from the room and returned before Mr. Brown could say a word with a pair of black mesh ballet flat women's socks.

"Best I can do, but they should fit."

"Thanks." Erland smiled and it comforted Patrice the blue eyes had not lost their twinkle in the face of what surrounded him, whether it was true or not. She had been in the Precinct for six years now and hadn't seen a better man show up for work in those seventy-two months than Michael Erland. He had lost eight pounds during the consuming hunt for Granderson and contributed the fullness of his pay during the time to help the grieving families of the terrible tragedy the monster Granderson had inflicted upon the community.

The Doctor left him to face Mr. Brown after a pat on the shoulder.

"You're gonna go home and sit there with an armed guard at your door and another patrolling the premises until I'm good and ready to talk to you."

"What about the memory loss?"

"Does it matter?" Mr. Brown failed to hide an iniquitous grin, leaving the room.

Erland smiled to himself as he affixed the socks and kept the thumb drive in the arch of his left foot. Whatever game Mr. Brown was playing he had no idea who he was playing it against. Erland might not've been a gambler and a game-player like Sierra, but he was a boxer and knew how to take hits to set up the knockdown counterpunch.

THIRTY-THREE

Against Nurse Kawada's best wishes, Henry Morell left his bed and waddled across the hall. There he saw two people bundled up in bandages and slings. The Nurse located him leaning against the wall and wore a scolding face.

"These are the survivors?" He asked.

She nodded and motioned for him to go back to his bed and he waved her off and stood next to a small woman who looked to be either Middle Eastern or Indian. Her name was Roshie and the other one was Mendholssen. They were the only living proof of the MCL and they were inches away from death considering the severity of their wounds.

"What did she break?"

"Spinal fracture...dislocated shoulder..." The nurse said in a cute accent, drawing out the words. It was obvious English was not her first language though she was very intelligent.

Morell swore and pointed to a dark haired young man with two breathing tubes shoved up his nose. A machine was doing the work for him and he looked as if he would never wake up.

"What about him?"

"Lung puncture and...cranial fracture..."

Morell swore again and sighed.

"Did that call come in for me yet?"

Kawada shook her head and nearly pushed him to get back to bed. He looked like something out of a horror movie, face cut and scraped with multiple lacerations, his neck colored purplish yellow from the snapping impact of the yacht explosion.

Morell shook his head like he was going to comply and Kawada busied herself with a tray of medical supplies for storage. When she wasn't looking Morell crossed the hall and took his things from the room where he had spent far too much time and although the badge and gun had been confiscated his phone had not and he gingerly traipsed to one of the rooms resident physicians used to catch a quick nap. Thankfully the room was dark and vacant and he found a set of civilian clothes that didn't fit too bad and freed himself of the hospital gown. A baseball cap of a team he didn't care for completed the escaping disguise and Morell casually shuffled out the hospital through a drafty side door to the stinging cold of a hedged lot. The hospital carried the eerie aura of death and light hung in the staggered yellowing orbs of industrial grade lamps and beyond the reaches of the lot was a deepening valley of power lines that caught Morell's eye and he followed them from their furthest point down a canyon of poky black trees as they ran back to his position and over his head, over the hospital and on to somewhere else. Morell wanted a cigarette in the cold and began walking around the side of the hospital along the hedge. The hospital was stashed in some rundown residential zone of greater Crescent and Morell had not only lost the river but the skyline as well and couldn't get perspective until he reached the busy State Route to see he was somewhere in Valley, Pill Valley as they called it locally, just east northeast of the big city lights.

He called Marland's number and walked east, as

the road paralleled the distant river, and his efforts
yielded no fruit. Morell cursed with a military flair at
the other numbers, billowing puffs of white heat came
from his lungs. Tabitha, Jimenez, Quinlan. No answer.
Even Rollins.

Morell's feet crunched frosty grass as the road
dipped to the loose spread of a small creek and
wetlands area that separated the road from a host of
apartment buildings.

There was one more number he could call, the
number of a man who he knew lived not too far away
and was as dependable as a pair of old combat boots.

The Crescent Modern Journal's dated square of
eraser-colored brick glowed in the bright lighting of the
new halogen bulbs like some kind of corner church.
Reston smiled a broad and toothy thing as he saw it and
ran to the door.

It occurred to him once at the door, that he had
no identification or key card or anything and he
frowned before crunching scattered gravel on the
pavement to see the side lot. Several cars were still
there, perhaps considering the day's events there was an
incredible political slant on the terror and damage, and
it quickly darted through Darren's mind how he had
missed the nearly diarrheic flow of television news
from his diet given the course of his actions. National,
local, even the British-speaking world news, it occurred
to him in the normal flow of life he had simply plugged
himself in like an electric car and sucked it all up in the
recesses of his brain. Surely the Governor had called a
press-conference, most definitely the Mayor, not to
mention CPD Chief Nolan and he had missed every
word, yet, been at the center of so much of it. It was
almost as if it had taken less out of him with the given
circumstances than if he had sat home with a box of

pizza and a case of beer, biting his nails as breaking news flash after breaking news flash flooded the screen with the aftershocks and fallout reports of Crescent's unending damage.

Reston let his hand harass the door and squinted to see past the lobby but the grime had been built up too thick on the windows. The journalist banged and banged again and finally let a thick sigh spill from his lungs and turned to face the coldness of the night. It had given him hope on the lonely march, knowing Kelly had chosen her own path, and with all that was in him believed Jessica Birchall was going to shock the world but he just couldn't be sure. It wasn't that easy.

Darren crunched gravel and let his head fall and the door whined and squealed. He spun quickly on his heel to see the disheveled and greasy appearance of Ted Mackie, bloodshot eyes and all behind a scruffy beard that was in modern fashion but never really worked for him.

"Where the hell have you been all day?" Mackie growled, a South Crescent-bred man all of his life he carried the harder edges of the dust and grease that it took to make a living.

Darren blinked at Mackie a few times. He was the Editor-In-Chief, right? He deserved an explanation.

"How much time do you have?"

"This whole place is falling apart and you make a joke? Didn't Barnett beat any sense into you or were you too busy..."

"It's a long story Mack." Reston came to face his boss who was frozen in a stance of halted movement. "And I'll tell it to you as it happened but you gotta do me a big favor."

If Mackie had answered the door with any patience it had run out.

"After sending you to the Libertarian Lounge

Party *I* gotta do *you* a favor? What'd you think your last three years have been, pal? You're a hack and you know it and any leverage you had from saving my ass from that falling crane is long gone."

Darren went to speak and didn't have the material. Had he saved Mackie's life from a falling crane? It was true, wasn't it? As true as his job was flying right out the window.

"You wouldn't believe me if I told you," And before Mackie could rebut with a litany of curses Reston held up his hand and removed the article from his pocket. "Now, you'll have to publish it under my name, and you'll have to get it in the press before Sunday's first."

Mackie was so taken aback by the demands and the subdued and calculated manner in which Reston delivered them that he listened.

"What is it?" He asked.

"Watch the Eleven o'clock news." Reston said with full assurance. "Then, whatever comes your way, you can call the shots with the percentages."

A ripple of something more honest than greed was evident in Mackie's face.

"What are you talking about?"

"It's the exclusive of a lifetime, *pal*." Reston tipped his eyebrows and turned back the street, crunching gravel.

"Hey!" Mackie frowned, trying to juggle between reading the hand-written article and thinking of just how much money Reston was alluding to. "Where are you going?"

Darren smiled.

"Home."

The restroom held an eerie silence and the overhead light hummed with the faintest buzz. Jessica

Birchall stared at her face in the mirror and cast aside what thoughts told her how pale and how tired and worn out she looked. She took a few deep breaths, hands braced on the pedestal sink and wasn't thrilled about her sinuses and the hints of scratchiness that was poking her throat. There would be no room for coughing and excusing herself or stumbling over the teleprompter, it was a moment that would be forever etched in the reels of history, and it had to be *perfect*.

There was a knock on the door and Birchall didn't even flinch. She was staring deep into the eyes that Francine had called jungle cat eyes and didn't see what every one was talking about. They were just brown, just hers, no different than the day she got them way back when. Birchall then stood with her back as straight as possible and opened the door to see Rose, one of the production assistants.

"Ten." She said as she left for studio one.

Birchall looked at the orange sponge-painted walls of the restroom as she shut the door to the restroom's solitude and let the sound of her heels striking the hall before her echo with the strict cadence drumming through her soul. She knew her lines, she knew the cues. She had done this a thousand times if she'd done it once.

She was ready.

Mills was the larger one of the two Homeland Agents with Farges but they were both thick and athletic-looking brutes and they stood behind Farges as he argued with Channel Two's lobby security guard.

"I am from the Department of Homeland Security, okay, I am a Regional Supervisor and have enough authority to send you to Mars if I want to." The nondescript looking man named Farges nearly shouted, his pale skin reddening. "And you are interfering with an ongoing investigation concerning national security and can go to prison for it!"

Mills and Dowen wanted to pick the guard up and throw him against the wall behind the desk he occupied since they had come to a standstill in negotiating the legality of breaching Free Speech.

"I can't let you by." The guard, a former volunteer fireman from Detroit whose name was Jones and had a strong southern accent. "Don't make me bring race into this now."

"I don't care if your skin is neon green!" Farges continued. "The woman in there who's about to go on air is going to jeopardize national security, is there some part of your brain that doesn't comprehend that? Now give us the key card or we will take it from you."

"Well you're breaking the right to free speech and now you're going to add assault? Whatever comes out of this station's already been cleared-we didn't get the Howard's Award of Excellence for sound effects."

"I told you already, the Agent that gave the clearance for this material is a fugitive of the US government."

"Well, I already called Mr. Hodge concerning that but I'll call him again."

Farges rolled his eyes with his hands on his hips and was a painfully unimposing figure in the brown sweater vest. He gave a nod to Mills and Dowen held the guard while Mills took the key card.

"You..."

"Save it for court." Farges pointed his finger and ran a hand through his hair before taking the key card from Mills and moving quickly toward the elevator. Dowen stayed behind for a brief moment to glare at the security guard and make sure he didn't alert the studio.

Farges eyed his watch and pushed out a tense

gasp of air as the steel doors rolled shut.

Christian Lowery opened the door to the narrow two-story in Ambler's Way and the keys made a hollow and louder than necessary sound in the lock as cheap and uncluttered newly purchased pre-fabricated homes usually did. Kimmie said something about needing to get a plant for the small foyer area but there was a set of stairs there and Chris ran big as it was and needed the room just to take his jacket off and set it on the tipsy side table, though he broke repetition's grip and left his jacket on.

There was the padding of feet from the room next to the hall that ran straight before him to the back yard and the patio, the combination of which was no larger than an area rug.

"Hey." Kimmie said in the slightly croaky voice he had always found extremely attractive, not that she needed the help in the slinky oversized white sweater and black leggings. She buried her small frame in his arms. It was a fabled existence, theirs, high school sweethearts, and all of it seemed to fade with the move to Crescent. Deep down Kimmie's heart had never left the beauty of the painted desert and he knew it by the fact she wore that Navajo silver and turquoise bracelet nearly every day, the one he had splurged to get their farewell night out.

"You're home *early*. It's good to see you." She said with a thankful squeeze of her arms. "Today was strange."

Lowery checked his watch. It was maybe three minutes to eleven.

"I guess I am." He rubbed her back and tapped it a few times, completing the embrace. There was nothing he could do at work anyway, considering the time of day and the chaos of the city.

"Is everything okay with that Officer?" She asked, and she had a naturally pouty face and Lowery kissed her once on the lips.

"No, but it will be." He took his jacket off and she assisted, spotting the obvious stain.

"Chris...what'd you do?"

"It's...I was getting some coffee and this Homeland lady bumped into me." Lowery looked at his pants. It wasn't bad but there was no way he could wear them tomorrow. "Those Homeland ladies think they can get away everything..." He muttered.

"I'll take it to the dry cleaners tomorrow."

"I thought Bri was coming over tomorrow."

"It's a *long* day, Chris, there'll be *plenty* of time..." Her tone was dredged in annoyance, since Saturday *used* to be Kimmie's favorite.

Lowery nodded, his mind elsewhere. Kimmie's face didn't lose any of its unintentional petulance as she watched him plop his weary frame on the couch and go for the remote. It was like clockwork. She wanted to cry if she wanted to scream but in the same token she admired how committed he was to serving the community and would make an excellent father if he ever got the opportunity.

Kimmie mashed her lips around choosing what to say as the volume of the television ever so slowly increased as she walked down the hall to the kitchen with its postcard-sized window of the flat symmetry of Verdant Lanes and all of its rigidly suburban glory. No one was ever home, no neighbors to chat with-everybody was out all day trying to be somebody and she was stuck at home learning how to needlepoint, hunt for new recipes, or window-shop for housewares she couldn't actually touch and feel on the internet. Even walking around the small neighborhood to one of their parks, little more than a basketball hoop and a swing set surrounded by a pair of alders and three juniper shrubs, the lack of love was evident.

Kimmie took the Panang Curry from the refrigerator and threw it in the microwave, knowing the true flavors of it would be destroyed but Chris would say it was great anyway and continue staring at the television as he ate it and told work stories with his mouth full and then ask her how her day was and not recall that she had said the moment he stepped through the door. The microwave beeped to life and Kimmie watched the little dish of prawns, peas and carrots spin around as the Channel Two News' cheerfully strident theme penetrated the peacefulness of the home at a volume appropriate for the near deaf. Kimmie wiped her hands on a dishrag and scuffed back to the living room to sit next to her husband. Nichole had a son, Michelle had a son *and* a daughter and now it was her turn. She was the middle child and they always got the raw bargain, right? In some way she felt like a military wife and the move from Phoenix to Crescent really set it in stone. After all of her efforts to force warmth and hominess into Five-Eight-One One-Hundred And Seventy-First Avenue Southeast, she still lived in an echoey, drafty off-white box with grass that just wasn't as green as the house next to it and another seventy thousand left on the mortgage.

Chris put his arm around his wife as she snuggled up to him on the couch. She felt sleepy to the touch.

"Good evening." Anchor Don Cramer nodded and continued in a deep and aged voice that fit the gray suit and red tie. "We begin tonight with a stunning new development in the Crescent Crisis-the revelation of the man behind the attacks, deemed by members of the US Government, as...acts of terror. Jessica Birchall has the story you'll see only here, Live on Two at Eleven."

Kimmie felt her husband stiffen around the ribcage like a hunting dog with a scent. It was as if some buried conviction of his was being psychically divined by the pretty albeit somber and sober Jessica Birchall as she spoke to a camera all of her own, standing slightly to the right of a grainy picture of a man in white whose face was legible but not clear enough to be memorable.

"Thank you, Don. Would you believe the murder at Fircrest Mansion I covered earlier this morning triggered a chain of events that would include a shoot out at PierHouse, a yacht exploding near the mouth of the Targus, a sixty foot trailer blocking half of highway Two-Eleven and the subsequent burning of the Mansion itself only hours later?" Birchall asked the camera, and America, with all of the conviction available to her delicate body, and the slow clarity of speech she had studied so well. "And would you believe that *one* man was behind it all? From a trusted source in the Department of Homeland Security I have learned the man responsible for all of today's destruction is a wanted domestic terrorist known only by the alias *Jupiter*, a moniker appropriate for a deity of war. The man you see in the picture behind me is that man-the most dangerous man in America."

Kimmie's eyes jumped between the TV and the eyes of her husband. They were locked on to the picture, as if trying to flip through the Rolodex of images to find a match.

"He is not only a cyber terrorist but a kind of arms dealer as well, trading information instead of guns, selling secrets instead of stolen weapons, and his tactics consist solely of intimidation, fear, and death."

The frames changed to helicopter footage and a voice-over piece rehashing the catastrophes-mostly PierHouse and the fire, spliced with close ups of the wreckage and bits of interviews from bystanders and first hand witnesses. Then there was a cut up of Chief Nolan and Mayor Geffington in their hope and promise speeches declaring to punish the guilty and fight on as Americans who stood tall in the face of any adversity.

The pre-taped feed ended with a pause and then a black screen and two voices were heard faintly in the background. Were they shouting? Chris squinted and the TV's volume was already maxed.

The camera feed quickly panned to Don Cramer who had his index finger to his left ear and was flustered, something he never was.

"Please get Hodge as quickly as possible." He said, looking down at his desk and took two papers and stacked them and looked back to the camera.

"I'm very sorry, we are experiencing some technical difficulties..." The two voices were male and shouting to get down or something similar, perhaps stand down. Lowery knew it because he was an LEO and there was a certain signature to it.

"Bear with me folks as we get this ironed out."

The live feed then jumped to a camera as it panned to the green screen stage right of Cramer's desk where a thick, suited man had Birchall on the ground as if she was a hopped up meth addict who had robbed a convenience store at gunpoint. He was in the process of cuffing her. Her papers were splayed on the floor to indicate she had been tackled or physically assaulted and her slight body wriggled under the man's grip.

"What about free speech!" Her voice could be heard in ambience as another man was removing the wireless microphone from her jacket as if it was the item she had stolen. "What about the truth!"

"Oh my God..." Kimmie sat up. "Chris, what's going on?"

"Shh..." His face was taught.

The thin man in a brown sweater vest who had taken the microphone tossed the unit to the soft tile floor where it rattled and rolled around until stopping feet from an unused dolly. Then it occurred to him the cameras were on and he shouted profanities about the cameras and ordered them to be turned off in a demonstrative way that included his badge and the waving of his arms as the muscle in the suit crushed the back of Birchall's fitted blazer and led her off screen. As the camera tried to follow her the man in the sweater vest ran up to it and pushed it down to the floor.

There was a split second of another frame, too quick to ascertain what part of the studio and then a few seconds of black.

A commercial for an erectile dysfunction pill followed abruptly.

"Chris, what just happened?"

"I don't know." Lowery stood, nearly bolting from the couch and taking Kimmie's breath with it.

"Wh...where are you going?"

"I'm going back to the Precinct." He said distantly as he was already halfway up the stairs for a quick change.

"No..." Kimmie pushed herself from the couch and turned off the TV, about to curse at the ridiculous litany of side effects. "You..." Emotions were getting to her, they had been pick pick picking all day, all month, all year-ever since the transfer from Phoenix. "You can't be serious!" She padded to the hall, eyes misty with tears.

Chris came thumping down the stairs in hoppity clomps, throwing his arms into a waterproof jacket after having grabbed a new pair of khakis without even taking his shoes off.

"Chris..."

Lowery stopped and saw the trembling face of

his wife as she tried not to cry.

"Chris I'm scared."

"Honey...don't be." He said leaning down and holding her by the shoulders but not hugging her. "You're fine."

"Chris, dammit, why are you going? I don't understand..." She threw her fists up and down as they were half hidden in a grip of sweater sleeves and then buried her head in them. "How can you...I mean, what can you do?"

"My case is a part of all this, baby. I need to do my part to save the country from this guy, look what he's done already."

"I..." Kimmie cried in choked sobs and Lowery held her, his face bent in thought. Part of him didn't want to go but it was such a small, quiet voice inside, one that he never listened to. Kimmie would be fine, she was a tough girl, she just didn't know it yet.

"I promise honey, when this is over..."

"I don't believe you..." She pushed herself away, eyes red and hopeless. "You're *there* more than you're *here*...it's like you...don't..."

Lowery sighed and took a step for another embrace and Kimmie crossed her arms and turned forty-five degrees. That was the end of it. She pushed a thick lungful of air from her chest and smoothed down her sweater, her jaw slightly jutted.

The Detective nodded slowly and then again as he stared at the pale wooden floor that ran from the front door to the back and wasn't even real wood.

He left the house and the door had the same hollow rattle it always did and he swore to himself once and once again with more spit and anger as he fished in his pocket for the keys to the Camaro to realize he had left them in his other pants.

Henry Morell entered the grounds of the apartment complex to see it was a flat and spread out stack of blocks no higher than two stories and abutted a soupy green wetlands area that couldnt've been larger than three acres. Glad to be clear of the slim shouldered main road that ran through Valley, Morell used his phone to quickly search from the records stored on it which apartment in the block belonged to Detective First Grade Michael Erland, only to find the man wasn't home. So much for being as dependable as old combat boots. Calling his number resulted in a dead end and Morell called the number again as he scuffed down the rickety steps to see a woman leaning on the post of a car port across the narrow lane that divided the two sides of apartment blocks as it ran in a long-winded and twisted circle around the span of the property. He wondered as quickly as possible why he hadn't spotted her on the way in. Examining her from the back and the gentle curves of her body in the whitish cast of the apartment lights reminded him how he'd been subjugated to a near death experience and had emerged on the other side of it somewhat unchanged. Beauty was beauty. Her hips twitched in the slightest, cocked as they were in her graceful slant and her left hand came from her body and flicked the ash from a fresh cigarette. Morell advanced with one thought consuming his mind.

The woman's body only improved with each step and his eyes darted up to the nearly full moon that glowed like a flashlight under a blanket behind a band of high cloud cover as if to thank his luck for the moment and the woman he was about to share it with.

"Could I bum a cigarette from you?"

She was wearing a furry hood and bent her head to reach into her jacket with her right hand, the left idly holding the cigarette to smolder and the twisting smoke

curled between them with random freedom. It made
Morell chilly to think of how warm it was inside of her
jacket, but his selection of clothes had been limited to
say the least, and some artificial warmth resonated
within him to think of being as close to her heart as that
pack of cigarettes had been. She shook the pack and
held it out for him to choose.

"Marlboro?" He asked. She nodded with a short
vibration of the shadowed face. "Excellent. My fav.
You have a light?"

She took the cigarettes back and produced a
cheap plastic one-time lighter from the same pocket.
Morell cupped the cigarette with his hand and sucked it
to life and his eyes rolled up to hers as the dancing
flame illuminated her face.

Morell's mouth fell open as the cigarette stuck
to his lip.

Those sapphire blue eyes were not easily
forgotten.

"Sierra?"

The lighter returned to the warmth of the
hooded jacket and she brought her index finger to
pursed lips. She flicked the cigarette again and tapped
her wrist where a watch would be and was not.

Morell nodded and was still at a loss for words
despite the thousands of questions making a play for his
mouth.

"Don't say anything." She added. "You'll
understand-we'll go from there. Do exactly what I tell
you or else all we've worked for will be wasted and I'll
be locked up somewhere with walls so thick I wouldn't
be able to hear a howitzer firing from the next cell."

Morell didn't understand but caught the gravity
of her voice and saw the honesty in her face. He
remembered their conversation on the way to the
Precinct what seemed to be ages ago.

Not a minute later a CPD squad car came thundering into the complex, squealing tires until coming to rest before Erland's unit. Sierra sidled along the post so that it ran down the middle of her back and with the nudge of her head directed Morell sit on the hood of a ratty Lexus sedan in the carport that was in the process of being tuned and painted. As the doors to the squad car whumphed shut Sierra lowered the cigarette to flick the ashes from it with a thin smile on her face that Morell read two ways as he was an interrogation specialist; the first being that she had never smoked a cigarette in her life and wasn't about to, and the second was that the image unfolding before him would answer enough of his questions to merit full support.

The frown was strong on Morell's face as the two Police Officers stepped from the vehicle and took a man from the back seat. Morell strained to see he was handcuffed and it was clear as the man spun in a slow three hundred and sixty degree turn to take everything in that it was Detective First Grade Michael Erland.

Morell went to speak and Sierra's face forbade it.

One of the Officers freed the decorated public servant from the cuffs and led him up stairs to his dwelling, the other stood by the car in guard mode.

"Now." Sierra reached into an outer pocket of her jacket and produced a switchblade, letting the knife flick to life with a sharp click. "This is what we're going to do."

THIRTY-FOUR

The whining chop chop of the helicopter blades slowed long enough for Jupiter and Jenkins to throw themselves on the frosty turf of Chief Katonah High's football stadium and they ran from the floodlights to a low fence. Jenkins was over easily being all of twenty-three and was able to help Jupiter with his bullet-grazed swollen ankle. In the darkness of the adjacent lot was the nondescript white van of team Ganymede.

Charlie was leaning against the hood with a toothpick in his mouth as the two approached, his eyes watching the sleek Sikorsky fly into the sea of night. Jenkins was admitted into the back of the van.

"Any sign of Killinger?"

Charlie dipped his head.

"I spotted his Mercedes on the other side of the school as we drove around."

Jupiter dialed the broker's number.

"Pinnacle building?"

"All set, the trigger's wired to your phone with an emergency circuit in the fuse box outside the Penthouse...what about Sugar Hill?"

"It didn't blow?" Jupiter frowned.

"No." Charlie confirmed.

Killinger answered before the hacker had time to analyze.

"I heard your entrance..."

"East lot, stadium."

"Right."

Jupiter stared at the phone, debating why Sugar Hill didn't explode. Courtland had answered his call, hadn't he? But then what had happened at Keller's? Marland must've stopped the explosion at Sugar Hill in someway and followed the trail to Keller's. It was his penultimate diversion, a savage blow to prepare the city for his knockout punch. To think of the public outcry at the death of so many innocent civilians, old men and women and children-it would truly have ripped the hearts from their chests and left them unprepared for what was to come. In reality, the purpose for the destruction was not to hurt or injure or kill, only to cover his tracks and create grand illusions and distractions while he committed treasonous crimes, the final of which being placed together piece by piece as he stood in the lot wincing from the pains of his ankle.

"What about Brown?"

"He's on his way too."

"I can't move forward without his confirmation."

"I know."

Charlie stood in the cold with his boss as the black Mercedes AMG rolled next to the van only decibels away from silence.

Killinger was unchanged from the last time Jupiter met him and his black eyebrows were inquisitive.

"Can I see it?" He said with his hands in the pockets of his overcoat. The muscle with him eyed Charlie and all of Charlie's handsome slightness and Charlie wouldn't give him the time of day behind the toothpick.

Jupiter fished for the CONSTANT memory card and held it out for Killinger to see and closed his hand when the broker tried to take it.

"Not till Brown shows up."

"How far out is he?"

"One can never know with Brown."

Killinger's jaw shot sideways and he blew out a puff of warm air. It was true. Brown's blessing was his curse. He had played both sides for so long he had lost any and all affiliation with the extremes and the cover of his motivational greed ran so deep it was as if he was a secret agent living a double life. Mr. Brown was one of the most powerful men in the world; a Homeland lawmaker and expediter with the ear of the President-a man so driven by money and wealth that he found himself in the company of the country's most dangerous men.

"I'll be in the car." Killinger said, looking around to the cold night and its empty stillness. Chief Katonah sat on a small ridge and the stadium was surrounded by oaks. It held a certain solitude and Killinger didn't like seclusion anymore than Jupiter liked busy city streets and large crowds.

The waiting wasn't a second past ten minutes but felt it much longer considering the intensity of what lay before the hungry men. Brown came from a sleek Lincoln that couldnt've been more than a month old and was flanked by Paul Chang. The dome light showed the presence of two men in the back of the car and the shutting of the doors left them to the silence of waiting.

It was then the meeting began, in the south parking lot of the football stadium with Brown, Chang, Killinger, his bodyguard, Jupiter and Charlie, their faces lit only by what light spilled from the field lights into the cold, hard concrete of the lot.

"How do you know it's real?" Brown asked and it was the first thing on his mind.

"What makes you think it's not?" Jupiter rebutted. If it wasn't, Killinger was gone and so was the money. In a way, Jupiter was still clawing from the bottom and wouldn't be in the clear till the money, in whatever form it would come, was his.

"The Detective, working with Marland. He was there when Reston got it from the box. He's been working with her."

"Who do you think I got it from?" Jupiter said with certain smugness.

"He never said..."

"Did you ask?"

"Not exactly-I didn't want him to get any ideas. He knew more than I thought he would but he was trying too hard to divert my attention from Marland, I couldn't figure out why."

"You're always too obvious." Killinger piped up, seeing as he was highly defensive over the money as was Jupiter. Brown's cut had nothing to do with the sale outright-he already had and would benefit over time from the largest corporation's contributions not only personally as they slept with the executive branch for top billing and the spillover fell to his lap, but privately, as envelopes passed under tables and nods led to bank deposits.

"Tell that to the President."

"He doesn't know to begin with." Jupiter scoffed. Charlie removed his toothpick and sniffed the air as a faint breeze puffed a strange scent his way.

"He will if you keep blowing everything up-I know you want to sell the information but you have to understand what the hell's going on from my side, you can't just go and do whatever you want. What did I tell you three months ago?"

"You warned me Homeland SAB had my number."

"You're damn right and how close has that number come to extinction today?"

Killinger held out a hand because Brown was easily hostile and never cared for Jupiter's demeanor when in actuality Brown knew how the country needed Jupiter. His attacks were paving the way for stricter surveillance regulations and the theft and sale of the CONSTANT cache of information would not only profit the three of them to no end, but ordain the creation of a revolutionary new system of surveillance the world had never before seen, brought about by the justified necessity of the war on terror's newest face.

"I'm still here." Jupiter said flatly. "And it's real. I checked it."

"Security?"

"You wouldn't understand it but I'll say that it was confusing enough wunderkind didn't know how to breach it."

Brown nodded and Charlie tried to follow the scent with a scowl.

"What was the proof?"

"Remember Al-Atabah? Libyan Security Force Captain?"

"Yes, very well. He went in hiding after the overthrow of the old regime-enough war crimes to last a lifetime."

"It has his complete Two-Zero Three Identity File and the un-redacted report of what *really* happened with Operation War Hammer. How much d'you think that'd be worth to the right hands on the open market?"

Brown smirked and his eyes landed on the faces of Killinger and Jupiter. Their demeanors were a mirror of his. They were like coaches with a host of new players the league had no idea what to do with.

"What about splitting it up then?"

"No." Killinger's smirk faded as he slashed a

leather-gloved hand. "The buyers have been sold the whole thing in its entirety and will purchase it as such."

"What about copying it?"

"That would take time." Jupiter crossed his arms. "I'd have to have a couple of mainframes and a laptop they don't sell in the local stores since my arsenal went down with the ship."

"We don't have the time." Brown conceded. "We..."

"We'll make enough money from the sale, gentlemen." Killinger interrupted. "There's no reason to deviate now, not when we're so close."

"Hold up." Charlie said and Brown turned his head to see the man sniff his shoulder near the back. "Do you wear cologne?"

"Yes, why?"

"What kind?" Charlie asked and the dead confidence of the handsome face under the swoop of blonde hair made Brown realize something was wrong.

"It's called Steele...it's by..."

"Does it have...brominated vegetable oil or glycerol ester of wood rosin?"

Brown's face was incredulous.

"How the hell do I know? What on earth are you..."

"Is your perfume tangerine or some kind of citrus?"

"No...not at all."

The toothpick switched sides in Charlie's mouth.

"Wait here."

Brown stared in some kind of disbelief as the leader of Ganymede stuck a course for the white van and came from it a minute later with a Geiger counter.

Killinger swore as the device clicked wildly on Brown's back and shoulder.

"Take it off." Charlie said as he reached in his pocket for a lighter.

"What's wrong?" Jupiter asked, voice still calm.

"His back has been patted with radioactive material hidden in some kind of cologne."

"What?" Brown watched as Charlie began to burn his jacket, the alcohol in the cologne acting as an accelerant, just enough to catch the affected area aflame. "Why?"

"It's a method of satellite tracking." Charlie jogged to the van for another pair of devices.

"Who uses that?" Killinger asked, having moved to the door of the car.

"CIA." Charlie threw the toothpick to the ground and clicked on a radio frequency scanner.

Less than three hundred feet away several feet higher in the stand of stripped oaks near the back of the stadium, the Texan CIA man named Loomis cursed as he shut off the directional microphone and shimmied across the ground to the trunk of a generous oak.

"CIA?" Jupiter frowned. "You said the CIA was out."

Brown shrugged.

"I guess not."

"Maybe they want the info too, they just can't pay for it."

"Shut up, all of you." Charlie said and wasn't afraid of hurting their feelings. He pointed the device along the horizon and spun slowly to complete a full circle. Then he set it on the top of the Lincoln and pressed a night vision scope to his right eye and spun again, slower this time.

"Anything?" Killinger asked, already prepared to have his bodyguard lay down rubber and escape the parking lot.

"Nope. But if this thing goes off again, run like

hell, you got it?"

The men nodded and held their comments since the conversation's abrupt comma had them all spooked. Charlie's failure to find an eyes-on-the-ground Agent couldn't remove the bitter taste of the clicking Geiger counter from their ears. Even if they couldn't find a listener, they weren't alone.

"There's nothing more to say...sell the merchandise." Brown broke the silence.

"Are you gonna change location?" Killinger asked with a distant throb in his voice.

"Why should I?"

"Because they've got a tracker on you-they can follow you."

"I just won't be there." Brown said. "I'll leave that to you two schmucks. I'm out until the sale's done. Then *I'll* call you, okay? Let's keep it calm. There's been enough damage done to give us time to get out. Don't make it any worse."

Mr. Brown's attentive green eyes were pensive on his burning jacket and he moved for the car, handing Charlie the radio frequency scanner.

"Thanks." He said. Charlie nodded and switched it off.

"I'll see you at the Arena, then." Killinger pulled up the collar of his vampiric overcoat and waited for his bodyguard to open the door to the Mercedes.

Jupiter confirmed with the tight bow of his head. None of them knew about the Pinnacle Building, except Charlie and the team. Not even young Jenkins. It was as almost as if they didn't want the violence they knew was so necessary-at any rate, Jupiter had little or no regard for human life but that of his own and had no problem in doing away with the lives of others for the macroeconomic purpose that never left the patience of his partitioned mind.

"Let's go." Jupiter said and Charlie peered into the tree trunks and the right angles of the football stadium for a quick second and debated flicking the RF scanner on once more to check but time was not his to do with what he wished and he quickly threw himself in the front passenger seat of the white van as it left for anonymity.

Burko and Rainey didn't like the assignment any more than Erland did, but it was procedure and they all knew that. Rainey led the Detective up the steps and couldn't help but feel sorry for the slump shouldered man. Whatever had happened to him had been somewhat beyond his control. Erland was one of the men that gave CPD a good image, and in a way, Rainey wanted to do his job keeping the whole thing hush hush for the Department's sake. But whispers of Homeland changed all that. Even with a city as large as Crescent, Homeland Security was a different animal entirely and whatever publicity, good or bad, fell on the city's finest, was on *their* behalf. Chief Nolan had been solid in his commitment to preserving the spirit of safety in the face of the *acts of terror*, as they had been dubbed, and was a bold voice for an infamous moment in American history.

"Listen, for what it's worth..." Rainey offered. Erland had his head down and lifted it only enough to glare a hole in Rainey's mind. "Okay, well...anyway, keep the door unlocked. I'll be right outside, Burko will be in the parking lot."

Erland didn't utter a word and admitted himself to the dark loneliness of his apartment with no uncertain shame. On the quiet ride over he had been debating his actions and the review of them was mixed. The trouble was, no line had been set before him, and finding out he had crossed that line made him question where. Remembering the moments in Tabitha's apartment, he determined it was on the count of stopping Jupiter and his network-without the knowledge that Jupiter's network had more people inside the government than anyone was aware of. When it came down to it, he had said yes to *Sierra Marland*, not to some suit or some dusty file folder, but to a living, breathing woman who had fallen into a space in his heart left vacant by the course of life. If say, Tabitha had been in Sierra's shoes, or poor Tallifer, would it have all worked out the same way? God only knew; probably not, and it would've stopped with his sending Quinlan into the tree. If so, the murder that began it all would've remained a mystery. But Magnolia Marland's murder had been solved and his sole purpose for being brought on had been accomplished and the sour taint of it all slept in the woven fabric of poetic justice. Tim Wolcek had been the one to commit the act but whoever else was in that room, save the blacked out Reston, was equally as responsible, and though Wolcek had been shot by one of his own, the others were still at large, and the fractured stones of justice were slowly sinking into the abyss.

It was cold in the apartment and Erland clicked on the oil heat which had a nice, comforting old sound and would fill up the drafty cracker box in the length of time he needed to let it all go and pass out in the rumpled sheets of his twin bed.

A thought of Sarina Veracruz and what on earth had happened to her with Jimenez tried to make an appearance in his imagination but there was no way he was going to listen. Some sort of severing had occurred between them and despite their moments in the living room earlier there was nothing more than that one night to connect them-given the situation they had spoken all the right words to each other but Erland knew damn well what was conviction and what wasn't.

Erland felt sore and old and his right eye throbbed. He took his shirt off and left the jeans and socks on, putting the thumb drive in his back pocket. Then he fell into the low twin bed and wriggled around in the ruffle of sheets until he didn't want to move anymore.

Burko squinted as he saw the shirtless man approach in a near drunken stagger. He had been standing guard in the cold for a few minutes and knew it was going to be a long night. His heavy flashlight was up quickly and the strength of the beam nearly knocked the man over.

"Whoa, hey! Stop!" The man begged with an outstretched hand protecting his bare skin from the bright light.

Officer Burko saw the man was bleeding and he ran to him from his position near the patrol car.

"Are you okay? What happened?"

"I got frickin' robbed, man!" Morell staggered and fell to his knees, holding his arm near the shoulder. A fresh cut was pumping out enough blood pool through his knuckles and drip down his arm. "I got..."

Morell dropped the switchblade dramatically and fell down sideways. The compounded nicks and scrapes and the horrid bruising of his neck from the yacht's explosion helped sell the idea in the heat of the moment.

Burko cursed and shouted for Rainey, who came thumping down the stairs, as he had been standing in the covered portion of the stairway to Erland's place, enjoying the noticeable temperature difference.

"What the hell?"

"This guy just got robbed, call an ambulance." Burko reached for Morell to sit him up. "How many attacked you? Where'd they go?"

"Is...it was just one guy...he took off that way.
He was wearing white shoes, white or yellow..."

"Get that knife in an evidence bag and stay with
him." Burko said as he stood to pursue.

"Hold on, what about Erland?"

"After what he's been through? He's gonna
sleep till next week."

Rainey shook his head and followed his
partner's orders. Valley did have its share of robberies
and stabbings but of all of the nights for it...

Erland woke quickly realizing he had passed
out. His breathing was heavy and his body was already
glazed with sweat. He fumbled on the nightstand for his
alarm clock to find less than three minutes had elapsed
since he entered the door and it scared him to the depths
of his spine.

The Detective shot out of bed and his head
reeled with a dizzy sickness that pulled at the corners of
his mind. Maybe the lack of adrenaline was letting it
creep in over a void of sleep, the STRIC-R and
whatever side effects it carried with it-ironically,
memory loss was the only thing he recalled Doctor
Patrice stating but it must've been some nasty drug
neither one of them knew the true power of. Perhaps the
reversal agent only stabilized him to a point of not
feeling the drug's dangers and that feeling was nothing
more than an illusion while the poisons worked inside
of him.

Erland stripped in the darkness as if the clothes
he wore were poisoned too and grabbed a fresh pair of
underwear, stepping in the cold white of the nearby
shower tub to rip the water. He sat down with his back
to the showerhead, submitting to the warming cascade
of liquid as it pummeled the weary muscles of his back.

The Detective let his bruised hands hold the heaviness of his head and the increasing heat of the water and the resulting steam flared the stinging sensation around his eye but the brokenness of being naked and covered with the steady stream of soothing liquid nearly brought him to tears. Erland took a few breaths and the moment he felt himself falling asleep he pushed himself to height and stepped from the shower, toweling off gingerly and pulling the fresh underwear on. The triple mirrors of the medicine cabinet facing the shower had since fogged and he opened the door he had shut by habit though it was a senseless procedure and wiped the mirror with the towel to see what the man from New England had done to his right eye. With the lack of perspective from the shut eye he pulled the two outside mirrors together like a bracket and squinted. He swabbed the fogged glass again and adjusted the angle to see a stunning face of blue eyes near the wall next to the bedroom.

Erland turned to behold her, leaning with her arms crossed in some statuesque repose. She pulled the furry hood back and the light painfully caught her beauty as it slept between repentance and remorse.

The Detective said nothing and closed the distance between them, wordlessly embracing her. He kissed her lips passionately, wrapping her body in his arms to squeeze its vibrant heat, feeling her spark and spirit seep into the marrow of his bones. His hand ran through her hair and around her hips and he found it on the subtlest cleft in her chin as their eyes met at kisses' end.

"You must've forgiven me." She said, her face breaking into the slight curves of an intimate smile.

"I guess it's because I understand why." Erland said and searched the cool, refreshing peace of her blue eyes.

"God, look what they did to you." Her hand

gently smoothed over his shut eye, the light from the bathroom shading his face. "I came when I could."

"You know..." Erland looked down and back up. "I could ask why you didn't tell me the plan but I would've argued with you if it would've worked or not. I forced you to blindside me...because...I guess *I* didn't trust *you*...but...I love you like I've never loved anything or anyone before...I don't know how to put it into words..."

"I *know* you love me, Mike." Sierra's face glowed and in all of the times he had seen her smile he had never seen the full joy of her teeth and the suggestion of crow's feet that pulled at her eyes. "And I love *you* with all of my heart-that's why I had to shut that side up-because of the promise..."

"Did you always trust me? Did you always know?"

"No." Sierra stuck out her bottom lip. "All of what I did is a calculated gamble-I thought my love for you had tainted the clarity of my vision, just like Maggie warned me."

"Is that why you asked if I would sleep with you? To see if I was committed?" Erland asked and he couldn't hide what disgust he held, not for her, or her actions, but for the way things had to be between a man and a woman. If he had a dollar for how many times what began in sex and ended in murder came across his desk he wouldn't live in Valley.

"Yes."

"And you knew I wouldn't?" Compassion entered his cheeks and jaw.

"Yes."

"Would you have asked me if you knew I would?"

Sierra sighed and shook her head. Some buried distress released from deep in her lungs.

"No...I would sacrifice myself a thousand times for my country, Mike, and the mission, but I would never *sell* myself. I watched Maggie do it more times than I could even count and I can't describe what it did to her soul...it was as if she would go to some detached place where she wasn't my twin sister anymore and she was some SAB machine." Sierra let her head drop against Erland's bare chest. "She did it so that I didn't have to. She was always out front. Always. I followed her and she took the blows. It was as if she needed me to stay the way we were *before* we got into this business, the way we were *supposed* to be, and she drew upon my simplicities, to remind her of what life was like. On long flights she used to just ask me to tell stories of when we were young, or talk about my foolish dreams of what the perfect life was." The jewel blue eyes connected with Erland's and the smile returned. Her arms locked behind his neck, resting on his shoulders. "Maybe that's why she warned me about...falling in love with the ideas in my head-she wanted me to find the real thing..."

They kissed again, tenderly, and there was a knock on the door.

"Hold on." Erland said and Sierra was hidden in the darkness once she switched the bathroom light off.

At the door, Rainey was flustered, like he had run without preparing himself to have done so and was slightly startled that Erland was naked save the boxers.

"Hey Mike, there's been a two-twenty, code three...don't tell that Homeland guy, but, we're just gonna take him over to the hospital, okay? It's only right over there-all the ambulances are out and the guy's bleedin' like a farm animal. It's not even a mile."

Erland smiled.

"Go for it."

Rainey nodded and clinked down the stairs with

a hurried hop step. Erland turned and didn't see Sierra in the darkness and walked to the bedroom. She had removed her jacket and taken a place on the edge of the bed.

Erland stood at the doorframe with his arms above his head. The room was in darkness. The apartment was in darkness. It was a purplish color of midnight northern sky, not the black of deep space. The ambient hum of the oil heater was distant enough to comfort and draw upon a cozy memory of the night before Christmas and the Detective didn't care that he couldn't see his own nose at the end of his face.

He could feel Sierra's desires pulling at heart and his lungs, at his hands and his lips.

"Time...creates value..." She said from the darkness, with the heaviness of reality.

"That's true." Erland held the doorframe.

"Maggie use to tell me that when we were having a hard stretch-when we'd put our heads together and cry about what our life had become."

"What happened to your parents?"

"Aveo Global Flight Four-Seventy-One from Morocco to Logan International Airport." Erland felt her reluctance, as if he'd dared to ask for an old dusty book high up in the unlit corner of a public library. "It was the eighties. There were a lot of hijackings...Libya wouldn't let them land...Spain wouldn't let them land...so they were gonna try Cuba. They didn't make it. The Atlantic's a big ocean...I think it's why Maggie chose the path for us that she did...so that someday we could get our justice..."

Erland knew he shouldnt've asked but it made sense why the twins became so close and developed into extreme opposites in their deepest cores while following the exact same outward pursuits and career paths. It was as if they had become the sole substance necessary for each other's survival and Magnolia's militancy and toughness as the firstborn not only allowed but *demanded* Sierra to develop into a soft and graceful woman whose skill set lived solely in the unfiltered power of her feminine charms and where Magnolia saw place for the fist Sierra would offer the suggestive twist of a backhanded word and yet, to keep the diplomatic and tactical weapon of Sierra's soul from losing its operational purity Magnolia had been the one to exercise the fullest potential of a woman's power over a man, and in a way, it further galvanized the hardness of what life had made of her soul. She had become the shield and the spear so that Sierra could remain a human being.

The Detective shook his head. It was all falling into place. He would drop dead if there was another woman in the world like Sierra Marland. And the fact that she had chosen to love him before even hearing his voice made him feel nothing short of invincible, despite the slow trickle of paralysis unknowingly working its way up his spine.

Erland took two steps to the bed and reached out into the darkness, his hand drifting toward the heat of her body and connecting with the silken black threads of her hair. His fingertips drifted over her forehead and her eyes, her cheeks and her chin.

"Sierra." He said. "When this is all over...will you marry me?"

She rose and the top of her head met his nose as their bodies came together.

"Yes Mike, a million times *yes*."

Erland felt weak and it brought a tear to his good eye to be squeezed in her arms, to be wanted and needed, chosen and spoken for by a woman whose loveliness no one would ever quite understand like he did.

"Can I tell you something I've been saving?" He asked, after the embrace had taken its course and the moment had been sealed in their hearts.

Her acceptance to his question was in her suggestive smile and her arms were locked around his hips.

"I wrote a poem for you."

He could feel her blush.

"What?"

"It was back at Fircrest...I used to think of random song lyrics when I was working in Mountain County...it gets lonely out there. I guess it started from boxing training, something to hold onto, like a mantra...anyway, as I got older I started to write my own poems, just one or two lines, in my head. They'd go away the second they were done but they helped me get through that moment, you know?" She nodded. "Anyway, when you came back from the Precinct and stood on the hill I thought to myself I'd never seen a more magnificent thing in all of Creation."

Her shoulders gave the smallest wiggle of anticipation. Erland spoke slowly.

"Your beauty lives in a thousand summers, rising up like new spring flowers, shining as only sunlight can in unbroken big blue sky."

The space of stillness reminded the Detective of the aloof hums of the oil heater.

Sierra let gravity pull her head to rest sideways on Erland's bare chest. Her face was damp. She sighed, aching for respite and the opportunity to devote herself to the heat of becoming one in spirit and silence.

"I can't say what I want to say, Mike." Her voice was breathy and soft, as he had never heard it before; void of all color and influence and somehow sounding younger than her age, which he had always believed to be no more than a decade below his.

"I know, baby."

"If I say it you'll say yes this time."

"Forever."

Sierra sighed again.

"There's one last move to make." She raised her face, glazed with tears, and a throb began to weave through the soft and breathy voice. "And if it doesn't work out, we'll die...I don't know if I'll ever have this moment with you again...for the first time I don't know what to do...I know what needs to be done but I don't know how to do it...I don't have any confidence in what I can do, Mike. I was never supposed to be in this position...you're all I have. I can't let you go."

The Detective ran spread fingers through her hair.

"I'm your husband now, Sierra. Trust me like you trusted Maggie. If all we have is each other then that's all we need, we have the power of agreement. There may be a hundred enemies or a thousand, but if we stand on the truth we *will* be vindicated, if not in our lifetimes then by history."

"But we have to end it, Mike. We have to *destroy* Jupiter and his network. He has the real CONSTANT. He's going to sell it. My contact in the CIA is trying to find out when and where and we have to kill them all. Jupiter, the buyers, *all* of them. We have to pull the trigger. There's no vindication for that."

"No Sierra, that's Maggie talking. You can't fight fire with fire, you have to fight it with water. At first the fire's too hot but in the end there's nothing more powerful than water."

Sierra blinked away the tears.

"What do you mean?"

"Water is knowledge. Knowledge is power. Let them kill themselves with their own words, let the world see what their evil has caused."

"How?"

"Let me get dressed and we'll talk about it." Erland moved for the light which didn't help either of their eyesight.

"Mike, that's what I'm saying." The tears returned. "I don't want *you* to get pulled down by *my* mess. You don't deserve it."

"What's *yours* is *mine*. We can do it together, just like we have been." Erland searched for the appropriate clothes.

"It'll *never* be enough, Mike. We'll *never* be able to get them all. Someday they'll come for us. That's why I want to take the fall and save you from it while I still can." Sierra's eyebrows twisted and trembled. "That's why I want you to take me in your arms and...make love to me, so that...for at least one moment of this doomed life I know that...loving you was more than I ever hoped it would be...and you would be able to live a normal life, knowing the real Sierra...not the one that went to prison for treason and murder."

Erland turned slowly and swallowed with great difficulty at the weak and broken vessel before him. The horror that had clawed at her face in the TMFOV had been exaggerated through mediation and the twists and turns of the hopelessly condemned operation were canyons never meant for her fabric to bear.

"Listen to me." Erland gripped her by the shoulders, his sparkly blue eyes radiating confidence. "No matter what happens, I love you. It's gonna be alright, okay? Don't talk that way-don't even think it."

Sierra nodded and Erland wiped her tear-stained cheeks.

"And when this is all over," His eyes were brighter than she'd ever seen them. "I'm gonna take you somewhere God only knows exists and make up for every day of my life I wished I knew you."

The fullness of her smile broke through the tears and they kissed once and then again with lingering lips to seal their final promise to each other.

"Alright then." Sierra freed herself from the choking emotions. "You get dressed. We've got to get going before the cops get back."

"Alright then." Erland echoed with a faint smile. "Go make us some sandwiches-I've got something to show you."

He pulled the jeans back on and patted the right back pocket, feeling the poky plastic of the thumb drive buried in the corner and took very few items of necessity from the drafty apartment, the new department issue laptop Brown had forgotten to have the Officers confiscate among them.

THIRTY-FIVE

Jessica Birchall held a brave face as Agent Farges had her booked into the County Jail for an overnight while he decided what to do with her and the damage she had caused. She ripped her arm from the sweaty, muscular grip of the large man accompanying him as the cold black bars of the jail door opened before her and shut behind her. When she saw the women she was occupying the small space with for the night she slowly turned back to the door, avoiding the feeling of being lost and alone.

"I want a phone call!" She shouted as the footsteps lost their volume. She couldn't see them but the squeal and clang of the door meant that the slight Farges and his enforcer were never turning back and the woman at the desk had been told to pay no mind.

Her eyes slipped along the bars and fell to the women. Prostitutes, drug dealers, shoplifters-the very constituents of a realm of business her Network exploited with endless self-righteousness.

"Hey..." A Hawaiian who looked strong enough to break Birchall in half over her knee called out as she was sitting against the wall with her legs arched. She was wearing flannel pajama bottoms and a ribbed tank top and just looking at her in the inhuman chill of the jail cell made Jessica shiver. "Do I know you?"

Birchall stuck out her lip and shook her head.

"I seen you on TV."

Birchall sighed at the inevitable and went to check her watch but they had taken it from her.

After thanking the Patrolman for the ride, Kelly stood on the curb and blew in her hands. There was something about Reston's house that stood out from the rest on the street, and the difference lived solely in her own eye. The journalist let the cold air burn her nostrils and she curled her short brown hair behind her ears as she examined the asymmetrical roofline and the overgrown bushes. It was the home she wanted to make her own-forget the rental on Thirty-Eighth and she was ready to admit she was wrong, which for some people, was an uncrossable bridge. Her last conversation with Darren left an indelible stain of conviction within her and at the end of the day, fear was the most selfish of thoughts. Meeting Rollins and seeing the Detective on the other side of the law had sliced through that fear because they were up against something far bigger than themselves as individuals and by working together she felt safe. The timed media assault left her vulnerable to the possibilities of her own thoughts and in retrospect she wished she could've been not only as strong as Darren but strong *for* him. He was out there, somewhere, alone. Her station wagon was parked on the curb and her head seesawed between it and the door a few times before the concrete walkway began to echo with her feet.

Kelly stood at the door and knocked. There was no answer. Her lips wrestled with each other as words of apologies formed and she tried the knob to find it was unlocked. She entered with reticence and attempted to feel for him in the silence of the split-level. She hated empty houses, empty *dark* houses, and the moment she returned to her own every night she was quick to throw on lights or music and most importantly the TV to drive all of the blackness and quietness out and the lonely echoes they had a way of creating. Kelly sighed as she leaned against the door, feeling its drafty cool pull at the back of her neck. Life had a way of being its own horror movie and she didn't want to be alone anymore in the same way she didn't want *him* to be alone anymore. There was balance there, somewhere, and Kelly reached into her jacket for a pair of hair clips and began the steady task of cleaning the house she would hope to soon call her own.

Detective Second Grade Christian Lowery pinched bloodshot eyes and cursed himself for the way he'd treated Kimmie as he waited for a red light to turn green. It was the job, wasn't it? That was no excuse-the billet in Phoenix had been a cruise through desert roads with murders so obvious they practically solved themselves. It was the money, the pressure, the *demand* to make it higher up the food chain that was ruining what he had grown with Kimmie in the desert and it was a chronic condition Lowery had developed since boarding the flight to Crescent. He could tell her he'd finish this one case and take a week off but he'd already used that line a few times and if he wasn't completely convinced beyond a shadow of a doubt that the murder of Homeland Agent Luis Jimenez had something to do with the Crescent Crisis and the acts of terror she would've said he was crying wolf. Deep down though, she knew, she had judged his reaction and that's why she had crossed her arms. It was her manner of toughing it out. He had seen it way back when his only interactions with the Police were lengthy wastes of time that ended in rejections. But they were kids back then.

The Detective cursed again, this time at the light. There was no one around for what seemed like

miles though it was impossible to tell in the brick and
mortar jungle and the red light wouldn't change.
Lowery shook his head and pressed his foot into the
gas. In the darkness of the intersection he saw a flash
and rolled his eyes. He would be taking that ticket to
court.

Lowery reached his desk by eleven thirty and
surveyed all that he had. He called Nguyen who was in
the Precinct and the clean cut Officer stopped by.

"What about her truck?" Lowery asked. "It's a
Two-thousand thirteen Chevy Silverado, red."

"Registered to Rodrigo Veracruz? Brother, not
husband."

"Yes. It wasn't in the driveway where she said
she left it."

Nguyen was dipping a teabag in a Styrofoam
cup as he sat on the edge of Erland's desk across the
room and frowned.

"No keys in her personal effects."

"You think the killer took her truck?"

"We'll sweep the area. Hopefully a traffic cam
got something."

Lowery rolled his eyes.

"A traffic cam got something alright..."

"Pardon?" Nguyen set the tea on Erland's desk.

"Nothing...gibberish."

"You know, I'm surprised to see you here...I
know it's best to do as much as you can when a murder
is fresh, but...with all that's happened today it'd be
good to go home and take it new tomorrow."

Lowery stopped himself from saying something
stupid. Nguyen had no wife or kids but he lived with his
parents and his brother's wife and two daughters in
spacious seven hundred thousand dollar house and he
was in one way, completely responsible for himself
being all of twenty-six yet his family was highly

dependent on him and was very close to him. He did his time and went home and came back the next shift always fresh and bright of countenance.

"...I think it's related...to all that's happened."

"Really?" Nguyen took a sip of tea. It was something fruity and he didn't care for it but it was all they had and was caffeine free. "How so?"

"Both of them worked Fircrest at separate times...they must've both known something...or seen something that made our great evil take them out just as they took out Fircrest. Maybe the convenience of their past relationship is part of the...cover up, the distraction."

The Officer's thin lips made an inverted u-shape as he nodded.

"To what?"

"Something like Fircrest. God knows what the point of all of it is. Davidson and half of Waterfront are scratching their heads about that damn yacht. I'm sure Lieutenant Ross knows more than he's telling me but if I don't need to know I won't."

"So...what about the burn victim?"

"He claims to be a thief who stole a security camera on behalf of the Mansion's owner."

"Are they responsible?"

"For the destruction of their own mansion?"

"No, the murder."

Lowery browsed his notes. He hadn't thought of it. Perhaps certain parts of the catastrophes were related and other happenings had either the misfortune or the good luck of occurring at the *same* time.

"Do you know who's handling Sugar Hill?"

"Romero said he offered to work with Symons from Eleven but the County wants to take it." Lowery shrugged with carelessness. "I don't know."

"It could be related too."

"The whole thing could be but we need a lot more than we have to be sure."

"Forensic work takes time." Nguyen reassured after finally becoming disgusted with the fruity tea.

"I know and we can't spare any more people!" Lowery let his head drop and spun in a tight arc in the chair, slowly and idly. There was no reason to raise his voice. He was thinking of Kimmie, still, and how he was going to make it up to her. Poof, case closed? It didn't even happen that way on TV shows. So she sat at home bitter while he sat in the uncomfortable office chair miles away staring at the type-A cleanliness of his corner enclave with no clear direction to the mysterious hand dealt him.

"I'll issue a BOLO for the Silverado and the nearest car will search in a two mile radius of the house. We'll find it." Nguyen pushed from the desk.

"Hold on." Lowery held up two fingers as he thought. "We'll do it together. We're going back to the house."

Nguyen watched the tall Detective push himself up and take a few of his notes and roll them up like a baton and then followed him to the motor pool.

Reston couldn't stop himself from shivering and had traipsed out in the cold night long enough considering the simple sweatshirt and waterproof jacket to merit the incessant state of numb shaking common to a hairless dog. The last clutches of Mossyrock had since departed and he was closing in on his own neighborhood and picked up the pace to a light jog; one so light it might've been a fast walk with a shoulder hiccup. He knew the limits of his relative laziness and life of alcoholism and wasn't exactly fond of the idea but was confident it would alleviate the chills. The air was a stinging, dry reality and after what felt like a mile but couldnt've been more than a block he wiped the trickle from his nose to see his sleeve was red. Disconcerting as it was it didn't stop him. Dr. Patrice had cleared him for a life of low-stress recovery and set an appointment for tomorrow afternoon to pump him full of a substance he couldn't pronounce and mentioned the word irrigation and little did she know what he had done since their last meeting. The demand put on his body was no where near the prescription and as soon as he wondered if the bloody nose was from that drug he told himself it was just the arid and frigid night air and a strong dose of dehydration.

By the time he reached his house several minutes later, he hit the bumper of Kelly's car and let his chest heave until the cooling effect of the sweat began to dip him back toward the chills. He felt nearly like a new man as he put his hand to the door and wanted nothing more than to collapse on the couch.

Opening the door brought the smell of food and a wash of light. Darren squinted, not remembering the state he'd left the house in and always liked to come home to darkness because it covered up all of his flaws as the house represented and bore fruit of them; his rattiness and laziness, his lack of care and life of procrastination.

Kelly was in the kitchen and he tilted his head to see her open the oven and remove a baking tray topped with two frozen dinners. His eyes drifted to the living room and how all of the magazines and books had been organized in stacks and arranged neatly along the walls and the spaces they had been cast across cleansed and cleared.

Darren let the remainder of the frosty wind leave his mind as he shut the door and the sound of it caused Kelly to look up and the homey smile that made dimples in her cheeks as she removed the oven mitts was worth more to Darren than the GTO or his job or the house itself. Even for a writer as he was, it was just hard to put into words.

The victim who had given his name as Hank Morrow was wincing from the cold and the pain shirtless as he was but in stable condition. Rainey escorted him to the waiting room and Burko checked in for expedited care. The man took a seat in the sparse seating area and Burko shook his head at the depravity. There was no good time for assault and armed robbery but this was the worst. Rainey made a comment about bringing the car around to complete the one-two exchange and an Officer would be by before the man's release, staffing permitting, to get a sketch of the man who had not only stolen a wallet, money and shirt, but gashed the man's arm.

Rainey left with a clink clink and Burko negotiated the particulars, signing a pair of waiver and release forms. He was prioritizing the man's medical care over those slated to receive treatment before him and even as it was a Police privilege it was not commonly used and had to be explained in the subsequent case report.

Burko turned once and then again quickly. The man who had called himself Hank Morrow was not in the waiting room chair. When Officer Burko asked around none of the patients in the waiting room had a clue what he was talking about which Burko's blood pressure didn't need. The thick-necked man felt the walls closing in on him for leaving Erland's apartment unguarded as the order had come from the man high up in Homeland Security and Burko forgot the alleged robbery victim and ran from the Hospital for the squad car. Once inside told Rainey to turn on the lights on and step on it even though Erland's apartment was maybe four blocks away.

The car screeched to a halt and Burko threw himself out of the grumbling vehicle with the primary-hued lights casting colors on the eggplant-toned walls of the apartment blocks. He took the steps in twos and found the door to Erland's unlocked as it was supposed to be only the Detective was nowhere to be seen.

Burko cursed and felt the heat under his collar at what furor and wrath was about to flow his way. The Homeland Agent with the green eyes looked to be the kind of man that could turn like mountain weather and Burko was more afraid for his job than that one time he had fallen asleep on duty with his car backed on the railroad tracks.

The GTO was a dream to drive, smooth and powerful and it smelled slightly of the colored tree dangling from the hood release latch as it covered old beer. Erland was on a path for the park and ride that sat behind the Hospital and through a foresty belt of trees and knotty bushes, adjacent to the long stand of power lines.

After selecting the length of three spots in relative darkness and dousing the lights, Erland reached for the laptop as Sierra produced the sandwiches she had made. The car chugged on idle and pushed fumes into the atmosphere.

Erland inserted the flash drive and while the computer's processor clicked to load the large file he eyed the sandwich. It was a smushed rectangle of rough and dry bread, nothing like the generous restaurant sandwiches responsible for forming the bulk of his daylight diet. It was his way to eat healthy at home and let the chips fall where they may while on the clock-there was no other compromise. He was out in the car far too often to worry about keeping a little mixed

greens salad cool in a plastic container and he burned
enough calories with the daily four point two mile jog.
By the time he came home he didn't care much about
flavor anyway and looked at the small pieces of bread
in disbelief that he had actually purchased them.

"It was the best I could do, considering." Sierra
held a comical smile to the corners of her lips.

"Gluten-free bread and organic turkey...grain
mustard? Fine with me."

"I grabbed a bottled water, too. You only had
one in the cupboard. We'll have to share."

Erland smirked at her from his further tappings
on the computer's track pad.

"Sierra," He sighed. "While that's a concept
that's entirely new to me I've been preparing for it for
quite some time."

Her joy was hidden in a mouth of sandwich and
the chewing thereof. Erland set the laptop between
them and the quality of the screen and the pixel count
gave them a clear and vivid picture of the short movie
of Fircrest cameras Rollins had pieced together.

"How'd you get this?" Sierra asked, with
amazement.

"Kelly Barnett gave it to me at the Precinct in a
very...surreptitious manner."

"She must've got it from Rollins." Sierra
studied the frames. The film started with the open bar.
Magnolia in all of her perfectly identical radiance was a
stunning figure in the teal Luciano Del Rey dress. In
certain lights, there was a near flip-flop effect of it, like
a custom painted car. Sierra washed what she had eaten
from her mouth and set the sandwich on the dash,
engrossed in the footage. Erland caught her eyes a few
times but was just as absorbed, not only for the physical
truth of it but because of Magnolia's mesmerizing
nature. He simply couldn't take his eyes off of her for

reasons he didn't want to analyze in the moment. She was Sierra, but she wasn't. There was a difference in her spirit, a singleness of purpose and a fluidity of movement and she danced through the static black suits and off white dresses with a symmetrical precision.

Darren Reston came up to her at the bar as it was adjacent to the main foyer only to the far left, dozens of feet from the hall to the kitchen. Magnolia was staring at the wall of bottles, no doubt watching for someone in the reflections they cast and Reston in some misguided confidence leaned against the bar on his elbows and began to banter. The lack of audio made the footage even more compelling.

Reston turned and drinks were ordered; shots, left on the bar. The bartender departed for another bottle of what had been ordered. Magnolia went to her clutch and was clumsy, bending down to get perhaps a tube of lipstick she had intentionally dropped and Reston could not avoid watching her from the compromising angle. A man in passing flicked a breath mint-sized item into Magnolia's shot and it had dissolved by the time she sat up and applied her lipstick over Darren's comments. She casually pointed to the staircase and his eyes went there with a smile. It was then she switched the shots and offered him a toast. After drinking Darren left the bar as did Magnolia; Darren headed for the staircase and Magnolia the opposite way.

The footage followed Reston and by the time he had scuffed up the staircase to perhaps find a space for privacy he was diverted by the obvious pains in his stomach and ran to the restroom just outside of the murder room.

The footage then cut to Magnolia on the second floor, reaching it perhaps by the servant's entrance, and her body language was hurried. She was obviously in some kind of evasion and it was made evident by the freckled man that followed her. He was drastically out of place, even in his tuxedo and had a dubious air about him. Magnolia came to a hallway of eight doors, a very long and narrow thing that lead to a dead end and froze when the man blocked her path. Erland could hear Sierra swallow a large knot and said nothing as her twin sister tried the knob of a door. The man began to run for her, drawing a knife. The door was locked and Magnolia pressed herself into another one and escaped certain violence as the man swiped at her, falling to his knees. He was up in a flash and entered the room as she had, shutting the door.

Sierra's eyes darted to the time signature on the footage and roughly forty seconds later Magnolia emerged, her only possession a key ring holding a single key. Her hands were tearing at the key ring as her body disappeared from the capture of the camera lens.

The film, with the perspective of the murder room, followed Reston as he waddled from the bathroom and fell to the couch on his back, his arms folded weakly on his chest. Not twenty seconds later his right arm fell limply to his side. Fifty seconds later on the time signature, Magnolia brushed into the room and shut the door. The time was ten forty-five PM. Both of them knew what was coming. Erland didn't debate holding Sierra's hand as it sat weakly in her lap. His hand was around hers, fingers interlocked.

Magnolia took the key as it was all she had and removed a small piece of paper from the bust line of her dress. Once the key was wrapped in the paper, she reached over Reston from the back of the couch and slipped the key down the front of his pants. It was then she made the sign of the cross and sighed, moving over to the small table with two dining chairs on it to lean for safety and clutch her abdominal region, as if she had taken the disruptive sedative given to Reston.

The door opened, startling her. Three men came in the room. Courtland, Pitts, and Brock, appropriately dressed in tuxedos as well. Jupiter followed them. He was wearing white from head to toe. The door shut and there was talking. The men were in a crescent shape around Magnolia, guarding the door, the window, and Reston. Pitts checked Reston by patting him down and shook his head. Jupiter only nudged his head while Courtland and Pitts held Magnolia by the arms and Brock removed a finger-sized hypodermic needle from a small wallet. Instead of injecting what they all knew to be STRIC-R in Magnolia's neck behind her ear, Brock performed the task with a quick jab to the same place where the stab wound was about to be.

There was more talking. Jupiter threw his hands up. He left. Courtland and Pitts kept Magnolia conscious as her head began to tip and her neck lose its control over what had become so heavy to bear. Brock took another needle from the wallet and jabbed Reston behind the ear and moved back to grab one of the dining chairs. The door opened and Tim Wolcek rolled through it, face pale and drawn out.

Erland felt the racing of Sierra's pulse through the tight interlocking of their fingers as her beautiful twin's life began its sacrificial end. They watched together as Wolcek coldly affixed the latex gloves and removed the carbon fiber spike from the left wheel of the chair, as it had been disguised as a spoke. He stood slowly and wobbled to the two men and the SAB Agent they held. The stiff fingers of his right hand steadied the target by the forehead as would a surgeon and the grace of her neck was exposed to the objectivity of the camera. Wolcek pierced her skin and slid the spike into her carotid artery and pulled it out. The blood that flowed from the wound was warm and rich and

Courtland placed her body in the position it had been when Erland found it nearly simultaneously. He sat in a crouch, watching her life bleed out, and removed the delicate golden necklace. Throughout this Brock had been trussing Reston up in the chair and set him near the window. Wolcek left for what Erland knew to be the bathroom and the others followed. The footage ended with the static image of Magnolia lifeless body and Reston set in deep freeze.

The Detective saw his bride to be's face and it was stricken with a suffering that was years in the making. She released the latch for the door and stepped out into the cold darkness of the parking lot, covering the staccato sobs of separation with her graceful hands.

Erland exited the car and made his way to her, his own heart heavy with sadness. God knew how many times he'd seen loved ones cry over the departed's closure even years later, but for Sierra to see it, so graphically and honestly and to realize how brave Magnolia had been, how trusting of her little sister.

Sierra's body was recoiling from the stifled weeping as Erland reached her and when he went to wrap her in his arms she shook her head and pushed him away. Before he said anything he understood why. Sierra took three steps and fell to her knees, vomiting.

Erland stood still and blew his breath in the air like a steam train, watching the woman he wanted to spend the rest of his life with be torn apart by the process he knew would change her existence forever.

The trunk of the car whined open and Erland turned and crossed the distance. It wasn't until he was within inches of odd angle of the trunk light that he saw the scarred face of Henry Morell. He was shirtless and his arm was interrupted by a bloody white bandage. He was rifling through a grocery bag of things Sierra had stuffed in the trunk.

He pulled out a shirt that was Erland's. It was green and yellow with broad stripes, not the most fashionable piece of attire in the Detective's wardrobe. Erland didn't remember the last time he wore it, perhaps college. It was tight on Morell.

"She thinks of everything, doesn't she?"

"She has to." Erland cast his head over his shoulder, seeing her rock back and forth with her head to the ground as certain cultures did when praying.

"She gonna be okay?" Morell took the slacks and tennis shoes that were in the bag. Again, they were old but clean. Then Morell saw the fullness of Erland's shut eye. The wound came from a serious beating and it conveyed in one second the Detective's commitment, despite his being somewhat of a normal guy-someone not trained for the job. The situation had harvested the extraordinary. Morell dressed himself quickly and took the thought further. The situation and Sierra Marland. He saw the way she looked at him and he was an Interrogation Specialist with two tours in Iraq under his belt. He spoke fluent Arabic though he never liked to talk about it and he could read faces like a menu. Between the two of them, there was something special, which was good, because they were special people.

"Yeah...she's as tough as they come. Her older sister died today, you know."

Morell nodded.

"Tabitha too."

An angry disbelief washed over the former Army Sergeant's face and he cursed through clenched teeth. He had grown attached to Tabitha's stoniness and commitment to the ever elusive perfect grade out over the months they had worked together.

"Who else?"

"Quinlan. Jimenez. Tallifer. Quinlan was dirty and killed Tallifer-I stopped him from stealing the evidence we collected in the Mansion."

"God..." Morell looked off into the trees. "Who the hell's left?"

"You. Me. Her. The rest are either dead or deactivated. It's a new game now."

Morell made a quick pursing gesture with his lips and his hands were on his hips, still getting over it.

"Boy she was right about you, wasn't she?" Morell cursed again, shaking off the uneasiness. As an Army Sergeant he had a different perspective on death, seeing it first hand-never being the one to cause it but always being the one to touch its many black holes of regret. His eyes went back to the bag to get his mind off of their once colorfully living bodies on the slabs of the County morgue. A small smile formed in the corner of his mouth to see the opened pack of cigarettes and the cheap lighter at the bottom of the back next to a small sandwich.

"She's sweet, isn't she?"

"Get in the car." Erland ordered plainly. It was good to know late in the game Sierra had someone Jupiter had forgotten about. "Back seat, by the way."

"Yes Sir," Morell nodded, then held out a cautionary hand to state that he was being serious. "I just want to say that you're damn lucky and from what I can tell you really deserve it."

Erland shook his hand with a firm grip. It was as close as he was going to get to a best man's toast.

"Get in the car." Erland said, his agreement of the statement residing in a gesture that wrinkled his eyebrows. When he shut the trunk of the GTO he saw Sierra, arms crossed, leaning on the hood of the car, gargling water. He stood next to her as she spit it out and watched as it began to freeze on the concrete of the lot.

"Take as much time as you need." He looked

her in the eyes and her spirit sat within the pools of blue.

"I don't know where I'd be without you." She said and took another swig of water. Erland kissed her forehead.

"It'll all be over soon."

Sierra breathed in deep with her eyes closed, receiving Erland's strength.

"I know."

They bunched into the GTO and Erland revved the muscular engine before pushing the sports car off into the darkness of midnight.

THIRTY-SIX

Officer Nguyen dropped Chris Lowery in the driveway of the brown house in the middle of East Hawks Lane and cruised the surrounding streets for the red Chevy Silverado.

Lowery stood in the sparse living room with the silence of his own thoughts and wondered what Erland would've done. The forensic team had taken blood samples and removed the slug from the wall, collected DNA and the like, but none of it would provide any revelations on the mystery man. Assuming for once, Lowery was wrong, then it was an open and shut murder. But where did the silenced Beretta come from? Where was Veracruz' truck and why were her keys gone? Why was her nose broken, the back of her shirt ripped and no sign of bruising found on either one of their hands?

And what about STRIC-R?

Lowery swore in the emptiness of the house. There was enough of an unanswered to save her from the charge of murder-just enough shadow of doubt to remain innocent until proven guilty-but the nature of her resistance to STRIC-R would reveal her lying about previous drug habits, however long ago they may have been. Her career as a K9 cop was over.

Lowery performed a browsing search of the house again. It was obvious Luis Jimenez, ready to move out and move on, was not a man of many possessions as it was, and the fact that he had nothing of value in the home further drove the notion home that he had been assassinated.

The Detective sat crisscross on the floor near the fireplace. There really was nothing he could do. Jimenez' autopsy was scheduled for four PM. It was as if he *wanted* there to be a third person, and not just for Veracruz but for the big picture, to be able to link some distant puzzle piece to whomever was responsible. And as he sat on the wooden floor he was beginning to wonder *if* there was a connection, to any of it. Was it a conspiracy or just a curse?

His phone buzzed in his back pocket and he expected it to be Kimmie even though it was his work only phone, an old flip model, she still had the number for emergencies. It was Nguyen.

"Tell me you found it."

"Yeah."

The Officer drove quickly to retrieve Lowery and he was nearly out of the car before Nguyen stopped it. The red Silverado was hastily parked with the right back tire on the sidewalk.

The Detective found it unlocked with the keys still in it. He had donned a pair of latex gloves in the car in anticipation.

"Anyone else available?" Lowery asked as the dome light clicked on and the dash gave off a repetitive ping.

"No."

"You got a camera?"

"No."

"Use your phone-mine's this old thing..."

"Right."

Lowery searched the truck for ten minutes with Nguyen's help and after all of the bending and grunting his tall frame into the painful positions necessary to examine every square inch of the vehicle his face was a shade of tomato and sick of the biting cold.

He cursed. It was clean-as clean as the day it was made from the factory.

"There's gotta be something!" He slapped the hood of the truck. Nguyen was sitting in the patrol car with the door open and the heat blasting, running the plates on the computer. Sympathy clouded his face but he was far too practical to be emotional. Despite how tremendously hard the Detective wanted to find something, if there was no evidence supporting this ghost man other than interpretive happenstance, then the decision would be in the hands of the judge and jury. It was also strange the media wasn't leaping from tall buildings to get a piece of the story and Nolan was more than likely sitting on it as long as tactically possible because of the suspect and the nature of the killing. It would come out soon enough, perhaps before the autopsy was completed. CPD didn't need anymore attention then they already had. At any rate, Veracruz' life had taken a dramatic left turn, and it made Lowery sick to his stomach that the obvious was a giant gaping hole large enough to drive a semi-truck and trailer through. Where was this mystery man's gum wrapper? Where was his mistake? Where was his humanity?

Lowery began to walk and made it as far as the street corner and to the red octagonal sign that stood tall against the yards of low bushes and the wide curbs of Mossyrock. Then he stopped and turned, the smirk he was seldom seen without having returned. He nearly ran to Nguyen.

"Chevy's have factory On-Star support, right?"

"You have to pay for it."

"But it's a brand new model-don't you think there'd be like a free trial period?"

Nguyen frowned.

"What are you getting at?"

"I'm not sure about this, but if the On-Star was activated when the alleged suspect took the car from the driveway and drove it here, then we'd have a voice recording."

"I thought they can only hear you if you call them."

"If it's on, it's on...the feed is recorded to a cloud and the algorithm can detect stress words or spikes in sound-anything that would indicate a crash or emergency situation where the driver would be unconscious and unable to answer a human dispatcher...I think."

"I'll get on it." Nguyen nodded.

"And do some door knocking when the sun comes up to find if any of these people have security cameras."

"Yes Sir."

Lowery walked back to the truck and placed himself in the driver's seat as he had done once before to check for prints and stray hairs and let out a sigh of contemplative relief. It was a long shot, but it was all he had to bet on.

The GTO rumbled and grumbled to a halt outside of a small two story with a generous side yard in the heart of Wayilow. A middle of the road Motorhome sat in the side yard and a white Mercury was dormant out front. The street was a long and narrow thing with houses of different generations built along it and held the obstinate privacy of normalcy. The house was off-white and had a for sale or lease by Hessler-Yeoung sign with detailed flyers near the mailbox.

Sierra knocked on the door three times and once

again after the space of a beat and the door opened. The house was in darkness.

"Welcome welcome to my humble abode." The west-Texas drawl filled the hollowness of the empty place. "Me casa es su casa."

The overhead light for the small foyer was a dated ceiling fan. The foyer split off two ways and directly above the entrance was the slightest sliver of a bannister from an upstairs hall. The rest was bad taste in blocky sheets of hastily painted drywall and something designers liked to call cathedral ceilings.

Morell was the last in and shut the door. Sierra was flanked by the two men and the man before them was a blonde in snakeskin cowboy boots and dirtied black clothing. He was no older than fifty but no younger than thirty-five.

"Well hello hello. What have we here?"

"Mark, this is Detective Michael Erland, CPD, Homicide and Homeland Agent Henry Morell, Crescent." Then Sierra glanced at both men. "This is my CIA contact, Mark Loomis, Extemp."

"Extemp? What's that?" Morell scratched at the old shirt.

"It's short for Extemporaneous." The man named Loomis hadn't moved a muscle, standing firm with his hands in his pockets. He was obviously in good shape and had a face that denoted he'd been around but was still pretty enough to pass off as several things that he inherently was not, though there was no denying he was born a cowboy. "It means without preparation-kind of like what's goin' on right now. You didn't say anything about your buddies, Sierra."

"I didn't know it would get to this stage...Loomis here," Sierra spoke to Erland and Morell, "Had his own CIA mission to retrieve CONSTANT-think of it like some strange third party contingency, only their idea was to stay back until they were convinced enough of the power players showed their hands."

"Like Brown." Erland nodded.

"More than Brown." Loomis' python boots made decisive clumps across the carpeted floor as Loomis walked a wide path. "The broker between Jupiter and the buyers, the buyers themselves and whoever is behind Brown."

"There's someone behind him?" Erland peered into the face of the Texan as he came to stand within arms distance.

"There's always someone behind the Brown's of the world, Detective. Brown isn't powerful enough or *smart* enough to make decisions by himself, he's just a micromanager. That's what makes him so dangerous. He has complete trust in the pipeline." The Texan eyed both of the men and observed their battered faces. "You boys look like you could use some refreshment." He held out his hand to Erland. "Thank you for what you did today. If you've made it this far with 'ol Marley here you must be alright."

Erland shook Loomis' hand and instantly liked him. Not that it was hard. He had charm in spades and the completion of the accent and the golden hair made Morell's attempts at boyish carelessness look like child's play.

"And you," Loomis moved to shake Morell's hand. "You probably don't remember a JSOC Mission code name Black Dagger back in two-thousand and three."

Morell shook Loomis' hand and a smile wove across his face and sat in the side of his mouth.

"How can I forget Black Dagger?"

"Who do you think the CIA liaison for that little gem was?"

Morell cursed and shook his head. Loomis eyes went to Sierra.

"We don't have a lot of time, Mark."

He held his hands out.

"Just being polite...let's take it to the kitchen. Y'all've bled for the cause and that merits a hot beverage and whatever else I can find in this dump."

Sierra cast a somewhat sheepish grin to Erland and he shrugged.

"Dan Bartleson told me personally about the operation about half a year ago." Loomis began, leaning on the bar with his arms flat and letting a loose wrist play with the handle of a coffee mug after the desired refreshments had been allocated. "He knew I'd been begging my uppers to get a deep cover op goin' as an arms dealer...the uppers are always thinking 'bout nukes but this Jupiter character just kept vaulting himself up the danger list and so they jumped on it to get the process of establishing a legend underway."

"Do you know who he is?" Morell asked. He had a microwaved pepperoni pocket and a tall glass of water, as well as a steaming cup of coffee.

"We have our guesses on an origin story but the short of it is, he's one of ours gone bad. We can't say for certain *which one* he is, but we know he's one of ours."

"What do you mean, one of *ours?*" Erland twisted his head in the slightest. All of it was new to him.

"Back in the eighties when we, and I mean the CIA, began to enter the new space race with the Russians-we never knew we'd be changing the course of history in the process. All of our hope was in our ability to advance technology *faster* than them, which we did, and we used a special *sages council* of the brightest minds from all walks of life to do it-some were engineers, others mathematicians, statisticians, you name it, we had the top of the pyramid. Many of them were newly immigrated as well. It was the second brain drain, the first of which being after World War Two. This time, the talent pool was more spread out-as you can imagine what kind of brilliant minds latched onto the newnesses of applied science in that do or die renaissance."

"What happened?" Morell said with his mouth full.

"They got jaded over time and one of three things happened. They went private, rogue, or died. Thankfully the middle was the minority."

"How many went rogue?" Morell swallowed.

"No more than seventy, no less than thirty."

Erland couldn't stop his face from twisting.

"You mean there's no less than thirty Jupiter's out there right now?"

Loomis nodded with gravity and took a swig of coffee as it had been laced with whiskey.

"That's our estimate. All of them were CIA at one time. I'm sure if we had enough time, we could narrow down who's who but in the end, they're too good to get caught. Plastic surgery, body doubles, foreign language mastery, you name it, these guys are all over it...their patience is our real enemy..." Loomis became introspective. "People think we just tap a few keys and a satellite spins around the earth and stops on a dime to take a picture of some lady's bare chest but they don't know how much it costs to move just one of those mirrors and cameras anymore than a centimeter. The state of the economy's affected what we can do with what we've been given and that's why they all got out. They were prophets of the social networking era, these sages, they knew what was coming and saw there was no good or evil to it anymore, like we had in our cold war with the Russians, just cash. They foresaw the exponential increase of computing power and the probability of handheld devices. They're already so far ahead it makes my eyes spin...but they're not in it for good or evil or the stars and stripes anymore. Just the money. That's why we can't get 'em. *We're* still in it for the flag. Our rules are different. We're just a bunch of dinosaurs and there gonna make us extinct."

Sierra returned from the bathroom and Erland could tell she had brushed her hair and fixed her makeup.

"I'm not going to kill Jupiter." She said as she sat on a bar stool.

"Good." Loomis nodded. "Brown doesn't need any more of a reason to lock you up and until we can catch him in the act he has all the authority in the world to do so."

"But what is he going to do now that *they* have CONSTANT?" Erland countered. Loomis had given them the particulars of the parking lot meeting and Sierra had left her options on the table.

"Nothing different." The Texan sipped. "If I know him, which I do, then he's going to make it personal."

"That was his threat to me." Erland confirmed. "I'm now a fugitive too...our plan was to make it personal for Jupiter and attack his privacy through the media."

"I don't think it really hit the nail on the head..." Loomis was distant. "Or else he'd be out of here."

"No, nothing's stopping him from making that sale. He wants to move up-CONSTANT's his ticket to the next level. He's still just a hacker at the end of the day. He doesn't have as much power as he wished he did." Sierra stood and moved to the tap for more water and paused once her glass was filled. "Did they talk about where it was going down?"

"I was flicking the power on and off and that point because they had an RF scanner, so all I got was at th...ena."

"Ena?" Sierra returned to the wooden stool.

"It's obviously the end of a word." Erland said to which Loomis silently agreed.

"We can search it." Morell offered. "Streets, businesses, you name it."

"Think we have enough time for that?" The Detective was contrary yet objective, and had a great deal of experience in hypothetical debate considering the vast expanse of his job.

"No." Sierra said, flatly. "It's something easy and wide open with a secret twist. Think about it. The buyers are going to be a diverse group, too afraid considering the merchandise *and* the day's events to be whisked away or stashed in some dark corner. It has to be somewhere they can feel safe to get out of if anything went bad and there has to be enough room for their bodyguards and entourages."

"Like the forest?" Erland offered. Katonah National Park was within thirty miles.

"I think it has to be in downtown Crescent." Loomis toyed with the mug and his tone was conciliatory. "That's where I'd do it."

Erland stood and stretched his neck, pacing. Loomis examined the Detective's face as it was hard to read with the shut eye.

"Talk to me Mike."

His face changed and he shook his head, staring at the ceiling.

"I don't believe it."

"What?" Loomis moved around the stubby bar as Morell finished the pepperoni pocket.

"The Winter Science Fiction Convention

Blizzardorama is slated to go all day at the Arena, starting at ten AM. Twelve hours of lights, noise, presentations, music-fourteen thousand expected in attendance. God knows how many will be in costume."

"It's perfect..." The light clicked in Loomis. "But how can we be sure?"

"I would bet all the money I have in savings." Erland's eyes were stony. "That's about forty-seven thousand bucks."

"You have to activate." Sierra said with some reservation and toyed with the rim of her water glass. Her eyes were slow in connecting with the Texan's face.

"Whoa, hold up Marley." Loomis pulled a cigarette from the pack in his pocket but didn't light it. "That's not some fast-food window order-it takes weeks to set up."

"You have to."

"What do you mean activate?" Erland cut in.

"Operation MERCHANT." Loomis said quickly but the intensity of his eyes were still on Sierra as the intensity of hers was on his. "She wants me to use my deep cover to get in as a buyer."

"But isn't that what you said you were doing?" Erland took a step forward to cut the eye contact between the two. "Jupiter's hazard made your superiors authorize your cover."

"Yes, that's right, but that's not what the debate's about. Deep cover is worth its weight in gold bullion, Detective, and mine can get me in anywhere I want."

"Then you can get in here." Erland insisted.

"Without question." Sierra slipped from the stool and stood next to her fiancée.

"But that's taking a legend eight months in the making that can potentially live for three to five years of limited operation and using it all up in one day."

"Mark, the whole reason you *got* your deep cover authorization was for CONSTANT's recovery *if the need arose*, you know that."

Loomis whistled air through grit teeth with his hands on his hips. He flicked the cigarette on the carpet as if he was disgusted that it was in his fingers.

"Sierra...this legend got me in with the Iranian nuclear program while you and your sister were waiting to trap Jupiter. They think I'm trying to get them U-231 and I'm only weeks away from getting some serious dirt for the UN Security Council."

Sierra's eyes narrowed. The situation with Iran and their desperate hunt for tactical nuclear capability was not only placing unreasonable pressure on Israel but threatening the vast riches of the Middle East and the tentative agreements between the ideologies of democracy and the regimes of old as the powers of the West tried to cultivate seeds of modernity, whether economically or politically, in the arid desert of an ancient Muslim landscape.

"You know how vulnerable this country will be if CONSTANT falls into the wrong hands? Just look at what happened today. This place is inches away from becoming a third world country under the right storm of events."

"Yeah," Loomis nodded and his intensity had not departed. "That's why this whole damn thing was such a risk...the downside's endless..." Loomis swore and shook his head. "It's the price paid to cut the cancer...the cost was counted long ago..."

"Who are the buyers?" The Detective interjected.

"I could only speculate agents of world powers, private contractors, representatives of global corporations-it runs the gamut between scary and really scary."

"Can you get in with them?" He continued.

The Texan put his hands on his head with his fingers interlocked and ambled around in a circle with his eyes to the ceiling.

"What the hell..." He said. "It's the worst of two evils." Then he came to stand within inches of Erland and Marland. "If we're gonna do it then it has to be *my* way. Comprende?"

"Yes." Sierra said without hesitation and Erland had no place to disagree.

"You." Loomis' intensity rested on the former soldier Morell. "You have any Army buddies in the private sector?"

"A few."

"Can they be here before eight?"

"Without question."

"Any of them on that JSOC mission I'd remember?"

"Hayes?"

Loomis smiled and the intensity that lit his eyes turned bright and nearly insane.

"Glory hallelujah." The CIA man turned to Marland. "You're gonna have to come with me."

"Where?" Erland stepped forward in the slightest.

"My plan, my rules buddy."

"It's okay Mike." Sierra assured and there was no rebuttal to the softness and confidence which was hers alone.

"She's gonna do a little raid on the prop house on Eleventh. We're going to hit this convention like the *pro*fessionals that we are. Morell, you and I are gonna recon the Arena while I make a few calls and worm my way into the auction and your Stryker buds get their tails up here."

"I'm staying?" Erland asked, confused.

"That's right, chief. "We'll be back before five, I'm sure of it."

"I can help." He insisted. Sierra had her hands in her back pockets and nudged her head toward the dark hall that lead to the bathroom. Erland eyed both Loomis and Morell and followed her. They stood alone in the lack of light and with the L in the hall, out of earshot of the two men.

"It's okay, Mike. You need the rest."

"I'm fine, Sierra, honestly. I know there's gonna be a lot to do and we still haven't determined *how* we're going to incriminate all of them."

"The less you know at this point, the better."

Hesitation crossed Erland's face and the shut eye twitched.

"I thought we weren't going back there, Sierra. I thought we had established what's mine is yours."

"It is Mike," Sierra said through a quick sigh. "It *is*. I guess what I'm saying is *I* don't know what he's going to do but I *trust* him. He's one of the best Extemp Agents there is-think of him like a...professional musician who can play any song or style without rehearsing. And he's giving up a lot to do this."

"Saving the country is giving up a lot? Since when? And what about what *you've* done? What about Maggie?"

"It's different Mike. God only knows if because of what he's doing to help us he'll find himself in the situation we're in."

"With the Iranians?"

"Yes, and whoever else he's formed bonds with- I know you have no prior knowledge to this world, but once a lie is discovered the grudge it forms *never* goes away. He's risking the *rest* of his life for this one moment."

"But he's saving the *country*, there's over four hundred million people here."

"I know Mike, I get it, but it was still a tough call for him."

"It was the only call."

Sierra placed her graceful hands on his shoulders.

"Mike, I love you, and all we have to do is play the game. Loomis is the coach now. We've got the footage of Maggie's murder and everyone on that tape is dead but Jupiter himself. I know you've got my back and I've got yours but you can't let your love for me ruin this."

Erland frowned and his voice was quiet.

"What do you mean?" Up to the moment, his love for her had *enabled* him to see past the pain of the present, living for the hope of a peaceful, triumphant outcome-never once did he think that such a beautiful thing could *ruin* the most crucial point of the operation and all they had worked for, all Maggie had done and sacrificed.

"I mean that you now have to promise to me what I promised to you back at Fircrest."

Erland swallowed. It was inevitable, and the difficulty of it was in the exposure of Sierra's weaknesses in his bedroom. She was *not* Magnolia, in *any* way, though they carried no physical differences between them and she was asking him to entrust her life and safety to Loomis and his variable set of gambler's dice as Erland had entrusted his life to her.

"Do you think something could happen to you?"

"I don't know Mike. I don't want to you freak out if it does."

"I won't compromise the mission, Sierra, but he can't compromise *you*. He can't *sell* you and there's more than one way of selling you. He doesn't know that you're not your sister, he hasn't worked with you today as I have. You're fragile and you're in no shape to..."

"I know I'm fragile, Mike, but this is it. The chips will fall where they fall. If we get CONSTANT and incriminate every bad apple in the barrel and I die in the process then you have to be fine with it *right now*-or else something *will* go wrong and you won't be able to do your part properly."

Erland swallowed hard. He was feeling like the weak one.

"You're asking me not to love you, not to *care* for you."

"No Mike." His betrothed's voice was soft in the hush of the darkened hall. "I'm asking *because* I know how much you love me and I know you'll say yes because you believe in the hope of the future like I do."

"But Sierra," Erland held her face in each of his bruised hands. "If you die, there *is* no future."

"And there won't be for anyone else born in this country if we don't give it all we've got tomorrow."

Erland grit his teeth and blew a lung of air from flared nostrils. He squeezed his love in his arms and felt her hold on for dear life. Her heart beat against his chest and he never wanted to let her go. But what was love? Was it selfish possession? Benevolent forfeiture and relinquishment? Was it a physical act of nature or was it just a word people threw around with no connection to?

The Detective kissed her forehead in the dark and Sierra raised her head to his. His lips brushed her face and their lips found each other for a string of passionate kisses stirred by the yearning of agreement that burned within their depths of their being.

"Do what you have to, baby." He said. "And I will too."

Sierra was silent and her hand wove around his face in a loving caress.

Then, she was gone, and her feet made no noise on the carpet as she left.

THIRTY-SEVEN

Sierra leaned against the door of the GTO as Loomis came from the house, Morell right behind. Loomis tossed the former Army Sergeant the keys and told him to drive. He had changed clothes to a nondescript outfit of urban earth tones, eschewing the cowboy boots for a pair of gum-soled sneakers and stood next to Sierra for a quiet moment as they watched their breath vaporize.

"What's wrong?" He asked.

"All I want is Jupiter."

"I know."

"And I am going to kill him."

Loomis shrugged and scratched the back of his neck with a lazy thumb.

"That's your call but it better be when all the dust's settled. Vengeance can produce bad timing, trust me."

"You know me, Mark." Sierra ran a hand through her hair and pulled up the furry hood.

"Not as well as I knew Magnolia-you ain't a clone of your sister but you sure do look like it. I'm sorry about her, Marley, I really am. It's a damn rotten shame."

"Did anything happen between you two last year in New York?"

"If only I was so lucky. Why?"

"She told me you were one of the good guys,

that you would do either one of us a favor at the drop of a hat if we ever needed to ask, that you'd go around the world and back and burn every bridge in sight if you had to. Why do you think Bartleson told you about our plans for CONSTANT personally? He knew you'd tell Peele and that would be the end of the circle-then you would have the same responsibility for CONSTANT we had, just from a different side of the firefight."

"I'm sorry about Bartleson, too. He was like a father to you two." Loomis avoided the crux of Sierra's truth, though it was accurate and as much as he had wished to have a more than professional relationship with Magnolia Marland is just wasn't in the cards for either of them. Magnolia was damaged goods, as it was, and she wouldnt've been able to have a healthy relationship with anyone but Sierra until she left the business for good.

"...He'll be alright. The worst part is he's worrying about me with all that happened to Maggie. He blames himself and he shouldn't. Responsibility is equality. We all signed the same contract and took the same oath."

"Well," Loomis looked off into the hanging darkness of the broad street and the carelessness of suburban Wayilow. "If your man in there can hang tough I think really think we'll get these bastards."

"Why do you call him *my* man?"

Loomis' smile was coy as he left for the passenger seat of the white Mercury.

"I may be dumb, Marley, but I ain't stupid."

Sierra Marland threw one last look to the plain two story with the motorhome in the side yard and fired up the GTO for the prop house on Eleventh.

The Detective named Lowery broke into a run through the narrow halls of the Precinct to find Sarina

Veracruz had been moved from room Five-Zero-Eight
to the overnight jail. An Officer named Timo was quick
to let her out and saved Lowery from saying anything
coarse or brash. Lowery pulled her out to the hall, away
from the ears of the two prostitutes and the one
domestic disturbance suspect.

"Did your brother pay for the On-Star system in
the Silverado?"

Sarina rubbed a hand across her face.

"God...I don't know. I don't think he would. He
saved every nickel he had to buy that truck."

"*When* did he purchase it?"

"End of August, beginning of September...I
don't remember."

The nod of Lowery's head was slow and
decisive. His eyes ran along the ceiling as he counted
days.

"There's the off chance that there is a voice
recording of the person that set you up."

The weight of the world fell from her shoulders.

"Oh my God..." Then her shiny olive green eyes
were on the Detective. "So then you believe
me...despite what the evidence says, what Chief Nolan
said?"

"Chief Nolan?"

"Yes, he came and saw me. He said he reviewed
the evidence and he's going to work out a deal with the
DA."

"What?" Lowery leaned closer. "That's insane,
Jimenez hasn't even been autopsied yet-he doesn't even
have all of the evidence."

"He told me he's thinking about the image of
the Department and how Homeland Security would
look worse than CPD for it in the long run considering
they're responsible for what's happened here today."

The redhead blinked, wanting to say so much

and nothing came out. Sarina was despondent and feeling the tail end of a very long day in which the largest roller coaster wasn't a wild enough metaphor for what had transpired.

"He told you all that?"

"Yes."

"That's not his place though."

Veracruz' eyebrows were bunched and she waited till one of the dispatchers walked past.

"But he's the boss."

"Ross said you hadn't even been charged yet."

"Why do you think they moved me?"

"What was it?"

"Murder One."

Lowery cussed and walked away, coming back quickly to bend to Sarina's height.

"There is no way the evidence supports murder one."

"He told me the stronger the charge, the more likely I'll get off and then he said he was going to work with the DA on the details-they're going to take it to Channel Two news when they're ready."

"But that's..." Lowery said and stopped, his mouth sealed before the innocent eyes of the young K9 cop. It was corruption in the way that it was more about Departmental image than a woman's life-more about working the system's loops and angles than the objectivity of factual evidence.

Veracruz shrugged.

"What can I do?"

"Have you seen Mike at all?"

"No, why?"

"Do you know what happened to him?"

Her face changed, as if it was hurt.

"No-is he okay?"

"He's okay but you know that he was working

Fircrest with Homeland, right?"

"Yes."

"I thought as much." Lowery stood to his full height and looked over her head to see that no one was coming. "Nolan said it himself-Homeland's responsible for everything that happened here. Mike got beat up really bad in whatever operation they were running and several people died-roughly about the same time as Jimenez was killed."

"You think that..."

"Yeah. I just don't know how to prove it."

There was a distant light in Sarina's olive green eyes.

"I'll tell you anything you wanna know, Chris, anything."

"It doesn't work like that. If there is a connection to be made I have to make it without you. Around you. *Outside* of you. Nolan tainted your testimony by running ahead with his half-cocked save face routine. He's convinced you'll get off free and CPD will only get a few weeks in the news and then it'll all die down. Your career's done either way, whatever happens."

"...I know..." Sarina was downcast. It wasn't the pay, it was the fulfillment of working with the animals. She had been responsible for training and handling four tracking dogs in her relatively short time at Precinct Three.

"I'll do what I can-just know that if I get this ghost guy *before* Nolan moves ahead with his witch trials you'll be off."

Veracruz nodded with gravity. She was aware Lowery was newly married and couldn't imagine what the family of *any* Law Enforcement Officer was going through with the day's events and the lengthened schedules they were demanded of to fulfill.

"Thank you." She said.

"You're welcome Sarina-I just want to do what's right, and if the evidence was there to support you killed Jimenez I wouldn't hesitate with a charge."

"I understand."

The smile that passed between them was perfunctory and once he saw that Sarina Veracruz was back in the shared cell he sulked off to call the On-Star people mulling over what Chief Nolan had done.

The Prop House on Eleventh was an old brick sewing factory that had since been refurbished and repurposed by a large film studio that shot a popular TV show in Crescent. The show was called *Magna* and followed a modern Robin Hood type character who wasn't as dashing as he was troubled and had a habit of saving comely women more than anyone else and his heart of gold was covered by an intimidating helmet and the rigidity of his office to save the city from crime of all kinds, especially that relating to the rich and powerful as they oppressed the lower class. Somehow, time travel was involved and the production value was more campy and kitschy than the novella it was based on but the show was very popular and was a launching pad for gorgeous, albeit not very skilled actresses to get creds under their belt on their way up the ladder to the big leagues of New York or Hollywood.

Sierra tried to recall the few times she'd seen the show as she removed the ventilation hood and kicked the grate from the old pipe that ran along the ceiling. It fell with a clang she wasn't worried about as her feet were on the floor with a swift movement. She had accessed the roof though the fire escape of the adjacent building block and the rooflines were close enough to hop between. The security on the building's lower levels was as pervasive as it was up to date but completely lacking when it came to the highest floor of the building, a stillborn graveyard of the bones of ancient sewing machines and racks of doubles, triples, and alternates for the costumes used in the show and enough space to mend them after certain stunts.

Her hands were quick through several racks to find Magna's costume. It was essentially a professional Superbike leather racing suit, all black with red and orange trim and piping, and the matching helmet was a slick combination of metal flake and airbrush work. Erland was roughly the same size as the actor who played Magna and though they would all be in costume to some extent, her delight was in choosing the Detective's. It took her maybe seven minutes to grab the other costumes and another three to stuff them into two giant laundry bags. The most complicated procedure of it all would be to leave the same way she came in.

Sierra found a small stool and it made a screaming noise as she drug it across the floor. The first bag was difficult to stuff through the small hole and was roughly twice the width of her body and had to be nearly twenty-five awkwardly bulky pounds. Several grunts and groans later the bag flopped from the ventilation hood to the roof. The second bag was easier as it held fewer items but she heard the clinking of heavy footsteps and the jingle of keys. Her legs were up through the square hole of the vent as the door creaked open maybe thirty-five feet away and there was no time to make it look as if she had never been there. Once on the roof, Sierra picked up the bags and ran, adjusting for their uneven weight, and dropped the lighter one at the edge of the roof, working up an underhanded swing to launch the heavy bag to the opposite roof with enough muscle to get it over and enough touch to save the more delicate elements of the costumes inside. She

counted the seconds from when the door opened and
was over the small gap in the buildings with the second
bag in under twelve. Wondering how long it would take
the security guard to see the evidence of the B&E was
not among her options and she ran with all haste to the
fire escape and began the tedious process of lurching
down the narrow and wobbly steps with the heavy bag.
Once the old laundry sack was secure in the back seat
of the GTO she made her way back up the fire escape
for the second bag and peeped her head over the
roofline to see the security guard poking his flashlight
around the ventilation hood and the surrounding area.
The flashlight swooped in a circle but wasn't powerful
enough to see past a couple of feet and the guard
reached to his radio to make a call. Sierra was away
with the second bag in a matter of minutes.

  "Mark." Her phone was at her ear.

  "Yes?"

  "I got the costumes. You almost done in the
Arena?"

  "Just barely got started-you go back to the house
and take it easy."

  "You sure you don't need a second hand?"

  "I've got Morell. I'm just about to begin
activation, so...I guess you should know."

  "I already know Mark, don't worry about it.
Whatever will be will be."

  Loomis was quiet for a moment as Sierra drove
somewhat illegally through Crescent for the house in
Wayilow.

  "That's why I want you back at the house...not
only to prepare yourself for what you have to do but if
you need some personal time, I understand."

  Sierra smiled to herself. Loomis knew what it
was like to face death so many times he had become
used to it. Morell too. And Maggie. But not Sierra. The

day had been an experience she would never forget and to spend what was left of it with the man she loved and had gone through so much with was not only the voice of Loomis' wisdom but a compassionate suggestion considering Sierra's physical safety and the dice roll thereof sat at the fulcrum of the operation's success or failure.

"Thanks Mark. I mean it."

"I'll see you at five. Or six."

Sierra tossed the burn phone on the seat next to her and sighed as the GTO slowed through late midnight Crescent on its path to Wayilow. She drove with one hand, the other on her forehead and as weary as she was, the specter of the unknown sparked like a fresh lit road flare in her mind. She just wanted to let it all go but she knew whether the pressure and the weight of American freedom left her shoulders or not was not within her control.

When Sierra entered the plain house she let its lack of fixtures and life speak to her. There was a calmness in it, an absence of the frenetic energy homes were usually hemorrhaging with and the heavy, junky objects that captured that energy. It made her wonder about her own home, the one she would build with Erland as she went to be with him in the upstairs bedroom. She wanted it to be a sanctuary, a cloister far away from the curses and opinions of the masses, a place where the only truth was the one they built together.

The Detective was bunched up on his side on an air mattress in the small bedroom the for sale or lease flyer was calling a master. Sierra removed her jacket and her boots, letting them fall to the carpet near the door and gently kneeled and slid on the mattress next to him as not to wake him. To see him completely motionless and to listen to the slow rhythm of his lungs as his soul was rapt to the great beyond of sleep blessed her to no end and she snuggled up close to him with her hand on his chest, her body a mirror of his, to meet him in the land where silence was the language of unity. For as much as she desired to taste love's perfect warmth she truly coveted stillness and tranquility more than anything else-to rest in Michael's arms as the softest symphony of rain pattered outside in the twilight of a new day, free of the mechanical ticking of time because to be loved was to be at peace, and if true love's purest peace wasn't heaven, then there was no such thing. It was that very fantasy Sierra related to Magnolia at the age of seventeen which caused Magnolia to choose the path she did, so that she could ultimately fulfill justice's revenge as a scourge of anti-terrorism and in the process cause Sierra to live a life that would not only support her sister with diligent comprehension but cause her to crave her deepest yearning in a way that she would never compromise it.

And not moments after she had closed her eyes, she too, fell into the boundless arms of slumber.

Tanya Wilson was telling herself it was safe to breathe in and out and let it go but from her time as a nurse she knew trauma was incapable of making a quiet exit. In fact, if it wasn't faced and dealt with, it could sit dormant in the depths of the human psyche and begin to cause medical conditions or worse, psychological conditions. A few of the staff at Regional remembered her and the presence of the Officer outside of her isolated room did nothing to encourage small talk and left her to the kaleidoscope of images in her mind, amplified as they were by the unhindered lingering of what she didn't know was called STRIC-R.

Her eyes opened quickly at the scuff of the door and startled her from a nap caused by a lapse of adrenaline. She was trying to stay awake and decipher what was what in her mind but nobody had answered the few questions she'd asked and left her to the unnerving solace of the secluded hospital room. How strange it was to be on the *other* side of it all.

Seconds from hearing the scrape of the door she saw the face of a kind black woman with very short hair whom she had a feeling was a Doctor.

"Hello." The woman came to check the IV drip and the EKG even though they both knew stability was a tender condition.

"Hi." Tanya croaked and her throat was still as rough as sixty grit sandpaper.

"You don't have to talk...I just wanted to make sure you were okay. My name's Anne Patrice, I'm a Doctor."

"M.D.?" Tanya adjusted herself to sit up but the angle of the bed wouldn't allow it and she fell back to where she had been when the Doctor entered the room.

"Yes."

"I'm an R.N."

"I know...try not to talk. I just want to let you know the man you helped earlier this morning is in stable condition and cleared of all supposition and suspicion of the murder at Fircrest Mansion."

Tanya closed her eyes and let whatever fear and confusion on the matter flee from her soul in a heavy sigh. Her sight danced around the acoustic tiles of the ceiling for a second and more clarity came into her face as her mind was furthered from the clutches of the impromptu nap.

"What is his name?"

"His name is Darren Reston, and he was injected with the same drug you were."

"Really?"

"Yes, do you remember?"

"I got the wind knocked out of me..."

Doctor Patrice was nearly disappointed and hid as much, noting the consistency in the STRIC-R victims. Instant knockout.

"It's okay...a Detective will be along later to get your statement and ask you a few more questions, you just try to rest."

"I can't rest." Tanya shook her head and Patrice beheld the forehead glazed with sweat and the greasy hair of the unfortunate victim of circumstance. The woman looked pale and lifeless though incredibly alert, as if her body and mind were separated somehow by a thin veil and didn't know they were trapped in the same vessel together.

"The ones who did this to you *will* be punished, Ms. Wilson, rest assured...I do want you to know that...the drug in your system is somewhat experimental in nature and the effects it has on the body are variable. Darren's amnesia was an extreme reaction due to alcoholism...is there anything you can tell me that might cause a divergence in your stability?"

Tanya turned her attention back to the ceiling. She was well aware of what drugs could do-narcotics, stimulants, analgesics, downers, uppers-not to mention the mighty concoctions of man-made synthetics that somehow targeted highly complicated bodily processes and either amplified them, manipulated them, or nullified them altogether.

"I have one kidney."

Patrice nodded and took the revelation in stride.

"Is there a reason why that wasn't on your medical records?"

Tanya's face was firm. She didn't want to say but the time for hiding the truth was long gone.

"I had a really tough stretch in my life Doctor...my fiancée died in a car accident when I was putting myself through medical school. I was overwhelmed by the debt...death is...very expensive-so is college..."

"Did you sell your kidney?"

"Yes..." Tanya turned her face to the wall, away from Patrice's kind brown eyes. "I knew that I'd be okay but if it was on my medical records I'd be passed over...anyone who wanted to know would know why and how...I couldn't live with everybody knowing. Just me..."

Patrice put a calming hand on Tanya's shoulder as Tanya continued to stare at the sponge-painted wall to her left.

"Thank you for telling me. You've done remarkably well considering..."

Tanya shook her head and the Doctor didn't remove her hand despite the burning guilt of the woman's confession.

"I did what I had to...not long after I did it my grandparents died and I got a substantial inheritance. Not enough to buy a new kidney..." A tear fell down Wilson's cheek. "It's one of those things, you know..."

"Try not to think about it..." Patrice offered. "I'm going to inform Doctor Jefferson." The Doctor paused before leaving. "I just got off-duty at the Precinct but if you don't mind I'd like to stay here and ask Doctor Jefferson if I can lend a hand in treating you."

Tanya let the weight of her head roll it over to her guest's pleasant face.

"Why do you want to?" The words were difficult to form with the dryness in her throat and her neck had become hard and stony. "Why don't you want to go home?"

The Doctor sighed as if asked why she believed in unicorns.

"Because I believe if I can go the extra mile for someone, it'll make a difference in their life-no matter who they are or what they've done."

She left with the scuffing of the door and Tanya smiled to herself, though it hurt to smile because of the stiffness in her neck and she felt herself fade to a reluctant darkness as the rhythmic beats of the machine that said her heart was alright became erratic and her vision fell into darkness as if sliding down a long and endless tube from which there was no escape.

The small office space with a desk unit in each corner was as void of place and time as it was the smell of Kimmie's delicious recipes and Lowery was reclining in his chair with his feet crossed on the cleanliness of his desk, waiting for the warrant to obtain the cloud copy of the Chevrolet Silverado's On Star recording. The stress ball was in his hands, being tossed back and forth, if only to pass the seconds and dissipate the intensity of his focus. Someone had bought it for him as a joke, a neighbor or some distant acquaintance, but there was a strange sense of fulfillment in squeezing the odd shape of the item as it was a gateway to heavy thinking.

Officer Towns poked her head around the doorframe as she was accustomed to doing.

"Warrant's coming through the scanner."

Christian Lowery kicked his size twelve shoes from the fake wood and was quick on the phone.

The first time he was placed on hold he stared at a small box of paperclips. The second time he went back to the stress ball.

"Detective Lowery?"

"Yes." He pulled up his chair and leaned low on his desk.

"My name is Robin Sanders, I'm in charge of

archival material-they can't hand you off anymore-I'm the end of the line."

"Yes, Ms. Sanders." Lowery allowed a quick chuckle.

"Mrs."

"Yes, um...did Mr..."

"Parvik?"

"Yes, did Mr. Parvik relay to you the urgency of the matter?"

"He did, and I want you to know that we will be able to email you the recording of the time period you asked for within the next ten minutes. Will that be satisfactory?"

Sanders could probably feel Lowery's broad smile over the phone.

"Thank you very much, ma'am."

"My pleasure...oh, and one thing Detective."

"Yes?"

"Does your car have On-Star?"

Lowery chuckled again.

"Yes but I don't pay for it."

"We can change that."

"...Maybe another time."

Lowery rolled his eyes as politeness wouldn't allow him to hang up on the woman and he fed her one yes after another until *she* ended the call. Then he was swift on the computer to learn that his lightning strike of an idea was little more than a few words but those few words spelled out the corner piece of a puzzle so large Lowery could barely push himself from the chair to tell his on-duty superiors.

Kelly Barnett left Darren asleep on the living room couch as she continued to clean upstairs. She had completely lost track of time and remembered Doctor Patrice's words in the Precinct about how he had been poisoned and needed rest. Their cozy dinner together had left a slightly odd feeling inside of her and she ran it over and over in her mind as she banished herself to work and forced him to relax. The moment she had hoped for had finally come and it was an exercise in servant hood, housekeeping, and care-taking. But that's what love was, and Kelly had resolved that in her heart after reporting on a story of a promising young fiancées and a car accident before she left the Crescent Times for the CMJ. The woman loved her scarred betrothed so much she remained faithful to him for three years even though they had never legally tied the knot and his physical state never progressed beyond a human vegetable before he finally slipped off one night. The story nearly brought a tear to her eye just to think about it and she stood with a sigh. She couldn't change his life in one day, and as much as she wanted to make his house clean and cook for him and repair his shattered career as a writer, it wasn't going to happen in an instant. It would be a long road of sunrises.

Kelly scuffed down the carpeted steps and smiled as the thought of those sunrises bloomed in her heart.

The light from the kitchen had been left on and she saw Darren lifelessly crashed on the cushy sofa, feet up on the small coffee table that had been freed of torn magazine pages and newspaper clippings. She stepped over his legs and sat down close to him with the squish of the cushion and ran a hand over his hair. His body resonated with some distant chill and a thought flared in her mind about grabbing a blanket but it paled in comparison to another thought too loud to ignore. Disbelief poisoned her face as her hand slid down to his neck where a delicate vice of fingers felt no pulse. Her hands snapped to his wrists and squeezed. No pulse. Finally she turned his head toward the light and pulled at his eyelids to see the once brown eyes darkened with the invincible ash and soot of death. Tears blinded Kelly Barnett as she fell across his chest and wept.

      Darren Reston was gone.

THIRTY-EIGHT

The sun was hesitant to rise beyond the tips of black evergreens and finally did so behind a thin sheet of clouds, casting horizontal slices of yellows and blues across the breadth of the sky. The early morning was a cold, crisp creation of harsh clarity, and frost lingering on the ground was crunchy underfoot.

Detective Michael Erland woke with a sharp intake of air and felt Sierra sleeping in his arms before the blurriness left his sparkly blue eyes. Any thoughts of it being a dream soon departed. Her head was on his chest and a slightly sweet and spicy smell drifted to his nose as he remained on his back to let himself warm to the notion of being awake for good. His eyes wandered over her as he was her body pillow and seconds after he began running his fingers gently through her hair she, too, awoke with a deep inflation of her lungs. Sierra nuzzled her head against his chest before making eye contact.

"Hey there..." She said. Her eyes were puffy and Erland knew the feeling of wanting to go another ten hours but having a prior commitment. It was an early establishment in his youth-the life of a boxer-and the hardest part about losing a fight was waking up early the next morning to face the lonely hills of hops for a jog, no matter what his body felt like.

Her face, as God had made it, was beyond

compare.

"I don't remember how we got here." Erland said. "But now that we're here I don't want to leave."

"I know." Her head went back to his chest and she shimmied closer. "When I returned from the Prop House you were out. Must've been five hours ago."

"Is whatshisname back yet?"

"Loomis?" Sierra yawned and was slow to cover it with her fist. "I don't know...I'd still be dreaming of a white Christmas if you'd hadn't woken me."

Her jewel blue eyes were simply captivating and the suggestions they held demanded addressing.

Erland took her with a strong embrace and rolled her over and smiled as he brushed strands of silken black hair from her face.

"Christmas, huh? Aren't you getting a little ahead of yourself?"

"Do you want to see what I got you?"

"For Christmas?" Erland frowned. "You really are ahead of yourself."

"No." She hit his shoulder and pressed herself up from the air mattress, slinking to the master bathroom. "Your costume."

She didn't shut the door and Erland sat up against the wall, seeing her shoes next to her coat on the floor and looking at his own clothes, how they reminded him of last night and strangely there was no strong memories of last night, as if it had never happened-just the knowing that it did. He released a lengthy groan and touched the tenderness of his ribs. The boots of Jupiter's henchmen had done their work well.

Erland was up to his full height and entered the bathroom with wobbly steps where Sierra had splashed cold water on her face and was brushing her teeth. The

Detective ran the same procedure with the cold water and winced as he braced his weight on the vanity to see the damage. His right eye was still dangerously swollen but he could see out of it, enough to squint at least.

"I hope the costume has a mask."

"We all have masks of some kind." Sierra said through a foamy mouth. "None like yours, though."

He stepped aside as she rinsed her mouth and she gave him a small towel for the beads of liquid on his face as she left for the stairs.

Minutes later she returned lugging a weighty laundry bag.

"I can't wait." He smirked as he leaned against the bathroom doorframe.

"You're gonna be a real looker." Sierra said, relieving the drawstring and removing the leather Superbike suit.

"You didn't."

Erland closed the distance slowly as Sierra laid out the fullness of the slick costume on the carpet near the air mattress. The Detective chuckled and rubbed the balding spot on the back of his head.

Magna was the epitome of every racing motorcyclist's dream and the show was fraught with dangerous stunts and squealing tires that put some movies to shame. The gratuitously gear-headed theme garnered the bulk of the budget and was the only purpose for the show in some critics' minds.

"I think you earned it when you stopped Quinlan from stealing those cameras..."

Erland went straight for the helmet. It was deep black with a famous reddish-orange nebulae airbrushed across its surface. The paint was metal-flake. The visor was a rusty chrome, artificially aged by the arts department to suggest time travel. The severity of the helmet was in the foam-composite ridges, venting and air-duct design that took the helmet from a traditional, full-face necessity to a nearly otherworldly artifact suitable for a star-fighter pilot or an intergalactic bounty-hunter.

"This is the real deal."

It was, the entire outfit carried a cost of a little under five thousand.

"It's practically leather body armor...you watch the show?"

"First season...the pilot was badass...then the acting really tanked...they film it here in Crescent you know-a few of the guys from Precinct Eight are consultants-not that the producers ever confer to them on Police procedure."

Sierra shrugged.

"No custom time trial bike with nitrous oxide to go along with it, but at least you look legitimate."

"Are all of our costumes going to be from the show?"

"Yeah. One stop shopping."

Erland smiled with sparkly eyes.

"What'd you get for yourself?"

"Something appropriate..." Sierra went back to the bag. Her costume was that of Aurora, a thief of greater skills than Magna.

"Aren't they adversaries?" Erland watched as she held the tapered blue leather pants and short jacket full of zips and snaps up to her body. A creamy white turtleneck and boots of the same color completed the stylization of Magna's foil.

"I don't know...does it matter? I just wanted something that would fit."

"Sierra, you'd make a garbage bag flattering."

His fiancée picked up the helmet that accompanied her choice and studied it in the light. The paint was a flip-flop chameleon treatment and held the strong motif of ice and blizzards as Aurora's character was a wooden composite of such themes, and diametrically opposed to Magna through competitive employment; although fate, or rather the writers, had forced them to work together on occasion.

"I got a cape for Loomis."

"That must be The Dreamer. The cape's purple, right?"

"Yeah."

Erland laughed and clapped his hands.

"You're gonna have a Texan wear The Dreamer's costume?" The Dreamer was a nightclub owner, a self-described entertainer, and owned a device that tricked Magna into rescuing people who didn't deserve to be saved, much to the chagrin of the audience. The Dreamer wasn't bad as much as he was selfish and egotistical. His attire was as flamboyant as it was fabulous. The mask was fashioned in an operatic, harlequin vein with an unnecessary amount of rhinestones.

Sierra shrugged again.

"No backing out now. Loomis said we're going to look the part."

"What about Morell and his Army guys?"

"They're going to be SWAT. Do they have a special name for them in the show?"

"No."

"Urban camo. They're in the second bag. Just the BDU's and boots. I didn't get all of the extras because Loomis will be bringing the real thing-they'll have body armor and the whole nine yards."

Erland swore quietly to himself.

"There's a little Magna inside of everybody you know..." He said, still gazing into the depth of the airbrush rendering of the brilliant nebulae. "A guy who lives in the future and goes back to save people he knows will die if he doesn't, each time weakening himself in the process. How many times would we've wanted to do that?"

Sierra gave him a quick hug because she needed it. Her mind immediately went to Magnolia and she didn't even want to think about Tabitha Grey and Ryan Tallifer.

"They're here." She said and left quickly.

Erland turned at the abruptness of her exit having heard nothing and went to the window to see bodies piling out of the white Mercury. Erland frowned. His ears were still, after all these years, his one sense that had deteriorated the least. Before he let it bother him he skipped downstairs to meet the new crew.

Joseph Hayes was a compact man, half an inch or so taller than Morell and both were shorter than Sierra, and much more than Erland and Loomis. Hayes was thick with muscles and still appeared, for all intents and purposes, as if he was *in* the military. Morell relayed to Mike and Sierra that he was a private military contractor.

"How are you?" Hayes said to each of them as he shook their hand and there was no question he was from gator country and spoke French only when intoxicated. His eyes were brown and there was a slight unpredictability to them. They learned he was an EOD during three tours in Iraq and made it all the way up to specialist four before losing his left leg from an IED. Erland was a tremendous study of body mechanics and language and couldn't tell in the slightest the man's left leg was a prosthesis, but it made sense considering the musculature of his chest, back and shoulders.

The man with Hayes and Morell was Ed McKinney. He was a wiry man and the smallest in the room but held all proper indications to lead Erland in assuming he was a human monkey. He was bald and had severe features that didn't aid his natural aloofness, but the positivity in his eyes and the grip of his hand let Erland know he was a man of extreme patience, focus and an immensely strong will. He ran a survival course in Katonah National Park and Erland smirked when he began to assume the man was a hunter.

"Are you gearing up for Elk season?"

McKinney smiled quickly.

"Yes. Are you?"

"I only hunt white-tail." Erland shook his head. "But I'd love to have a go at elk."

"Rifle or bow?"

"Rifle."

"I want to get into recurve bow hunting-I'm one-quarter Apache."

"Fellas..." Loomis cut in with his broad hands. "Save it for the lodge. We've got work to do."

Sierra heated up frozen pizzas while Loomis discussed the game plan with the rest of the group. He had the schematics of the Arena on a laptop computer and guesstimated what areas would be best for the sale considering size and ease of exit.

"How sure are you the sale's gonna be here?" Hayes asked and already looked to be in battle mode, having begun to chew gum with a mechanically repetitious grind of his strong jaw.

"Before we scoped the place out? Fifty. Now, one hundred and fifty."

"What changed?" The former specialist crossed his arms.

"Morell and I saw one of Jupiter's possible associates down there with a handful of men scoping out the west side just before we left. He didn't see us. His name's Charlie Norstrum-he's a former Special Forces, now a PMC."

Hayes swore.

"Charlie Norstrum? He'll recognize me."

"I know you two used to work for the same PMC outfit last year in Nicaragua. You'll be all covered up though, just try not to speak. You're running a support role as it is."

Hayes took a swig of water from a half-empty bottle.

"Charlie's a bad dude. He's smart as hell too. I hope you've got a few contingencies. If your target has more men like him then it just got a lot harder."

Loomis smiled even though Erland had been in the corner wearing a skeptical face the entire time.

"Don't worry buddy, I've got it all figured out."

Erland listened to the plan and grit his teeth at its possibility. He'd been on stakeouts and stings and even a few undercover operations, but never something with as much wide open caution-to-the-wind variability and complete self-assurance as the ultimate finale of Loomis' CIA Operation MERCHANT. But what did he know? He was only a Homicide Detective, as they had told him. He was the ball boy and they were the pro athletes. With as many times as he had tried to volunteer a form of a strategy he finally got the hint.

As Sierra removed the pizza from the oven, she caught a look in Erland's eye she hadn't seen in him before, standing where he was with a guarded posture in the corner of the empty living room, away from the tight circle of strategists and kept what thoughts his demeanor provoked inside to herself. She was submitted to the demanding accuracy of Loomis' great magic trick and that was the way it had to be. Somewhere within the gears of her mind she knew it was too late to confront or question what final decision Erland had made about the mission and the woman he loved with a simple and wholehearted conviction and his face was a product of pain-whether it was for the thought of losing her or the fact that he was going to pull something wild out of his sleeve she couldn't tell and she resolved within herself to trust Erland with her life as he had trusted his to her.

"Okay." Loomis began once the wrinkles were addressed. "This small convention room is the most ideal place to do the sale. It's small, open, and directly adjacent to multiple service entrances while still being secluded from the rest of the Arena. It can be easily secured and maintained throughout the course of the sale. The greatest risk we run is the communication-we will be unable to communicate in any way-so everybody will have to do their job to perfection. I'll have a small AV button camera on me but the hard drive will only record eighty minutes, so if it goes longer Erland will be backup."

"Hmm?" Erland stepped forward with a slice of pepperoni.

"The convention room is uncovered and exposed to the slope of the rafter work that girds the roof, and will be unused until five PM when the Arena crew will begin to set up a VIP meet and greet. Detective you'll be up there with a hand-held camera and a silenced Winchester 70."

"What would be the conditions to use the Winchester?" The Detective said with food in his mouth.

"If we have an OK Corral situation, take out who you know to take out. Just make sure your aim is as good as the Mountain County Sheriff's Department records say it is."

"I go to the rifle range once a month and hunt white tail twice a year."

"Well, human beings aren't white tails, and some of them'll be wearing body armor under those suits, so go for the head. And once you know we're in place, you'll have to hoof it to get in position. You up for it?"

Sierra gauged his face and it was flat behind the pizza. Loomis was CIA Extemp and the occupational hazards of such was a necessity to use people as a means to an end, leaving them in a worse position than they were before-if they were still alive after the process of being deputized by the spontaneous Loomis. Erland was in an open Officer Involved Shooting case and had escaped house arrest issued by Mr. Brown who carried Executive Office backing. If the right hands latched a hold of him it would take a pretty powerful lawyer with a giant rabbit's foot to get him off of doing time in federal prison considering Mr. Brown *was* a lawyer and knew the full extent of the law he carried with him. In the same manner, Loomis was putting his life on the line not only in the operation but with the Iranians, seeing as if his cover was blown and he did make it out alive under the nose of all the guns pointed at him, the Iranians would respond in wrath to find out they had been courting a lying two-faced CIA operative-especially with all he had done to get in with them.

Erland inquisitively pointed a lazy finger to his right eye, the very same eye that would be looking through the scope of the Winchester if need be.

"I can still see."

"Howabout your legs? Your lungs? I know you were loaded with STRIC-R and beaten within an inch of your life. You'll have to climb to the top of the Arena and navigate all the tresses and girders like a ninja."

"I can do it." Erland nodded and the faces of the soldiers were tense. The eyes of the room were on him in silent judgment. They knew he was tough but they also knew he wasn't a *soldier*. Every one in the room had served the military but him and with the gravity of the situation it wasn't something they were avoiding.

"Well alright." Loomis mirrored Erland's gesture and moved on with the plan. Sierra watched the Detective carefully as he went for a second piece of pepperoni and he caught her eye and winked.

Her legs crossed as she sat on her ruby red jacket to protect her behind from the chilly floor, Jessica Birchall continued to listen to Leilani's life story.

"I di'nt know how to get off the big island, you know? Bot' my brothers were in jail 'n I di'nt see a way out of da life."

"How'd you get over?" The flight from Honolulu to Crescent couldn'tve been cheap.

"I stole da money...Five O's been lookin' for me. I guess you can't run forever."

The door to the holding room squealed open and Birchall didn't even turn. Her eyebrows were twisted in compassion and the full attention of journalistic investment. Leilani was born the youngest of a man who only wanted sons and had a failing construction business on the big island that hemorrhaged debt-driving his sons to lives of petty crime with his youngest left in the middle.

"Ms. Birchall." A Sheriff's Deputy came by to release her as the electronic door lock filled the hollow cell with a grinding sound stirred the two prostitutes to wake groggily.

"Yes?" Jessica turned and the Sheriff's Deputy motioned for her to rise.

"You're being released."

Birchall responded quickly and silently, grabbing her coat and not even bothering to dust it off.

She turned to see the Hawaiian's pleading eyes.

"I won't forget your story." Birchall promised and as she followed the Sheriff's Deputy, she honestly meant it. There had to be some way out for the poor girl, and though she looked older she was only nineteen.

"There's some people here to see you." The Sheriff's Deputy was a beer-bellied man with a good, albeit lackadaisical nature about him.

"Really?" The reporter asked, wondering why she wasn't in handcuffs because Homeland Agent Farges had thrown around the word *treason* nearly as much as he had the actual charge of *criminal defamation*. Birchall didn't know as much about the law as she wanted to but no extent of education could have prepared her for the Deputy's opening of the doors that separated the jail from an adjacent hall.

Digital cameras clicked and flashed as a small and noisy mob of her peers were waiting with vocal recorders and cell phones in outstretched hands. The group surged to her position behind the Deputy and unleashed their flurries of questions like a Desert Storm rocket barrage.

Birchall squinted against the repetition of the flash and turned to her right to see the slowly advancing frame of a slight man in a sweater vest whose name was Farges. She wanted to run but there was no where *to* run-only questions, questions, and more questions, and the irony of it gave her a tremendous shiver at eight o' clock sharp that Saturday morning in early November she knew she would never forget.

The Texan was alone in the motorhome adjacent to the plain house in Wayilow, sitting before a Hollywood artist's display of mirrors, lights, and make-up; props and artificialities necessary for transfiguration. Mark Loomis was *not* the man of the legend, and every bit of west Texas soldered seamlessly into the fabric of his being had to be flawlessly covered by a con so solid it could fool his own mother. He twisted his head to take in the dyed light brown hair with touches of gray, hair that was once blonde and free, masculine and caught in tight curls, now straightened, slicked back and slightly receding. With a small sigh he began the job of altering his face. It required patience and skill to convincingly change the unique lines of a mug he'd seen so many times but part of the career *was* being someone else and he had divided his personality in a way that the young man who signed up for the ROTC because he shed a tear whenever he heard TAPS on a trumpet was still alive and locked away for safe keeping. His compartmentalization of who he knew he really was enabled him to do seemingly unspeakable things in the name of truth, justice, and the American way-and more importantly the safety of all those who knew no better.

Loomis applied glue to all of the skinplants, as they were called, little more than flesh-like silicon and fixed pairs underneath his brow near the edge of his eyes and another pair parallel to his nostrils. The last pair of skinplants fleshed out below his bottom lip, giving his face a widened, puffy and slightly unhealthy appearance. A seemingly minute skinplant was applied to the bridge of his nose. All of these additions were expertly covered in makeup. Finally he removed two contact lenses from a small case of many, items that would muddy the color of his eyes to signify aging. The finishing touches of makeup were in shadowing beneath the eyes to which Loomis played around with different expressions, slowly returning to character like an old iron horse huffing and puffing to leave the station on slick steel rails carrying the weight of thirty loaded cattle cars behind.

There was a knock on the door and Loomis hollered for entrance. He was surprised to see Erland of all people and kept it to himself.

"Where's your bike?" Loomis asked as Erland occupied the doorway and said nothing, taking in the transformation.

Erland looked down at his costume and shrugged.

"It's a low budget operation."

"On the contrary," Loomis hadn't changed his voice yet, and the rich west-Texas drawl didn't fit the face it fell from. "No expenses spared." Loomis stood and offered his hand. "The name's Mic LaCosta-jus' call me The Merchant and I'll call you when I gots my hands on what you wan."

Erland shook his hand, frowning slightly at the perfect New Jersey accent and then again at the cold fish handshake, which was not so much as an unmanly gesture, but just an impatient touch of hands as if there were more important things to do.

"Your legend?"

"Yes Sir." The Texas drawl was back and Loomis sat down again.

"How long till you'll be ready?"

"Heck, ten minutes."

"Are you in?"

"Not yet ol' boy." Loomis leaned forward to touch up the skinplants around his eyes, seeing as they were the most problematic with the slightly histrionic facial movements Mic LaCosta was known for. "Timing's everything."

"...I..." Erland was focused on the floor. "I just want to let you know I'm grateful that you're doing this...I know it's dangerous for you."

"You only live once..." Loomis tossed the

applicator brush to the small laminate table top and sighed. "You know how deep this legend is?"

"No." Erland shook his head and a wrinkle ran through the CIA man's face as if to ask himself why he was about to say what he was.

"I became a Muslim to get in with Iranians." The Detective's face showed concern as he listened. "I was born and raised a certain way, you know...I guess I'm doing this so Mic LaCosta can die...can't say I ever liked being him." Loomis demeanor changed as he stood up and went for the costume, which Sierra had left in the laundry bag. "You're aware of the social climate in the Middle East, Iran is public enemy number one-even the Saudis are scared of them. If they get tactical nuclear weapons there's no telling who they'll send one to."

"There'll be more Agents, more opportunities."

Loomis shook his head.

"No...I *am* Mic LaCosta, I've been in these people's homes and seen their family photos, not only do they think I'm a complete sampler of junk food America which they find strangely comedic like some kind of toy, but they think I'm *one of them*, and they think I'll get them a nuke if it's the last thing I do because they're convinced I'm just as crazy to see the return of the Mahdi as they are. You'll never understand, thank God, but I know Magnolia would, and Sierra to a certain extent, and if this whole debacle with Jupiter wasn't more of an immediate threat I would've just shaken y'all's hand and said good damn luck to 'ya."

The Texan removed the flowing purple cape and the harlequin mask from the laundry bag.

"What the hell is this?"

"Low budget operation." Erland echoed.

"My dad would kick my ass if he saw me

wearing this." Loomis shook his head. "Pa's a retired two star General. Air Force. His name's Mike, too, by the way."

"You're not wearing it." Erland shifted positions and his leather suit squeaked. "Mic LaCosta's wearing it."

Loomis touched his nose and pointed with his head tilted and was back in a New Jersey state of mind.

"You're sharp you know that, you're *really* a bright one."

"Sierra picked it out for you."

"Oh she's a sweetheart, a real doll, y'know?"

Erland nodded and left with a mild concert of leathery creaks and croaks.

"We're ready when you are."

The CIA man smiled and waited till the door was shut to place a call he knew Erland would be unable to bear. Even if the numbers came up wrong on the green felt the operation would still work. He wasn't risking a life for failure. Not his life, at least.

THIRTY-NINE

Killinger reached his phone before the first ring had ended its cyclical chiming noises but didn't answer until he remembered where the number was from, which took another three rings.

"LaCosta?"

"Damn Mr. K, I just grew five new gray hairs waitin' for you to pick up."

The broker was in a large hotel room on Fourth and his bodyguard was outside in the hall. Still, his neck bent forward slightly and he walked with light steps to the patio and wouldn't speak until the sliding glass door had shut behind him. The building had a view of the river and didn't cost as much as usual, considering.

"I told you, I can't get you a nuclear weapon or U-231. We can't risk meeting again, you know how the CIA are monitoring anyone even *closely* related to Iran."

"What, the G-men are after 'ya now?"

"No, and I'm going to be extremely busy today."

"I know-I wanna get in."

Killinger's naturally arched black eyebrows came together.

"What do you mean?"

"I wanna get CONSTANT-on behalf of the

Iranians-they figure they can trade it for a nuke or leverage the bureaucrats in Washington and put 'em in a bad spot, make 'em back off until they become tactical."

The broker braced his weight which wasn't much on the railing.

"How'd you know?" He asked after the space of several heartbeats in which he had debated hanging up and calling Jupiter-seeing as Jupiter had already given his blessing to the names on the list, the VIP's, as they would be referred to.

"You know how connected I am's'n I was in the area when everybody jus'about wet their pants to get SAB Agent Marland."

Killinger was quick. Not as quick as Jupiter but his brain was still making money in the stock market let alone his less than legal dealings, and with the current state of economics, his position in the DOW was rare-all on the count of his analytical brain.

"Where is she?"

"Now now boyo this is the part where we haggle n' stuff."

"The auction's closed, it's too late. The seller is a very careful man-he's vetted everybody against his databases."

"I'm sure...after seeing him on the news...he'd like the cloth Iran can put up...n'if he ain't into cloth, we can find him somethin' shiny in the royal vaults..."

Killinger felt himself slipping into the deep end of the pool. LaCosta was a brutal bargainer, cold-blooded and ruthless, as was Jupiter-only LaCosta's loyalty to and backing from the Iranians and their gold made him a favorable candidate for an *unreasonably* large sum for the Aladdin's cave of classified American information CONSTANT truly was.

"Here's the deal," Killinger leveled, voice void

of all defensive mechanisms. "It's Jupiter's call, not mine."

"I have Sierra Marland. I picked her up in the industrial district after some kinda shootout went down. We'd been tailing her since the local LEO's gots their BOLO's for her and waited till that helicopter left to pick her up."

Killinger turned quickly, thinking he heard a noise behind him and saw only the plain hotel room behind the glass. He knew about the shootout and the helicopter-it was purely factual and the only other person that could've known about it was Sierra Marland. Jupiter was convinced everyone else had died and his teams had swept the area but it was an easy place for a professional to hide.

"Is she okay?"

"Couldn't be better. I had to beat a few'a my boys wit a baseball bat to keep them away from her though-she's *fine*, if you know what I mean."

The broker sighed.

"What are you offering?"

"This is it, straight up, take it or leave it. Lemme come in as jus'another one of the boys and I guarantee you some royal bank, man, righteous bank and as a token of good faith I'll give you Marland wit no strings attached, do with her what you wanta."

"I'll call you back." Killinger went back inside and sat on the bed, staring at his phone for a space of seconds. It was his decision as much as it was Jupiter's-they were splitting the money down the middle. Brown wasn't part of the deal physically but was in theory, and Killinger would bet all he had on the man's greed-especially with a dealer as reputable as LaCosta. Mic LaCosta was a real bastard and could afford to be with the cushion of Iranian Secret Service on his six and a small band of cutthroats and killers gathered from the fires of international conflict zones in each pocket.

"Why are you calling me?" Jupiter asked calmly, after the broker had finally worked up the courage to overcome his own paranoia. "You're not supposed to call me until nine."

"It's about the sale. A new buyer wants to sit at the table."

"Absolutely not." Jupiter responded, not the slightest chance of hesitation in his voice.

"Hear me out."

"It's not the agreement and you know that."

"It's LaCosta, Lawrence, and he's got Sierra Marland."

Jupiter was quiet for the time it took Killinger to stand up and pace around the large bedroom which had suddenly become claustrophobic.

"How?"

"He said he picked her up after the shootout. He was in the area and started looking for her after the BOLO-I told you Brown was too clumsy."

Jupiter held out his hand on the other side of the call for Killinger to be completely silent-the hacker had to think. He had to methodically break down the timeline and the probabilities and statistics, sift through what was perfectly true and what was too perfect to be.

"What about the CIA?"

"LaCosta's not CIA."

"I know, but they're glued to everything the Iranians touch."

"They were onto Brown, too, and he's not going to be with us."

"How do you know he has Marland, what proof has he offered?"

"None." Killinger sat down on the edge of the bed again. "But you know LaCosta, the guy's a radical right wing Muslim with Garden State street smarts-if you don't want Iran..."

"It's not about who gets CONSTANT...it's not about how much...it's about the timing, and the fact that he's got Marland."

Killinger shrugged nearly helplessly and reloaded.

"...What happened at Keller's?"

"Marland's plan backfired. She tried to bait me with CONSTANT and take me out. The cost was high but look where we're sitting."

"So she was vulnerable-LaCosta said he was tracking her since Brown included the Police."

"That's entirely possible but I don't like it."

Killinger felt the fracture in Jupiter's stance open wider. Seconds ago he had been adamant.

"You know how badly he wants to be the one to bring nuclear capability to Iran, after all of what this country's done to him. They want CONSTANT to leverage their position against the US-and they have more gold than you could imagine. Four hundred some tons in their royal vaults-I'm sure he can get them to cough up some of it."

Jupiter was quiet. There were no more arguments to be made.

"Tell him to be there at ten and bring Marland-if he's pulling something we'll shoot them both dead on the spot."

The broker stood and nodded an unnecessary amount of times.

"I understand completely."

Killinger nearly flew out the sliding glass door to make the call back to LaCosta to ensure the Iranian money would be on the table in the VIP conference room at ten and if LaCosta was in the market for some kind of strange double cross he was going to be the first to go.

Loomis ended the call and sat on the motorhome's uncomfortable bed, tapping the phone on his leg like a drum stick. Erland was right. It was the Arena-with thousands of freaks and fan boys all geeked up, it would be a veritable madhouse; a miasma of bodies and colors and costumes. The Detective was sharp-smart enough to nail Granderson, a man who'd left no evidence at a quadruple homicide-certainly his mind could handle what was about to happen.

It wasn't his mind Loomis was worried about, and he didn't have the courage to ask the Detective because never knew what it was like to feel the same way about somebody as they felt about you, and as much as he didn't want to screw up what Erland and Marland were experiencing, he was given no other choice.

The CIA Extemp Operative grabbed a few things from the motorhome he didn't want his compadres to know about and called to let them know, even though it wasn't yet nine o'clock, it was time to leave the bland home in Wayilow for good.

Detective Second Grade Christian Lowery was unaware he'd dozed off until the rap at the door shocked him back to cognizance. Armstrong was bearing two cups of free sour coffee he had found somewhere, as was Armstrong's prerogative. He probably wasn't the best for an undercover assignment, seeing as he was a stingy-looking baby-face with a buzz cut and had the mark of the government stamped all over him, but Armstrong was *extremely* observant, so much so they called him Falcon-Eye, perhaps because the other two more popular birds of prey were already famously taken. He was from Vice and had cut his vacation short with the Crescent Crisis as the news stations were in a hurry to call it and Lowery had to fill in what points of the case Lieutenant Ross didn't care to expound upon on the count of being so busy. Sarina Veracruz' death in custody during the night had been a terribly bitter pill to swallow in the midst of all that had happened and while the desperate necessity to solve the murder of Luis Jimenez had since disappeared, what connection perhaps fused that event to the greater scope of the Crisis remained. Even though Veracruz had built up some sort of resistance to whatever drug she had been subjected to, the poison preyed on her deeply stressed immune system, the end result of which being kidney failure.

Lowery took the coffee and set it in the center console of the early millennium Red Ford Explorer Sport as it lay dormant in the flat and spread out lot of Municipal Arena. The back was loaded with surveillance equipment, both audial and visual, strictly of the handheld variety, as well as a pair of Kevlar flak vests-the Lieutenant wasn't taking any unnecessary precautions.

Armstrong checked his watch.

"It's twenty till. Shouldn't this guy show up soon?"

Lowery shrugged. His lottery ticket had paid off only to fund an even stranger speculative sweepstake. The archival recording of Veracruz' truck detailed a phone conversation between a nasal-voiced man who Lowery was convinced was the killer and an unknown on a cellphone, relating to the man a time, and a location.

Municipal Arena, ten o'clock.

The grey of it all was what sold Lieutenant Ross and after Lowery told him of Nolan's decision to move ahead with charges of Murder One, those grey areas quickly cleared up and somehow in Ross' mind the

finding of this man would solve everything and so
conveniently so at ten o'clock considering the judicial
process of Veracruz' criminality would've began
promptly after lunch-not that it mattered with her tragic
misfortune.

But since their arrival at seven-thirty, the steady
volume of people had made it increasingly difficult to
profile and theorize who the man on the recording was
and what he was supposed to be doing. In some ways,
and no thanks to the glorified power-nap on the couch
in Ambler's Way, Lowery felt completely disconnected
from the true Detective work of it, as if he was going
through the motions. It had nothing to do with Kimmie
and how she had locked the door to the bedroom, it was
something about the mass of costumes flooding the
highly anticipated yearly ingathering-seeing as the
event was bi-yearly and the summer convention was
held in Minneapolis of all places. There was a
tangible...happiness, all around, as if the Arena was a
pilgrimage site and he was supposed to keep an eye out
for the one apple in the entire barrel who truly *was* in
disguise. Was it another terror attack? Teams had found
the explosives at Sugar Hill Elementary-Semtex, a
Czech made plastic explosive, set to a remote trigger.
And when Ross made a motion to question Erland
about the planned destruction to see if he had learned
anything of the sort, he found that Brown had been
holding out on him about Erland's absence. The
insanity of it was beginning to get to him and
Armstrong's incessant snapping of innocuous
photographs was fraying what was holding his nerves
together.

Lowery took a swig of the coffee. It tasted as
sour as it smelled. What he really needed was a tall,
frosty mug of ale and a good damn football game.

"See anything?"

"Nope." Armstrong shook his head. "Not that I know what I'm looking for. Lotta spandex, though, let me tell you, I do *not* miss the eighties."

"I'm still too young." Lowery chuckled though his heart wasn't in it and fired the car.

"What are you doing?" Armstrong asked, and not in a pushy way, though his face had a habit of appearing pushy, perhaps it was the haircut and the way his nostrils were naturally flared.

"Riding around the Arena."

Armstrong agreed. The Explorer Sport was getting chilly.

"Drive slow." He said. There were five other cars at the event, mostly traffic cops and PEO's, only *fourteen* Officers for an event suspected to draw fourteen *thousand*. CPD was *drastically* understaffed and they were seeing just how much. If a bomb threat was suspected, where was the SWAT team, the bomb squad, the dogs, all of it? Why was Lowery searching for a ghost of a man when he had no idea what to look for? His mind immediately went to Nolan and the scuttlebutt about his problems garnering funding from the city council following last year's increases. The general consensus was that the council had given CPD more money with the stipulation that it go straight to giving the Precinct buildings a face lift, and had nothing to do with hiring more Officers or purchasing better equipment. Even with the city council's skinflint donation above the standard, only a few of the smaller Precincts had received the fullness of the upgrade. Lowery was trying not to be bitter about the situation and the swirl of issues it was stirring inside as he slouched in the seat of the Explorer Sport and wound around the northeastern entrance. Terrorism, the council holding back funding to fight terrorism from the Chief of Police, the Chief of Police robbing one of his

Officers of due process, that Officer involved in a murder and dying in custody, his wife in the deep end of rejection, and nearly fifteen thousand geared-up nerds and geeks foaming at the mouth for the science-fiction and comic book mania of *Blizzardorama*.

"What was the name of the guy that's running security?" Lowery nearly mumbled.

"Herkin."

"Weird name..." Lowery threw a wave to a pair of Officers as they stood by one of the gates, thick with fan boys and their equally as frenzied wives or girlfriends. "Tell him to keep an eye out."

"Already done." Armstrong nodded. It was one of those phrases that meant nothing and said a lot. Sure there was some fear hovering around the building but it was hidden in and amongst a last-night-on-earth sense of moment-seizing fury, and if they were all going to die, they were going to die together, as superheroes and creatures of alternate dimensions, living the life they wanted to instead of waiting for the next calamity to strike cooped up in their apartments with their hands glued to a TV remote or smartphone.

"How many's he got on staff?"

"Herkin?"

"Yeah..." Lowery mumbled as the Explorer Sport pulled around to the west entrance, which was thick with trucks and service personnel tasked with building some of the stage and lighting elements of the small concert set for the evening.

"About a hundred yellow jackets and another thirty plainclothes."

The Detective stopped the Explorer and grabbed one of the telephoto-lensed cameras before his de facto partner could, and took a tight angle on one of the loading bays.

"Isn't the FBI supposed to be here too?" Lowery

clicked a photo.

"Would we know if they were?"

"You'd think we'd get a heads up but no..."

"Do think they're looking for who we're looking for?"

"How the hell do I know, Chris?" Strange, it was, that Armstrong and Lowery shared the similitude of a name and Lowery might as well have been asking the question of himself.

"I asked *do you think*-you know you could use some time off, it really helped me. This job, it's not..."

"Hold on." Lowery said and squinted to at a procession of bodies.

"What is it?"

"I don't know."

The Detective handed the camera to Armstrong and put the Explorer in gear for a closer look.

The killer named Denison loitered between four comic book stands and felt odd in the Galactic Paratrooper helmet he had stolen from someone in the bathroom. Other than the white and black plastic of the identity cloaking apparatus, his appearance was unchanged from the murder of the Homeland Agent in the house on East Hawks Lane. It was as generic as it was modern in a black three quarter trench coat and slacks and he was distantly thankful there were plenty of half-hearted attendees like him who had only ventured to stick something goofy on their head to show their support. He was free to browse the comics as well because of the leather gloves he was wearing and the cold temperatures of the crisp Saturday morning further authorized their use. As the digitized numbers of his multi-function watch drew nearer to the hour he snagged another helmet from a display table and switched in a slice of darkness created by a star galaxy-

themed photo booth. He also removed his reversible
jacket, changing it from black to brown, and pocketed
the gloves. If there were any cameras concerned with
his presence, they would be none the wiser, and
Denison exited the spreading space of the Arena. The
turf football field was covered in an industrial rubber
carpet and made host to hundreds of stalls and kiosks of
everything from displays of rare and limited run toys, to
movie props, to first edition comics, and meet and greet
photo booths. Near the west entrance crews were
building a small concert stage, testing fog machines and
laser lights and the buzz of the atmosphere was
captured in the thousands beginning to mill about in
otherworldly attire. Municipal Arena was a flattened
dome of antiquated construction and the exposed steel
rafters and girders had to be two hundred feet above
ground. Lights were multitudinous, yet the size of the
Arena sucked away much of the wattage and there was
a dimness and lack of sharpness blanketing the floor.

Denison dipped behind a pair of dull yellow-
jacket security guards as they rifled through two
unscrupulous-looking teen's backpacks with a gruff
hastiness and he worked his way quietly through the
gray concrete of the service track that ran around the
Arena to one of the designated and not yet occupied
VIP spaces, located in a stretch of rooms that were used
for dressing, waiting, conferencing, and other faculty
and staff necessities common to Arena life. Some of the
rooms were in the process of being transformed for
their later duties as the evenings more prestigious and
anticipated events would rely on them. Each and every
one of the rooms had been built with twenty-four foot
high walls yet none of the spaces had ceilings, and
while it had saved money thirty-some odd years ago
when the Arena had been constructed, complaints about
the lack of ceilings had been filed over time, due to the

complete absence of sound diffusion, which, for some athletes and performers was essential. The room chosen for the rendezvous was a long rectangle of stark white with snagged blue carpet and a dark laminate table of the same shape surrounded by enough banquet chairs to merit the comfortable seating of fourteen. It was connected to a small anteroom that was bereft of accessories but unfortunately cursed with the same carpet and Denison was stopped at the open door by a burly man in a suit and a blonde man with a scarred chin who wore all black. Neither were in disguise, but masked their features somewhat with oversized women's sunglasses.

Instead of removing his mask, Denison held out his thumb for the blonde man who pressed it into the face of his smart phone. The screen flashed like a photocopier and the three men waited for a span of twenty seconds till Denison was admitted.

Jupiter was sitting crisscross on the floor with his head against the wall in meditation. Kirke was pacing and Jenkins was madly striking keys as he tried to investigate the parameters of the CONSTANT memory card. Two large black duffel bags were on the floor to the young hacker's left. Denison stopped in the doorway and blocked the light from the next room, causing Jupiter's eyes to open.

"Are you ready?" He asked. Denison nodded. Jupiter's head bowed to Jenkins and Denison waited for the young hacker to break his attention from the laptop at his fingertips to hand the killer a red file folder with the pictures of his next two targets. Detailed information had been printed on the picture's reverse side.

Denison nodded once he had studied the two images and then removed a lighter from his jacket and began to burn the red file folder and its contents.

"If you can," The killer asked, waiting to drop the spreading fire in his hand to the ground till the last possible second. "I'll take fifty-thousand for each."

"Money will not be a problem." Jupiter said without opening his eyes, his voice as calm and placid as ever still trapped in the midst of his meditation. "It's location. You have to take both of them out as if they were standing shoulder to shoulder."

"And you promise to arrange this?"

"I don't promise as much as I guarantee its probability." The most dangerous man in America was back in white, which would've been a foolish thing if he had not worn the classic theater mask of tragedy which lay dormant at his side. "Just set your nest across the street from the Pinnacle building and you'll get your chance, but considering the situation you'll only have two shots. If you can't get them both at the same time you don't deserve the money."

"I understand." Denison acknowledged, his voice nasally underneath the mask. He smiled to himself as he hit the door where the burly man and the blonde man stood guard and gave them a nod of good luck.

Charlie glared at the man behind the woman's glasses as the man left and was swallowed in the circulation of bodies hundreds of feet down the concrete track. Charlie tapped Killinger's bodyguard in the chest several seconds later as the broker named Killinger rounded the stretched out corner of the concrete track with a cadre of men in suits black and blue suits and monkey masks and their entourage of bodyguards, dressed to the nines as Homeland Tactical Assault.

Lowery scrutinized the cars and trucks surrounding the west entrance like a hunting dog unsure of the scent sneaking through the air. Dozens of people were breaking the small snapshot of space Lowery was trying to pause in his mind.

"What is it man?"

"It was this one guy, I didn't feel right about him."

"What'd you mean?" Armstrong turned in his seat, looking past Lowery's head and then back to him, the parsimonious lines of his face tightening.

"It was..." The Detective began and then smirked. "Do you know much about sci-fi?"

"No."

"Neither do I...I just...you know those masks, like the Phantom of the Opera?"

"The happy and sad faces? Those things creep me out."

"Yeah, me too. I saw a guy dressed in white, head to toe, he was wearing one. I don't think those are sci-fi, you know? I mean, they're creepy like ghosts, but a ghost isn't...*sci-fi*, is it? He looked like a ghost-not a ghost, I mean..."

Lowery's face changed as if he had been playing hide and go seek with the truth and stumbling over his own words to communicate what was brewing inside in the process. The lack of sleep and the stress of the day had only compounded the effects of monthly overwork and all but severed certain cognitive functions he always relied on being so quick. His phantasmal recollection of the figure in white was because his *introduction* to the figure in white was just that-grainy and disturbingly stoic, caught in a trap and suspended in time, like a specter on a security camera would be for that one, frozen moment.

Security camera...*helmet* camera?

The Detective ran it over once more in his mind, through the contraptions his IQ used to analyze flat images and transfer them to real life human bodies. Behind it all there was the knowing Erland talked about and cursed it more than he praised it.

Instinct.

The words of Jessica Birchall were warbly as they floated back to him.

And would you believe that one man was behind it all? From a trusted source in the Department of Homeland Security I have learned the man responsible for all of today's destruction is a wanted domestic terrorist known only by the alias Jupiter, a moniker appropriate for a deity of war. The man you see in the picture behind me is that man-the most dangerous man in America...

Lowery reached for the radio to contact the other Officers scattered around the grounds. Armstrong's hand was quick on his wrist and his grip was crushing and vice-like.

The confusion that began to bloom in the Detective's face lasted for only a split second as his de facto partner landed a punch squarely on the redhead's right temple, the force of it sending his head against the window. Lowery crumpled into the steering wheel, tripping the horn and Armstrong pulled him back again to see his head was floppy and loose.

"Sorry man." Armstrong took the Detective's badge and gun and secured his hands together directly in front of him through the gap in the steering wheel with the Detective's own handcuffs. Then he buckled Lowery in and made damn sure the seat belt was locked at the shoulder and tight across the waist. Armstrong took the radio and tossed it in a dumpster along with Lowery's badge, gun and the keys to the Explorer Sport as he made his way into the procession of staffers and service personnel coming and going from the west entrance to locate head of security Herkin and tell him access ways to the VIP rooms were not to be disturbed for the next hour and a half despite what the schedule said. The rooms would be under a joint CPD-Homeland investigation for potential bomb threats and they were going to keep it quiet to prevent mass hysteria.

FORTY

Magna, as portrayed in alternate costume number three by Michael Erland, stepped from the motorhome nearly a half a mile away from the Arena's east entrance and hitched up the guitar gig bag on his shoulder. Erland had always considered guitar his favorite instrument in music and knew the greatest players in the world would've had a hard time finding notes on the Winchester 70 stuffed inside the bag. His back was sore and stiff as he walked, especially his lumbar region around the kidneys and he blamed it on the air mattress. Sierra's presence had been a sponge full and ready to be squeezed and the only thing he could recall about waking to feel her in his arms was a childish sensation akin to being bundled up and walking home through winter dusk in Garden Grove when the streets were deserted and fresh powder fell from the lavender sky. Perhaps it was the last time in his life everything had fit into place and all was right in the world. That Christmas his parents began the argument that would conclude in their divorcing each other months later and the used boxing gloves he had been given as his one and only gift were fashioned into tools of catharsis for years to come. Erland let a thick and heavy sigh stretch from his lungs as the looming monolith of Municipal Arena became larger and more of a tactile reality. Its sound and shape and color were lodged deep in his psyche and the Arena looked no different than that one night in April many years ago. He had superstitiously avoided returning to the site as it was a grave, of sorts. So much pressure had been on him for that final fight of the Golden Gloves tournament, so many words of tainted hope and encouragement; the tangled tentacles of others and their perverted desire for his success. Their voices had been syrup in his bones and glue on the soles of his shoes; the small town boy against the purebred generational byproduct of Tijuana and East Los Angeles. Hugo The Hellhound Marquez had toyed with him like a cat and stretched the technical and clinical punishment for the full twelve rounds only to catch him on the chin seconds before a ring of the bell would end the fight. Some youthful zeal in The Machine Gun Man's mind told him if he could go the distance, the judges would've given him victory on a split-decision, and while time and maturity determined that to be false, it was a horrible blow to be so close to the end of the fight and lose by knockout. In fact, it was the belief of some that Erland's heroically valiant and gutsy effort had only made The Hellhound's masterful performance *that much* more impressive and Hugo Marquez was in the Golden Gloves Hall of Fame on the count of that epic pinnacle to his perfect amateur career. Erland knew as his stride was swift and confident in the leather Superbike suit that consciously avoiding the site of his professional boxing career's death had gained him nothing. To turn one's head was to be afraid and Erland was surprised it had taken him so long to realize how weak he had been in addressing the depth of the scar that night had created, when it was only the painful burial of his difficult youth. In truth, it was a seed that died unto itself and what shot up through the soil of life was the chance at out of state college, the complete detachment from family ties, and the path of an outsider that would lead him to Law Enforcement and save him from getting married or having children and if his life as a Detective was going to end there was no better place on the planet for it to go down than the Arena. After studying death and murder for so long the Detective finally knew what could possibly drive someone to take life in justifiable manslaughter, if there was such a thing, and he loved Sierra Marland so much he would lock and load the Winchester 70 in her defense, no matter who stood in the way. The decades of being a loner were over, as were the years of being CPD's Mr. Reliable, and if it was a damn selfish choice, then so be it.

The group of monkey masks totaled thirteen in number and each one was admitted with the nod of Charlie's head after a pat down from Killinger's bodyguard and a thumb scan on the smartphone. Charlie peered through the women's glasses to see a tall man in a gray suit speaking with a handful of security guards hundreds of feet away and was confident the man would perform his part of the bargain, as everyone on the take was supposed to but seldom did. It seemed they were working with a makeshift bannister of some kind and there were logistical issues with the stage hands and the bulky items they were on schedule to set up. The strategy of the event planned on the limited space in the loading bays being vacated by a certain time and no doubt the security guards were working with the CPD Detective named Armstrong to figure it all out in the wake of whatever yarn he was spinning before their eyes. The bodyguards of the buyers club were a physical presence in their Homeland Tactical Assault getup, replete with M-4 carbines and Charlie let his free hand play with his lip as the suits filed in the room, one thumb scan after another and had his thoughts on the spread of it all-how many were truly involved and to what level they understood but before he could become philosophical it was time to close the doors.

Killinger stopped the former solider with a hand on his shoulder.

"Has LaCosta showed yet?"

Charlie glanced down to the hand on his shoulder which was promptly removed.

"Who?"

"Jupiter knows."

"LaCosta, you said?" Killinger seemed nervous to Charlie but compared to Charlie, just about everyone was, save Jupiter himself. "Nah, if he wasn't on the list I can't let him in."

"Jupiter knows." Killinger reiterated and began to unbutton his thick black overcoat before taking a seat at the head of the table. Charlie didn't shut the door and leaned on the frame with a visual angle on the roundness of the dimly lit concrete track that ran around the stadium. He knew of Mic LaCosta by reputation, and how he had taken vengeance upon the United States for their abandoning of him and his ailing grandmother during Hurricane Sandy, how he had found a *new* calling from his life of crime and had become a ruthless character-perhaps a bit *too* ruthless at times, overcompensating for some fear or weakness. Charlie had his streaks of cruelty and it was somehow always tied to efficiency, even though he hadn't taken life before today since the war in Afghanistan and as it had been a historically hostile civilian but an unarmed civilian nonetheless, he knew what it meant to be burned by the country he gave his life to and instead of facing public humiliation he had chosen the life of anonymity as a brother of illegal arms-a hired gun, a nomadic mercenary.

Just as the table of monkey-masked suits was ready to begin, four figures came from the east, winding around the track with purpose. Charlie removed his shades.

The leader was a man in a showy purple cosplay creation complete with a flowing cape and a thin harlequin mask of bejeweled brilliance. Behind him, two counter-terrorist soldiers with gas masks and body armor down to knee and elbow pads walked with a woman between them, and a flinch ran through Charlie's scarred chin. The woman was in sky blue leather pants and a tight motorcycle jacket of the same material and something about her was familiar in a way that it reached deep inside of a place where no one was allowed to go. An intricately airbrushed helmet covered her head and before Charlie could tell the misguided geeks how their presence was unauthorized it became clear to the former solider their destination was the room he stood guarding. Killinger brushed past Charlie, bumping into him. The broker offered no apologies and rushed to meet the man in the ridiculous purple outfit and they shook hands. Charlie left his post and made his way around the table as some hushed form of small talk was passing between the monkey masks and the former solider found his boss on the floor in meditation.

"There's somebody here, Killinger said his name's LaCosta?"

Jupiter nodded.

"Is he alone?"

"No, he's with a woman and two men dressed like CQC Anti-Terror."

"He has a sense of irony..." Jupiter stood up without the bracing of his hands, as if he'd performed the maneuver a thousand times. As he stood however, he put his hand to his heart and his head dipped down for a second or two.

"Is he legit?"

"We'll know soon enough..." Whatever tremor it was had passed. "The woman is supposed to be Sierra Marland."

Charlie's handsome face was hard.

"How the hell..."

"If it's fake, we'll know..." Jupiter steepled his fingers. "Otherwise, LaCosta will be a contender to win CONSTANT on behalf of the Iranian Government."

Charlie let his head fall and his eyes stare at the black combat boots that added a few inches to his height. Muslims were supposed to be his enemy, it had been bored into his skull with a diamond-tipped drill, but somehow he didn't care anymore, the allegiance to what he once called home so far removed from the present. Iran was one of the enemies of America, whether officially or unofficially, and he was no longer American. He was a soldier of fortune, and they had no home-no border.

"Tell me what to do." He said and listened as Jenkins took one of the duffels into the rectangular room.

When Jupiter had finished speaking he sat down again and closed his eyes.

The Dreamer, as portrayed by Mark Loomis passed a tense look to the smoked chrome visor of the icy blue motorcycle helmet. At each of Sierra's elbows stood Morell and McKinney, respectively, and the tactical shotguns slung tight on their backs were fully operational death machines if it came down to that. Killinger told Loomis to wait for a second and he kept silent and activated the CIA-built AV recording camera he'd embedded into the harlequin mask. The Texan threw a thought to Hayes who was out in the lot with the motorhome and Erland, God knew where he'd gotten to and as Loomis let his head naturally drift up the sloping arch of the Arena's roof he noticed how high up the girders and the catwalks to maintenance them were. Killinger popped from the door only for a second and motioned them in with a quick gesture with his fingers. Loomis and Sierra were admitted and Killinger's burly bodyguard was thick in the doorframe and his posture encouraged the two tactically-camouflaged urban warriors remain outside. The bodyguard shut the door behind him and that was that. Morell crossed his arms and walked to stand next to Killinger's bodyguard and McKinney silently did the same.

Erland's breathing was labored as he stuck his feet into the ladder. His walk had been brisk all through the Arena and he'd taken the stairs to the executive suite level whereupon it was a small maze of grimy corridors to reach one of two access points to the roofline catwalks. Sweat was pouring down his back as if he'd entered the third mile of his traditional four mile run and it didn't matter whether the Detective blamed the leather or the price of the newest IPO on the S&P 500 for the sweat and the difficulty he was having with the ladder because it was the truth and nothing would change it. He paused and debated ditching the helmet as he was getting tired of his own breath fogging the visor and took the moment he had to cinch up the guitar bag strap as it had become dangly. The more he told himself he was making progress the further away the catwalk became and when the slight bend of the roofline ran through the ladder his grip grew tighter with the achievement of each new handhold.

Erland allowed himself a quick heaving of his lungs at the end of the catwalk once the feat of reaching

the top had been realized and he slowly removed the
rifle from the bag and threw his helmet inside.
Thankfully the ladder wasn't far from the room Loomis
believed to be the one in question. Getting back down
in a hurry would be a rough trek, but Erland took his
steps on the catwalk slowly and cautiously as the open
topped rooms became visible. Sight through the scope
of the rifle was like some strange doll house and Erland
found the room, having dropped to one knee. It was a
long and boring rectangular thing, and the table that
seemed to be its sole purpose was filled by men in
monkey masks. One seat was empty, and the scope
travelled to see a thick bodyguard flanked by Morell
and McKinney. Erland nodded to himself. He searched
the table again and the corners of the room though the
flattened angle prohibited vision of the near corners of
the room and Erland let his winded weariness release in
a single puff as the importance of Sierra's blue figure
on that scope rose to the forefront of his mind. He
debated moving closer. He was as physically close to
the room as he could be, catwalk permitting. His right
eye left the scope and stung with the puffy, throbbing
irritation as was expected and the Detective spotted a
small maintenance track running around the bend of the
roofline. He went back to the scope and found no
evidence of Sierra or Loomis, seeing as they were both
incredibly hard to miss and the shut door in the center
of the room's far wall spoke volumes. The small size of
the room prohibited him seeing more than the far corner
of it and Erland determined he would ruin the mission if
spotted on the maintenance track that ran not thirty feet
from the top of the open-ceilinged rooms. That and it
was perhaps a ten minute ordeal to be in a position
capable of viewing *both* rooms with perfect clarity and
secrecy. The Detective attempted to further steady his
breathing as he rose and slowly continued along the

catwalk, his full attention on the burly bodyguard outside the door whose eyes were no doubt, constantly searching behind the oversized sunglasses.

Loomis was quiet as he stood before the man known only as Jupiter, who was seated crisscross like some kind of far eastern statue with his palms facing up. The lack of sound in the room was tangible, considering it was a pervasive hush stabbed with bits of loudspeaker announcement spillover or a spike in Killinger's voice as he outlined the parameters of the auction to the men seated around the table. There was a single duffel bag on the floor on the right wall and the blonde man named Charlie Nostrum was standing directly before Loomis near the wall opposite the door, with his arms crossed and the sole of one of his boots flat against the wall as the leg it belonged to was bent and perpendicular to the wall. Sierra was a statue behind Loomis with her arms behind her back in the security of a zip tie. On the floor, near the duffel bag there was a pile of ash. How easy would it would've been do shoot them both and take the memory card. But MERCHANT wasn't as much about CONSTANT or Jupiter as it was about the men in the monkey masks, a veritable *community* of clandestine country-controlling criminals, a council of corporations and conglomerates with enough cold hard cash to buy anything and everything in the world *but* peace because it was chaos they thrived on, competition and conflict, like a hand cranked dynamo their gears generated only as much power as the muscles of simple economics could provide, and it was their world now-theirs to shape, these thirteen kings of culture, the very tip top of the wicked pyramid, an all-seeing eye of fame, fortune and self-preservation.

"It'sn' honah ta meet 'ya." Loomis said in

LaCosta's Jersey bite.

Jupiter nodded to Charlie without opening his eyes and Loomis stood still as Charlie wordlessly walked over to the duffel bag and zipped it open, turning on what Loomis knew to be a highly specialized RF scanner and it brought him back to the strained moments at Chief Katonah. Something inside Charlie then snapped, because he lashed out at the woman in light blue and with his hands on the shoulders of her jacket, he sent her flying into the wall opposite the door. Loomis turned his head quickly and when he looked back to Jupiter the man's eyes were open and deadpan upon the dazzling detailing of the harlequin mask, and the diamond cuts where their eyes met. Neither man blinked as Charlie manhandled Sierra, banging her feminine frame against the wall and pulling it back to launch a knee to her stomach only to continue the cycle against yet another wall, feet away, and Sierra, compromised as she was with her hands behind her back took the beating with nothing more than a series of grunts and groans. After nearly a minute of pummeling which was in some way playful to Charlie, the former soldier ripped the helmet off of the woman's head and drug her over to Jupiter by her silky raven black hair.

Sierra winced and steadied her breathing. Jupiter broke his gaze and uncharacteristically shot up from his position of rest, startled by the purity of the blue eyes he saw, perhaps having prepared himself for the exact replica of the hardened machine he had ordered to death in the seclusion of Fircrest Mansion. He put his hand to his chest for a moment and let his eyes dart to and away from her face a few times, like a foot testing the temperature of water. Then he slid his arm around Loomis and pulled him to the corner, away from Sierra.

"If you are who you say you are, then it's an honor to meet *you*." Jupiter nearly whispered. "If not," He bent in and ripped the mask from Loomis' face, letting it fall freely to the floor where it bounced to the corner. "You'll be just as dead as her."

Loomis nodded.

"I gotsit, no problem."

He didn't bother going for the mask-yet.

Jupiter spun and jerked his head. Charlie let Sierra's hair go and returned to the duffel back, bending on one knee to manipulate something involved and slightly metallic in sound.

"So *we* finally meet." Jupiter crossed his arms. "I hope this encounter is longer than the one I had with your sister. I relish the chance to speak with a worthy opponent about this game we find ourselves in."

Sierra rolled on her stomach and came to her knees, her chest and lungs still recoiling from the dizzying effects of Charlie's pushes and shoves and the tightness of the jacket didn't help her search for breath.

"Why did you kill my sister?" She asked, flatly.

"I didn't. Tim Wolcek did."

"You authorized it. You're the only one left alive who had a part in it."

"True...but hell would freeze over before she would tell me where CONSTANT was, what she had done with it and all."

Sierra's full lips pursed and there was some reserved contentment in the smile that came as a result.

"I bet it burns you to know the guy on the couch had the key all along and the Agent you had to watch the bank was as dirty as city storm drain. You could've had it one two three. All of your planning to out-*plan* us and there it was like a ripe piece of fruit."

Jupiter shrugged.

"I'm surrounded by incompetence." Charlie

turned his head and went back to his work in the duffel
bag as if he didn't hear what had been said. "Except for
now. You've whittled me down to the bare essentials
and backed me in a corner. You thought you had me
dead to rights at Keller's but you know how hard it is to
catch a man that always has a way out."

Sierra's lips were pursed again.

"So what's your way out this time? Will you
give me the pleasure of knowing before you throw my
body in a dumpster?"

Jupiter grinned, a movement his face had not
been required to do for some time and it was a hideous
thing in the fact that it was raw and unpracticed, just as
confused as it was honest.

"Onward and upward. I'll become one of the
men on the catwalks instead of one on the factory floor.
The air's different up there. The dialogue's different.
The money's different, all of it. I won't be hunted or
outlawed. I'll be..."

"You'll be dead before you hit the billionaire's
club." Sierra leaned back on her knees and began a
steady but subtle rocking as if she was counting, or
keeping her feet from cramping.

"Why?"

"CONSTANT *can't* be copied. I'm sure you
know that. If anyone tried it would delete itself. That *is*
its security. That and the hunt for it."

The sickening grin spread in its unadulterated
perversion. The face of Jupiter was as insane as it was
void of emotion, his eyes flat black pushpins and his
eyebrows thin and dark, like the receding hair above the
blunt forehead.

"Too little, too late."

"Wait, whaddya mean?" Loomis stepped
forward. The mask was in one of his hands, the other
beginning an arc of demonstrative gestures that would

increase if the conversation continued to move the way he supposed it would.

"She's grasping, LaCosta."

"No, it's true." Sierra shook her head. "CONSTANT can only be *accessed* by standard and traditional computational devices-it can only be *copied* by the secure MINAS machine in the Homeland building in D.C that created it."

Loomis looked between the two faces.

"I can't buy that. The Iranians would string me up by my balls."

"You don't have to, LaCosta, you were never supposed to."

Loomis frowned. It was a necessary wrinkling of his eyebrows but even the man behind the skinplants and hair dye was confused. What was Jupiter up to and what the hell was Charlie taking so long to put together from the duffel bag? Its signature was a metallic clicking, just as random as it was repetitious.

"Wha...what are you saying?"

"Two things, LaCosta, and you will do them or you will die."

The brutal stare had returned to Jupiter's emotionless eyes. Loomis nodded quickly, full of cowardly surety, or at least the best he could muster. Sierra's eyes narrowed and darted to Charlie.

"I don't wanna die...don't get me wrong, I'm nadda 'fraid to, all them virgins waitin' for me and all, I 'jus don't wanna go yet."

"Relax." Jupiter said as Charlie stood with two silenced pistols he had obviously built from bits and pieces sewn into the lining of the bag. One he handed to Jupiter, the other he kept for himself in a tight angle next to his body.

"Wha'do I have ta do?"

"You're going to, using your influence of

Iranian gold and somewhat...unstable religious disposition, drive up the price of the auction."

"But..."

"No buts...CONSTANT can't go for any less than a billion dollars, you understand?"

The nervous nod returned and nearly shook Loomis' body.

"Yeah, yeah."

"Timing is everything, and Killinger will prompt you on when if you're unsure. You can stop once we've hit a billion. You won't be able to leave the auction till everyone else has, but you will do this for me, won't you?"

Loomis pointed to Sierra.

"What 'bout her?"

"You will kill her." Jupiter flipped the gun in the air, and, having caught it by the silencer, offered it to Loomis. The CIA man's hand was hesitant to take it and his eyes were on Sierra's long enough to see the slightest negation of her head. In a perfect world, Loomis could put a bullet in Jupiter's chest and get one into Charlie before the solider of fortune could take him down and Jupiter's use of the silencer was almost *begging* for it, a last chance temptation to see if the opponent of the most violent and cerebral battle of his life had one last trick up her blue leather sleeves. He was a damn genius, and submitting to Sierra's desires, he took the gun by the handle, tentatively.

"I'm not afraid to die either." Sierra said, after fluffing her hair with a shake of her head and adjusting her posture so that it would be a strong and dignified execution.

Loomis placed the mask back on his face and pointed the weapon at her stomach.

"No no, stick the gun in her mouth. Put those clever brains on the floor. I wouldn't want you to miss."

Loomis wore a pained face and eyed Charlie. He was just as dead as she was if Jupiter's wishes weren't met-Charlie wouldn't miss. He *couldn't*. For the briefest moment the Texan wondered about Erland. His gun was silenced, too, and with a steady hand he could take anyone in the room out with extreme prejudice. Loomis held that hope and stepped forward. Sierra opened her mouth, her eyes locked onto Loomis'. He swallowed a breath and slid the silencer over her tongue and closed his eyes behind the mask and pulled the trigger.

The click of the bolt was a deafening sound to Loomis' ears and the recoil of the forty-five caliber pistol snapped through his hand and up his wrist. A single shell casing plunked to the ground before Sierra's body fell back with a scrunch of tight leather. Loomis blinked his eyes open to see what he had done and was shocked to witness the beautiful woman on her side, her chest heaving wildly and not a single ounce of blood on the floor.

She was alive.

Jupiter chuckled as he took the gun back and squeezed off three more shots Sierra's way as she worked her jaw with a moan to see if it was broken or not. Pain said it was as close as it could be without actually being broken.

"Blanks." Jupiter said and gave the gun back to Charlie. "Being an arms dealer you'd know the weight of a loaded gun, I couldn't risk such a bluff. I had to see if you were serious or if our little sorceress over there had finally found a way to do me in, seeing as I gave her an opportunity."

Loomis didn't dare release a sigh of relief even though he wanted to hook himself up to an oxygen tank after what may have been.

"So you're not gonna killa?"

"Not yet, she's too valuable, and when the time comes, I'll leave that to Charlie."

The Texan watched with reserved agony behind the mask as Charlie drug the woman to the corner of the room and stared her down with the silenced forty-five in his confident hands. There was no question Charlie's pistol was loaded with live ammunition.

"You'ra bastard." Loomis told the hacker as they moved to the door to begin the bidding for an item Jupiter knew was tainted and not worth the price of admission, seeing as its failsafe had been built to counter Jupiter's greed, *not* his hacking skills and was the shell of the memory card itself, *not* the program or the cache of information. Whoever purchased the memory card and attempted to download it onto a hard drive would find the unstoppable chain of self-deletion as destructive as performing arson on the Federal Reserve. It would stand to reason a buyer would *check* the memory card and even carry equipment to do so, but specialized units were necessary to copy the information and only after the liquid money had been transferred could they begin the process. They would rip their hair out and take razors to their wrists to learn that the man responsible was *long* gone and the man who'd brokered the deal knew nothing about it and whoever bought the cursed item would suffer the consequences of the ice age to what was left of their liquid assets as a result, for the men at the table were only agents of their respective branches and genres, tools of the higher powers they served, and they were just as expendable as the bodies that would be sent to replace them after they failed.

FORTY-ONE

The Verdoro green Pontiac GTO, free from its tow chains behind the motorhome, had been parked directly in front of the Beaver Monterey. Hayes checked his watch and studied the parking lot. The Arena's space for cars was a confused circle of one-way lanes and dividers and Hayes had broken a few rules of etiquette to reach the seclusion near the east entrance where strictly VIP vehicles were allowed. It was only a matter of time before some lackey yellow jacket inquisitively approached the motorhome looking for a VIP pass in the broad space of the dash. It was for that very reason Hayes stepped into a light jog with the slightly odd gait the prosthesis gave him to investigate the red Ford Explorer Sport that had either a malfunctioning alarm system or a young child trapped inside, playing the horn like a musical instrument. Either way it would draw unnecessary attention to the motorhome, seeing as the SUV was but a hundred feet away. The windows were foggy and Hayes zipped his jacket against the chill and learned the reason for the Morse code-like bleats of the horn. A red-headed man was seemingly locked in a precarious position and was repetitively poking his head into the steering wheel's center without looking up or changing the rhythm. Hayes tried the door to find it was locked. The click of the plastic wasn't enough to cause the red head to stop and Hayes banged a fist on the window. The man ceased and tried to peer through the window, and then with a great strain, smudged a bit of clarity into the frostiness with his shoulder. To see the face on the other side of the glass was neither friend nor foe gave Lowery a pause that lasted no more than a second.

"Get me out of here!" He shouted and the man leaned in, cupping his ear. "I'm CPD! I'm a cop!"

The man pointed to the lock but since the Explorer Sport was an older model chosen for the undercover operation *by* Chris Armstrong himself, the power locks were non-functional. He had already tried using both his shoulder and his teeth to get at the cylindrical lock and the seat belt had been cinched too tight considering his large frame and the position of the handcuffs for that to be a reality. Nothing worked, not mashing the gas, tearing at the wheel, trying to lay the seat back; nothing but the horn.

When Lowery turned he saw man had left and he quickly began to punch the horn again, even though the craning position terribly strained his neck muscles. Thankfully the mechanical clicking of the lock stopped him from mashing the horn and the door was open in a matter of seconds.

"Thank you," Lowery said after swearing and then eyed the man up and down. He was a tough looking man and had militaristic features.

"Who are you?"

The lock-pick kit in the man's confident hands went to the handcuffs.

"Joe."

Lowery was in some form of disbelief as the restraints fell to the floor of the Explorer. He rubbed the redness from his right wrist as the man released the belt.

"Joe, you'll be getting a medal for that. I'm a

CPD Detective and I gotta call one of my Officers."

Hayes' hand was muscular on Lowery's shoulder and he had a flashback of when Armstrong decked him.

"Not yet, Detective." The man said and explained to Christian Lowery exactly why.

The table of monkey-masked men was silent as Killinger began the bidding. Each of the men had been given a smart phone synched to Jenkins computer and he was a forbearing figure behind Killinger in case any technical difficulties would present themselves. No seat was available for Loomis and he stood by Jupiter and Kirke near the shut door, leaving Charlie and Sierra alone in the room.

"One last time gentlemen before this procedure becomes irreversible, the bidding will begin at zero with strictly twenty-five to fifty million dollar increments." Killinger's heavy black eyebrows were arched and his professionalism prevented him from showing the glee working its way into his pale face. "I will present the item, and the rest is up to you. The bidding will stop when the price is set for exactly sixty seconds. Your devices will lock if a new bid is not placed before sixty seconds and the auction will be over. As you also know but I am obliged to say, payment will be in non-printable liquidity, preferably gold, and will be exchanged for the memory card at a set location arranged for the following week."

Jupiter reached into his pocket and placed the CONSTANT memory card on the table. There were nods behind the monkey masks to finally see the item in question.

"Would it be possible to witness a demonstration?" A blue suit in the far corner asked politely. If he was to be described in a manner that

differentiated him from the other monkey-masked men
in the room it would be a properness of posture and
cleanness of enunciation and dictation that was his
alone.

"What do you wish to know?" Jupiter asked
before Killinger could speak.

"I wish to know the home addresses of the
Executive Board of Directors of TerraSpace Defense
and Dynamics, and the last phone number each of them
called on their private lines."

Jupiter shook his head and Killinger was paler
than usual. The monkey mask nearest Killinger turned
in some kind of devastated frustration and stowed it as
fast as possible. Loomis couldn't help but wonder if *he*
was from TerraSpace Defense and Dynamics and the
man who asked for the test was a competitor.

The hacker reached for the card and gave it to
Kirke who walked it to Jenkins. Loomis observed all of
it behind the mask, even though his mind was fractured
in its division of interest, wondering what Charlie was
doing behind the closed door, and the objectivity of the
camera embedded into his mask would make no
mistakes. He was grateful for this damming exploitation
of CONSTANT but it would also take up precious time
in the camera's recording space and he wanted to get
the fullness of the auction more than anything else-most
importantly, who would be the one to purchase it.

Jenkins typed and typed on his laptop after
inserting the memory card into a USB-connected
device. Then he nodded to Jupiter who walked slowly
to the screen. This freewheeling demonstration was
throwing a wrench in Killinger's style but Jupiter was
only using the broker, just as much as the broker
thought he was using the hacker.

"CEO William J. Harstock Jr., 337 West
Tempeda Boulevard, Quozecha, Arizona, 480-919-

7522."

The man in the corner nodded slowly and Jupiter threw a glance to the man whose face was burning with rage behind the monkey mask.

"COO Denise Whittlef, 418 West Tempeda Boulevard, Quozecha, Arizona, 480-377-1751. Shall I continue or does the demonstration suffice?"

The man in the corner cast a sinister pair of eyes to the one sitting near Jupiter who might have been tempted to rip the memory card-reading device from the computer and make a run for it.

"No, the demonstration will suffice. I'll begin the bidding."

Jupiter stood next to Killinger as the first fifty million by the man in the corner was immediately raised to a hundred by the man who was visibly distraught and doing all he could to refrain from drawing the attention of those who still couldn't tell. Loomis figured the man was caught in a sordid affair and some sort of blackmail was going to be a factor in driving the price up. Whatever the case, he wondered if it was worth a billion dollars, because that was the demand of a man who at this point, was in complete control. Loomis' Extemp strategy rested on Erland's judgment now, even more than Sierra, and he refused to let his vision float up to the rafters. This was *his* moment, as much as it was in the small room with Jupiter's near-deadly test of faith, and *all* of the back-breaking work on the legend of Mic LaCosta was for the now and left to the trigger finger of the Homicide Detective.

The man in the corner bumped the price up to a hundred and fifty and nearly forty seconds went by before Loomis clicked it up to five hundred. There was a gasp from one of the suits and a chuckle, perhaps he had come with only five hundred million prepared.

Jupiter's demand for tangible liquidity would no doubt alienate certain players and certain tiers, seeing as many rich and powerful men and women's wealth was merely on paper, and their assets and projected net-worth's were inflated digital numbers. Every representative in the room came with some *substantial* liquidity but the real bidding war would only be between two or three in the end.

Seeing Loomis jump the bid by so much was a necessary cut of time, and a man to his left clicked it up to six twenty-five, which was his max.

"And that's in platinum." He said.

Jupiter nodded and Loomis waited twenty seconds to knock the man off at six fifty.

The man behind the monkey mask swore and tossed his phone on the table. The monkey mask who was being blackmailed hit the bid up to seven hundred million. Loomis couldn't help but laugh darkly to himself. Seven hundred million to the man more than likely from TerraSpace Defense and Dynamics. That was pocket change in perspective to one of their radical new military robotics patents or contracts. It was a great deal of liquidity, but absolutely nothing compared to those inflated numbers that took years of restructuring and tweaking to fulfill.

"Chinese gold." The man from TSDD said smugly. "Better than any other gold on the planet if you ask me."

It was then Loomis did it.

The bid flew to one billion exactly.

The man from TSDD shook his head and Loomis noticed the reserved satisfaction of the monkey mask in the blue suit at the far corner of the table. Loomis turned his gaze to Killinger who was nearly levitating. Loomis didn't know that Killinger was set to get half the money and would never see a penny of it and Killinger wasn't aware of Jupiter's threat to the man in purple to raise the price as he did.

"Iran-ian gold." Loomis said, in LaCosta's nearly sing-song Jersey diction. "N' they've got five-hundred tons of it."

The monkey masks on the table all turned to him as if he was out of order. It let Loomis know that he was the *only* representative of a foreign country and the rest were corporate raiders with just as much at stake nationally as internationally.

"Do you know how much that weighs?" The man who had stopped bidding at six twenty-five asked.

"No, I'm jus' doin' as I'm told ta." Loomis shrugged in the ridiculous purple costume and couldn't help but smile at the layered ironic depth of such a statement.

The man near the computer from TSDD clicked in a number and tossed his phone on the table as if it was broke.

The number was one point six billion.

"If anyone can take it from me," He said with his arms crossed. "Then they damn well deserve to."

Loomis' eyes narrowed on the man. Perhaps there was some personal conflict with the one occupying the corner who'd asked for a demonstration, but Loomis guessed some far-right patriotism if the man *truly* was from TerraSpace Defense and Dynamics had won out. TSDD had contributed mightily to the campaigns of right-wing constitutionalists who desired to see a wall divide the southern border of the US and the company was based in the Arizona desert near Phoenix. It would've gone without saying they were heavy donors to first amendment rights and campaigners, but the basing of TSDD in the greater Phoenix area made all the more sense. In some way, Loomis was glad CONSTANT was going to someone

who wanted to *protect* America, albeit in an antiquated
us and them sort of way, instead of *exploit* it like Jupiter
would've been apt to do had he not desired to rise
above and become something more. On that train of
thought, Loomis was still worried that the hacker had
more to offer Crescent, and thus, the country, and if the
broken fractures of the government would only find a
way to agree with the powerful ancillaries of the small
independent militaries of companies like TSDD to
protect the land as administrations continued sending
their young overseas to die the country would have
more balance. Yet the division grew larger, forcing
situations like the one unfolding before Loomis' eyes,
where an evil man was ultimately profiting on the
selfish desires of rich and powerful men who took it
upon themselves to shape the country to be the way
they wanted it. There was some shortcoming, some
flaw, Loomis decided, in the government's framework
that forced this position upon its amazingly wealthy
private sector. Sure there was a lust for power and gain
but it was the *why* of it Loomis had never fully grasped
until the moment CIA Extemp told him was the only
moment that mattered-the now.

"You got me." Loomis said as LaCosta and the
man in the monkey mask nodded in a broken way.

The bid held for a minute of silence and just like
that, without trumpets or fanfare, the complete databank
of Homeland Security's clandestine national
information had been sold.

The man stood.

"We'll be in touch." He said and began the
unemotional procedure of the departure of the monetary
sages council of the future.

Jupiter watched as the monkey-masked bidders
and potential buyers left one by one until only Loomis
remained. They would meet up with their bodyguards

and leave as nonchalantly as they arrived with
Detective Armstrong securing their exit. Killinger had
kept his mouth shut and his muscular bodyguard
entered the rectangular room, leaving Morell and
McKinney outside. Charlie entered the room and shut
the door behind him. Loomis tried to look into the
sliver of space behind Charlie's body to see Sierra and
did not. A silenced forty-five was in Charlie's hand and
he threw the one Jupiter had used to scare Sierra to
Kirke.

"I can't believe it." Killinger shook his head and
blew out a sigh. "We did it."

Killinger turned his gazed to Jupiter who
shrugged. Charlie put four silenced rounds in the body
builder and he fell awkwardly to the corner and
smeared the white walls with red. Before Killinger
could speak Charlie shot him in the neck and the broker
stumbled back into the wall and made a clutch for
Jenkins with what little life remained in him. The young
hacker deftly dodged the falling body and gave him a
brief glance before returning to typing.

"Well," Jupiter said to Loomis as both Kirke
and Charlie fixed their guns on him. "This is the end of
the road for you, if you want."

"If *I* want?" Loomis tilted his head a smile
peeled across his face, his voice still stuck in Jersey.
"What makes you think I'm the guy that's in danger
here?"

"How do you figure?" Jupiter crossed his arms.

Kirke's leg took the silenced bullet from the
Winchester 70 and it pushed him against the wall
screaming. He dropped the gun that may or may not
have had live ammunition in it as both hands attempted
to stop the bleeding. Morell and McKinney heard the
screams and entered the room with shotguns up and
cocked.

"I don't screw 'round. If you thought I was afraid you's not as smart 's I took youta be."

Jupiter blankly gawked at the two dead by his order and the squirming Kirke as his blood seeped into the blue carpet and his breath was a violent wheeze between clenched teeth. Charlie's face was tense and inquisitive as he looked to his boss-not for guidance, but for some nonverbal cue so that he could save his own skin and for once, Jupiter wasn't the coolest figure in the room. That was a debate between Charlie and Loomis, who were sizing each other up.

"What do you want?" Jupiter asked with a small quiver in his voice. "Part of the cut? One point six billion in gold weighs over twenty-four tons."

"No. I want Sierra Marland back. You can have your money."

Jupiter's face fell completely at the release of Loomis' New Jersey arms dealer.

"Who are you?" He said.

"Mark Loomis, CIA Extemp." The blonde Texan removed the mask. "And everything you've done and said has been recorded and you're going to rot in hell for it."

"Is that so?" Jupiter asked with some deviant grin and Loomis questioned where the quiver in his voice had gone. Loomis frowned. The man never stopped the gamble. Everything with him was a play, an act, a magic trick and to square off toe to toe, one illusionist to another was an exercise in the insanity of chance and who had momentum the moment the music stopped.

It clicked in Loomis' mind why the young hacker Jenkins hadn't ceased typing and the Texan's eyes rolled toward him as Municipal Arena's power transformers arced and popped and the already dimly-lit Arena was shrouded in a cape of darkness. A consensus of screams and shouts erupted from the floor of the Arena hundreds of feet away. Loomis couldn't see his own hand in front of his face and there was a series of grunts against the rustling of cloth. A strong grip ripped at his shoulder and he found himself flying over the table and colliding with one of the banquet chairs in the darkness of deep space. The sound of struggle flared to his left and one of the shotguns sparked and flashed a high-angled boom in the darkness. Loomis didn't know what direction was up and as he clutched for his bearings his hands touched the warm liquid of blood on the floor.

A woman's voice shouted in some muffled distance, perhaps the bellowing of a name. The clarity of it called out to him and gave him Sierra's position-from that he ascertained the location of the door and the narrow choke point between McKinney and Morell Jupiter would have to pass through to make it out alive.

"McKinney! Morell! Status!" He shouted as he kicked the chair aside and groped for the table.

"Here!" Morell called out.

"Here!" McKinney echoed. They had not left their flanking of the door, statues in the dark despite what danger could befall them. Loomis guessed them to be twelve to fifteen feet away.

"Both of you, in the hall, now!"

Loomis pressed himself on the table and walked across it, hopping down to what he would believe was near the space between the wall and the table. His feet were wide as he leapt to the ground and caught the length of a human leg and the brutal cracking and breaking of the ankle and tearing of the ligaments in the knee was a sickening sonic signature. A young male voice cried out in pain and a clunky crash of some heavy object rattled two feet away .

"Loomis!" Sierra called from behind the door.

"Hold on!"

The Texan reached down the length of the man's body to feel for his head. A second later the young hacker named Jenkins had been knocked unconscious. Loomis threw his wild physicality into the door and it splintered open.

"Sierra!"

"Here." Her voice was soft in the darkness.

"Are you up?"

"Yeah."

He came to her voice, hands out and stopped when he felt her body and his hands went to her shoulders.

"Morell and McKinney are in pursuit. The kid's down. I'll stay behind and secure his computer."

"I shouted for Mike, he should be coming down."

"He should stay, it'll be a death trap him trying to make it down in the dark, in his condition."

Sierra brushed past him, heading for the wall where they both knew one duffel bag had been lying in wait.

"There's gotta be a flashlight in there, and a knife or something."

Loomis' hands were greedy in his search and found both. The flashlight was a blinding LED model and Sierra's hands were free with the swipe of a box cutter in a matter of seconds. He left her to search the bag and returned to the rectangular room of the laminate table to blind Kirke who was barley alive with the intense beam.

"Where'd Jupiter go?" He asked.

The man shook his head weakly. The light dipped to Jenkins and Loomis took his computer. It too had a concussion but the hard drive would be a gold mine. The light went back to the corner where he remembered Jenkins and the duffel bag being during the sale.

"Is CONSTANT secure?" Sierra called from the next room.

"Yes." Loomis answered, tearing the memory card from the USB-connected reader, and as he did, it occurred to him he was dealing with a man whose slight of hand was as practical as it was legendary. Loomis swore. If it was a dummy card the possibilities of the real one's location were approaching infinite and with each dark second that passed the probabilities were multiplying themselves like a virus. Sierra hopped over Jenkins as she came from the small anteroom with a second flashlight and something that looked like rolled up paper.

"We have to get him."

Loomis let a heavy breath go as pandemonium would be capturing and enslaving the miasma of event-goers in a matter of seconds if it hadn't already. Their voices of confusion were beginning to spill over the twenty-four foot walls of the rectangular room. Whatever tender threads of false peace and hope had been fabricated in the hearts of the Blizzardorama constituents to overcome the tragedies of yesterday's acts of terror had since torn and the violent stampede to the pale light of safety was bound to leave its own mark of destruction.

"McKinney and Morell split. Hayes is in the parking lot with the Beaver and the GTO. I'll stay here-you meet up with Erland. Chase him down by any means necessary-don't talk to anyone about what's going on unless they're one of us. Lord knows who he's got planted here."

"That's the plan?" Sierra asked the tired eyes behind the darkened contacts.

"That's the plan."

Sierra held out her hand and Loomis shook it.

"God bless you, Mark." She said with some finality and he nodded wearily. Her movement was quick and decisive and she was nearly at the door before Loomis stopped her.

"Hey." He said and tossed her the silenced forty-five that Kirke had been physically unable to retrieve since taking the thirty-ot six round to his femoral artery. Her jaw still ached from the shock of the recoil. She caught it with two hands and began removing the silencer as she pressed into the darkness of the concrete track in a dead run.

FORTY-TWO

The flash and concussion of the transformer's explosion rocking the near corner of the building startled Lowery and he spilled his coffee as a result.

"What was that?" He said, wiping his mouth with the sleeve of the waterproof jacket.

"Transformer." Hayes said and swore as he stared at the ground for a second. Then he came close to Lowery, his eyes large. "Everything I told you comes down to this, okay?"

Lowery tossed the cup toward the Explorer Sport, letting it splash on the ground.

"Go ahead, I'm listening."

"Jupiter's going to try to escape. I'm going to follow him at a distance in the motorhome. Wait for Erland and Marland, they'll take the GTO. We'll be in touch with each other. Once that happens and *only* once that happens, you get in there and find Loomis in the room I told you about and make sure he's secure."

"What if Armstrong gets to him first? Jupiter could have more guys."

"Don't worry about that. Just get all of the Officers you can to secure Loomis and that room, it's your top priority."

Lowery cursed as he wiped his lips with his sleeve again. Then the hysteria caused by the booming explosion and lack of power began to roll through the

Arena like a thick wave of glue and the west entrance
became blurred as the stage builders and service
personnel clogged the exit with their bulky equipment
and the yellow-jacketed security guards were caught in
some sort of sandwich in between.

"There he is." Hayes pointed with a keen eye
after some twenty-seconds of watching the exit. The
man was nondescript of face and hair and arrogantly
clothed in white Lowery could definitely see the
similarities between him and the figure frozen in Jessica
Birchall's interrupted report, even at such a great
distance. The fact that no one else noticed him was a
tribute to the panic he had caused and his blonde
bodyguard escorted him from the throbbing fingers of
overwhelmingly distraught fans and event-goers as their
numbers attempted to spill into the parking lot.

"What about the men in the monkey masks and
the fake Homeland Tactical Assault, who follows
them?"

"Leave that to Loomis." Joseph Hayes said as
he made a hopping run for the motorhome. The bidders
club had since dispersed into greater Crescent, though it
had been only minutes. "I gotta go before this place
gets too crazy. See you on the other side."

Lowery jogged to the GTO and watched, wide-
eyed as the costume-clothed hundreds trampled each
other in a race for safety. The ominous threat of terror
was lodged in their hearts and even Lowery himself
was prepared for the top of the Arena to crack and
smoke with the detonation of heavy explosives. The
sound that came from their lips was a wild and frantic
staccato of self-preservation and the Detective wouldn't
take his eyes off the mass of bodies cascading from the
narrow west entrance in hopes of seeing Erland and the
Homeland SAB Agent by the name of Sierra Marland
accompanying him; or, as Joe Hayes had described

them, Magna and Aurora.

Detective First Grade Michael Erland was taking his body to the limit as he slid down the ladder. He had snagged his helmet and left the rifle and crawled the length of the catwalk on his hands and knees the moment the power cut. Jupiter was always a step ahead and Erland had feared he picked the event for the safety found in numbers because there was something else at stake, something beyond the sale of CONSTANT and pushing himself from the ladder he began to work his way slowly through the dark maze of the service rooms, reaching for the pathetic penlight Sierra had made sure was in his back pocket. The going was slow and the thick old walls diffused the chaos to a dull and distant torture and did not help the rhythm of his heart. Ever since he'd entered the Arena he'd felt beyond taxed and had fallen to a physical level he could only describe as exhausted and spent. Yet the thoughts of Jupiter getting away made the aches and pains of his lower back and the gluey sap sticking to the inside of his throat seem so meaningless.

Once he reached the executive level he saw an intense LED beam bouncing across the broad carpet.

"Sierra!" He shouted and the beam froze. Then he sprinted with all he had.

"Mike!" She came to him and they embraced quickly and breathlessly in the darkness. He could feel the shape of a gun in the small of her back. "CONSTANT is secure." She said as their free hands were interlocked and their feet were taking them toward the stairs.

"Loomis?"

"He's in the room. Two bodyguards are down as well as the broker. The tech is unconscious."

"Hayes has to be gone by now."

"We'll know once we get to the GTO."

"You okay?" He called as she was ahead of him, her legs like pistons down the stairwell.

"Yeah..."

"I couldn't see you." He said with the remorse present in his voice she tried to hide in hers. It was as if she was ashamed at herself for what could've been, and how boldly she was ready to die when the life-long desire of her heart was ripe for the taking.

"Charlie threw me around but I'm still here."

"Yeah..." Erland echoed. He hadn't wanted to kill anybody, and was dealing with the fact that the man he purposely shot in the leg was no longer alive. It was a wrinkle he didn't need floating around his subconscious and it took all he had to keep up with Sierra Marland. She was possessed by some inner motor, the gear-ratio of which was set to a level he hadn't seen in her before and the scrunch and squeak of leather ended with a blast of double doors at the top concourse of the Arena's field level seats, from which a long ramp carried them to the curve of the concrete track and a thick surge of bodies.

"This way." She said and took a left, hitting a door that ran down a tight set of stairs to the Arena's plumbing system. Navigating the linear flow of pipes wasn't as difficult as it was tedious and the stench of the submarine-like rooms and spaces of pipes and valves was a hideous fetor of aged fecal matter and unreasonably powerful cleaners and chemicals. They were free of the plumbing in a matter of minutes and the light of the outside world was as welcome as it was harsh and cold. The GTO was in sight.

Erland took a split-second to catch a breather and Sierra was already running toward the GTO and he pushed his heavy legs to work, catching up with her nearly sixty feet from the car. A tall, red-headed man was standing near the GTO, faced the opposite direction with his hands in his pockets and something about him held a familiarity to Erland and the man turned once he heard the squeak of leather and the huffing of lungs at work.

It was Christian Lowery. The surprise on his face to see Aurora and Magna as described manifest from the emptiness of the small side parking lot was mirrored behind Erland's aged chrome visor. He took his helmet off as Sierra moved for the driver's side and shook Lowery's hand.

"Chris, what the hell are you doing here?"

"Long story," He said, still stunned that the man he knew as a tireless Detective was as deeply wrapped in the days events as the man who incited them all. "Joe Hayes got me up to speed-I have to go get every available Officer to secure Agent Loomis."

"Here." Sierra called out, stopping Lowery. She tossed him one of the cell phones that had been stashed behind the rear driver's seat. "Give this to him."

Lowery nodded and flashed a quick salute and broke into a loping jog, heading for the confusion of the west entrance and the scatter of semi-trucks and service vans that were congesting the mass exodus of Blizzardorama fans.

Erland still felt beyond winded and fell in the car as Sierra began to strip to her underwear. There was no way Jupiter could spot them in the rear-view mirror in their leather. Wherever he was going and whatever he was planning had to be discovered in complete secrecy. If Jupiter sensed the slightest threat there was a chance one of his alternate plans would take over and what future act of terror he had planned would stay dormant. A change of clothes had been prepared for each of them behind the seat and Erland went for the cell phone instead, his interplay with Sierra operating on a symbiotic level in the heat of the moment.

"Hayes? Where are they?" Erland asked, shutting the door and beginning to undress slowly and with difficulty. The stiffness in his body which began in his lower back had spread outward and all of the running had given him a headache.

"They haven't left Vernon...approaching fourteenth."

"Train station." Sierra said as she slipped behind the wheel and fired the car and Erland watched her with a nearly stupefied face as he could barely hear Hayes himself-then he noticed the phone was out, in his hand, on speaker mode and he never remembered doing that. Sierra took the phone and placed it in her lap as she threw the GTO in gear and the V-eight responded to her lead-footed pursuit. Erland began to change his clothes and the difficulty of it made him sweat more than the running had. Sierra drove like a State Trooper in pursuit and before he wondered where she learned how he found himself sick to his stomach. The GTO lurched to a stop at a red light that would've been too dangerous to breach and Erland caught the door handle just in time. Whatever was in his stomach left in a hurry.

"You okay?" Sierra asked as he shut the door.

"Yeah..." He wiped his mouth with the belly portion of the t-shirt he had worn under the hot leather jacket. He turned to Sierra and her blue eyes were as full of vibrant beauty as they were distant sadness. It was as if she knew something he didn't, or perhaps that she felt responsible for something that was to come because of the choices she had made.

"Hang in there." She said, in tan cargo pants, a teal t shirt and a level II body armor vest lined with Homeland markings. Her hair was in a ponytail and Erland's head reeled with the disconnected sickness trying to grip his body. How quickly she was capable of change-if only he could shake what had been creeping upon him with the same facility as she switched voices and faces. The forty-five Loomis had taken from Kirke and given to her was now dismantled on the floor where the clothes had been waiting for them and both were now armed with H&K's.

"I'll be fine." He said and reached for his seat belt. Sierra revved the car and hit the green light with a squeal of tires.

"They're in a black Mercedes." Sierra shifted and passed a string of cars. "And they turned onto Cherry from Fourteenth. I don't think they're going for the station."

"No." Erland sighed and tried to blink some focus into his perspective and continued dressing so that he looked exactly like Sierra, only his t-shirt was black and smelled slightly of vomit.

"What are you thinking?"

"I think he's going to cover his exit from Crescent with a big bang."

"Another bomb?" She asked and Hayes gave crossing of blocks like a countdown timer.

"Thirteenth."

"Yeah, that's what I'd do if I were him. It gives him enough time considering the mess at the Arena. Loomis wasn't aggressive with Jupiter, but he wanted the buyers just as much as the seller, and he backed Jupiter into a spot where he has to react with something big to cover his exit."

Sierra nodded.

"He's got Jupiter's computer, too. I'm sure that cop..."

"Lowery."

"I'm sure Lowery's got him secured by now."

Erland put his hand on his chest and sighed as the facades of buildings and street lamps began to blur like some kind of lullaby.

Lowery pushed his way through several groups of fans that were clustered at the garage-like door of the west entrance. They were screaming and shouting in their cell-phones and he surmised they had been dropped off in groups either by bus or by friends or family. His height gave him perspective and he was able to get inside to the darkness quickly. The backup generator had been tripped by one of the service personnel and a small series of runner lights around the stadium and bluish white pinpricks of the same scattered here and there gave the Detective enough illumination to navigate the concrete track that ran around the outer bowl of the Arena. His eyes narrowed as he saw a pair of CPD Officers jogging past a line of yellow-jackets and he pushed through the yellow-jackets, shouting to the Officers.

"Chris Lowery, CPD!"

They turned and came to him, telling the four yellow jackets that were after Lowery to stand down. The Officers were named Taldo and Wellman, and they were both men in their forties.

"Detective, Nichols has been trying to get a hold of you." Taldo spoke as he was the more naturally assertive and had a thick mustache.

"I know, I'll explain later. Where's Armstrong?"

"We don't know. We've been trying to secure these rooms but we have to make sure everyone's out of the field area before we can."

"Give me your radio." He told Wellman who complied. "You two come with me. And if you see Armstrong, don't hesitate to pull your Taser."

The Officers followed as the Detective's large gait ate up the concrete and he explained exactly why.

Sierra came within three cars of the Mercedes on Cherry. Hayes had pulled the Beaver off a few streets back and was circling around the other side to block the Mercedes in on Sierra's command.

"Still think it's the train station?" Erland asked and as Sierra gave the question a cursory glance she could see his forehead was glazed with sweat and the space underneath his eyes darkened and run-down. He was fully dressed and ready for combat as she was but looked as if he would pass out the moment he stepped out of the car.

"It can't be Mutual Partners Bank..."

"No...it has to be something bigger...something that would mask his escape and take so long to clean up we wouldn't have the resources to track him."

Sierra ducked her head low and checked the skyline.

"What would be the most...symbolic building of Crescent?" She asked, stifling a curse that two cars had pulled off and there was only a small electric car between them.

"The Pinnacle Building." Erland said blankly as he cocked his H&K Forty and stuck it in the hip holster.

"The van..." Sierra nearly gasped as if she had missed it entirely and Erland studied her eyes as she did, though he only got the side of her face and the blueness was blended with remorse.

"Don't take it so hard." He said and coughed. "We're gonna make it right. Whatever you missed or think you did wrong it's over now. It's gonna be okay. We've got 'em dead to rights."

"Not just yet." Something hard set in Sierra's jaw and wouldn't leave. "Not just yet."

The Detective spotted the Pinnacle Building not three hundred feet away and could feel Sierra thinking in the moment.

"Let's have it."

"At the next light, we'll get out and shoot the tires. Then hit the back window and I'll toss the smoke grenade in the car." Sierra patted the bulge in her cargo pants leg pocket. "Call Precinct Four right now and tell them to get every available unit to the Pinnacle Building."

Erland nodded and then held a dumb gaze.

"We're fugitives."

"Just call 911 and tell them there's a bomb at the Pinnacle Building."

He did so as traffic slowed for the next intersection.

"Think it'll work?" They came to the red light and Erland coughed.

"It better." Sierra nearly growled and tapped Erland on the shoulder twice with her fist. He drew his pistol and rushed from the car, nearly falling to the sidewalk. He was able to catch his momentum and ran into a newspaper dispenser to fall into a lurching crouch. From the cover of the steel container he squeezed off three shots into the back tire and one of them rewarded his efforts with a deafening pop and the Mercedes sagged to the right before the engine responded to Charlie's foot. Sierra stood behind the open door of the GTO and shot four jacketed hollow points into the left side of the car in hopes of hitting the rear wheel as the blonde goosed the throttle with controlled roars. The car responded in a wildly unpredictable arc of rubber smoke and Sierra paused before stepping from the safety of the door and firing two bullets into the left front tire. The Mercedes jolted again as sparks flashed with the connection of steel and concrete and Charlie's flooring of the gas pedal fishtailed the Mercedes until it sideswiped the electric

car with a crunch of glass and plastic and shot straight
into the tarp and scaffolding ensconced entrance of the
Pinnacle Building.

"Stay in your car!" Erland yelled to the driver of
the wounded electric vehicle and ran a dizzying angle
toward the right hash of the destroyed entrance to
crouch and wait for Sierra behind the puffing clouds of
his pulse. From his flipped viewpoint of the street, he
could see traffic had come to a complete halt and sirens
wouldn't be far behind. The Mercedes had utterly
collapsed the tiered scaffolding and was laid to rest in a
steaming heap, having ran headlong into a thick marble
enclave near a half-built fountain. Sierra surveyed the
static image and ducked down behind a displaced piece
plywood as Erland advanced cautiously to meet her.

"There's no good way to do this." She said.

"We could wait for the cops."

"We don't have the time. It's us or the
building."

"But there's only two of us, we can't possibly
find them unless we know where they're going."

"We have to try. The cops'll be here any
minute, and once they're here, SOP will nearly
guarantee that bomb'll go off."

Erland looked her in the eyes even though his
gaze was blurry at best.

"Okay." Was all he said and Sierra vaulted over
the fallen scaffolding, her gun taught in her grip as she
scanned the devastated lobby and took cover behind the
empty black car. Her eyes darted for the elevator lights
and found one of them rapidly climbing floors.

"Mike, stairs!" She shouted as he made it over
the scaffolding with difficulty. Sierra rushed to the
giant bank of elevators and hit the button. She reached
inside the first one that opened and punched in a route
for one of the higher floors and followed Erland toward

the stairs.

"They didn't take the elevator?" He said as she passed him up the cubic zigzag.

"Not on this floor. They wanted us to-so we'll let them think we did. They can't be far."

"Wouldn't they plant the bomb in the foundation?"

"The foundation's probably already wired to one of the higher floors-I'll bet you he's gonna wait for his precious helicopter to get him out of it and since he doesn't have his computer they'll have to do it the old fashioned way."

Erland swore. She was dead right and he could barely keep up. Each stair bit into his joints and ligaments as if they were a hundred years old. His kidneys felt like he'd been holding a trip to the bathroom for a week and the first floor was a deep reality check. It was a large food court, barely lit by the windows that weren't boarded up. If Jupiter had more men, they would've cut Sierra and her fiancée down with ease.

"Sierra." Erland stopped at the elevator bank. "I can't do this."

"Yes you can." She said and hammered the elevator button with her fist. "But you're going to have to gamble with me."

"How so?" Erland gasped for breath, bent over with spread legs.

"I'll be dammed if they're not headed for the top floor and we're going to play a little game with them."

Erland twisted his head to see the hardness set in Sierra's face as it competed so incredibly with the tender blue eyes that could only watch her love helplessly crumble and succumb to the brutal poison of STRIC-R that was beginning to wrap its paralytic effects around the core of his mind.

She took two steps and stood him up with her arms on his shoulders.

"Don't give up now." She said. "It's the final round, and nobody's gonna knock you down because I'm in your corner, okay?"

Erland nodded as he heard the plan and blinked away the burning sensation eating away his weary eyes as two separate elevators doors opened and they parted ways.

FORTY-THREE

     Mark Loomis had secured the young hacker Jenkins with the strap from the duffel bag and sat on his knees in the corner with wary eyes toward the door since the backup power had kicked in. The CONSTANT memory card was in his pocket and he wished there had been another forty-five in the bag even though Morell and McKinney were due to return soon. Jupiter was a man of a thousand contingencies and he half expected a band of his henchmen to invade the eerie stillness of the room at any second. Loomis checked both of the bodyguards with a cautious glance. The bulky man near the door was long gone, Charlie had made sure of that and the one Erland had shot from the catwalk still had a chance but his pulse was faint. The thirty-ot six round had done a number to his femoral artery and blood had soaked the carpet. Loomis returned to his spot and hunched when he saw the beam of a flashlight.

     "CPD!" There was a shout as the razor of light caught angles of body parts and displaced banquet chairs and Loomis saw the black shape of a service weapon.

     "CIA!" He shouted back. The figure stopped and blinded him with the light. Despite the backup power the space was still dim and dark.

     "Hands up!" The voice was nervous as the light

darted to the dead and dying.

"Mark Loomis, CIA, get your Officers here now!"

The CPD man stood stoically and the light dropped back to the faces of each man for an ID. The moment he advanced slowly and Loomis caught on to his actions, he clenched his teeth. The man was not holstering his weapon.

"What happened here?" He said, not ready to give his motives away yet, and perhaps Loomis was just being suspicious-if he was a local LEO he would've been too, with all of the messes Homeland Security had made, all of the death and destruction, he would be leery of some guy throwing out a three letter acronym in a room of dead bodies too.

"Operation MERCHANT." He said, rising.

"Stay where you are." The light and the pistol were back on him from the frozen CPD man. Loomis could see he was in a cheap suit and had angular, nearly gaunt features. The man's eyebrows came together as the light caught the flowing purple of the cape.

"I'm undercover."

"So if I asked for ID you wouldn't have any?"

"Nope."

"Then if you are who you say you are you wouldn't mind coming down to the station with me while we process this crime scene and determine your involvement in it."

Loomis shook his head.

"This is way above your pay grade, Officer."

"That's Detective to you." The man still hadn't moved, blinding Loomis as best as he could, and began advancing ever so slowly.

"Detective?"

"Armstrong."

"Well, Detective Armstrong," The Texan

attempted what charm he had left. "Have you ever heard of a man named Mr. Brown?"

"No, should I have?"

Loomis paused.

"Why haven't you called for anyone?"

The gun kicked as it fired and Loomis closed his eyes. His left arm burned with a searing pain and he fell with a thud, clutching it.

The man advanced and kneeled on Loomis' legs, pinning him. Armstrong stuck the barrel of the gun on the Texan's chest in the tender space right below his rib cage. A bullet there would cut through all of the soft stuff and shatter his spine.

"Where's CONSTANT?" Was all he said.

"What?"

"Three seconds and I pull the trigger."

Before Loomis could answer the man reared back as if struck by lightning. His arms were wide and he dropped the flashlight as he attempted to stand against the clicking. He staggered for footing and lost it as he stepped on Loomis' leg and collided with Jenkins, becoming entangled in a pair of banquet chairs where his body undulated from the force of electricity running through it.

"Loomis!" A masculine voice rifled through the room.

"Here!" He shouted back, sitting up. The Detective had only nicked his arm and it was a shock more than anything.

"You Loomis?" A tall redhead asked as he surveyed the room with quick eyes and the two blue jumpsuit CPD Officers with him secured the traitorous Armstrong.

"Yes," He nodded with hesitation. "And you are?"

"Chris Lowery CPD-I work with Erland. This

jerk knocked me cold and locked me up, if it handnt've
been for Joe Hayes I'd still be there."

"Ah..." Loomis stared at the blood pumping
from his arm and when he looked back to the Detective
the tall redhead was eyeing his costume.

"I was told to secure the room. Thank God I got
here in time. Hayes told me exactly where it was. I
don't know what you were working with Erland and
that woman from Homeland but I know it's all related
to that man at PierHouse. I'm working the murder of
the Homeland Agent on East Hawks Lane."

Loomis nodded slowly as the Detective reached
in his pocket for a cell phone.

"For me?"

"Yeah. I'll get a few more Officers over here."

"No, wait." Loomis ordered as he began search
the numbers in the phonebook. "We can't risk it-not
yet."

"What's going on? I can help."

"No, we don't know who's on what side yet.
Armstrong proves that, doesn't he? And he knew a
whole lot more than you think he might've. You saw
the Homeland Tactical Assault and the monkey
men...this mess is larger than you could ever imagine."

Lowery put his hands on his hips and his eyes
went around the crime scene. Before he could say a
word, Morell and McKinney entered the room with
shotguns raised.

"Hold up!" Loomis shouted.

Taldo and Wellman both drew their weapons
and there was a tense yelling match of exclamatory
expletives until both parties realized they were on the
same side. Morell and McKinney removed their masks
and Loomis put the phone to his ear. The Officers stuck
Armstrong in the anteroom and began poking around
the duffel bag and the burnt papers.

"The Pinnacle Building?" Loomis said with dread in his voice. "Alright...yeah, we'll be there."

"What is it?" Lowery reached for his radio.

"Mike and Sierra speculate a bomb threat at the Pinnacle Building-Semtex, just like Sugar Hill-high probability. Pinnacle also has a helipad-that's how Jupiter, the guy responsible for all of this escaped the firefight at Keller's."

"Pinnacle's on Cherry. Precinct Four is right there."

"Yeah, but we gotta go. Hayes is a former US Army EOD, make sure your men let him handle the explosives."

Lowery nodded and was about to step into the hall and call it in when Taldo came with a fraction of a burnt photo and his flashlight.

"Chris, ain't that Chief Nolan?"

Lowery took it and tipped it toward the light. "Holy..."

Loomis remembered Mr. Brown's collection at the Airport. Himself. The two from the FBI. The tiger women from State, and the Chief of Police with a handful of tough, paramilitary-type cops. His mind was trying to work and the throbbing pain in his arm wasn't helping.

"What d'you make of it, Sir?" Taldo asked Loomis who shrugged.

"I don't know but if he's not at the Pinnacle Building I'll be shocked."

Lowery's face was grim and he ran out of the room to call dispatch.

Mr. Brown was in a Homeland Security safe house in a condominium high rise on Schwartz near the intersection of Eleventh recording Rollins' damming testimony against his fellow SAB team of the Marland sisters and the boss of it all, Don Bartleson. In the seclusion of a nearby bedroom, Jessica Birchall patiently awaited her turn to testify against Sierra Marland and the threat of imprisonment for treason had forced her to do so.

"Excuse me, Mr. Rollins." He said as his phone buzzed in his pocket. He left the small and nominally furnished living room before answering and the voice on the other end of the line froze his blood. Paul Chang, who was recording the testimony stayed behind with Agent Farges and Mr. Brown instructed Mills and Dowen to accompany him with their sidearms to the Pinnacle Building.

The slight man behind the imposing desk tipped his head as he listened to the interdepartmental lingo from both Siller and Harrington, the FBI Agents he'd come in contact with after Brown's meeting at Bay County Airport. There wasn't a bone in his body that particularly enjoyed the bureaucratic side of the job, but Crescent Chief of Police Nolan was the kind of man that was able to be exactly what the person sitting across from him *needed* him to be in the space between handshakes. He was a suave and confident man with silver tipped dark hair and a weak cleft chin and downplayed his intelligence with ready sarcasm. Underneath it all he still carried the burden of being physically undersized his entire life and held up a hand.

"Gentlemen, I *know* the Crisis has really tested our limits as a department and I can only reflect your concerns with the way Homeland Security has handled their responsibilities."

"Will you testify?" Siller asked, the more aggressive of the two, although they both carried a harder edge behind close-cropped hair cuts and suits of the same nature.

"I will most definitely...*objectively* answer any and all questions directed toward me in a judicial forum *concerning* Homeland's handling of the Crisis."

"However?" Siller asked, detecting Nolan's reservations as Harrington gazed out the window which held a view spanning the waterfront and the wide-scale clean up effort of the aforementioned disaster.

"However, I need some...extra muscle in convincing the City Council just how understaffed CPD really is. I know this is your first time visiting Crescent and I wish it were under different circumstances, but I must stress to you that CPD gets half of what other larger and more prestigious cities like Chicago and New York get, monetarily speaking. I'm no prophet but I don't know how many times I've told that pack of suits on Eighth and Cherokee *in confidence* that this city *could not* handle a major catastrophic event and I'm not running to the nearest reporter to tell the City Council I told you so but I sure as hell did."

"What do you mean extra muscle?" Harrington turned his attention from the window to Nolan.

"I mean pressure from the State Legislature. The political fallout of yesterday is going to ripple through the Capitol Building for years to come-not to mention the Rubik's cube of possibilities and variables that begin today and end God knows when. Keep in mind, both of you, that November isn't only an important time for Crescent, it's important for the state, and for whatever cities and states you two live in, and I want to use the Crisis to radically change Crescent's monetary policy concerning the safety of its citizens. Whoever's in leadership after Election Day needs to see it the way I see it. They need to see the Waterfront from this window and know that it could've been prevented."

Siller and Harrington were silent and gave each other a thoughtful, albeit juggling glance and Siller pulled at the tight knees of his slim tapered pants.

"While what we're asking of you is much further down the road from what you're asking of us, it's also a lot easier. There's no downside-you have no relation to Homeland despite their having a small observatory presence in this city because of the location of the Federal Reserve-whereas *we* don't really have the luxury of partisan campaigning and if we *do* choose to proceed and are...misinterpreted, the whole Bureau gets a black eye, not just one of us."

Nolan shrugged.

"I know it's not an easy situation but I *can't* scratch your back unless you wax mine." His head tipped and his eye brows jumped. "Understand?" An uneasy silence passed across the table. "It's not that I won't, it's that I can't. You see your position as desperate because Homeland's taking your money, your bullets, your talent...I get that. But you represent a Federal Bureau-a corporation. *I'm* a small business owner and if I don't get what I need, Crescent will slowly begin to lose *all* of the money and prestige it's taken so long to earn. I'm not going to bore you with the history of this place, but we didn't get anything we didn't earn, and to see PierHouse get shot up really does a number to the psyche of these citizens. This is the *only* opportunity I'll have to make my case to those in power to do something about it, and all I'm saying is, that if the FBI's *observational* opinion of this matter was to reflect mine about the hand I've been dealt, my *professional* opinion would have no choice but to agree with theirs concerning Homeland, *because*, Homeland made my job *that* much harder in relation to my lack of staff, and if, God forbid, the situation were to arise again, I would much rather have had the FBI in my foxhole, let alone twenty-thousand more on staff and a couple of hundred million dollars for what they call toys and we call tools."

Siller stuck out his bottom lip and nodded. Nolan was a smooth speaker and accented the right words-perhaps a law degree was stuffed under one of his multitudinous community accolades.

"Just be ready when we call you." Siller said as he stood. Chief Nolan stood as well.

"I'll be right here." His smile was as warm as it was a fabrication of careful practice.

"And make sure not to let Homeland's retainer lawyers trip you up-it'll be a lengthy tribunal, I'm sure of it." Harrington added as he was the last to rise from the comfortable plush leather seats Nolan had placed before the imposing and intentionally regal desk.

The FBI men saw themselves out and Nolan went to the window, squinting against the odd low angle of the cold late-morning sun.

The phone rang and he answered it quickly. His eyes were beady as he received the information he was given and the phone hastily crashed back to the base unit as he made a rush for his heavy overcoat.

Erland steadied his breathing as his head spun and he fought gravity against the dizzying barrage attacking his equilibrium. The gold and brown elevator hummed with a constant mechanical whine and Erland blinked to focus his eyes on the small red angles of the climbing numbers on the black screen above the massive panel of buttons. The moment he wondered if he was dying he saw Sierra's stern face flash in his mind and he knew, if he was dying, he wouldn't feel anything-he would just fade with the lights and the noise like the night the Hellhound caught him across the chin before the final bell. What he was experiencing was the rise from the wooden stool to enter the magnetism of the ring one last time, and the dizziness

and stomach sickness, the aching of his joints, lower
back and kidneys-that was all just residual, that was the
journey. To let it over take him now was out of the
question. He didn't back down to a sure loss then, no
matter what he had told himself in that ring, and he
certainly wasn't going to now. His nostrils flared for the
clearing of his clouded mind with a rush of air and he
gripped the H&K Forty tight as he took his position on
the left side of the elevator with his hand reaching
across the space of the door, ready and waiting to press
the button that would hold the steel doors shut until the
perfect moment for a devastating counter punch.

Her eyes attentive and focused on the numbers,
Sierra's inner clock was counting the time elapsed
between floors. The final destination was numbered
seventy six and if she was wrong in her gamble, there
was no return from it. Perhaps Erland knew it when his
sickly eyes connected with hers, as if he had come to
grips with the improperly treated curse of STRIC-R.
They were doomed and even if they were finally
deemed the heroes of the Crescent Crisis there would
be some civil hell to pay. The people of Crescent
deserved the truth but Sierra knew as sure as Magnolia
was dead and gone they would never get it. The system
just didn't work that way. Loomis' presence validated
her efforts to a point where the grown ups would begin
to step in and argue for their children, and while
Homeland was a broken family and she was something
of a foster child to it, the CIA was well known for
adoption. But if her and Mike blew to bits with the rest
of the Pinnacle Building, there was no doubt in her
mind the easy shroud of infamy would forever rest on
her grave, and in some way, wasn't much of a contrast
to the ambiguity of anonymity she expected if the CIA
ended up sponsoring her after all. The depth of the

corruption remained to be seen and Sierra was trying to push away from her brain the box of horrors the Crisis really was. It was only the beginning of a much more brutal storm, a long and undying fire that would claim the lives of countless others as the bitter grip of the clandestine elite either bought or killed their way to absolute power. Thinking was her greatest strength, and as she took the smoke grenade from her pocket, eyes ever watchful on the floor number as it soared, it had to be the furthest thing from her mind. She had to *be* Magnolia, for once, and do the very thing that got her into so much trouble over the years-react. It was in their polar extremity they found harmony and for once she had to embrace the reckless abandonment of *Magnolia's* gambling, the mud on your face girl of cuts and bruises who used to dominate the frosty fields of St. Severine's Lacrosse tournaments as if it were the only thing that mattered in the world-a vicious attitude that found its refining furnace in the Shotokan Dojo and lived fearlessly in the relentless snow globe of ops. Sierra had to look death in the eye and close the distance between with a brutal war cry.

Sierra closed her eyes and took a deep breath as the elevator stopped. She popped the ring on the smoke grenade, letting it drop and rattle to the corner and sent the elevator to the next floor, sprinting for the stairs as the thick steel door pinged shut.

The ringing pops of handgun fire hadn't been heard on Cherry Street since the Clons gang turf wars of the nineteen twenties. The staccato explosions gripped Precinct Four and the crashing of car glass and plastic had only sealed the panic in their response. Within minutes Chief Nolan had been notified and three block radius around the Pinnacle Building had been sealed off as every available unit that wasn't awaiting procedure's hesitant direction was busy clearing out the surrounding buildings.

Lieutenant Bynum, a decidedly Norwegian looking woman in blue jeans and a puffer jacket, was talking with Nolan on the radio as she stood behind the safety of her carpool Ford.

"Sir we have to either escort this man in as per Detective Lowery's instructions via the CIA operative," She said with a strained voice as Joseph Hayes stood with clenched teeth and fists to her left. "Or you have to give me a plan of attack on the building..."

Bynum shrugged to Hayes as she listened. An item-filled khaki green messenger bag was slung over his shoulder.

"Yes, but the CIA believes there to be a bomb..."

Bynum frowned at the answer the warbled voice nearly spat over the radio. It was soft, almost as if he was intentionally trying to avoid damage by waiting. But the Pinnacle Building wasn't PierHouse. It was a desperate rope bridge to cross a canyon. Loomis was positive Jupiter had run out of options and was hastily running to pull the plug on some master scheme he had set for a future date, just to cover his departure from the city he had changed forever. Joe Hayes saw the turmoil stretch across Bynum's pleasant Nordic features and she ruffled her short hair in the back before a switch flipped in her heart, deep down in a place that had questioned Nolan since the day he took the job.

Bynum tossed the radio onto the seat and faced Hayes eye to eye.

"I'm gonna get sent to Qualaps Correctional for this but if there's a bomb in there I'll be damned if I'm standing right here when it goes off. I can't risk the safety of the other Officers but I can take you in myself while they hold the perimeter. The Chief's on his way, bomb squad is on its way. All I want to do is *know*, understand? No heroics, I just want to *know*."

Hayes' answer was cut by the garbled blades of a hastily approaching black Sikorsky S-76.

"Is that one of ours?" Hayes asked as his eyes drifted to the Officers inspecting the Verdoro Green Pontiac GTO.

"I don't think so-not that anyone would tell me."

Neither one could see the helicopter as it cut along the rooftops of the North's prosperous skyline.

Bynum turned her attention to the former solider.

"Ready?"

Joe Hayes pushed his neck to each shoulder and the cracking sound that it made seemed to shoot some adrenaline into his eyes.

Bynum raised her hand held walkie as she crossed the barrier and began to jog the distance toward the destroyed entrance. She slashed a hand across her neck and traded a grip on the walkie for a tight one on her Glock 17 and she instructed the weaponless Hayes to stay back as she stared down the iron sights of her service pistol. The rubble that lay before her was as telling as the diamondbacks of poker cards in a pair of hands across the table and she pushed herself toward the breach of the door, all in.

FORTY-FOUR

     Lieutenant Bynum paused in the eerie quiet of the half-constructed lobby. A black Mercedes Benz was a wreck of bullet holes and broken glass and the space carried the perfume of burnt rubber and motor fluids. She looked to the marble and gold ensconced bank of elevators, twelve total, all in a straight line, and noted the numbers above the doors. Strangely, four of them were in use, three sent to floor seventy-six, one to seventy-five. Suddenly the chopping blades of the helicopter made sense. The man reportedly responsible for every single detail of the Crisis had escaped the CIA's attempt to catch him at the Arena and was going to retreat back behind the gray blanket he had cast above the city via the newly renovated rooftop. Christian Lowery had nearly screamed his guts out in relating the gravity of the situation to Bynum and she nervously toyed with her wedding ring as she was accustomed to. She had already jumped two feet into the rapids and the heavy truth of it was pulling her down the current. The situation was a split-second affair, she had to act quickly.

     "This way." Joe Hayes settled into the trot-like movement of a desert soldier scanning rooftops as he cut through a dusty city. Even without a gun, Hayes instilled a great deal of confidence in Bynum and she felt safer with his presence. She had the sense the building was completely deserted save those in the CIA operation attempting to track the terrorist in the race to the helicopter.

Hayes took them past the elevator bank and up a pair of wide stairs and around a long glass and tile hall that stretched the length of the east wall.

"What are we looking for?" She asked, completely trusting his lead.

"Access to the foundation."

"What about the elevators?"

"No, we don't have the key or the override. We'll have to find the service entrance."

"That could take ten minutes." She said as his pace increased.

"It could take an hour." He called back and was quick down two steps as the spreading space of a large ballroom area stretched before them, impressively eating up six floors in an inverted and tapering triangle of blue glass and was host to unreasonably large modern art paintings and an incredible system of lights to show them. The space was obviously being prepared for a millionaire's banquet slated for the Eve of the New Year when the remodel would be finished.

Bynum stopped at the crown of the stairs for a second. It was overwhelming. No wonder the owners of the building had been keeping their work secret. The volume of glass and soaring angles of architecture was a feat of engineering and Bynum fell into a quick jog as she spotted Hayes poking his head down a series of corridors.

"Talk to me!" She said and soon gathered the reason why. The small and secluded corridors drove into the core of the building directly opposite the elevator bank. The doors lead mostly to restrooms but also utilities, security, and storage.

"Got it!" He shouted and she caught up within

seconds as he was trying the door with a lock-pick.

"Do you have a permit for that?" She asked, nearly breathless.

"Ask Lowery when you see him." Hayes opened the door and pressed into the dark. Their flashlights were bouncing beams of stark white and the hall ended with backside access to the elevator bank. Hayes' feet clanked on the catwalk as he flung the door wide for Bynum and his sword of light jumped around the greasy elevator shaft, lit only by recessed runners. His eyes were hasty.

"Here!" She shouted as he had missed the narrow ladder and she waited for Hayes to go first, casting her light seventy-six stories up where the beam faded and lost clarity in a dense fog of white smoke slowly spreading from one of the elevators.

Charlie's handsome face was cold in the empty hallway as he took cover behind one of the pale and dusty colored marble pillars of the top floor penthouse built specifically for Eric Island, the CEO of Pacific Holdings. He cursed and if he knew how to pray he would've prayed that his boss would hurry the hell up with the detonation sequence. In contingency, the four hundred and eighty kilos of Semtex were set to blow on a timed digital failsafe hard-wired to a long string of detcord. Jupiter had desired to hold the building for ransom and blow it anyway as a final show of extreme power to mask his transition from terrorist to one of the ruling elite, but the absence of his computer had nearly taken his breath as he ran from the Arena for his life and never in all of his time of service to Jupiter, domestic or abroad, had Charlie Norstrum seen the man so distraught. Even as the thumping blades of the helicopter and the promise of fire support of Team Ganymede became an increasing ambient crescendo it was as if the man was contemplating some sort of suicide-Charlie knew it because their last dosage of STRIC-R had been stashed in the fuse box with the detonator.

Charlie swallowed as his internal clock ticked off the seconds. Sierra Marland was no rookie, and the mercenary in him wanted to sink his teeth into her and regretted leaving her alone at the Arena. It had been Jupiter's orders but Jupiter had made a mistake with her, *and* the arms dealer. He had believed a legend that was nearly too good to be true and was dearly paying the consequences-a man who lived in the shadows had become the fox in a hunt that would never cease.

The hired gun's view of the elevator bank was compromised by his flattened angle of it and he stared down the length of the hall with narrowed eyes. The golden elevator bank was a threshold, and beyond it, the stairway to the helicopter, and he was simply a sitting duck guarding Jupiter's arming of the detonator in the L shape of the hall behind him, just outside the door to the CEO's penthouse in what little cover the pillar provided.

The grinding whirl of the elevator's rise ceased and he frowned as a thin finger of white smoke curled from beneath the door, the draft of the box's construction sucking at it as it began to pour into the six foot wide hall of pale marble. What began as a strand grew like some ghostly genie and the recessed pot lights cast uneven shafts of yellow through the anamorphic creation of thick chalky smoke as it spread and swelled. Charlie swallowed and the ping and roll of a door snapped his attention to the elevator near left and he squeezed two hollow points from his Glock into the gold-plated frame. As he attempted to rectify by peeling to his right for perspective the blocky shape of a man surged from the smoky outline of the door, bullets ripping from his pistol. Charlie ducked and made himself slight as the lead flew wild and by the time he counted ten in clockwork constancy, he realized the brilliant hammer and anvil of the set-up. His gun attempted to rise in defense as Sierra leapt through the cloud, having rushed up the stairs. She collided with him and he felt his ribcage compress against the unyielding strength of the marble pillar. The shooting ceased and a knife-like pain rifled through his chest and before he could decide if his lung was punctured or not, Sierra was on the balls of her feet, hands ready in loose blades. Charlie pushed himself up and fought the wheezing and the tightness of his pulse. They had lost their guns and the white smoke forced its way around them. Charlie closed the distance with two steps and threw a thick and looping right. Sierra slapped his arm and he spun with the carry of momentum and the moment he regained perspective she was gone. Charlie blinked through the billowing haze and let his eyes jump back to the linear track of pot lights and their yellowed beams. Regaining composure he sidestepped to the elevator bank and Sierra appeared in front of him slashing and hacking with razor-like hands. She drove him back as he blocked each and every assault and she feinted a devastating punch and slid in her stance, whipping her foot into his rib cage. Charlie crumpled against the heavy golden door and Sierra teed up on his face with another flick of her foot. The edges of his vision blurred and his hands tingled with paralysis and the last thing he saw was her foot frozen in space before it crushed the broken ribs into his punctured lung for good.

Erland winced to peer through the smoke and turned his back, unevenly rushing down the hall to the rooftop stairwell, dodging pillars as they appeared from

the cover of the fog. The noise of the helicopter was
deceptive and he knew the helicopter wouldn't leave
until Jupiter was on it but Erland was just as nervous
concerning the reinforcements tasked to retrieve Jupiter
as he was about Jupiter's detonation of the bomb. The
Detective scanned the space frantically for some object
that would impede the reinforcement's progress and he
found it with a wall-mounted fire hose unit. He worked
quickly as the wall of smoke began to pull its way
toward him and the Detective made a knot in the
bracket of a door handle he had learned from his
grandfather. It would take some herculean strength to
tear the thick fabric of the hose and the confusingly
tight knot it had been manipulated to represent. Erland
turned and pushed down a wave of nausea. Was it the
smoke? The running? The adrenaline? He lurched to
one of the pillars and tried to breath deep, coughing in
the unforgiving cloud of white. There was no escape
from its disorientation, no hiding from its confusion. He
had to get to Sierra, he had to get to the stairs. His back
was a stiff plank, sore and worn out and his kidneys
were one sharp movement away from exploding inside
of his body. Erland pushed himself into the fog with an
unbalanced stagger with the invisible timer of STRIC-
R's diabolical powerlessness counting down to
permanency.

　　　His hands sweaty and nervous, Jupiter ran
through the complicated process of arming the
detonator. The device itself was a scientific calculator
with a high-speed computer processor chip and the
necessary on slash off sequence was an involved string
of numbers that belonged to a personal signature code
he had created. One incorrect number and the
explosives in the foundation would detonate and the
precaution required to enter the locking code was a

luxury he didn't have. Still, his fingers worked their fastest and their trembling reminded him of his first database hack. That's what the meditation was for, to put him in a place of perfection, where his weak heart beat strong and immortal and his fingers hammered keys of letters and numbers with mechanical precision. He coughed against the spreading fist of white chewing its way down the hall and squished himself into the small corner of the L shape to finalize the sequence.

Seven. Five. Eighty-one. Six. Four. Eight-two. Five. Three. Eighty-three. Four. Two. Eight-four. Three. One. Eighty-five. Two. Zero. Eighty-six.

Function.

The crushing grip of an arm silently snaked around his neck and began to clamp. The arm spun him left and right, disorienting him in the white fog of the smoke grenade and his throat made gurgling noises as he reached for the calculator. He only had to press the on button, that little yellow on button in the top right corner of the keypad. His arms stretched as it became harder to breathe. Then he pried at the grip with his trembling fingers and braced his legs against the floor. The body behind the arm was light in weight and responded to his reaction by wrenching backwards to arch his posture. The move failed as Jupiter twisted away from the choke hold with as much luck as anything else and threw himself to the fuse box, pressing and holding the yellow button before the spike of a well-trained foot flicked into his kidney. Unable to dwell on the pain flashing through his body the kick struck again, this time the entire shin with the rigidity of a steel pipe as the swipe caught him on the tender skin covering the back of his knee joints. Vulnerable in a bruised kneel on the cold marble floor, a hand swept from the fog with swift confidence and palmed the back of his head, smashing his face against the wall below the fuse box panel, denting the painted drywall with a crackling depression. Inches away from a concussion with the dull and sense-deafening pain flooding his brain, Jupiter offered no resistance as Sierra Marland stood him up by the epaulettes of his white jacket and hooked her right foot around his and deftly spread his legs, pushing down on his shoulders with her hands. She tucked her left leg into her chest and with the raging face of her sister Magnolia, smashed her foot against the angle of his knee. Jupiter screamed in agony as the brutal assault had torn the complete set of cruciate ligaments in his knee and he fell, clutching in futility at its now horizontal angle.

Sierra stood over him, lungs a series of tight compressions as the scream for vengeance held court with the necessity of justice. The scythes of her hands folded to clenched knuckles and Jupiter was one punishing shot to his Adam's apple away from a horridly painful death, where the tortured voice of his pain would be caught in a crushed windpipe, unable to escape as he choked to death. Perhaps what physical torment she had inflicted upon him would communicate the feeling of loss he had burden her with and the cycle would be complete. Jupiter's once calm face of eastern mediation was an animalistic display of anguish and suffering and fear was a specter tainting his jagged view of the woman before him as she fell back into the thickening cloud of smoke.

Erland waited till the clear air of the stairwell surrounded them to speak. He could see Sierra was visibly as distraught as she was given to some wild and punishing rage and his hands touching her and guiding her to the staircase reeled her in from the deepest lake the human soul had to offer.

"He armed the bomb." She said, emotionless.

Erland cursed.

"It must be on a timer, long enough for him to get to the helicopter."

Sierra released her heaviness and blinked herself to the quicksand of reality.

"Charlie's dead. Jupiter almost. Leave Charlie and take Jupiter in the elevator to the ground floor-I'll go and describe the trigger to Hayes."

The words fell from her mouth and she turned to leave and Erland wasn't having it. He had been following the manic slipstream of her momentum and there was no way with the definitive threat of the bomb minutes away he was going to leave her to such heroics. He had submitted to her reason and her will and it was time to leave the ring. They had taken their lumps but the fight was over, no sense in trying to play for extra credit.

"No Sierra, you're coming with me. Screw the building, let's get the hell out of here!" His words were as bold as his voice was weak and stressed.

"Baby, there's a chance we can save it!" Her face was sympathetic and a harsh contrast to the steel in his blue eyes.

"I'm not leaving you up here." He said.

"You don't have a choice." She shook her head and made a move to re-enter the smoke. He held her back and she turned.

"Just in case." He said and handed her two guns he had stuffed in the waistband of his pocket. Charlie's Glock and her H&K Forty.

She nodded and kissed him on the forehead after an appraising glance. He looked moments away from death and in that viewpoint lived the conflict of her actions. STRIC-R was going to take him. The building was going to blow. What difference was there in killing Jupiter and avenging her sister? What would it amount to once their doomed bodies fell under the immense weight of the walls that surrounded them? History was going to forget them. Their work would turn to dust as their bodies would, and for a moment she put her options to the scales of value and looked to her adoration for guidance.

The faintest microdot of sun-shiny blue left in her fiancées' eyes held on to their secret hopes with an undying grip. The light spoke to her about what *will be* not what *could be* and it was the same light Maggie saw in Sierra's eyes that had been responsible for choosing their paths. It was the hopelessly naive dream of blissful, romantic love and even if his body was unaware of it in its decay of STRIC-R driven degradation, Detective First Grade Michael Erland's spirit still hungered for the partnership of golden rings and an endless seashore that was theirs alone.

She kissed him on the lips.

"Go. I'll be right behind."

The Detective smiled wearily and took the steps in twos and entered the fog.

The former EOD man cursed at the placement of the Semtex. The foundation was a solid concrete block God knew how many feet thick and the Pinnacle Building was built from columns of steel, rebar and concrete. The wisdom of the distribution of the Czech made explosive that functioned much like C-4 and was used primarily in construction demolition provoked a litany of curses colored with a military flair.

"What is it, what's wrong?" Bynum said as her feet hit the flat hardness of the foundation slab. Her flashlight danced around the pillars and beams and spotted the systematic wrap of the Semtex.

"It's a puzzle, there's no way we have enough time. There's hundreds of kilos down here and they all look hardwired to a remote detonator." Hayes light followed the maze of wires that ran from the clusters.

"That's all I wanted to know. I'll get them to evac the area." She reached for her radio.

"It won't work down here, get topside, now!"

The pleasant-faced woman made a move for the ladder and stopped. Hayes hadn't twitched a muscle. He was frozen and glued the shaft of light he was staring down. The extensive nature of the explosive strategy had him completely baffled but something deep inside wondered if it was a bluff for the simplest and hastiest bomb there was.

"What about you?" She called back.

"Go!" He roared as he shuffled in through the dark and Bynum threw herself at the ladder. The cast iron rungs were freezing cold to the touch and even for a woman who worked out three days a week and held a reasonably physical job, the six story ladder was by no means easy, and the Lieutenant focused her every ounce of energy on the frosty handholds as Hayes' footfall ran into diminuendo.

Sierra hit the second speed-dial.

"Hayes, I'm at the trigger, where are you?"

"Foundation." The response was rimmed with the hiss of static. "Nearly...beam is...with Semtex." The Homeland Agent shook her head in disbelief. "What about the trigger?" Hayes inquired. "Talk to me."

"It's a scientific calculator. He's armed it but there's no timer." Hayes swore, and not at what she said, at something he had seen. "What? What is it?"

"There must be...five hundred kilos of...in the...southeast corner. It's possible the rest of the charges are dummies. This...cluster could send the building...right across Eleventh..."

Sierra grabbed the calculator and twisted it.

Messy guts of wires connected it to the fuse box.

"It has to be hooked to the main power source." Her mind raced as the smoke curled around her and forced a few coughs. "I'll have them shut down the grid."

"No!" Hayes shouted as if he had broke into a run and the static amplified its hissing. "Power surge'll set it off prematurely...generators will keep it going anyway. Get the hell...and have them evacuate...on Eleventh to the southeast!"

Sierra's eyes blinked in the confusing smoke as she speed-dialed Mark Loomis.

"Yeah, go."

"It's gonna blow any second, evacuate the southeast of..."

The nearly pneumatic rattling of a high-powered machine gun of European design startled her and she dropped the phone, and watched in horror as the flimsy back separated from the plastic husk and the battery clattered on the floor.

Sierra cursed and took the two pistols in hand. Jupiter's reinforcements were coming for him. She attempted to steady her breath but the pace of it ever so slowly increased as the door to the sky top stairwell was smashed open, the tough fabric of the fire hose having been torn to shreds by the armor piercing rounds. Sierra bowed her head as she listened. Her vest wouldn't stop one of their bullets, however many there were, one or a hundred, and the combination of the fire hose and the thick smoke set the reinforcement team on extreme edge and she could only discern the faintest of combat boot footsteps above the beat of her own heart and the throbbing of her neck.

Sierra Marland squeezed her eyes shut and thought of her dear sister but there was no answer, no face, no voice, no memory. It was as if she was finally gone and the image that had replaced her belonged to the reassuringly American features of Michael Erland. Not the sickly colors of a poisoned man but the easy smile of only hours ago, when she had awaken beside him on the air mattress. She released her fear of losing such a lovely thing and pivoted on her foot from behind the cover of the L shape and squeezed the triggers of the pistols as hard and as fast as possible. The recoil of the guns sent the bullets zipping wildly into the fog and she made a desperate surge for the stairwell before the guns ran out of ammo and the support team, wherever they were with their automatic weapons, sent return fire. Split seconds from the exposure of the hallway, the surviving members of Ganymede let their assault rifles buzz as bursts of seven point six two millimeter rounds zipped through the white cloud. Sierra paused at the notched seclusion of the doorway to the stairwell and bit her lip as she gently and quietly opened the door to freedom, shutting the haphazard grind of gunfire behind her. As quickly as humanly possible, Sierra flew down the steps and opened the doors to three elevators on floor seventy-five, sending each one of them to a random floor before squeezing into a fourth.

Kalil and Greene rushed down the stairs with their FN-P90's high and tight. The smoke had been as unanticipated as the loss of Ritter. They were expecting Jupiter and were cognizant of his pursuit but had been unprepared for the seventeen hollow points sent their way through the smoke screen. Greene paused at the door and kicked it wide for Kalil who whipped his gun left and right and turned his attention to the elevators. He swore as he watched five of them descend in number.

"Back to the helicopter." Kalil said. If Charlie were still alive, he would've said the same thing. They

knew how much time they had having checked the
scientific calculator hard wired to the fuse box and at
the moment their own lives were the only thing they
could save. Jupiter was long gone.

   The Detective blinked with burning red eyes as
he watched the digital number slip lower and lower.
There was no forcing it and the speed in which it fell
was its own. In some ironic way it was a mocking
mimic of the detonation timer, and Erland could only
wonder if Sierra had taken an elevator yet. She said she
was...
   Erland fought a nearly paralyzing wave a nausea
that seemed to be squeezed from some organ deep
inside and the light-headed result was impossible to
fight. It was as if the elevator was a spinning cube, a
hamster-wheel, and he tumbled backward like a
submarine captain would once subjected to a crushing
depth charge. His head took a knock and the small
world of the fluorescent-lit walls spun and danced in
narcotic dissonance. There was no pattern to it, and it
made him something he never was.
   Afraid.
   He was losing control of his senses and his
skewed spectrum of vision fell on Jupiter. The man was
watching him, slumped in the corner of the elevator,
just as he was, and the terrorist seemed to gain some
clarity the Detective would've sold a winning lotto
ticket for. Jupiter's right leg flared in an inhuman angle
to his side and his face twitched with pain as he reached
into his jacket for a small, black wallet. Erland stared in
dismay as the wallet seemed to shrink and grow at the
same time and the gravity of the situation thundered
upon his mind a waterfall of meaningless thoughts that
collided with an endless echo of voices and faces
caught in conversation. The hacker's hand was

trembling beyond the point of salvation, an equal mix of physical paralysis through brutality and exhaustion and the unrelenting avarice of the moment. What scared Erland more than the nightmarishness of his spinning reality were the black eyes of his adversary, connected to a hyperactive mind locked in a physically impaired body, possessed with the primal instinct to exact a survival kill.

A needle came from the wallet and Jupiter nearly dropped it. Erland shook his head and tried to push himself up but the unreasonably square cube of the elevator wouldn't stop stretching and bending. He was in every way, as helpless as Jupiter. The hacker couldn't move much below his waist and steadied the needle between his index and middle fingers, ready to squeeze his thumb as hard as possible to load the Detective with a final dose of STRIC-R. Jupiter didn't plan on him and didn't know where he came from, and for the moment, didn't care. It was his lasting revenge on Sierra for besting him at their brutal game. She had come for him once and he was the only one at her side to help take down the great and mighty hacker and his power of perception needed no more ammunition to end the life trapped in the elevator next to him.

Jupiter swallowed the hard truth of his bodily pain and concentrated with the grandeur of his natural endowment to do so. The Detective's vital organs were protected by a bullet proof vest and which left his legs as the next best target, though a direct shot in his neck would be severely fatal, since he was already experiencing the unraveling of STRIC-R degradation. Having studied the drug carefully he knew Erland's physical impairment only ran so far-much of it was purely psychological, and unlike his own wounded body and horribly twisted leg, Erland actually could fight back. The problem was the angle. They were both stuck to the corners of the elevator, and while Jupiter could touch the Detective with his right hand, he would have to perform some kind of excruciating lunge to plunge the needle home. A twisted smile crept across Jupiter's face and he jabbed his left several times at the man to gauge his reaction. The Detective's features had fallen into turbulence and the feinting of the needle was as disorienting to him as it was deadly and perilous, like a hooded cobra poised to strike. Jupiter paused and worked up within himself the fortitude to kill the man, knowing what pain it would case him to do so.

The hacker pushed from the wall with his right hand and wheeled his left in a crescent. Erland pushed from the wall and kicked the hacker with vicious force for fear at the greedy shape attacking him and the Detective squeezed himself to full height as the man in white's final screams of pain were stillborn by the needle protruding from his neck.

The elevator closed around him and he plunged into a deep and endless black that he was powerless to fight and his body sunk to rest next to Lawrence Alexander Fydorvsky, the American born first generation Ukrainian immigrant known only as Jupiter.

FORTY-FIVE

Sierra Marland pried at the elevator doors as they pinged wide and rushed to the next available set of doors, pressing the button to open them only to find the elevator empty. She didn't have the time or the patience to play the game and the next set of doors held the same chilling reality. Had he taken the stairs? She couldn't call him, he couldn't call her. Where was he? There was a thumping of footsteps and a swishing of cloth to her left.

"You still here?" Hayes hitched up the bag. "This place is gonna blow any second!"

"We have to get Mike!" She screamed and the terror on her face snapped the former solider to arms. He too began to press the buttons for the elevator doors.

"Over here!" He shouted and she closed the distance to see two bodies splayed lifelessly like a yin and yang symbol on the elevator floor.

A curse gargled in Sierra's throat as her eyes stung with tears. Hayes was quick to get Jupiter even though the last needle of STRIC-R had been released into his neck. Sierra struggled to raise her fiancée as his weight was dead and cumbersome.

"You got him?" Hayes asked, feet ahead as he the muscles of his upper body had easily shouldered the hacker like a sack of potatoes. Sierra grunted and fell into the Mercedes having drug Erland backwards and lost her bearings.

Hayes ran over to her.

"Come on, grab his arm, both hands. He'll live. He's okay. Come on."

Sierra did so and between them they drug him across the floor in a loose crucifix. Hayes kicked aside what debris had fallen in the way and the harsh light of day was a blistering and blinding joy.

"Come on, come on." Hayes shuffled, feeling the pressure on his prosthetic leg. Sierra squeezed the salty tears from her eyes as the half-circle of police cars and SWAT personnel stared them down behind weapons at the ready. Lieutenant Bynum rushed from the cordon to help and a cavernous thunder pealed from within the ground, the shockwave of it sending everyone within a three block radius either to their knees or their hands and face. Loomis and Lowery collided with Mr. Brown and Chief Nolan near the SWAT command vehicle and Hayes was up in a flash, dragging Erland and Jupiter by the collar. Sierra pressed herself to height and sprinted to follow as the Pinnacle Building began to groan and wail under the immense strain of its inevitable structural failure. Sierra turned to see the tower lean with a dense grinding and snapping series of explosions as it tilted toward the corner of Eleventh and fell under the burden of gravity's unyielding truth.

Loomis covered his face as the deafening crunch and crush of glass, wood, and concrete tore through Eleventh and Cherry and the rushing cloud of dust and filth swept across the city block.

Loomis grabbed Lowery's arm and began to pull him amongst a stir of wheezes, coughs and radio chatter desperate to coordinate some kind of damage assessment. Strings of buildings and businesses had been utterly demolished and the swathe of destruction would echo through Crescent for years.

"Sierra!" He called out and she looked up from the prostrate body of her beloved. Lowery's face bent to see Erland flat on the ground and he ran off for the EMT's and the ambulance a congested three-hundred feet away. "Is he alright?"

"He's alive." Her eyes were lakes of sorrow. "But he's *not* alright."

"We'll get him to the hospital-I've got a specialist waiting."

Sierra fell to her knees and braced her hands on her legs, letting her head drop. Loomis squinted past her to see Jupiter lying alone, needle sticking from his neck. He cursed and Chief Nolan approached with Mr. Brown, both of them stone-faced in the aftermath as CPD and first responders rushed to their duties.

"Sierra Marland and Michael Erland..." Brown said and Loomis knocked his head toward Jupiter.

"That's the man?" Chief Nolan asked.

"Chief, this entire site is the jurisdiction of the Department of Homeland Security, and..."

"This site is a damn warzone and if it hadnt've been for these two you deemed fugitives we would've never captured the man responsible, let alone recovered the CONSTANT memory card with the *full* effort of the CIA, CPD, and those two *fugitives*."

Mr. Brown turned to Nolan, his attentive green eyes beady behind his glasses.

"I'm operating on the orders of the Executive Branch, and while I am grateful for CPD cooperation, I wouldn't overstep my bounds if I were you."

"No one's leaving my sight till I am damn well good and ready for them to-these people are going to get the medical treatment they deserve as American citizens whether you think they're terrorists or traitors and there's not a damn thing you can do to stop me.

Homeland is no longer welcome in this city and you are powerless to change the fact!"

Loomis bit his lip. There wasn't. Mr. Brown was spinning on a log in the middle of an icy lake surrounded by CPD Officers. Nolan wasn't aware of the extent of Mr. Brown's actions and he never would. The piercing high-pitched whine of the fifty-caliber rifle bullet burned the air before ripping into Crescent's Chief of Police, body armor and all. Loomis froze as the man's blood splattered on his own body. The bullet had cut a jagged swath through his heart and lungs and even more startling to Loomis than the gory reality that lay before him was that the second bullet from the rooftop adjacent Mutual Partners Bank sliced into Mr. Brown the exact same way. Loomis stood between the carnage and stared at his hands and his legs as both men's liquid life had stained him crimson red. A frenzied stir of voices began to hoop and holler and Loomis knew they would never find the shooter and his timing couldnt've been better. For a moment, the Texan of CIA Extemp wondered why the elite sniper had refrained from killing him too, but the thought quickly faded as he turned and stared at the unconscious man in white lying face up on the ground. The voices and shapes of bodies continued to flutter in flurries around him and the hands of first responders whisked him away to the pair of ambulances heading for Corazon.

Doctor Patrice left the operating room where she had been assisting Doctor Jefferson and the Specialist Mertz in treating Detective Erland's STRIC-R poisoned body. The somewhat experimental procedure had run eight hours and Patrice slumped next to the beautiful woman with the tearstained face. She was hunched on the floor in front of the line of seats in the waiting room, hugging herself, perhaps praying, perhaps thinking, and the kind Doctor's heart was heavy to see her so. Michael Erland was a good man and didn't deserve the hand he'd been dealt.

The woman's blue eyes were deep with virtue hidden behind tears and she rose to sit next to the Doctor. It was Sunday at four in the morning. The woman had been at the hospital since arriving with the Detective in the ambulance from what the media was calling The Pinnacle Site, a tragedy of international interest. Dozens of people had spoken with her since then, all of them in an official capacity, and she had barely moved a muscle through the entirety of those conversations, her mouth a full, albeit unfeeling red line. Her attention was not in her brief and harsh choice of words, but on the doors of the room where she assumed her love lay in a mess of tubes and beeping medical devices.

"Give it to me straight, I can take it." She said, not making eye contact.

"He's the only case we know of so far to have survived the first forty-eight," Patrice began, "And while Doctor Mertz is reasonably doubtful about the next seventy-two, Jefferson is extremely optimistic."

"What about you?" The blue eyes were on her.

"I don't know." The Doctor shook her head. "We just finished the beginning stages of a rare procedure. You see, STRIC-R affects the way blood vessels interact with organs and once the drug has entered the body, every blood vessel is infected. However, the *new* blood vessels the body produces are not only *un*affected, but *immune* to STRIC-R-one of the problems is the organs' interaction *between* the two, as well as some of the psychotropic and analgesic extremities of the narcotic spectrum, but if the body can refill itself *before* critical organs are irrevocably damaged it can make a *full* recovery."

Sierra blinked and twisted her head. Sleep deprivation diffused her thoughts but could not rob them from her.

"What about a blood transfusion?"

"Far too dangerous. Organs in this type of critical condition are very sensitive to foreign blood and there would be a high probability of the transfused blood becoming infected."

"So the only answer is in his own blood?"

"Yes. We're keeping him on life support while we drain his blood and process which red and white cells are infected and which are immune. The immune blood is re-routed straight to his heart as we wait for more to be produced."

"What about long term affects?"

"The bulk of the damage done to his organs is reparable through careful dieting and exercise and we've done what we can to gently stimulate an increase in his blood cell production without taxing his body in any way, but I'm afraid the damage to his memory is slightly permanent."

Sierra's eyebrows twitched.

"What do you mean...*slightly* permanent?"

Anne Patrice sighed.

"You know enough about STRIC-R to know what it does. What I'm saying is that he will remember what he will remember and he will forget what he will forget. It will be permanently deleted. That which isn't *can* be recovered. Careful psychological treatment will be able to unlock clusters of memory or scenes that surround what he *does* remember but until we're absolutely positive his body has *fully* healed, we'll be unable to remove him from the induced coma, and simply *can't* know the full extent of his mental damage."

The beautiful woman buried her face in her

hands. Patrice touched a hand to her shoulder and the woman turned away. The Doctor smashed her lips together and pushed her weary body up to fade into the dimly lit and sparsely populated halls of the ICU. Regional was seeing most all of the cases the Crisis had caused and the powers that be had selected an older wing of Corazon to attempt to treat Alexander Fydorvsky. He had been beyond saving and Erland had taken his place as the guinea pig and the seclusion of the isolated wing had been heavily exploited by various offices and titles requiring Sierra's undivided attention and her response to all of them had been nil.

A series of footsteps clip clopped with an unmistakable cadence and Sierra raised her head from a pillow of fingers. Mark Loomis stood with his hands in the pockets of a pair of blue jeans and his Sherpa-lined coat was necessary against the snowy chill that had blown over Crescent and all but killed several cleanup efforts. Weariness was a pleasure he couldn't afford although he looked dead tired and he squat-kneeled and clasped one of his Texan-sized hands around the pair of hers, tipping the brim of his buffalo pelt Stetson back with the other.

"How's he doin'?"

She shook her head.

"I know he'll pull out of it. He won't be a vegetable..." Sierra was brave to plug the levee of emotion. "But I'm afraid he won't...remember me."

Loomis sighed and rose to take a seat next to her.

"I'm gonna talk now." He said in his calmest and most soothing West Texas drawl. "So you just listen and don't say a word. First of all I've been busy since you've holed yourself up in here. I've gone to bat for you *and* him. We're about to write the past, present, and future of this whole thing and we get to decide what is fact and what is fiction."

   She turned and he shook his head, continuing.

   "The CIA has privately taken *full* credit for the recovery of CONSTANT and scored extra points for righting Homeland's wrongs. The CIA has also been tasked by the President himself to secretly investigate the extent of Homeland's corruption with the Corporations represented at that bidder's table and whatever spill-down that relates to it. The FBI will absorb the bulk of Homeland's duties in the interim and will make *official* inquiries into the Department's personnel-think of it like a witch hunt. If CIA finds them guilty, the FBI will get the praise for taking them down and their demise will feed the public's outcry for justice. The FBI is also captaining the hunt for the shooter responsible for killing Mr. Brown and Chief Nolan and so far haven't had any leads in the matter. An Agent named Siller is in charge. Ultimately they're just another statistic to the Crisis' stat sheet and Jupiter is suspected to be responsible. We've learned a great deal from his computer with the help of his protégé Jenkins, seeing as he took a reduced sentence over the death penalty in exchange for his cooperation. We've been able to completely corral the rest of Jupiter's crew and are delicately working on a case against the players at that bidders table and will move in on them when the time is right, but that's a different animal entirely and a great deal of work remains to be done. Detective Michael Erland has been placed at the very top of a list of heroic CPD men and women and will be forever remembered for his influential role in the Crisis, even though the public will never really know who he was or what he did-notwithstanding the Granderson case and what he had accomplished *before* the Crisis. You, Sierra Marland, and your sister Magnolia, as a result of your self-sacrificing patriotism and tactical expertise in the Crisis, have been officially *adopted* by the CIA and your operation to get Jupiter with Don Bartleson has been backstopped as a CIA sponsored affair. All of your non-military service records have been sealed and your time at SAB has been filed away at Langley. Welcome to the Company." Loomis smiled wryly as he offered his hand.

Sierra took his grip and matched it with her own.

"Ye shall know the truth..."

"...And the truth shall set you free." Loomis finished the motto of the CIA, a passage from the Holy Bible, specifically the Gospel of John. "At least the truth we make." He clapped his hands and rubbed them together. "You two are free to be who you are."

Sierra's eyebrows squeezed together.

"Mike's in a coma."

"And that's exactly what I mean, Marley, the CIA has been pioneering psychological research for years-especially in the field of memory loss and memory *gain*."

"What are you talking about?"

"When his body's done with the medical treatment, and you know that guy's as tough as they make 'em, it can go through a tried and true *psychological* treatment that fleshes out what he does remember and if he doesn't remember anything, *creates* whatever you *want* him to remember. In other words, you don't have to be afraid of him not recognizing you, because you can carefully fabricate his reality down to the fact that he could pass any polygraph in the world with the truth you've given him. In many ways, it's a good thing-he can know you for who you *are* and he doesn't have to ever know who you *were*. All of your records are done and gone, you're just a normal person now, just like you always wanted to be."

Sierra's expression changed from painful acceptance to violated confusion.

"How'd you know that?"

"Maggie told me during that operation in New York in one of our...quieter moments. She said she had a twin who was nothing like her-she talked about you as if you were the greatest human being to ever walk the earth. She idolized you and doted on you at the same time because you were what she always wanted to be but never could. Instead of causing her sadness it gave her great satisfaction, almost like she was your parent. I already knew she had a twin, but I didn't know anything about you. I wasn't surprised that you just wanted to be a real, *normal* person and that's why Maggie relied on you so much, because for all intents and purposes, you were. You didn't carry the baggage she did and she told me if I wanted to be in a serious relationship with her I should track you down. The first time I met you, though, I got the message that there already was someone special, even though you hadn't met the good Detective yet. I'm perceptive enough to understand people's souls to the extent that I know the real thing only happens in fairy tales but ever so often if people are patient enough...and mature enough, they find that person that unlocks a secret in their heart, even if they've never laid eyes on each other...it's as if they already knew each other from a past life and they've been walking through amnesia waiting to remember what always was."

A single tear fell from each of Sierra's feminine eyes.

"He can't forget you, sweetie. You're now and always will be Sierra *Erland*."

The seat made a scrunching noise as he leaned toward her and kissed her on the forehead with remarkable tenderness.

"If only Magnolia would've known," Loomis whispered. "She was the one for me, just as Mike's the one for you."

The blue eyes watched the Texan as his python skin boots took him into the dimness of the hall of doors and his escape from Corazon's ICU was a clip clopping stride of broken confidence caught in the rebellious lighting of a cigarette.

FORTY-SIX

The pickled white beach house of two stories and a veranda sat behind a scruffy string of beach grass that rippled with the slightest puff of Atlantic Sea breath, as if an invisible hand was constantly divining from it music of dry rustles and hisses. The lithe form of a woman in a one-piece halter top swimsuit of ivory walked barefoot and free through the tawny sand and her footprints ended near the curving foam of the tide as it swooshed and broke from the deep horizon and spread across the endless strip of sun-bleached brown.

"It's like a dream, isn't it?" A voice called behind her and the woman let the sunlight behind the rippled scraping of clouds warm her bones against the ocean breeze of early June.

"Yes...only it's *not* a dream."

The woman turned and walked to the man who was sitting on a parched hunk of driftwood. An empty bottle of Red Stripe was lodged next to him in the sand. Her eyes were the same color as the sea, and he wanted to take her in his arms and make love to her, as he had every day of the month thus far, because she was the most exquisite and divine woman he had ever laid eyes on and the beach house was theirs, as was the beach, and the identical rings of pure and simple gold they wore on their left hands.

"Oh..." Sierra said, interlocking her fingers

together over her head. "I forgot your beer."

"That's okay." Erland shrugged and held out his hand. The graceful fingers pulled him to height and they began to slow dance in the sand to the tidal rhythm. Sierra let her husband's body heat continue to warm her as the sun began to touch her back and a sigh floated from her body like a wayward kite as she nestled her head against his neck. After a full medical recovery, Loomis' prescribed CIA-sponsored psychological program had been accepted by Michael's mind with open arms, and while he remembered the night of the murder and traipsing around the forest and some large house as he had called it, he had no recollection of the events following it until the first Sunday of December, where he woke in the hospital from injuries sustained during the Crisis. Sierra, with Loomis and a Doctor by the name of Jikan, had carefully crafted a simple falsehood in the months that followed, leaving Erland to believe he had miraculously survived the destruction of the Pinnacle Building, which was a good thing, because he was going to retire that very day and set in motion the marriage of his fiancée on what she had described as the ideal Christmas wedding. Michael was easily able to write off the blur of his police days just as easily as he nodded at the reality of a past boxing career-so he believed the path of life went-time waxed and waned in seasons and since the season of CPD had passed he had gladly moved on. He *did* remember Sierra, but forgotten how they had met. The story was they had become acquainted at the Precinct, weeks before the Crisis and she was a semi-failure of a writer attempting to pen a fantastic tale on cops and killers and had been profiling him ever since the Granderson case which he was shown news articles of. She was given access to watch him interrogate a suspect and the faintest flashes of his impactful first recollection of her in that two-way mirrored room sealed the story. As was Jikan's theory, Erland had no problem believing their *facts* to be true because they were in a way, lifted *from* the truth, built around it and with its general guidance, and Sierra's shining face and confident voice faithfully at his side through the process reassured him that everything she said was completely and utterly God's truth.

Her mind told her it was a lie, a *good* lie but a lie nonetheless, and her heart told her it was a clean washing of the slate, a true sea change as much as it was the truth that always lived in the depth of their hearts. Like the sea, driftwood and green weeds from the past would wash up every now and then, but Jikan was more than confident in Sierra's ability to convince Michael of anything she wanted to and in more ways than one he trusted her as a child trusted his mother. After all, she was the sole reason he was alive, in his own eyes, and that was just the way Jikan had planned it. To Sierra, it was absolution, and they would live a simple life on the edge of a never ending skyline, trapped in the obscurity of normalcy and the molasses paced-life of Liberty Boughs. In honesty, Sierra knew Michael didn't really care for his memories and showed no desire to chase them, and his emergence from death's door had left him a mild and mellow-mannered man who smiled and laughed as much as he shrugged, a vessel completely void of the dense burdens of his cursed responsibilities as a Homicide Detective now free to receive the cleansing air of the daily Atlantic sunrises as the gifts they were. Sierra *was* his world, now and forever.

"Do you want a beer?" He said as they danced and his hand slid down her back and pulled her to him so their bodies touched from head to toe.

"I don't think I should."

"Why not?" He asked, peeling his head away to behold her lovely face.

"Because I'm pregnant."

Michael Erland's heart skipped a beat as the joy spread across his wife's mouth and lit her face with the incandescent grace of a woman bearing the seed of life.

A wheeze of air left his stomach as if the heavyweight champ of the world had socked him square in the belly and he stared at her in awe as her smile ended in a wide display of white teeth.

His lean arms swallowed her up and he squeezed her body, feeling for the newborn soul buried in her womb with the depth of his spirit.

After their embrace had run its course of silence, Michael gazed in her eyes for the space of a tidal crash before lovingly kissing her lips until his throat became dry and choked with emotion.

"Come on." He jerked his head to the left and felt chilly and winced at the mottling of peeling and cracking clouds blowing across the warm sun. "Let's take a walk."

"What should we name her?" Sierra asked, after several steps.

"Her?" Michael asked, with more comedy than anything, seeing as his eyes were growing harder and harder to see out of and he figured the walk would make the tears leave because he felt like latching his arms around her and sobbing till next week. The truth of it all and the look in her eye made him weak with an aching satisfaction he was unable to process in the moment. "How do you know it's a her?"

"I know." Sierra nodded. "Call it a...woman thing."

"What about one of the characters in that book you're gonna finish some day?"

A laugh of spontaneity and genuine delight

bubbled from her throat.

"Like what?"

"You know." He shook her shoulder with his right arm and wiped his eyes with his left. "That girl who saves the world, the one that looks exactly like you-you little narcissist-not that I blame you but you could've at least changed her hair color or something."

"Oh...Magnolia."

"Yeah, Magnolia, don't *oh* me, you know exactly who I was talking about-the one that falls in love with that emotionally scarred prizefighter like you broke the creativity bank on that one."

Sierra's smile was as sly as it was fulfilled.

"What if it's a boy?"

Erland shrugged.

"Well, if it's a boy, then we'll have to wait and see what he looks like, you know? I'd hate to give him a name that he couldn't grow into."

"Yeah..." Sierra nodded and watched their feet as their steps dented the sand in harmony.

"This calls for a celebration." Michael said, sucking in as much sea air as his lungs could hold.

"We don't really know anybody to invite over for dinner or anything."

"No, we'll go out tonight and I'll buy you something pretty at that boutique the movie stars send their personal assistants to find them a real eye catcher for the next award show."

"Mike, you don't have to. You know I'm easily pleased. Just being with you is my idea of..."

"No really-it's not everyday you get pregnant, you know? Live it up." He pinched the subtlest cleft of her chin. "Live it up. Especially since I won't be seeing you so thin for awhile..."

Sierra shook her head at him and laughed.

"If it is a girl," She said as she looked up to the

sky and shaded her eyes. The sun had broken free of the thin blankets blowing across its purity. "I want to name her Grace."

Her husband waited a few steps before nodding in agreement.

"Grace it was, grace it is, grace it shall be."

Sierra welcomed a chilly swirl of Atlantic peace as the beach ended and their steps pulled them up through the lumpy mounds of jagged green grasses, and with the piercing light of the golden June sun at their backs, husband and wife walked in silence to the pickled white two story house they called home.

ACKNOWLEDGMENTS

Thank you God for your gift of life and for your grace
and love and all of my gratitude goes to you.

Thanks to those members of my family that encouraged
me to write and publish knowing what was in store for
me if I persevered. Thank you for your patience and
support of all kinds during the process.

Thank you Laura Gordon for such excellent work on
the cover design.

Thanks to the beta readers and to those fine people who
inspired characters naturally occurring in this book.

Finally I thank *you*, sincerely, for reading!

I should add that I was born and raised in the greater
Seattle area and drew heavily upon that experience for
the setting of this book, while at the same time creating
a fictitious place that resembles and resonates with
other parts of the US.

www.ingramcontent.com/pod-product-compliance
Lightning Source LLC
Chambersburg PA
CBHW032248020726
47495CB00001B/15